# A TIME IN GOVAN

David Graham

First published in the United Kingdom in 2014 by
The Cloister House Press

ISBN 978-1-909465-21-3

Design and page layout by David Graham

# CONTENTS PAGE

**A TIME IN GOVAN – MAIN BOOK**

CHAPTER 1    TO GOVAN A WEAN IS BORN
CHAPTER 2    A WEE GAMBLE
CHAPTER 3    LIFE AT WEST DRUMOYNE
CHAPTER 4    VOTE FOR ME
CHAPTER 5    PLOTTING AND PLANNING IN GOVAN
CHAPTER 6    THE SAD HIGHLANDER
CHAPTER 7    A GOVAN MAN IN HIGH OFFICE AND RELIGION
CHAPTER 8    CHANGING TIMES IN GOVAN
CHAPTER 9    WATER ROW MURDER
CHAPTER 10  DO NOT VOTE FOR THE LAIRDS
CHAPTER 11  WOOLWORTH ARRIVES
CHAPTER 12  GOVAN PRIDE
CHAPTER 13  HMS DAPHNE AND ROUGH JUSTICE
CHAPTER 14  ONCE A STEPHENS MAN
CHAPTER 15  RAZORS
CHAPTER 16  A GOVAN WEDDING AND FAIRFIELDS
CHAPTER 17  LET US HASTE TO KELVINGROVE
CHAPTER 18  ABE
CHAPTER 19  HARLANDS POTTER
CHAPTER 20  GOVAN HIGH
CHAPTER 21  THE MAN BORN TO BE A SHIPYARD OWNER
CHAPTER 22  POWER TO THE GOVAN PEOPLE
CHAPTER 23  MEETING WITH A MADMAN
CHAPTER 24  HARLAND AND WOLFF
CHAPTER 25  GOVAN HIGH FIRE
CHAPTER 26  GOVAN HIGH – BELLA
CHAPTER 27  OH DR BEECHING!!
CHAPTER 28  FAREWELL GOVAN

# ACKNOWLEDGEMENTS

*THANK YOU TO THE VAST NUMBER OF PEOPLE WHO MADE THE PUBLICATION OF THIS BOOK POSSIBLE.*

- **Family members Sue and Stuart.** Both have done a fantastic job and I will always be grateful.
- **Marilyn Kilgour**– Map of Central Govan.
- **Benburb Football Club.** To all at Benburb Football Club including past and present committee's. To the many Benburb supporters who have provided great company and also provided interesting content.
- **Yore Publications.** For the provision of two Partick Thistle pictures.
- **St.Anthony's Football Club.** Always responded promptly to requests for information. Excellent Historian in Alistair Hay.
- **Colin Quigley.** Acumfrae Govan Forum. Providing a picture of Alec Crawford one of my all time favourite players.
- **Chick Mc Gee.** Sunny Govan Forum
- **Jimmy Strang.** My Govan Forum. A more helpful man it would be difficult to find. Provider of countless bits of Govan information
- **Mitchell Library.** Providing photo's of Govan yester-year.
- **Evening Times.** For making archives available.
- **Elder Park Library.** Providing information from yester-year.
- **Govan High School.** Ian Mc Cracken at the school for providing photo's from Govan High past.
- **Mary Weller.** Providing Govan High School badge.
- **Chris & Val Munro.** Years of help and information through the 'On Tinto's Slopes' Blog.
- **Les Smith.** 'The Mountblow Bankie' For the provision of the Tinto Park photo.
- **Ian Grant.** A true gentleman who provided much key information over the years.
- **Rab Cairns.** Providing the Plantation Park photo.
- **Pie & Bovril Forum** Providing the photo's of the 50 pitches and Moore Park.
- **Jock Shaw articles site:** An excellent site dedicated to a great footballer.
- **Lady Govan** : Very good blog dealing in past and present Govan.
- **Plus countless other individuals who helped and encouraged.**

# *PREFACE*
## *A TIME IN GOVAN*

*A Time in Govan is a book divided into two parts.*

### *PART 1:*
*Is a fictional story of Govan people during the important period dating from just after the war to late 1963. Many of the true key issue's which affected Govan during this period are covered , ranging from politics to murders and from social events to court appearances.*

*The author uses a fictional boy called Derek Wilson to enable many of my personal memories to be provided. These include a fractured family upbringing to school and general life in Govan.*

*Strong theme's are the demise of the Burgh in terms of employment with the loss of many Shipyard jobs. Also the enormous spirit of togetherness by Govan people despite obvious religious, social and political differences.*

### *PART 2:*
*Is true records and stories from the football world. Of course there have been many books written on the game. This book has a bias towards Govan , Govan players and teams. It covers the top teams but also covers players and teams from playground to World Cup Final. Again Derek Wilson appears to detail how he graduated from a diabolical bad footballer to not quite such a diabolical bad footballer*

*A brief explanation on a few of the Associations within Scottish Football if I may.*

***Scottish Senior Football*** *(Rangers as example) had virtually all the top teams in Scotland competing in two divisions at the time.*

***Scottish Junior Football*** *(Benburb and St.Anthony's as example) is effectively Non League part time football. At the time the quality was good and many top players started their careers at this level. Ignore the 'Junior' tag, the players could be any age group.*

***Scottish Amateur Football*** *Teams who do not get paid for playing.*

***Scottish Juvenile Football*** *Teams which have a loose age restriction. The six Juvenile Geographical Regions often had differing age bands but when playing in the Scottish Juvenile Cup they agreed a compromise (either under 21 or 23).*

*The rules were quirky. For example if the age group was under 21 then a players father was allowed to play in the same team as his son.*

*Could only happen in Scotland could it not !!.*

*I sincerely hope you enjoy the book and thank you for reading it !!.*

# CHAPTER 1

# TO GOVAN A WEAN IS BORN

It is a bitterly cold February evening as Ruth Wilson makes her way in intense discomfort to the Maternity unit at the Southern General Hospital. The race is on to get the expectant mother to the delivery theatre for the birth of her baby. The year is 1948 and Great Britain is in the grip of austerity following the end of the Second World War three years earlier. At Ruth's side is her father Robert 'Boab' and her brother Jack. Until a very few weeks before no one knew that Ruth was pregnant; she had kept it secret and the 'bump' only became apparent in the final 3 weeks of pregnancy.

Boab is a long time widower; since 1932; in his early 60's and looking forward to his pending retirement from Stephens Shipyard. He is a foreman in the Instrument Shop and is much respected by all. Ruth's mother was Elizabeth Lutton (known as 'Lizzy') and she hailed from Benburb; a small County Tyrone town in Northern Ireland. Boab and Lizzy had previously lived in the Gorbals area at Caledonia Road amongst squalid conditions. They had three children Robbie the eldest son, Ruth and Jack. The addition to the world's populace duly arrives and Ruth is delighted to hug her newly born offspring. Two weeks later in a middle floor tenement in 31 Daviot Street, West Drumoyne the initial joy of the birth has given way to some serious discussion's on a way forward. The boy has been called Derek after a close relative uncle and 'wee Derek' lies in his pram oblivious to the talks going on above his head in the tenement living room.

Boab, Robbie and Jack are far from happy and the arguments have reduced Ruth to tears. 'Where the hell is he ?' Robbie says enquiring as to the whereabouts of the father. They all know who the father is but are totally dismayed at his lack of presence or seeming interest in the birth of his son. 'Leave it Robbie' says Boab. He continues 'Ruth Tell Welsh to get 'F**cked . He will never be welcome here and he is completely and totally banned from this hoose'. Robbie and Jack have been supportive of their sister; buying a pram and lots of the babies clothing. Robbie and Jack are in agreement with their father and both say 'We do not want to see him aroon here'.

Meanwhile at the other end of Glasgow in a Bridgeton pub ; Jimmy Welsh leans up against the bar. 'Another half and half' please ' . The bar keeper says 'Dae ye no think ye have had enough Jimmy ?' 'No I have not !; do yea want serve me or not ?' The bar keeper moves across the bar counter to serve another drinker while Jimmy's mind goes further into stupor and memories come flooding in from the brain cells. Jimmy had been a Sergeant in the Black Watch and had fought in campaigns across North Africa and through Europe.

1

He had been a brave soldier and much commended for his courage. His thoughts were not with the war victory but now with the fellow soldiers and support units who had been lost during the war years. He finds it difficult to talk about the War to anyone and his eyes already yellow from the alcohol are swelling with tears. Welsh calls out 'Barman , give me another drink !. Richard the Bar Owner has been summoned by the barman. Richard has a good way with Jimmy; being one of the very few people who could reason when drink had scrambled the faculties. Richard says 'Whit is the matter wi ye Jimmy; ye are no yersell over the past few weeks. Is it something I can help yeh with ?'. Wid yeh like a wee sub ? . Is it money ?.

Is everything aw right wi Joan and yersell ?'
The words penetrate through the drunken fog in Jimmy's head and he manages to drag himself up to an upright position.
'No it is nothing like that thank you Richard ' The bar door opens and Jimmy staggers down the pavement on the short journey to the 4th floor tenement room he shares with Joan his wife.

Joan is waiting for him as he eventually staggers up the stairs helped by neighbour Billy Dawson. On the way up he had stopped at each landing. On the second floor landing he sat down and keeled over, his head hitting a tenement door of the Dawson family and Billy Dawson has opened up.
'Here Jimmy ye are in a hellafa state again !.
Lets help ye up the sters !' Joan helps him in and is relieved that their two wee children William and Mary are still fast asleep.

Several months later it is dawn at 31 Daviot Street.
Robbie is preparing his sandwiches to go to work. A metal 'billy-can' is filled up. This is a silver coloured container split into two with lids at each end. In one end is tea and in the other is sugar.

A small bottle of milk is packed into his khaki coloured bag which is soon strapped down and he descends the stairs on his way to Fairfields Yards. Jack is next to rise and he is soon on his way to McEwans Brewery where he drives the delivery lorries. Ruth has a put up bed in the living room with Derek in the pram adjacent.
Ruth has had a variety of jobs over the years. Her favourite was the Light factory on Shieldhall Road; near to home and the best payers she had worked for. Unfortunately with the arrival of Derek this job had gone and the pay off money has already been used up.

Ruth had effectively taken over the mantle of her mum in providing the 'wumin' element to her father and brothers. Within 31 Daviot Street, Boab had the larger bedroom and Robbie and Jack shared the slightly smaller bedroom.

The 31, Daviot Street tenement had its own bathroom and also a scullery where the washing and cooking were carried out. One other household resident was Darkie a jet black cat who scratched constantly at the wooden legs of the scullery table.

Boab is reading some documents relating to his pending retirement. It was a devastating loss to him when his wife Lizzie died. He frequently looks at one of the very few photographs of her. Lizzie was only 32 years when she died.

In the harsh conditions of the Gorbals, life for a woman many succumbed to a variety of illness's and it was TB that took the life of Lizzie just a few days after the family arrived in West Drumoyne. In the weeks prior to her death she had been in high spirits; after all ;the brand new tenement had its own bathroom, scullery and two good size bedrooms as well as a good sized living room. She had been planning with Boab exactly how the tenement was going to be.

In another part of Govan a family meets in the 3rd floor tenement flat in Shaw Street to celebrate a double birthday. The Leslie family are very close. Alfred Leslie works in Harland and Wolfe as a Riveter. His wife Marie has a long association with the Circus and helps out with the Kelvin Hall presentations during the mid winter in Glasgow.

The couple have two sons; identical twins Jim and John in their mid 20's. Both have an interest in the Circus and Jim works virtually continuously for the Circus Production as a clown. John is also versatile and is a reserve to stand in as a clown during the busy Kelvin Hall programme. . Both the twin brothers have a slight defect in their eyes which makes them look off centre. However the slight impairment means that they can move their eyes virtually together and they use it to good effect when they are performing at the circus. They frequently look at the children in the front rows of the audience; put their eyes together and gain plenty of laughs from the parents as well as the children.

John has another part time job working in the Pawnshop of Cox's in Golspie Street. The Pawnshop is owned by Abraham Finklestein. Finklestein has changed his name by deed poll to Arthur Boulton Cox conscious that a more Christian name may be more appealing to the mostly Christian Govanites. Everyone who visits the Pawnshop knows him as simply 'Abe'.

John is usually on the counter valuing the items brought in and providing the receipts giving the pawn customer 21 days to recover the item. Abe rarely goes on the front desk. Mr. Murdoch from Napier Street brings in a gold looking watch to pawn .

He overspent the previous Friday night in the Govan pubs and needs a short term loan to see him through the week providing food for his wife and baby son. John looks at the watch and offers 5 Shillings. Mr.Murdoch replies 'Five shillings !!.

3

It has got to be worth more than that son ?'. John replies 'Sorry Mr.Murdoch but it is not real gold and that is the current value of that metal'. Mr.Murdoch shouts around the corner into the back office ' Hey Abe, can I see you ?'. John says ' Mr.Boulton Cox is extremely busy at the present time with an important customer. However I will see if I can attract his attention and show him your watch Mr.Murdoch'.

John looked around the corner into the tiny back office where Abe is alone. Abe puts up a finger having heard the conversation at the front desk. John says ' Mr. Murdoch Mr.Boulton Cox has indicated that as you are one of our better customers he will offer 6 shillings'. 'Aye aw right' says Mr Murdoch and the pawn paperwork is completed.

As Mr.Murdoch walked out of the shop two uniformed policemen come in and John opens the thick metal door to let them through to the back office. Abe says 'Nice to see you again PC Mc Cabe and PC Elliott'. PC Mc Cabe says ' Anything arrived this week Abe that may help us'. Abe says 'Not this week PC Mc Cabe. All we have is run of the mill items mainly watches and jewellery mostly poor quality stuff'. PC Mc Cabe says ' Have you had anything from Gibby this week ? He seems to be quiet at the moment'. Abe says ' No not had anything in from Gibby. Would you both like a cup of tea ?'.

Ruth does not see Jimmy Welsh very often. They keep in contact through her close friend Nan Sillars who passes messages between them. Ruth looks down on wee Derek and remembers the times around a year previous when he was conceived. It was 1947 and Britain had just experienced the worst winter in 100 years. May had arrived and Ruth was in good spirits; a bit of genuine love had appeared into her life.

For Jimmy Welsh and Ruth Wilson normal days started differently. He was a Scaffolder and a Govan Building site required him to work at high level. Joan his wife was apprehensive of him working at high levels when he had drinking bouts. However he re-assured her. ' Joan, Darling, This is a big fast track job, I will have no time to have any drink'.

'Jimmy the money sounds good and we need it'. Joan said. 'Joan darling, my whole world revolves around you and these two kids; they are everything to me.

Prior to getting married Jimmy and Joan had met a number of times at several Dance Halls around Glasgow Central. Both were expert dancers with perfect poise and grace; rarely a wrong step.

They enjoyed each others company on the evenings out they had. Now with the arrival of William and Mary the nights out were restricted in particular for Joan. Jimmy was thick set ; a perfectly groomed black moustache and black curly swept back hair always immaculately combed. He was conscious of his appearance and was rarely seen without a nice jacket and tie.

4

He was very charming to all he met and had a knack of getting good quality jobs despite not being particularly well qualified. It was while he had a job in Harland and Wolfe providing structures for the boats that he met Ruth. He had been in the Brechin Bar near Govan Cross when Ruth came in with her father Boab. They got into conversation and the subject of Ayr came up. Ruthie said she had never been there.

Boab had to leave to go to Suppliers in Helen Street and left Ruth and Jimmy chatting. Jimmy asked if he could see her again and they arranged a meeting at the Plaza picture house a few days afterwards.

The relationship blossomed until one day Jimmy said 'Ruthie would ye like to spend a weekend with me and we will go to Ayr . Ruth said 'That wid be great Jimmy but what aboot yer wife ?' I have had enough of her, she does not understand me and all she does is scream at me'. said Jimmy.

The plans were made. Jimmy left Joan with a big brown suitcase saying he was off to work on a sizable job in England. He came out of the Bridgeton tenement and hailed a taxi. The short journey to Central Station took a bit longer than expected. A tip was given to the taxi driver and Jimmy carried his suitcase over to the platforms and looked for the Gourock departure platform.

Meanwhile Ruth had told her father and brothers that she was going away with a few friends 'doon the watter'. She walked up to Cardonald Station. Jimmy had told her he would be on the second carriage and sure enough as the train pulled in to Cardonald he is looking out of one of the windows. He comes off the train gives Ruth an embrace and helps her on to the train carrying her bags. 'Come in here Ruthie` and he takes her to the carriage where he has his bags.

Ruth is besotted with Jimmy and sits opposite.

The train to Gourock gradually empties out the Friday night passengers as it passes through the South Clydeside stations. By Langbanks Jimmy and Ruth have the carriage to themselves.

Ruth looks a picture having spent virtually all her limited money on a new dark coloured jacket top with matching skirt and her hair is curly with the latest style. She had been working on her hair for days to get it right.

Jimmy stands up and unhooks the leather strap holding the train window up to its highest point. Just as the window is lowered the train passes through a short tunnel and smoke enters the train cabin at pace. Jimmy rubs his eyes and with a handkerchief starts wiping the soot from his face. Ruth looks at him and a small smile quickly becomes laughter from them both. Ruth helps him remove the soot and they both embrace. The train pulls in to Gourock and the couple  head off to a Bed and Breakfast.

The next morning is very sunny and the couple  catch a bus along the coast road to Ayr where they check in to another small Bed and Breakfast

Within a short period they are both walking hand in hand along the promenade at Ayr. Ruth is aware that Jimmy is married but he says Joan and he are finished in all but name. He says that he has been working extensively in various parts of England and only came back occasionally. However now he felt settled and was looking to live permanently in Scotland and with anyone apart from his wife.

As they walked along the Ayr seafront holding hands and occasionally stopping for a long kiss and embrace, Jimmy said 'Ruthie I have never been so happy !. I must confess I have had a few girlfriends plus of course a wife of sorts and I hope that does not upset you !'.

'Jimmy, with a good looking man like you I imagine you wid have a few winches but am jist pleased its you and I' said Ruth. As they walked along the promenade Jimmy spots an Ice cream stall.

'Wid ye like an Ice Cream Ruthie ?' 'Ruth says 'Aye I wid, but jist you let me pay fur them'. Ruth had never very much money but would give her last penny to anyone who needed it more than herself.

When she had a home help job prior to the better money at the Lamp Factory at Shieldhall Road she would occasionally buy groceries for the pensioners she was looking after who were sometimes in some need.

The ice creams are licked to prevent the next forthcoming drip falling from the 'pokey hats' Jimmy looks over to a large house set back from the promenade. In the garden three children play on their swings.

'Ruthie, that will be us in due course !. A hoose down here in Ayr and you could look after the wee yins. ' he says 'Aw Jimmy that wid be great. 'Dae ye like my brooch Jimmy ?. This wis ma maws' and Ruth points to the brooch on her lapel. 'She was so pleased with the brooch when she was alive and said it brought her good luck'. Jimmy's mind is now elsewhere as he looks out to the sea and does not reply.

The weekend over Jimmy heads south to England still with the same suitcase while Ruth returns to West Drumoyne not knowing that the seeds of conception have been well and truly planted. Ruth says 'How can I keep in touch with you Jimmy ?'. Jimmy says ' I will come and see you at 31 Daviot Street three weeks today.

I promise you I will be there. I cannot wait to see you when I get back !'. Three weeks later Ruth has got herself dressed up and has a new hairstyle. She paces backwards and forwards within the tenement. She goes to the window but still no sign of Jimmy. She thinks ' He did say seven o' clock..

Perhaps I heard him wrong and it was seven thirty or even eight o'clock. Boab sits reading his paper but is taking more notice at his daughters impatience waiting for her man to arrive for the date. Robbie sits in his chair smoking and also reading a paper. At eight thirty Ruth goes into her fathers room and changes back into her 'normal' clothes

6

She thinks 'What could have happened ? and goes through endless possibilities , becomes upset and has a wee greet. Her handkerchief wipes the tears from her eyes and she is already thinking beyond 'her man'. She had spoken enthusiastically at the Lamp factory to her fellow lady workers about Jimmy and now she was thinking what to tell them when she returns to work on the Monday.

The following week Ruth was taking her turn to scrub the common tenement stairway. She used whitening to make them look spotless. Also she cleaned the walls thoroughly. All the women in the close took turns religiously to keep the close clean and it showed. Just as she arrived at the bottom entrance hall she heard footsteps behind. She turned round and saw it was Jimmy. He stood there in a nice suit and a gleaming smile. In his hands was a large bouquet of flowers. He gives them to Ruth and says 'Ruth, Sorry I could not make it on Friday. The job ran on and on. However we finished it and I am back now. It is great to see you again !. Do you forgive me ?.

Ruth says ' Jimmy they are lovely flowers and of course I forgive you. There was nothing obviously you could have done about your job over-running'. Jimmy says 'We will set up a method where we can keep in touch properly'. Eighteen months later and it is closing time at Cox's the Pawnbroker. The three balls outside the shop are blowing in the wind. Abe and John go to the back room . Abe removes a wall panel and behind are three Chub Security Safes. Abe says ' Right John I will put a code in again and see how long it takes you to get it open'. Abe gets ready to start his stop watch.
He says 'Ready'. John says 'Yes' .

 The watch is started and Johns starts turning the dial on the front of the safe. Abe says '30 seconds' ; John has already heard two clicks and listens carefully as he moves the dial gently more to the left than the right. 'One minute' says Abe. John has reached for clicks and on the fifth the safe door is opened. Abe says 'One minute and eighteen seconds.
If we allow three minutes then we should be ok'.

He writes down the result on a note book beneath the shop ledger. Abe continues 'With the next job you will have two new lookouts. Bill Eadie is bringing them in from Edinburgh. He tells me the men have done a few jobs before of a similar nature and are sound. We will meet up with them next week in Edinburgh. They want £150 each providing we get a result

'Jimmy Welsh is standing at the bar within the Bridgeton Arms. Richard the pub owner is discussing the political results and delighted that the Progressives are doing well in Glasgow and the Conservatives generally in Great Britain. Although Bridgeton is near Parkhead and the home of Celtic it has many 'blue' area's with a predominantly Protestant populace.

7

The Bridgeton Arms clientele are almost entirely of the protestant/Rangers persuasion. Jimmy Welsh is of staunch Orange belief and is a Freemason as is Richard the barman.

Jimmy has an intense hatred of Catholics long beyond the point of any reason or understanding. He is a formidable fighting man and once was a boxer for a short time before war set in. On certain occasions Richard had used Jimmy's services; usually with a drink quota as payment; to sort out any trouble within the pub.

Jimmy has had a few drinks but is not drunk as he steps out of the pub. Almost immediately he is face to face with a man he was certain threw insults at him a week or so previous and then ran off when Jimmy made his move to get him. Jimmy wasted no time in exacting revenge .

A fierce punch to the solar plexus had his perceived adversary gasping for breath from his severely flattened lungs. A perfectly timed right hook had the unfortunate man sprawled on the pavement. Richard and a few of the pub regulars came rushing out after hearing the commotion and pulled Jimmy away before he landed his next blow. 'Jimmy whit are ye dae'in ?' said Richard. Jimmy replied 'I said to this Celtic man I would get him and now I am going to beat him to pulp'. Richard said 'Jimmy this man's not a Celt; he is Kenneth McDonald and he is a regular at the Church of Scotland in Shettleston'.

Jimmy is surprised. Kenneth is being helped into the pub and can barely walk. Jimmy is speechless for around a minute at which point he says ' Tell Kenneth I am sorry about that and the work over he took was intended for someone else'.

He gives Richard a pound note and walks off. Richard produces another pound from his own pocket and goes in to give the unfortunate Mr, McDonald two pounds for enduring the mishap.

Derek has a friend in the back court of 31 Daviot Street. Jean Kenealy is also 2 years old and her father Dick has bought a playpen. Derek and Jean play away happily oblivious to the works going on around 20 yards away.
The doorways to the air raid shelters are being bricked up by Glasgow Corporation Bricklayers.

The shelters are known as 'Dykes' and have fulfilled their use. They had 4 quarters for families but over the post war years have become a toilet for both cats, dogs, humans and the smell is appalling. Ruth, like Jimmy Welsh, is also very staunchly Protestant and comes out into the back court with some bad news as she saw it. Helen Kenealy (Jeans mother) is told that another Roman Catholic family is to be moved into adjacent Tormore Street.
Ruth says, 'The Protestant families are the only wans dae'in the cleaning. It is disgusting !. They will no get away wi putting a Catholic family in No.31' .
No.31 Daviot Street is a tenement which houses 6 families .

Ruth sees less and less of Jimmy at this time. Boab, Robbie and Jack have met with Jimmy but are still of the opinion he is probably not the best company for Ruth. Ruth thinks differently and fends off criticism of Jimmy with 'You should gee the man a chance !'.

However as the year passes by Ruth has secretly given up any hope of a relationship with Jimmy Welsh. She has settled down into a routine of looking after Derek and occasionally earns money by helping out friends with elderly parents doing home help duties. One day she is walking home from helping out with Mrs. Weir a very elderly lady who is very generous and appreciative of Ruth's help. Her family of sons and daughters are also very appreciative. Ruth walks past a group of three youths and one yells out 'Are you a pro (Prostitute) Ruth. Wher is your wee protestant bastard today ?' Ruthie recognises them immediately as three undesirables who she has had arguments with in previous times.

Ruth walks on and takes no apparent notice but is hurt by the remarks. During this period the Roman Catholic Church makes great virtue of the fact that their religion makes family life including marriage a centrepiece to stability. At this time having children outside wedlock is much more rare and the children born into this situation are more likely to be the exception rather than the rule. Ruth thinks 'The one thing which is certain with all mankind is that no person has control over the circumstances of their birthright. You are born into an individual situation whether you are Protestant, Catholic, Muslim, Rich or Poor and you must get on with it. I hate the preachings of the Churches'. Ruth knows the three 'undesirables' as Gibby, Junior and Bernie.

It is a Saturday in late 1952 and Ruth is taking Derek into Govan. The No.4 bus arrives at the Shieldhall Road shops and Derek is helped on to the Glasgow Corporation double decker.

Soon they are at Govan Cross and Ruth has decided to treat Derek with some toy soldiers and marbles. The soldiers are made of lead; each has a rifle pointing forward and they are identical.

While in Govan Ruth visits a number of the shops including the Co-op stores where she tries on various coats and shoes. She has a little bit of money at this time and looks for some bigger clothes for Derek.

News from around Govan is good with the battle for Ship orders seemingly being successful. Rumours fly around that there may be some more jobs at Harland and Wolff. On Ruth's return to Daviot Street; Jack is waiting to give her some news.

He has decided to emigrate. His employer McEwans are not the best to work for and he has decided his options are better in Canada. He has already a job lined up and will soon be on his way to Toronto. He tells his sister not to worry as he will be sending money back to help with Derek.

Ruth and Derek walk slowly along Shieldhall Road until they come to Drumoyne School. They look through the railings and see the school children at playtime. The girls are playing hopscotch on chalk squares the boys are playing football with a tennis ball. Ruth says 'Derek that will be you soon son.

In a few years from now you will be gawn in ther and becoming a clever wee boay. You will be learnin aw sort o things and when you leave you will be clever and educated. You will have a lot o money and a hoose by the seaside at Ayr. You will have three kids from a beautiful wumin and have swings for them as well. Wid yea like that Derek?'
Ruth kisses Derek .

**GOVAN FAIR**

**MISS DOIG'S DRUMOYNE SCHOOL CLASS CIRCA 1955**
**A SMASHING BUNCH OF CLASSMATES**
**THE AUTHOR IS BACK ROW 2nd FROM LEFT**

GRANDAD BOAB AND THE
AUTHOR  CIRCA 1953

RUTH (right) AND NAN SILLARS
VISIT CENTRAL GOVAN  1946

Photo 1

THE BACKYARDS OF DAVIOT ST.   WEST
DRUMOYNE CIRCA 1950
THE AUTHOR ON LEFT ; JACKIE PARKS
ON RIGHT; JEAN KENNEALY IN PEN

THE INVERNESS STREET SWING PARK.
AUTHOR IS ON RIGHT CIRCA 1953

THE ORANGE WALK ARRIVES AT
CARDONALD PARK. THE DICK FAMILY
WITH TWINS WILMA AND NORMA.
CARDONALD RAILWAY STATION IS
ABOVE RUTH'S HEAD.

JIMMY WILSON  (ON THE LEFT ), THE
AUTHOR'S  FATHER.
(JIMMY WELSH IN THE BOOK)

Photo  2

# CHAPTER 2
## A WEE GAMBLE

Ruth is sitting at the living room table when she suddenly bursts out laughing. On the table she is reading the latest weekly Govan Press edition. She calls to her father Boab. ' Hey Da come in here and read this. We have some dafties in Govan. Listen to this. Two court cases:

Case I: At 250 Langlands Road a housewife was cooking in the kitchen. She heard a noise in the living room and went to see what was going on. As she entered she heard a call from the fireplace 'Coo-eee' followed by a big cloud of black soot.

In dock Matthew Dowie the chimney sweep said he brushed the wrong chimney and offered to clean the housewife's house.

The housewife had moved out the house due to the mess and refused Dowie's help. Baillie F Clark fined Dowie £2 or 20 days in jail.

Case 2; Alex. Brown of 33, Copland Road, decided he would conduct his own defence. The prosecution alleged that Alex. Brown had entered a ship cabin through a porthole measuring no more than 20 inches in diameter. Once inside the cabin he opened some drawers and took £4 and 6 shillings. Brown said that the court should discount the fact that he had numerous previous convictions for theft; on this occasion he was innocent of all charges. He maintained that he entered through the porthole in order to apply for a job on the ship. When apprehended by the crew he denied the theft of any money. Baillie Joseph Mc Kell rejected Brown's defence and fined him £2 or 20 days in jail.

Govan like the rest of the Clydeside Shipyards is doing well in winning orders for ships. An order for two large tankers has been received by Harland and Wolff. Fairfields has received an order for 4 Cargo ships totalling £25 million pounds.

Ruth approaches the entrance of Cox's Pawnshop with Derek in hand. As she enters the shop which is empty she sees John Leslie at the counter. John says ' Ruthie, you have made my day ! Of all the lovely wumin that I like to see in Govan it is you ! Ruth says 'Away ye go John !' John says 'Now what is it'. He looks at the gold necklace and bracelet and then continues 'Same again Ruth. £4 and 21 days ?' Ruth says ' That would be great John. Hopefully I will be back before then'. John completes the paperwork and hands the forms to Ruth. He says looking at Derek ' Hello Derek. You are growing up to be a smashing wee boy. Wid ye like a wee sookie ?' From behind the counter he produces a small lollypop which he hands to the small boy having first obtained the nod from Ruth. Ruth says ' Thanks John yer a charmer. Ah bet you get aw the lassies efter ye !.

11

John says ' Naw Ruth, I am a confirmed bachelor !'.

They both laugh and Ruth and Derek leave to catch the No.4 bus back to West Drumoyne. As Ruth leaves John notices the clock has gone past 5.30 pm and walks round to the front door. He turns the door sign to 'closed' , locks the door and goes in to the back office where Abe sits. Abe says ' Well my boy you done well on Saturday'.

I have counted £945 and 10 shillings excluding the lookouts. So the split is this . The two Edinburgh boys doing the lookout you paid £150 each.

This leaves this amount of money which we always split fairly and evenly. You have £445 and 10 shillings and I have £500 save us going to all the trouble of calculating my boy'.

John says 'The agreement Abe is always 50:50 so re-count !'. Abe says 'All right John. I have never been a mean man you know that '£473 for you and £472 and 10 shillings for me. 'When we go to the Restaurant on Friday you can buy the meals !.' John says 'Are you Jews all the same; obsessed with money ?'. Abe says ' How can you say that ?'. He continued ' I have told you before. Govan folk work to live. Jews live to work. We are a hard working race that put a lot of extra effort in which is why we are invariably successful'. Abe smiles as he counts out the money into two separate piles.

The UK economy is mixed and doing well from the results received The country exported £214,389,000 worth of goods made up of items like Locomotives, Shipbuilding, Aircraft, Wool and Tobacco. The standards of ships leaving the River Clyde is good and all workers strive to maintain the tradition of 'Made on the Clyde' meaning excellence.

However a lot of strikes, particularly dockers in England, paralyse the country and Rolls Royce at Hillington has a massive walk out of 3,000 workers following the sacking of a few shop stewards.

Gambling is illegal in Great Britain and any betting must be organised away from the eyes and ears of the Police. Many Gambling clubs are set up in a circumspect fashion and one of these clubs, based on the ground floor of 24 Woodlands Terrace, has an exclusive clientele of some of the City's top business men and gamblers.

Every Saturday fortnight they arrange to have a gambling evening and the event is greatly enjoyed by the people who attend.

The unofficial gambling club owner John Mitchell has opened his safe which housed the previous Saturday's takings. He cannot believe that the takings were as small as they were at around £3,000.

He thought there was at least another £1,000 or so taken. He cannot report the issue to the police but contacts the other club owners to see what could be done. Had they a thief in their midst ?

The owners met a few days later. Mitchell advised that the money had been put in the Chubb safe that evening immediately after the close at around 4 o' clock in the morning. There was no sign of a break in or had the safe been blown. However the suspicion is that a considerable amount of money had been taken. The group reviewed the people who were in attendance and all appeared to be well known to each of them. 'Who on earth could have stolen money from the club ?' says Mitchell.

At Govan Cross there is a commotion. 34 year old Denis Mc Colgan; worse for wear with liquor; is staggering around with a baby in his arms.
He had arrived home at 45, Burleigh Street, when he had an argument with his wife and told her to 'beat it'. As he walked around Govan Cross he became abusive to anyone who approached him including police officers who were summoned by his wife. Mc Colgan claimed he was taking the baby to his mother to look after his wife had left the tenement flat.
Mc Colgan was fined by Fiscal Mr. D. Brown Mc Farlane £1 for being in charge of a child under 7 while drunk. In addition another fine of £1 was imposed for being drunk and disorderly.

The tramcars and buses pass by the doors of the Bridgeton Arms. Nan Sillars who is Ruth's best friend and also lives in 31 Daviot Street goes in to the pub and asks for Richard the owner. Nan has an office job not too far from Bridgeton Cross and is the 'go between' with Ruth and Jimmy Welsh.

She has been through the same exercise many times before by delivering hand written 'messages' in an envelope. Ruth sends plenty of messages to Jimmy but only occasionally do any come back. Nan says to Richard 'Ruth was asking if you have been passing on the messages; she has not heard from him for a while.Richard says, ' Nan I will put your message with the others. Jimmy is in England at the moment and is due back tomorrow. I am sure he will get in touch '.

The next day Jimmy Welsh enters the Bridgeton Arms. He opens his wallet and shows Richard around £100 in pound notes. 'Look at that Richard. I have just given Joan money as well as presents for Willam and Mary.' What are you having Jimmy, the usual . 'Yes a 'Half and Half' .

Some hours later Jimmy sits at the bar; eyes bleary and has to be helped to his feet. 'Its time to shut Jimmy, do you want help Jimmy is unable to respond as he is completely drunk. Richard and one of his barmen help him to the nearby tenement in James Street and up to the fourth floor. Joan opens the door and sees Jimmy. She says calmly ' Thank you Richard. Bring him in'.

William and Mary are both standing adjacent to their mother. Jimmy is packed straight into bed. Joan takes his shoes off but leaves him to lie in his clothing and pulls the blankets over him.

She will sleep in the living room settee.  Richard says 'I am sorry Joan I should have kept a closer eye on him or told the barmen to'.  'Do not worry Richard, it is not your fault'.  We have been looking forward to seeing him for two months and he is as bad as ever.  He said he had not touched a drink while he was in England' said Joan.

The next morning Jimmy wakes up and sees Joan with her arms folded and looking worried.  'Jimmy I have packed your bag and I want you to go'.  'Why Joan I have only just come back !.  You know how much I have been missing you, William and Mary !'.
You three are the only thing I have on this earth, I could not live without you'.
Joan says 'I have had enough Jimmy.

You promised you would stop drinking and you haven't'.  'You can take your money with you as well, I do not want it'.  She throws the money that Jimmy had given her the previous day at him'.  Joan is an attractive blonde lady who has returned to her job as a Secretary in one of the Renfield Street offices. Unknown to Jimmy she has had an affair with a work colleague and the balance of favour and love has tipped against Mr.Welsh.

John and Jim Leslie were twins and both had attended Govan High some years before.  Jim had followed his mothers interest in the Circus and enjoyed travelling with the group and the animals.  Both were masters of the quick clothing change as clowns and disguise .  John had followed his fathers career into Harlands and Wolff Shipyard as a welder and served a five year apprenticeship.  Having finished his apprenticeship he opted to take time out from his chosen trade and work part time for the Circus and take a job in Cox's Pawnshop in Golspie Street, Govan.

Over time; the shop owner Abe and John had devised innovative ways of earning extra cash for the business.  This was robbing the safes of Gambling Clubs which were illegal.  They calculated that the club owners would not report the robberies to the police.  However the planning for each robbery had to be perfect and in every case it was.  Abe had attended courses on money safes and in particular the most popular make Chubbs.  In the back of the shop they practised on opening the popular models prior to any robbery.

Abe who had worked for some years in London in various Jewellery and Pawnshops was able to get a supply of second hand safes delivered through his contacts.  John learned all the code cracking techniques.

He had on two occasions used his welding skills of oxy-acetylene to burn open the more sophisticated safe lock.  Abe was a gambler and visited most of the many gambling clubs around the Glasgow City Centre area.  During his gambling evenings he was able to survey the premises.

He assessed the locks and usually visited the Cashiers to top up with money to continue his gambling.

14

Most establishments had Chubb safes and Abe was confident that any Chubb safe could be opened. He always had a good look around the smaller gambling clubs weighing up the security weak spots.

At Bridgeton, Joan has given Jimmy one last chance. William and Mary are pleased as they love their dad but get frightened when he has had drink. Joan thinks she has made the wrong decision. Jimmy has told Joan that he will be making one final visit to the Bridgeton Arms to say sorry to Richard before giving up drink completely. While in the Bar, Richard hands Jimmy the messages he has received from Ruth via Nan Sillars. He says 'I forgot to give them to you the other night until it was too late. I remembered later on but did not want Joan to find them in your pocket.' Jimmy opened the most recent message. ' *Dearest Jimmy, as you have not replied to my previous six messages from Nan I assume we are not to see one another again. Just to tell you I have enjoyed all our times together and love you dearly. Derek is growing fast and has your black curly hair. He still does not know who you are but some day I am sure you will be able to meet him. Loving you always, Ruth*

In Cox's Pawnbrokers in Golspie Street the 'shop closed' sign has just been displayed. Abe and John are surveying their largest forthcoming project. Abe says. 'Well John this one will set us up for years. It is not going to be easy this time. So lets review the problems.

- The Gambling Club in Hope Street is located on the third floor.
- The outside windows are tough glass and they also have inside windows. In between they have bars.
- Each weekend they have a large clientele and the money goes into the Cashiers office. The weekend in question when the project goes ahead will see some of the top gamblers from all over Scotland converge to the club.
- The windows and doors within the Cashiers Office have an alarm fitted to them. The latest technology has a thing called a timer. Once you break the circuit the alarm does not sound at the building instead it alerts the Security guard on the premises. He is then able to get reinforcements and operate a switch to allow the bells to operate. As the robber runs out on hearing the bell the club enforcers will be waiting for them. The Cashiers Office Safe has anti flame protection which rules out burning a way in. The code is changed daily so it will take at least an hour to open the door.
- At weekends following the gambling a guard is placed permanently outside the door. The guard is Joe O'Donaghue a sturdy Irishman who sleeps in the alcove adjacent to the Cashiers Office.
- The front door to the Cashiers Office is securely locked.

Both Abe and John have been preparing and surveying the 'Project' for at least 10 months. Abe says to John 'Are you confident ?'. John replies 'Nae bother !'. Govan people of contrasting age groups were treated to events;

- An Old People's outing was arranged by the Fairfield Committee and 21 coaches took 700 pensioners on a trip to Largs.
- A free children's pantomime, 'Red Riding Hood', was performed in the open air at Bellahouston Park in front of a large number of Govan youngsters

At Linthouse Sir Murray Stephen was discussing the latest intake of apprentices. The company were proud of the apprenticeship scheme they had in place. The apprentices had some of the most skilled engineers to learn from as they proceeded around the various departments as part of their training.

The Shipyard owner was a very keen yachtsman and visited the drawing office to see the outline of his own personal yacht he was having built. However that was some way off as the shipyard worked hard to fulfil a full order book.

At Govan Courts seasoned housebreaker Michael Mc Millan (33) of Burndyke Street appeared. He was accused of carrying a jemmy when stopped in Govan Road near Hoey Street. His defence was that he was drinking in one of the Govan pubs and got drunk. He must have picked up the jemmy in the Govan Road gutter. He was sentenced to imprisonment for 60 days.

After 10 months of planning Abe and John are ready to put their plan into action. The Gambling House in Hope Street has attracted the biggest selection of gamblers in Scotland for an evening at the Casino.

The police are aware of it but as several of their high ranking officers are keen gamblers and present they will not be taking action. The two 'Enforcers' are in place. Brothers Jack and Andy Bell are best known for violence in Glasgow. Both carry knuckle dusters in their pockets.

They are dressed in immaculate fashion. Black suits with waistcoat. Well Brylcreamed swept back hair. Gleaming well polished shoes. They were professionals at their trade which was usually scaring people.

John Leslie had done his homework. He had made a few visits to the building and in particular the Boilerhouse below.

In the guise of inspecting the Riser cupboards for rodents and cockroaches the Boilerhouse staff had allowed access on two occasions some months previous. John followed the Riser shaft which carried the heating pipework and electrics from the Basement Boilerhouse to the floors above.The Riser had a steel ladder which allowed access to the floors above.

The steel ladder was also used as a fire escape from the floors through a heavy door at each level. On the top gambling floor the door was alarmed on the inside, although in a fire situation the door could be opened to allow escape.

16

On the Sunday morning after the Gambling evening, John arrived outside the Boilerhouse with a small lorry and his two accomplices. He had previously changed the number plates on this lorry.

Inside the Lorry he had two heavy flat metal plates.

The Boilerhouse door was easily opened as John had discreetly taken a cast when the Boilerman gave him the set of keys in order to do his survey. Once inside the lorry contents were off loaded and taken into the empty Boilerhouse. The Boilermen did not work on Sundays.

If by some chance they were to return then a bogus Purchase Order would be produced to confirm the works were to take place.

John went to the long ladder which led all the way to the top floor and upwards to the roof space. The Cashiers office was served by a ventilation fan in order to provide the minimum 20% fresh air requirement in the case of sealed rooms. A thin mesh was cut as John left the top of the iron ladder and climbed into the roof space.

An access hatch leading to the ventilation fan was in the Cashier Office. This was accessed normally by a tall pair of steps. Outside the Cashier Office door Joe O'Donaghue was asleep with several glass beer bottles adjacent to the comfortable settee he was lying on.

John dropped a long rope down the Riser which was caught by his two accomplices.

In a large bag they put a pulley set used widely in the Govan shipyards. John pulled up the bag and then fitted the pulley securely over the top of a strong metal beam. The bag was lowered down and a long rope was hauled up to the top.

This rope was attached through the pulley and now anything could be raised or lowered. On the third delivery upwards John was provided with a rope ladder and a small tool kit via the new pulley/rope assembly up the Riser. John moved across the ceiling and was easily able to lift the access hatch upwards and into the ceiling above the Cashiers Office. He tied the rope ladder to the beams and climbed down and into the sizable Cahiers Office.

Outside Joe had been rudely awoken from his sleep by the Bell Brothers. Jack said 'You should nae be asleep Joe. They took a lot of money at the gambling last night and you should be alert'.

Joe said ' They have no chance of getting through the door; I am a very light sleeper. '. John was inside the Cashiers Office having climbed down the rope ladder. Suddenly he saw the Cashiers door handle go down; operated from Jack Bell on the outside. Sunday was a very quiet day in Central Glasgow.

The cinema's were all closed and most Roman Catholics attended Chapel. A sizable percentage of the Protestant population also attended Churches and the sound of Church bells rang over the rooftops of the city.

Ruth did not go to any church but was staunchly Protestant. She was preparing a cheap Sunday dinner of tripe. Boab was reading his Sunday papers and the in depth report on the Queens Park game before a lunch time bus ride to Govan for a 'pint'.

Meanwhile, at Hope Street the locked door to the Cashiers Office did not budge and Jack Bell and his brother were satisfied that nothing was wrong.

They told Joe to stay alert in view of the considerable amount of money inside the safe. Within the Cashiers Office John now focused on the heavy door which had an emergency Fire Exit sign fitted. The door was alarmed and a break in the circuit would set the alarm off .

As the Bell brothers came out the front door of the Hope Street offices, Andy suggested that they take a look around the building. They went in the back court looked up at the cashier office windows and saw nothing untoward. They then walked round the corner to where the boiler house door entrance was located and also saw nothing.

The lorry had been moved by John's two accomplices Ray and George from Edinburgh to a quieter spot away from the building. The Bell brothers then went to a nearby Bar for a Sunday drink and cigarette.

John traced the cables by standing on a chair and following them around a ledge. He then got a penknife and carefully stripped back the insulation without breaking the conductor on the cable. At another point on the opposite side of the door he repeated the same bit of works. He then got a length of cable with a small crocodile clip on each end. He attached the crocodile clips onto the very low voltage conductors.

The heavy Emergency door could now be opened without the alarm going off. The door was opened and he looked down to see his two accomplices in the boilerhouse. Ray and George came up the ladder and into the cashier's office. The safe was sitting on a strong metal frame.

The three of them tilted and lifted the safe and frame slightly and four casters with rubber wheels were fitted onto the lower frame. The three pushed the safe assembly very slowly and carefully towards the Emergency Exit door. Outside Joe was again asleep and the three daring robbers could hear his snores. This gave them a comfort. While John had been successfully entering the cashier's office, Ray had climbed the riser ladder and fitted another strong pulley on the metal roof girder. Already attached to this second pulley were the heavy metal plates which would be used as a counter balance.

The whole safe  assembly had several ropes attached. Between the three robbers they carefully lowered the assembly down the riser and towards the boilerhouse.

At the half way point the flat plates, guided by George, passed the safe travelling slowly down. The safe was lowered gently to the floor.

The trio then used the safe as a counter weight for the heavy plates and carefully lowered them to the boilerhouse floor.

Outside it was mid afternoon and the trio were going to wait two hours until darkness before bringing the lorry back for its rich collection.

John retraced his steps. He went inside the Cashiers office and closed the emergency door. The alarm circuit was now re-engaged. John carefully removed the crocodile clips and placed a cable clip over the top of the bare wires.

With a small brush he moved the shelf dust over the stripped cable. He repeated the same exercise with the other crocodile clip. He then climbed the rope ladder and pulled it up carefully. The ceiling hatch was replaced and John put all the equipment and rope ladder into a bag. This was lowered all the way down to the Boilerhouse via the pulley. The Pulley's were taken off and the mesh into the false ceiling re-fitted carefully to look solid. The Pulley's were then lowered and John came down the ladder to the Boilerhouse. The trio then cleared up any sign of their presence in the Boilerhouse and packed the safe into a wooden crate.

Once the streets became dark the lorry arrived driven by Ray.

The lorry was taken to a quiet spot just outside the City Centre for the evening. The two Edinburgh Accomplices caught a train back to their home city. John slept in the lorry.

The next morning  there was a delivery to  Golspie Street. John and Abe struggled with the safe weight but managed to move it past the counter, into the back and then behind the wooden panelling where it would stay for at least six months.

The next morning the unofficial Casino owner Joe Loizou arrived at the top floor offices. Joe was a flamboyant Greek character and his objective was to set up Gambling Establishments around the UK.

When Gambling was legalised then he would be in pole position. John was beaming and thanked Joe for all his hard work in guarding the Cashier's Office. He pulled out a roll of notes and gave Joe O'Donaghue £20. The Irsishman thanked him profusely and then went off for a well earned rest.

John Loizou entered the Cashiers Office. Something was missing.

His jaw dropped.

# CHAPTER 3
## LIFE AT WEST DRUMOYNE

Coal', 'Coal', 'McKechnie's coal'. A Coal Lorry turns slowly off Tormore Street and into Daviot Street. Ruth summons the Coalman from the window. 'Whit wan dae ye want' shouts up the Coalman. 'A bag of the back wans' says Ruth. The coal lorry load is divided into three with the better quality coal at the front and the lesser quality coal at the back. He trudges up the stairs and has a leather shoulder pad. He leans down and the coal is emptied in one swoop straight into the coal bunker. He shakes the bag of any remaining coal into the bunker and Ruth says 'I hope the coal is a bit better than the last lot which was a bag of rocks.'

She pays him and off he goes. Opposite the coal bunker which is in the scullery there is a table. All four legs show signs of being scratched by the cat 'Darkie'. Ruth looks at the scratches and thinks that it has now been a week since 'Darkie' went missing. Then a lady chaps at the door. 'Hello are you Ruth ?' 'Aye' says Ruth. 'Jist to say a bit of bad news I think.

If Darkie was your cat as I have been told he was run over in Berryknowes Road a few days ago. ' Ruth is saddened and thanks the lady for taking the trouble to tell her the news. She decides never to tell Derek about Darkie and leads him to believe he has found a new home with other cats in the house for him to play with. The scullery has a wringer for the washing and a 'washing board'.

It also holds the cylinder for the back end boiler with the fireplace in the living room at the other side of the wall. West Drumoyne is approximately one mile south west from Govan Cross. It was built as an estate for shipyard workers in the 1930's and had decent quality tenements. Virtually all had inside toilets in a bathroom and at least two bedrooms, a living room, a scullery and a reasonable size entrance hall with storage space. They were a far cry from some of the squalid conditions in many of the central Govan tenements.

The scheme was probably unique at the time in that it had no pub or no church of any denomination. The nearest churches were St.Constantines and the 'wee free' Church of Scotland in Moss Road. West Drumoyne was served by two separate shopping parades; one on Shieldhall Road and one on the corner of BerryKnowes Road near the entrance to Cardonald Park. One small factory dominated the estate that being Cockburns ; an engineering factory on Meiklewood Road.

An Italian family own a café on the corner of Meiklewood Road and Berryknowes Road. . The owners are Italian brothers Andy and Peter who are well established in the area. The café is extremely popular and next door they also have a fish and chip shop. When Ruth has troubles of any sort Andy and Peter are always one of the first to offer help.

They are well tuned in to the scheme grapevine. It is said that during the war they had been upset by the Italian Government support for Hitler. During times of hardship they would cash cheques or drafts for many of the West Drumoyne residents.Some months previously Andy had heard that things were tough for Ruth. In an amazing act of generosity he and his brother offered a free meal at the café for Derek and even the occasional dinner at their house in Crookston. A focal point of the scheme is often the swing park between Inverness Street and Meiklewood Road.

It is on the corner of the swing park that a long blue car sits. A man walks towards the car and chaps the window. 'The rear window drops down and Michael accepts a bit of paper and some money. The window closes again. The owner of the little betting business is Pat Mc Shane who lives not too far away in a semi-detached house which faces on to the 50 pitches changing rooms. Ruth sits in the park with her friends and neighbours and they discuss all the local gossip. At the opposite side of the park is a swing section with park-keepers hut in a well kept green surrounded by gardens. Ruth tells her friends about Derek. The other maw's give the progress report on their children when they see a figure enter through the park gates. It is Mr.Donnelly. He always wears a dark coat and a black hat,

He has a bad limp and needs a walking stick. Under his arm he has a bundle of comics and beckons all the kids in the park. He organises races and the comics are the prizes. The winner gets the 'Toppers' the second place the 'Dandy' and third place 'the 'Beano'. Mr.Donnelly frightens some of the children occasionally as he grunts a bit when he speaks.

John Leslie stands looking out to seaon the quay of St.Hellier on the Channel Island of Jersey. He has one foot on the quayside rail and is smoking a cigar. It has been over six month's since the audacious robbery of the Hope Street Casino and he awaits the arrival of a large heavy wooden crate.

The safe which had been stolen in the robbery was hidden behind a wooden panel in the Golspie Street pawn shop until the last week. In front of the wooden panel were three smaller safes. A few days previous a lorry had transported the Safe to Tradeston for loading onto a cargo ship destined for France, en route it is scheduled to stop at St.Hellier. Abe the owner of the Golspie Street pawn shop has arranged with his acquaintances in London for the wooden container to be taken to Simmons an Island metal workshop. The safe will be forced open and the contents removed. Afterwards the Chubbs safe will be destroyed to avoid tracing. Abe has an account at one of the Island banks popular with people who wish to avoid paying the Great Britain mainland taxes. Simmons workshop is on the outskirts of St.Helier and well sheltered; the owner is a long time friend of Abe. The safe is opened by drilling through the lock with a large electric drill. The lock is soon disabled and the safe opened.

John cannot believe his eyes at the amount of cash and other valuable items inside.The items include watches, rings and other jewellery probably given in as desparate gamblers tried to reverse their mounting losses.

John counts the money with the Simmons owner in the back office of the small engineering firm. £12,500 is counted.

The owner rings Abe and agrees to dispose of the additional non cash items. Simmons take £1,000 plus 50% of the value of the various assortment of jewellery. John is given a ride back into St.Hellier and makes a visit to the Island Bank where Abe has an account where he deposits the cash.

He walks slowly down to the quayside at St.Hellier lights up another cigar and draws heavily on it. His glasses have a slightly thicker than normal lens to try and offset the slight eye impairment he has.

He is satisfied and will have a good drink in the Scottish bar in St.Hellier before returning to his hotel. Tomorrow he will be making the long journey back to Govan.

Around Glasgow the local elections are in full swing. However apathy rules and in most wards the turnout is between 30 and 40%. The Progressives retain power with 58 seats ahead of Labour with 53 seats. They were delighted at hanging on in Pollokshaws and Parkhead.

In Govan courts the leader of the Scottish Workers Republican Party (SWRP), Peter Mc Intyre was in dock. He was charged with abuse and assault of his political rivals. His party faced a hefty fine. After the party was fined Mc Intyre said he had already resigned from the party and apoligised for his actions. The judge asked 'Who is now in charge ?'. Mc Intyre said 'No one. I was the only member and I have resigned. The party is now defunct !'.

Large crowds attended a launch at the Harland and Wolff shipyard as Princess Astrid of Norway came to launch the Oil tanker Bolesta. The yard had anticipated the crowds by building special stands which were filled hours before the launch. The Princess was met by the Lord Provost of Glasgow at the Central station and driven to Govan. Huge cheers went up as another quality ship was launched onto the River Clyde.

With the new Glasgow Council back in place an announcement was made that Balarnock would see a lot of housing development.

In the Evening Times there was a report about an assault. Taxi Driver Wesley Mc Causland (32) picked up four young passengers to drop off in Govan. On arrival he was attacked and hit over the head with a blunt instrument. He managed to stagger to Govan police station to report the assault and the theft of £14.

Jimmy Welsh is happy in his job and things are a little better with Joan at home. He suspects that Joan is probably having an affair and is constantly thinking of what to do.

If he confronts her he knows he will get it with both barrels from Joan about his drinking. If he says nothing then things will tick along as they are; a marriage without any real affection or love. He chooses the latter and calculates he should be able to enjoy himself a bit more. Jimmy has more money in his pocket and plans to offer Joan a holiday down in Blackpool with William and Mary.

That way they could be together and hopefully start to patch things up. He says to Joan. 'Joan, since I have had this new job I have saved up some money and I think we should all go on a holiday to Blackpool'. He shows her the adverts in the papers. Joan is immediately interested. 'Jimmy, that would be great I am sure William and Mary would love it !. There is plenty for them to do down there and they have a Pleasure beach with all the rides.' Jimmy is pleased knowing he taken his first small step in recovering his marriage to Joan.

The Welsh family arrive in Blackpool after a terrible journey on the 'Holiday Special'. The journey has taken some 8 hours with diversions through many towns they had never heard of in Cumbria and Lancashire. During peak times, 'Holiday Specials' were often put up sidings to let the scheduled trains, who had priority, go past. 'At last' says Joan as she arrives at Blackpool Central Station.

The family are soon on their way to Lytham St.Annes where they have booked in to the Squires Gate Holiday Camp. The Camp Reception is reasonably efficient and they are soon in their chalet.

In Blackpool the Welsh family spend some time at the Pleasure beach. The gentler rides provide enjoyment to the two children. The camp offers waitress service in a big restaurant to the campers plus good night time entertainment. Jimmy and Joan enjoy the dancing and win a small prize during a competition. They also offer supervision of children up to 15 and the offer is taken up one evening to allow Joan and Jimmy to sample the dancing at the Ballroom below the Blackpool Tower. The couple board a tramcar and head down to Blackpool Centre along the seafront from Squires Gate. Joan says ' I am looking forward to this Jimmy. I have always wanted to dance here. They say the Ballroom is great, far better than the Locarno' .

Jimmy and Joan are not to be disappointed as they go through the steps in perfection for the Fox-trot, Tango and Pasodoble. On the way back to the camp on the top deck of a tram car, Joan says ' Jimmy that was great !. When we get back to Glasgow we must go for nights out at the dancing again' says Joan. Despite being a stockily built man Jimmy is an excellent dancer ; quick on his feet with expression and poise. Soon they are back at the Squires Gate Holiday Camp. It was in a Dance Hall that the couple had met many years before and their love of dancing sustained the relationship for several years. Just before the war they were married in a Registry Office.

23

Married life was put on hold as Jimmy fought as a Sergeant with the Black Watch. His unit spent some of the campaign in Northern France before a decisive push into Germany saw an end to the fighting. Joan helped the war effort by working in the Springburn area helping make munitions. It was round the clock work and a lot of shift work was required. After the war the couple resumed life in their 4th Floor tenement flat in James Street Bridgeton. Within a year of returning home from the war. William is born and some 15 months later Mary arrived.

'Joan, you are still one great dancer !' says Jimmy. Joan replies 'You too darling !'.

Jimmy says 'Joan I was meaning to ask you something' 'Yes Jimmy, what is it ?'.says Joan. 'Are there any men in the office where you work and have you had a relationship with any of them ?. Please tell me honestly'. says Jimmy 'Yes Jimmy there are plenty of men in the office but no I have not even thought about having a relationship with any of them' says Joan and continues ' Jimmy, It is hard being married to you when you drink so much. A lot of other women can stay at home and look after their children. Because of your drinking habits I have had to go out to work and also bring William and Mary up.' Joan continued. Over the past number of months you have not drank so much and things are better, so lets hope it continues. '

At 31 Daviot Street, Derek has learned to yoddle, mimicking artists from the radio. He is very good but Boab is getting fed up. 'What the hell is going on here Ruth. Every time I want to sleep he starts yoddling.' says Boab. 'Do yer yoddling outside Derek'. Ruth says. Derek descends the stairs of No.31 and is in a world of noise.

Soon he is joined by a few other boys and for a while West Drumoyne sounds like the Swiss Alps.

If yoddling came on the scene amongst the boys of West Drumoyne quickly it finished equally quickly. Derek has been to Dr.Duff's surgery in Langlands Road and a tonsil removal surgery is recommended. It seems to be the same diagnosis for many of the children in Govan of the same age.

Dr.Duff is a middle aged doctor and highly professional. Ruth says 'Derek you will be gauin to the Southern General to have a wee operation. Afterwards you will be getting the best ice cream you can ever have '.

A few weeks later Derek goes into a ward and gets changed into his new pyjamas which his mother has recently bought him. He is joined during the course of the day by around a dozen or so other children. In the morning all the children are gathered and asked to sit on two beds. The covers are drawn around the beds. The first child goes down to the operating theatre for the tonsil removal. Approximately half an hour later another child is taken for the op. Derek looks through a gap in the curtain when the second child returns. He is unconscious with blood still pouring out of his mouth.

24

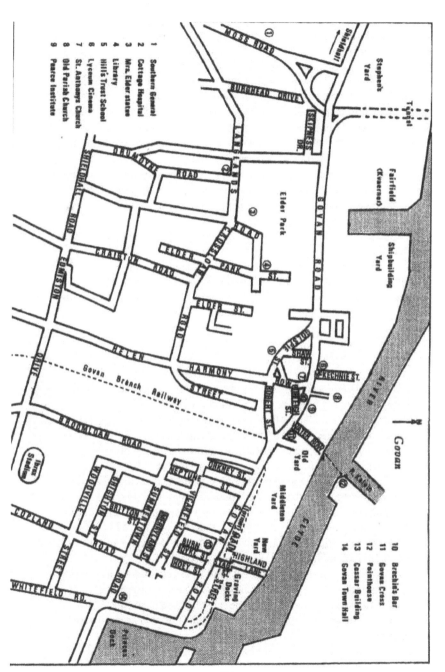

1  Southern General
2  Cottage Hospital
3  Mrs. Elder statue
4  Library
5  Hill's Trust School
6  Lyceum Cinema
7  St. Anthony's Church
8  Old Parish Church
9  Pearce Institute

10  Brechin's Bar
11  Govan Cross
12  Pearcehouse
13  Caesar Building
14  Govan Town Hall

25

This is certainly not going to be a bundle of laughs thinks Derek. Derek's turn comes and he is taken for surgery. A towel face mask is placed over his head , the chloroform administered and soon he is asleep.

It is in the evening that Ruth and Boab arrive and Derek is barely conscious. His mother says ' Hiv they given you yer ice cream yet Derek ?'.

A week or so later Ruth goes with Derek to the shops on Shieldhall Road for the weeks supplies. At one end there is a fruit and flower shop with an ironmongers shop next door. Beyond a stairway to an upstairs flat is the shop of Jimmy the Butcher; a jolly and very popular man.

Jimmy is always happy and calls Derek'Curly' when he sees him. The biggest shop is in the centre of the shopping parade; a Co-op grocery store. When Ruth enters the shop she queue's and is soon being served by a young fair haired man.

He goes and gets all the groceries on Ruth's list and pats the butter with flat wooden bats before serving up. At the end of Ruth's list he counts up very quicky the pounds, shillings and pence on a bit of paper and writes it on a bill which Ruth takes to a cashier in a glass booth in the centre of the shop.

There she pays and gets the award to go on her Co-op account. A cake and bread shop also owned by the Co-op is next door. Derek's favourite shop is next that of the Post Office which doubles as a newsagent.

The shop belongs to Mr. and Mrs McCutcheon and Mrs Cook is usually the main server. Mrs. Cook is the wife of one of Benburb Football Club committee members who helps pick the team. Ruth usually relays the Bens news back to Robbie, Jack and Boab; who they are playing, what the team is likely to be, new signings; in fact anything about Bens football club.

The last shop in the parade is a Drapers. Two ladies have a thriving business selling wool, some garments and a lot of threads and needles. Ruth goes into this shop once a week; as much to gossip as anything else and always buys something even if just a thimble.

It is over six months since the Pawnshop in Golspie Street carried out their 'project on the Gambling Club in Hope Street. One day Mr.Mc Cluskey , an elderly Govanite, enters the shop and puts on the counter a wooden walking stick. Abe is on the counter and says 'what can do for you Mr. Mc Cluskey ?'. Mr. Mc Cluskey says 'Look Abe at this; the quality of the wood and the roondness of the handle. It must be worth a guid pawn'.

Abe says ' Well Mr.Cluskey, lets have a look'. He gets out his magnifying glass and looks at the item. 'We do not normally take walking sticks Mr.Cluskey. I can see an inscription on the barrel. It seems to say 'SGH' !.Mr.Mc Cluskey says 'That is right Steven Gerald Harper an auld relative o' mine'.

Abe says ' The only SGH I have ever known is Southern General Hospital !.

The Govan Press reports that a lot of the Elder Park Library books are getting stolen—500 they say. They are blaming the Govan High pupils who take them to replace the books they have lost. Other items reported ; Fairfields has just got another £5 million order for 4 ships . It says to 'Supply 4 Ore carrying Ships from Liberia'. American firms are providing 50,000 more jobs for Scotland it says. Jimmy Gould is in trouble again. He was convicted of Breach of the peace. It says 'James Gould (29) of 383 Moss Road assaulted a polis man in Langlands Road near Greenfield Street. He punched him in the belly and got 6 days in prison. Magistrate Langmuir says Gould had a deplorable record'.

DI Roy Fletcher has made a circumspect visit to the Hope Street top floor offices to try and get some clue's as to the robbery six months previously from the gambling club. He asks John Loizou ' Have you got a list of members of the club who were there on the evening of the robbery ?'. John says 'Yes, Andy and Jack have had a look at them and there is no obvious candidate. Virtually all of them are keen gamblers !'.
Roy Fletcher says ' I am not interested in the ones who were here. I am more interested in the ones who were not. Can you give me the list of these names and brief note on what you know about them'.

Fletcher then looked around the Accounts office. He looked at the doors and checked the door and window alarms all of which worked perfectly. He was puzzled and scratched his head. After a few minutes looking at the wall panels he looked upwards and saw the access hatch to the roof. He said to John 'Is that hatch alarmed ?' Joe said 'Not that I am aware of. It only goes up into the Ventilation Fan area'. Roy says ' Can you get me a pair of steps long enough to look above the hatch'.

Roy climbs up and raises the wooden hatch. Above he hears the noise of the Fresh Air Fan and also the noise from the Boiler house coming from the ground floor level. He moved over and saw the less than substantial mesh that led to the riser which went down to the Boiler house. Roy Fletcher climbed down into the Accounts Office and the looked at the entry doors to the area. He focussed on the Fire Exit door which led out to the Riser. Roy called for the steps and traced the cables which were connected to the door switch.
He brushed away dust with his finger until he found where the copper conductor was showing through the cable insulation. He now knew how the robbery was carried out and a short visit to the Boilerhouse confirmed his suspicions.

In Golspie Street Ruth with Derek are walking towards Cox's pawnbrokers with her latest set of items. Behind her there is a lot of noise as a lorry with a man shouting into a loud hailer bids for the Govanites votes. It is Jack Nixon Browne the Unionist candidate. As he drives along Golspie Street some Govanites give him a wave. He acknowledges with a wave back and then gives the V for victory Churchill salute.

Ruth enters Cox's and joins the queue for pawning. Some of the people in the queue say 'What a commotion oot ther !' Ruth moves up the queue and reaches the counter which is manned by John Leslie. John says' Ruthie, you have made my day. Now dae ye remember when we used to sit together at the back of the classes at Govan High ?' . Ruth says 'Ach away ye go John; that was a long time ago'. John says; looking at Derek; 'Hello Derek, dae ye want a wee sookie ?' After waiting for Ruth's approval he gives Derek the small lollipop.

Ruth says ' I bought these three matching hand painted geese from Mrs. Morrison's shop on Govan Road. Unfortunately the nail you are supposed to hammer in to fix to the geese to the  wall is not very good and they are likely to fall off. Mrs. Morrison says they are the finest  porcelain geese ye can get anywher.

So how much are ye gauin to offer John ?' John says ' Look back here Ruth 'John pushed the door back and there stacked up was around 100 virtually identical geese. 'Sorry Ruth we already have too many'. Ruth says ' Awe right John; ye can hiv ma earings and took them off'. John looks through his magnifying glass and says 'Five shillings Ruth ?' Ruth says 'OK John'. John prepared the paperwork and Ruth had a sum of money to tide her over for several more days.

DI Roy Fletcher and John Loizou had a meeting over tea in a Central Glasgow café. Roy says ' We now know how the robbery was carried out. From the police records there is no indication of where the safe has gone. The trail is cold. We have looked at the list of people who were not present on the evening of the robbery and there are no known proper criminals'. John says ' Roy we have done everything you asked and even bought the safe you recommended from the company you wanted us to go through. We have bought the same safe again and would like some assurance that there will be no repeat !'.

Ruth has just completed her shopping at the Shieldhall Road shops. She has a blether with Mrs Horn and very quickly they are joined by other Govan women for a blether, the way only women from West Drumoyne know how. Suddenly there is a noise. It is Jack Nixon Browne the Unionist candidate coming down Shieldhall Road on the back of a small open backed lorry with his loud hailer. A few people wave to him from either side of the road and he waves back followed by a Churchill V for victory salute. He passes the group of women at the Shieldhall Road shops. The group of women all wave and the he asks the  driver to slow down and stop. Jack says 'I trust you will be voting for me on Thursday Ladies ?' They mostly reply 'Yes, Jack and good luck !'. Jack says 'Thank you. I was just saying to my driver a minute ago what a charming bunch of ladies at the shops'.  He thanks the ladies again and drives off to greet the next set of West Drumoyne voters.

The gathered group of women continue to discuss what they were blethering about before before commenting on politics. All five ladies say how dashing Jack is. Mrs Horn says 'He is obviously very well educated and has done a lot of work bringing the issue of housing in Govan to the fore. I went to his meeting and he says he would help the Govan people with the Protestant work ethic. Also he says that a Conservative-Unionist government would look to restrict the entry into Scotland of so many Irish folk. Jack looks so confident and assured' just the sort of man we need in Govan'.

The 1951 General Election is destined to be as close as the 1950 General Election where Labour gained a very small majority. Glasgow has become a key political battleground with a number of very closely contested seats.

At 31 Daviot Street, the Wilson family are having their tea and the subject of politics comes up. Robbie says ' From what we can make out Govan is going to be a very close run thing. A lot of people are saying that the Govan result could decide the entire election. Nixon Browne holds a wafer thin majority. Glasgow has 8 Labour and 7 Unionist MP's. Jack says ' I do not like the way Nixon Browne is dividing the Govan folk with his unashamed appeal to the Billy Boys. I will be voting Labour'.

Boab says ' I agree Jack it would be good to get Browne unseated'
Ruth says 'We are not exactly spoiled for choice in the Glasgow seats; just two candidates in Govan and in most of the other Glasga seats. Why is that Robbie ?'. Robbie says ' It seems that the Liberals have withdrawn their candidates after making a deal with the Tories. There are a group calling themselves 'Independent Liberals' who say they will support the Tories rather than Labour.

Also Clement Davies the official Liberal leader has made a deal with the Tories so that he will support them. In return the Tories have dropped their candidate from the Montgomery seat to let him win'. Ruth says 'They shouldnae really be allowed tae dae that !. Awe the wumin aroon here seem to like Nixon Browne. He has a way which appeals to the ladies and of course the Protestant voters. I will be voting Labour anyway'.

At Cox's Pawnshop John Leslie has just closed up for the evening. He and Abe both go into the back office. They are having their quarter year meeting and some serious issue's to discuss. Abe says 'Well we might as well start and take the subjects in order:
1) Mrs Smith. Abe says 'Right we know the issue. William Smith was convicted for bashin' his wife. The reason was that she had pawned his smart suit in order to provide clothes for the weans. He was given the choice of £3 or 20 days in jail and he paid the £3-. He has told Mrs Smith to get the suit back and she does not have the money. We have had countless people asking us to help. This is a fairly easy one John. We run a business not a charity shop !'. John says 'Whit !.

We have got to help here Abe. You know what like Smith is; he is a f\*\*ck\*ng brute. Mrs Smith is always outside Fairfields every Friday after he has been paid to get some money off him before he goes to the pubs. If we ignore Mrs. Smith then our business reputation will be in tatters. All of Govan will know about it'.

Abe says 'Business is Business my boy'. John says ' Look Abe. We can easily afford the cost of this pawn so f\*\*k you I will pay for it myself !!'.
2) Benburb Football Club: John says ' I have seen the plans at Tinto Park for the Bens new cover. It is rubbish !!. They have a cover for about 200 people at the top of the Drumoyne terrace. The collections they take will never achieve a decent stand.

They send the boys around with the sheet each week to catch the coins. With the money we made from our last project I would like to help them build a quality stand'. Abe says 'Well with your part of the funds, you can do what you like John. Are you sure you want to do this ?. You will never be a proper businessman my boy !!'.

John says 'Abe I support the Bens. Mr.Mc Vicar has tried his heart out and he needs help'. Abe says 'OK, very well. Now how do you propose we give him say £2,000 without us having every policeman in the country paying us a visit ?'. They both sat quiet for a few minutes.

Abe says ' I must be mad. How about this ?. We ask Mrs. Smith to go and see Mr.Mc Vicar at the next Bens game. We get the money and a suitcase which we will handle with gloves and emphasise to Mrs. Smith that it must remain a secret. Mrs Smith will present him with the case and tell him that it is a wee collection towards the stand from folk and business's around Govan. She will tell him we hope to see a really good covered enclosure'. They will have to modify their plans but I cannot really see that being a problem'.
John says' I thought you were a Jew Abe. That is brilliant !!'.
3) The Circus: Abe says ' John, I am unhappy about you having two months off every year on account of the Kelvin Hall Circus !'.
John says ' Well George covers and does a good job does he not ?'.

**SOUTHERN GENERAL HOSPITAL**

**GOVAN ROAD**

**THE VOGUE CINEMA**

**GOVAN TOWN HALL**

Photo 5

# CHAPTER 4
## VOTE FOR ME

Jimmy Welsh enters the Bridgeton Arms and orders a whisky. The barman serves him the drink and he is soon joined by Richard the pub owner. Richard says 'Well Jimmy who is going to win the election ?'. Jimmy says 'Churchill. I hope he is the next Prime Minister. Labour has kept this austerity going too long and it is stifling the country. We still have food rationing and we are in the 1950's !. The sooner they are gone the better. Cannot see where all this nationalisation is taking us and besides there are too many Catholics involved with Labour in Glasgow'.

In Govan the Labour candidate is a local Govan man, Jack Davis, who narrowly lost to Nixon Browne in the 1950 General Election. Davis has the central Govan votes in the bag and campaigns mostly around the shipyards where he is popular. The door opens at Cox's Pawnbroker's shop and in walks William Gibbons (known to everyone as 'Gibby') much to the annoyance of John who is on the desk. 'Hello John. Wait to see what I have for you pal. Feast yer eyes on these'. John says ' Gibby you smell. When is the last time you had a bath?'. Gibby says ' Never mind that. Look at these. How much can you pay ?'.

Gibby put three items on the desk. A brooch; a watch and a charm bracelet. John looked at the items and got out magnifying glass to look at the charm bracelet in particular. He says ' Where did you get these Gibby ?'.

Gibby replies ' I found them in the drystone wall down at the far end of Shieldhall Road. You know I widnae steal them John' and burst out laughing. John says ' I do not like your hyena laugh Gibby; you are an idiot'. John says 'I will ask Mr.Boulton Cox to cast his eye over the items'. John went into the back office and said quietly to Abe ' The charm bracelet looks interesting. Gold on every charm. It must be worth a lot of money'. Abe looked at the bracelet and said 'Offer him 5 shillings; I will phone London and get a value on the bracelet'. John went back out to the shop front. He says to Gibby ' These items were not stolen in any way Gibby were they ?'. Gibby says ' Absolutely not John; honest. You know me'. John says 'That is the problem Gibby, I know you and I do not like you. Nothing personal you are just an idiot !'. John says 'It is fools gold so we will give you 5 pounds for the bracelet. Three Shillings for the watch and Three Shillings for the brooch'. Gibby says 'Is that awe ?. Alright I will take it '. John gives Gibby the money and says 'That should get you a bath Gibby'. Abe listens to the conversation and when John returns to the back office says ' You certainly have a way with the customers John !'. John says 'Abe that charm bracelet must be worth a bit'. The phone rings and Abe gets confirmation based on the information provided that the bracelet is probably worth several Thousand pounds. Abe says ' I will ring PC Mc Cabe.

Mr. Mc Vicar the Benburb Secretary cannot believe his eyes when he opens the suitcase. A typewritten note tells him it is a secret donation on behalf of local business's and Govan folk. He is overwhelmed as is the entire Benburb Football Club committee. The plans are re-submitted and approved. As the stand only overlooks Drumoyne Bowls Club, where several of the Bens committee are active members, no objections are raised. However, it is likely to be a few years before the project progresses.

The Govan Press announces with pride that the new Benburb Football Club covered enclosure will be the envy of all the Junior Clubs and probably most of the Scottish senior clubs. The stand plans are impressive and the Bens supporters are going to be dry while watching the football matches at Tinto Park.

Election day arrives with Jack Nixon Browne still confident. The polls open and a large turnout of voters cast their votes. At the conclusion of voting the count starts and indications are that the voting for Glasgow and Govan in particular will be close. Jack Davis of the Labour Partyis also confident that he could win. During the pre-election period the Labour Party has persuaded the Communist Party candidate to stand down and this should cancel out the Liberal voters who will probably switch to the Unionists.

The Govan count goes on and on. A re-count is ordered. At the Shieldhall Road shops a number of people are gathered waiting for the Evening Times to arrive with the result. The radio has announced that the Govan result is a re-count requested by the Labour candidate; the indications are that Jack Nixon Browne has once again won the seat on a wafer thin majority. The result is confirmed. In Glasgow no seats change hands and Labour win 8 and the Unionists 7. Labour obtain a quarter of a million more votes than the Conservative and Unionist Candidates combined and over 48% of the total votes cast. However the addition of the Independent Liberals plus the official Liberals mean that Clement Atlee's Government has been defeated and Winston Churchill is the new Prime Minister.

**GLASGOW GOVAN:**
JACK NIXON BROWNE (CONSERVATIVE/UNIONIST) 20,936 (50.29%)
JACK DAVIES (LABOUR) 20,695 ( 49.71%)
**NATIONAL:**
LABOUR 48.8% 295 seats
CONSERVATIVE, UNIONIST & INDEPENDENT LIBERALS 48%
321 seats
LIBERAL 3% 6 seats
PC Mc Cabe arrives at Cox's the Pawnbrokers shop. Abe welcomes him in and ushers him into the back office behind the counter. He pours the policeman a cup of tea. Abe says ' Gibby brought these items in yesterday.

a watch and a brooch. The watch is ten a penny and good quality. It would be impossible to know where that watch came from. The brooch has an initial stamp on it although difficult to make out'.

PC Mc Cabe returns to Orkney Street police station and hands in a bag with one item. He says to the sergeant. 'Gibby has been up to his tricks again. He handed this brooch into one of the Govan pawnbrokers. He says he found it inside a dry stone wall'. The sergeant says ' This will be hard to prove as we have had hundreds of low value brooches handed in. Let us see what he hands in next time'.

John is having his last day at the Pawnbrokers before going to his second job at Kelvin Hall for two months. George the stand in pawnbroker is already at the desk.

John says to Abe ' This invitation from the Glasgow Pawnbrokers Association. It says to celebrate 100 years they are hiring a cruiser to sail from Broomielaw down the River Clyde. Sounds good Abe !.
Are you going ?'. Abe says 'No !'. John Says 'I will definitely go it sounds good. Dancing as well as Drinking., Women and Song. What could be better Abe ?'. Abe says 'I rarely drink and I am a confirmed bachelor so no thanks !!'. John says ' I know a couple of wumin that you could go with Abe. You wid love it; let you're herr doon so to speak'. Abe says ' No thank you John. You go and represent the shop. It is good that they have these occasions. The Glasgow Pawnbrokers Association does well. We are the biggest Pawnbrokers Association in the whole of Great Britain apart from London. Glasgow people are well tuned in to the Pawn broking trade.

John returns to his Shaw Street tenement flat where his mother has good news for him. She says 'Look John, you hiv a new clowns outfit. It is identical to Doodles. Jim emerges from the back room in a similar outfit that has been made for his twin brother John. His mother says 'No one can ever replace Doodles the Clown of course. He brought such happiness and joy for thousands of Glasgow weans for decades.

But you two together can remind the customers of Doodles. You can do most of his tricks and you both now look like him. So for this year Jim you are Boodles and John you are Foodles'. Both the brothers started practising juggling with 3 balls in the air followed by passing the balls between themselves at high speed.

Alfred the father arrives in from the Harlands & Wolff Yard and sat down ready for Evening meal. He watched his sons doing all sorts of tricks with the balls. He says ' Funny thing today at the yard. We had a visit from a Detective Inspector called Roy Fletcher. He was asking who does the welding and uses the torches. It seems that there was a robbery some months ago in Central Glasgow when the robbers stole the safe. He was asking in case any of us had been asked to open it'. John listened intently and suddenly dropped one of the balls.

Jimmy Welsh and his wife Joan are arguing. Joan does not like the amount of time Jimmy is working away from Glasgow and wants him to get a local job. Jimmy puts out the feelers and lets his fellow brother Masons know of his interest in finding a new job. He visits the Bridgeton Arms where Richard has asked to see him.

Richard says 'I have a wee bit of good news for you. If you have a word with Bill over there. He is looking to take on a moulding tester at his works. You already have your name on the job if you want it.' Richard continued. Jimmy says 'That is great Richard'. Richard replies 'Now Jimmy, if you get the job you will have to moderate your drinking. I will keep an eye on how much we give you and we stick to it' says Richard. 'Aye that's great Richard thank you' says Jimmy.

Jimmy Welsh starts his new job in Springburn at an alloy supplier to the various firms nearby.

Jimmy is met by Bill the business owner very warmly and taken down to his place of work. Bill enters the workshop and calls the Foreman's name. 'Kenneth, please come and meet James who will be helping us out for a while '. When Kenneth appears he is in shock as is Jimmy Welsh.

It is Kenneth McDonald who Jimmy had once beaten up some years back. Once the initial shock had worn off; Bill says 'Do I take it you two have met one another before ?. Kenneth said 'Yes we have; I believe it was around the Bridgeton Cross area was it not James ?. Welcome on board; we need to start work on testing and clearing as many castings as possible over the next few months'.

John has started his 2 month spell as a Clown with the Kelvin Hall Circus. He is walking along behind the Elephants as they travel slowly from Partick to the hall. The shows start with performances twice a day. Both Jim and John enjoy the occasions and play to packed arenas.

The advanced bookings were at record levels with the Christmas—New Year period already sold out. The two month period for John as a clown soon passes and he returns to his desk at the Golspie Street pawnshop of Abe.

In a Central Glasgow Restaurant John Loizou and Roy Fletcher discuss developments on the missing safe from the robbery over a year previous. Roy says ' This robbery was well planned and the trail is stone cold John. Obviously the robbers have kept a low profile and left no clues.'

John says 'So you are giving up.

We have just lost the money and the safe'. Roy says ' Don'talk to me like that Loizou. I will catch the robbers at some stage. That is what I am paid to do. The only problem we have at the moment is when they are caught they do not get the justice they deserve. The Scottish force caught and had convicted 16 murderers last year. Guess how many got hanged ?'.

John says 'I do not have a clue'. Roy says 'Just f**cking two. Two !'.

I have offered my services to help the hangman carry out the executions but got turned down. I hate criminals and would like to see them pay the ultimate price. We have an unsolved murder from a few years ago when a night watchman got hit over the head during a robbery and died a few days later. Whoever did this robbery may well be paying for it with his life if we can link both crimes'.

Ruth reads the Govan Press and is asked by her father Boab, who is smoking a pipe, if there is anything of interest. Ruth says; 'Not much. There is a good wee story about a great wee piper ,12 years old, from Copland Road School. He has won just about every competition going and has been invited to be the honoury piper for the Knightswood Highlanders Association. His name is Kenneth Mc Donald; his parents must be very proud of him. Some talk about why Govan High School does not do so good with the Dux awards.

I think they won it every year when I wis ther !' Boab says 'Naw they didnae; you are thinking of the Duck award. So what else ?'. Ruth says ' Ther wis a lot of trouble at a house party in 28, Kellas Street wher a few men got battered'. I see they caught the Nylon guy. His name is Sam Craig aged 30 years apparently. I bought a pair of stockings from him down on Govan Road. He rolled them up his arm and they had a lovely seam. A lot of wumin bought the stockings which he put in a bag. When I got back here the stockings had no feet in them !. He got fined £3 or 30 days in jail by Boss the Fiscal'. Lunch time at Boulton Cox's Pawnshop sees John and Abe discussing the Circus events. John says 'You should have come Abe; I would have got you a ticket'. Abe says ' I thought about it but was too busy. What did they have this year ?'. John says ' The clowns were under Reco who has been a great replacement for Doodles. Jim and I were Boodles and Foodles in memory of Doodles' This year we took a lot of children on rides on top of the Shetland Pony; they loved it. They had a Ladder Strongman this year and some great horses and dogs.

The Clowns were brilliant of course but oor jugglin looked poor compared to the proper Juggler'. Abe says 'I will come next year'. John says ' Have you got any family at all Abe ?'. Abe says ' Yes, they are in London. However we had a fall out some years ago and we have lost contact. I still have some business friends who help me with some of the items we acquire of course'. John says 'Remind me how ye managed tae finish up in Govan Abe ? Abe says 'I worked for a trainee valuation clerk in a jewellers shop in Hatton Garden for a while then got a job in a Pawnbrokers. They had a chain of shops up and down the country. A vacancy arose in Glasgow at this shop in Govan and they sent me up to take it on. I had never been to Glasgow before but felt up for the challenge.

The previous pawnbroker had become very ill and actually died within a few weeks of me arriving in Golspie Street. That was around 25 years ago and I have been here ever since.

The Pawnbroker group which owned the shop went out of business before the war. The administrators felt it could be kept as a going concern and they sold the shop to me for one pound'. John says 'Do you not get lonely Abe ?'.
Abe says 'No. I have my record collection and love all kinds of music. I play postal chess and also like the Arts'.

The Fairfields Shipyard and Govan was a sad place when John Whitelaw aged 55 was gassed when the head blew off a Gas Cylinder in the engine room on a new ship. One hundred workers were evacuated and great acts of heroism were displayed in trying to save the trapped people.
A week later there was celebration at the yard when the largest ore carrying ship built in Britain, the Omi Hill, was launched.

At Govan Courts a number of cases were presented. John Fraser, a motor car demolisher, boarded a tramcar with a huge Great Dane dog. Fraser was said in court to be worse for wear with drink and was persuaded by the conductress to go upstairs with the dog. However after a few minutes he came back down the stairs and stood on the boarding platform denying passengers the right to board or get off the tramcar in Paisley Road West. Fraser said ' It wis the dugs fault he is just not used to travelling on tram cars. The Fiscal Campbell fined him 30 shillings or 14 days in jail with 14 days to pay the fine.

At the same Court hearing three boys aged 13,11 and 10 were admonished after they admitted climbing the Plantation Parish Church roof to catch pigeons All three had to be rescued by the Fire Service.

All three claimed they done it because they were threatened by three older boys who said they would get a good 'leathering' if they did not climb.
Five drunk men were singing 'Glasgow belongs to me' on the underground between Copland Road and Govan Cross. One of them; for no explainable reason suddenly smashed his fist through the door panel glass. Bruce Lyden was fined £3 or 14 days jail by Baillie Ralph Stark.
Ruth went with Derek to the shops on Shieldhall Road for the weeks supplies. At one end there is a fruit and flower shop which sells one penny chipped fruit to the children with an ironmongers shop which sells everything imaginable next door. Beyond a stairway to an upstairs flat is the shop of Jimmy the Butcher who remains a jolly and very popular man.

John Leslie requires female companionship for the forthcoming Pawnbrokers Riverboat trip down the River Clyde. He walks down Drumoyne Road in his best suit and a bunch of flowers in his hand. He is exceptionally well groomed and knocks the door of his most recent girl fiend Sandra Chalmers.
Sandra opens the door and sees John with the flowers. She says 'what are you dae'in here John ?'. John replies ' Sandra I hiv been missing you !'.

At that moment Sandra's mother Helen comes out from the living room and stands behind her daughter. She puts her back foot on the bottom stair and listens to the conversation between John and Sandra. Sandra says ' Wher hiv ye been ?'. John replies ' Did ye no get that message I sent up wi the wee boy ?'. Helen butted in ' Ther wis nae message John !'. John says ' So ye didnae get the message. You wait till I see that little'. Sandra says ' The flowers are lovely John. I came down the shop a few times but Abe said you were not in. I asked him to tell you I had called in. Did he not tell ye ?'.

John says ' Abe gets confused sometimes Sandra !. Anyway Mrs Chalmers. Is there any way ye could forgive me for this obvious misunderstanding and allow me the pleasure of inviting you daughter out wae me' . At that point he brought from his back a second bunch of flowers which he gave to Helen. He says ' Mrs Chalmers , you must know how I feel about your daughter. I know this small misunderstanding may have blotted my copybook but if ther is any way and anything I can do to make up then I will move mountains.

Now if you could both think aboot it and I am sure you will both give it careful consideration then please come down the shop or ring us. You have one fantastic , beautiful daughter ther Mrs Chalmers and I can see so many features in yersell wher she got her looks from'. John says goodbye and walks back to his home in Shaw Street. At the Scaffolding firm of John Henderson's in Springburn the husband and wife team which own the company are worried. John Henderson has a thriving business and his wife Sheila plays a vital part in the Management and Administration.

Sheila says ' John, that accident in Edinburgh where three men fell 60 foot down a shaft when the scaffolding collapsed has me worried'. John says ' Sheila that was bad; two men dead and one critically injured. There have been several other accidents recently around Glasgow although fortunately none fatal'.

Sheila says 'I felt happier when Jimmy Welsh was in charge of the Safety issue's. I have been told that a couple of the younger lads we have are taking the odd short cut. One accident due to negligence and we will have no business. We should see If we can get Jimmy back'.

At Fairfields Yard there is much celebration as the yard continues to secure orders for large ships. However a few clouds are appearing on the horizon for the River Clyde shipyards. The British economy is being stifled by a shortage of steel. Albion Motors have laid off workers while awaiting stocks to be replenished and the Shipyards are also suffering.

By contrast the defeated nations in World War 2 have been given considerable help to recover their economies. West Germany had help to quickly get Industrial production started and has a freely accessible steel supply. More ominously for the British Shipyards, Japan has unlimited access to Steel and is already winning orders around the world.

A high profile fighter for the Clydeside shipbuilding industry was Sir James Lithgow.

He was the Chairman of Fairfields Shipyard in Govan and a host of other Shipyard related companies. He also had his own shipyards in Greenock/Port Glasgow. His father had been a part owner of the yards. James Lithgow had a chance of high academic education but chose instead to become an apprentice in the shipyard. Amongst the top management at his companies he was much liked. Amongst his workers he was respected and loathed in equal measures. In any situation he expected anyone who met him for a meeting to be fully prepared with facts. If not the meeting was cut short and the member of staff or workforce told to get out and stop wasting his time. It was said that people waiting to see him were often trembling awaiting their turn to present their case.

On technical matters he had an ability to grasp things quickly and realise the consequences and implications involved in decision making. In his time he accepted some strong technical innovations in his yards which improved the quality of the ships. He much respected some of the workers who would debate things with him on technical matters.

He was not so ready to debate wages with Communists and always drove a hard bargain with the Trade Unions. In addition he and other Shipyard leaders often annoyed the workforce by not acknowledging liability when accidents were due to a fault with the Shipyard procedures.

However, he was a key defender of the Clydeside Shipyards and when, at the age of 69, he passed away at his Glendoch House home at Langbanks he was much mourned. He was to succeeded by his wife until his son William had completed his training period.

A man in a blue grey suit and open neck shirt is stood in the dock of a Courtroom in Edinburgh. He had been expecting to be executed during this very morning but a very late appeal by the defence had bought some time. James Smith had been convicted of the murder of Martin Malone in the Hibernian Club on Royston Road, Glasgow. He had stabbed Malone to death with a knife and also inflicted a serious knife wound to a man called Louden who had survived the attack.

During the trial Smith did not deny that he had stabbed to death Malone at a dance in the Hibernian Club.

However he claimed it was self defence; a claim that was rejected. However the defence were confident their late appeal would succeed.

After all it was found within the last day that the Prosecution had withheld the fact that a second knife belonging to Malone had been found on the Dance Floor. This supported Smith's claim for self defence. Smith's defence wanted as a minimum a re-trial.

The assertion rocked the Scottish Legal system and threw them into turmoil. A re-trial would make them look ridiculous with the situation that the prosecution withheld such a key bit of evidence. Also, the defence team looked amateurish for not asking on their clients (Smith's) behalf, whether someone had not found the knife. The top Scottish judges decided to conduct the appeal in the same way that the jury might have provided the verdict had they known the facts. The execution of Smith was put on hold and he had to wait several weeks to get the verdict on the appeal.

In Govan an elderly lady enters the Boulton-Cox Pawnshop in Golspie Street. It is Mrs O'Hare and she has come to speak to the Pawnbrokers about a silver crucifix she pawned some weeks before. Today is the day the pawn must be retrieved. Abe was at the desk and greeted Mrs O'Hare warmly. 'Nice to see you Mrs.O'Hare, have you come to get your crucifix ?'. Mrs. O'Hare was nervous and immediately went down onto her knees and put her hands in the prayer position. Beneath her head scarf her brow was furrowed with worry and tears ran down her face. She had a well worn coat and her think stockings were wrinkled.

She said, 'Please Abe, can you extend the pawn for another week ?. That crucifix has been in our family for at least 100 years and was given to me by my mother. I have only thrupence I can give you at the moment'. At that moment she bowed her head which almost touched the floor. The queue looked on to see what reaction Abe would provide. Abe thought hard and knew he had to make a decision. He says 'OK Mrs O'Hare we will extend the time period by one week. Please come back and we will discuss it then'. John who was on the next counter smiled.

After the shop closed John said to Abe ' We are not running a charity shop here Abe !! , this is a serious business !'. They both laughed.

A few weeks later James Smith returned to the courtroom in Edinburgh to hear the results of his appeal. He wore the same smart clothes he had on at the start of the appeal. After a very long winded statement read out in court by the judges; Smith had his appeal turned down and a new execution date was set. The execution was duly carried out on the re-arranged day. Smith did not have many sympathisers; after all he openly admitted he went into the Dance Hall with a knife. He did not have the best reputation. After the execution at Barlinnie Prison a notice was placed on the board at the bottom of the hill approaching the main gates.Only a few very sad family members and relatives were there and his father was the only one who walked forward to see what the notice said. He read the statement and walked back to give comfort to the group as they walked away from the prison. At the Glasgow Central Police HQ; Detective Inspector Roy Fletcher was in bubbly mood as he told them how events unfolded at the execution. Although he was not part of the execution party he had been given the job of serving up Smith with his last meal. .

He told his fellow officers. ' I knew he was guilty and it was right that the appeal was rejected. That is how you deal with murderers'.
He scoffed down his breakfast and seemed calm.' One of the police officers said ' Did he say anything to you Roy ?' . Aye. He said, Do ye want bit of toast ?'.
Another officer said ' I think he should have had his life spared; it was a blunder by the Scottish Law System which was really on trial with the appeal.
Alternatively he should have had a re-trial. Malone was also looking for trouble '.

Fletcher says. 'I got invited to the post execution gathering. They said how professional everyone had been and that everything was carried out to the book. We all had a good drink as well; Glasgow is rid of a vicious murderer.
Three young boys boarded the No.4 bus at Paisley Road Toll destined for Govan and went upstairs. Two stops later they decided to get off the bus just as the conductress was coming up the stairs to collect their fares. As they passed on the stairs the two bigger boys made grabs into the conductress money bag. Each took between one and two shillings. The conductress managed to grab one of the boys and a shout alerted other passengers. Two men caught the other two and the bus did a detour to drop them off at Govan Police Station.
In Court The Fiscal Superintendent Boss advised that two of the boys were aged 9 and the other who was with them 7. The seven year old was immediately dismissed from the court. The father of one of the other boys said ' I give him a f**kin good hiding so he wulnae be dae'in that again Superintendent Boss'. The father of the other boy said his son was always well behaved and quiet so it was a surprise that he committed the crime. Both boys were admonished and put on probation for one year.
In the shipyards there was much dismay as the new Government budget announced a reduction in the Steel subsidy from £7,900,00 to £4,500,000 as they pointed the direction of the Nation's future. Much comment was made with further announcements that subsidies in Racing cars would be increased from £25,000 to £40,000; Hotels from £175,000 to £375,000 and watch making and Jewellery from £12,000 to £25,000.
The last announcement was a subject of discussion on the Pawnbrokers Association Riverboat Cruise on the River Clyde. The Waverley paddle boat left Broomielaw and sailed down the river. John Leslie and his girlfriend Sandra stood on the deck looking at the sights along the riverbank. Approaching Govan they passed the Dry Docks where despite being a Saturday work was being carried out on two ships. Ahead John and Sandra could see the large Govan car ferry making a crossing. A few of the passengers on the ferry were waving. However something caught John's eye which annoyed him. An elderly couple were sitting in their car. The rear window was opened to provide a cooling breeze in the warm day. John recognised Gibby adjacent to the back door of the car reaching in and bringing out; very circumspect; the ladies handbag.

He brought out the purse and took some notes before putting the purse back into the bag and the bag into the car. John called out to Gibby from the low in the water Waverley .He shouted up 'Put that f**cking bag back Gibby !'. However the noise of the ships drowned out John's shouts. Sandra said ' Forget it John for now. Let us just enjoy the day and we will report the theft to the police later on'. The couple leaned up against the rail as the Waverley passed by Fairfields.

They sailed past Renfrew Ferry and the waves from their ship went up the slipway. Old Kilpatrick, Bowling and then past Dumbarton Rock. The first stop was Craigendoran where a number of passengers disembarked heading for nearby Helenburgh. A number of passengers got on to have a day trip to Arrochar.

The Waverley set off and serenely turned into Loch Long and onwards to the second and final outward destination, Arrochar.

The Pawnbrokers Association members moved across the road from the pier and on to The Arrochar Hotel. The tables for lunch were laid out and table name tags helped the group  find their places for the meal.

Sitting opposite John and Sandra  were a very friendly middle aged couple. Peter and Cynthia Moriarty Tigwell. Sandra was a bit worried about the protocol and being in such exalted company. Cynthia immediately picked up on Sandra's concern and re-assured her. John said 'I have told her not to worry Cynthia but she does anyway'.

As the day wore on various toasts were given; awards presented. Peter asked John ' How is Abe these days ?. Have not seen him for a while'. John says 'He is still working hard Peter.

He could not make it today so you are stuck with me !. Are you a Pawnbroker ?'. Peter says ' I have many occasions to deal with Pawnbrokers; hence the invitation. However I am the owner of the Boswell Art Galleries in Boswell Street'.

John says ' Very renowned of course Peter !'. Peter says ' Yes we have some superb oil paintings and business has been brisk. Of course we have a few that are virtually priceless including the 'Sad Highlander' by Iain Irvine.

John says ' I imagine having a painting like that in your Gallery must be a security nightmare !!'. Sandra and Cynthia were discussing the dresses some of the other ladies were wearing for the evening. Sandra said 'I wish I could afford a similar dress to that lady over there. It makes her look very elegant'.

John and Peter continued their discussion. Peter says ' Security is of the highest possible. The Gallery and adjacent Studio are on the top floor; there is only one way to get to the top floor and that is by lift.

The lift access to the top floor is by a key switch issued only to security cleared people. The lift lobby is manned 24 hours a day by a security guard and all the windows and doors are alarmed. Now here is the clever bit.

When the alarm is triggered it starts a thing called a timer but it does not sound the alarm straight away, only at the security company. Instead it sounds the alarm ten minutes later and as the thieves run out the police are there to nab them. Ingenious do you not think John ?'.

John replies 'Brilliant Peter. Only a mug would attempt to rob your galleries.'. Peter said ' Yes John. It is a brilliant system and we were provided with it by 'Glasgow Secure'. They were recommended by Scotland's foremost Detective Inspector Roy Fletcher'.

The wine flowed throughout the day into early evening and John and Sandra were on the dance floor The music was provided by a small band of musicians with black bow ties and black suits.

In late afternoon the Waverley was ready for the return trip. After they arrived; John and Sandra boarded the pre-arranged taxi for the journey back to Govan. At the Pawnshop on the following Monday morning John told Abe about the evening and said 'Abe, I think we may have another project coming up !'.

Jeannie and Patrick Deveney of Blackburn Street did not get on well. They argued constantly and one day Patrick ,a labourer, started to chase his wife around their first floor tenement. She escaped and as she ran down the stairs Patrick threw two milk bottles at her. The bottles missed and Jeannie fled to the safety of her mothers. The next day Patrick turned up to Jeannie's place of work and offered her an ultimatum. 'Get back home and look after our five children or I will kill you !'.

A compromise was reached whereby the children went to live with Jeannie's mother while Patrick and Jeannie stayed together for one week only to see if they could patch things up.

A few days later Jeannie's mother, worried about her daughter, knocked on the door of the Blackburn Street tenement and there was no reply. The police were called and on entry found the body of Jeannie Deveney. she had been strangled with Patrick's necktie. Patrick Deveney was soon captured and the subsequent trial lasted just a few days. 'Guilty' was the verdict and Patrick Deveney was given the death penalty.

Golspie Street pawnbrokers ,John and Abe, had the ticket for a number of pawns by Mrs.Deveney. On reading the Evening Times paper John says 'Well Abe, it looks like we have a pawn which will definitely not be collected. What a shame it came to that with 5 children as well. We will sell the necklace and other items and give the money to Jeannie's mother. She will need it !'. Abe smiled and said 'You are a soft touch John !'.

Peter Mc Cafferty was on his way along Govan Road and passed the Govan Cross subway. He was on his way to his home at 26, Helen Street. He decided to enter the Subway and went down the steps to the platform. At the edge of the platform he kneeled down and put his legs over the edge; moving to a sitting position. The stationmaster shouted at him and reacting very quickly switched the power off to the subway railway track.

Within a few minutes Constable Chalmers arrived. Peter jumped down onto the railway track and started to run out of the station towards Merkland Street. Constable and stationmaster gave chase first alerting other police officers to go to Merkland Street station. A number of policemen arrived just in time to see Peter Mc Cafferty arriving in the station. As soon as he saw them he carried on along the tunnel heading towards Partick Cross.

Constable Chalmers and the Govan Cross stationmaster arrived at Merkland Street and joined the now growing posse after Mc Cafferty. After several minutes he was caught and taken to Orkney Street police station. In Govan Court Fiscal Boyd asked Mc Cafferty if he was playing a game of 'Chase the Hare' as he was charged with Breach of Peace. He continued 'Were you drunk?'. Mc Cafferty said 'I must have been. I cannot think of ever having done such a stupit thing'. He was fined £2 or 20 days imprisonment.

It is the day of the execution for Patrick Deveney at Barlinnie Prison who was convicted of the murder of his wife Jeannie. When the sentence was passed he moved quickly from the dock downstairs; he wished the sentence to be carried out quickly. On the morning of the execution, Detective Inspector Roy Fletcher has for a second occasion managed to help by carrying the condemned man's last breakfast to his cell behind two burly prison officers.

The sentence is carried out and Fletcher again attends the post execution gathering. The group go through the procedures and all agree how professional the Scottish machinery of justice operates in such matters. They thanked Roy Fletcher but says his services will not be required for future executions as they have a dedicated officer in place .

The next day Roy Fletcher tells his fellow detectives and police officers of the occasion. He says ' These guys are the true professionals' One of the other detectives says ' I must confess there are times when I could strangle my wife; especially when she visits Lewis's'.

They all laugh. Roy describes how he carried the breakfast tray to the cell. He says 'The breakfast smelled fantastic'. I took it over to Deveney and said 'Here is your breakfast !'. One of the policemen listening said 'What did he say ?'. Roy says ' He said he was not hungry and just wanted to get things over with'.

The same policemen says ' So what did you say Roy ?' I says 'Well you will not mind me eating your breakfast then. I will produce a full report on the food quality. He did not say anything'. Roy continued ' The breakfast was fantastic, probably one of the best I have ever had. As he was led away with the Priest I said to him 'So long Mr.Deveney, I could recommend the Black Pudding !'. One of the detectives said 'You are sick Fletcher !. I am not surprised they will not be asking you back to Barlinnie Prison again for any more executions'. The notice board outside Barlinnie Prison displayed the paper which said the execution had been carried out. There was no person reading it as Patrick Deveney died having few friends; especially around Govan.

# CHAPTER 5
# PLOTTING AND PLANNING

At the back of the Old Harmony Bar a group of men are discussing politics; the group comprises mainly of Labour Party activists and Trade Union officials. They are reflecting on the previous General Election defeat in Govan by the Unionist candidate Jack Nixon Browne. The most prominent of the group is John Gillespie, a shipyard worker who is both a Trade Unionist and an active Labour Party man who is still in his dungarees having just arrived from Fairfields Yard. A middle aged man, weather beaten face and very articulate. He is plotting. 'Well Guys; I have only got over the re-count last time round. However I got over it and we must move on. The unseating of Broon starts noo.

We must plan from now what we have to do to replace him with one of oor ain. Joe a short man with glasses says. ' I thought it was going well. Jack Davis our candidate talked in front of big crowds and was well received all along Govan Road'. Another man present says ' There lies the problem. He was well received along Govan Road but not in the other wards in Govan.

John Gillespie speaks. ' I had a look at the amount of money each candidate put into the election campaign. In Govan we raised barely £400. Broon declared over £700 and it was likely he had a lot more than that.
He had more leaflets and better quality loudhailers than we had'. A few of the others suggested that they only made a little difference. Gillespie came back and says ' the little difference was winning and losing. We lost after a re-count. Every little advantage counts'.

Joe looks over his spectacles , sips his beer  and says. 'Let us face a problem which we do not like to talk about !. This election in Govan is not about politics it is about religion. The wards divide almost into religious groups. A third of the Govan population are Catholic live near Govan Road and they virtually all vote Labour. The better off Protestant areas to the south of Govan; Mosspark, Craigton and Cardonald etc vote Unionist 'en bloc'. The bit in the middle where the poor Protestants live decides the election. Gillespie says ' Where are we talking about Joe ?' Joe says 'I would say the West Drumoyne scheme decides the election.

They vote mainly for Broon especially the women. Quite a few of the skilled tradesmen vote Labour but there are not enough off them'. Gillespie says 'Drumoyne itself is almost 100% Unionist.
When I go there they chase me when I tell them I am the Labour agent'. Joe says ' West Drumoyne has got to be a target ward. Firstly, we must try and get more of the women to change the voting habits of a lifetime. To do this we must get the priests to stay away from the scheme.

They should only go there if necessary. I have already spoken to the Chapel and they have agreed although they are not happy. Secondly we must move the agenda away from Religion and focus on class. The comparison between the lot of the West Drumoyne folk and the lot of Nixon Browne'.

Gillespie says ' It makes sense. We will not get a Labour victory unless we get more Protestant votes'. Joe says ' The second point is we must have a good candidate; someone who appeals to a broader section of the Govanites'. Gillespie says 'One thing that will work against us is the end of austerity. The Tories will equate Labour with austerity and themselves as the party that ended it. There must be some women in West Drumoyne who would consider voting Labour and getting us a victory !'.

At 31 Daviot Street, West Drumoyne, Ruth is sitting at the table reading the Govan Press. Derek plays on the floor with 20 lead soldiers all identical . She says to Boab her father 'Da, I was doon in Govan last week and the Labour man was saying they want to help West Drumoyne. I told him it was not before time. He says he thinks they will get Nixon Browne out at the next election'. Boab says 'It would be good if they did ' he spends too much time doon in London wae his pals and not enough time in Govan. The Shipyards are becoming short of materials; especially steel.

In the Boulton Cox pawnbrokers; Abe asks John about his project. John gives him details and asks Abe about paintings. Abe says 'Peter Moriarty Tigwell does a very good trade at the Boswell Galleries. He always presents 'The Sad Highlander as his top painting. It is always prominently displayed and he even has a light shining on it. John says 'What is the Sad Highlander ?'. Abe says ' The Sad Highlander is a painting by Iain Irvine . He painted it around 70 years ago and it is worth a lot of money. There are replica's of the painting which are also good and Peter has a couple behind the gallery.

The painting depicts Bonnie Prince Charlie being led through the streets of Inverness on a horse after the Battle of Culloden. The Highlander who leads his horse has a very sad face hence the name the "Sad Highlander". He seemed to know it was the end of the man born to be King'. John says 'How much is the painting worth ?'. Abe says ' A minimum of £20,000'. John says 'If someone wanted to dispose of a painting like this one for reward and remain circumspect ?'. Abe says 'Amsterdam'. So what obstacles have we got to overcome' Abe continued:

- The Boswell Galleries are located on the top floor.
- The only access is by lift and a special key to operate.
- All doors and windows are alarmed.
- There is a Security Man on Reception 24 hours a day.
- The windows have bars and the doors very thick.

Abe says 'So how do we do it ?'.
John says 'Nae bother !'.

A young lady enters the Plaza Cinema on Govan Road with her friend; in fact it is the sixth evening in a row she has attended with a different friend. Miss Margaret Thomson aged 32 was able to tell her latest friend that was her appearing in the film 'The Kilties are coming'. Margaret lived at 32, Peniver Drive, Govan and was proud of her small part in the film.

On Govan Road there was a commotion. Chris King was driving his bus and tried to overtake the bus driven by John Gibson. Gibson saw some glass on the road and swerved to avoid it forcing Chris King to perform an emergency stop. Both drivers got out of their cabs and had a fierce argument. King says 'We will settle this man to man when we get back to Govan Cross;.

When the drivers arrived back at Govan Cross they went to the drivers room and King immediately sets about Gibson.

King delivered some fierce punches knocking out Gibson who was quickly rushed to the Southern General Hospital. In court Fiscal Robertson sentenced King of 30 Copland Road to a fine of £5 or 30 days in prison.

Abe and John have had a busy day on the counter of their Golspie Street pawnshop.

Abe has struggled throughout the day with breathing problems and coughs at regular intervals. John has told him frequently that he should consider cutting down on cigarette smoking. Abe usually does for a few days then returns to his normal habits. His fingers are stained with nicotine. It is questionable whether he will be at work the following day as he wheezes loudly.

It is approaching closing time and two friends of Abe arrive. The taller man is Roger Joseph, the other Moshe Steinberg. Moshe is an Orthodox Jew and wears a hat as well as sporting a lengthy black beard. John opens the narrow door to the back office to let them in as Abe says 'Hello Mr.Joseph , come on through !'. Roger walks through but makes no acknowledgment to John. Similarly with Moshe.

Roger sits down and says to Abe. 'How is business Abe ?. Moshe will tell you we have had some fantastic income over the past few weeks. At Tradeston we get a 25% commission on every deal in a new coffee brand for making the proper arrangements Supplier to Customer'.

Abe struggles for a few seconds to catch his breath and says ' That is good Roger'. John goes to the front of the shop and puts the closed sign facing outward. He goes to the back office and says ' Sorry to interrupt Abe. I am off to practice for the Circus tonight. Goodbye Mr. Joseph and Mr.Steinberg'. Both Roger and Moshe totally ignore John's farewell. He closes the shop door and heads to Drumoyne Road to see Sandra for an hour before going for Circus performance practice.

46

The next day Abe has arrived for work. John says ' You should not have come in today Abe; you are not a well man'. Abe says ' I will be all right John !. John one reason I made a special effort to come in today was to apologise to you. I did not like the way Moshe and Roger did not show any respect or manners to you.

Please do not think all Jews are like this they are not. If you ever meet my Rabbi you will find a totally different person. He despairs with the Rogers and Moshe's of this world.

He feels we are the chosen people and we should behave accordingly'. John says ' They are a strange couple of men Abe; but you need not apologise, it is not your fault. The Orthodox fella does seem particularly strange. I have seen him read a book and almost stoat his head off a wall before.

The one thing I did not like was the fact that they saw you are not well which was obvious and the first thing he talks about is your business. A Govan person would always enquire after your well being first and probably offer to help you if they could. This type of Jew seems to be only interested in business and, if I may say so, are very arrogant with it'.

The River Clyde shipyards continue to receive large volumes of orders. The Liners orders are drying up but they have been replaced by cargo vessels.  In the Linthouse Shipyard office of Sir Murray Stephen, he sits behind his desk with the apprentice manager and several departmental managers. They are carrying out a revue on the training of the next batch of apprentices.
Sir Murray says' We are losing many of our better skilled engineers to yards abroad. We must consider the training of our lads and make it top notch. OK, I like the idea we currently have of scheduling them for a fixed period in most of our departments.

You department managers have an important role here in putting yourselves out to encourage them. Who knows in a few years time they could be well earning over £1,000 per year. The one day release at Stow College is good also and they can progress to the appropriate Craft City and Guilds Certificate. The quality of the finished apprentices at this yard is second to none and we must make a big effort to keep them on when they finish. Thank you for your efforts'.

The gates  at Govan High School opened and the entire number of pupils came out in two's. They were not going too far; a short walk along Langlands Road to the Vogue Cinema. Awaiting them on the stage was the Lord Provost of Glasgow Tom Kerr accompanied by George Blair the school headmaster and his assistant Mr. Bell. On stage they were presented to the two head pupils Isobel Beswick and Campbell Mc Lelland.
Provost Kerr spoke about the Govan Fair, its traditions and the importance of the event to the burgh of Govan.

He commented on the success of the School's football teams and the work put in by the hard working teachers. Over many years Tom Kerr was a staunch supporter of the Govan High school; he had of course been a former pupil. He was held in affection by most of the Govan populace having represented the Fairfield ward as an independent Labour councillor. He loved Govan and was an officer with Benburb Football Club.

At 31 Daviot Street Boab asks his daughter Ruth where his second waistcoat chain is. Ruth says ' Aye Da ; I pawned it for a few days' Boab says 'Whit, yer not that hard up ur yeh ?'. Ruth says 'Aye but I will be able tae get it back on Friday when I get some money'. Boab says ' Whit is fur tea ?'.
Ruth says 'Tripe again I am afraid' .

Ruth says ' I wis speakin tae a Labour guy doon in Govan. He thinks like others that his party should do mer fur the people of West Drumoyne. He wis sayin that we will be getting a new Candidate and definitely one with Protestant leanings'. Boab says 'Whatever religious leanings we are we should vote on who looks after us best. It is definitely not Jack Browne the Unionist we need.

The countdown to Derek starting school has begun. Ruth has got him new clothes and shoes to wear ready for the first day. However it is a summer Friday morning and there is a commotion at the door of the first floor landing tenement at 31, Daviot Street.

At the door are around 6 members of the McHarg family and they are angry. Ruth is trying to appease them but having no luck.
The McHarg's live on a corner tenement on Meiklewood Road opposite the swing park. They are probably the largest family in West Drumoyne with 4 boys and 4 girls.

The children sleep 4 to a bed with head and feet alternate at each end of the bed to give more space. However as the children get bigger one or two are waking up with feet in their face. Mrs Alice Mc Harg arrives and talks to Ruth. They get on well and have always been friends. 'Ruth that is an awful thing Derek has done !, He could have taken Jim's eye oot'. Derek had got into an argument with the McHargs and thrown a stone at them. It caught the youngest McHarg on the top of his shoulder narrowly missing his head. 'I know Alice I have already battered him and told him not to do anything like that again.' Ruth had hit Derek around the legs and also around the head. She was fuming with her son.

Mrs. McHarg has blond hair and a reddish face from being in the sun. Ruth summons Derek to the door. She says 'Derek, Say sorry to Mrs McHarg. Derek still tearful after his thrashing says 'Sorry Mrs Mc Harg I did not mean it to go so close'. The one lesson that Derek learned from the episode is never get in a fight with a big family especially one like the McHargs.

With them if you picked a fight with one you were up against them all. Soon Derek and the McHargs were on good terms and they helped out in a protective way when the need arose.

Ruth has attended a school meeting for parents of the first years. The first years are 5 years old and attend half a day only. 'Derek you will be pleased !. Your teacher Miss McLaughlan was my teacher when I was at Drumoyne. Derek, having Miss McLaughlan is a great thing. She will give you plenty of education and you will become clever !.

Derek walked through the gates for the first time of Drumoyne School in Shieldhall Road. On arriving at the classroom they are greeted by Miss McLaughlan. She ushers the children in and over to a giant Dolls house in the corner. Derek cannot get near it with all the girls having prime position. Miss McLaughlan is sweetness and light to all the mums and says how pleased she is to be teaching their little boy or girl. She was well versed in the art of assurance provision to the parents. However, as soon as the mums are out of view from the Drumoyne School gates the atmosphere changes. 'Now sit down children and be quiet. A noise still existed but this was silenced by a crack of a wooden ruler on the desk. The smiling face had changed quite suddenly and the 1st Year children soon knew they were in for the learning

The year is 1953 and the King dies. There is a Coronation and all the children at Drumoyne school are given a tin of sweets with the face of Queen Elizabeth on the front. Derek thinks immediately that once the sweets are gone he will have a first class tin to put his bools in' .

Drumoyne School is proving to be hard work for Derek. Miss McLaughlan has shown the children the strap a very thin tawse to inflict punishment. 'You do not have to worry children, only bad behaving boys and girls will get punished'. Miss McLaughlan is a middle aged lady.

She is tall and has pointed features and Derek thinks she looks very similar to a witch he had seen at the pictures. Derek is struggling to grasp things as fast as Miss McLaughlan would like and the day of judgement duly arrives. All the children, bar Derek, have got a small piece of work with numbers correct. 'Get out here Derek !'. 'You have obviously not been paying attention.

Put out your hand ! '. 'Whack' a single strap on the hand for Derek who is stunned'. The school bell goes for a milk break. Derek does not want any of the other children to see that he is crying so decides to run and run and run. Around the playground he ran and he was going to tell his mother about this.
Lunchtime arrives and Derek is met at the gates by his mother. She can see he is unhappy and has been in tears. 'Whits the matter Derek ?'. 'Maw I got the strap today, but I did not do anything '. Ruth said ' But ye do not go to school to do nothing and whacked him on the legs'.

'Miss McLaughlan is a good lady and a first class teacher. She taught Jack and me. Now you get back in there tomorrow and start listening to what Miss McLaughlan is saying and stop dreaming'.

Robbie has moved to Canada to join Jack and seek a better life. He finds it hard to settle but remains for the time being in Toronto, Canada. Robbie and Jack send Derek parcels of comics; the pages on the Canadian comics are huge in comparison to the Scottish issue's.

At 31 Daviot Street, there is a bit of excitement. Ruth has been struggling getting back into work after 5 years out looking after Derek. Now a potential breakthrough has come along . Ruth has been offered a job at Jimmy Deakins Laundry over in Partick . Jimmy Deakin is a relative of the Mc Dougal family who live opposite No.31 in Daviot Street.

Ruth is excited. 'Derek son, this is going to be great ! A job at last !. There will be more money coming in again. We will get doon to Govan and get some decent clais frae the Co-op. You can have a good pair of sandles, trousers, shurts and a new set of braces. I will be getting a new skirt and matching top, a good quality jumper and a nice blouse. I will be one of the gallas girls, won't that be great Derek ?'.

Ruth starts her new job which is near the Merkland Street subway station. Ruth has got the bus to Govan Cross, one stop to Merkland Street and then along the Clydebank Road to Jimmy's premises. The Laundry is set underneath a tenement block and the first impression Ruth has is the amount of steam coming out of the door. Inside there are a couple of ladies working on the presses and an elderly man doing fetching and carrying.

Jimmy welcomes Ruth and introduces him to the 3 other staff members. It is a tiny laundry and clothes piles up everywhere. Jimmy says Brenda and Ella are good workers. Auld Jock over ther is useless. He is slow and his eyes are bad. He has to wear thick glasses which get steamed up at various points in the shop'. Once you are up and running, we will pension auld Jock off'. Ruth looks around at her new environment. Perhaps not the best but it is a job and it provides more money than the pittance offered by the 'broo'. After the first few days Ruth is exhausted. She sits down next to the fireplace and stokes the fire in a dream.

'How is the job Maw ?' says Derek. 'Hard work son'. Boab comes into the living room and asks Ruth the same question and gets the same answer. 'Some of them bags of laundry are very heavy. One of the ladies has a bad back so she cannot help and the other is permanently on ironing and pressing. So it's me and an old guy who lift the clothes around. Jimmy is nice though and keeps everything ticking along. They are very busy so I should have the job for a while yet. Boab says 'I have had a wee note from the school Ruth fur ye' . Ruth opens it and a message says it offers the parents the chance to speak to the teachers on the last day of the teaching year.

50

A meeting of the Trade Unionist officials takes place in the Old Harmony Bar. It is unofficial but John Gillespie a Labour Party official is listening intently. The local party are proposing to fight the General Election on purely class grounds and try as far as possible to keep religion out.

Frank Mulvenney is a Communist and very popular with most around the yard. He is a good speaker at meetings and seems to have a grasp of politics.

Frank has been given a slot to address the audience which grows by the minute as workers arrive from the yards. He says ' so, at long last we are going to fight an election on class ! Not before time ! The people that run this country are a total disgrace; they think they are better class but they are not. There is a college in England where the class folk have to put there names down when they are born. Yes when they are born !.

It does not matter whether they are intelligent or not they will go to this particular college. Now the college want them to stand out and guess what ?'. John Gillespie says 'What'. Frank continued 'They dress them like penguins to make them look different from everyone else !.

Most of them are inbreds because they cannot be seen to mix with the rest of us. Hence like most inbreds they are f**kin dense !. The fact they dress them up as penguins gives the game away. It is an insult to the penguins who have more f**kin brains !'.

The whole pub roars with laughter. Frank downs some beer and continues 'Aye there are a few intelligent ones in this group. It is said 10% are normal and the other 90% abnormal. Now hear this.

They have their own song and there own game. It is a wall game they have invented and do you know the score of this years match ?. Dae ye ?. I know it was 0-0. How do I know it was 0-0 ?. Because it has been 0-0 for the last 200 years. This stock are no capable of scoring a goal !!. They are dense !. Now if ye go doon tae the 50 pitches the teams there have no problem scoring goals. The pub again burst into rapturous laughter.

We are normal people; they are abnormal people by and large. The shipyards produces men who work hard and have fantastic skills which should be better rewarded as I have said many times before. The college I refer to produces people who rule this country. Why ? Because the working classes allow themselves to be divided and it is easy to pit one worker or group off against another.

If the people of Govan fight the election on class then Browne can start packing his bags. There are more poor people in Scotland than Lords and Lairds. Lets work hard, stay united and put the boot up their pin striped backsides !'.

The people in the pub roared their approval. After the noise had died down John Gillespie said 'What about Tom Kerr; the Lord Provost ?'

Frank said 'Tom is a good man that is for sure. However, he has been bought off with title and no longer holds the ambition to help us '.

John says 'There is talk about boundary changes and we are not sure how these will affect us. Unlike the last elections when former Labour MP Neil McLean was de-selected causing a split; this time we will be united behind one man whoever he is. Let us hope he is good and prepared to look after the interests of the Govan folk'.

Frank says' Sorry to have to disillusion you guys. I think the incoming Labour guy will probably be like the others !'.

At Jimmy Deakins laundry there is a commotion a few days later. Jimmy has summoned the four staff together. 'Jock, whit are we going to do with you ?. The other day you gave Mrs McKenzie's washing to Mrs Mc Kendrick and now this pointing to a huge pile of clothes on the floor. Jock has very thick glasses that look like the bottom of milk bottles.

Jock says 'I am sorry Jimmy, The 66 ticket dis look identical to the 99 ticket and I thought they were the same order !.

Ruth says 'We should be able to sort it out Jimmy. The first lady with the 66 ticket has two girls and the 99 ticket has only one son. I have seen each of them in the outer clothing when they have come in the shop before so that is easy'. Jimmy says 'Fair point Ruth but what aboot the men's simmits and long johns.

' I am afraid all we can do is get all the items nicely folded and let the first of the two ladies pick out her laundry order.

Jimmy handled the situation brilliantly saying sorry to the first of the two ladies who duly picked out her laundry items. He provided her with a voucher to Jimmy Deakins Laundry with the first six items washed free. When Ruth returns home later that evening she tells her dad Boab of the mix up. He laughs and has to put his pipe down.

Ruth turns up to the school having agreed with Jimmy Deakin about the time required off. Jimmy is understanding and Ruth works on later in the evening. Miss McLaughlan is all sweetness and smiles to the mothers as she always is; charm personified. She says 'Ruth, Derek has done well in his first year; he is a bright wee boy. At the beginning I had to give him a wee strap because he thought he was here to play and not learn.

He was alert at playtime but not in the class. Ever since then he has improved and is good with numbers. I am very pleased with him and I am sure he will do well once he goes into Miss Doig's class.' 'Ruth says ' Miss Doig !. As well as you she was also one of my teachers !.

Derek will go through school with all the same teachers I had !. Another one Ruth is Mr Scott the music teacher . 'Now is he not a fine looking man?.' says Ruth.

They both laugh.  So Derek's path to the next year is set at Drumoyne School.
Ruth relays what Miss McLaughlan has said to Derek who is pleased. I am
pleased your doing well Derek, keep it up. Then you will become clever.
Perhaps one day a man will come into my life and you will have a brother and
sister.  Perhaps our family will have a good house down at Ayr with swings in
the garden facing the sea.  Just perhaps Derek.
In the distance down Shieldhall Road there was the faint sound of drums
followed soon by flutes and pipes.

It was a sizable Orange Walk walking down the road towards the Shieldhall
Road shops from the Craigton Road crossroads. The sides of the roads had a
fair number of people clapping and cheering them on. Just before the Shieldhall
Road shops they turned left and marched around the swingpark.  It was a
spectacular sight of colour with huge banners and red,white and blue aplenty.

Derek was fascinated by the drum major throwing a large baton in the air,
catching it and twirling it round behind his back. The bands kept coming, one
after another, the top floors of the West Drumoyne tenements were a sea of red
white and blue and through the open windows the tenants cheered . The
brilliant sunshine made the occasion more colourful as they wheeled right
down Meiklewood Road.

Soon they were at Andy's Café and crossing the road into Cardonald Park;
onwards past the 50 pitches changing rooms; a left turn up towards the Plots
and then the march ended with a big rally in the big field next to the railway
line. For the most of the residents in West Drumoyne it was good
entertainment.

However for the minority Roman Catholic and Southern Irish tenants  it must
have been a miserable day.
Ruth had an intense hatred of anything Roman Catholic. The reasons were
difficult to fathom. Perhaps her mother Lizzie Lutton; who was a Northern Irish
Protestant may have had the influence.

Whatever hatred Ruth started with would have increased with the viewpoints
of Jimmy Welsh who was part of the parade walking through West Drumoyne.
Like a flock following the Pied Piper many of the West Drumoyne tenants
followed the Orange march into Cardonald Park and several hours of
entertainment was provided.  Jimmy Welsh was at the march. Although not  so
involved with the Orange movement, he supported the 'cause'.

Ruth and Jimmy met up at the Orange Order gathering in Cardonald Park and
caught up with the latest news.  Jimmy was saying how much he had missed
Ruth and how he had gone to Blackpool, reluctantly, recently  with Joan but
only to benefit the kids.
Ruth told him of the good holiday they had at Millport.

Ruth says 'I think Derek will make a good Orangemen when he grows up. He does not play with any Catholics yet'. 'It is important to remember the reasons we are who we are' said Jimmy. 'Our brothers and sisters in Ulster are us and they need our support Ruth', he continued.

Of course all references in regard to the rights and wrongs of the Orange Order were above the head of Derek. However, advice of a different kind was forthcoming to Derek which was to balance up the scales in his views forever. It came from other sources.

Boab, Robbie and Jack attended the gathering but only for the social aspects of it. There they met the neighbours from the estate. All three supported the Protestant cause in Ulster but all three had a totally different viewpoint on Roman Catholics. They told Derek to ignore their mother and play with whoever he wants. 'Ignore the fact that they are Roman Catholic' says Robbie. 'Treat them just as you would anyone else and do not discuss religion. Just play with who you like' he continued.

The gathering over, the West Drumoyne residents returned home in early afternoon; the various Orange Bands boarding busses to take them back to various parts of Glasgow and beyond.

Derek started his second year at Drumoyne School with Miss Doig his new teacher. Miss Doig had previously had Ruth and Jack as pupils many years before and was polite to Ruth. She was a career teacher, thoroughly professional and had the class content set out after many years of practice. She wore a broach and had swept back hair. One feature which soon became apparent was the first lessons were not reading, counting or writing. They were manners and respect. Miss Doig produced a small book of stories which she read out and explained. The first short lesson was 'Respect all other human beings'.

In particular she emphasised the respect that should be shown to the Roman Catholics at the St.Constantine School. ' They are ordinary children like you are and they are good people'.

So the second piece of advice from two totally different sources at an early age shaped Derek's viewpoint of the religion differences. Miss Doig rarely, if ever, mentioned the word Catholic unless it came up in a school context. She went on to manners and gave examples such as always hold doors open for people and never put dirty feet on the train seats etc. Under Miss Doig Derek and the rest of the class flourished and learned very quickly. The pens were wooden with nibs and there was an inkwell on each desk. Practice after practice went in to writing and chanting out the times tables. Nothing scientific just complete repetition until it was engrained in the mind.

Ruth wants to go into Govan catching the 4a bus at the Shieldhall Road crossroads bus stop.

As they pass the Govan High School buildings on the right Ruth says 'Look Derek, in some years time that is the school you will be going to when you leave Drumoyne. They will make ye cleverer than you are now'. They pass the Vogue Cinema, the Elder Park library and soon come to slow traffic. Govan is a busy place.

The streets are packed with people on a Saturday morning visiting the shops along Langlands Road and also in Govan Road. As the bus eventually reaches Govan Road they must stop as the tramcar in front stops to allow the passengers to get off. In the distance Derek can see the Plaza picture house with a big board on the wall displaying the films currently being shown Derek I have wee surprise for you' says Ruth. You know we lost Darkie a while back, well Robbie, Jack and I have decided to by a budgie'. They visit the pet shop in Shaw Street and emerge with a green budgie with a yellow head'.

Ruth had recently left her job at Jimmy Deakins laundry after being offered a position as a home help. Her help rota took her to a variety of usually old ladies in various parts of Govan and also Cardonald.   Ruth say's ' This is a great wee budgie Derek as she carried it out the shop in a cage covered by a towel. The man was saying it is great wee whistler !' Derek is carrying a box of Trill budgie food and excited at seeing his new pet. A green and yellow Budgie quickly named 'Joey.

# CHAPTER 6
## THE SAD HIGHLANDER

The moment of truth has arrived. John and Abe are about to carry out their first project into the world of Art. The Boswell Galleries, which is owned by Peter Moriarty Tigwell and his wife, are located high above Boswell Street in Central Glasgow .The only entrance is via a lift which is key operated to the top floor Gallery. Abe stands circumspect in a doorway on the opposite side of the street from the gallery. It is 10 o clock at night and Glasgow streets are still busy with the pub drinkers.

John enters the block opposite Glasgow Central Station and when there is no one about easily forces the door lock. He closes the door behind him and climbs the stairs to the roof. The fire escape door is easily opened and he produces a small torch from his pocket which he shines on the ground. He walks over the roof tops and enters the Lift Motor Room above the Boswell Galleries. He shines the torch onto his wrist watch; all so far has gone to plan. The preparation and surveys had taken weeks; the execution of the first phase had taken just a few minutes.

Ten minutes later he looked over the top of the roof parapet and Abe immediately saw his torch signal. The reply was to operate his lighter and both were now in communication. Geoff the night watchman sitting at the building security desk was reading the latest edition of the Evening Times.

He had some catching up to do also with the daily papers. John entered the Otis Lift compound and opened the big control panel. Relays 36 and 37 on the circuit board were large and could be unplugged. At 11 o'clock; Geoff raised himself from the seat and called the lift. It was the two hourly inspection of the Boswell Galleries.

John was waiting for a signal from Abe who had seen Geoff walk towards the lift. Abe lit his cigarette and John went scampering back across the short section of roof into the lift motor room.

He had his stop watch ready and once the lift doors had closed John knew that 12 seconds later the Night Watchman would be between the first and second floors. At precisely 12 seconds John pulled Relay 36 which stopped the lift and the motor stopped. Relay 37 disabled the call alarm.

Geoff felt the lift come to a halt and started pressing the buttons. He pressed the call button but nothing happened. The telephone which was activated by the call button did not operate. He was relieved the lights were still on. He called out 'Its Geoff here !. Level 2'. However with the building empty he realised no one would hear him. He sat down on the carriage floor of the lift.

John lifted up the wooden cover and looked down the lift shaft. He was skilled at climbing with ropes from his circus work.

He put a sack around his shoulders and lowered himself down until opposite the doors of the top floor gallery; just one floor down from the lift motor room. He had the 90o key to unlock both the top and bottom latches. From his sack he produced two car jacks and after prising at the top and bottom of the doors slipped them into position. He then used the tommy bar to open the doors a small movement at a time; first top then bottom.

Soon he was able to enter through the door into the Art Gallery. The Sad Highlander was facing him lit up by a light above the picture. John produced a cheap copy of the portrait and exchanged it with the genuine article. How long would it be before Moriarty-Tigwell would spot the change he thought !. John then retraced his steps; the whole project had taken around quarter of an hour. He cleaned up any grease from the ropes. Soon the Lift shaft doors were closed and John with the car jacks and portrait was looking down the lift shaft. Geoff had not heard anything or detected any movement in the lift carriage. He gave out another call, ' Level 2, It is Geoff here.' John was about to embark on the part of the job he feared most; re-instating the relays. He pushed in Relay 37 first. No problem. He pushed in Relay 36. A few blue flashes but the relay stayed in and the lift was now operational. Geoff was relieved as the car came up to the top floor.

John put the hatch down and made his escape across the roof. Abe was waiting for him in an appointed space in Boswell Street in a car and off they went. Geoff entered the Galleries and after a cursory look around re-entered the lift praying there would be no more mishaps.

John and Abe were delighted as they opened the Golspie Street Pawnshop the next day with the Portrait of the sad Highlander. Abe said 'George has agreed to work for a few weeks in a month's time. We will make arrangements for a trip to Amsterdam'.

At Govan Courts a couple appear in front of Justice Donald. The wife alleges that husband used jujitsu on her. The husband alleges that the wife threw a bottle at him. Both alleged similar instances and the wife said she had been assaulted.

The trial went on for several minutes.

Justice Donald intervened and said ' For the sake of your children are you both prepared to let bygones be bygones ?'. They both looked at one another and slowly a smile appeared on each face. A few minutes later they left the court hand in hand.

Cowiesons one of the larger Building Contractors started shedding labour due to shortages of materials; an on going feature.

'. At 31, Daviot Street Robbie and Jack have returned from Canada and seem set to remain in Scotland. A few weeks after the Orange parades, Derek asks 'Who is the soldier on the horse ?' Ruth replies 'That is King Billy son, on his horse. He beat the Catholics and they didnae forget it

It is a shame they could not get a hundred or so King Billy's and get them to ride down the Irish Channel doon in Govan.

Daviot Street does not hiv too many Catholics and long may that continue '.

'Ruth that is stupit talk; stupit talk. You know as well as we do that the Catholics have nae chance of getting many of the jobs in Govan jist because they are ...... Catholics ! ' says Jack.

'Welsh likes the Orange  Order Ruth. All we are saying is let Derek eventually think things through for himself ' says Robbie.  Boab says ' Well we are not a religious family and Christ almighty, is the Catholic Church any worse than some of the other churches in Scotland? Some of them folk are weird to say the least.

Robbie was  well read and had a good if not excellent knowledge of history and also in particular politics. He said ' A lot of the stuff the Orange Order put around is not entirely true. Somewhere through time the facts get mixed up and we have what we have now.  Firstly, William of Orange (King Billy) was not the great fighting leader depicted on the banners.

He did not win any battles at the head of an Army apart from the River Boyne.' Robbie continued, ' At the Battle of the Boyne King Billy was opposed by the man he took the throne from; King James. William`s army was around 35,000 and James` 25,000. In relative terms this was a big battle for the period; both armies had many foreigners.

At least 5 or 6 thousand Frenchmen fought for James alongside an Irish Catholic army and a considerable number of Dutch, English and Scots  joined the Ulstermen on Williams side. William`s army was better equipped and had a slight advantage in soldier quality; some of the foot soldiers on James side were little more than peasants with pikes.

Despite such a huge number of soldiers and the type of battle fought the casualty figures were very low on each side with a combined total of just over 2,000 lost. So the 'Up to our knees part of the song' is a myth. Once the battle went decisively against them the Irish Catholics fought a skilled withdrawal all the way down to Dublin.

After the fighting the talking started  and the Irish Catholic landowners were given back their land. The one big loser in the battle was James.

He fled the field of Battle and it is said he arrived in Dublin before anyone else and quickly sailed to France. William of course fell off his horse not so long after and was killed.

It is also likely that the Pope at the time backed the army of William of Orange as they were both part of the 'Grand Alliance'; a group of interested parties and countries united to counter expansion by France.

It is the Top Floor landing on the tenement block of James Street and Jimmy has arrived at the door of his flat to find his suitcase outside the door. Joan has had enough of his drinking and she wants him to go. Since leaving his job as an alloy tester in Springburn Jimmy has had some casual work with John Henderson, his former business partner, who runs Henderson and Mc Coll. Prior to the war Jimmy had a small stake in John Henderson's business. However immediately after the war John bought his share in the business, with Jimmy Welsh struggling to re-adjust to life outside the forces. John has a flourishing business with a number of good contacts in Glasgow Corporation and also the Commercial buildings in Central Glasgow.

His work standard is good and he has a high regard for Jimmy. When they were in business together, Jimmy did a lot of the site erections and put great emphasis on Health and Safety. He outlawed 'bombing' where the scaffolder throws poles and struts into a space which has been left clear.
He insists the poles/struts/castors must be passed down by hand to hand. John is aware of Jimmy's problems with drink and insists that he does not go anywhere near a site while under the influence.

Jimmy adheres strictly to the request. The drink problem he has causes frustration to all that know him. He could go several months without touching a drop. Even in the Bridgeton Arms, Richard provides him on occasions with soft drinks for weeks on end. However, once he starts drinking he does not seem to be able to stop and a spiral of drunkenness lasting days occurs. The brake which ends things is eventually running out of money.

Now Jimmy has to find somewhere to stay for the evening. Joan has told him to come back once he has sorted his drink problem out. He staggers back to the Bridgeton Arms and Richard opens the door as they are beyond closing time. Jimmy explains what has happened. Richard says 'We will put ye up for the night Jimmy and sort things out tomorrow'. He has a bed made up in the bar seats and Richard and his wife go upstairs to the flat above the pub.

The next morning Richard and Jimmy discuss the options then Richard says. Nan was in yesterday with another wee message for you from Ruth. 'I was just going to contact Ruth through Nan' says Jimmy. 'Instead I will go over to Govan and see her' he continued. Derek is starting to go through the routine at Drumoyne School. Bell summons the children to the classroom.

The school is bitterly cold and the classroom doors are a bit of a hazard as the winds sometimes make them slam. There is talk of a wall and glass being built as a shelter for the classroom doors, providing a corridor. Everyone thinks that would be a good idea as even with the doors shut and the radiators at full heat the classrooms are cold. The teachers tend to always wear pullovers and woollies during the winter.

Just prior to morning playtime a crate full of small milk bottles arrive and straws are issued to the class. They have a small knife which the teacher uses to cut through the bottle seal allowing the straws to be inserted into the bottle.

At lunchtime most of the class go home and a small number stay to have the school meals. Derek always goes home and returns after around three quarter of an hour to play 15 minutes or so of football in the playground. Afternoon playtime is usually 15 minutes and again a football session unless the weather is really bad. Four o clock bell ends school for the day and the children return home to their nearby homes.

It is to Govan that Jimmy Welsh has arrived and he has asked to see Ruth that evening through the contact Nan who works in a nearby office in Bridgeton. He then is put in touch with a landlord who has properties around Govan.

There he is provided with 'a single end' at 20, Craigton Road opposite the McGregor Memorial Church. A single end is a single room with a wash sink and a small alcove where the bed is usually located. It will take him a few days to get decent furniture and bed covers so he plans to return to Richards for a few evenings; Richard having already made the offer. Ruth and Jimmy meet outside his pending new abode. 'Ruth I have decided to leave Joan !' he says.

'As I have said to you before, she does not really understand me and I am afraid I have tried to make the marriage work for long enough'. he continued. ' Well Jimmy this is a bit of a surprise'. 'What prompted this to happen ?' 'Ruth I have felt for a long time that she needs to calm herself down.

Sometimes she is demented and shouts. This upsets William and Mary'. Ruth says 'Jimmy are you sure you are telling me everything ?' 'Of course Ruth' he says and continued 'I must go to pay the landlord his rent; I have rented the flat for three months.

I will see you outside the Lyceum tomorrow night at 7 o'clock.'

When Jimmy arrives at the landlords, he is shocked. On top of the 3 months initial rent, he has an item at the bottom called 'Key money 10 shillings. 'What is this ?' he says. 'Key money, always payable in advance !'. Jimmy pays up and then gets the tramcar back to Bridgeton

### *FROM THE PAPERS:*

- To the south of Govan the skyline is altering. A huge structure of apartment blocks called Moss Heights is being built. A certain amount of discussion preceded the building of the structures between those in favour of Corporation Housing and those in favour of Private development.

- Tremendous sadness descended on Cardonald . Five year old Joyce Margaret Mc Clelland of Bucklaw Terrace, drowned on the beaches of St.Ives in Cornwall. The local Cornish people were shocked and raised £50 for the little girls funeral expenses.

\*        At Glasgow Sheriif Court William Bow Murray was sent to prison
for 11 months after pleading guilty to assaulting 3 policemen in Helen Street.
Prosecuter Fiscal said a disorderly crowd had gathered at the corner of Helen
Street.

When asked to disperse the police were showered with bottles and other
objects. Murray had run away but was soon caught by the police officers.
Murray's friends had tried to get him free and continued to throw bottles and
missiles at the police. Murray was ushered into a nearby close but continued to
fight on with the police officers.

Murray claimed that had no re-collection of the incident and had been having
just a wee drink with his friends.Albert Charles Morrow returned home from
his job as a bar waiter late one evening the worst for drink but he could not gain
access to his tenement flat through the front door. He decided to climb the rone
pipe and soon he had entered a bedroom through the window. Two young girls
on hearing someone enter their bedroom screamed and pulled the covers over
their heads. Morrow made a dash for it but was soon caught. Being his first
offence Ballie Johnston fined him £5 or 20 days imprisonment.

\*        25 year old labourer Peter Rattray demanded that his step mother go
out and get him a newspaper. When she refused he threw his dinner on the
floor. He then set about his father for refusing to give him money to buy drink.
Fiscal Mc Kinnon at Govan Court said it was a very serious assault offence and
sentenced Rattray to 60 days imprisonment. Rattray's father said he would be
allowed admission back into the house.

\*        Albert Knowles and William Greenwood died at the Harland and
Wolff shipyard. Both were working in the central section of the ship when they
were overcome by carbon monoxide fumes. Heroic efforts were made to save
the men by fellow workers. The pair were extracted from the ship and rushed
to the Southern General Hospital but were dead on arrival. Plumber Walter
Green (34) who had made a valiant effort to save the men was also rushed to
the Southern General but was soon released.

Mrs. Black of 56, Fairfield Street liked her tea. However, on many mornings
when she opened the tenement landing door the milk delivery was not there.
Arguments ensued with the milkman and both parties soon established that the
milk was being delivered but disappearing before Mrs. Black could collect it
from outside her door. Mrs Black decided to monitor the situation by watching
the milk delivery through a small vent hole above the door.From there one
night she watched next door neighbour James Higgins steal a pint of milk. She
awoke her husband and the next morning they confronted James Higgins. At
Govan Court Higgins had told his wife to pay for any  milk taken from the
Blacks but she had forgot. Fiscal Boss and the court said it was a particularly
mean form of theft. Higgins was fined £1 or another option of 10 days in
prison.

The increase in traffic volume was bringing problems. A collision of some sort seemed to happen in Govan every week.

The worst junction for collisions was that between Copland Road and Edminston Drive. However the biggest source of continued accidents were with the Corporation Tramcars throughout the city. This was causing considerable concern.

Elsewhere in the City the Gorbals riots saw bayonets and chisels used and a huge number of people were up in court. There was a fear expressed that the riots may extend to Govan. However these proved unfounded and life in the burgh continued much as before. Most Govanites were in work and the main concern was loose masonry falling from the crumbling tenements in particular around Neptune Street.

Mrs Jean Whyte of 6, Neptune Street said that corporation workmen had gone onto the roof and thrown a lot of chimney rubble down onto the back courts and no one had been back since. She had written to the factor by registered letter but no response.

Her neighbour Mrs Agnes Smith also complained that her chimney stack had collapsed in a gale. The police spokesman said the Master of Works had climbed onto the roof to make it safe.

The Iron ladder access previously attached to the chimney is sticking up in the air like a circus act. Viewed from Orkney Street there is a slight sag in the roof and guttering where the chimney had collapsed.

# CHAPTER 7
## A GOVAN MAN IN HIGH OFFICE AND RELIGION

Tom Kerr was Lord Provost of Glasgow and was a Govan man through and through. He hailed from the Fairfields Distict of Govan and had been a pupil at Govan High School. He championed the poor and sought his vehicle to do this initially through the Labour Party. Things were not all to his liking in the Labour Party so he joined the Independent Labour Party and fought the Fairfield ward. He fought the election with his fellow ILP candidates including Manny Shinwell on the manifesto overleaf.

Tom Kerr was tall, thin and always well groomed. Virtually all the ladies found him handsome. He was a fierce debater on politics or anything you wished to discuss. Tom pledged to represent the people of Govan as equals; Protestant and Catholic; Rich and Poor; Employed, Skilled and Unwaged.

He won the election easily and through time worked his way to high office when he eventually returned to the Labour Party fold. Once Tom Kerr was elected to the Lord Provost post he worked tirelessly to bring the people of Glasgow together. He never lost an opportunity to promote Govan. He also made countless visits to the local schools. He always tried to encourage the children to achieve better things and made as many visits to the local schools as he could. Any excuse would do like planting a tree or opening a re-decorated classroom. He also visited Benburb Football Club on a regular basis and with Bill Struth the Rangers manager served for a while on the committee. Many photographs of Tom Kerr show him in his top hat.

However, it is in 1920 that Tom Kerr first entered the town council and he was awarded a testimonial at South Govan Town Hall just prior to Christmas in 1952 for his sterling work. Among those attending was political opponent and sitting MP Jack Nixon Browne. The music was provided by the Arion Choir. Tom Kerr loved music and given opportunity would sing the occasional popular song.

At the end of 1952 Tom Kerr provided the annual Glasgow Lord Provost message.

*'The Cultural side of Glasgow is all too often pushed into the background because of the industrial nature of our community. It is true to say however, that large as our community may be, we are a kindly and warm hearted people and to all of you at this time and particularly to any visitors who may be in Glasgow at the beginning of this New year I extend best wishes for a Happy and Prosperous New Year.*

### TOM KERR—LORD PROVOST

Business is slow in the Golspie Street offices of Pawnbroker A.Boulton-Cox. John and Abe are puzzled. It is some weeks since they carried out an audacious robbery in the Boswell Galleries.

Both had felt that the replacing of the 'Sad Highlander' painting with a good quality fake would have soon been noticed; or at least after a few days. However nothing in the news had indicated that the robbery had taken place. John and Abe had made arrangements to go to Amsterdam and sell the painting at an auction.

With George helping out in the Pawnbrokers shop John and Abe had travelled to Amsterdam with their painting. Both were sitting in a café overlooking the canals and enjoying a meal and drink. They had already given the painting to the Art auctioneers. Abe said ' It would be interesting to see how much we get. John said ' Well so far so good.

We have arranged the sale through an intermediary (which is commonplace) and hopefully things will go through quickly and easily. Abe says ' I know all the auctioneers well John. They are true professionals at their trade'.

John and Abe continued to enjoy the remainder of their meal amongst the Amsterdam Canals. At that moment they both looked out the window and saw a sight they were not expecting. Cynthia and Peter Moriarty Tigwell were walking arm in arm slowly along the opposite side of the canal. John said 'Gee Whiz !!. Now what Abe ?'. Abe said 'Leave it to me John, just finish your meal and enjoy the wine !'.

The next day John and Abe decided not to attend the Auction. However, unwelcome visitors to the auction were Peter and Cynthia Moriarty Tigwell. The auction started and Peter and Cynthia noted that 'The Sad Highlander' was one of the exhibits to be sold. Both looked at one another. Peter said 'It is probably one of the copies Cynthia. We will soon find out !'.

Peter stood up and said 'I say !. That is either not the Sad Highlander or it is a painting that has been stolen from our galleries!. We own the Sad Highlander !'. Almost immediately the Auction ushers moved in and ejected Mr.and Mrs. Moriarty– Tigwell from the Hall amid much noise and shouting The Auctioneer said ' As you are aware, every item on auction here is thoroughly vetted and we have never had to attend a verification exercise for 150 years. Let the auction continue !'

The crowd burst into applause; the auctioneer bowed in appreciation as the auction resumed.The Sad Highlander fetched a good sum. John and Abe received the money from the intermediary and paid them a good commission. John said 'I see your intermediary was a Jew !' Abe said Yes Jews are good businessmen John.

Did you notice the little bit of extra detail that a Govan man would miss ?'. Yesterday we told the auctioneer that we had been warned that someone would come in claiming they owned the 'Sad Highlander. True enough they did !'. Abe looked at John smiled and winked his right eye. John also smiled and offered his hand. They shook their hands together sealing another successful project.

# Municipal Election.

## FAIRFIELD 31ST WARD.

## THE LABOUR CANDIDATES.

"As a Socialist, and the nominee of the Independent Labour Party, I have been selected to contest the Fairfield Ward as one of the Candidates of the Local Labour Party. I have been resident in Govan for over 20 years and during that time I have taken a keen interest in the public business of the town. My time and energies have all been spent in the working-class movements for the Social betterment of the whole community.

I do not wish to draw any distinction between men and women's questions, because essentially they are one, but I am convinced and have always advocated that women should take their full share of public work.

Mrs. M. BARBOUR.

FELLOW ELECTORS,

For more than 4 years I have represented you on the Town Council, during which period I have consistently directed my efforts towards Municipal expansion and improvement.

During my period of office I have been approached by hundreds of electors seeking advice, and in many cases believe I have been of some assistance. My views on Municipal and Labour questions are well known to every elector. My record in the Town Council as a working-class representative will stand the closest examination.

On this occasion I am seeking re-election, and the men and women of Fairfield, if they again honour me with their confidence, may rely on my devoting the same attention and energy to their interests in the Corporation as I have done in the past.

E. SHINWELL.

I seek your suffrages as a Socialist believing that in Socialism alone lies the solution of the problem of Poverty. I contend that poverty is the greatest evil that man has to combat and the battle is only necessary because a small portion of society believe that want is irremovable or alternatively that it is necessary for their continuance in power. As an advocate of the cause of the poor I offer myself as a candidate at this time. Incidently, I am a member of the I.L.P. and the Trade Union and Co-operative movements.

On the clear issue of Socialism versus Capitalism I ask you to vote on the 2nd November, and I shall accept your decision as being sincerely reached.

T. A. KERR.

## To the Electors.

FELLOW CITIZENS,

On the invitation of the Labour Party, which comprises the Trade Unions, the Independent Labour Party, and Co-operative Movement, we are contesting Fairfield Ward at the forthcoming Municipal Election. Everything points to a complete Labour victory and in consequence the opponents of Labour have become seriously alarmed. This fear has called forth every form of gross misrepresentations which occupy the most prominent place in those reactionary news sheets which are at their service.

Jimmy Welsh has moved to Govan and lives at 20, Craigton Road in a ground floor tenement 'single end'. He hears of a vacancy at Harland and Wolff shipyard. Jimmy has an option of working on a contract basis for John Henderson but he has turned it down for the time being.

He is not totally convinced his future is in scaffolding.

Derek had a novel way of scaling the Air Raid shelters that were built between tenements. He would put his back against one wall and his feet on the dyke wall opposite and by pressing against the wall and moving his feet upwards a step at a time he was soon on top of the dyke. However, it caused damage to his clothing and his mother was none too happy.

Half way through discussing the problem with Derek Ruth noticed a couple of well dressed children from further up Daviot Street on their way to Sunday School. 'Derek I have an idea. I think you should go to Sunday School, maybe that way you will be keen to keep a decent pair of clothes on your back. The next Sunday Derek went down to the Sunday School held at the 'Free Church of Scotland' on Moss Road.

The Church Minister was the Rev. Bartram Potts. The Sunday school teachers were young Christian helpers but at the end of the school Derek was told not to come back again as he was too disruptive.

On arriving home Ruth asked Derek 'How did yea get on ?'. 'OK' says Derek. 'But they said that I was not to go back next week. I was playing a bit with Bernie '. Ruth butted in 'So yea didnae behave yerself !. Robbie overheard the conversation . 'Leave it Ruth, if he does not want to go or they don't want him, then so be it'. That was to be Derek's first and last attendance at Sunday school.

Paul O'Callaghan is preparing for an interview at Harland and Wolff's. The O'Callaghan family live in a semi detached house in Cardonald. Mary is Paul's wife and they have four children two boys and two girls. John the eldest son aged 10 and Francis the youngest aged 6 . They have two girls Theresa and Joanne aged 7 and 8.

The couple are devoted to their children and each Sunday they are immaculately dressed to attend Sunday morning mass at Saint Anthony's on Govan Road. They could attend other Chapels but as they had lived in Govan previously they continue to go to Saint Anthony's.

Paul has worked hard as an Electrical Engineer and wherever he has worked he is very highly regarded. Work is beginning to dry up at the small Marine company where is employed on the Electrical section at Hillington. 'Good Luck Paul !' says Mary as she kisses her husband on the cheek when he leaves the house.

At Harland and Wolff the preparation is on for the interviews.

The successful candidate must be capable of testing, and if required, rectifying faults on the new ship`s electrical system. Consistent with Harland and Wolff, everything must be to the highest Marine Electrical regulations. The interviewers are Derek Drummond Chief Electrical Manager supported by Bill Haynes and Bob McNicol. There are four candidates on Drummonds list ; Bill Smith, Brendan Coyle, Paul O'Callaghan and James Welsh.

Drummond is a portly man wearing a nice suit and a waistcoat. He says to his two Foremen' We must get the right man today gentlemen'. I will take the lead role, Bill you ask the technical stuff and Bob you tell them about the job requirements.

Drummond summons the first candidate who is already waiting.'First Candidate please' A half hour passes and Bill Smith leaves having been told his experience at a local factory changing the light bulbs is not really what is required.

Brendan Coyle has had reasonable experience as an all round electrician but after half an hour it is already evident his credentials do not extend to circuitry testing. He is told that the yard will be in contact with him soon but he is aware that the job offer looks remote

Paul O'Callaghan enters the office with a pleasant smile,
He is in his mid 30's with dark hair and a grey suit with waistcoat plus a shirt and collar. He has a sizable box in one hand and a series of sizable folders in the other. Mr.Drummond welcomes him and introduces him to Bill and Bob. The job scope is outlined and Paul listens intently, pulls a pen from his inside pocket and makes notes. After hearing the job outline Paul is asked to provide his qualifications. He opens the sizable folders section and displays a series of Certificates. Many are Marine Engineering and Electrical Regulations and Theory.

He also has a Certificate for Testing of Ships electrics he obtained while working as an Electrical Engineer on board a Cross Channel Ferry. Paul explained that in addition to the qualifications he already had he was studying at Stow College on Submersible Electrics.

Bob Mc Nicol asked what was in the sizable box he had brought in. Paul opened the box and inside was a complete electrical tool kit. A range of screwdrivers, pliers, cutters soldering iron were amongst the collection. In addition he showed the Meggar he used for earth leakage testing. He opens another smaller wooden box and inside was the latest range of AVO meter with the leads. The whole kit was impressive. Excitedly Paul says that he puts money away each week from his wages to fund his kit.

Paul then opens up more of his folders and shows the drawings he has produced from Design to Final Issue on Electrical Circuits; virtually all on Marine Engineering. Bill Hayes is charged with asking the technical questions and Paul provides perfect explanation with add ons for his answers.

The interview ends and Paul leaves. Bob and Bill think they have a first class candidate but have a little doubt at the back of their minds on how Derek Drummond would see it.

The last candidate is James Welsh who had learned about the job through his friend Richard Crozier at The Bridgeton Arms.

Drummond who was previously 'non plussed' with the previous three candidates beams as Jimmy enters the room.

'How are you James, I have heard a lot about you !'. 'Extremely well Derek, I am a well respected man around the city these days'. 'Welsh is well dressed but has no tools or certificates with him unlike Paul.

The job outline is provided and Jimmy Welsh says 'No problem with that job spec.'. Bob says ' Reagrding your qualifications James have you brought them with you ?'. 'Actually No; I was working down in England recently and am currently awaiting much of my equipment to be sent up'. Derek Drummond says ' That is no problem James !.

No doubt we will see them in due course !.' Can you give a brief outline as to your Electrical experience James says Bill. 'No problem' says Jimmy 'I constantly take an interest in electrics' he continues.

A few weeks back I was involved with the electrics at the Bridgeton Arms when the place was in darkness.

No one had a clue but I immediately located the fuse box and once the fuse wire was replaced hey presto the lights were on again.' 'That is marvellous James ' says Derek Drummond, showing real initiative in a crisis.' he continued.

Bob asks James 'How would you go about fault finding on circuits ?'. 'No problem' says Jimmy 'The key is always to break the circuits into two sections. Use Kirchoff's Law ! If you cannot find the fault in the first part of the circuit you will find it in the second !'. ' Self evident James' says Derek Drummond. The interview is soon over and Jimmy was on his way back to Craigton Road.

Meanwhile Paul arrives home at Cardonald and Mary asks 'How did you get on Paul ?' . 'I thought I did quite well Mary, but you never know with interviews, I would really like the job '.

Back at the yard, Drummond looks over his glasses at his notes. 'Well Bob and Bill I know you will agree with me that the decision is clear cut. Can you ask the secretary to write to James Welsh and tell him to start on Monday. Also ask her to write the other three a Dear John. Well that concludes the interviews for today gentlemen thank you for your guidance !. Bob says 'Mr Drummond, I was very impressed with Mr.O'Callaghan'. Could we not employ him ?' Drummond says ' Yes he came across as not bad, I will give you that.' 'The concern I have is harmony. It is essential that the ships are built within a good timescale. The Electrical section all seem to be as one'. 'I noted that O'Callaghan went to St.Gerrards'

Drumoyne School has called for an assembly in the main hall. Today there is a visit from the Reverend Bartram Potts. Potts is a tall thin man with the little bit of hair he has swept back and he wears shiny rimmed glasses, a black cloak and dog collar.

After a while reciting passages from the Bible he asks a question 'Who is the man with the long white beard in the bible ?'.

Quick as a flash Derek's hand goes up. 'Father Christmas Reverend Potts' Derek replies when asked.

The Reverend Potts then completely loses his calm. 'What sort of answer is that child !. How ridiculous !. What is your name ?.' 'Derek' the boy replies. 'You should be ashamed of yourself Derek and please do a lot more reading of the bible'. The minister was clearly rattled and the assembly soon broke up.

The Reverend Bartram Potts was someone who was in a permanently bad mood. He had been involved in the Korean War during which had a bit of shrapnel removed from his brain.

On returning from Korea he managed to get a post at the 'Wee Free' Church of Scotland in Moss Road. Once every few months he would visit the local Primary schools within the radius of his Church.

On returning to the class, Miss Doig sat down thinking hard on what to say to Derek and the rest of the class. Her hands clasped over the front of her face. Then she said 'Derek there is a lesson for you to learn today !'.

'Do not answer a question, unless you are 100% certain that you know the answer, when Reverend Potts asks. Derek then asks 'Miss, can you tell me who the man with the man with the long white beard is ?' . The Reverend Potts had not got round to answering the question he had posed.

Derek it was obviously St.Nicholas' replied Miss Doig. 'Please Miss. I think there was another man in the bible who had a long white beard' said one of the girls in the class who attended Sunday School. 'Moses had a long white beard as well' she continued.

The unthinkable has happened at No.31 Daviot Street and a Catholic family has moved in. The Johnson family have taken over one of the two ground floor flats.

The previous tenants were an elderly couple who moved to the next close and a flat on the top floor away from the street noise.

Ruth is dismayed and complains to the Factor on Berryknows Road. Tony Johnson and his wife Rose have two children Ronnie and Sarah who are at pre school age 4 and 3. When Rose offered to introduce herself to Ruth, Ruth completely blanked her.

The same response was given to Tony . Each tenant in the close took turns to wash the stairs and Ruth took her turn in sequence and also cleaned the area around the Johnson flat. Rose Johnson came out and thanked her but Ruth totally ignored her.

Boab, Robbie , Jack and Derek all spoke to the Johnson's but not Ruth and no amount of persuasion would change her mind. All the other tenants in the close got on well with the Johnson's. Tony was very keen to get the small garden at the front of the close outside their windows looking nice and after several months it looked a picture, easily the best in Daviot Street.

With Darkie the cat no longer around, No.31 Daviot Street started to get some visitors and not the welcome kind. Mice appeared from the many cracks in the wall brickwork. To counteract them Robbie purchased a mouse trap. Each night it was baited with a bit of cheese and sometime during the night the trap operated loudly.

The mouse was despatched into the ash from the living room fire grate and on down to the midden. The procedure went on for a week or so before a second trap had to be purchased but fortunately it never reached the need for three traps.

Jimmy Welsh arrives at the door of Joan's tenement a bunch of flowers in hand. Joan opens the door and asks him in.

She says 'Thank you Jimmy that is lovely but I think it best you still stay away for a while. We cannot take any more'. Jimmy says 'I have a place for 3 months and will try to sort things out and then come back and see you'. He returns to Govan and surveys his new abode. There is a lot of noise in the backyard with kids playing. The sole window in the single end only faces the back yard. He has a toilet at the end of a long narrow passage way. John and Abe have returned from Amsterdam very circumspect and continued serving and working in the Golspie Street Pawnshop. It is now beyond closing time and they are alone. John says ' Abe I cannot believe we have so much money'.

Abe says ' So much is never enough John; that is what you will learn my boy !. Anyway now for our little celebration !'. Abe went to the safe cupboard and pulled out two bottles of whiskey and around six bottles of beer. He continued ' I do not drink much but this is special'.

He went over to the customers unclaimed goods and produced a good quality record player which he plugged in. He went to his large bag and pulled out a large record.

He said ' Let us have some decent music John !!'.

The turntable on the record player was spinning and Abe lowered the needle onto the black record. The song was 'Hava Nigella'.

**HAVA NAGILA**   LET US REJOICE & BE GLAD

Hava nagila, hava nagila;      Hava nagila ve-nis'mecha;
*Repeat*
Hava neranena, hava neranena;     Hava neranena venis'mecha;
Uru, uru achim;    Uru achim belev same'ach

The song starts slowly and both John and Abe are downing their drinks. As the record music gets quicker Abe stands up ; puts both his hands in the air and struts down to the end of the office. Not to be outdone John quickly follows and both repeat until the record is finished. Both sit down and continue to drink for 10 minutes. John says ' that was f**king brilliant Abe. Lets do it again !'. The same celebration to a fantastic piece of music played loudly was repeated. Two hours later both Abe and John were lying slumped back on their chairs oblivious to the rest of the world.

Bill  Haynes and Bob McNichol who were involved in the interviews at Harland and Wolff learn of a good Electrical Technician's job that has become vacant due to retirement at one of their suppliers Ford's Marine in Hillington.

They phone up John Ford  and tell him of Paul O'Callaghan and provide details of contact. They give Paul a glowing reference. The owner of the company goes to Cardonald and knocks at the door of the O'Callaghan family. Mary answers the door. 'Hello I am John Ford the owner of Ford's Marine in Hillington' Can I speak to Paul please ?'. 'Oh come in please' says Mary. 'Paul will be home soon'.

They discussed the Harland and Wolff interview and Mary says ' Yes Paul was disappointed. He felt the interview had gone well and it was a job he would really have enjoyed. However things have moved on a bit.

I will let Paul discuss it with you Mr.Ford'. Ford observed how well behaved the O'Callaghan children were and how clean and tidy the house was.  Paul arrived and they discussed the vacancy.  Paul says 'I was disappointed about the Harland's job. However, I had written for another job in Barrow, England and I have been offered the job. Mary and I will be looking at houses down there at the weekend, the company is paying our train fares.
So Mr. Ford, thank you and also Bob and Bill; if things do not work out then I may well be coming back to see you'.

At 20, Craigton Road Jimmy decides to go for some entertainment and instead of a bar he goes to the nearby Vogue cinema at the end of Crossloan Road. Picture Houses are very popular in Govan and in particular the Lyceum and the Plaza in Govan Road. They tend to get the most recent releases and the night out offers good value for money.

As well as the main film most performances have a 'B' movie and in addition often a cartoon as well. The Lyceum usually has queues outside and once inside, often every seat is taken. On some occasions the patrons are offered standing down the sides until a seat becomes available. These are usually spotted by the usherettes who shine the torch at the vacant seat.
The Vogue also gets the recent films fairly quickly whereas the Mosspark on Paisley Road West and the Elder get them second time around.

One day Ruth enters No.31 and Rose blocks her path. Rose says 'Ruth, can I have a wee word with you please it will only take a minute'. What do you want' says Ruth. Rose says 'I notice that all the other wumin tenants in the close take their turn at cleaning the stairs and walls. I would like your permission to help you all ! If you wont let me help then Tony and I would like to pay for the cleaning stuff'. Ruth is stunned and does not know what to say. 'Well I suppose if you want to help there is nothing wrong with that'. They both smiled and thereafter were on very good terms.

Some days later Derek sees Rose and Ruth having a discussion and laugh at the entrance to the tenement. When Ruth comes upstairs he says 'I thought you did not like Catholics Maw ?' 'I don't but Rose and Tony and their kids are not proper Catholics !'

During school holidays a lot of the Drumoyne boys would go to Cardonald Park to play various games mostly football. On occasions they would meet up with a few Mormons from USA. They were always friendly and trying to introduce their form of football to the sessions.

One day they arrived and around 16 boys of varying ages were split into teams for American Soccer. It made quite a pleasant change. Around 6 of the boys were Catholics; within 15 minutes of the game starting two young Roman Catholic priests from one of the local chapels appeared and immediately summoned the 6 Catholic boys away from the game. Clearly someone had told them that they were involved with another non Roman Catholic religious group.

The game stopped awaiting the return of the 6 boys for around 10 minutes. Eventually the game re-started again without the 6 Roman Catholics who went back to the West Drumoyne estate. Once the Mormons had gone as if by magic all 6 re-appeared and football continued with the British rather than American form.

At the end of the game all the boys sat down and had a short discussion, in particular about the Mormons and why the Catholic boys had to leave the game. They had been told not to discuss it with any of the 'Non Denomination types' even if they asked.

Derek brought the subject up with Ruth , Robbie and Jack. Ruth of course had a strong view about anything involving the Roman Catholic Church.

However, she said that Tony, Rose and their kids were good Catholics. Jack felt the whole affair was stupid and the Priests should not have got involved. ' They seem to try and totally control the lives of the ordinary Catholics '.

Robbie felt that virtually all Catholics are no different from any of the rest of people in Scotland. He said 'I cannot see why this nonsense exists at all.

If you go to England or virtually anywhere else in the world people just seem to accept that they have a religion of some sorts. In the west of Scotland too much is made of what religion you are.

If the Catholics want to go to their chapel so be it'. Ruth says ' If the Pope had his way everyone in Scotland would be Catholic !'. Jack says 'He has nae chance of that whatsoever. However, something needs to be sorted out with employment. If you have a Catholic name or have gone to a Catholic school you have a far lesser chance of getting the better jobs in Govan'. Derek says 'There are more Catholics now than before. I like the ones I play with, I do not see any difference'.

Jack says 'What about the Rangers ?. They will not sign a Catholic.' Robbie says 'Yes that is true and it is a disgrace. They say they have not had one good enough . What a poor answer that is !. Jack says ' Celtic have no problem signing Protestants and even the Ants do not seem to bother either'. Robbie says 'The Bens have always signed Catholics ever since I can remember !. At any given moment it always appears to be half Protestant and half Catholic.' Jack replies 'Aye, and the best Bens players are usually Catholics. For some reason they seem to play better for a blue jersey'. Robbie says 'The people that run the Bens and the Ants are a calibre above Rangers and Celtic, they always have been'.

- Bellahouston Harriers Athletics Club were formed in 1892 by a group of Postal workers and had their headquarters in Govan Baths. One of the founders of the club John Mc Diarmid was still involved and the club still flourished. Occasionally one of the better athletes reached a standard to take part in the AAA Championships in London. However in Scotland they had a good record with other competing clubs and enjoyed the Athletics competitions as well as the Rangers and Police Sport events at Ibrox which were always well attended by spectators. The club celebrated its 60 years anniversary with a Dinner-Dance at the Cranston's arcade Rooms.

- William Houston (48) boarded a bus on its way to Govan. He went upstairs and started shouting and bawling at the fellow passengers. He moved around the seats and sat beside some of the passengers. When sitting beside one gentleman he produced an open razor. 'Gie us 5 bob fur a drink ' he said. When the man refused he moved on to other passengers. In Govan Court, Houston was jailed for 30 days for using abusive language and brandishing an open razor. Houston said 'It was the act of a fool as I was worst for wear with drink. I did not mean to harm anyone'.

- The Shipyard owners meeting saw the results for present shipbuilding and the future. Britain still had a 41% share of the shipbuilding orders. However with a world economic slump the requirement for shipping saw changing patterns. There is big demand for Oil Tankers and less demand for cargo and passenger Liners. Some of the Clyde yards had orders for as long as 5 years but beyond that things looked uncertain.

Four boys climbed onto the roof of St.Columba Church in Copland Road. They were spotted and the police arrived. Three of the boys came down but one boy aged 10 refused to budge. The Fire Brigade were called after the boy slid down the slates to the gutter. He was rescued. In Govan Juvenile Court Baillie Roberston ordered payment to be made for each boy of 10 shillings or 7 day detention. The Copland Road residents reported that while the boys were on the roof many slate tiles had fallen onto the pavement below.

John and Abe say their farewells for the evening outside their Golspie Street Pawnshop. John is off to see Sandra; Abe is off to the Pearce Institute for a game of snooker. The next morning in the pawnshop Abe says ' You will never guess what John !!' John said 'What' . Abe says 'I beat Mc Intosh at snooker last night'.

John said 'Mc Intosh, Govan's finest snooker player !!. Tell me more Abe'. We played for 5 shillings with the loser also paying for the light and I won. Mc Intosh gave me 28 start'. John said ' I see you probably played one of your tactical games Abe did you not ?' 'Yes' said Abe.
John said 'Let me guess !.

Your tactical game. You stood behind the pocket Mc Intosh was shooting into and chalked your cue ! You blew smoke all over the table when it was his shot! You coughed up as he was about to cue1; and so on. Am I right ?'. Abe said ' Well it was a tactical game. I won on the black with a fluke as well. Shot to the middle and the black hit the jaw and went in the opposite pocket. McIntosh was very sporting and paid up straight away'.
John said 'How is the team doing these day Abe ?'. Abe replied ' They had a league table on the board. It looks like they are half way up. The Union Club are top.

Horatio Nelson Weir (33) was a small man by stature barely five feet tall. He was walking along Scotland Street when he had an altercation with 23 year old Allan Leslie (a hammer man) who was over six feet tall. Suddenly Weir pulled an Iron bar from inside his coat and hit Leslie square on the forehead causing him to bleed. To Weir's astonishment Leslie was not unconscious and started to punch Weir.

In a short time Weir was on the ground and Allan Leslie was punching and kicking him until he was unconscious. At this point a crowd had gathered and restrained Leslie just as the police arrived. Both men were taken to Southern General Hospital; Leslie to have 8 stitches in a head wound and Weir for treatment to a broken jaw. The police officer picked up the iron bar which fell out of Weir's pocket.

In Govan Police Court Weir and Leslie both pleaded guilty to breach of the peace. Weir, who had several similar previous convictions, was fined £5 or 20 days in prison. Leslie was fined £2 or 20 days in prison.

# CHAPTER 8
## CHANGING TIMES IN GOVAN

Derek was sitting at the living room table with his mother Ruth at 31 Daviot Street, having returned from school. Ruth is reading the Govan Press and in particular the Deaths and Orbituary's column's. She was checking to see if any of her old home help customers had expired. Derek was quite excited and said 'Maw, you will never guess what ?'. Whits that Derek ?' Ruth replied continuing to read the paper. 'I got 3 stars today for good work !'.

Ruth replied still reading the paper 'That's great son' . Derek went on 'Maw it was not one or two stars, it was actually three !', easily the most I have ever had !' . Ruth said to Derek 'Derek I am going to see your father tonight at Craigton Road. I might be moving away from here'. Derek said 'When will I meet him ?'. 'Soon' Ruth replied.

Derek had been doing well with Miss Doig as indeed had the rest of the class. He could not believe how lucky he was to have a class of such nice kids. Yes, occasionally they had their scraps and Derek was usually the worst offender but always they made up and moved on as kids do. Derek felt part of the Drumoyne School class ever since the time he had Rheumatic Fever and many of them came to his tenement to enquire about his well being. Ruth predicted Miss McLaughlan and Miss Doig were going to be good; she had already had them many years before. However, when Derek said he was having music lessons the next day and said Mr.Scott was the teacher. 'Mr.Scott', she said 'He was starting out as a music teacher when I was at Drumoyne ! He is fantastic the best teacher of all time and also very good looking !'. Derek said 'Yes I always enjoy his lessons they are brilliant and I cannot wait to attend them`.

The next day Derek went down in the two by two formation to the main hall at Drumoyne School. Mr Scott said 'We will go over the songs we have done so far. You have all done so well boys and girls that I have had a word with the head teacher and we will let your Mums and Dads in for 20 minutes or so when we have our next session and they can hear how well you are doing'. At that time it was rare for parents to be allowed to witness any activities in Drumoyne School. However, Mr Scott had obviously been very persuasive.
He went on 'I did say that only the best singers will be allowed in the Drumoyne School choir. You have all done so well that we have a very big choir indeed , you are all in it !

Needless to say everyone was happy with this decision.

Two weeks later a considerable number of the age groups (probably only excluding the two youngest classes) assembled in the Drumoyne School main hall.

Mr Scott had already had the practice session and the children knew exactly where to go. Essentially they were in four groups. The Girls in two sections strong and not so strong voices. The same make up was provided for the boys although the number in the strong voice section was smaller.

Essentially the better singers were in the strong voice group and Derek was in the weaker.

A sizable number of parents came to watch including Ruth .

Mr Scott introduced the short performance:.

'The first song the Drumoyne School choir will perform is 'Oh Shenandoah' Each line of the song was performed by a different section of the choir. The lower notes by the weaker singers the higher notes by the stronger singers. The opening lines of the song were by the weaker voice girls and they sounded brilliant with their pronounced Govan accents. All the groups were pleased with the production.

After that the group gave another good performance of Kelvin grove. 'Let us haste through Kelvingrove bonnie lassio'.   This song was to be the lead one in the next term. Two other similar songs were performed.

At the conclusion the parents gave a polite applause and they broke up for lunch time. Derek did notice most of the mothers had handkerchiefs stuck firmly to their noses and eyes including his own mother.

Derek and his mother walked back to Daviot Street. As they walked past the Inverness Street swing park  Derek said 'Whit is the matter Maw ?' Ruth dissolved into tears. 'Derek that was so good back there and I am so proud of you. I am no much of a maw to yea and I should of said more to you the other week when you got the stars'.  Derek said 'Maw, it does not matter. I have you, Robbie, Jack a great school and good friends.

- There was a worrying trend in the Govan Firms in regards to accidents. A plater Alex Graham of 141 Neptune  Street was awarded £1,260 when the jury under Lord Blades found Blair's of Woodville Street liable for the accident. Mr. Graham was struck by an iron bar after the sling which attached it to a crane snapped. The injuries included many broken ribs and a kidney had to be completely removed.
- Three workers at Govan Dry Docks fell 30 feet when the long plank of wood they were sitting on fell to the floor of the basin. They were Thomas Mansfield of 113, Neptune Street; James Brown of 35 Marlow Street and Richard Scanlon of 25, Hoey Street.
- The men were chipping the side of the vessel. Fortunately, all three received only minor injuries and were soon discharged from the Southern General Hospital.

76

- Nine men were hurt at the No.3 Graving Dock in Govan when a rope holding their scaffold broke and they plunged 25 feet to the floor. The men were employed by Harland and Wolff. One of the injured men heard the rope snap but before he could properly warn his work colleagues, the scaffold had fallen at one end and the men were thrown down. The injured men were : Eddie Mc Millan of Dunn Street, David Milligan 339, Moffatt Street; James Mc Intyre of 12, Dunsmuir Street; David Mc Lean , 134 Burden Avenue; Peter Mc Dermott of Eglington Street; Eddie Fitzpatrick of 49, Templeton Street; Thomas Mc Cabe of 63, Fulton Street; Daniel Lennie of Grace Street; Joseph Mc Laughlan of 29, Hoey Street.

At the next music lesson in Drumoyne School, Mr Scott told how proud he was of all the children in school for their efforts at the last large session. Next time we will make our lead song 'Kelvingrove' but we will also include the others. So practice began with the new lead song .

Mr. Scott provided music lessons to virtually all the Govan schools in a rota basis and it is likely that most former Govan school children would immediately think of their former school on hearing the main two songs.

It was perhaps ironic that both the songs Mr. Scott chose as his main proved to be very prophetical in a Govan sense. Both songs were about people leaving places they loved and moving on to something uncertain.

.At the Boswell Galleries Peter Moriarty Tigwell has telephoned DI Roy Fletcher  for a discussion on security. Peter says ' Nice to see you again Roy !!' They shake hands. Peter continues 'Roy, I have a problem. I believe the Old Highlander Painting has been stolen !'. Roy says ' Is that not it in its usual prominent position?' Peter says ' the one on display is a copy. It is not the real one. We have moved the viewing rope away from the picture and put extra lighting on the picture to ensure seasoned art viewers cannot see it properly. I want to know how this painting was stolen. What happened to the Glasgow Secure Alarm system ?'.

Roy Fletcher's face went crimson. 'The only access into this Gallery is by lift. The fire exit sounds as soon as the door is opened.  What do the security guard's notes say ?'.

Peter says 'Nothing Roy. The only thing of note was the lift played up one evening several months ago and the security guard got stuck for a short period. However nothing was taken when he checked'.

Roy says 'How can I gain access to the roof ?' Peter says ' I will show you'. The pair  collect the keys and walk down Boswell Street and access the rooftops from the end building stairway .

They soon cross the roof and enter the lift motor room. Roy says 'Is this motor room always locked ?'. Peter says 'Yes'. Roy says ' The lock is easy to open'.

As the pair enter the Lift Motor Room Roy lifts up the wooden hatch above the lift shaft. They both look down the shaft and immediately conclude how the robbery took place. Roy says ' This has the hallmarks of a criminal gang who have carried out several other robberies. On one robbery they killed a night watchman.

When they are caught they will hang for that crime.  Peter says ' by co-incidence we went to Amsterdam and saw probably what was the Sad Highlander being sold'.  Unfortunately, when we tried to trace the seller no one was able to help, such is the close network of the Auction trade.

At  Glasgow City Chambers  Lord Provost Tom Kerr is sitting at his desk and strumming his fingers on the desk.

The Iowa Girls Pipe Band from USA were late for their welcome to Glasgow meeting with the Lord Provost; The Lord Provost does not like lateness. He summons one of his secretaries to his office and says the meeting has been cancelled.

The lateness cancellation was not unique for the Lord Provost as he felt lateness was disrespectful.

At the Old Harmony Bar the Trade Union officials are having and informal meeting. The feedback they are getting is that for the forthcoming General Election there will be a few boundary changes to Govan. These would appear to favour Labour. John Gillespie and Frank Mulvenney update the gathering group of shipyard workers. John says 'It seems that Jack Nixon Browne is looking for a new seat'. Communist trade unionist Frank says 'Good riddance to him. A coward'.

John says , ' it seems that Govan will be getting John Rankin as a candidate. He is the MP for Tradeston at the moment; that seat is also affected by boundary changes.  Either way we want a Labour MP for Govan'.

Derek has crossed the Berryknowes Road  at Andy's Café to the Cardonald Park entrance and a large crowd of younger children with their parents have gathered in front of a small open booth.  They all shout out excitedly  as a puppet with a rolling pin hits another puppet around the head 'That's  the way to do it !'  Punch and Judy had been performed at the same spot over many years and provided good free entertainment for the West Drumoyne children. Adjacent to the performance stood the Old People's Club which Derek's grandfather Boab had helped with in its formation years.

Cardonald Park is a large expanse of ground on the perimeter of West Drumoyne.  The eastern extremity was Berryknowes Road and an incline took it to Cardonald Railway station. The southern perimeter of the park was the railway track west bound along the Clyde towards Gourock.  At the western extremity of the park  was a less used branch railway track  which joined Shieldhall under a road bridge. Shieldhall Road formed the northern part of  the park and was the home to countless football teams in an area known as the '50 pitches' .

Heading eastwards along towards the Shieldhall Road crossroads, Finbury Road ended the football parks . Going along Finsbury Road brought you to a 90 degree bend and onwards from there brought you back to the Cardonald Park entrance.

Cardonald Park had two very large fields near the eastern extremity; one had held a sizable Orange parade a few years previously. In pre second world war days many of the older Drumoyne estate residents said it hosted cricket matches. Derek liked to watch the steam engine drawn trains go by and waved to them along with his friends. He made a few moves on occasions to get down to the track but with eyes like a hawk the signal box operator down the track was quick to come out his cabin. He pleasantly told any children who strayed in this direction 'Get to F*** away from the track ya load of bampots'!.

The biggest field also played host to Drumoyne v Cardonald at football. A very informal match with teams selected from which side of the track you lived. It started off at 17 a side and just got bigger with age ranges from 5 to 21 years. The players would put down there jumpers/jackets and even shirts, when it was warm enough, to form the goalposts which finished up about 4 feet high and had a wide circumference. The matches sometimes lasted about six hours in the summer evenings with players going off for tea and returning later. Along the track from Cardonald Station was the signal box, previously mentioned, with the pulling the levers to the sound of bells. A regular sound for the West Drumoyne and Cardonald residents were the steam trains. The signal box always seemed to have a massive amount of coal available underneath the cabin and both the two signalmen guarded the coal supply diligently.

The area in front of the signal box was a large series of allotments, one of which was owned by Derek's Uncle Wullie. Wullie was keen on his plot and grew a wide variety of produce. Cabbages, potatoes, tomatoes and runner beans were among a wide range of vegetables.

Derek often visited the plot with his mother and came away with a good bag full each time. Wullie was well set up in a small hut and brewed tea for his visitors. A favourite for Derek was the peas in the pod. Each year all the allotment holders would take their produce into a large barn on the site where it was judged for prizes . In addition much of the vegetables were sold, giving the purchasers a good deal and the allotment holders a nice income. One day Ruth and Derek are with Wullie in his plot. There is a lot of noise and all of a sudden a man with a stick is bellowing at a few passers by who are walking near the plots. 'Get to f*** oot o' here; I'll be calling the polis tae get ye arrested !'. Wullie says 'That is Mr.Turner, he is slowly going mad ! We had a few thefts a year or so back so every time someone walks past or is in the plots that he does not recognise we get this nonsense'. The passers by look at Mr.Turner in bemusement and walk on into Cardonald Park. Wullie continues 'The plots are not as popular as they were immediately after the war ' pointing to a few vacant fenced areas.

I think folk are a bit better off these days and can get their vegetables from the new supermarkets that are coming in. Ruth says ' If you do not mind me saying so Wullie you seem to have lost a fair bit of weight '. Wullie says ' Yes Ruth, I have not been well recently and things are not going to get any better. I will work the plot for as long as I am able as I love this wee allotment. I won quite a few of the prizes the other week'.

Ruth says ' I am sorry to hear that Wullie !. Please keep in touch and let us know what is going on'. Wullie was to pass away soon after Ruth's visit to his plot from a cancer related illness.

The plot gradually fell into disrepair after not being looked after.

Further along the main railway line there was a large lake but it was not a natural lake. From the side it looked like quite pleasant with a white perimeter which you could easily envisage as sand. However the water was green and the whole area was contaminated from dumping of toxic waste by persons unknown. All the Drumoyne children were warned about going anywhere near this area of Cardonald Park.

At 31, Daviot Street Ruth has put on her coat. Boab says 'Where are you going Ruth ?'. ' I am off to Mc Crindles with Derek; he has got toothache ' she says.  Derek and his mother arrive at McCrindles in Langlands Road. He is greatly discomforted by two teeth that his mother says were going black. Dr McCrindle the dentist has concluded the teeth are to be pulled.  Ruth says 'I brought you a handerkerchief Derek'. 'Thanks Maw, can we not put this off for a week or so ?'.

'Naw it must be done son. Derek is dreading the visit, a normal check up was usually bad enough but a couple of teeth out was grim. They both went in and the receptionist ushered them into the waiting room on the ground floor.
Dr. McCrindle always seemed to be late which made the situation worse.
Finally the call came and Derek was on his way up the stairs to the surgery.

A big dentist chair awaited with the mouth rinse refreshed. Above the chair which looked out over Pirie Park there was a light which beamed into the patients mouth. A huge needle was soon on its way to the gums at the back of Derek`s mouth, the dentists thumb pressing down firmly on the needle holder till it could go no further.

'Right' said Dr.McCrindle. 'Hop down and go downstairs while your gums become numb' he continued.

Derek went downstairs and back to the waiting room where Ruth was waiting reading a magazine.  Suddenly the front door of the surgery burst open and in came Joe McGurn in great discomfort. Joe worked as a riveter in the Fairfield yard and arrived with his dungarees on with a bunnet and scarf.
'McCrindle, are ye up ther ?' he shouted up the stairs. ' It's Joe McGurn here,I am in f******* agony and dyin doon here !'. The assistant came down and asked Mr. McGurn to go in the waiting room.

Joe's teeth looked like a piano with a black gap for every two whitish teeth. 'Ah need tae get up ther quick' he cried holding his jaw. After completing the appointment for the lady being treated both Ruth and another patient agreed to allow Joe McGurn upstairs to have his gum numbed ready for the probable extraction. .

Mc Gurn had an intense dislike of the needles and a lot of noise and movement came from the surgery.. ' Christ almighty whit ur ye dain tae me McCrindle ?' When he finally came down Derek went up to have his two teeth extracted. The dentist chair was never the most appealing prospect for anyone. However,

Doctor McCrindle's technique was perfect and Derek was soon on his way home with a mouthful of blood being held in by a handkerchief.

At the Pearce Institute a snooker match was about to take place. The Glasgow Snooker League title favourites Union were taking on the Pearce Institute in search of frames to strengthen their challenge.

The Union club had 6 good players capable of compiling good breaks. The Pearce had one good player, McIntosh , and 5 other average players.

The Pearce players awaited the arrival of their opponents. The money was put into the snooker table pay machine slot by the Pearce manager. The door to the snooker room swung open and in walked the Union club.

All six players were dressed as snooker professionals. Black waistcoats, immaculate trousers very well pressed, white shirts and well polished shoes. Two of the players, the Quinterman brothers, were well known for countless business deals. Both were over six foot tall, strongly built and had their own cue boys who walked into the Snooker Room ahead of each player.

Each of the cue boys was dressed exactly as their player, waistcoat white shirt , creased trousers, shiney shoes. Each cue boy was a middle aged man, small in stature, around five foot tall. As they walked ahead of their Union Club player they held the black wooden cue box at exactly a 45o angle.

The younger Quinterman was the best player in the team and hence played first. His cue boy removed his cue from the case and wiped it with a damp cloth. McIntosh for the Pearce was always on first. McIntosh went to a wall where around fifty long metal cue cases were hanging. He unlocked his case and brought out his cue. A large crowd packed the room ; the tension mounted. Safety shots seemed to go on for an eternity.

Mc Intosh was formidable on his own table and Quinterman could not get a potable shot. Mc Intosh left Quinterman a difficult chance at a pot. The tall Union player smiled; he had his chance. The large number of players watching were hushed. Quinterman seemed to cue for an eternity; he shot but the ball jangled in the pocket. Mc Intosh was around the table in a flash and quickly compiled a 40 break before snookering Quinterman. Quinterman got out of the snooker but set up Mc Intosh who compiled another heavy break and the Pearce were a frame up.

Quinterman was stunned. Mc Intosh offered his hand of friendship and to buy his opponent a drink which was accepted. The second frame saw the Pearce player win on a black ball finish to give the Govan side a 2-0 lead. All the remaining frames were very tight and the Union clawed back for a 3-3 draw. At the end of the evening the players of both sides adjourned to the bar.

Just down Govan Road the Lyceum Snooker Club hosted many exciting snooker matches played for money. The Govan hustlers usually offered the casual player a match and allow there opponent to win. 'Kin we have a wee game for money pal?'

An offer of a money match was often taken up when the hustler's play improved by 100%. Unlike the Pearce Institute an occasional match of fisticuffs followed the snooker at the Lyceum club.

| Glasgow Snooker League | Pl | W | L | D | F | A | Pts |
|---|---|---|---|---|---|---|---|
| Shawlands Victoria | 8 | 7 | 1 | 0 | 36 | 12 | 14 |
| Union Club | 8 | 6 | 0 | 2 | 34 | 14 | 14 |
| Radnor Park | 8 | 5 | 0 | 3 | 30 | 18 | 13 |
| Rutherglen | 8 | 5 | 1 | 2 | 32 | 16 | 12 |
| Pearce Institute | 8 | 4 | 3 | 1 | 21 | 27 | 9 |
| Southern Victoria | 7 | 4 | 3 | 0 | 22 | 20 | 8 |
| Scotts Welfare | 7 | 3 | 3 | 1 | 22 | 20 | 7 |
| Vulcan | 8 | 3 | 5 | 0 | 21 | 27 | 6 |
| St.Francis | 8 | 2 | 5 | 1 | 17 | 31 | 5 |
| St.Mungo | 7 | 1 | 6 | 0 | 16 | 26 | 2 |
| Princes | 7 | 1 | 6 | 0 | 15 | 27 | 2 |
| Kelso Royal | 8 | 0 | 8 | 0 | 11 | 37 | 0 |

At 2, Sharp Street, Govan, Hugh Gemmell (38) was coming home happy. He was singing and trying to play his mouth organ despite being very drunk. As he reached his tenement landing he fell over and his head hit against the neighbours door.

Mr. and Mrs Short came to the door and were greeted by a storm of abuse from Gemmell who was lying on his back. At Govan Police Court Hugh was fined £5 or 30 days in prison. He admitted many previous convictions for similar instances; Gemmell said to Fiscal Cuthbertson he had been off the drink now for 6 weeks.

Jimmy Welsh arrived home at 20 Craigton Road, his new abode, following a day at Harland and Wolff. He was unhappy and realised that he was out of his depth in the job that fellow brother Freemason Derek Drummond had 'engineered' for him.

He made a cup of tea and lay down on the bed within the single end tenement and listened to several boys running through the close corridor from Craigton Road to the backyards. He put both of his hands behind his head looked at the cracks on the ceiling and reflected on his present changed set of circumstances. Jimmy Welsh was born during the First World War in the East End of Glasgow the only son of William and Jane Welsh. William Welsh was a steel worker and had spent his entire life working in the various Steelworks around Parkhead and Springburn. Jimmy left school at 14 and was soon employed as a Scaffolder with the firm John Henderson. From the start he was very keen and soon his strength and agility were coming to the fore.

The company expanded rapidly after the depression in the 1930's and Jimmy was soon helping John Henderson quote for projects, such was the demand for their services.

Jimmy Welsh was able to save a considerable sum of money and when John Henderson required capital for new equipment he offered Jimmy a 20% stake in the business responsible for the smaller projects. The main company was John Henderson but Jimmy was thrilled to bits to run Henderson and Welsh for John.

He was a very keen footballer and also an exceptionally good dancer. It was while dancing at the various venues across Glasgow that he met Joan and they were to become dance partners. His original dance partner was Sheila Gorman who subsequently married John Henderson the business owner. Jimmy's father, William, was an Orangeman and Jimmy was very keen to join. He was initiated into the Order with the secretive ceremony. He took his membership of the Order seriously and was keen on attending the various functions and marches. However, his business partner John Henderson was a member of a different secret society; he was a Freemason.

One day when John and Jimmy are discussing business the subject of the Orange Order and the Freemasons came up. John suggested to Jimmy that it may be in the business interests for him to join the Freemasons. He did not have to join he emphasised and the Masons would not actively try and persuade him to join. He was told he had to make the application if he wished to join. Jimmy thought about it and soon came to the conclusion that to further his business interests he may be better off in the Freemasons as opposed to the Orange Order.

Both the Freemasons and the Orange Order appeared to have very similar rituals. The difference between the two was that the Orange Order strove hard to ensure a strong Union of Britain with Northern Ireland firmly part of it. Also, it had firm religious value's and definite anti Roman Catholic views were expressed on a regular basis by its brethren. The Freemason's tended to be more middle class with good quality throughout. Jimmy remained a member of the Orange Order but not as active as previous.

He joined the Freemasons but remained only at the First Degree Craft level. In the years running up to the war, Jimmy Welsh worked hard on his fitness and played a lot of football as well as the occasional boxing session. A number of his friends persuaded him to sign for Strathclyde club who played at Springfield Park near Parkhead. He was an instant success playing at inside right and the Strathies started to win on a very regular basis.

Jimmy's relationship with Joan blossomed and they were permanent partners in various dance competitions. Jimmy proposed marriage and Joan accepted despite deep reservations from both her parents.

They were professional people and somehow the idea of their daughter with a scaffolder was not really what they wanted. They had met previous boyfriends of Joan who they thought were better suitors for her hand in marriage. However, Joan was besotted with Jimmy. The family reluctantly agreed to the wedding but refused to finance a church wedding. The wedding was held in a Registry Office but Joan's parents paid for the hire of a room in the upper class Central Station Hotel.

Joan and Jimmy rented a tenement flat which was in reasonable condition. However, no sooner had they moved in than World War 2 broke out. Jimmy immediately volunteered and was soon in the Black Watch. After long intense periods of training, the Regiment were impressed with Jimmy's fitness and leadership as a soldier.

Over a relatively short period he was moved up through the ranks and promoted to Sergeant. He had several postings on various missions abroad. However, the most intense action was reserved for the final two years of the War when the Black Watch, with several other Regiments, pushed through Germany.

After VE day Jimmy stayed on in the Army for a short while before returning to Glasgow and Joan. William and Mary were born within 18 months of one another. However the character of Jimmy Welsh changed markedly after the War.

He did not return to playing or even watching football on a regular basis. He was struggling with the situation in the tenement and his mind seemed to drift. John Henderson gave him his old job back but he was frequently absent; certainly not the enthusiastic individual he had been previously.

He seemed to drink more and also to gamble. To enable him to have some money John bought his share in the business offshoot he was supposed to be running. Joan and Jimmy started to argue.

In his single end at 20 Craigton Road, Jimmy moved out of his thoughts; he was feeling sorry for himself. Joan should really have been more understanding and given him a    second chance. The situation made him unhappy. Also making him unhappy was the situation at Harland and Wolff.

It took the Electric section all of a few days to realise that he was not an electrical man.

84

The ploy of introducing a 'self checking' system and 'peer to peer' questioning so he did not have to be involved was not working. Key decisions had to be made to enable things to progress and his in tray of Memorandum's was piling up. He overheard a few of the workers calling him a 'chancer'. He decided to tell Derek Drummond that he would be leaving one weeks hence and apologise to him.

A tramcar came down Craigton Road and arrives at the corner by the McGregor Memorial Church. There it slowed down and turned right followed quickly by a left turn on its way to Govan. Derek had been to Hogansfield Loch several times by the No.7 Tramcar. On the first occasion it was with his grandfather Boab and on other occasions with his mother Ruth or one of the uncles.

Tramcars were popular and the streets throughout Glasgow had overhead power lines to which the green and yellow livery cars were attached. The best seat on the tramcar was the upstairs front which was almost semi circular and gave great views.

Along Govan Road there was a good view of the Dry Docks over the wall. Paisley Road Toll was a busy junction and the tram went onwards through Tradeston and Central Glasgow. Eventually, a long time later, the Tramcar reached its terminus destination at Hogansfield Loch. Hogansfield Loch near Stepps was a popular spot for Glaswegians and the small loch provided opportunities for boating or sailing boats. Derek`s latest small yacht had a long piece of string attached after previous memories of Elder Park. When the tramcar reached its destination the conductor turned over the wooden seat backs to make them face forward.

On the return trip good views of Central Glasgow were obtained from the upstairs front section as the tramcar went downhill. On reaching Govan the overhead power connectors sometimes came off the overhead power cables and the long pole was required to enable the conductor to re-connect.

Around Glasgow there was a growing number of road accidents and a high proportion involved Corporation Transport in particular Tramcars. Discussions were made to look for other options for moving Glasgow people around the city.At the top end of Copland Road a gang had arrived with a mission. The gang were called the Dukes and they wanted a fight with the Peppers from Cessnock. Some local youths said that the Peppers were not around but if they wanted a fight then they would be able to help. With the attraction of a scrap a number of youths were quickly assembled and the Dukes came off second best until the police arrived.

At Govan Police Court Fiscal Charles James McArthur noted that virtually all of the accused were in their mid teens. Twenty were involved in the fighting and eight were caught by the police officers.

Each were fined £1 for breach of the peace. The supposed leader of the Dukes, Richard Stewart (18), said they were not a gang. The Fiscal asked him why he wore a belt around his neck. Stewart said he wore it around his neck because it did not fit his waist. He had taken it off in the pictures.

Two queue's were forming outside the Lyceum on Govan Road. One queue was for the Stalls; the other for the Balcony. Suddenly, they all became concerned when across the road and from an upstairs tenement a man was throwing bottles out of the window. Fortunately no one was hurt.
In Govan Police Court James McKee pleaded guilty. When Fiscal Charles James McArthur asked McKee who had two previous convictions for breach of peace what prompted his actions. McKee said ' I went oot fur a wee drink and when I got back hame I fell asleep. When I woke up I couldnae get the front door open'. The Fiscal said' Yes so what has that got to do with your breach of the peace ?'.
Mc Kee said 'I threw the bottles oot the windae in order that I could attract some attention'.

With the re-start of the Circus season at Kelvin Hall John Leslie has re-joined the group as one of the clowns. He will be performing alongside his twin brother Jim as Foodles and Boodles at some of the shows. However, his role as a clown this season will be lesser due to a larger than usual number of clowns being available. However, he has offered to help with the considerable number of support roles.

The Kelvin Hall is within easy reach of Govan. When the weather is good John and Jim use the Govan Ferry across the river and walk up the hill to Kelvin Hall. The circus is at the far end of the hall and like previous years there are queues to obtain tickets for the shows.
The shows are all very popular. Bears riding motor-bikes; Collies going through their paces for obedience. Two sisters on the trapeze.

Horses have a prominent role in this years circus and thrill the audience. As always the clowns prove to be extremely popular and Charly Wood steals the show on his uni-cycle.
At the Golspie Street pawnshop of Boulton-Cox , Abe is struggling for breath and wheezes.

His fingers are nicotine stained and he asks George the assistant to man the counter. He knows the cause is probably smoking but he is addicted. Abe looks down at notes he has taken during a recent evening he spent at one of the smaller Central Glasgow gambling club.

Whilst there he surveyed the entry points into the building. He knew entry and exit should not prove too much of a problem. However what he did not know was how to access the safe. He and John had decided that trying to blow the safe door was impossible due to the noise. A safecracker had to be sought and risk plus costs were higher.

Bill in Edinburgh was contacted and a local safecracker with only two previous convictions some years previous was offered. Abe was weighing up the options before he was to discuss the project with John once his Circus period had finished. Ruth prepares her make up. Jimmy Welsh has bought two tickets for a dance at the South Govan Town Hall. The event has been organised by the QuarryKnowe Street Masonic Lodge. A few bands provide the music including the Johnny Dryden Old Time dance band, P.Moran's Band and the Merry Mac Band.

Jimmy has paid the entry of two shillings each. Ruth is taken around the floor by Jimmy and knows the steps to most of the tunes. Where it is possible Jimmy teaches her the basic steps on a few of the others. Ruth is in her element and happy with what she sees is 'her man' . Jimmy is dressed for the occasion and enjoys the evening and the dance evening is a total success.

Around Govan local events frequently were reported in the Evening Times and the Govan Press. These included :All the children are pleased. To celebrate the Queen's Coronation all children are to be given a newly minted half crown. An apprentice plumber, 20 year old William Douglas, was climbing on the tenement rooftops high above 947 Govan Road. His job was to replace some lead that had been stolen. Unfortunately, he slipped on the tiles went over the edge and fell onto the pavement below. William of 98 Neptune Street was rushed to the nearby Southern General Hospital but was found dead on arrival. The young man was very popular along the Govan Road area and many Govanites were distressed by his death.

John Armstrong was a grandfather at the age of 36 years. He was a hawker and lived in a horse drawn caravan with his family of wife and four children and a grandchild. The authorities have asked him to move his caravan on under the trespass law. He has refused.

In Govan Court Prosecuter-Fiscal Mr.James Robertson asks Armstrong why the caravan has not been moved. Armstrong appearing with his family replies that he does not have a horse. PF Robertson asks how he got it there and Robertson replied that he had a loan of a horse but could not afford to buy one and perhaps the police could help him move it as it was heavy. Robertson was fined £1 or 10 days in jail.

Arthur Wilson arrives home late one evening at 93 Blackburn Street. He is very drunk and as he passes each tenement door he kicks out and shouts abuse at his neighbours.

The Plantation police are called and he is taken to the Plantation Police office. Some time later he is taken to Southern General Hospital where he is found to have two broken ribs.

Wilson says that he did not have the broken ribs before he went to the Plantation Police Office and his wife would vouch for that.

Wilson was fined £4 for breach of peace or 20 days imprisonment.

67 year old Andy Brown of Weir Street was arrested 3 times in 36 hours for being drunk and incapable on Govan Road, He was fined £2 and allowed 8 days to pay.
The police officers retrieved a bottle of surgical spirit from his pocket. Thomas Keenan (61) also appeared in court. He had gone home after drinking but his wife would not let him in. Hence he returned to the pub. Some time later he was staggering along Govan Road when he was arrested by two policemen.

He was fined 5 shillings or 5 days in jail by Bailie John Mains for being drunk and incapable. Keenan rustled through his pockets and could only find 4 shillings. Bailie Mains put his hand in his own pocket and said to Keenan 'I will give you the shilling you need'. Alan Russell (17) of 7, Tormore Street, West Drumoyne went down to Govan for a party where he accepted drink as a 'dare'. On the way back he opened the window of the Mc Garrigle house and cut the sash cord. When confronted by the owner he threw stones at the window breaking four panes of glass. He shouted obscenities in Helen Street and assaulted George Smith, a passer by from Kellas Street. Smith was punched and head butted. He then shouted and swore all along Langlands Road. Russell was fined £10 or 60 days in jail for disorderly conduct and assault by Bailie Cuthbertson with 28 days to pay.

John returns from his Clown role at Kelvin Hall and sits in the Golspie Street pawnshop with Abe. It has just gone closing time. Abe is excited about his new 'project' . John listens intently then says ' Are you f**kin mad Abe ?.
You are breaking every rule that we set ourselves. The planning detail must be a bit more than what you have provided. There are third parties coming in from Bill Eadie in Edinburgh who we know nothing about. We scrap it and wait for a better opportunity'. Abe thinks long; his pride hurt.

He says 'I am sorry John, you are right of course. Anyway how did Kelvin Hall go this year ?'. John says 'Abe, it just gets better and better every year. The thing Jim and I love best is to see the joy in the faces of the kids.
They love seeing the elephants, tigers and of course the artists. They are all brilliant. It is a great experience being part of it. Jim and my mother are there virtually every day. The money is good and helps of course but the happiness that the Kelvin hall Circus brings to so many people in these times is what gives them the greatest thrill'.

Roy Fletcher is excited. He has had a breakthrough in trying to find out who has been behind the Boswell Street Art theft and the Gambling Club robberies. He tells his fellow Detectives. 'I am getting good information from Edinburgh at the moment.

A convicted Safe blower has a possible job coming up in Glasgow. He has had his sentence reduced for co-operation in identifying the people behind robberies in both Edinburgh and Glasgow.

So far we have rounded up half a dozen or so and we will soon have them behind bars once they appear in court. It seems a guy called Eadie is the provider of the specialist skills. We will allow things to develop and then collar him'.

At the Old Harmony Bar on Govan Road, plotting of a different kind goes on. Frank Mulvenney and John Gillespie sit in the corner drinking; workers come in at a steady rate. The yards have just closed for the day following the sound of the hooters which resonate all over Govan.

Within minutes the table where Mulvenney and Gillespie sit is full of men in dungarees wanting to know the progress of politics. Many ask for Mulvenney to give one of his regular amusing speeches . Mulvenney replies ' Awe right, awe right' you've twisted my arm. Now I know you have all heard of the Duke of Portsdale down in southern England. Well, he is in to his sport is the Lord and he likes Fox Hunting.

He assembles the hunt on his land, they have 300 horse folk, the wumin's faces look like horses and off they go. 2,000 dogs in front of them to chase after the wee fox and tear it tae ribbons when they catch it.

The Duke Portsdale is so fat he has to be helped on to his horse and his big fat a**e bounces up and doon on the saddle. He shouts 'Tally Ho' and aft they go. They spot a fox and they all give chase.

The Duke lags behind with wumin in tight white troosers ; even bigger fat a** es than the Dukes; and every bit as stupit.

Over hill and dale they go until they see what's left of the poor wee fox lying in front of the dogs. The shout 'Tally Ho', rejoice and off they go back to the local country pub. That is whit they call sport and that is whit they call efficiency. Awe that number of folk an dugs to catch a wee fox. Noo in the shipyards the rat catcher feels disappointed if he disnae bag at least a 100 rats a day.

That is whit yae call efficiency. The Duke goes shooting but misses every time. Hence his flunkies fire wae him and shoot doon the burd and say it was the Dukes shot. Wan day his electric lights failed and his caretaker guy wis oot. The Duchess wanted him to check and replace the fuse for the lights. He went doon tae the basement and found a screwdriver.

He wis havin trouble and took a long time. The Duchess finally came to see him and said 'Darling you might have a better chance of replacing the fuse if you use the screwdriver the right way round'. The Harmony Bar was in uproar with laughter.

Gillespie and Mulvenney were surveying the political situation. John says ' The turnouts at the local elections are poor; just 33% voted in Govan. The apathy is terrible. If we are to win the election we must get the Govan folk more interested'. Frank says 'The workers struggle is ongoing. The capitalists will not give up their ill gotten wealth easily. Only a Communist society will work where everyone is equal'.

John says 'I do not like the Unionists or Tories. However Churchill and many of the upper folk learned a lesson in the war. That is they need the British people behind them and in particular the working classes. That is why they are palatable at the moment. Unfortunately when this generation moves on the replacements are likely to be every bit as nasty to the workers as they were in times gone by'.

John says ' That is why we need the dice to be thrown and a new set of leaders put in place to favour the working classes'. Frank says ' John, You know as well as I that is never gaun tae happen. The Capitalists and the Communists like the smell of power and they will not give it up without an almighty fight'.

A meeting opened in offices of one of Glasgow's leading bankers. The opening statement was read out on behalf of Sir Harold Yarrow of Yarrow Shipbuilders.

In it Sir Harold cited extreme competition from foreign yards who were producing vessels at lower prices and with better deliveries.
To get the Clyde Shipbuilders back on track a better Industrial Relations was required coupled with a lower tax regime. The present taxation on the Yards was leading to lower investment.

A knock on effect from the decline in orders from British Shipping was the British Merchant Navy. The share over the decades of world trade had dropped to 21% well behind the USA. In its peak the British had over 30% of the trade. The Merchant Navy complained of high taxation and higher wages being required to be paid to the sailors in post war Britain. Coal remained a very profitable export and the British Mercantile Marine brought the country £150,000,000 in foreign currency.

## *GOVAN SNIPPETT'S:*

- The Co-operative Shop in Sheildhall Road had a very sturdy Safe. One Friday evening a few safe blowers gained entry to the shop and set off a massive explosion. The safe remained firmly closed.
- Scottish Unemployment reached a 10 year high with 3.9% of the population out of work. This was almost twice the national average 2.2% and the decline in shipbuilding was causing concern for the Govan folk.
- The Govan Ward Committee put on an occasion for the Old People of Govan. At Govan Town Hall they had a Dinner and a Concert and all were given £1 each.
- At 58 Holmfauldhead Road tragedy was unfolding. 24 year old Amie Mackie was found on the floor in a gas filled kitchen by her mother. She was quickly transferred to the nearby Southern General but all attempts to revive Amie failed. The death was attributed to gas poisoning.

# CHAPTER 9
# WATER ROW MURDER

A large crowd has gathered at Govan Cross. TV cameras are being set up and newspaper reporters push through the crowds. There has been a murder at No.1 Water Row. Govanites ask as they arrive 'Who wis murdered ?' or 'Whit happened ?'. A man answers both questions. Mr.McZephyr has been murdered and they are looking for his flat mate.

Mr.McZephyr was the name of a radio character in the 'Mc Flannels' a few years previous. The voice was that of George Mc Neil and he owned the flat where his pyjama clad, badly decomposed body was found. Mc Neil , who was 47, was a youth leader and was employed as a welfare executive at Fairfields Shipyard.

The police announced immediately that they sought his flat mate 24 year old John William Gordon. Gordon was a tall fair haired freelance writer and it was thought he was abroad. The police were contacting their counterparts in France and Spain where it was thought Gordon had fled.

A Tunnel between Linthouse and Whiteinch is the objective of Lord Provost Tom Kerr. He intends to move heaven and earth to achieve the objective which he hopes will benefit Govan in particular and Glasgow as a whole. He leads a deputation of several Labour MP's to Westminster to press the case for the Tunnel. Also in support are the Clyde Navigation Trust, The Chamber of Commerce and the Scottish Council. Transport Minister Mr.E.T.Lennox-Boyd listens carefully to the arguments put forward.

John and Abe are putting the finishing touches to the plans of their latest 'project' . They have a concern that the Waterloo Place project will need extra 'watchers'. Bill Eadie 'the Edinburgh contact and usual provider of helpers and watchers' they suspect is under surveillance from the police. The Govan pair they have been recommended to seem to be amateurish. Bernie and Junior are small time criminals around Govan.

They usually stay one step ahead of the police. John will meet them at a neutral meeting house and be heavily disguised in a dark room. He will outline the project without giving too many specifics and threaten them as to what happens a) If they are caught and b) If they spill the beans on the project once it starts. They meet in a dark empty house on Paisley Road West. They sit on the floor and John details the contact arrangements. They will be by messages left in a few of the telephone boxes along Paisley Road West. The directory page 100 will tell them where to meet and what they have to do. As a clown John is used to quick change routine's and keeps his two accomplices in control. For the first time Abe and John are concerned but feel the risk of using Bernie and Junior can be controlled. Abe outlines the plan. 'John, this one is a ground floor establishment at the rear of a Restaurant Bar. The rear door is alarmed and the windows barred.

Details of the murder in Water Row continue to emerge. George Mc Neil was found in his pyjamas; his head beaten by a heavy object. His savings bank account had money taken out. Cheques were cashed from his account and in both cases the description of the man withdrawing the money matched that of John William Gordon . The passport of Mc Neil was also stolen. News came through from Spain that a man had been arrested in Gerona resembling the description of John William Gordon. He was apparently heading to Tangiers.

John William Gordon had a large number of addresses while in the UK and had an association with the secret Research Establishment at Harwell in Berkshire. John was tall fair haired and very confident. He was well liked by most who met him. His job was listed as a freelance journalist. The British Consulate established that Gordon was going to Tangiers to meet Carl Kuhamski in connection with his top secret Harwell work.

More details emerged about George Mc Neil, the murdered man. He had been employed as an officer at the Pearce Institute for 3 years before taking up his post as Welfare Officer at Fairfields Shipyard. He enjoyed his Radio Work and his youth officer duties. He had fame for his part as Mr.Mc Zephyr in the Mc Flannels broadcast from BBC Broadcasting House in Glasgow. It was said in the press that he had been killed by maniac force blows.

Gordon, when confronted with the news of Mc Neil's death, said ' I heard that George had been shot but I have nothing to do with it. I heard he had gone to France prior to that'.The Scottish Justice system wanted Gordon back to Glasgow as soon as possible for questioning.

There was much rejoicing around Govan when it was announced that Lord Provost Tom Kerr had been successful in his bid to have a Clyde Tunnel built. The Lord Provost continued to meet a large number of guests in the City Chambers.

To break the ice with poor relations with the Russians he invited a party of 26 to the Chambers .

They included Doctors, Teachers, Artists, Trade Unionists and others.

Tom Kerr greeted them all and burst into song with the 'Volga Boatmen' which brought smiles to all the faces of the Russians. In return a few of the Russians recited works of Robert Burns.

In Govan Police Court a 70 year old knife grinder is conducting his own defence and the court is in uproar with laughter. Charles Rae has been accused of being a Pedlar and not having a Pedlar's License.

The Prosecutor Fiscal was Inspector Sharpe and Baillie Brown and Bailie Valance  listened intently. Rae said 'The Police Constable said tell that to the Marines. I said I am not telling it to the Marines, I am telling it to you. !'. Rae produced a sheaf full of papers and presented them to the court. He said ' These documents prove I am a knife grinder with my own regular customers.

I am not a pedlar because I sell nothing but my labour. I have to do that to live !'.

He continued ' The Pedlar's Act of 1871 was for the sole purpose of dealing with undesirable persons moving from town to town with dunnage. They offer goods for sale. I am a skilled craftsman !'.

Baillie Valance said ' Nobody is disputing your skill and, certainly, nobody is saying you are an undesirable Charlie ! Part of the definition of a Pedlar is a person offering his skill in any craft. You did this and you must have a license'. Ballie Valance found the case proven. He said 'All you have to do is buy a license for 5 shillings as you leave this court. Then you will not have to come back here quoting chapter and verse about Tinkers, Pedlars or Candlestick makers'. Rae joined in the laughter and said 'I will get the certificate; I just thought I did not need one. Thank you your honour !'.

In Waterloo Place it is the monthly Ladies gambling evening. Gamblers frequently come outside the back door to chat and smoke. However, the ladies gambling field to see who wins the big prizes has been whittled down and the last four ladies are at the table. The audience crowds round; this is the crucial part of the evening.

Through the back door three more persons enter and immediately turn down a short corridor and into the Gents Toilet.

With the gamblers at the table there is no one in the Toilets. John, Bernie and Junior go beyond the last WC and John produces a screwdriver and removes a wooden panel very quickly.

All three go behind the wooden panelling and John pulls the wooden panel back into place. John has a beard glasses and a wig.

Bernie and Junior both have false moustaches. They are in for a long wait in a very confined space. The night wears on, the gamblers thin out and leave the club. It is now quiet and the three emerge from the panelling. John replaces the Panel. They look down the longer corridor and see Joe O'Donaghue.

He is locking up the front of the premises having already secured the back door. Joe goes to the office and sets the Glasgow Secure door alarms. Joe is merry having had plenty to drink from the many guests at the club. He leaves the club into Waterloo Place on his way home.

Joe is a devout Roman Catholic and must sober up to attend the 11.00 am Sunday Mass the following day.

Once Joe is gone, Bernie watches the back door while Junior is the lookout on the front door. John easily opens the lock into the office and the Chubb Safe is one he is familiar with.

He will try and listen to the giveaway internal clicks which will provide him with the combination. He needs silence but every few minutes a bus passes and drowns the noise spoiling his hearing quest.

John has come prepared with a strong drill to use if the combination cannot be obtained. Half an hour has passed and he is still struggling to hear the clicks. Bernie and Junior watch intently the street outside.

Drunks sing and occasionally a police officer moves them on. For Bernie and Junior this is their big moment in the life of crime. They are going to be rich beyond anything they have ever had. John is still working on the combinations and thinks he is close.

He produces his note pad and pencil. Left 2 5 and 8  Right 7 9 and 3. Only one number is now required. If in doubt with a Chubb safe the number 0 usually provides the open safe option. He starts the combination's and enters the numbers. Now for 0 and a louder click is heard; the door has opened. John looks at the bundles of money in the safe. However, he notices that there are several batches that appear to be cleaner and more uniform than the rest. Most cash money going across a gambling table or in a day to day transaction becomes dog eared with just some new notes. He is suspicious; a sizable amount of jewellery is in the safe also. Anything from watches to earrings to bracelets have been given up in the evening and previous weeks.

Abe would have little difficulty in processing the merchandise through his contacts in Hatton Garden and Jersey.

The last obstacle is to exit the premises without setting off the burglar alarm. John goes to the Glasgow Secure box.

He has a key to open it and smiles as he makes the adjustments. He changes over a few wires on the timer and puts a different setting on the dial. He disables the mute button. The trio are ready to leave. Waterloo Place is quiet. However, a passing car shines its headlights into the doorway and Bernie sees John's eyes. They are not normal and he is slightly cross eyed. The disguise is perfect but Bernie now knows that his main accomplice has an eye impairment.

The next morning the staff arrive at Waterloo Place. As soon as the door is opened all the bells which are very loud sound off. The police are called and Roy Fletcher is soon on the scene.

The bells cannot be silenced by pressing the mute button. John Loizou the gambling house owner is soon on the scene and is furious with Roy Fletcher. He says 'Roy if this is what I think it is, you and I are going to have some serious discussions. Glasgow Secure who you recommend have let us down again.

This timer system is rubbish !'. John discreetly goes into the office. The safe is closed. He opens it and as he feared the contents are gone.  Roy says ' John ' All is not lost. I will speak to you later about this. The robbers are just about to be caught !'.

John William Gordon was back in Glasgow and soon appearing at Glasgow Sheriff Court charged with the murder of George Mc Neil.

The Empire Glasgow has the toughest audience in the world to please. Some artists had been known to be reduced to tears as they are booed off the stage. However, one new artist has captured the imagination of the Glaswegian's; he is Frankie Vaughan who sings with pianist Bert Waller.

The queues outside the Empire are long to see the former Leeds United colt footballer and boxer. Glasgow had taken Frankie Vaughan to the city's heart and he was a regular, welcome visitor.

Thomas Leeming (30) wanted his partner to return to him. He threatened Annie Fitzpatrick (25) he would cut her hair or break her legs if she did not. Leeming went to her lodgings and took scissors from the mantelpiece during an argument and cut several locks of hair.

In court Leeming claimed that Annie had a tendency to run off and not care for their two young children. At this time he was caring for the children after she had once again run off. Police Judge Smith told Leeming not to indulge in any more Sweeney Todd barber activity and not to threaten. The sentence was deferred for 6 months pending good behaviour.

Tom Kerr, the Glasgow Lord Provost, opened an extension to the Mitchell Library with Lord Rosebery . The Lord Provost was very active and his prowess extended to some impromptu singing and piano playing to audiences who probably not expecting it. Kerr  always said his second football team was Rangers; Benburb were his first and he was good friends with the Rangers manager Bill Struth. Both had served on the Benburb committee in the 1940's. It was fitting that Lord Provost Tom Kerr should be asked to present Bill Struth with a Portrait of the Rangers manager by C.D.Chapman at the Glasgow City Chambers.  Bill Struth had joined Rangers as a trainer in 1914 and became manager in 1921. He had a leg amputated around a year previous and despite illness the 77 year old had steered Rangers to Cup and League double.

At an Education Exhibition at Bellahouston, Tom Kerr gave an insight to his schooldays.

He said ' I left school two weeks before my 13th birthday. I see a number of my school teacher friends in the audience. In order to convey to you something of the bonhomie that now exists between teacher and pupil. I can assure you that voice of the headmaster  terrified me more than the thunder of Jehovah. I can only tell you of the awe, reverence  and terror that the teachers held for me'.

Tom Kerr went on to say how delighted he was that so many choirs were taking part in the festival.

A few weeks later Lord Provost Kerr was offered a Knighthood for his services to the public which were considerable. He declined the offer.

The Lord Provost spoke out to encourage more boys to play football. Tom Kerr believed that football generated a good principle for physical activity as well as building teamwork essential for the workplace.

He called on the authorities to improve the school facilities to cater for more football to be played and that included the Rugby playing schools.

No sooner had the remark been made than a fierce attack on him came from Allan Glen's School Rector Alexander Mc Kimmie.

He says These are vicious attacks on our school and with the avowed intention of forcing us to play football.'.

The remarks sparked a huge Rugby v Football debate and the strength of attack by Mc Kimmie brought many to ask him to apologise to Tom Kerr the Lord Provost. Mc Kimmie refused but was then asked by the town clerk to substantiate his remarks. Around Govan Allan Glen's was being seen as very aloof. Some years previous they had played football and been successful.

At 31, Daviot Street, Ruth still lives with Derek, father Boab and brothers Robbie and Jack. She sees Jimmy Welsh at 20, Craigton Road on a frequent basis and helps him with his housework and washing. Ruth has just returned from a few home help jobs she has being carrying out in Central Govan.

She says to Boab ' I have doon tae Govan today. The hooses doon ther are terrible and getting worse. The family with 5 kids opposite the wumin I wis doing work for are living in awful conditions. Their tenement comprised of two sizable rooms but no bathroom. A large sink was used for most purposes. The first floor flat had 5 families and two toilets on the landing to suffice.

Around Govan there are many similar tenements offering the same very limited space. The re-generation of housing stock seemed to be taking an eternity and virtually all the families concerned yearned for something better. The area's around the middle of Govan were particularly challenging for the families and in particular the 'Wine Alley'.

As well as housing, concerns were being expressed about the security of employment and in particular the shipyards; things were gradually slowing down. When an order was secured Govan was a happy place but firm orders seemed to be drying up with Harland and Wolff at Govan Cross in particular seemingly feeling the pinch. The shipyard had its own railway spur which saw a small steam engine train deliver and remove equipment.

The traffic would be stopped on Govan Road, a gate would open and a steam train would emerge from the yard crossing Govan Road with the Plaza picture house on the left and Govan Cross on the right. Nearing the end of the day if a train came out it was followed by many workers presumably relying on their workmates to clock them out.

One day while Derek was home his mother Ruth noticed he was scratching a lot. When she looked inside his shirt there was a considerable number of red spots. A visit to Doctor Duff in Langlands Road quickly diagnosed measles and he was told not to go to school for at least a week or two.
In the event, virtually the entire class at Drumoyne School was off with the same illness; surely one of the most contagious and unpleasant experiences. Endless Calamine Lotion eventually did the trick and the pupils began to drift back to School.
Derek was enjoying school and was taking special interest in the history lessons especially The Old and Young Pretenders. The story of Flora Mc Donald saving Bonnie Prince Charlie from capture and the loyalty of the highlanders captured the imagination of the class.
Drumoyne School is becoming ever more interesting with an excellent Miss Doig teaching. Some of the lessons are repetition especially the times tables $2x2 = 4$; $2x3 = 6$ Right up to $9x8 = 72$ and $9x9 = 81$. All the class chant out the tables parrot fashion but also have a good grasp of the counting in detail.

- Fairfields Shipyard were concerned about the theft of brass from their premises so a trap was set to establish who was guilty of the thefts. Brass fetched a good price. One evening a prime suspect Alexander Mac Farlane a ships plumber was stopped in Saracen Street with a bag of metal over his shoulder. Admitting the offence in Govan Police Court James Robertson the prosecutor Fiscal fined Mac Farlane £10 or 60 days in jail. 'Stealing from your employer is a very serious offence'. Mac Farlane was sacked.Also at Govan Police station

- Chief Detective Inspector James Morris retired after 18 years at the Govan Division. In his time he solved many crimes and was responsible for the hanging sentence on two murderers.

- James Marshall (29) was sitting on the top deck of a tram car. A man got out of seat and said to him ' Hey, You and I are gaunae have a fight !'. An argument ensued and commotion erupted on the tramcar. The challenger Robert Herson (49) and the challenged James Marshall got off the tramcar and went into the backcourt of a nearby tenement. A large crowd gathered to watch the fight including women and children before the police arrived. In Govan Police Court Herson who had 11 similar convictions was fined £4 or 20 days imprisonment. Marshall was fined £1 .

- Mr. and Mrs Joseph Roberston of 34 Mc Kechnie Street celebrated their Golden wedding Anniversary on the same day as the Govan fair. They recalled the many parades through Govan over the many years they were together. Most of their family had moved abroad although there son was home for the occasion.

- There was a huge man at Govan Cross and he was about to retire. He was 17 stone Tommy Black who had been 33 years in his job as points man. He had to control traffic on the private railway line from Harland and Wolff into the Govan Mineral Yard where it crossed Govan Road. His hobby was singing and he was bass singer at White Memorial Church choir. Tommy helped children to cross the Govan Road to the Plaza Cinema and was employed by the Govan Police.

Three old men were arguing outside the Pearce Institute about football. The arguments became more heated and the Institute Caretaker called the police. In Govan Police Courts Fiscal Charles MacArthur asked 76 year old Stephen Monaghan what the argument was about and why did he use his fists. Monaghan of 155 Neptune Street says 'I didnae use my fists !. I know mer aboot fitba than these other guys. In fact I have forgotten more aboot 'fitba than they ever knew. We awe hid a wee drink'. Monagahan was fined 10 shillings.

Jimmy Welsh is a Freemason and he occasionally has a drink problem. However, no matter how drunk he gets he does not divulge any secrets of the Brotherhood. Jimmy joined many years ago when he had a small share in the business of John Henderson. Jimmy serviced a number of clients most of whom were Freemason's when he was active as part of Henderson and Welsh Scaffolders.

He meets with a number of his former customers at the meetings and they discuss everything and anything that comes along. Most are of a similar persuasion; mostly middle aged, Conservative/Unionist biased and many are very sociable.

The Masonic Halls are well kept up in appearance and the meals and drinks with the company after ceremonies are greatly enjoyed by Jimmy. He is always willing to help with fundraising efforts to help needy causes. The actual Ceremonial parts involving rolling up trouser legs, nooses and other rituals did not bother Jimmy and it appeared that the Lodges he now attended usually Kinning Park or Govandale were recruiting new members on a regular basis.

The membership in Scotland was well on its way to reaching around 100,000. It appeared that many Protestants were drifting away from the attendance at Churches in favour of a good class of Working Men's Club that might give them a leg up when the situation arose.

When, with Joan, Jimmy would attend the Ladies Night but Ruth would probably be very unlikely to attend if asked. She felt more at home in a conventional Working Mens Club or a nice pub.

She knew little of the Freemason's except that Jimmy attended occasionally the various Lodge meetings. He would receive letters on a regular basis on plain envelopes and had a chest under the bed with his Masonic Regalia.

.

Definitely not in the Freemason's were Robbie and Jack. Both never had the inclination to join and were contented with life outside the Brotherhood. Life at 31 Daviot Street went on as usual. The Corporation had sealed up plenty of cracks in the wall to prevent the mice coming in and it seemed to be doing the trick. One day the door knocker goes and Derek answers. A tall swarthy figure with a turban is standing in front of him. He has an open case full of ties, cravats, stockings and silk.

With a huge smile he introduces himself politely and offers his wares. Derek says 'My Maw is not in at the moment'. That was the first time Derek had seen anyone other than a white person.

Robbie is continuing in a job in the Fairfield yards as a labourer. He is not over enchanted with the job but at least it is work. Robbie was a qualified toolmaker but never really got into the swing of an organised workforce anywhere he was employed. He tended to work for a while, save up plenty of money and then quit his job. With the money he had saved he would go and enjoy himself until it run out and then the process would start all over again.

Unfortunately, when work was less plentiful, he could be on the 'broo' for a wee while until something turned up. Robbie was a rebel and a non conformist. He read books as though they were going out of fashion in particular non fiction. Socialism was his politics and most of his views were well left of centre.

Robbie was once conscripted into the Army and spent some time in Libya although not on active service. There were few subjects that Robbie did not seem to know about and he followed the news ardently on the television, radio and in the papers. Robbie had Communist party sympathies for a while. Like most of the family, Robbie supported the Orange principles against Republicanism although he did not belong to either the Orange Order or the Freemasons.

He had no grievance with Roman Catholics but disliked the Roman Catholic Church. That said he, like the rest of the family, had no great affinity to the Protestant churches. Robbie, to sum up, was a quiet man; content in his world of books and enjoyed what Scotland had to offer. He did not like Jimmy Welsh because of the way he dealt with his relationships to Ruth.

A few storm clouds were beginning to gather over the Govan Shipyards by way of employment. Industrial relations at the yards were never 100% going back many years or even decades. Older workers often recalled the battles of previous times with the employers and in particular the 'Red Clydeside' strikes during the Great War of 1914-18. Just prior to 1914 the Trade Unions had negotiated an increased deal by collective bargaining. As the War started the employers asked for the increase to be postponed due to the Emergency situation as everyone was helping in the war effort.

Western Scotland had the highest number of volunteers for the forces per head of population in the UK and they fought and often died bravely amid horrendous losses. However as a contrast to the volunteering they also had the highest number of people opposed to the war. Disputes were numerous; some of which were understandable. The Fairfields workers some 10,000 strong walked out when the Housing Factors started throwing families out on the streets for unpaid rent arrears. . It transpired in many cases the reason for the late or non payments was that the man of the house was on the front line in France or Belgium. The issue reached the very top of the Government circles and they conceded that the rents would be frozen until the end of the War. Buoyed with is success the Trade Union movement throughout Glasgow pressed for a wage increase. This went down badly with the rest of the UK who felt that the Glasgow Trade Unions were unpatriotic and the media of the day felt they were traitors.

The Prime Minister Lloyd George came up to try and resolve the issue.
In a famous meeting he probably lost the debate but afterwards sent in the troops to restore law and order. The result was many famous protesters like David Kirkwood and Manny Shinwell got arrested and with others went to jail for short sentences. Another frequent bone of contention was the recruitment of lesser qualified staff to carry out works previously taken on by highly skilled staff.

On the one hand the Shipyard owners wanted to reduce its costs and could not afford to permanently have the highest graded workers on the highest wages even when the order book was low.

The Shipyard workers saw it as the thin end of the wedge and felt that if they were to leave their jobs they would have difficulty finding work elsewhere in times of recession. Trust between the two sides was never high and the same situation existed into the 1950's.

Jimmy Welsh has made a return to the Bridgeton Arms to see Richard and many of his old friends. He surveys the issue's of the day as he reads the Evening Times newspaper. 'Look at this Richard'.

House building at an all time high since the Unionists have come to power. The economy is powering ahead and Labour's Austerity programme for everything is finishing thank God. Only businessmen with the true Protestant work ethic will turn things around.

Jack Nixon Browne the MP in Govan is doing great stuff in the Houses of Parliament. The next election will be a walk over for the Conservatives.

Richard says ' Yes, things are improving but there are still a lot of people that believe in the Labour people'. Jimmy says ' The figures speak for themselves. People's standards of living are increasing. If the Communists in the yards would only give the Government a chance then they would see a difference.

They think they are skilled and educated. However they do not seem to realise that the present Government members have been educated in the highest standard schools and Colleges. They know how the money markets work; how to see that the speculations and investments benefit everyone. The profits are filtered down to the business's through investment in the countries industries.

From these investments comes the jobs and prosperity'. Richard says ' You are right Jimmy. What would a guy in dungarees know about getting investment, he would not know where to start. The country would disintegrate into chaos. Labour seems to support the two extreme positions of Communism and the Roman Catholic Church. The ordinary hard working people in the middle who go out and work hard are the one's they should claim to help'. Jimmy says ' Just look at that 9,160 houses have been built in the first three months of this year. Over the UK the figure is 345,000 an increase on the Governments target of just 300,000. Life could hardly be better for many people. I imagine the improvement will soon be arriving in Govan'.

John Leslie is spending an increasing amount of time with Sandra. He loves her to bits and is planning to propose to her. He has thought about the engagement ring he wants to buy. He has of course; unknown to Sandra; accumulated a considerable amount of money from his 'projects' with Abe. The following Saturday he plans to take Sandra into Glasgow and spend some money on her in the various clothing shops; Sandra loves looking smart and has a good taste.

Sandra and John were on top of the No.4 bus on its way from Govan to Glasgow Central; John was accompanying Sandra to look for clothes in the Glasgow shops and Sandra was in her element. To Lewis's they went; the ground floor displayed gloves and Sandra's eyes were affixed.

She said to John ' I wish I could afford some of these gloves !'. They are lovely'. John said 'Sandra, We have had a really good week at Abe's. I have brought out some money for you to spend. Come over here !'. From his pocket he drew out two hundred pounds. Sandra says ' John, you do not need to spend any money on me that`s not fair !'. John says ' Do not worry Sandra; I cannot think of a nicer young lady who I would like to spend my money on.

You are lovely and you will look a wee bit better in the gloves'. Sandra smiled ' OK but if you run out of money let me know !'. John says ' Do not worry Sandra you have a budget of £200 to help me spend !!'. Although she felt a bit guilty Sandra was looking at some of the clothes she thought she would look smashing in and gain John's approval.

She bought black turquoise Rayon gloves for 4 shillings and 11d and a colourful floral frock at 30 shillings was then purchased. Sandra liked all sorts of jewellery in Lewis's and she purchased a few brooches and earrings from the cheaper ranges at 1 shilling and sixpence each.

She went over and smiled at John 'Could I try on the stockings ?' John says '
I thought you would never ask'. The sample bear brand of 15 denier stocking
was tried by Sandra in the fitting room and she came out to show John. His
heart raced and at 8 shillings John thought he had a bargain. He said 'I will
give you some money and you can sort out the frilly knickers to go with them'.
Sandra blushed and said 'John !'. The couple had a lunch in a restaurant before
going to C and A Modes and the cycle of selection and try ons by Sandra went
on.
Filled with bags of wrapped parcels with brown paper and string, the couple
returned to Govan.

A project for Govan Schools had been organised. Lord Provost Tom Kerr
wanted all Govan children, totalling several thousand, to know about the Govan
Fair and its origins on its anniversary. Twenty one schools heard various
speakers outline the same text and speak about the Fair. The route for this year
would take the fair along Langlands Road, Burleigh Street onto Govan Road,
along to Copland Road, Edminston Drive and disperse at Broomloan Road.
A fireworks display was organised to start at Cardonald Park at 10pm in the
evening and a large crowd was present. The carnival Queen, Anne Andrews, of
Govan High School was crowned by Mrs. Kerr, wife of Tom Kerr and Lady
Provost of Glasgow.

A huge sum of money was collected for charity which was distributed
between the local hospitals and institutions. Benefiting from the collection were
Southern General Hospital , David Elder Hospital and the Hawkhead Assylum.
John has met up with Bernie and Junior in the dark at the same empty house in
Paisley Road West. He is again heavily disguised and gives them specific
orders. 'You are being paid for your work which you have carried out well.

I suggest strongly that you do not change your spending habits for at least six
months or a year. Even then be careful. The polis are on the look out for anyone
who has more cash than they usually have. Do I make myself clear ?'. Junior
and Bernie both said 'Yes'. John gave them the money owed for the project
and it was more than either Junior or Bernie had ever held in their hands.

What John did not tell the pair was that the money they were being provided
with was likely to have the numbers recorded; the notes had several batches of
consecutive numbers not consistent with cash at the table gambling.

The trial of John William Gordon was arousing enormous interest around
Glasgow and much discussion. Ruth says to her father Boab' What do you
think about Gordon ?'. Boab replied 'Well he is an interesting character.

The evidence does seem strong against him and I think he will be convicted
unless other evidence comes out at the trial. Ruth says 'Well there has been a
development in tonight's papers. A guy has admitted the killing of George
McNeil . He is currently locked up in Hawkheid Mental Hospital'

The first is he knew Mc Neil having worked with him at The Pearce Institute for a while; also second, he has murdered before in similar ways to this murder !!'. The trial starts in front of Lord Sars the Judge. The first part of the trial is spent looking at the Robert Matthews confession. Several witnesses stated that it could not have been Matthew's as he was seen in the Hawkhead Mental Hospital at the probable times of the murder. Also he was prone to telling lies. The Jury are quickly asked to discount the evidence and confession of Matthews.

Gordon had little in the way of an alibi. He had cashed the cheques belonging to McNeil, he was seen in the tenement flat at the time and the case against him became compelling. A character reference, Mr George McLeod of the Iona Community group, spoke highly of Gordon and could not believe he was capable of carrying out such a terrible crime.

The trial was short and the mainly women jury were soon asked to deliberate and provide the verdict. It was by a majority, said the foreman. 'Guilty of Murder !'.A number of the women jurors wept as the verdict was read out; the suspense caused by the interest in the trial was immense. Lord Sars donned his black cap very briefly before removing it which was unusual.

He sentenced John William Gordon to be hanged by the neck until he was dead. The execution date was set for 21 days from the end of the trial. Gordon stood impassively as the verdict was read out.

In Govan Police Court they were having problems. Nicholas Cook (47) was staring straight ahead. He was being accused of being disorderly on a stair. Baillie John Mains said 'How do you plead !'.

A court official said 'He is stone deaf and dumb'. After a few minutes they brought in a Braille board and a big writing pad. Nicholas wrote on the board and the letters were difficult to understand. However, it was established it meant 'Not Guilty !'. For a time Nicholas waved his hands around trying to make himself understood. On other occasions he stared straight ahead as the court tried to attract his attention. The trial was postponed to enable a method of communication.

On the River Clyde, no fewer than six launches were scheduled for one week. Mathieson's of Oslo order for an oil tanker was fulfilled by Harland and Wolff. The launch was performed by Mrs. Mathieson the owners wife.
John Brown's at Clydebank launched the passenger ship Arcadia at 28,000 tons for the P and O line. The Greenock dockyard launched the oil tanker Alva Cape.

Three other smaller yards down in Ayrshire provided the other three. Ardrossan Dockyard launched one of the passenger steamers 'Maid of Cumbrae' the last of the four 'Maid' boats built. The Troon Ailsa shipbuilding Co. launched the cargo motorship Pearl and the Fairlie Yard launched the in shore minesweeper HMS Cosham.

In a large house at Morpeth on the outskirts of Newcastle Don Lipton has arrived home. He is serving an apprenticeship at Fairfields and is following in the footsteps of his father James. His father also served an apprenticeship on the River Clyde with Fairfields some years previously.

'How did you like your apprenticeship at Fairfields Don ?' says James. Don replies 'I enjoy my time in Govan although I would not like to live there. The apprenticeship is good and it will always probably be a good reference'. James Lipton left Fairfields yard after his apprenticeship and did an enormous amount of travelling. Apart from a the period during the 2nd World War, he was involved in major construction projects. He started as a project engineer then project manager and became a senior figure in a Multi-National Construction operation.

'Well my lad you will never get a better training than on the River Clyde. When I was young and could not get in the yards for an apprenticeship in Newcastle my father suggested to me to try the Clydeside yards. I was lucky and learned a lot. It is not just the job skills you learn in Govan, it is all about life as I am sure you have found out `. Don and his father both laugh. Don says 'What makes me laugh is that they come straight out of the yards into the pub on a Friday night and drink together, still in the overalls that they have been working in. They are very closely knit and very funny, a sense of humour second to none. Sometimes, when you walk down Govan Road you see men in dungarees who looks so ordinary.

When you are working beside them in the shipyard you realise what fantastic skills they have. You learn about everything from the design, the large steel sections, the hull, the motors and machinery. After that, as the boat nears completion, the fitting out of the luxury parts and quarters. The list is endless and a massive number of trades work together to get a ship built.'

His father says 'that is where they are at their strongest is in their teamwork, they are all inter-dependant. I bet they pulled your leg with your Geordie accent !' Don says 'Yes they did. They said Geordies are really Scotsmen but with their brains knocked out'. His father laughed 'Yes that is what they said to me !'. The only thing that spoils it is the constant 'them and us' attitude of some of the Trade Unionists coupled with a few reactionaries on the management side. If that could be sorted out Govan could expand their shipbuilding yards'. Don said 'It is not going to happen Dad'.

Ruth was upset with the pending execution of John William Gordon. She said to her father Boab 'Its no fair. I am not even sure he killed George McNeil. I do not even think Lord Sars thought he was guilty'. Govanites were organising petitions asking for clemency. The petition was being signed by thousands all over Govan as the Burgh was upset by the verdict. Gordon thought his situation was hopeless and did not appeal. The execution date was set.

At Shettleston unbelievable numbers were signing petitions requesting clemency for 24 year old John William Gordon. An early count revealed 14,000 to add to the Govanites numbers.

A prison officer at Barlinnie Prison was fumbling with nerves as he tried to get the key in the door lock to open. He quickly succeeded and a group of men were moving down the corridor towards the condemned cell. The pace was brisk and at the front was a tall man. He was followed by prison governor Sir William Kerr and the prison chaplain walking together. Behind them were two prison officers.

The pace was brisk and within seconds they were at the door of the condemned cell. The prison officers inside the cell were aware of the arrival and opened the cell door. Inside John William Gordon stood up from sitting on his bed to face the group. The tall man at the front of the group said. 'Are you John William Gordon ?'. Gordon replied unflinching 'Yes'.

The tall man was Lord Provost Tom Kerr and he read from a piece of paper. He said ' I have today received a letter from the secretary of State of Scotland. The contents say that Her Majesty the Queen has granted his request for clemency. Do you understand this ?. Gordon looked impassive and said 'Yes'. At this point the visiting party immediately left the cell.

Gordon's reprieve was met with much relief around the City of Glasgow. However far away to the north of Scotland at Inverness Gordon's mother answered the door after delay to newspapers who told her about the reprieve. She said 'Thank God my prayers have been answered !. I have been awake constantly for days and ate nothing due to stress. I hope they move John up here nearer Inverness so I can seen him'.

# CHAPTER 10
## DO NOT VOTE FOR THE LAIRD'S

The 1955 General Election was fast approaching. In the Old Harmony Bar, John Gillespie, the Trade Unionist and Labour Party member, sat content. He discussed the election progress with just two weeks to go and felt Labour would win Govan by a handsome margin. He says to a packed and interested group of Shipyard workers. 'Govan looks as though it is in the bag. John Rankin will be our MP'. Gillespie had every right to be confident. The boundaries had been changed and Govan had joined with Tradeston. John Rankin was the MP for Tradeston. Jack Nixon Browne had moved from Govan to be a candidate for the re-vamped seat of Craigton. The boundary changes meant he should be more comfortable winning his new territory than the old Govan seat. Apathy was rife throughout the two seats and the predictions were for a lower turnout; favouring the Unionists. Election meetings previously well attended had many empty seats. The years of austerity after the war, blamed on the Labour Party, had given way to a slow gradual improvement in living standards under the Conservatives and Unionists.

Gillespie and his fellow Labour Party members had campaigned throughout Govan on a class ticket; probably unknown to John Rankin the MP. They told the Govanites not to vote for the Lairds and the upper classes. In the final few weeks of the campaign they were canvassing almost entirely in the Craigton seat trying to dislodge the former Govan MP Jack Nixon-Browne. Browne felt he should win easily and was confident. Labour felt they were closing the gap on him and were confident a shock result was on the cards. Jack Nixon-Browne was used to close run elections and that little bit of extra appeal to the wumin voters may sway it his way. He held a rally in front of the Moss Heights which was well attended.

Encouraged by Robbie, Derek has joined the junior section of the Elder Park library. The children`s books are upstairs in the library. Derek likes any books related to boats and enjoys a series of books on tugboats. Virtually every time he hires out a book he descends the stairs and the librarian, a stern elderly gentleman, says 'SHHHH' You could hear a pin drop in the Elder Park upstairs library. One day Ruth is at 31 Daviot Street tidying the house and doing the washing. She is in the stairs blethering to Helen Kenealy and Mrs Johnson. All of a sudden Derek comes into the close at pace looking flustered. He says 'Maw, If Mrs O'Brien comes tell her I am no in !' ' Hold it Derek, what has happened ?' Derek looks out from the close and sees that Mrs O'Brien is still not in sight. 'Maw, I took my stamp album back from John O'Brien' he said excitedly. `We had an argument about religion and I said things I should not have but it was his fault.

I have two stamp albums, my best one which has all my best stamps in it. My other one is for swoppies. Anyway, a few weeks ago I lost it. Today we were looking at stamps and John brought out my stamp book. I said it was my one and asked him to look at the name on the second page. He opened it up and the second page had been torn out. I told him where all the stamps were in the album but he still would not give me my stamps back. I called him a f****** thieving ******. He said that in his religion he is not allowed to steal it is a sin. If he stole he would have to confess but if the theft was property of a non Catholic then he would be cleared of his sin. So I took the book from him. He ran off to get his mother and the other boys are saying I am for it'.

Ruth says 'Well Derek, you should not have sworn at him. Besides you have enough stamps to open your own stamp shop so why bother ?'. 'Maw I do not like him stealing the stamps from me' replied Derek. Mrs. Johnson says 'Do not worry Ruth I will speak to Mrs O'Brien when she comes. Derek is right, John should not have stolen the stamp book; John is wrong to steal from anyone. Roman Catholic or not, it is a sin and he will have been told that many times before. The priest will definitely tell him that if he brings that up at confession'. Ruth and Helen both say to Mrs. Johnson that they are pleased with her offer of help. Derek says 'OK I will give him the stamp book' Mrs Johnson says 'No you won't Derek it is your stamp book and you should keep it. I will tell Mrs. O'Brien that John will not be getting the stamp book.

Mrs Johnson says ' We are Roman Catholics and we believe in our religion. At times we feel we need guidance when difficult issue's come along. I find Confession a good way of getting that guidance especially when I think I may have made a mistake. The priests are good in Govan and they usually give good advice. A few of the younger ones occasionally do not always give the best advice but I suppose that it to be expected'. Mrs O'Brien duly arrived but after a short conversation with Mrs. Johnson went away.

At Drumoyne School the class went through the usual routine. Miss. Doig picked passages from the Bible and explained the meaning of certain chapters. The class had read both the Old and New Testaments at least twice over as reading exercises. The class was encouraged to read and write a lot and great emphasis was placed on the shape of the letters. Nibs on the wooden pens were constantly used and the ink levels went down quickly. The class are excited by a school trip to Calderpark Zoo. The day arrives but the whole trip proves to be a disappointment as torrential rain and high wind mean a lot of standing around in tea rooms and shelters.

The visit is eventually cut short by a few hours as a class full of droon't rats board the bus. However, the weather was much better when a number of local councillors and school board people visit the school.

The school assemble behind Miss McLaughlin's class to see a number of trees being planted followed by some speeches. On this particular day Derek is going to sample a school meal for the first time. Like a number of boys he wants more time playing football in the playground. The meal has round potatoes from a scoop on top of mince beef. Then follows pudding with custard.

The results of the Glasgow seats in the 1955 General Election are being announced. Glasgow Govan has once again been a two horse race. The veteran Labour Candidate and former Tradeston MP looks supremely confident. His Unionist counterpart knows the game is up from looking at the bundles of votes.

### GLASGOW—GOVAN
J. Rankin—Labour—24,818
A.G.Hutton—Unionist—15,216
Labour majority 9,602 on a 79% turnout

Tension mounts for Jack Nixon-Browne at the Glasgow Craigton count. It is very close and a re-count is requested by the Labour candidate Bruce Millan. The indications are that Nixon Browne has just about squeezed through yet again. The re-count figures are offered to the two candidates and Millan accepts defeat.

### GLASGOW—CRAIGTON
J.N.Browne– Unionist—19,120
B.Millan—Labour—18,910
Unionist majority 210 on a 79% turnout.

In Glasgow Labour won 8 of the seats and the Unionists 7.

Elsewhere in the country there were very few seats changing hands. Those that did change went from Labour to the Conservatives. Anthony Eden who had taken over from Sir Winston Churchill was re-elected Prime Minister for the Conservatives.

### 1955 GENERAL ELECTION
CONSERVATIVE AND UNIONISTS—345 seats ( 49.7%)
LABOUR—277 (46.4%)
LIBERALS—6 (2.7%)

Mrs Jesse Gibson of 101 Plantation Street was standing at the corner of Ballater Street. Suddenly some stones came hurtling down from above and knocked her to the ground; the adjacent tenements were crumbling like many others in the Govan area. Many were shored up and some families were being moved from the most dangerous ones.

At Craigton Cemetery, the Statue to Sir William Pearce was badly damaged. The statue was made of marble, bronze and stone and the damage was estimated at £10,000. The complaints were numerous and the local residents were incensed by the vandalism to such a nice memorial. The Police set a trap. Soon they found two youths trampling over graves and firing stones via a catapult at the Pearce Memorial.

In Govan Police Court 17 year old John Mc Menamin and a 16 year old friend appeared in front of Judge A Mc Pherson-Rait. The older boy was fined £5.00 or 30 days in jail. The parents of the younger boy were ordered to pay £5 with 28 days to find the money.

The shipbuilding and steamer trip results confirmed a trend. Clyde sailings were well down and some of the steamers were being withdrawn from service. The huge Ocean going Liner orders were also all but disappearing. For the first time in a long time the Clyde yards tonnage had dropped below 400,000 tones compared with 750,000 before the Second World war. Individual Yards saw Lithgow's at Greenock still the leader of the shipyards in terms of tonnage output.

**Lithgow's (5 vessels) 50,595 tons    John Brown (3 vessels) 43,900 tons**
**Fairfield (2 vessels) 34,500 tons    Scott's (2 vessels) 34, 421 tons**
**Alex.Stephen & son (2 vessels) 33,046 tons   Harland & Wolff (3 vessels) 28,657 tons**
**Denny & Brothers (7 vessels) 27,714 tons  Blythswood Co. (3 vessels) 26,515 tons**
**Chas.Connell & Co. (2 vessels)25,261 tons  Wm Hamilton & Co.(3 vessels)22,041 tons**
**Greenock Dockyard (2 vessels)19,682 tons  Barclay Curle & Co. (2 vessels)17,800 tons**
**Lobnitz and Co. (3 vessels) 5,490 tons George Brown & Co. (3 vessels) 4,813 tons**
**Ailsa Co. (3 vessels) 3,295 tons  Wm Simmons & Co. (1 vessel) 3,000 tons**
**A & J Inglis ( 4 vessels) 2280 tons James lamont and Co. (3 vessels) 2142 tons**
**Ferguson Brothers ( 2 vessels) 1,844 tons Yarrow & Co. (6 vessels) 1,562 tons**
**Fleming and Ferguson (3 vessels) 1,519 tons  Scott and Sons (2 vessels) 532 tons**
**Ardrossan Dockyard (1 vessel) 508 tons**

Ruth has returned home to 31, Daviot Street from a days work as a home help. She gives her father Boab some news on an issue which is upsetting many Govanites. She says 'Da, I just signed another petition !'. Boab replied ' So jist who is aboot tae get hung this time ?'. Ruth says ' Naw it is nothing like that. A family from doon in Govan has just moved in to an empty hoose in Cardonald. They have arrested them and they might be going to jail. Seems a bit unfair as the state of some of the hooses in Govan is awful'

At 6.00 am in the morning the police storm a terraced house in 369 Tweedsmuir Road, Cardonald. They arrest 8 men and two women for trespassing. The action was brought by the Western Heritable Investment Co. of Bath Street, Glasgow.

Later in the same day all ten were bailed at £1 each to appear at a later date. The eight were James Mc Culloch (47) , George Abercrombie (30), Bole Mc Gibbon (30), Henry Curran (29), Norman Dunlop (23), William Mc Queen (23), John Mc Daid ( 21), Karl Mc Culloch (19), Margaret Boyle (34), Janet Devine (19).

The group of ten had taken up residence to protest at the pending removal of the original squatter William Crawford (26) and his wife

The ten were charged with trespass and all pleaded not guilty.

A few days later, at Glasgow Sheriff's Court, Crawford appeared and an agent Mr.Donnelly, presented his defence. He said the property owners had asked them to leave the house and Crawford promised to do so. Crawford argued that as he had no where to go and the weather was exceptionally cold, he decided to stay where he was.

Sheriff Hay decided to put a deferred sentence on Crawford and gave him 6 months to find an alternative house and vacate the property in Tweedsmuir Road.

The other accused were advised by their agent to plead guilty and they too were given a deferred sentence.

The case aroused much interest in Govan and before long Crawford was being given much support from the Govanites.

A few days later, seven men were charged with squatting in a similar manner as the Cardonald case. Charlie Mc Donald (23 and Angus Bowie (23) were found squatting in 133 Elderpark Street without the owners consent. Johnston Bradshaw Addison (24) was found living in a property in 66, Copland Road, James Dickson (22) living in 62, Elderpark Street, Francis Patrick Carr living at 110 Neptune Street. Two other men had similar charges and all were allowed bail of £1. Subsequently a deferred sentence was imposed and the accused ordered to remove themselves from the houses.

Bernie counts his money in preparation for booking his trip with Junior to London. He is £10 short to pay for the Excursion to the UK capital. He thinks perhaps just one of the notes from the bundle hidden behind a drawer panel would hardly be noticed.

At the Glasgow Central Police station Roy Fletcher is told that a bundle of notes handed in to the Clydesdale Clearing Bank contains one from a robbery some months previous. The notes were traced to the booking hall of Central Station. The most promising lead of several was a man who talked about going to the Cassanova Gambling Club in London's West End. . The ticket issuer could not remember what he looked like. The name provided could not be traced.

Roy Fletcher alerted his counterparts at New Scotland Yard on the London Embankment.

# CHAPTER 11
# WOOLWORTH'S ARRIVES

Ruth is pacing up and down the first floor tenement at 31 Daviot Street. She is due to be off shortly to an interview for a position at the new Woolworth store due to open a few weeks hence. Ruth says to her father Boab ' I really want this job Da and I am a nervous wreck'. Boab is reading the paper and taking in the content that is a Queens Park win. 'Do not worry Ruth you will get the job; of that I have no doubt !' `Dae ye think so Da !' says Ruth now drawing heavily on a cigarette. 'No problem' says Boab continuing to read the paper.

Ruth turns up for the interview at Woolworth's in Langlands Road. The shop fitting works are in full swing in order to meet the store opening deadline. Once inside Woolworth's Ruth is directed down a partitioned off passageway which leads to a corridor where there are 12 seats lined up against a wall at the far end. The first 4 seats are occupied by other hopefuls. Ruth sits down on the 5th seat already a bundle of nerves. This was the best job she had ever applied for. The young lady in the seat beside her was reading a book, wearing glasses and was smartly dressed. Ruth got up and put her bag on the seat. 'Could you look after my bag please while I go outside for a fag' 'No problem' said the young lady.

Ruth went outside and walked up and down Langlands Road for 5 minutes before returning inside the Woolworths store. When she arrived back she noticed there were now 7 seats occupied but no immediate sign of her bag. However, she noticed that it was sitting in chair 8.

She went and retrieved the bag and walked back up to speak to the young lady who was supposed to be looking after her bag. 'Thought ye were supposed to looking efter ma bag ?' Ruth said.' The young lady said nothing and continued to read her book. Ruth says ' I will tell you what, I will go in before you !'. Just then a young lady came out and asked for the next interviewee. She had a clipboard and a piece of paper with around 20 names on it.
'I am Fiona McTavish`. The girl with the clipboard looked down and said 'Yes, there you are on the list' and ticked her off'. Can you come this way please 'she continued.

The first few candidates in the chairs moved up but Ruth looked at the young lady with the glasses sternly. The young lady had briefly made a move but sat down and Ruth moved in to the now vacant seat ahead of her.
At the Cassanova Club in Mayfair area of London some detectives have arrived from New Scotland Yard on the Embankment near the Houses of Parliament.

They had forewarned the Croupiers to make sure they keep the pound and ten shilling marked notes separately from the games where Bernie and Junior had played. The bundles were examined but not one of the numbered notes was found.

The call went through to DI Roy Fletcher in Glasgow; he was surprised and disappointed. He thanked his counterpart in London. Bernie and Junior spent a few days in London while the undercover policemen, allocated to trail them, were recalled.

A few days later, Roy Fletcher was given some news that some of the marked notes had arrived at one of the Glasgow Central Banks. It was established that they came from the suspected Waterloo Place gambling club. The gamblers were identified as two aspiring entrepreneurs from somewhere in South Glasgow. Roy Fletcher was furious especially when one of his fellow officers quipped. 'It must be the first time that money has been stolen from a safe and then found its way back into the same safe !'.

Ruth has reached the first seat in the queue at Woolworth's awaiting her turn to be interviewed. The interview panel for this first day of interviews is stronger than usual as the Company are training the newly appointed shop supervisors on interview procedures. In the selection panel of three there is Louise Crampthorn-Pemberton who has come up from a National office in Swindon, England where she is Chief Personnel Manager for the country. Bob Anderson is chief Personnel Manager for the Glasgow Woolworth stores and is the second interviewer. The third interviewer is 25 year old Eleanor Donaldson who is to be the Senior Store Supervisor. The first two interviewers plan to pass on the interview process technique to Eleanor and a few of the other supervisors as well as the Store Manager for subsequent interviews. At the outset of the interviews Louise said to Bob and Eleanor in a soft spoken very correct English accent 'It is very important that we get the right candidates for the job from the off. Otherwise the reputation of Woolworth's could be damaged'.

Ruth enters the room having been ticked off on the applicants list. She says 'Hello, I am Ruth !'.She sits down clenching her bag tightly, knuckles white with fear.

Louise says 'You are Mrs. Wilson, yes I see you are on the list'. Ruth says 'Naw, its Miss Wilson, I am not married!'. 'I see' said Louise.

Bob said 'Thank you for coming Miss Wilson, I will give you a brief outline on our plans for the store and the type of person we think would be suitable'. Ruth said 'Thank you'. Bob outlined the plans for Woolworth, Govan 'I feel the store has good long term potential. The Burgh has been crying out for a store like Woolworths for quite some time'.

He continued to give a short outline of the companies goals. 'Have you any questions so far Miss Wilson' 'Naw, that sounds great Mr. Anderson, I would love the job'. 'Over to you Louise' said Bob. 'Well Mrs.Wilson. Have you got any children ?'. Ruth replied 'Its Miss Wilson and yes I have one son, Derek'. Louise sighed and said 'Hmm' looking at Bob and Eleanor. 'Have you had any experience whatsoever in working in shops ? continued Louise.

'Yes' said Ruth and continued 'I worked in Jimmy Deakins laundry. If you contact him he will tell ye I was a good wee worker.' 'Will you require to have time off if your son is ill ' asked Louise. 'Naw' said Ruth adding nothing to the answer. The interview went on for another few minutes. Ruth stood up and pulled out a photo of Jimmy and one of Derek from her bag. 'That is my man Jimmy,who I hope to marry some day, in his army uniform; he was a Sergeant in the Black Watch. Derek goes to Drumoyne School and that is him at the back' . The panel looked at the photos and Bob said 'Thank you Ruth for sharing those with us'. With the interview completed Eleanor guided Ruth to a small temporary room opposite to await the decision.

At Drumoyne School  many afternoons are spent in Pirrie Park as a good spell of weather prevails over Scotland. Derek  and the rest of Miss Doig's class play as the school teachers bring chairs and watch while having a blether. Pirrie Park is a large expanse of fields behind Drumoyne School. It has both black ash/red ash and grass football pitches as well as a red ash hockey pitch. The single pitch on the right hand lower field has a small raised area of terrace. It was said Scottish League football was once played there.

It is possible that this was the Langlands Park ground of former Scottish League club Linthouse before they moved to Govandale down by the River Clyde in the 1890's. Occasionally, Derek goes down to the field to watch Govan High play and they win virtually every match, having a number of very talented players.  The playing surface was a credit to the grounds man for the pitches, from the side it looked like a billiard table.  During Summer months this field is laid out for the Govan High Sports days.

At Woolworths the interviewers were giving the short verdict on their latest applicant. Louise said 'I think she is completely unsuitable, not really the Woolworth image. We need bright young talented ladies on our counters. For all we know Miss Wilson will never turn up for work due to problems with her son. I believe in married life and wives staying at home looking after children'. Bob gives his verdict ' For the third applicant in a row, I disagree with you Louise. I believe Ruth would be an asset to our Govan store. She said she never had any time off because of her son, apart from when he had Rhumatic Fever and, that apart, has not had a day off sick for many years and I believe her'.

Louise is annoyed and says 'Well I have gone along with the last two Bob but really the standards may not be as high as we should be getting. Most of the candidates cannot speak properly and I assume it is a combination of Gaelic and English. Govan does not seem to be the home of the most intelligent people on earth. Is there any proper education in the Burgh ?'.  Bob says 'Louise, that is the way they speak around here. Ruth would not be selling to your London Oxford Street customers, she would be selling to Govan people and they definitely do not have any trouble understanding one another ! .

They think their English is good enough. Also, Govan has three schools, all with good reputations. The Roman Catholics have about 25 to 30 % of the Govan population and they are served by several Primary Schools and St.Gerrards the Secondary school. The rest (70% +) go for the regular School Board Education. In Govan's case it is Govan High and Bellahouston Academy. Their pupils come from a sizable number of Primary Schools in the Burgh'.

Eleanor said 'I went to Govan High and it was a good school when I was there. All the Primary Schools in Govan have a good reputation for having good teachers.'. Bob said 'Getting back to Ruth Wilson.

I see she has worked as a home help for a lot of her life. Looking at what she wrote down as her wage she is easily affordable. In fact her wages are so poor that I do not know how on earth she survives with a boy on that income. Eleanor for the 3rd Candidate in a row, you have the casting vote. Could you see Miss Ruth Wilson fitting into your shop floor team ?'.

Ruth leaves the interview and goes outside Woolworth's, she is still a bundle of nerves and hoping beyond hope that she gets the job. A job in Woolworth's would be a step up from a laundry lady or a home help.

She lights up a cigarette and blows the smoke skywards. On the way home she decides to go past 20 Craigton Road and see if Jimmy Welsh is in. He has asked her to let her know the result.

At Woolworth's the Interviewers are packing up. All 20 candidates turned up and they have come to their decisions. 'Now lets re-cap' says Bob. 'From the list all No's apart from 4, 9, 12, 13 and 20 are we agreed ?' 'Yes` replied Eleanor and Louise. Bob says that was a good day, 5 recruited already; interest in the jobs has been amazing. Louise says 'Well I will never forget Govan Bob'. It is pronounced 'Guvin' Louise not 'Go van.

They are a very close knit community with a massive population of over 100,000 condensed into a very small area of only one or two miles. In the circumstances they must get along together and most of them seem to know one another. My guess is the ones that were successful here today will be known all over Govan by tomorrow.'

She smiled and went outside to enter a waiting taxi on her way to the Central Station Hotel, Glasgow  where she will stay for the evening.

At 20, Craigton Road the door opens and in walks Ruth. Jimmy is surveying papers in front of him outlining what pub he would be soon visiting in Govan. 'Well Ruth ?' Ruth burst into tears ' Jimmy I have never been so nervous in my life, that was awful' He gets up and comforts her.

They had this English wumin in there asking me all sorts of questions. She sobbed then continued ' You will never believe it ! You remember Ella Donaldson from Inverness Street who we bumped into last week ?'

'Yes' replied Jimmy. Ruth continued, 'well Ella was on the interview team ! We did not say anything throughout the Interview but at the end when she showed me into a wee waiting room she told me that I already had the job. She came back about 5 minutes later and told me I start in around 3 weeks time. It is about 3 times more money than I get now` Jimmy says 'I told you that you would get the job Ruthie. Whu hay !'. They danced around the room pleased that things had gone well. 'We are out for a celebration tonight Ruth' said Jimmy.

After about 5 minutes Jimmy went back to his list of pubs and said 'Right Ruthie which pubs am I still banned from; here is the list Ruth said.

Watsons at the Govan Cross Subway— You are OK there

Commercial Bar at Govan Cross—Banned.

Waverley in Langlands Road– Your ban must have expired by now.

McLoughlin's Bar, Langlands Road– You would not be welcome in there.

Boar's Head, Langlands Road– You are OK there.

Old Harmony Bar– You would not be welcome there.

Lyceum Bar– McKechnie Street– Not really proper drinkers in ther Jimmy.

The Stag– Govan Road– Banned  Weavers– Warnock Street—You are OK there.

Sheeps Head & The Cosy Corner—both Harmony Row– You would not be welcome there.

Jimmy says 'Watson's it is Ruth'.

Mrs. Catherine Smith decided she would take a shortcut through Craigton Cemetry. As she was walking along she heard the sound of footprints behind her. She walked quicker but the steps behind her also were heard to go quicker. It was two men and they were on a mission of robbery. Suddenly, they hit Mrs. Smith on the head with a heavy object and she fell to the ground.

The men grabbed her handbag and ran off. Two men passing saw the incident and gave chase but lost sight of the attackers on Paisley Road West . Mrs Smith was taken to the Southern General Hospital and had three stitches in a head wound.  Her bag was found a few hours later in Wallside Avenue. £1 and ten shillings had been taken.  Govan CID said they were after two youths aged between 16 and 20 years old.

John and Abe are having their lunch in the pawnshop. John is reading the Evening Times and says 'How about this Abe; crime is down with the exception of safe blowing'.

Abe says 'That is great news John; we can now feel that much safer walking around Govan !' John continues to look at the paper and says 'Bad news for the yards, orders are down again. However, with what they have got and a few orders in the pipeline they should be ok. You remember Neil Mc Lean the Labour MP. He left £3,365 in his estate'.

- The No.7 Tramcar was on its way back to Bellahouston via Govan. Suddenly, the driver had a problem as his tram started to slew off the rails. Fortunately, no one was hurt and the cause was found to be a 4 inch bolt that had fallen off the Tramcar in front on the rail. The traffic was delayed by one and a half hours as the Corporation vehicles tried to get the Tram back on the rails.

- The draw for the much coveted Glasgow Snooker League Individual Championship was made. The Pearce Institute players made up the Govan entry and they were paired as follows. H.Burns ( East Kilbride) v J.Miller (PI): W.Mitchell (PI) v P.Hampson (St.Mungo); P.Anderson (Commercial) v D.Mc Intosh (PI) ; A.Nelson (PI) v G.Carnegie (Union); W.Green (PI) v E.Paton (Commercial)

- Lord Provost Tom Kerr was at the march past in John Street, Glasgow as 8,000 students took part in a Charity Day. The Students divided up into many groups to venture into the various areas of Glasgow to collect for good causes.

- Two Govan men were summoned to Govan Police Court. As they entered the court they both smiled at Bailie Roy Cuthbertson. Both were to receive the Royal Humane Society Parchment for Bravery award.

While bathing at Douglas in the Isle of Man, 20 year old Pearl Howe got into acute difficulty and was drowning. Without fear John McCart a 55 year old Tram Inspector, after spotting the danger to Miss Pearl, swam out to save her. On reaching her he managed to keep her and himself afloat long enough for help to arrive.

Joseph Clark (45) a tug boatman of 61 Langlands Road was on holiday in Withernsea, Yorkshire. A woman and two girls were in difficulty out in the sea. Three men waded out to rescue them when high waves came in. One of the men who could not swim, drowned. Another was almost given up as lost when Joseph Clark made an effort to save him. He managed to reach him and carry him to the shore. Artificial respiration was applied for 15 minutes to Hugh Mc Indoe. He started to respond and slowly recovered.

Both men were highly commended for their very brave actions.

Henry Stewart (38) of 480 Helen Street was watching television with his wife in their living room when the door went and two of his wife's aunts came in. All four settled down to watch the television. Suddenly Stewart started to make the aunts unwelcome. He asked his wife to tell them to leave and when she refused he threw all three out into the garden. He pulled the clothing of one of the aunts and punched her on the face. In front of Fiscal Mr.D. Browne Mac Farlane, Stewart was very well dressed. He had been married for 13 years and the incident was out of character. The Fiscal asked if he had been drinking. Stewart replied he was a non drinker. However, he did say that he was under the doctor due to stress at work.   Stewart was admonished.

In the Old Harmony Bar, plotting has begun against a proposed Government Policy. John Gillespie and Frank Mulvenney read the latest proposals. John says 'Well this one has gone down like a lead balloon. The Mr.Osbert Peake Pension plan for the Tories. Apparently, we are all living too long and the Pension pot cannot afford to pay us any more. The proposal is to raise the men's retirement age to 68 years and the wumin to 65 years '.

Frank says ' That is what you get with a Tory Government !'. John says 'I wonder what has happened to all the taxes that we have paid !' Frank says ' Look who is on the committee, Mr Iain Mc Loed, Mr Henry Brooke and Mr. Marples the Road Construction Company owner. My guess is that the Pension money is probably going to be paying for the roads.

If I was a Capitalist and not a Communist I would have shares in Marples. Sad thing is, the Pensioners will be paying for it once their money is withdrawn'. John says 'You are too cynical Frank. I do not think they will ever be able to get these sort of proposals through. Apparently, even some of the top Tories feel it is harsh'.

An 11 year old boy was watching a Saturday morning matinee at the local cinema. Suddenly, he felt a sharp pain in the back of the neck.

It was a staple fired from a catapult by one of two boys further back in the rows of seats. The injured boy was taken to the Managers office to have the cut in his neck dressed. The attendant went back into the cinema and saw the two boys firing iron staples from catapults at various people in the front rows.

They were taken to the managers office. At Govan Police Courts Police Judge John Scott fined each of the boys aged 13 and 14 years the amount of 5 shillings. In the same cinema two boys gained access by climbing through a ventilator. They then had access to the 1 shilling and six pence seats. The two sixteen year olds were each fined 5 shillings. Both fathers were in court and said that they both had been given a thrashing and would not do it again.

A Govan woman appealed to the court for protection from her ex husband in order to bring up her three children. Mary Graham said she was struck on the face by the ex husband of Mary Boyle, James Langan a 31 year old bus conductor.

The assault was at 141 Neptune Street, Govan. Mary Boyle and Mary Graham were good friends. Mrs Graham said the blow knocked her hearing aid out.

Langan claimed that he wanted to see his children and was struck on the head with a milk bottle by Mrs Graham.

He had to go and receive stitches to stop the bleeding. Langan said that both women were liars and he did not strike them.

Baillie James Bennett found the charge 'Not Proven' at which point Mrs Graham burst into tears and said 'Not proven ! What is the law for ?' At this point she ran from the court.

Beatrice Mc Morrow of 93 Broomloan Road was worried when her husband had not returned home by 2.00 am so, with her 19 year old son, she went looking for him. They tried 35 Golspie Street where Michael's brother lived and found the door open. The tenement was in darkness but they could hear snoring.

Beatrice struck a match and found Michael sleeping on a mattress on the floor with another woman. She was shocked and screamed and screamed and screamed. Michael jumped up from the mattress and kicked his wife in the neck with his bare feet trying to keep her quiet. Beatrice went outside and continued screaming and shouting 'Call the Polis !' At this point virtually every window in Golspie Street opened with the residents hanging out wondering what the commotion was.

At Govan Police Court, Michael Mc Morrow (47 years) told the court ' I have been married 24 years sir and this is the first time I have ever been tried for wife assault'. Judge David Johnstone said 'This is not a Court of Morals. I hesitate to send you to jail for a first offence so you are fined £5 or 30 days imprisonment with 21 days to pay'.

In Govan Police Court Patrick Donnelly (59) an unemployed steel erector was accused of attacking his wife Mary. They had 13 children. In court Mrs Donnelly said ' He tried to hit me with a kettle of water, I ducked and then he punched me in the face knocking my glasses off'and threw me out '. Fourteen year old daughter Mary confirmed her mother's story of the assault in their Cook Street home.

Donnelly said 'She is a liar'. Constable Alastair Mac Kay said he called at the house and Mrs Donnelly was sober. 'Donnelly called out 'He is a liar !'. Police Judge Andrew Donald told Donnelly ' Cross examine the witnesses in a proper manner or I will hold you in contempt of court'. Donnelly said he had not worked for 8 years. Judge Donald said 'You look a fit enough man to me. I think you may be lazy. You are sentenced to 30 days Imprisonment'.

Leo Reid always had a problem with drink. At his daughters wedding, his wife hid the drinks left over to prevent him getting drunk. When Leo, a 53 year old building trade labourer had drink, he made everyone's life a misery.

When his wife and two grown up sons went out, Leo searched for the left over drink and found it. When the wife and sons returned he was drunk and abusive. He threatened to beat them all up but the sons restrained him. After a while Leo went out and down into the back court. He started shouting and swearing and throwing stones at the window. The sons, after a struggle, managed to get him back in the house.

Leo Reid appeared at Govan Police Court with a sticking plaster over his eye after the struggle with his sons. He said ' I appear here like this because of my sons'. Judge Mac Pherson Rait said 'It is because of you that you appear in front of this court. Your wife and sons have tried everything and you still are a nuisance'. Reid was fined £2 for breach of the peace.

James Lowther (39), a labourer, did not treat his wife and 8 children very well. He beat his wife Elizabeth after dragging her over the kitchen floor by her hair while the children watched. Some time later she arrived at the Southern General Hospital and among her injuries were bruising to the hand, a black eye and multiple abrasions to the face. In addition he threw a bucket of water over her at their home in 9 Clachan Drive.

In court Lowther said that given the opportunity he would never lift a hand ever again.

Bailie James Bennett said ' think yourself lucky you are getting it. The sentence will be deferred for 6 months`.

On her way home from Woolworth's Ruth decides to call in and see if Jimmy Welsh has arrived home from work. At 20 Craigton Road she chaps on the door and Jimmy answers.

'Jimmy, whit dae ye think aboot aw this wife beatin aroon Govan in the papers. Jimmy says ' Well it is only a small number, most families live happily enough'. Ruth says ' well look at the case of the man that pulled his wife aroon the fler wae the herr o' her heid in front o' her 8 weans !' .

Jimmy smiled and said' Well we only hear one side of the story'. Ruth said ' The judge let him aff with a 6 months deferral. That was ridiculaous !'. Jimmy said ' well I was reading the other day that the British husband is the most hen pecked in the whole world'.

Ruth says ' And jist who come up with that ! A man I suppose'. Jimmy says ' well many men are feeling the pressure a bit at the moment and require a bit of understanding Ruth'. Ruth says ' I give up' . She then opened the door and was gone. Jimmy called her back but Ruth said she would see him at the weekend. She walked down to Crossloan Road and along to the bus stop opposite the Vogue Cinema. Being a stage stop she saved a few pence from taking the bus at the Central Govan stops. She boarded the number 4 and was soon back in West Drumoyne.

At 31 Daviot Street Robbie, Jack and Ruth have shared the cost to get a television. It is an Ekco model and the shop offers a service plan which is accepted. The agreement is to cover breakdowns and to get a once per year service.

This comprised mainly of replacing big glass valves and cleaning the inside of the screen of dust.

The Ecko duly arrived and all the five in the household watched with excitement when the TV man switched it on. Nothing happened. Boab says to the TV man ' It looks like you have your first breakdoon'.

The TV man says ' Just wait, it takes the valves 4 minutes to warm up'. Sure enough the television came to life and the family had a night of entertainment. They got out the newspapers to see what was on the two channels. BBC and ITV.

Govan Town Hall was popular. Ruth and Jimmy noticed that an event was to be staged at the Hall that would attract interest throughout Great Britain. Ruth says ' Look Jimmy, Govan will be on the TV. It is the big table tennis match between Scotland and England from Govan Town Hall. We must go !. When the cameras film the crowd I will be able to wave and my pals in Drumoyne and Woolworth's will be able to see me. I will be quite famous !'. They both laughed.

When they arrived for the match they were ushered to seats at the back of the Main Hall which was packed with enthusiastic Govanites wanting to be seen on the TV. The first match started after the announcer introduced the players. The English No.1 made short shrift of his Scottish opponent and soon the announcer said 'England win by 3-0 and lead the match by 1-0'. A short while later it was 2-0, then 3-0 and eventually 9-0.

Coming out Ruth says ' Whit a shame that Scotland did not do so well'. Jimmy says `yes, looking ahead the hall has a good programme. They have boxing which we will go and see and also wrestling'. Derek might want to go and see the Bruins'.

In the 1800's, a Tramcar service was available to patrons at the Govan Town Hall. If a concert was on, the gentry and the wealthy, many of whom lived at Ibroxholm (south side of Paisley Road West, would board their horse drawn carriages and travel the short distance home.

Others attending the concert would board a horse drawn carriage run by the Ibrox Tramway Company either to Paisley Road west or down Copland Road and on to Govan. The speed of the journey would depend on how many people were on the tram and how tired the single horse pulling it was.

The Vale of Clyde Steam buses also ran a service from Paisley Road Toll to Govan. The usual fare was 1 penny.

At the Pawnshop in Golspie Street John and Abe are sitting in the back room. It has been a relatively quiet day for business. The door opens and in walks Moshe Steinberg and Roger Joseph, friends of Abe. As they enter Moshe points without words to John to the door in order that they can both gain access behind the counter. John obliges and both walk through with no thank you or acknowledgement to John.

Moshe says to Abe 'How is business Abe ?'. Abe replies 'Average'. Roger has had some fantastic deals and more importantly mark up's'. A customer walked into the Pawnshop and John went to serve him.

Abe, Moshe and Roger were all members of the Giffnock Synagogue. Moshe and Roger operate an Import/Export business in Tradeston. Abe makes both his visitors a cup of tea and they discuss the many characters at the Synagogue. Abe says 'I hear Ephraim Groundland is going to Stockport to take over the Synagogue there.

120

A big miss as a potential Rabbi and also for his music talents'. Moshe says the Jewish Music and Drama productions are winning all the competitions at the moment around Glasgow'. Abe says 'I have seen that; obviously very talented groups. I must try and see a production'.

When they have gone Abe can see John is not happy with the attitude of his friends. Abe recognises John's unhappiness and says' I know John; they are difficult characters'. John says with a glint in his eye ' I think we have a project coming up !' Abe looked at John and smiled.

There is a commotion at Water Row next to Govan Cross. The cars and motor transport are beginning to back up along Govan Road in both directions. The motorists and other travellers were showing their impatience and started sounding their horns.

29 year old James Wilmot had jumped the queue to get on the ferry by at least three cars. The Ferryman had seen him and asked him to back his car off the Govan Ferry and join the back of the queue.

Wilmot refused. The Ferryman and several other motorists told him that if did not move they would call the police officer. Wilmot said they could do just that but he was not for moving. The Police arrived and James Wilmot stayed put claiming he was in his proper position on the ferry. The Police ordered the ferry to depart with Wilmot still on board but questioned and cautioned him at the Partick side of the river.

In Govan Police Court, Wilmot was charged with taking actions likely to cause a breach of the peace.

Witness John Rooney a travelling foreman said 'there was a lot of horn blowing and when the ferry moved off there was a queue down Govan Road. If the police had not arrived I would have been inclined to punch him on the nose'. Wilmot said he had got out of his car to post some letters while waiting for the ferry and other people took his position in the queue.

One lady got excited and started shouting. Judge Joseph Mc Kell said that the case was proven and fined Wilmot the maximum fine of £2.00. He said his behaviour was supercilious.

Jimmy Welsh has returned to his former home in James Street, Bridgeton to see his estranged wife and his two children William and Mary. He brings along a bunch of flowers for Joan. She thanks him and makes him a cup of tea. Jimmy says 'How is it going Joan ?'

Joan says 'Very well Jimmy. William and Mary love you to bits and would like to see more of you. I think it would be in order if you came every two weeks or four weeks'. Jimmy says ' Joan, this breaks my heart, is there no way you would have me back. .

I have all but given up drinking '. Joan says ' Jimmy I have another man in my life now and we will be moving from here.

You will still be able to see our children; life must go on. A friend of mine says she saw you dancing a few times down at South Govan Town Hall to the Merry Macs. Apparently, the lady you were dancing with was called Ruth. Is that so ?'. Jimmy says ' Yes Ruth comes to the dancing with me'. Jimmy is upset by the news that Joan now has another man and seemingly out of reach.

He walks down to the Bridgeton Arms and is recognised by Richard the bar owner who says ' Hello stranger, hows Govan ?'. Richard pours Jimmy a pint and puts it on the counter. Jimmy says ' Not too bad Richard, just came over to see William and Mary. Joan wanted us to get back together but I have told her no way whatsoever !'.

Richard says 'Well the country is certainly getting sorted out with the Tories and Unionists in charge. Record number of houses being built and Rab Butler has a surplus as Chancellor.

Compare that to the austerity we had under Labour; nationalise everything in sight and the rest of us have to pay for it. Trade in this pub has never been so high because most people have money in their pockets'.
Jimmy says ' I agree !. However, in Govan they tend to cling on to the old way of Trade Unionism and actually believe the Communist doctrines. Communism can never work. There is far too much restrictive practices in the shipyards, they seem to think they have a job for life. Who would ever employ these guys ?'

Adverts wanting skilled and highly skilled engineers and tradesmen appear in the Scottish Newspapers.

The exodus is on throughout 1955 and Govan is losing many of its skilled shipyard workers. A total of 32,000 leave Scotland with 8,500 to Australia, 3,300 to the United States, 16,000 to England and the rest elsewhere. With a population of just 5 million Scotland had approaching 2 million people emigrating in the first half of the 20th Century.

A Govan wife fed her baby and returned to bed at noon; in the bed was her husband. He said she should not be coming back to bed at this time and was lazy. They argued so he kicked her out of the bed. He then got out of the bed and kicked her on the legs and body before pulling her around the floor by her hair. The neighbours knocked on the door to find out what was happening. When he opened the door he threw his wife out onto the landing.
In Govan Police Court the husband admitted the offence of wife assault and got a deferred sentence of six months by Police Judge, John Storrie.

# CHAPTER 12
# GOVAN PRIDE

The competition was intense. James Burns wanted to retain the much coveted title he had won the previous year. His Plaza cinema near Govan Cross had after all been awarded the prize ahead of countless cinema's in the Scotland West district. Jim and his staff kept his cinema spotless which meant they was always in contention for the cleanliness category. Courtesy and service to the patrons was second to none as was management efficiency and staff relations. They were a team in the cinema and it showed. When the announcement came it was close. Alas the Plaza was voted second behind the Regal in Paisley. However, James was pleased and thanked his staff for their efforts.

Two 13 year old Govan High schoolboys were walking along the front at Lochgilphead and saw a young girl fall into the sea . Within seconds she was being dragged out to the open sea by the currents. Both boys in their full clothing dived into the sea and kept the young girl's head above the water. She had been face down and unconscious in the water. Once ashore she was revived with artificial respiration and recovered. The boys were invited to the City Chambers by Tom Kerr the Lord Provost and were presented with Corporation Bravery medals.

Govan Constable Lyle Mc Millan saw the plight of an elderly man caught in a fire. He bravely entered the flames and rescued the man and was also presented with the Corporation award for Bravery.

The Ferryboat from Whiteinch to Linthouse was nearing the end of its crossing. 72 year old pensioner Malcolm Crosby was standing at the back of the boat when suddenly he toppled backwards and fell into the River Clyde. A boy on the steps at Linthouse saw what happened and raised the alarm. Gilbert Lawrie the ferryman quickly manoeuvred the ferry around and, with engineer John Clark, put out the pole hook and pulled Mr.Crosby in unconscious. He was revived and taken off to the Western Infirmary.

John and Abe were sitting in their Golspie Street pawnshop plotting the final details of a project. In front of them was a wooden telephone box with a handset and receiver fitted. From the bottom was a pair of twisted VIR cables with crocodile clips on them. John says 'My survey is almost complete'. John has been watching the Tradeston Import Export building where Roger Joseph and Moshe Steinberg work. He has religiously watched the movements of people entering and leaving the building over a few weeks. The pattern is the same.     Moshe Steinberg is an orthodox Jew and is always the first to arrive. From high up on the large warehouse opposite John has noted his arrival times. Just down the corridor is the telephone exchange for the buildings in the vicinity of the many Tradeston Warehouses; the telephone engineers rarely attend the exchange. Abe has his script prepared and they are almost ready.

John picks up a paper and reads the headlines, he says ' have you seen this Abe. Scarface Teddy Martin has escaped from Peterhead Prison. He is not to be approached. I imagine he will be heading to Govan as we have a lot of men with scars on their face !'. Abe smiled.

Ruth arrives at 20, Craigton Road. Jimmy is ready in his suit and they are off to South Govan Town Hall for the Old Time Dancing again to the popular Merry Macs. Ruth says ' I am looking forward to this Jimmy; you are a smashing dancer'. Jimmy says 'You are not too bad yourself Ruth'. The South Govan Town Hall is packed and Ruth seems to know just about everybody. She says ' This is ma man Jimmy' as she introduces her dance partner.

At Govan High School a lady art teacher is about to go to break. She puts her diary with a £5 note and two one pound notes into her desk. She is being watched as she walks along the corridor to the Teachers Rest room. A 14 year boy enters the classroom and goes to the desk; he takes the diary and the money.

The teacher finds the diary missing and immediately reports it to the Headmaster. The desk is easily accessible as it is near the washing up basin and pupils frequently see the teacher opening and closing the desk.

The classes who had art lessons on the day of the theft were addressed by the Headmaster; all denied the theft. Soon the diary was found in an adjoining classroom. The pupils were asked to help and soon one boy was on his way to the Headmaster. The pupils had reported that suddenly he was spending a lot of money on sweets and in particular chewing gum.

The head asked him to empty his pockets but found nothing. He was asked to take his shoe's off and a £5 and £1 note were found plus some coinage. The police were called.

At Govan Juvenile Court the Procurator Fiscal James Robertson told the boy that it was pretty low offence almost akin to robbing a blind man. His guardians said he was a member of the BB and a teacher at the Sunday Bible class. He was put on probation for 2 years and ordered to return the 18 shillings and 4 pence to the teacher.

Moshe Steinberg arrives at the Tradeston Import/Export building. His black beard is being blown in the wind and he holds his black hat down in case it blows off.

He has not been the first person to arrive at the door at this particular morning. In the entry hall an hour earlier, John had left a number of the 'marked number' £10 notes on the floor with an elastic band around them.

The notes were suspected by John and Abe as potential plants by the police during a previous 'project'. The numbers of the notes were recorded and the Glasgow Police had asked the banks to advise them immediately they arrived back. John was on the third floor of the adjacent building watching the entry pattern of Moshe.

Around 30 seconds after Moshe went into the doorway and saw the notes, he went back to the entrance. He looked left, then right and went inside. Around 30 seconds later he looked out again to see if anyone was there; he then put the money in his long coat.

John went down the corridor to the telephone room where Abe was sitting with his telephone box. Two hours passed and the Tradeston Import/Export offices filled up. John, on the lookout for a chance visit from the telephone engineers, signalled to Abe who picked up the receiver and dialled Glasgow 1212, the Central Police number. He asked to be put through to Detective Inspector Roy Fletcher. Roy's phone rang and the reply was 'DI Fletcher here'. Abe, with a disguised voice which he had practiced said, 'A tip off. Write these numbers down. You will find 6 of these £10 notes in the Tradeston Import/Export office. Mr. Moshe Steinberg knows all about them'. Roy Fletcher says 'Who am I speaking to ?' Abe says ' The line is a bit crackly in his disguised voice and then hangs up. John says ' That was brilliant Abe !!'. They both laughed.    John was in a police uniform and sticking the ends of his eyes out to disguise his crossed eyes. Once his policeman hat was on he put the peak down low and  asked Abe how it looked; Abe said 'Great John'.

From their vantage point they were able to see a police car arrive with a Black Maria; Roy Fletcher got out of the car. Around 10 minutes later Moshe Steinberg was dragged out and put into the Black Maria.
The staff of the office were surprised and came out to see one of the company leaders being bundled off. John and Abe waited another hour. Then Abe phoned the Tradeston Import/Export office and said ' Can I speak to the person in charge'. Roger Joseph answered. Abe says 'hello this is Glasgow Central Police here, you may be aware that Mr Steinberg has been brought in for questioning regarding stolen money' Joseph says 'Yes I am'.

Abe says 'Well it seems he may be in the clear. What we need quickly is a sample of £800 in notes so we will send a policeman around to collect the money. When he arrives ask him to give his name, it is PC Smith and ring us here on a special number Glasgow 1398 to confirm identity'.

Joseph says 'OK we will do that'. John changes over the telephone cables to enable Abe to receive the incoming call and then goes down to the office where he is met by Roger Joseph. Roger asks him his name and phones Glasgow 1398. Abe answers and says 'PC Smith has arrived I take it, that is fine. We will give the money to Moshe when he is released in around an a hours time. Roger gives John the money.

John returns to his vantage point and changes into his normal clothes. Abe packs up the equipment into a bag. They both catch a number 4 bus exactly on time and are soon in the Golspie Street shop where George has been manning the counter for the week.

A debate was continuing in Dunbartonshire Education circles. It revolved around the use of the 'Tawse' or strap in schools; in particular Primary Schools. The debate was heated. The supporters of abolishing the belt punishment gained support from the ruling Dunbartonshire Council Labour group and they wanted corporal punishment for those under 11 to be stopped. The Education Committee issued the instruction to the teachers to implement the ban some months later.

Immediately, there was considerable opposition to the instruction; Lenzie Academy was one of the first to voice their opposition.

They said ' the first scholastic action a teacher takes is to buy a strap; they are not issued by the Education board. In Secondary Schools only the headmaster would be allowed to use corporal punishment and he has to keep a record of how many strokes he has administered.

In the Govan schools the strap was very common and not likely to change. The Dunbartonshire initiative was watched with much interest. The motion was passed by the smallest of majorities 12 votes to 11 votes.

The Teachers claimed that they were not consulted properly. They claimed that they had a deputation from pupils wanting the belt rather than lines saying that it was 'all over there and then'.

Two weeks later there was an acrimonious meeting between the Education Committee and the School Headmasters. The Heads claimed:

- We have had a deputation from 20 boys at Renton Public School by head Mr William Wood. They want the Tawse re-instated.
- Mr Wood said since the ban, catapults, fireworks and slings had been brought in. Also one boy had brought in four .22 bullets and sold them for two pence each.
- Mr. Wood claimed a pupil burst a bag when the teacher was on the blackboard and 'said Ye cannae dae anything tae me !'.

Other examples were given. The decision of the Dunbartonshire Education Council was under pressure.

A week later the decision was reversed by 15 votes to 9 votes. The teachers claimed how hurt they were with the previous decision to abolish corporal punishment. Mr Monaghan of St.Patrick's High School felt more consultation should have taken place before the previous decision.

He said 'in this all teachers in Scotland are behind us'. A teacher said at the meeting 'You should remember that it is the teachers who have to deal with the pupils in this matter'.

Scotland remained as having one of the most draconian systems in Western Europe in respect to Schools Corporal punishment.

Jimmy meets Ruth outside Woolworth's one day at lunch time and they go on a walk to Elder Park. As they walk down to Govan Road, three young men pass by and one shouts out ' another man Ruthie, I hope ye telt him of the others' The other two laugh. It is the same three young men that had come into Woolworth's some months previously and had made adverse comments to Ruth.

They follow Jimmy and Ruth west towards Elder Park. They run past and shout 'Hiv ye telt him you'r a pro Ruthie'. They then stop and allow Jimmy and Ruth to pass, Ruth was about to say something when Jimmy says ' Don't Ruth just keep quiet. Let us cross over' . They then walked past the gates of Fairfields yard and along opposite Elder Park. Jimmy moves Ruth to the edge of the pavement to allow her tormenters to pass on the inside if they wish. Sure enough the young man who was calling out says 'Ruthie, who is yer man noo !' The three move to pass the couple on the inside of the pavement kerb and the Fairfield yard wall. The two who laughed most were allowed to pass. Then, suddenly, as the thick set young man who had been making the adverse comments passed, Jimmy made his move. His right arm came out like a telescope and instantly was firmly cupped around the neck of Ruth's tormenter. Within a second Jimmy had the young man crashing against the wall and his hand was lifting him upwards. Jimmy received a blow on the side from the young man but did not feel it. Once against the wall Jimmy's second hand was also around the tormenters neck and he was raising his victims feet off the ground.

He said to his two friends ' Do not come near or I will choke him !'. The tormentor was totally at the mercy of Jimmy who had his back pinned against the wall and was slowly raising his feet off the ground making him choke. Jimmy says `now I am a well respected man around this city, what is your name ?'. He lowered the young man down to allow him to tip toe a bit more firmly and allow some more air through his neck. 'Bernard ' He could not complete the second part of his name. Jimmy says 'Bernard. I sincerely hope we do not have to meet again'. Bernard was in serious trouble, his face was red and his arms were limp against the wall. Jimmy smiled and felt someone pulling at his back. 'Jimmy leave him, you will kill him !'.    It was Ruth franticly trying to pull him back. Jimmy allowed Bernard to fall to the ground just as several people arrived at the scene. Bernard was lying on the ground desperately trying to recover his breath. His two friends were hurling abuse at Jimmy. 'Ye could have killed him ya mad b******d. '. The other people arriving started to help Bernard. One said 'You could have strangled him !'. Jimmy said 'No, I was only trying to help him breath. Have you not heard of vertical resuscitation ?. It is time you went on a First Aid course !'. He patted Bernard on the head and said 'You will be all right now Bernard'. One of Bernards two friends said 'We are going to the polis, you're mad !'. Ruth said to Jimmy `C'mon, we have got to get out of here quick'.

Jimmy moved towards the pond direction but Ruth ushered him straight on and then sharply right behind trees and bushes where they could not be seen from Govan Road. Jimmy asked 'Who were these guys Ruth ?'.

Ruth says 'His name is Bernie. His two side kicks I think off as laughing hyena's; whatever Bernie says they just laugh. They are called Junior and Gibby. Some years ago when I was a home help I was asked to look after an elderly lady in a bungalow in Paisley Road West.

She was an English lady, a widow and had a bit of money. Bernie was a delivery boy for the local butcher on Paisley Road West and the lady, called Susan Hargreaves, was one of his customers. One day Bernie offered to bring other items of shopping to Mrs. Hargreaves and she accepted.

Initially there was no problem and he always got a good tip. On occasions, depending on the value of shopping, Mrs Hargreaves would tell him to keep the change. As time went on he would take the money for the forthcoming weeks shopping and not bother returning any change even when there was obviously a considerable amount of cash to return. Mrs. Hargreaves then made sure she only gave him a little more in cash above the value of the shopping and things settled down. One day he delivered some shopping and Mrs Hargreaves left her purse on the kitchen draining board. When Bernie had gone she discovered at least £5 was missing and her purse was in a different position in the kitchen.

When I started to work for Mrs. Hargreaves the following week she was relieved that she would not need to deal with Bernie again.

The following week Bernie came to the door asking to do the shopping. As agreed with Mrs. Hargreaves I answered the door and told him she did not require his services for the shopping messages and also the supply of meat. He was very unhappy about this and asked to see Mrs. Hargreaves. Mrs Hargreaves said to him that now she had a home help there was no need for him to put himself out with the message items. Bernie was waiting on me with Junior and Gibby by his side when I left Mrs Hargreaves. Bernie says 'Did Mrs. Hargreaves say anything aboot me ?' I said 'No'. 'I am sure she owes me some money for the last few weeks shopping' says Bernie.

I said ' I will ask her the next time I come over and if you ask the butcher to prepare the bill I am certain she will honour it. As you are aware Mrs. Hargreaves is elderly and is sleeping at the moment so I suggest we all go off home now'. We moved off and I went to the bus stop to catch the No. 23 bus to Govan. A week or so later Bernie and his hyena's were waiting for me and started accusing me of influencing Mrs. Hargreaves against Bernie.

I said ' That is rubbish'. However, Bernie got more and more agitated and then accused me of stealing money from Mrs. Hargeaves. I said 'If you believe that then we can go down to the police station along Paisley Road West and sort it out. I have never stolen a penny in my entire life and I will not have you accuse me of that !'.

Slowly but surely we saw less and less of Bernie and his two hyena. Mrs. Hargreaves was a wonderful lady and very kind. I thought I had seen the last of the trio but after Derek was born occasionally I had to walk past them and of course endure abuse. Since Derek was born they are the only people that have ever made any adverse comment on him being born out of wedlock.

Everyone else has been very kind and virtually everyone on the West Drumoyne scheme knows Derek as my son and go out of their way to be kind to him.'

'Well Ruth, had I known that ten minutes ago I would have killed him and that is no word of a lie' said Jimmy.

Ruth says 'Bernie lives in Cardonald and I believe his parents are quite nice by all accounts. However, he is a wrang wan'.

Abe and John are in good spirits. The last project in Tradeston had been successful and after closing time at Cox's Pawnshop in Golspie Street they sit down . Abe produces a bottle of Whisky and brings two glasses.

Soon they are sipping and sipping and sipping. John says 'That is great stuff Abe !'. Abe went over and brought out his favourite 78 inch record. Soon it is playing on the turntable of the record player the needle initially making the sound and soon the tune Nava Tehilla was inspiring them as they got more and more drunk. Abe says ' John I would like to say I have never been happier in my far too formal life'. John says ' We have a great time with this Pawnshop and of course with our wee projects'.

The loss of top shipbuilding engineers was beginning to take some toll on the yards. Many left for better posts elsewhere because poor management did not spot the individual's potential.

David Lyon Mc Larty worked in the yards and he was good. He was promised some form of recognition which was not forthcoming from a stuffy management. Recognising he was getting nowhere he applied for a job in China. From there he moved to Australia.

His engineering know how, learned on the Banks of the Clyde, went into the construction of the New South Wales Dockyards one of the biggest enterprises in Australia. With Mc Larty at the helm and Director of Engineering and Shipbuilding a lot of the River Clyde Shipyards were switching their business to Australia and not returning.

He built the first passenger and then cargo vessels ever to come out of Australia. The lay out of the yard was exactly what he would have had in the Clydeside Yard. It had much acclaim .

He did not forget the employees and they received a substantial bonus from the £2,500,000 turnover achieved in the first few years.

Other talented Engineers were departing for foreign shores probably never to return.

William Innes a 39 year old Labourer went to the cinema. He was drunk , he liked women and he felt frisky. He sat beside a 36 year old lady in the stalls. Conversation was tried but no luck. He then put his arm around her neck and rubbed his leg against hers.

The lady got up and moved to another seat some distance away from Innes. He then moved down a few rows to where a lone 62 year old woman was watching the film. By this time his movement were being watched by the manager  who was soon joined by a policeman. He tried conversation with the lady; it failed. He then put his arm around her neck and touched her knee at which point he was arrested.In Govan Police Court Police Judge Mrs Jamesina Anderson said 'It is terrible that women cannot go to the pictures without being molested by someone like you. Considering you have had a previous conviction you are lucky not to be sent to prison. Innes was fined £7  or 30 days in jail.

Alexander Edoni ran a very popular café on the Govan Road.  Some weeks previously he dismissed a lady from employment at the Café. The ladies husband Alex Mc Rae and son Ian felt Edoni had treated Mrs Mc Rae shabbily. They broke windows and assaulted Edoni.  The Café owner was taken to the Southern General Hospital with two black eyes, bruises to the body and a cut above the eye. He was sent for an x-ray to determine whether he had broken ribs.

The Mc Rae father and son were each fined £5.00

The Harland and Wolff workers formed a choir. After some practice they put on a concert at Finnieston for their fellow workers. It was a success and they entered the Glasgow Music Festival Competition. They gave a good account of themselves and achieved third place.

Ruth reads the newspapers and sees that Bruin the Boat builder is appearing at the Govan Town Hall; Bruin is a cartoon character who has a column in the newspapers. His best friend is Pingo the Penguin and Hugo the Hippo. Derek is excited when his mothers says he is to get a treat.

The Govan Hall is packed with children for the performance and everyone is entertained to the maximum. Songs, Magic and small competitions captivate Govan`s children who are members of the Bruin Club.

In Govan three men are in a café and  are licking their wound; Bernie, Junior and Gibby want revenge. They want to know who the man with Ruth is and what revenge they can take. Bernie says ' I thought I was gaun tae die when he put his hands on my throat. Junior says ' We wait for a wee while and then we strike and strike hard'.

A Tram collision at the junction of Holmfauldhead Drive and Govan Road saw the Tram collide into the shops after hitting a milk lorry and a private car; the  No. 27 Tram was several feet inside a shop.

With glass showering all around him the driver was lucky to escape injury. The conductress was badly shaken and taken to the Southern General Hospital but later released.

Junior and Gibby are on a visit to Govan to do shopping of a different type; they operate a good routine for shoplifting in Govan. They identify what they want to steal, usually from either the Co-op or Woolworth's.

At Woolworth , when there is a suspected shoplifter, the shop tannoy blares out 'Staff announcement. Mr.Mc Swift' to the front door please'.

The store security and stock men immediately move through the store to chase and apprehend the suspected shoplifter. If Gibby has taken something he rushes out of the store and bumps into Junior who is going in the opposite direction and transfers the stolen goods. Gibby always allows the chasing pack from the stores to catch him up. He usually says 'Whit's going on !. I am trying to catch a bus !'.

Obviously they do not find the goods and he is let go. However, the stores are getting wise to shoplifters

The larger stores in Glasgow are sharing information on who they suspect as shoplifters. They have more security officers patrolling the stores and good techniques for mingling with shoppers while monitoring suspects. However, in Govan where the rewards are not so great, it is essentially 'grab and run'.

At Govan Police Courts a few days later James Davidson was convicted of the robbery with two other men and sentenced to 60 days in prison. The sentencing of the two older men involved was deferred.

A taxi driver was in a hurry when approaching the level crossing in Govan Road near Summertown Road. Around 15 to 20 people were said to scatter when the taxi sounded his horn and went straight through.

A police constable Robert Robertson of the Govan Police station was present and sounded his whistle after the taxi but he refused to stop.

Some minutes later the taxi was seen coming back in the opposite direction and stopped by PC Robertson. Taxi Driver James Stark (30) pleaded not guilty and said the crossing was empty when he crossed; the police constable was mistaken.

Baillie John Mains found the case 'Not Proven'.

In Govan there is a stirring in the night behind 870-872, Govan Road. Three thieves were using a muffled hammer and chisel to remove bricks and gain entry into the Cooper and Co's Store.

They were being watched by some young Govanite boys. The thieves gained entry into the store and took 36 bars of chocolate and 6,540 cigarettes. The watching boys were contemplating 'Shall we tell the polis ?'

At Govan Police Courts a few days later James Davidson was convicted of the robbery with two other men and sentenced to 60 days in prison. The sentencing of the two older men involved was deferred.

# CHAPTER 13
## SS DAPHNE AND ROUGH JUSTICE

It is a very sunny day and Ruth and a few of the West Drumoyne mothers decide to take Derek and the other children on a trip on the No.23 bus to Linthouse. They will go across on the ferry, walk along the other side of the river at Whiteinch, cross back over to Govan on the Partick/Govan Ferry and back on the 4A bus to Drumoyne.

At Linthouse a few large ships sail past delaying the crossing of the passenger ferries. The swell from the boats dances up the steps reaching almost half way up. As Ruth looks down at the calming river she is aware of a terrible disaster not so far away at Stephens many years before, frequently told to her by her father Boab. Boab had worked at Alexander Stephens and Sons for many years and talked about what he was told about the tragedy.

A memorial in Govan remembers the events.

In 1883 the SS Daphne was launched from Alexander Stephens. Around 200 men and boys were on board and it was a happy day to start off with. The ship was sent towards the River Clyde with the two drag anchors restraining the ship from entering the water too quickly.

The crowd on the bank watched; many with family and relatives on the ship. They were excited and waved. Suddenly the port anchor moved some 60 yards while the starboard anchor stalled at 5 to 6 yards.

A swell on the River Clyde caught the ship tilting it over. Initially, it seemed to correct itself but another wave from the River Clyde at high tide caused the Daphne to capsize. All the loose weight had been thrown to one side of the ship and most of the people on board were trapped under the ship as desperate efforts were made to get them out of the water.

Some managed to get to safety but most were drowned. 124 men and boys died at the scene with those on the bank watching on in horror. The ship was re-floated some days later and taken to Govan Dry Dock. The subsequent enquiry cleared the Shipyard of all blame amid accusations of a cover up However, some key recommendations were given.

A)      On launching, a ship must only have on board the minimum number of people to operate the vessel.

B)      All hatches must be closed on launch.

C)      All equipment on the deck must be securely fastened down.

The three failures above were contributory to the disaster

On walking along the Whiteinch side of the River the mothers blethered on the topics of the day. A few months previously William Gordon had been pardoned but a few weeks earlier, a woman in England called Ruth Ellis, had been hanged and the country was now sharply divided on the issue of Capital Punishment.

In the case of Ruth Ellis there was no doubt that she had committed the crime. She shot 5 bullets into her ex lover David Blakeley, stayed at the scene and waited for the police to arrive. At the Old Bailey the trial was short before Justice Havers advised the Jury that the only thing they had to consider was whether Ruth Ellis had pulled the trigger or not.

No manslaughter or any other verdict would be acceptable. Inevitably it was very quickly a Guilty verdict and Havers donned the black cap. Ruth Ellis was an attractive platinum blonde. She had moved to London and soon became a model attracting many rich men. David Blakely was a motor racing driver and friends of Mike Hawthorn one of the top drivers.

He was wealthy and enjoyed the high life but he treated his women badly and had a stormy relationship with Ruth Ellis. Sometimes they got on well but on other occasions Blakeley became very violent. On one such occasion he punched Ruth in the stomach causing her to lose an unborn baby. A few weeks later Ruth Ellis on seeing him leading the high life with other women decided to take revenge.

A day after sentence was pronounced Ellis decided not to appeal against death by hanging. She wrote several newspaper articles for the popular papers with the money going to help her children who were being cared for by her loving and supportive parents.

Flowers were arriving at her Holloway Prison Cell; the nation was stunned. A change of defence team brought very late hope of some sort of reprieve. They petitioned all the top figures in the Establishment for help but to no avail. They garnered nothing from petitions containing tens of thousands of signatures. On the day of the execution Ruth Ellis woke at 6.30 and had breakfast; she was calm throughout. She gave her glasses to the warders who she got on well with and said 'I will not be needing these anymore'.

The execution itself was mercifully quick; timed at 12 seconds from the time Ruth walked into the chamber had a hood put over her head. With her hands and legs bound, a rope was put around her neck and she was instantly killed when the trap door opened.

At Whiteinch Ruth said to the other women. 'That wis terrible whit happened ther'. If she had had been in France it would have been a crime of passion and she would have got a jail sentence. Another mother, Helen, says' her defence team was useless'.

She widnae have got hanged in Scotland, we tend to let everybody off unless it is really cut and dry.

The English Law system is Barbaric; these auld duffer judges seem to think it is something to be proud off condemning people to death'. The mothers were in agreement on one thing, that Capital Punishment should be abolished.

Ruth says 'Well with the outcry over this, perhaps the death of Ruth Ellis will help stop them sending people to their death so readily. You notice it is never the rich and famous that go to the gallows. Now if Blakeley had shot Ruth Ellis would he have been executed ?' . All the mothers in unison said 'Naw, nae chance'. The Govan Car Ferry had just arrived and the group were heading back to West Drumoyne.

Jimmy and Ruth have planned a holiday and are off to Port Rush in Northern Ireland . Ruth is pleased because they are booked in to a good quality hotel; The Royal Court. Bed, breakfast and evening meals have been booked and they are not to be disappointed. Port Rush is a peninsula and both find it the perfect place to relax.

Jimmy soon meets up with a local Orange Lodge member and they are drinking in the local Lodge for a few evenings.

Jimmy and Ruth are both staunchly protestant and feel at home in a town where mostly the same values are shared. With the marching season in full swing they both board coaches to a few of the smaller town gatherings. One evening they both walk along the sea front and discuss things. Ruth says 'Jimmy, I am so happy we are here.

I have not enjoyed a holiday like this for a long time. Is it nice to be away from Govan for a few weeks ?'. Jimmy replies 'I also enjoy this, I just wish we could have more holidays'. Ruth says 'If you were to try and cut down on your socialising and drink then we would be well off.

It is ridiculous you are living in Craigton Road, with the combined wages we have we should have something better'. Jimmy says 'Ruth, I have tried and tried and for long periods I seem to beat it. Unfortunately, when I start I cannot stop and you know the rest'.

Ruth says 'Jimmy, there must be somewhere you can go to get treatment. If you carry on you will become a full blown alcoholic. When you are drunk it is unbearable'.

Jimmy replies ' I know Ruth. I will try I promise and I would like to spend more time with Derek. Ruth says 'He likes football . Perhaps you can help him with that and go to the odd Rangers game, he would enjoy that'. The couple arrive back at their hotel and go straight to their room. They get ready for the evening meal by changing in to more suitable formal attire.

At the evening meal Ruth enquires about the situation Jimmy has reached in concluding a divorce settlement from Joan.

Jimmy says, 'Well Ruth, Joan is a woman you cannot trust. In marriage everything should be shared, I gave that woman everything but when it comes to the divorce she feels I should not have a share of the house !

Anyway the divorce will soon be granted and we can be together properly'. Ruth says. 'Jimmy , it is great being with you the way you are now; I am very happy and it is a smashing holiday. However, if the drink problem is not resolved then we will not be staying together, I will be moving elsewhere'. Jimmy says 'Ruth, I will be cutting right down on the drink from now on you do not have to worry about that !'. He puts his hand on top of Ruth's as the first course of soup is brought to the table by the well dressed waiter.

The following day the couple go to Benburb in County Tyrone so Ruth can see where her mother was born. It is a lengthy journey and they arrive around mid afternoon. Ruth looks around various points of the village especially around the centre and envisages her mother at various points looking at shops and buildings some years before.

They walk a mile and visit the scene of the Battle of Benburb; clearly the winners of the battle were not what Jimmy Welsh expected. 'Ruth, we have tramped a mile here to see the one battle that lot ever won !.'

Ruth envisaged that her mother would have looked out on to the nearby river at some point while she lived there. She looked at the brooch her mother had given her when she was a little girl at Drumoyne School and was in thought for around 10 minutes. Jimmy put his arm around her and the pair walked off on their journey back to Port Rush.

The British Medical Association were worried. The conditions in which the British populace worked and lived were not all they should be.
A survey had to be carried out on one of the poorer parts of the UK.
Surprisingly, Govan was chosen.

Central Govan had 35,000 souls living in 9,200 dwellings. It had 132 registered factories employing 8,000 people; the sizes of the factories varying from employment of a few people going upwards to around 750.

The report found that most of the big employers provided 'good' conditions. However, the smaller premises were found to be, in many cases, 'poor'. Hygiene was a major concern and the lack of separate washing facilities and cloakrooms for staff was commonplace.
Only two out of 465 Govan Road shops met the required criteria including eating establishments.

Most damning in the report was the poor ventilation, poor heating, overcrowding and poor lighting. As a consequence of poor working conditions the people who were employed in the establishments had poor health. They suffered a lack of iron plus anaemia; particularly the women.

Dental care was bad; in particular the younger workers. Personal hygiene was cited and a whole host of criticism's was given in a lengthy detailed report.

At the Golspie Street Pawnshop John and Abe are having lunch and John is reading the BMA report in the paper. He says to Abe 'Have you seen this Abe ?' Abe says 'Yes John and before you go any further we are one of the two good premises !'. John thought for a minute.

He said 'Abe I have some news for you and a favour to ask !'. Abe said 'This sounds ominous John ! How can I help ?' Abe ' I am on the Queen Mary 2 on Saturday for the Jazz Festival and Sandra is really looking forward to it. Please do not laugh but I intend to go down on one knee in the middle of the dance floor and ask her to be my wife !'.

Abe says ' John !!. What fantastic news; I will not laugh of course, why should I'. He got up and moved over to John and said 'Many congratulations my boy ; I am delighted for you.

Sandra is a lovely lady and you are both well suited'. Abe shook John's hand warmly. John said ' That is the first part of it Abe !'. Abe said 'Yes, there is more ?' John said ' Abe, Please sit down'.

Abe sat. 'Abe, I would like you to be my best man !. Will you please agree ?'. Abe looked stunned, his eyes opened wide and tears began to run down his face'. John said smiling ' I take it that is a yes Abe !' Abe got up and hugged John and said ' Of course I will be best man. I have never done anything like that before but I would love to be involved'.

Lord Provost Tom Kerr was in his City Chambers, his time as the top Glasgow man was rapidly coming to an end. He was about to carry out one of his last duties.

He invited 27 youngsters to receive special medals from the City of Glasgow. The events included General Knowledge, Boxing, Table Tennis and Swimming. Where the youngsters had achieved something special, the Corporation had rewarded them with a medal which bore the City of Glasgow coat of arms on one side and the National Association of Boys Clubs on the other.

When asked what he would like to do after his term as Lord Provost was over, Tom Kerr said ' I would like to go back to Govan and stand for election as a Councillor for the Fairfield Ward'.

On hearing the news the opposition Progressives immediately withdrew their Candidate as a mark of respect. In the event Tom Kerr was not going to get a clear run. Two other candidates fought good campaigns.

Fairfield Result:
Tom Kerr (Labour) - 4,103 votes
J.Mackie (Independent) - 772 votes
G.Greig (Communist) - 431 votes

At a school in Dunoon the headmaster Archibald Leitch Smith was taking class. A ten year old girl Priscilla Anderson was having some trouble with arithmetic . He asked her to come to the front of the class and work on the blackboard. The young girl had two more attempts but got the answer wrong. Smith lost his temper and hit her around the head. The girl went home but, fearful of consequences, did not tell her parents. Her mother noticed that she was constantly rubbing her ear and when she pulled back the girls hair the mother noticed that her ear was black and blue. The mother went to the police.

In court the headmaster advised that he had been teaching all his life and had a boil in his eye at the time of the incident. The Fiscal D.Copeland agreed that things could be quite difficult for a teacher. However, the case was found against the Headmaster and he was fined £5.00.

Airdrie Academy pupils were given a questionnaire to take home for their parents to complete. One of the questions related to corporal punishment in the classroom and the teachers were in for a surprise.

210 favoured the continuation of Corporal Punishment by means of the tawse. However, 325 said that a withdrawal of school benefits or lines was a better option. They did not like the idea of their children being beaten by teachers; public opinion, as in Capital Punishment was shifting.

Joe Cook was a cook on the Queen Mary. One day on the high seas he had some drink and then some more. He was soon drunk and the frying pan he was using caught fire.

Another cook Edgar Spink became irritated and, with the help of some others, put Cook out of the kitchen. Joe Cook lost his temper and when re-entering the Galley threw a frying pan full of oil at Spink. Spink was taken away to receive attention for burns. At Southampton Court Cook was full of remorse and blamed the incident on having too much drink and losing his temper.

Cook lost his job and returned home to his Govan Road home. The judge fined him £10.

Tom Kerr had officially retired but his influence and memory lingered on for several months. In Paris the French authorities re-counted the occasion when he invited a group of French children into the Chambers and set up an impromptu concert with Mr.Kerr playing the piano. His fame for hospitality had gone beyond the UK shores.

At Govan Juvenile Court a mother was at her wits end with her 10 year old son. She said 'I am heart broken'. The boy was accused with two other 9 year old boys of breaking up drain pipes in a yard.

The mother continued 'He is just as destructive in the hoose. He pulls the fire onto the floor cuts up the curtains and soots the beds. . He will not take a telling' and I have given him a good leathering as well'.

The boy was fined 10 shillings and the two 9 year olds 5 shillings each.

The Queen Mary 2 Riverboat shuffle was well on its way down the Firth of Clyde. The Jazz Music was second to none with the Bill Paterson Quartet and the clarinettist Tommy Corrigan of the Ayrshire Jazz Band proving extremely popular. The night wore on and John was beginning to become nervous.

He had primed the compere when to stop the music for a few minutes while he would go on one knee and ask his long time girlfriend for her hand in marriage. He thought it would be a formality and she would say yes. However, something at the back of his mind suggested that wumin can be unpredictable.

Sandra was standing next to John. He said 'Wait there a minute Sandra ! The music stopped at the appointed moment as arranged with the compere. John had the floor to himself and a bemused audience waited to hear what he had to say. John had rehearsed his little speech.

He walked over to Sandra and brought her onto the floor. He then went down on one knee like a knight of old and said 'Sandra, I love you; in front of all these people I would jist like to say I want to marry you. You are special and I want you for my wife !'.

Sandra smiled and in 2 seconds flat it was a done deal. Sandra in tears said 'Of course I will John'. The crowd around the floor all burst into applause and the music re-started with many of the men stealing a kiss from Sandra and congratulating John. John and Sandra both went up on deck.

The breeze meant they both put on scarfs and coats. John said ' I have never been so happy Sandra'.

Sandra said ' Wait till I tell my mother when we get back'. John said 'Do you think she will be pleased ?'. Sandra said 'You are fishing for compliments John !. You know she loves you. She has always said that you can tell that you are such an honest person and so genuine'. John smiled.

In return for some pocket money Ruth has got Derek into the swing of carrying out some shopping for the family.

She has taught him that into the one bag goes the milk, one bottle at each end of the bag, the loaf in the middle with the bread rolls. Robbie likes the flat sausages from Jimmy the Butcher and occasionally has the link sausages. Derek has at least one 'piece and jam' a day and loves them.

The Shieldhall Road shops seemed to have the friendliest staff you could wish to have. In the fruit shop they still sell off 'a penny chipped fruit' to the children near the end of the day and Derek gets some on most days.

A bit of worrying news is that the elderly lady Mrs. Sillars (mother of Nan Sillars; one of Ruth's best friends) is not too well. They live in 31 Daviot Street immediately above Boab/Robbie's flat.

Nan has had to give up her secretarial job near Bridgeton and manages to get a job as an usherette at the Elder Cinema. The Elder Cinema is a small theatre located in the next street off Govan Road behind the Lyceum picture house.

As a general rule the Lyceum, Plaza and the Vogue Govan cinema's get the pictures not too long after they are released. The Elder and the Mosspark picture houses tend to get the same pictures but a few weeks later.

If a film goer was to miss a film at the bigger picture houses then it was to the Elder or Mosspark they would go. Nan initially finds the working hours a little difficult to get used to but soon settles in. Her role is to walk down the aisle with a customer and shine the torch at a vacant seat. The beam of the torch usually highlighted a substantial amount of smoke in the cinema.

Once the cinema goer was settled into their seat then she would await the next customer. At Intermission Nan would don the Ice Cream tray and walked down to the front to sell the ice's and drinks to the customers.

The Drumoyne School teachers set the class out in order of academic ability. The pupils with the best results are over at the back and the seats are normally reserved for Peter McLaren, Norrie Greig and Gillian Shaw. Derek is usually somewhere in the middle. The bottom double seater desk has only one seemingly permanent occupant; a girl called Maria Benson.

For a short time some of the other classmates would make fun of her. She was invariably poorly dressed and on occasions absent from school for short periods. Maria lived in Balbeg Street across the road from the school. Derek talked to Uncle Jack about Maria one day when he came over to visit. Jack said ' It sounds like Maria has problems at home.

Whatever happens, even if you are ridiculed by the rest of the class and even the teacher you must support her, talk to her and offer help. You must always support the weakest person in your class !'.

Derek took Jack's advice on board. However, it seemed that all the other members of the class had been given the same advice; especially the girls. Maria was treated well after that. From what was learned, Maria's mum was a single parent and desperately ill.

After school she had to spend time caring for her mother, a tough job for an adult but even tougher for an under 10 year old. Maria had a lovely smile and all the class liked the days when she smiled and generally seeing her cheerful. Janet Brown of 331, Hillington Road was a good conductress. When the tramcar stopped near Summertown Road she helped an elderly lady to get off the tram and over to the pavement.

When she re-boarded the tram she was confronted by 24 year old John Stark of 772, Govan Road. He said 'You are not going to throw me off this tramcar'. Janet asked him 'What are you talking about ?'

139

After an angry exchange of words Stark was asked to go upstairs as all the seats were taken in the lower deck. He refused and at this point the conductress sounded the bell to stop the tramcar. The driver came round and an altercation started.

Stark threw a fish supper in the face of the tram conductress and followed it up with a punch to the head and face. At this point he ran off pursued by the driver and a few of the passengers. A passing police van noticed the chase and soon were also in pursuit of John Stark; he was eventually cornered in the stairwell of 4 Copland Road and arrested.Janet the conductress was taken to the Southern General Hospital and detained overnight suffering from shock.

In court Fiscal Mr.Grindlay said it was a shocking and unprovoked attack. 'Perhaps a spell in prison will bring you to your senses'. Stark who was married with two children had a previous breach of the peace conviction and was sentenced to 30 days imprisonment. James Mac Gregor was a 21 year old painter and boarded a bus which had both a conductress and an inspector on board. He was asked for his fare of 2 pence but refused to pay.

The inspector and the conductress tried to persuade him to pay but without success. The pair asked him to provide his address if he had no money and he could pay later; he again refused and the police were called.

The policemen said that unless he paid he would be arrested. He got out two pence from his pocket and threw the coins at the inspector. The policemen immediately arrested him.

In Govan Police Court Mac Gregor was fined £2.

The Tramcars were being involved in a disproportionately high number of accidents. The No.7 from Craigton to Riddrie collided with a bakers van at the junction of Craigton Road and Shieldhall Road. 15 year old George Gibb in the Bakers van, who hit his head on the cabin roof, was soon ok but the chocolate cups and other bakers sundries were scattered all over the road.

It was announced that tramcars were to be phased out with no new ones being ordered to replace the existing fleet.

At 76, Copland Road, Mary Edwards was running herself a bath. She was taking her clothes off when she heard a scuffling noise at the window so she opened the curtains and saw a man was standing on the window sill peering in. She grabbed him by the raincoat and he entered the bathroom before punching her. Mary had bruises to the arms, face, body and her spectacles were broken. Mrs. Edwards son, who heard the commotion, came to his mothers rescue and after a violent struggle the intruder was held down on the floor until the police arrived.Peter Best (27) a local motor driver was told by Fiscal Mr.W.A.Grindlay that there had been a number of complaints about a peeping tom in the area.

To reach the window sill Best had to climb over a four foot wooden fence negating the defence plea that he was drunk.

Best was heavily fined and given the option of 60 days imprisonment.

At the Rob Roy Bar it is the middle of the night. The bar, situated on the corner of Elder Street and Govan Road, is quiet but at the rear of the pub there is activity. Thieves have descended into the space behind the pub entering from a close in an adjacent street.

Quietly, using muffled hammer taps, they knocked out the brickwork and climbed into the Bar cellar and from there they passed out boxes of whiskey They then made a hole in the ceiling of the cellar and entered the Bar. They blew open the safe and took money from the various charity boxes.
Later that evening the safe was blown open at the Fairfield Working Men's Club in Uist Street and money taken.
Govan CID called in the finger print experts.

Govan workers were being tempted away to foreign shores. New Zealand placed regular adverts in Glasgow newspapers.

They offered over £11 for a 40 hour week plus overtime and free passage for men aged under 45. In particular they needed Moulders, Boilermen and Blacksmiths. An exodus of the skilled Govan tradesmen was continuing. Tragedy struck outside 67, Clifford Street. Church Officer for Bellahouston Parish Church, Robert Mc Kittrick, stopped to light a cigarette. Almost immediately masonry from above fell down on him and he was rushed to the Southern General Hospital but died shortly afterwards. It was said to have been a million to one chance; on the roof workmen were trying to repair a damaged chimney stack.

The workmen had warned residents to watch out earlier in the day.
A conductress was in a good mood as the tramcar she worked on moved along Govan Road. She issued a ticket to passenger Gordon Dow (21) of Lettoch Street whereupon he immediately threw it on the floor of the tram and ordered the conductress to pick it up.

The conductress refused, so Dow spat in her face. When Dow was leaving the tramcar he pressed up against the ticket machine of the conductress releasing many tickets from the ticket machine.
He then spat on her face again at which point the conductress stopped the tram. A combination of passengers helped detain the spitting passenger until two policemen arrived.

In court Gordon Dow pleaded guilty. He said he had never been as drunk as he was at the time, having attended a wedding.
He apologised to the conductress and said if their was anything he could do to make up he would. Baillie Thompson fined Dow £5 and said
'These girls must be protected in carrying out their public service'.

In Aitkenhead Road a  22 year old conductress was collecting fares. Neil Judge (44) of Lettoch Street said the fare was too much and an argument ensued. A brawl between the two started and Judge scratched the conductress`s face until it bled. Two passengers jumped on Judge and restrained him until the police arrived.

At Govan Police Court Judge was sent to prison for 10 days after apologising saying he was worse for wear with drink.

Alex.James (53) who was drunk, got on the wrong bus at Govan Cross. The journey started and on asking for the fare James and the conductress realised he was on the wrong bus. The conductress said he would have to go back to the terminus and get on the correct bus. An argument ensued and a lot of bad language from James was forthcoming. The bus driver on arriving at the Hillington terminus summoned the police. At Govan Police Court Baillie Carruthers said his behaviour was disgusting and fined James £2 with an option of 20 days in prison.

Catherine Davis (18) was a bus conductress. As her bus approached the next bus stop, she noticed that three young ladies were waiting to board along with other passenegers. Her heart sank; these particular three had caused trouble on the bus on previous occasions. She asked the three not to board but they ignored her and got on board.

The conductress refused to take the fare of the three young ladies. They sat three to a seat, had a sing song and annoyed other passengers. Catherine tried to reason with them but without success and an argument ensued.

The conductress had had enough and took off her ticket machine and launched into the three young ladies.

At Govan Police Court Catherine Davis was in the dock accused of assault. Baillie Joseph Vallance weighed up the evidence and recorded a 'Not Guilty' verdict. A counter charge against the three young ladies for breach of the peace was also dismissed.

Ruth is on her way home from work and calls in at 20, Craigton Road to see Jimmy. Ruth says ' All the shops along Govan Road are improving their hygiene, plumbers are fitting wash hand basins and the lavatories are being upgraded.

I think it was a bit unfair of the British Medical Association to provide that report. You would think that awe the folk workin there had plooks, pimples, piles and bad teeth.

Nothing could have been further from the truth'. Jimmy says ' Well the BMA have come out quite a few times since to say that all High Streets, not just in Govan, have the same problem.

At least Govan is doing something about it'. Ruth says ' Whit are ye getting spruced up for Jimmy. Not the Mason's again ?'. Jimmy says 'Yes Ruth, we have a deputation coming tonight from another lodge'. Ruth says ' Och Jimmy they are a foosty lot '.

Jimmy says 'Ruth they do fantastic work behind the scenes for charities and all entrants to the brotherhood are carefully vetted. Now would you like to come to a whist night at the lodge to raise funds ? Ruth says ' Naw, I cannae think of a more boring way to spend an evening'. Jimmy brushes his shoes and then brushes down his jacket as Ruth departs. Jimmy will soon be on his way to Govan Town Hall.

At Dyers Bakery in 31 Greenfield Street, an acrimonious parting of the ways occurred between the owner James Dyer and bakery van driver Donald McLellan. Some weeks later Dyer who was a Master Baker noticed that a number of his regular customers had moved their business to the new company who employed Donald McLellan.

Dyer was incensed and went to the house of McLellan. An argument ensued and a number of people gathered to see what was happening. Dyer threatened McLellan and said ' I will cut your throat ear to ear if you continue to approach my customers'.

Ballie Ballance stated that although Mr Dyer was a highly respectable man there was no excuse for him making the threats to Mr McLellan. He was fined £1

With the end of the tramcars announced, a discussion by Glasgow Corporation took place to establish a place to scrap the trams. The decision was Elderslie depot near Paisley. Once a tramcar was scrapped it made its last journey to Elderslie where the fitters stripped out everything that could be re-used including the stairways, metals and all the electrics. These items were sent to Coplawhill tram works.

The entire process was scheduled to continue over a 5 year period.

In Govan a lot of people head towards Linthouse and the Stephens Shipyard; it is the launching of a ship destined for Vancouver in Canada. The 'Princess of Vancouver' is an order for the Canadian Pacific Railway Company and the launch is to be carried out by Mrs.Arkle wife of the European Office General Manager for CPRC. The ship is a Car/Railway/Passenger ferry and is 388 foot long and a gross tonnage of 7,000.

The inside of the ship is quality with cocktail bars for the passengers which are luxurious. The Govanites give a huge cheer as the ship moves down the slipway and into the River Clyde.

## THE SS DAPHNE GOES DOWN AT LINTHOUSE

*The day dawned like any other one,*
*The mother yawned and kissed her only son,*
*Watching as he slowly spread his wings,*
*Anxious as she cut her apron strings,*
*The father walked beside his little boy,*
*The offspring spoke of dreams of hope and joy,*
*Apprenticed to his father would be hard,*
*Aboard the SS Daphne in the yard,*
*His pride a lass was ready for her naming,*
*The Clyde alas so greedy for the claiming,*
*When champagne bubbles drenched the hull,*
*The sky had turned a deathly dull,*
*Then down the slipway trailing chain,*
*The cheering crowd all wet with rain,*
*Foghorns blaring in celebration,*
*Tugboats waiting in anticipation,*
*In the blink of an eye the scene was changed,*
*Him in the sky had another arranged,*
*Into the river the steamship splashed,*
*With one dreadful lurch all hope was dashed,*
*Hope and dreams of the deep blue ocean,*
*As Daphne was listing a circular motion,*
*The woeful day wore on and on,*
*The mother knew all hope had gone,*
*The father she had come to cherish,*
*Among the ones who were to perish,*
*The offspring scarcely in his teens,*
*Remained with her in all her dreams,*
*The day has ended but him above,*
*Will hold the souls within his love.*
***POEM FROM THE LATE JOE SHARP-GOVAN POET***

**photo 7**

# CHAPTER 14
## ONCE A STEPHEN'S MAN

Govan Old Folk once again had a treat; in fact all 900 of them. Each were invited to Govan Town Hall where they were given a dinner and a concert with a sing a long. At the end of proceedings each elderly person was given £1. This was donated by the 29th Municipal Ward.

At 110 Blackburn Street, Plantation, two families who lived on the same landing did not get on. Alfred Dobbin Wood (35) and his wife Mary (34) disliked Thomas Stewart (43) and his wife Margaret (45).
The two husbands met on the landing one day and Stewart accused Wood of casting aspersions on his family.

Wood punched Stewart knocking him to the floor then both wife's joined in the scrap . Mrs Stewart hit Wood with her shoe causing bleeding and the event descended in to a complete free for all. The Fiscal at Govan Police Court fined both husbands £3 each. Both of the wives were admonished.
James Mc Garrigle had attended the funeral of his father in law. He got into an argument with his brother in law at the post funeral drink at 129 Paisley Road West. The argument descended into a fight and both finished up on the landing. The police were called and they were both arrested. At Govan Police Court Mc Garrigle was fined £2 by Baillie Vallance. His brother in law Harry Marsh did not turn up and a warrant was put out for his arrest.

There was a commotion outside 227 Summertown Road and around 200 people had gathered outside. The police arrived and found a lot of noise from the second floor. Water was pouring down the landing and when they entered the tenement flat they found four men and five women in a fight.

Empty bottles, wine glasses and broken tumblers lay scattered around. The local residents rushed into the fray once the police arrived and helped with the apprehension of the fighting drinkers.

The 11 accused said they had been attending a birthday party, Helen Deighan said the party was to celebrate her 21st Birthday.

The Police Judge asked if she got the key to the door amid loud laughter.
Four men were fined £1 and the other seven accused were admonished.
John takes Sandra down to Shaw Street; he has arranged for his mother Marie and his father Alfred to meet his bride to be. He has no fears about the meeting going well as both his parents, he knows, will take to Sandra like ducks to water.

Marie offers a'Wee cuppa tea' and Sandra accepts. Marie asks Sandra a few questions before Alfred says ' Didne ye be askin silly questions Marie ! Marie says 'Well John wisnae a chip off the old block gauin doon oan his knees tae ask fur yer hand !' Albert, you jist wisnae like that !'. Albert says ' Aye bit it wis different in those days Marie ! '.

Marie says to Sandra ' I am so pleased fur yea both and look forward tae the wedding. It will be great and I cannae wait'.

The following day in the Golspie Street pawnshop Abe is sorting things out with John and discussing the wedding. Abe says 'Where are you both going to live John ?' John says 'Not finalised things yet Abe; still looking'. Abe says ' John I think I may be able to help here if you are interested. I have a friend who has just vacated a house in Mosspark Boulevard, he wants me to look after it for a while and only lease it out to reputable tenants. Would you be interested ? John says ' Not half Abe. I will discuss it with Sandra tonight but I am certain she will be over the moon. If you could arrange it Abe that would be fantastic'.

What Abe did not tell John was that he was going to purchase the house. Helen Chalmers and her daughter Sandra boarded the No 4 bus at Langlands Road destined for Glasgow City Centre. The mission was the forthcoming wedding of Sandra to John Leslie. Lewis's in Argyle Street was the target and mother and daughter looked at the wedding dresses on offer. They were both fussy.

The Tiara had to be right with the veil; the shoes the perfect match to the dress. The dress hang had to be right and the lingerie carefully considered. The measurements were taken and Helen bought countless smaller items to be stored in the 'bottom drawer' until after the wedding. The father, Bill Chalmers, fortunately had budgeted for the day one of his two daughters got married and he himself was keen that there was no hitch on the wedding day. He liked John and they both had become good friends, his daughter could hardly have a better suitor he thought.

Ruth and Jimmy were regular visitors to the Govan Town Hall as they had a new café with a small band and many events. Among these was weekly wrestling which attracted good crowds. Ruth liked the 'Black Panther' but tended to get bored as the evenings wore on. Typically there were four bouts and on one occasion the wrestling programme was Ray Hunter (Tasmania) v Reg Williams;  Jim Lewis v Eric Sands;

Don Mendoza v Alf Rawlings;  Jack Proctor v Bill Howes.

The Govanites took to Wrestling and there was a clamour for Boxing also to be held at the Town Hall.

A young choir was in full practice. It was the Govan Junior Gaelic  Choir and they were rehearing for the The Mod of Ancontumm Gailheadach  held in Aberdeen. 422 children had entered the competition from all over Scotland under Conducter Donald Grant and they were looking forward to the day out and the competition.

14 year old twins Pat and Eva Mc Niven met the famous 86 year old Aberdeen Mod veteran Peter Mc Cracken Mac Donald.

The Highlands and Islands competitors claimed many of the top prizes but Catherine McNiven from Govan managed third prize in the prestigious Gaelic Folk Songs category.

Mrs. Agnes MacCormack went along to a wake paying last respects to the dead man. The family of the dead man did not want Aggie to go into the room because they felt she had put a curse on him.

She said ' I didnae' and pushed past the family into the room with the coffin. The family followed and a row ensued. Mrs McCormack said she only wanted to have a wee prayer with the dead man but as the row developed Aggie started to shout, curse and swear. The police were called.

At Govan Police Courts Mrs MacCormack was fined £2. She said 'I don't usually have a drink due to my blood pressure. I will not touch a drop again !'.

A twelve year old girl was giving evidence against her father who was on a charge of assaulting his wife at Govan Police Court. Baillie John Mains said to the girl 'Why have you got red varnish on your finger nails ? She replied 'I play by myself varnishing at times. Both my parents know I do it !'. 'Does not the school say anything about it ?' says Baillie Mains. The girl replied 'Sometimes they check me, sometimes they don't'.

The father was found guilty of striking his wife. The row had started when the 12 year old girl had said she was not going to school.

Baillie Mains asked `does either of the parents have any authority over the girl? ` The father said 'She does not do what she is told and does what she likes'. The girl said 'I was only joking about not going to school; I like school !'. The case awaited a probation officers report.

There was a row in Helen Street with around 30 youths involved. A number of plain clothed policemen moved in following numerous reports of disorderly conduct. The youths scattered but four were caught.

At Govan Police Court William Rice—Labourer (22) of 57 Copland Road and Sam McFarlane—merchant seaman (18) and two other 16 year old boys all admitted causing the disturbances.

Judge Adam Templeton fined them all £1 each ; the low penalty taking their ages into consideration.

Ruth and Jimmy were walking through Elder Park to see some events to celebrate the 70th anniversary of the Park being opened. Ruth says 'Mrs Elder must have been a very kind lady Jimmy giving Govan Burgh a nice park like this'.

Mrs Isabella Elder purchased the 36 acres of ground in memory of her husband Mr David Elder in 1883 at the cost of £37,000. Jimmy says ' I think Govan owes a lot to these people for giving them so much employment over the years and it`s a shame the Communists in the yards are trying to wreck the dreams the Elders had with their strikes. The Elders would be turning in their graves if they knew what was happening`.

John and Abe are working in the Golspie Street Pawnshop. Abe asks ' How are the wedding arrangements going John ?'. John says ' I must admit I am getting a wee bit apprehensive. As well as Sandra's mum Helen arranging lots of things, my mother is also arranging things but she will not tell me what'. Abe says ' I am actually looking forward to the wedding I think it will be a great day'. PC McCabe came into the shop and John ushered him through the door and into the back office offering a cup of tea. PC McCabe gratefully accepted the offer and produced a long list of stolen goods.

He says 'There seems to be a lot around the Govan area this month especially houses in Paisley Road West. My guess Gibby has been involved so if he comes in please check the list '. Abe says ' Is it not time you were able to pin something on Gibby ?' PC McCabe says 'Gibby is as slippery as an eel and I think Bernie and Junior cover for him too much. However, he has upset a great many people so he could have a few people after him'.

Abe says 'What other things are happening in Govan ?'.

PC McCabe says 'A month or so back we had the honour of trying to arrest a local drunkard up at Bellahouston. We all took a few punches from him before finally we subdued him and got him down to the police station. He has countless convictions. Anyway, the local minister turned up at Govan Police Courts and says he is now in Alcoholics Anonymous so he got spared the prison sentence and was only fined £5.

We went to another situation when there were a few hundred people outside a tenement. The man went beserk inside the house and started throwing everything out of the windows; he was drunk but was strong.

He had beaten his wife up who had tried to stop him and I thought he was going to throw a few of us polis oot the windae but we managed to subdue him. His wife says he had just received his holiday bonus.

Well thank you for the tea and if you are offered these items please give us a call'. Abe says ' Yes we will do that'.

Lord Mountbatten was the guest of the Clyde Navigation Trust and sailed down the River Clyde inspecting the ships under construction. As he passed Fairfields he saw the troopship Oxfordshire (20,000 tons) and the Empress of Britain (26,000tons) built for the Canadian Pacific Co. within the Fairfield Basin. The two ships cost £10,000,000 combined to build.

Ruth has seen a couple of familiar faces walking through Woolworths . It was Bob Anderson and Louise Crampthorne-Pilkington who had been present when Ruth got employed many months previous. Both still remembered Ruth and came over to where she was serving. Bob says smiling' You do not seem to be so nervous today Ruth !' Louise also smiled. Ruth says ' Hello !!.

147

Naw I cannot think I have ever been as nervous as at that interview ! . I wanted the job so much '. Bob says 'Has it met up with your expectations Ruth ?'. Ruth replied 'Oh yes I love the job and I love the people that work here and most of the customers. Thank you both for giving me a chance'.

Bob says 'No problem Ruth, we are pleased you seem to be getting on well. It was evident at the interview that you were perfectly suitable. Was that not so Louise ?' 'Yes exactly' says Louise.

A few minutes later Ruth is asked to go to the Personnel Department. Eleanor is there on her own and she says ' Ruth we have had a call from the Southern General Hospital; your father has bee admitted. Please feel free to go ! Ruth caught the No.23 bus and was soon at the hospital. Her father Boab was not looking well but was sitting up in his bed and he was pleased to see his daughter and smiled.

Boab had been employed at W.Stephens Shipyard in charge of the instrument workshop for many years until his retirement a few years before. He had been active in getting the Old Age Pensioners Club opposite Andy's Café on Berryknowes Road opened. Boab was on the committee and helped organise several functions and days out.

He liked the club which was barely 5 minutes walk from where he lived. Ruth departed after spending a while with her father. Robbie and Jack had arrived and they kept their father company. After Boab was left alone he went for an operation which was felt would be routine. The next morning Ruth was again summoned to the Personnel Department at Woolworth's. Eleanor was again there to greet her but this time looking sombre. She said 'Ruth I have some terrible news !!'. Your dad Boab has died.

Word soon got around about the death of Boab who was 71 and countless people fromStephens came to the house to pay respects. The coffin with Boab was brought to the house one day before the funeral and on the day the neighbours paid their respects as the hearse dove off down Daviot Street, Tormore Street, Meilklewood Road and into Berryknowes Road. As the Funeral procession passed the Old Peoples Club all the pensioners stood, head's bowed with their bunnets removed.

At Craigton Cemetry Boab was re-united with his wife Lizzie, who had died some 25 years previous, in the same grave. In the 1930's the family could not afford a headstone and the same situation existed at this funeral.

The shipyard named Alexander Stephen's had been a fixture at Linthouse and provided employment for thousands of men over a great number of years. Alexander Stephen was not a Govanite and in fact came from Moray in the North East of Scotland. The first records of the company show Alexander starting their association with building ships in 1750 not long after the end of the Jacobite Rebellion and Bonnie Prince Charlie's crushing defeat at Culloden.

His brother William managed to escape the redcoats and together they started building boats. They built a small yard at Burghead on the Moray Firth and one of the greatest shipbuilding enterprises was born.

Alexander's father was a farmer with a small holding near Lossiemouth and helped in many small ways. Initially, the yard built fishing boats, whalers and trading vessels for the south seas. Their nephew William was brought into the business and he quickly learned and developed many skills associated with shipbuilding. William started up another yard in Aberdeen near Footdee. He had the skills to develop ships features that other shipbuilders felt were impossible. William was a swarthy man and was noted for his continuous swearing; to compensate he turned partly to religion. William's son, William Junior, on returning from the Napoleonic Wars opened another yard at Arbroath. However, it was not a success and almost collapsed the entire Stephen's enterprise with the father, at the age of 69, trying to save it by fending off lawsuits. The younger son, also called Alexander, came to the rescue by agreeing to clear all debts over a period of time. He moved all the shipyard enterprises to Arbroath and after a number of years down the coast to Dundee where he built the world famous Panmure Yard.

In 1850 Alexander decided the best place to build ships was on Clydeside as Glasgow was becoming prosperous with the arrival of tobacco and cotton. He left his son William in charge of the Dundee yard and set up a yard at Kelvinhaugh/Yorkhill Wharf on the Clyde.

Stephen's yard suffered a number of setbacks including a fire and mud slides around the yard. Alexander had enough and moved back to the Dundee yard. He left his two younger sons James and Alexander in charge of the Clydeside yard. The third Alexander was a shrewd progressive businessman and not afraid to try something new.

He allowed his workers to introduce a co-operative and allowed them a building to operate out of completely free of charge. With the co-operation of his workforce he started building iron composite ships with an iron frame and a shell of wood. They built one of the first composite screw steamers and, probably illegally, sold it to the Confederates in the American Civil War. It sank 37 Northern Ships on the Shenandoah.

The most famous of the ships built at Kelvinhaugh was one of the smallest. No other shipbuilding company in the world thought that the order and specification was possible. The ship was to be a small schooner weighing just 70 tons. It was to be called the Aurora Del Titicaca and the order was to be placed by Senor Germino Costa of Peru.

The order had to be completed in 1869 and the schooner available for trading on Lake Titicaca which was 12,500 feet above sea level in Peru.

The components of the ship had to be no longer than 18 foot and light enough for carrying up the torturous roads to the mountain top. The Stephens engineers met the spec` and the ship was carried up the mountain bit by bit. It was re-assembled easily on the lakeside and ready to sail on time.

When the Kelvinhaugh lease was due to expire Alexander Stephen junior looked around for an alternative. Initially he thought Barrow may be a good option but eventually settled for Linthouse; he bought the Linthouse Estate for £32,000.

Some of the finest Clippers in the world have been built at Stephens, many of them for racing across the Oceans. Stephens adapted the yards for building steamships made of steel. They also built up an impressive client base over the years which includes City Line, Anchor Line and Allan Line. In addition there was Clan Line, Fyffes, Elder, and Dempster Elder, all valued customers.

William George Murray was a man who believed in order around his house; he set a roster for his children to clean the windows and on the wall he had a list of Do's and Don'ts. In front of Baillie John Inglis he said the roster, for example the 20 windows, was to help his wife. The three children aged 17, 13 and 7 all do their bit.

Mrs Murray felt the discipline William exerted over his family was too severe. On a recent occasion he chastised the 13 year old daughter and when his wife objected he punched her on the arms and body.

Murray was admonished and Baillie Inglis said 'Just go easy with the roster !!.They can be a bit irksome when other things need doing'.

In early morning Govan there is a loud crash. Driver Betty Cope (26) has seen the tram she is driving collide with a permanent way tram. The whole tram front is stoved in and Betty is eventually cut free and taken to the Southern General Hospital in serious condition.

In Paisley Road West there is a collision between a tramcar and a motor bike. The pillion passenger William McGregor aged 11 is safe and comfortable in hospital but the motor cycle rider, his father, has been killed outright.

Tramcars continue to be the greatest source of accidents in Glasgow and many welcome the day they are removed from the roads.

At the Golspie Street pawnshop, Abe and John have just turned the shop sign to `closed`. Abe lights up a cigarette and blows smoke into the air. He gets two bottles of beer from the cupboard and two tumblers. Carefully he pours the contents in the tumblers and with John they talk about everything and anything. Out of the blue John asks 'Are there any poor Jews Abe ?'.

Abe replies 'Of course there are'.

John says ' You do not seem to see many !'. Abe says 'That is because we work harder my boy !' They both laugh.

John says ' I was waiting on that one Abe !'.

Abe says `We have as many poor Jews as any of the other Faiths. We try and help them by having a few events throughout the year. At the Giffnock Synagogue next week we have the Festival of Passover. We give the needy clothes, foodstuffs and money. Also, we give out bread, eggs, sugar and ceremonial wine'. John says 'That is impressive Abe !'.

Down at the Old Harmony Bar John Gillespie and Frank Mulvenney are standing at the bar discussing the affairs of the world. Soon the topic revolves around Capital Punishment. Frank asks John his view on the subject.

John says ' I think it should be abolished !!. Since the Ruth Ellis execution most folk want change. The Labour guy Sydney Silverman seems to have a lot of support for the Bill including a lot of Tories'.

Frank says ' It will probably get through the Commons but will it get past the Lords ?'.

John says 'probably not because it is a punishment that only affects the working classes. The upper classes would never face execution'. Frank says 'That is what is wrong with the system !'.

John says ' The Communist system is even worse Frank. All the indications are that many are sent to a remote place in Northern Russia called Siberia never to return !'. Frank says 'That is Western propaganda'.

John says ' Capital punishment in Scotland is rare; they usually find some loophole to change to life imprisonment. The ones that get hanged usually deserve it in anybody`s book. In England the Laws seem to give little protection to people being charged and they seem too quick to get them to the gallows. Bad mistakes are plentiful like Evans and Bentley. The trouble is you cannot reverse the mistakes they make. Britain is apparently the most barbaric regime in Western Europe. Your Soviets out in Russia are probably ten times worse than Britain'.

Frank says ' I do not think so. It was said Stalin had to put his foot down to get rid of people trying to reverse the revolution'.

The barmen said 'This is heavy stuff guys dae ye want another drink ?.

Frank says 'What do think about John Rankin?'.

John says ' He has done well with his transport initiatives. Since transport was Nationalised the country has had an operating surplus of £221,000,000 a great achievement. Now the Tories are in they will probably De-nationalise it, make a big loss and the general public will pay for it'.

Frank says 'That is why you need the Communists !. They fight for the workers rights'.

# CHAPTER 15
## RAZORS

Following the death of Boab the Wilson family had some decisions to make. Robbie, Ruth and Jack are present as is girlfriend Maggie and also Derek. Maggie has visited the house on several previous occasions and is well liked by everyone she meets. She is always well dressed and very pleasant. However, she has a secret that has so far has been kept between Jack and herself and from the family at 31 Daviot Street.

Jack announces that Maggie and he have a wedding date set and they have managed to obtain a Clydebank Council tenement flat in Glasgow Road, Clydebank. It has two rooms only but will do as a start. Jack says he will make a short announcement which those present should know ' Maggie is a Catholic !'.

Ruth is stunned. 'I do not believe it. I have been nice to Maggie all along and now this, awe naw !'. 'Ruth listen' says Jack. Ruth continues ' I suppose we will have a hoose full of priests for the wedding, I will look ridiculous with the neighbours !'. 'Listen Ruth' says Jack.

Robbie says 'Listen Ruth'. Jack continues 'Maggie was born a Catholic and wants to remain a Catholic. We have discussed it through and through'. Maggie stays quiet.

'Maggie has not been to Chapel for countless years. I am a non Catholic but I would not give you the time of day for the Protestant churches.' says Jack. Robbie says 'What does it matter what religion Maggie is Ruth they want to be together and that is that !'. Jack says 'We have looked at the strengths and merits of the Clydebank schools and the Protestant schools are by far the better. If we have children they will not be brought up in any particular faith. The wedding is in 6 weeks and it will be in Govan Registry Office. I will be leaving soon to live my life with Maggie; that is where I want to be !'

Ruth has calmed down and Robbie asks 'What is happening now that Welsh is back on the scene Ruth ?'. Ruth says' Jimmy has got a single end down at Craigton Road as you probably know and I would like to move in with him'. 'And what about Derek ?' asks Jack.

Derek says 'I would prefer to stay here with Uncle Robbie ! . All my friends are here, I like my school and I am happy. The place at Craigton Road is too small anyway. I have already been there'. The family agreed that Ruth would visit Daviot Street once per week to do washing and house cleaning. Derek offered to do the daily shopping at Shieldhall Road. So the wheels were set in motion. It is launch day at Harland and Wolff shipyard. An order from the British Phosphate Commissioners is launched and with good weather a good number of Govanites have turned out. They line up at the bottom of Water Row to get the best views. A large crowd has been allowed into the shipyard to see the launch and among them are Jimmy Welsh and Ruth. .

Derek Drummond the Chief Ship Electrical Engineer is there `backslapping` with the main launch guests and playing an excellent host. He breaks off to speak to Jimmy '.'How are you James ? . I heard you have been working down at the Southern General'. Jimmy says 'Very well Derek, I am sorry I could not have stayed longer with you'. Derek says 'This ship is called the Tristar a small Passenger Cargo vessel. We have orders for another three similar vessels'.

Govan is blessed with a spell of good weather and Derek is attentive as Miss Doig announces to the class that the following term will be taken by Mrs.Dewart. She says if the class get through the work quickly then its down to Pirrie Park for the afternoon. The work was quickly over and the group plus several other classes were soon running around Pirrie Park. The teachers brought chairs with them and soaked up the sun. All the children in the class enjoyed the summer days at Pirrie Park, a lasting memory for all Drumoyne School pupils in years to come.

While the boys run around it is noticeable that quite a few of the boys have warts on their hands and arms. The teachers call a few over and inspect the infections; a number of the boys claim that they are spreading and ask for cures. The teachers have the solution to the problem. 'Tell your parents to get some vinegar and a needle, that is the best cure. As quick as the warts arrived they seemed to disappear with or without the 'cure' being applied.

Jimmy and Maggie duly got married and moved to Clydebank. On the day of the wedding they threw coins from the wedding car on their way to the Registry Office. Ruth had already moved in with Jimmy at 20 Craigton Road while Derek and Robbie re-adjusted to life in a less occupied No.31 Daviot Street tenement. The house quickly had a new addition.

A blue and white budgie came to occupy the cage previously bought for Joey. The name given was Billy the Budgie and what a little gem he was. He would fly down on to the carpet when he was let out and knock the marbles around the floor with his head. He tried to copy many of the whistles Derek trained him with. Once out he would always try and land on Derek's shoulder.

A smashing little friend who went on to have a very long life.
Jimmy has been to Watson's Bar and is the worse for wear from drink. He staggers through Govan with eyes pied.

He is slowly but surely making his way towards Craigton Road and the betting is will he make it before he collapses down drunk.

As he passes Hills Trust School three onlookers take an interest. It`s Bernie, Gibby and Junior. Junior says ' That's the guy Bernie !.' Bernie says 'Lets follow him'. The three remain circumspect as they watch Jimmy stagger all the way to 20 Craigton Road. Junior says 'plans must be made !'.

Nine year old Patrick Mac Farlane liked sliding down the banisters in his tenement as opposed to using the stairs.

His mother sent him for milk and within minutes heard a cry as Patrick lost his balance on the banister and tumbled 50 feet to the bottom of the stairs at 201 Paisley Road West. The neighbours rushed out to help and Patrick surprisingly was relatively unscathed . He was taken to the Southern General Hospital for observation.

## SNIPPETS:

- The Summer months saw some additional sporting attractions. At the White City Stock car racing was proving to be popular and drawing big crowds. In addition horse show jumping took place at the venue with a few of the Scottish prime events being contested.
- A former Harland & Wolff man passed away. Robert Allen had spent 47 years with the company having joined the Belfast factory. He fought with the Irish regiment in the First World War.

A letter to the Glasgow Press Offices caused much debate on the conditions within the Clydeside Shipyards.

J.Gemmill wrote:

' *Your editorial on the Clyde and its shipyards was a welcome relief from the gloomy and dismal utterances we often hear from some Clyde shipbuilders. For the last 100 years or so, our shipyard workers have been the finest craftsmen in the world. They still are; but what conditions they work in !. Much shipyard work has to be done out of hours or under very little cover in all weathers or in the ship itself in confined spaces. Foul air with mixed fumes from electric welding, river fires, paint, red lead and in a noise which leaves most workers slightly deaf.*

*Some hardship is inevitable but many conditions could be improved. In most yards there is nowhere to wash, nowhere to keep clothes or tools and no compensation if they are spoilt or lost. Hardly any yards provide medical observation or treatment such as violet ray and there is usually only the minimum of ambulance facilities. The minimum legal standards are lower for shipyards than they are for factories.*

*Re-equipment of yards to keep pace with modern developments of construction has been a piecemeal affair. We need a real drive for modernisation and planning. That the world's best shipbuilders should also be the highest paid is only justice, but the future of the Clyde yards cannot be assured by better wages and conditions or increased production. None of these will prevent slumps or unemployment.*

*The future of the Clyde depends on trade expansion and full employment.* '

John and Abe are beginning to be more and more aware of the countdown to John's wedding. The pawnshop will be closed on the Saturday of the wedding and the notice has already been placed in the window.

Abe has got a suit for the occasion but will not tell John anything about it except that he was fitted out at the W.L. Thompson and Sons shop in Union Street, Glasgow.

154

John has bought a smart suit at Lewis's for his wedding. Helen Chalmers has left nothing to chance for Sandra' s wedding and the big day will soon arrive.

The school strap debate continued with arguments and counter arguments. It was argued that the reason that Scottish children learned their 3 R's quicker than their English counterparts was due to the use of the strap. This theory was put forward by three University Psychologists Professors. Vernon, Mr.O'Gorman and Mr. McLellan.

Mr.William Campbell of the Educational Institute of Scotland contested the findings and said that the reason for the 8 year olds achieving better results was that the teachers were better trained. Scottish teachers had a three year training period to their English counterparts two. He concluded ' The strap should not be used to drive up standards and only be used for class discipline'.

Lanarkshire Schools County Education Committee had a meeting to decide the future use of the tawse in classroom's. This was after an increasing number of parents had suggested that it should be done away with completely.

Recommendations were put forward for consideration including:-

- Secondary School girls should not be given the strap in general. If it is felt corporal punishment is necessary then it should only be after consultation with the head teacher or advisor.
- Pupils should not get corporal punishment because they may not have achieved the required result in lessons.
- Infant children should not get the tawse.

Back in Govan the teachers at all the schools completely ignored the guidelines and felt that lack of discipline in the class would hinder the learning process.

A 12 year old Govan boy was caught stealing from a multiple store in Langlands Road.

Appearing in front of Govan Juvenile Court his mother said 'He can neither read nor write and goes to a special school. If I keep him in he just climbs down the drainpipe'. Judge James Johnston says ' The only cure is to give your son plenty of the strap !' . The boy was admonished and discharged.

The barbers shop at Greenwell Terrace was a popular and noisy establishment on Saturday mornings. Many Govanites would sit in one of the six or so chairs and talk away to the Barber. The queue system was always shambolic especially if you were a schoolboy.

The Barbers immediately identified the regulars who were good tippers and of course the waiting schoolboy would be unfortunately overlooked. 'Sorry son I didnae see ye there!'

Ruth would usually let one or even two of the queue jumping situations go before. 'My wee boy here is next, thank you !'.

The smaller boys sat on the board provided by the barber to get the required height for the haircut. Many of the regulars would have their faces foamed as they chatted with the barber who sharpened the razor on the strap hanging from the wall. Ruth always said she thought most of the men in the Barbers shop talked rubbish about everything. 'They moan and groan about the slightest setback in their lives Derek. Make sure you do not grow up like them. There are many people worse off than we are '.

Ruth is sitting in 20 Craigton Road watching the television doing some knitting and darning socks. The coal fire is roaring away and she is thankful for where she is. Ruth looks up at the clock which is approaching 10 0'Clock and she expects Jimmy will be soon arriving from having a drink at one of Govan's pubs. It is a misty, cold evening as Jimmy walks up from near Govan Cross and as he walks through Harmony Row he is passed by three men going in the opposite direction.

He walks on but is aware of footsteps behind him. He looks round but can see little through the mist except possibly a shadow. He walks on and hears running footsteps behind him. Again he turns round and again he sees nothing.

Just as he turns round the corner into Helen Street, he feels both his arms held one by each of two men. A third opens a razor and runs it across Jimmy's face. He struggles with them and finally breaks free but in a flash they are gone. He sees them fade into the mist and he hears the footsteps running. Another noise he hears is a strange laughing; one which he has heard before. However, his immediate problem was to stem the large flow of blood from his face. He is in shock and feels bitterly cold as he sits down on the wet pavement. A passer by sees him and thinks he is drunk.

However, he looks down and sees the flow of blood mixing with the water on the wet pavement. 'Ye will be aw right pal !. I will take good care of you. We must stop the blood'. At this point two other passers by arrive and Jimmy is being treated by all three as they valiantly try to stem the flow from one of his cheeks. One of the three runs off to get help.

Two hours later Jimmy is in the Southern General Hospital, his face bandaged and awaiting the arrival of a police officer. At 20 Craigton Road Ruth is becoming concerned; it is past midnight and no sign of Jimmy. She hopes that he is not too drunk and possibly fallen over. In recent times he has been happiest using the pubs around Govan Cross. She gets her coat and scarf and wraps up warm before going out into the chilly air.

Jimmy is visited by a police officer who requests a statement. Jimmy tells him he was attacked by three men who had scarves around their faces. Two held his arms while the other cut his face with a razor. The policeman wrote down the notes quickly and asked 'Do you know anyone Mr.Welsh, who would want to carry out this attack ?'.

'No' said Jimmy. 'You have no idea what their motives may have been; do you know anyone who may have a grudge against you ? ' said the policeman. 'No' said Jimmy. 'He continued 'I cannot think of anyone'.

Jimmy arrives at 20 Craigton Road at exactly the same time Ruth has returned from Govan Cross where she has been looking for him. 'Jimmy, what has happened ? Good God almighty !' .

Drumoyne School was now teaching dancing and Mrs. Dewart's class was enjoying the lessons. A gramophone was blaring out various tunes including the Gay Gordon and the pupils danced around the main hall in pairs. Within Mrs. Dewart's class Derek was invariably sitting beside Janet Daniels as they always seemed to get the same marks.

Not too surprising as Janet allowed Derek to copy her answers when he got stuck. As a result when it came to pairing off the boys and girls for dancing Derek and Janet would be together. This went on for quite some time; the pair on the same desk and always paired off together at dancing. As with everything at Drumoyne School this bit of information fed back to Derek's mother Ruth. One day at 31, Daviot Street, Ruth said 'I hear you have a wee lassie Derek !'. Derek went red faced and bashful. 'Naw maw, that is not true'. Ruth said ' I hear her name is Janet , Derek !'. Derek replied ' Maw Janet sits beside me in the class and we are usually paired off for dancing'. Ruth says teasing and smiling 'Is she yer girl friend Derek ?'. Derek went very bashful . 'Maw Janet is nice and her friend Lizzie is nice as well. All the boys in the class would like to be Janet's dance partner so I am lucky. I think Janet would probably prefer some boy better than me'. Ruth says 'I am only teasing Derek, but it is nice that you can be friends and get on with the lassies'.

So the dancing lessons went on within the main hall. 'Forward one, two three, four.'. The following months were proving to be extremely difficult in Derek's life. Derek was returning home from school when he was absolutely drenched in a deluge of rain. Soon he feels unwell, having trouble breathing and developing a very high temperature. Doctor Duff is called and Derek is soon asleep seemingly for an eternity. He has Rheumatic Fever and is in bed, mostly asleep, for around 10 days. The fever started to ease and a procession of his friends arrive at the tenement door asking about his well being.

Ruth shows them in and Derek has a huge lift from the visits and recovers fairly quickly after that. Life should have been returning to normal after the trauma's when Ruth suddenly saw Derek scratching his chest. On removing his top clothes she noticed a lot of red spots which was very quickly diagnosed by Doctor Duff as Measles.In addition to Derek half the class had also contracted the illness. Calamine lotion was applied in liberal fashion to try and get rid of the spots but the temptation to scratch is almost continuous. It takes some time for the very contagious illness to pass and life returns to normal at Drumoyne School.

Derek is pleased to be playing football again with his classmates in the playground. However, one day he is chasing a ball at full speed towards the wall which has now been built in front of the classrooms when he falls over the bottom step and goes headlong into the brickwork.

A huge cut appears over his right eye and he is quickly sent to the Southern General Hospital for stitches. A week or so later with the cut healed Derek goes back to the Southern General Hospital to have the stitches taken out which proves more painful than expected. Another month passes and Derek takes a short cut through a few back gardens in West Drumoyne. He trips over and unbelievably puts his hand on top of a broken bottle. Four more stitches are sewn in and another painful removal of the stitches a few weeks later.

With the death of his grandfather, two nasty illnesses and two sets of stitches Ruth is becoming concerned. 'Whit next Derek ?. You are not having much luck at the moment. However, things will turn around, they always do !'.

The door of the Golspie Street pawnshop opened and in walked Gibby. John greeted him with the disdain he held for the man with tightly packed ginger hair and loud hyena laugh. 'What do you want Gibby ?'.

Gibby says ' John, I hiv jist come in tae say 'Congratulations' on yer weddin coing up. Fine lassie is that Sandra !' .

John says 'I repeat what do you want Gibby'. Gibby says 'Awe right, awe right, feast yer eyes on this John; must be worth at least £100 ?'. John looked at a Swiss Clock produced from beneath Gibby's coat. ' John says 'where did you get that Gibby ?' Gibby says ' Somebody gave it to me and asked me tae seek oot a reputable pawnbroker to get it valued !' John says ' I will get Abe to put a value on it; he knows more about Swiss clocks than I do'. Gibby says 'Watch this John !'. He pulled a lever at the rear of the clock and immediately a lady in a brides dress came out.

She backed into a door and from the other side the brides groom came out. 'Gibby says ' Now would that not be a good gift to someone soon to have a wedding ?' John had already written out a receipt for the clock and gave it to Gibby. He says 'Come back in three days Gibby and we will give you a value on it!'.

The newspapers and TV continue to have Capital Punishment as a main topic. Hangings are beginning to almost completely dry up in Scotland and reducing in England.

The House of Lords have retained Capital Punishment but only in a selected number of cases. The main one is murder in pursuit of gain.

A letter to the newspapers in Scotland in support of Abolition of Capital Punishment.

*' The arguments both for and against capital punishment are strong but I feel, after long consideration, that I must support the move for the abolition of the death penalty. I do this with the fullest sympathy for all who have lost their lives through murder and all to whom this has caused sorrow. I have seen several people condemned to death for murder. To take another person's life is terrible but does the execution of a murderer help ?.*

*This is not '' Sob Stuff''. It is hard to overcome the feeling that ''justice'' (in this case is it not more like revenge ?) must be carried out. But we must do so. I have no statistics but I wonder how many of the 'scheming murderers' are actually sane. ,*

*Britain in many ways is one of the most progressive countries in the world. I believe that Britain is one of just a handful of countries in Western Europe which still retains Capital Punishment. I believe that no one would respect Britain less if the death penalty was abolished.*

*The method of execution is irrelevant ; someone's life is still taken. Abolition may not come immediately, but I do not think it is too trite to say ' It is coming and the sooner the better'.*

At 20, Craigton Road Ruth is attending to Jimmy's cut on his face. It is bad and the black stitches have a yellowish surround. 'Jimmy, I think you are going to be scarred for life.

They are deep nasty cuts'. Jimmy says. 'The doctor said they might be able to use new surgery to improve the cut. It involves taking skin from my backside and grafting it onto my face'. Ruth says 'Either way Jimmy, this is going to take some time. I will come down to the Southern General when you have the stitches taken out'. Jimmy replied 'I am not looking forward to it Ruth !'.
Ruth says ' Have you still no idea who could have done this Jimmy ?' . Jimmy says ' No, there were three of them and they had scarves over their faces' Ruth says 'my money would be on Bernie, Gibby and Junior, they have a motive especially Bernie'.

Jimmy says 'Ruth, they had scarves over their faces as I said and it is going to be difficult for the police. However, I am sure things will turn out ok'.
At 26, Cairnhill Circus, Cardonald Mr Taylor has financial problems and it is getting him down. It is also getting the rest of the family down including his 20 year old daughter Betty. Betty decides to do something about it. She advertises that she will marry the first man who can provide £100. She will give the money to her father and he will be able to clear his debts.

To the press Mr.Taylor announced, 'The whole thing is off; there is no way I would allow Betty to be involved in such a thing. I will clear my debts even if it means eating just a crust from the floor each day. Since the mother left after I lost my job. Betty (who also does not have a job) has been helping me bring up our children. We will survive !'. In the meantime Betty had three offers of marriage.

159

## CHAPTER 16
## A GOVAN WEDDING AND FAIRFIELDS

John is standing outside St.Mary's Church at Govan Cross. It is his wedding day and there is a large crowd of wedding guests and well wishers in attendance. The service is now less than half an hour away and Abe is having a laugh with many of the guests and in top form with his wit. John has never seen Abe dress so smartly for anything and he looks the part in his suit.

Suddenly, there is noise from beyond the Pearce Institute. John's mother Marie had promised John he would have a few surprises; he recognises the sounds immediately. It is the noise of the clowns band who are leading a small procession down Govan Road. Appropriately, the small clowns car follows with the clowns waving to all the children who wave back cheerily. A large number of children scheduled to go into the Plaza ABC minors have just been told the show has, for the first time ever, been delayed by a half hour.

The tall men on stilts come along and Govan Cross comes to a virtual standstill. The police are able to keep the transport moving and keep the wedding guests away from harm. The scene is one of colour and happiness and the clowns are keeping everyone amused with juggling and acrobatics. A few lucky, smaller children are given a ride on the clowns car. Ruth is there and wishes John well saying how lucky he is to be having such a smashing bride as Sandra.

John and the wedding guests are summoned into the church by the minister, the organ plays and the guests take their seats. John and his best man Abe go to the front and the respective families are adjacent and behind. The Church is packed as both families have many friends and relatives. The clowns are respectful and go to the gallery and stay circumspect.

Sandra arrives and gets out the car. All the wumin in the crowd outside say how beautiful she looks and what a lovely veil, dress, shoes and pretty young bridesmaids. It was the perfect day; sunny and joyous.

The wedding is over in half an hour. The car departs with money thrown out of the car windows for the children to collect; 'Scramble' is the cry that goes up.

Clowns are up to high jinx afterwards waving the happy couple away to the reception at the Central Station Hotel in Glasgow. For a little while afterwards they entertain the guests which is warmly appreciated before the little car makes its way back up Govan Road past the Pearce Institute.

The Govan wedding is over and the reception for many guests takes place a few miles away in the City. The next morning John and Sandra are on their way to Jersey on their honeymoon for two weeks.

A train journey to Southampton has a first night stopover followed by a ferry trip to the capital of Jersey, St.Helier.

Jimmy Welsh is talking to his fellow freemason at the Govandale Lodge, Jackie Flawcett, in a café in Central Glasgow. Jackie told Jimmy that he had been requested by John Henderson, Jimmy's employer, to try and help in the situation. Jimmy explained to Jackie how the scar on his face had been inflicted and also that he wanted revenge and had not told the police too much about the incident.

The story he gave was that he went to separate two guys brawling and one pulled out a razor and tried to slash the guy he was fighting with missed and caught Jimmy.

Due to the fog he did not see who it was and they both soon disappeared. 'How can you take revenge Jimmy if you do not know who was involved and why did you not tell the police ?; says Jackie. He continued 'You and I know that Brother Kennedy and the Brotherhood will not want to be dragged into anything sinister !'. Jimmy replied ' I know Jackie. I think I know who inflicted the scar because I recognised the laugh of one of the three as they ran off.

I had a set to some time ago with three morons in Govan Road and I guess this was their way of getting revenge'. Jackie said 'Jimmy, you should not go after these people unless you are 100% certain they were involved. You should let the law deal with it. What do you know about them?` 'The main one I think is called Bernard McGillogy, his two pals are called Junior and Gibby' says Jimmy. Jackie gets out a notebook and writes down the names as Jimmy gives a description of the three. Jackie says ' I know one or two people, probably like yourself, who are in good positions within the police force and crime detection. I will see what I can find out ' . I have your address so I will write to you again and arrange another meeting. One thing you must not do is take the law into your own hands. Let the law take its course, it is always the best way '.

Abe has paid a good price to Gibby for a Swiss Clock. The price is half of the real value of the clock which Abe quickly realises is very rare. He calls PC McCabe and tells him about the sale and asks if he knows if anything has been reported in terms of missing Swiss clocks. PC McCabe rings back and says he is not aware of anything being reported in terms of a Swiss Clock. Abe is now free to sell the clock and make a good profit.

Predictably, the letter from 'Let them Live' on Capital Punishment got a sharp response from people with the opposite view. 'Punishment should fit the crime' was typical of letters on the subject.

' *It seems incredible that after two hideous crimes have been committed in this area we should have a person signing himself as 'Let them Live' stepping forward to defend the actions of barbaric misfits in our midst.*

*This is obviously one of the rapidly increasing number of misguided intellectuals who are prepared to reject out of hand principles of disciplined citizenship that have been achieved and proved effective for thousands of years of trial and error.*

161

*'slashers' and 'coshers' who escape murder charges by a hairs breadth to
manipulate their cowardly weapons with more weight and reckless abandon.
From the leniency viewpoint our laws at present are severely stretched. Just try
and picture the future if this stretching goes on, with these psychiatric
intellectuals housing murderers in open jails to come and go as they please.
When they slip up again their beastly actions are explained away by lawyers
who plead away the criminals the lack of 'mental and physical co-ordination'.*
**Signed: Punishment should fit the crime**

Abe bids farewell to his latest customer retrieving a pawned item from his
shop. To his surprise the next visitor is Peter Moriarty-Tigwell from the
Boswell Galleries. Abe welcomes him and asks that he comes through to the
back of his office. George is requested to take over at the desk. Abe makes
some small talk and makes Peter a cup of tea. He then asks ' What do we owe
the pleasure of this visit Peter ?'. Peter replies ' 'Abe do you remember that
Swiss clock on the shelf at the Gallery ?'. Abe says 'Yes Peter, vaguely !'.
Peter says ' Well it has gone missing from the gallery. We have looked
everywhere but with no luck. I think we were distracted and someone took the
opportunity to remove the clock which was near the Gallery entrance'.

Abe says ' Well I never, nothing is safe these days !'. Peter says ' Normally I
would leave it to the police. However, their detection rate is poor and Detective
Inspector Fletcher usually tries to encourage us to buy more security from his
reputable Glasgow Secure company. If you are offered it Abe please let me
know, I would pay a good price to get it back'.

Abe says 'If it comes our way you will be the first to know Peter'.

Derek is happy with his classes under Mrs.Dewart. Mrs.Dewart is proving to
be as religious than Miss Doig and the class are soon again reading the bible. It
fulfils two purposes; one is it helps the class with reading and also much of the
bible meaning is discussed by the teacher. Each pupil is asked at random to
read a passage from the bible and this continues for a while until they have all
read at least one paragraph out to the rest of the class.

Then Mrs.Dewart discusses meaning. One of the first topics is the Good
Samaritan. The question is 'Would you stop and help the person in trouble ?'
The answer was unanimous 'Of course we would' said the entire class. Mrs
Dewart introduced the class to money and during the weekly dinner money
collection day, each of the class were asked to act as shopkeepers giving
change and understanding values of coinage.

The girls in the class played a wide variety of games. Skipping ropes as
singles or as a group when sometimes they had four jumping at once. Bouncing
a tennis ball underleg against a wall and catching every time. The boys
continued mainly with football in the playground and Derek was now getting
the occasional goal for his side

Sandra and John return from their honeymoon and move in to their new home in Mosspark Boulevard. When John returns to the Pawnshop Abe updates him with events and in particular the Swiss Clock received from Gibby.

A few days later John phones Peter Moriarty—Tigwell and tells him that a clock answering his description may soon be on the pawnbrokers list. Peter agrees an amount for John to work within during the purchase and a good profit is achieved by the Boulton Cox pawnshop in returning the Swiss clock to its rightful owner.

As Abe puts the phone down to a customer he suddenly has a coughing fit and has trouble breathing.

John and George go to his assistance but Abe recovers and is soon serving customers again. John says ' Abe, I have seen a programme on television that says smoking is not really good for you. You smoke heavily. Perhaps you may feel better if you reduced the fags !' Abe looked at John and smiled ' You are probably right John'.

Plans are afoot for the conversion of the No.7 and No.11 Tram routes to trolleybuses. The cost for both routes is £687,000 and it has been recommended by the Glasgow Transport Committee. The No.7 travels from Craigton to Millerston and the No.11 from Mount Vernon to Linthouse. Approximately half the cost would be for the purchase of the new trolleybus and additional cabling would be required as well as the removal of some sections of track. With a high birth rate in the late 1940's there is a considerable stress on the schools. Many schools are badly overcrowded and the teachers are feeling the strain. Many retired teachers are being re-recruited to help out and without them the Glasgow Schools would be on the verge of collapse states the report on the City Education. Glasgow estimates that most classes are in the order of one teacher to 45; 50 or even 55 pupils. 14,000 extra pupils added to the system and a shortfall of qualified teachers in the order of 700.

The Circus season restarts at Kelvin Hall and once again John has a more limited role. For the most part he helps his mother in the booking office and Sandra also helps during the busy periods. His brother Jim still helps behind the scenes and likes being a clown.

At the end of January the lions, tigers in special cages ponies and horses are on their way to Switzerland via the Harwich - Zee Brugge Ferry. The three Elephants are the last to depart on their way to the continent. Jim Leslie travels with most of the other clowns and helpers. He enjoys the Zurich Show in Switzerland show and has built up a network of friends at all the destinations. Adverts were appearing in the main Glasgow Newspapers from foreign shores. Canada seemed a popular destination for a lot of the more skilled and educated Govanites. The SS Castel Felice sailed from Greenock to Canada for just £56 Tourist class. A first class travel on the same boat was priced at £78 from Scotia Transport in Bothwell St.Glasgow.

A group of women are standing outside the gates of Fairfields Shipyard. It is Friday and the day that wages are paid. Most of the women want to extract some money from their husbands before they enter the pubs along Govan Road. The hooter sounds and an army of workers exit the yards; the workday over. The wives almost by instinct home in on their man and the money out of the packet is handed over.

The founding of Fairfield's Shipyard revolves around the name of one man, Robert Napier. Napier was a skilled man in shipbuilding and was not afraid to teach his gift of skills to others. It is said Robert Napier was born with a hammer in his hand.

John Elder and Charles Randolph, the founders of Fairfields, were both Napier trained. In fact John Elder's father worked alongside Robert Napier as an engineering manager.

The young John Elder started in Napier's office before going to work in England. He came back and was in charge of the Napier's drawing office. In 1852 the young Elder decided to start his own company and he teamed up with Charles Randolph. Randolph had also been Napier trained but left many years before to pursue a career in developing machines for mills and factories.

John Elder and Charles Randolph were soon to develop engines to propel ships and constantly improve them. Their engines were gaining much acclaim in the shipbuilding industry and before long they had produced the ultimate engine known as the 'compound engine' which saved over 30% in fuel. This revolutionised the whole shipping trade and opened up vast trade opportunities for steam propelled vessels.

Randolph and Elder decided that in addition to building ship engines they wanted to expand into building the entire ship.

They bought Robert Napier's 'old yard' on the south side of the River Clyde and started making hulls as well as engines. The orders flowed through the doors for ships and within five years the company moved to new premises further down river at Fairfield. Within two years the yard lost its two founders. Charles Randolph retired in 1868 and just one year later John Elder died at the relatively young age of 45 years.

His death left a huge gap at the top of Fairfield as he was much respected by all the workforce and brilliant as an engineer. Innovative , enterprising and intelligent he was a great loss to Clydeside shipbuilding.

With Randolph he had started a small engineering company and developed it into a major shipbuilding player on the world stage.

Mrs Isobella Elder the widow of John Elder decided to purchase a piece of land across the road from the yard and dedicate it to the people of Govan who both she and her husband had tremendous respect for. Elder Park and Elder Park Library were given in his memory.

After the sad death of John Elder another Napier trained engineer took over the running of the company; an Englishman by the name of William Pearce. If there was ever a 'natural' replacement for Randolph and Elder it was William Pearce . He had enterprise and drive and was soon an expert in everything shipbuilding. In 1879 the yard built the 'Arizona', over 5,000 tons, 465 feet long and capable of 17 knots; easily the largest ship built on the River Clyde at that time. The ship was soon nicknamed the 'greyhound' and broke the speed record for crossing the Atlantic eastbound.

William Pearce soon became Sir William Pearce and the shipyards name changed from John Elder and Co. to Fairfield Shipbuilding and Engineering Company. Success continued at Fairfields yard right up until the First World War. In 1916 a super large submarine was built at the yard named simply as K 13; the number was to prove unlucky. During trials in the Gareloch the funnel hatch failed and with the boat just having submerged a frantic effort was made to rescue the crew. Under 80 feet of water Mr. Mc Lean, who worked in the submarine department at the      Fairfields yard, skilfully manipulated the angle of the boat by use of the air compressors.

He manipulated the angle of the boat to lift the fore end above the water. 46 of the 80 men on board were then rescued. After 57 hours underwater Mr.Mc Lean was still using the Air Compressors to kept the entombed men alive. Above water fantastic efforts were being made to get the required apparatus to the scene to help. A large steel hausser was placed under the vessel and it was raised enough to get a portion of the hull above water. The hull was cut and all the men on board escaped. The vessel was re-floated a few weeks later and resumed its programme for the war. However, before it was re-launched a major decision was being made at Whitehall Gardens in the Ministry of Defence Building. A meeting on the 8th Floor with all the Admirals and Sea Lords present decided a new name was appropriate and changed K 13 to K something else.

In the Second World War most Fairfields built ships survived; the most notable exception being the Athenia. After the 2nd World war the yard completed many quality ships and not so long ago Her Majesty the Queen launched the Empress of Britain. A quality ship from a quality yard.

John Sloan a 30 year old brass dresser aimed a punch at his wife, missed and hit their 3 month old baby instead. The baby was taken from their home in 6 Hoey Street to the Southern General Hospital for treatment. Sloan was drawing £4 a week sick benefit and when he returned home he offered his wife £3 and 18 shillings.

The wife refused to accept it from Sloan who was worse for wear with drink. He went out of the house and returned later when he offered his wife 3 pence. An argument ensued and he threw an empty wine bottle at his wife, missed and it smashed against the fireplace.

He then punched and kicked his wife. John Sloan was sentenced to 20 days in prison by Baillie Gray at Govan Police Courts. Sloan says 'I think I may have lost my temper!

Jimmy Welsh and Jackie Flawcett have their second meeting to discuss the incident that led to Jimmy having his face cut with a razor. Jackie gives an update on what he has found out. 'Jimmy I have had a word with a few people in the police force who are on the square and close friends. Firstly, all three of the people you mentioned are known to crime.

Bernard Mc Gillogly is a burglar and an opportunistic thief. He has already been given a few short sentences after being convicted of house burglary, usually when the occupants have been on holiday, from better off houses in Crookston. Gibbons is a shoplifter and very deft at it. He has been stopped on numerous occasions after darting from stores but when apprehended no goods have been found on him. The third one is Junior.

He is well known to the police and can be violent. He has been in possession of a razor, a bicycle chain and even a sharp knife when stopped. He is suspected of inflicting serious injury on quite a few people in the past. He has had a few short sentences for hitting people with his chain causing terrible injury. A nasty piece of work. `From what we hear you were lucky when you attacked Bernie that there were many people around. Junior plays the jackdaw like Gibby but he is bright and very dangerous.' Jimmy says ' thanks Jackie, so now what ?'. Jackie replied by saying ' The last thing you must do is attempt to get revenge on them; leave it to the police.

If things escalate and you murder one of them then there is no guarantee the judge will be able to save you from the gallows. The last thing you want is to be swinging on the end of a rope by the neck in Barlinnie on account of these guys'. Jimmy replies 'I am grateful Jackie for the information.

Tomorrow I go for a skin graft where they take a section out of my backside and graft it onto my face. I am not looking forward to it'. Jackie says ' Jimmy, You will be interested to know that the three of them are under suspicion of two crimes and it looks like there is finger print identification pinning Bernie and Junior to a burglary in a big house at Crookston. Gibby has also been caught with stolen goods in his pocket after being apprehended outside Lewis's in Glasgow.

He claims that he does not how the watches got in his pocket there but there we are !'. Jackie winked at Jimmy and they both smiled. ' Jimmy asked ' What are the chance of Junior and Bernie getting convicted ?'. Jackie says 'Pretty good I would have thought. We will have to wait and see`.

John and Sandra have settled into their new home on Mosspark Boulevard. Sandra frequently looks down on the wedding ring that she received on her wedding day; she loves it and shows it off to everyone she is friends with.

She asks John 'Where did you buy the wedding ring John ?'. John says ' If you work in a pawnshop you do not have to buy such things Sandra !' Things went silent for around 5 seconds when John smiled. He said ' Sandra, would I do such a thing ?. I bought it ,with my mother present, at H.Samuel in Union Street. She helped me choose it'. Sandra says 'It is lovely, as is your mother'. Around West Drumoyne there are plenty of Davy Crockett hats as the Battle of the Alamo is played out in the tenements. What starts as fun turns into arguments then back to fun again. 'Your deed; naw am no; aye ye ur a got ye; Some little girls came out with Davy Crockett hats on much to the dismay of the lads.

'How can ye be Davy Crockett if ye ur a lassie ?' The reply was 'Am no Davy Crockett; stupit am his wife !'.
Fess Parker, the film star who played Davy Crockett, arrived in the UK and the cinema's filled up as a consequence to see the Davy Crockett film.
At the Elder Cinema in Rathlin Street there is a commotion. Five youths worse for wear with drink arrive outside the cinema and want entry. They are refused and start cursing and swearing.

They are moved outside but return and force their way into the cinema itself where they continue to curse and swear. A number of the patrons are unhappy and an altercation starts.The police arrive and arrest all the youths. At Govan Police Court , Baillie William Meikle said to the accused ' You could have caused a riot involving women and children`. James Herrity (17) of 183, Neptune Street, admitted disorderly conduct plus assaulting two police officers and was fined £10.
Kenneth Reid (19) of 48 Clydeferry Street; James Mc Kinnon (18) of 65, Nethan Street;
Joseph O'Rourke (18)of 185 Sandwood Road; Daniel Kilbride (18) of 25, Nethan Street ;
and Malcolm Bennet (17) of 52, Fairfield Street all admitted disorderly conduct and were each fined £7.
A 16 year old youth was ordered to pay £5 or spend 20 days in a remand home.
At Govan Police Court a 70 year old white haired man appeared in the dock and almost immediately he broke down and cried.
He was charged with disorderly conduct on a bus.
After he had recovered sufficiently, Baillie John Mains asked him to make a plea. The old man said ' I do not know what to plea. I suppose I am guilty as I was drunk. The day before the incident I was with my wife when she was knocked down and killed by a bus. I was by her side when it happened'.

Baillie John Mains admonished the accused and he was discharged.

12 year old Janette Stewart was sitting in her home at 16, Golspie Street when a housebreaker came in. Seeing Janette he attacked her with a poker and the girl had to be taken to the Southern General Hospital for stitches. The assailant escaped empty handed and Janette was helping the police in the efforts to apprehend the house breaker.

Within the ground floor flat at the 20 Craigton Road tenement Ruth was still coming to terms with the noise from the children playing in the back yard. There was very little if any grass and in summer days washing in abundance was draped over the various washing lines. Ruth and Jimmy were having an argument. 'Jimmy you could have taken the windae oot !' referring to a brawl he had in the Rob Roy Bar on Govan Road the night before. 'I know Ruth but as I told you before I was aiming at Smith and not Charlie McGhee' referring to a chair he had thrown. Ruth says 'Jimmy that is unacceptable ! You must control your drinking better. Every time you have so many drinks you seem to want to fight with everyone. It has to stop !'.

Derek had long adjusted to the new arrangements and enjoyed getting the papers at the newsagents. He would have a brief chat with Mrs. Cook who would tell him about the Bens news. He also collected a comic virtually every day and enjoyed reading them all. The Beano, The Dandy, The Knockout, The Topper, The Wizard, The Eagle were all read ardently. On Fridays it was the Govan Press and he would read the match report on Benburb about three times. Occasionally, he would enter the weekly competition for children. This was two almost identical pictures and you had to spot the difference and send in your answer to the Govan Press offices.

Govan Cross was a focal point in Govan. It was a small Burgh Cross in comparison with others. Govan Road ran west to east parallel with the River Clyde.

The north part of the cross was a short roadway to the Govan ferries. The south was a dog leg road which served as the main Govan Cross bus terminus.

The 4A (later numbered 34) was a popular route and went across southern Glasgow via Drumoyne, Cardonald and Mosspark. The number 23 had a stand further round and served Govan Road west, Linthouse, Drumoyne, Cardonald and on towards Crookston. The No.4 bus did not stop at the terminus but on Govan Road. Its destination was Shieldhall Road at the Garage. The 'wee' single decker 25 bus was for workers going to the Hillington Industrial Estate. There were two ferries across the river from Govan. The larger ferry carried cars and other vehicles as well as passengers. The Passenger ferry was a small vessel with cover at the middle of the boat. The steps up to Water Row were treacherous in wet weather. In peak times they sometimes put on two passenger ferries.

It is night and very dark as William Gibbons makes his way along Water Row from the ferry. He looks round and has had an uneasy feeling that he has been followed for some time. He sees no one other than a few shadows which may have come from the river lights. Suddenly two men grab him into an alley way. 'Hello Gibby son; how ur yeh dae'in' says one man. Five minutes later there is a splash in the water of the River Clyde.

At a café near Glasgow Central Station Jackie Flawcett and Jimmy Welsh meet to discuss the body found in the river at Govan that morning. Jackie says ' They say it is 'Gibby' Jimmy. Not official yet of course but that is what everyone in Govan is saying to the newsfolk. A couple of guys said it was that wee b***ard Gibby and there were 20,000 suspects as to who would possibly want him done in !'. They both laughed. Jackie continued 'Nobody liked Gibby or his two pals and he has obviously upset one person too many. The Govan folk seem to have a way of dealing with these guys !' Jimmy says ' I dare say there were no witness's !' They both laughed.

Jimmy says 'I imagine the other two will be taking note, hopefully'. Jackie says ' They had both been told by the polis to watch out for themselves and that was before poor Gibby lost his footing and slipped into the Clyde'. Sadly, they seemed to get some money from somewhere, got themselves a really good lawyer and got off the Crookston house robbery charges.

A crowd has gathered at the top of Water Row to find out more details on the poor unfortunate who has been fished out of the River Clyde. PC Mc Cabe walks up the Row from the Govan Ferry terminal. Bill an older man with a bunnet says ' Hey Mc Cabe, who wis it ?' 'We think it is William Gibbons but await formal identification to be carried out' says PC Mc Cabe. Bill says 'Gibby eh !. That thieving wee ba***rd. Well there wulnae be many mourning his passing. So whit happened ?'

PC Mc Cabe says 'Strictly off the record Bill it looks like an open and shut case. He slipped down the ferry stairs. It is apparent from all the bruises on his head that he hit his head on the ferry steps on the way down. !' Bill says ' Well if by any chance he wis done in tell us who done it and we will give him a medal !'

Ann a middle aged lady who likes to know everything that is going on in Govan overhears the conversation. She says ' So poor auld Gibby ! At least we wulnae hiv to cling onto our purses anymore when he is aboot. That laugh he had wis something else. Everytime you heard it ye knew someone was looking for something he had just stolen'.

At 20, Craigton Road, Jimmy has returned from Glasgow and tells Ruth about Gibby. Ruth says ' Obviously he upset someone once to often. Who was it who done him in Jimmy ?'

Jimmy says 'How would I know Ruth ! I do not mix in such company. I am a well respected man around these parts'. 'Aye Jimmy I know, now who wis it ?'. Jimmy smiled 'Ruth I do not know. The official version is he fell down the ferry stairs with his head stoating around as he went down. He was unconscious as he entered the water. That is all I know'. Ruth says 'I wonder what Bernie and Junior are thinking about at present'. Jimmy says ' Junior and Bernie are a target for a few hard men who are after them; the are keeping a low profile. At least that is the last I heard from Jackie Flawcett'.

In the Golspie Street pawnshop there is a gap in the customers and Abe and John are talking. Abe says ' John would you like to do some training ?'. John says ' Why are you asking Abe ?'. Abe says ' I had a telephone call from an old friend in London. We got talking and he said he has been working all the hours under the sun and needs help. He is excellent at valuing items; in particular gold. He has been unable to recruit a suitable candidate. I told him that you may be able to help him for a week. From that you will gain some experience which can do you no harm'.

John says ' Well that sounds a good way to learn and of course it is only for a week. I will discuss it with Sandra tonight and let you know tomorrow'. Abe says ' There is something else John !! If circumstances change around here in the future I would like you to take over the business'. John is surprised and says ' What sort of thing is likely to happen Abe and do you not have some family ?'. Abe says ' I have told you before John ' I do not have a good relationship with my family. They will crawl out of the woodwork when I die wanting to know how much money I have. Two bits of my estate I want to go to you are the Project Account and the Business. The rest of my Estate I have still to decide'. John says ' Abe , we are talking a long time in the future and things will change before then`.

The next day John confirms that he will be able to go and help his friend in London. Abe makes the arrangements and John is booked in to a good quality hotel near the City of London. Abe's friend is called John Sykes and works near Hatton Garden. Abe advises John that both he and John have mapped out a short training course on Valuations.

At 20, Craigton Road Ruth is looking at the Govan Press she has just brought home. Her first read is the obituaries column and one name immediately catches her eyes.
'William Gibbons' . Died on 2nd May '1958 after a tragic accident on the Govan Ferry steps. Funeral at St.Anthony's Chapel.

On the day of the Funeral the hearse moves slowly along Govan Road before pulling up outside St.Anthony's Chapel .
The pole bearers, including Junior and Bernie, carry the coffin inside. Among the small gathering of people is Ruth.

She looks at some of the flowers being taken in from the hearse sent by the close friends he had.
'From the Ward 3 Correctional Unit at Hawkhead Phychiatric Hospital.'
' From the Govan Police Station. ' Good Bye Mr.Gibbons'. '
' So Long Gibby, Govan shopkeepers Security Staff'.

Ruth walks off and at once somehow feels sorry for the man. She bumps into Joan one of her former colleagues from Woolworth and they have a 'blether' about Gibby. Ruth says 'I feel a wee bit sorry for him Joan. Yes he stole but you wonder what went wrong.'. Joan says 'I could not stand him. That ginger curly hair and always open neck shirt made him look scruffy all the time. I doubt whether he ever had a bath; it is said that when he went Harhill once, John the poolkeeper used up his quota of chlorine 1'. They both laughed. Joan continued 'You are too soft Ruth'.

Harland and Wolff were ready to launch the ship Southern Princess, a 7,900 ton motor vessel. The pilot was waiting for the fog to clear and receive advice from the Clyde Navigation Trust. He turned round and to his horror the ship was on its way down the slipway with no hope of stopping. The H & W solicitor contended in front of the Marine Court that the Shipyard manager contacted Renfrew for the weather report and based on information received allowed the Launching Ceremony to proceed.

Fortunately, no accidents were to occur and H & W were warned to take more care on launching. The case against them was proven and they were fined £2.

Industrial relations on the Clyde were becoming more strained. At Harland and Wolff four older riveters were dismissed as they were deemed too old to carry out the job of riveting. The Clyde Riveters Committee (Upper Reaches) convened a meeting and gave due warning to H & W of their concerns and the likely outcomes.

Mrs. White at 38 Fairfield Street was not happy. Her husband James had ordered her out of the house after an argument. She left with her six year old son in her arms. She returned later and went in to the bedroom and hit James twice on the head with a poker. Mr. White rushed out the house in just a raincoat over a shirt and started shouting and bawling at his wife outside while bleeding from head wounds.

As it was 2.00am in the morning the neighbours called the police. When they arrived James was still bawling and shouting. The police took him to the Southern General Hospital where four stitches were inserted in his head wounds. Later he was arrested and charged with 'breach of the peace'.
In court Mrs White was asked if she heard him outside. She said she had heard nothing. Mr. White said ' I cannot win here !'. The case was proven and James White was fined £2.

171

# CHAPTER 17
## LET US HASTE TO KELVINGROVE

Drumoyne School has one male teacher in addition to Mr.Blair the headmaster and his name is William Park. He is about to become famous and get at least half an hour in the front of Scottish television and BBC television cameras.

A By Election has been called for the Westminster Constituency of Glasgow Kelvingrove on the opposite side of the River Clyde from Govan. Derek has arrived home to 31, Daviot Street and put on the television. It takes around 5 minutes for the valves to warm up and a face he recognises is on the screen; Mr. Park, a teacher at his school! Ruth and Robbie are both sitting reading. Ruth is reading a newspaper at the table, drinking tea and smoking a cigarette. Her brother Robbie reads a book whilst sitting in an armchair in front of a warm coal fire. He smokes a pipe making the living room full of smoke.

Derek says ' Mr.Park is a teacher at Drumoyne School, what is this politics he is discussing ?'. Ruth says 'He is standing as a Candidate in the By Election at Kelvingrove but he has no chance whatsoever'. A few days later and William Park is the first candidate to lodge his papers with the Sheriff at the County Buildings in Glasgow. He is to be the Independent Labour Party Candidate and the newspaper reporters are there to obtain a quote or two from him.

Mr.Park says ' Well at least I will be first at something !. The first to lodge my papers for the By Election !'. He is then asked 'Why are you splitting the Labour vote at the By Election ?'. Mr Park replies ' It is the Labour and the Tory Candidates that are splitting the vote !'. There are three major policies in which we are different from the Labour and Tory candidates. That is the H Bomb; Conscription and Unilateral Disarmament'. The reporters ask 'What about your campaign ?'. Mr.Park replied ' I will not be taking anytime off from my teaching job at Drumoyne School except for the last few days and the day of the count. I will be doing my campaigning in the open air for the most part '.

The Independent Labour Party was founded in 1893 and for the most part was closely associated with the Labour Party. Its early roots were based on some religious principles and a buffer against the stronger views held by the Orangemen and the Irish Republicans. As the Labour Party evolved, the ILP produced many good candidates who were to make an impact in elections. Known as the 'Red Clydesiders' during the 1920's, they had success in the general Elections with over 30 MP's. Among them were John Wheatley, Emanuel (Manny) Shinwell, Tom Johnston and David Kirkwood. Also, of course, there was Govan Fairfields Councillor and Future Lord Provost Tom Kerr. The leader of the group was James Maxton.

Both the elected Labour Governments in the 1920's were a big disappointment to the ILP so they proposed their own programme for change. This was soundly rejected by the Labour Party at the time. The programme had 8 points:.

1: A Living Wage. Incompletely applied.
2: A substantial allowance of the Unemployment Allowance.
3: The Nationalisation of Banking. Incompletely applied.
4: The bulk purchase of Raw materials.
5: The bulk purchase of Foodstuffs.
6: The Nationalisation of Power.
7: The Nationalisation of Transport.
8: The Nationalisation of Land.

In the 1931 General Election the ILP Candidates refused to take the Labour Party Whip and just 5 got re-elected. Outside the Labour Party the parties support began to wane and in the 1945 General Election, a Labour Landslide, just 3 ILP members were returned; all in Glasgow. Jimmy Maxton the leader died shortly afterwards and soon all the MP's were gone.

Television viewing results produced an unexpected winner; Amateur Boxing was easily the most popular programme. Unfortunately, if a lot of people were watching Boxing on TV, the audiences were poor anywhere in the suburbs of Glasgow. That was with one exception—Govan. Good crowds turned up at Govan Town Hall for the occasional Professional Boxing Shows and a prize bout for the Benny Lynch Trophy. The boxers who fought for the title were Frankie Jones (Wales) who beat Dave Moore (Belfast) at flyweight in 5 rounds.

Arthur Donnachie from Greenock made a winning start to his professional career with a win over Jackie Horsman from West Hartlepool.

Danny Mac Namee also made his Professional debut and boxed a draw with Jim Cresswell from Clydebank after a great fight.

Dave Croll (Dundee) outpointed Jimmy Mc Ateer (London).

Tony Mc Grory (Greenock) was beaten in the last round by sustaining a cut eye against tough Ray Mann (Gold Coast).

Also from the Gold Coast was Harry Haydock who outpointed Jim Mc Guiness from Wishaw.

Bus Parties from Dundee, Greenock and Lanarkshire turned up and saw the 6 bouts.

Many Govan men seemed to enjoy their Boxing ; Ruth and Jimmy Welsh usually were regulars at the Friday night Wrestling at the Govan Town Hall.

The very first political live debate on television was soon to be screened. It was being screened on both BBC and ITV Channels. The By Election was caused by the death of Mr.Elliot the Unionist MP. His wife was the new candidate and defending a small 3,000 or so majority.

The two By Election front runners Mrs Katherine Elliot the Unionist Candidate and Mrs. Mary Mc Alister the Labour Candidate were tetchy about the people who would be doing the Interviews and the questions they would be asked.

The Liberal Home Rule Candidate Mr. David Murray paid his deposit with brand new £5 Bank of Scotland notes and immediately went out campaigning. The Unionists were complaining about the Socialists heckling their candidate at meetings.

The tension mounted with three candidates on the TV debate. The fourth candidate Mr.Parks seemed relaxed having spent the day teaching at Drumoyne School.

At the debate most neutral observers thought that Mr.Murray and Mr.Park were given more hostile questions than the two lady candidates. Both Labour and Unionists agreed Mrs.Mc Allsiter was the winner of the first debate.

The second debate on the day before the poll a full scale row erupted between Mr.Murray and Mrs.Elliot causing the Unionist candidate to seek an apology via her solicitors on several of the Liberal Home Rule Candidiate accusations.

Mr.Murray said that on election day he would be flying a light aircraft over the constituency in the effort to gather votes.

The result was announced with Mr. Park still as jovial as ever.
RESULT:
Mrs. Mary Mc Allster (Labour) 10,210
Mrs. Katherine Elliot (Unionist) 8,850
Mr. David Murray (Liberal—Home Rule) 1,622
Mr.William Park ( ILP ) 587

The following week many of the teachers and parents including Ruth told Mr. Park that they thought he had done well and he thanked them and greeted them with his usual smile. As a part time politician he had done well in front of the National media.

An issue which did not have as much attention as it should have had was exposed by a letter to the national media from a Govan man.

*' I have just been reading that the President of the Scottish Old Age
Pensioners Organisation, in his presidential address, appealed to the Trade
Unions to back us in our fight for a better standard of housing.
Why Not ?. Our fight is their fight also. They forget they will be old someday
themselves and they surely see how their Fathers, Mothers and Grandparents
are being treated at the present time. £2 a week to eke out an existence with
the high cost of living. Of course the Government is trying to put one across by
saying they do not have to retire at 65. They can work on as long as they like.
That is very nice but where is the employer that is going to employ men
between 70 and 80 ?. Not on your life, an employer wants his pound of flesh
and he makes sure he gets it !.
There is no union that can afford to pay out a retirement benefit to all its
members. Don't get caught napping !!'.*
### ANDREW MURRAY

Upstream from Govan there is a lot of movement in the waters around
Glasgow Green. The top Glasgow school rowing teams are there coached to the
hilt and preparing for the forthcoming Regatta. However, there is one other
School which competes every year and has a proud tradition in Rowing  -
Govan High.
They are defending the long boat title they won the previous year and are
expected to come under a serious challenge from Allen Glens for the
St.Mungo's Quaich Trophy. Rowing is popular at Govan High and they always
provide good opposition at the various Regatta's. No fewer than 57 School
Crews take part in the most recent Regatta's—a record.

### SNIPPETS:

- The Govan Labour Party moved a motion at the Labour Party
  conference wanting sweeping extension of Nationalisation without
  compensation. However, it did not receive sufficient support from many
  Trade Unions at the conference. Mr.Harry Selby (Govan) who has a
  hairdressing business in Parliamentary Road says in favour of the
  motion, ' recall the spirit of the pioneers  and their faith in
  Nationalisation.

- A Painting of Mr.Tom Kerr to commemorate the work of the 'father' of
  Glasgow Corporation was proposed. To save money Tom Kerr
  suggested just a photograph which he had already received was
  sufficient. The cost of the portrait would have been £1,000. The council
  agreed to set aside somewhere in the region of £100 on the suggestion of
  Mr.Tom Kerr. This money was to be used as a reward to children who
  achieved something special.

Abe and John discuss the days events in the Golspie Street pawnshop. The demise of Gibby seems to have made life a bit easier with the blood pressure of the average Govanite considerably lowered. John says ' Gibby did not always act alone Abe, I wonder if his friends will be worried ?' Abe says 'Well if they are not then they should be. John I had a call from John Sykes down in London where you went the other week. He liked your attitude and work ethic. He asked me if you would like to help them out for a month. His firm would pay the travel and hotel costs and obviously a higher rate of pay than you get here for the duration. I said I would ask you. I told them that you had recently been married and obviously Sandra would have to be consulted. They said that Sandra could go down as well for a week and they would pay for that as well'.

John says ' John Sykes was an amazing man. He showed me the Guildhall in the City of London which seems to be the home of many 'Livery Clubs'. He told me a lot about gold and he even got me into the Rothchilds Bank gold room, there were countless bars of gold in there. The chap in there was saying that the gold in there is virtually a permanent feature; the only thing that changes is the label on who owns the gold. I will ask Sandra but I think she will let me make the decision on an issue like that'.

At Cardonald there is a discussion between two very worried men, they both suspect the razor attack on Jimmy Welsh had a bearing on the death of Gibby. Bernie says ' You have got nothing to worry about ! He may suspect me but with us wearing scarves they will not be able to pin anything on us'. Junior says ' I was half expecting a visit from the polis but between us we could confirm alibis'.

Bernie says ' The fact that there was no visit from the polis means they do not know who done it, although I guess they probably suspects us. Gibby did say that he thought he will be after us, especially me. I suggest you do not go anywhere near either Ruth or him for a while; one thing is for sure, I do not think Gibby's death was an accident !'.

Over the period of a few years there had been a number of accidents around Govan and occasionally in the shipyards. HMS Blake had been standing within Fairfields Yard for some time after completion of works because the owner had still to take ownership of the Cruiser. It took 5 fire engines and a fire boat a number of hours to put the large fire out. As in a number of cases Fairfields did not disclose the cause of the fire.

At the offices of the Scottish Machine Tool Company in Woodville Street damage estimated at around £3,000 was caused by a big fire. The fire was discovered by a patrolling policemen. The caretaker Patrick Mc Elhinney and his family were asleep in the house next door until awoken by the policemen.

Sarah Duncan, a two year old, was crawling around the tenement landing in Wick Street, Govan. Suddenly, she went through the railings on the landing and fell 60 feet to the bottom of the stairway. Her 19 year old mother who was talking to a neighbour on the landing could only look on in horror. Sarah was rushed to the Southern General Hospital with a fractured skull and her condition was described as poorly.

There were numerous tram accidents around the Govan area. One occurred in Govan Road near Lorne Street. Five people were taken to the Hospital including :
Joseph Zborroski (45) head injury; Isa Mc Ghee (46) 61 Uist Street—shock Elizabeth Paton (54) 189 Crossloan Road—shock; Catherine Collins (12) 6, Logie Street—Facial Injuries; Mary Austin (73) injury to side and shock.


John discusses the work in London situation with Sandra. Sandra says 'It sounds good John and if, as Abe says, it will help with the valuation of Gold items then it will improve your career ! Also, I like the idea of a week in London. I will take in the sites while you are at work and we can go out in the evening.' The arrangements are made and John departs to London from the Central Station.

Abe does not feel well one day, a recurring cough is starting to give him concern. He knows the cause is almost certainly smoking and his fingers are stained with nicotine. However, he is addicted to tobacco and cannot stop the habit of around 30 cigarettes a day.

A middle aged Govan woman Elizabeth Longmore was at her 2nd floor window in 22, Burghead Drive. She leaned against the window and before she knew it, she was tumbling to the ground. She was rushed to the Southern General Hospital where her condition was later reported as 'fairly comfortable'.

An explosion in the engine room of HMS Blake was considerable. 20 men were trapped and frantic efforts were being made to get them out of the Cruiser berthed in Govan Dry Dock. Poisonous fumes meant the rescue teams had to wear breathing apparatus. The initial blast was considerable and blew men around the engine room. Of the 20 men 12 were released after treatment and eight were detained with serious injuries. Anthony Carr 95, Golspie Street; John MacKay 102 Kintra Street; Robert Mc Loed 113 Brighton Street; Patrick Hart 277 Summertown Road; David Leishman 121 Carrick Road; John Reid 54, Wanlock Street; Hurdy Mc Kenzie 12 Tarland Street; William Foley 106 Neptune Street.
Carr, Hart Reid and Foley were on the critical list.

Within three days Anthony Carr and Robert Mc Loed had died from their injuries.

Five workmen were slightly injured when scaffolding collapsed outside an office block in Helen Street.

At 20, Craigton Road Ruth and Jimmy discuss the seemingly endless stream of accidents. Ruth says' There seems to be too many accidents Jimmy. That boat HMS Blake is jinxed. Jimmy says ' Most accidents are caused by carelessness by the people involved themselves. I work in the scaffolding trade and we have never had a serious accident for years. We take care when we erect scaffolding etc. and go through a check list.' The gasses in the engine room of HMS Blake should have been monitored'. Ruth said 'who is responsible, the yards, dry dock or the workmen? Jimmy said 'The employer is responsible for the safety of the workmen. However, shipyards and dry docks are dangerous places to work'.

Govan, being a close knit community, was deeply saddened by a seemingly endless run of accidents and a tragic loss of life. However ,they were unprepared for one of the saddest events.

At 31 Copland Road, four very young children died in a fire in a tenement room and kitchen. The mother, Mrs Trevitt, had left her four children alone while she went across the road to a laundrette. A fire started and the four children in the tenement all died.
Robert Trevitt (4), Phillip Trevitt (3), Rosemary Trevitt (2) and Phyliss Trevitt (5 weeks) all perished.

Heroic efforts were made by neighbours to save the children but they were beaten back by the intense heat and flames.
John Trevitt was summoned from work and gave comfort to his wife.

This accident stunned all of Govan and provided one of its saddest days.
At 20, Craigton Road Ruth is in tears as she reads the Govan Press. She says to Jimmy 'That poor wumin and her weans. I think Govan has a curse on it at the moment'.

Accidents continued for some weeks afterwards including:

A tramcar collided with a bus on Govan Road near Clachan Drive. One man, Edward Caffrey of 5, Hutton Drive, Govan sustained bad head injuries and died after admission to the Southern general Hospital. Others injured were Helen Winning (27) of 73 Tradeston Street (shock); Hugh Henderson (49) — tram car driver; Duncross Road Pollok (shock); Josephene Marshall (28) 1240, Govan Road (shock); Rebecca Park or Nelson (54) 32, Peniver Drive (body injuries) ; Pat Smith (20) Renfrew -the bus conductress (shock).

It was announced shortly afterwards that the tramcars would soon be withdrawn from the Govan routes and, in view of the high number of accidents, Govan folk were pleased.

A letter was sent into the Evening Times following yet another tram collision; it was entitled 'These Trams are a menace'.

*' In the controversy over the suitability of our trams I would be inclined to scrap the lot. Recently I was a passenger in one of the post horse type which, after a skid of 50 to 60 yards, crashed into the rear of a stationary bus. A private motorist would have had the Road Traffic Act thrown at him if he could not have stopped his car in a fraction of that distance. Why are these decrepit relics not road tested like taxi's are ? If they are tested then perhaps someone could tell me the standard of safety required !'*

*R.O'Neil*

At the Golspie Street pawnshop Abe and John are discussing the amazing amount of accidents around Govan during the year of 1957. John says ' Hardly a day seems to go past without some accident or other. I went up to Kelvin Hall last night with Sandra to help my mother in the ticket office and afterwards we watched a bit of the show. I told Sandra how good some of the acts were including the Tiger Trainer Frank Carloss. Last week the Tiger flicked out a paw and cut him on the chin; on Saturday a Leopard slashed him across the face. I said I was sure everything would be OK. Then he was directing the Tiger on the pedestal when it suddenly bit one of his fingers off !!. He wrapped a handkerchief around the finger and amazingly carried on the act until the end'.

Sir Murray Stephen owner of the Stephen's Shipyard issued a statement.
' A shipbuilder takes a gigantic gamble these days. The yards gamble when they give a fixed price to a buyer. The buyer gambles that he will get his money back within 20 years of the vessel's life. Win or lose the Government takes its commission from both sides with 50% in tax.

Not much encouragement here for an industry that has done so much for Britain in both peacetime and wars'.

Sam Mc Ilwraith was walking around the streets of Govan . Behind him was his faithful friend pulling the cart; 'Dinkie' a 9 year old Shewbald mare. Sam shouted out to the countless tenement windows above 'Any old Iron, any old Iron, best prices paid !' Dinky was popular with all Govanites in particular the children.

At the last Govan Fair competition Dinky won 1st Prize for the best turned out horse. The children liked giving Dinky the occasional sweeties and her favourite was lollipops. One day at Gower Street the horse and cart were in collision with a car. The cart was damaged and Dinky got loose but got her legs trapped under the cart. She was badly injured and had to be destroyed. Another victim of the seemingly endless Govan accidents.

# CHAPTER 18
## ABE

It is the Friday before John is due back from London on his one month of work learning the skills of gold and also diamond evaluation. Abe is in his Pawnshop and is not feeling well. George takes the opportunity during lunch time to enquire. He says' Abe would you like me to take you down to the Southern General ?' Abe says ' No, I will be alright soon but thanks George'. Abe is relieved at the end of the day and locks up the shop before going home.

On the Monday morning Abe opens the shop seemingly recovered from his illness on the Friday evening. John arrives and serves the waiting Govanites with items to pawn. Once the initial queue has gone Abe says ' Did you hear the news John ?' John says 'Whits that Abe !'. Abe smiled and said 'We now have a Jewish Lord Provost for Glasgow !' John smiled and said 'Whit ! . Well at least we know no money will be spent over the next three years !' Abe says 'His name is Myer Galpern !'. John says ' The City of Glasgow seems to full of Jews Abe'. Abe says 'Yes there are quite a number of Jews is Glasgow; I believe 20,000. We have produced a book for the first time in Scotland called 'Hashanah'. John says ' I would buy it but I cannot afford it on my wages Abe !. Fair play most Jews seem to work hard and put a lot of effort into business'.

Abe says ' John I received a call from John Sykes in London. I think he would like to offer you a job'. John says ' John was a great help when we were down. He showed Sandra and I some of the houses around London so I think he was hinting a bit'. Abe says 'John and I go back a long way and we still do a bit of business'. John says ' What would happen to this business if we moved to London Abe ?' .

Abe says 'George and I would carry on for a while. The demand for pawnbrokers will go down as people become better off'. John says 'I will talk it over with Sandra. She loved it down there'.

Around Govan music blared; Elvis Pressley was making his mark and the Govanites loved Rock and Roll, in particular the younger generations. At No 31 Daviot Street Robbie and Derek listened a lot to the radio and watched the TV when decent programmes were on. With just two channels to choose from the TV was off more than it was on. The only way music could be played was with an ancient gramophone with a big horn and an open turntable. Not being electric, it had to be wound up and invariably the large records got slower within a few minutes.

This prompted another crank on the handle and before long the music sounded as it should have done. When he was alive Grandfather Boab had assembled a small collection of records and particularly liked Rogers and Hammerstein. Oklahoma was one of his favourites.

A few days later Derek was back at school and his last year at Drumoyne had started. Mrs Dewart explained that over the course of the year 4 exams on every subject were to be taken. From the results the pupils would be assigned to the appropriate class at the Govan High School. The routine has started again. The milk tops get pierced and straws inserted. The milk is drank and almost immediately the bell for playtime rings. Out into the playground and the football games start with either a tennis ball or a punctured plastic ball.

The plastic balls when new lasted around a day before they punctured and then became very hard. Eventually, after two weeks or so, they split and it was back to a tennis ball. Mr Park has picked his school football team and Derek is unsuccessful. However, he is quite happy to support the team as a few of his near neighbours Bernie Quinn and George Mc Cleary are in the side.

Mrs Dewart proves to be an excellent teacher and the pace of learning by the class improves. All seem certain to get good marks on virtually every subject. Derek reflects that he is lucky to have such a good school and a great set of classmates. The only problem child Derek thought was himself as he sometimes gets involved in scraps when he should not. This gets him a deserved few whacks of the strap when some classmates tell on him. He calls them 'Clipes'.

The Govan Fair Queen, Maureen Keenan of Copland Road School, was crowned by Miss. Freyja Longley- Cook, daughter of Vice Admiral Longley-Cook, of Fairfields Shipbuilding Company. The fair was hugely attended and the floats seemed to take an eternity to pass. Few of the people at the fair noticed a man falling as he left the pawnbrokers; it was Abe. An ambulance soon arrived and he was on his way to the Southern General with severe breathing problems. John received a phone call later in the evening from the Hospital. They advised that Abe was being operated on and was unlikely to see visitors for a few days. John was requested to phone during the following day.

At Bellahouston Academy achievement was rewarded when Helen Mac Kay and
Alexander Mac Lean received the Dux awards.
Stephen's Boys Club beat off a lot of competition to win the Chris Campbell Memorial Shield two years running. The award was for the best all round club within the Glasgow Union of boys clubs.

The club leader Mr.J.Hunter plus leaders and 30 boys were invited to visit the Hague in Holland staying at a Youth Hostel.

A few days have passed and John gets permission to go to the Southern General and see Abe. On arrival he is asked to see a Senior Nurse and Doctor and he is given some very bad news. The Nurse says ' I am sorry to say Mr.Boulton-Cox is unlikely to survive until tomorrow. You can see him for a short period once we have attended to him'. John is stunned, he cannot believe it . 'He says 'Thank you I am sure you have done all you can'. The nurse and doctor say 'We are terribly sorry, he did say he wanted to see you Mr.Leslie'. John says 'Excuse me'.

He goes to the Gents toilet and looks in the mirror. His eyes have tears which makes it difficult for him to see. So a decision has to be made for probably the last discussions with Abe. A normal conversation with banter or a comforting conversation due to the terrible situation. He asks himself 'What would Abe want ?'. The answer was obvious.

John took a handkerchief out and blew his nose. He left the toilet and met again with the nurse who took him down to the bed. Abe lay with his eyes closed; his body seemed to have shrunk as the covers were almost parallel with the bed showing how thin he had become.

John says ' There ye are. I was looking down the ward for the biggest nose. I came along here seen the nose and look who wis underneath it ! Abe opened his eyes and smiled. His eyes had red lines but they soon seemed to sparkle. He moved his hand from under the covers and offered a handshake. John gripped his hand tightly. Abe said 'John listen !. As you say in Govan I am b**gered When I am gone there is a letter in the top drawer in the shop. I have left everything to you except some money to the Glasgow Jewish Actors.

My family deserve nothing, they have shown no interest in me'. With the money I suggest you consider a move to London and work with John Sykes. He will see you all right'. They spoke for several minutes about the projects and the countless laughs they had had together. Abe slowly went into a deep sleep. John sat in the chair and he also began to nod off and outside darkness descended. John was dozing when the Nurse asked him politely to leave. The next morning John arrived at the pawnshop and within ten minutes the inevitable telephone call was received from the Southern General.

A funeral had to be arranged. Within another few minutes the Rabbi from the Giffnock Synagogue had called. He said ' Do not worry John we will see to the arrangements. Abe has already told us what to do. You and your good lady will be very welcome.'

At 20, Craigton Road, Jimmy Welsh is looking at some papers he has received from Joan's solicitor. He has filed for a divorce but Joan has surpringly refused to entertain it and wants him to return to her and their children William and Mary. Ruth asks him ' What are you going to do now Jimmy ? , are you gawn tae go back to Joan ?' .

182

He puts his head in his hands and says 'No Ruth I will not be going back, I am happy here with you. However, I must see her and try and resolve the situation'.

Jimmy goes back to James Street in Bridgeton and sees Joan, William and Mary. He says 'Joan you asked me to leave because you did not like me drinking. Now when I want a divorce you refuse it !!'. Joan says 'Jimmy, you are with another woman and probably having a great life. I have had to bring up William and Mary on my own. It is hard and you have not provided much money'. William and Mary are pleased to see their father and tell him about their school and friends.

Joan says 'Jimmy I think we should give our marriage one last chance for the sake of William and Mary. They need you here at this important time in their lives and I feel certain your lady friend would understand that !'.

At the Synagogue Abe's funeral takes place within a few days of death. The Rabbi immediately assigned a 'shomer' (watchman) to stay with Abe until his funeral.

When the funeral party returned to Abe's home, John was greeted by Abe's long time friends Roger Joseph and Moshe Steinberg. They asked 'Do you know anything about Abe's arrangements for his finances'. John says 'It is not the appropriate time to discuss these things'. Roger says ' We will come around the shop tomorrow and help you sort things out'. John says ' Roger would you like to step outside for a minute I may have something interesting for you' The pair walked outside into Abe's well kept garden. Roger said 'Yes !' at which point John landed a fierce blow on the chin. Almost immediately the Rabbi and Sandra came rushing out and held John's arms. The Rabbi said 'Do not worry John this will go no further !'.

Sandra says ' I did not know you had a temper like that John !'. The Rabbi said ' Roger and Moshe can both try anyone's patience'. The funeral was over. John returned to the pawnshop with Abe's key. He opened the top drawer of Abe's desk and sure enough there was a large envelope with John's name on it. Inside there was a long letter from Abe to John telling how he had enjoyed their relationship.

He thought of John as much as a son as being a business partner. Apart from outstanding bills and a donation to the Jewish Youth actors, everything was left to John. The sum was enormous and added to the money they had made from their 'projects' John could move to London with the knowledge that he and Sandra could afford a very good house. As John read the letter he felt very sad that he had lost a true friend.

He was thinking ahead on how to spend the money. Uppermost, was the move to London and the start of what seemed a good opportunity. Also he wanted to visit a clinic in Switzerland and get his eyes corrected.

# CHAPTER 19
# HARLAND'S POTTER

In West Drumoyne Derek is talking to some of the Govan High pupils about his pending move upwards from Drumoyne Primary School. Tommy Mc Donald says ' unlike what you hear there is no dunking of heads in the toilet on the first day. Most teachers are not bad although watch out for Mr. Mathers the Music teacher. He is just pure mad. Apparently, when he was in charge of PE, he had the boys running around the playground at Dysart in their tee shirts and shorts when it was absolutely freezing cold with sleet. Watch out for him and the Deputy Head Bud Neil'. They are both vicious ba** a**s. It is a Saturday afternoon in Govan and Derek has joined the queue outside Harhill Baths affectionately known as the 'Steamie'. He has a towel under his arm with swimming trunks inside. Eventually he enters the red brick building and the pool is packed full of bathers. John the pool keeper calls for everyone to move away from the corner of the pool  deep end. He shovels in some more lime to combat any bacteria that may have survived his previous addition. Most swimmers are having trouble seeing and exit at the shallow end to reach the showers hopefully being able to get there eyesight focussing again. Suddenly, there is a cry from the pool and a 10 year old boy is in trouble.    John hands one of the children his burning cigarette 'Haud that son !'.  He gets a long pole and offers it to the splashing, panicking boy who gratefully grabs it before John pulls him in. 'Ther wi are pal; yer safe now !'. He retrieves his cigarette before bellowing at a couple of teenage boys who are chasing one another around the pool. The changing cubicles are all full and John moves each batch of clothes to one side and under the seat to allow for more swimmers. Derek jumps in and swims a few lengths. Harhill Baths is popular and very busy. As well as bathers they have the 'Steamie' where women bring their washing and have a good 'blether'. Inside the swimming pool the noise is intense as the Govan youngsters enjoy themselves. All too soon John calls the swimmers out when their time is up. He beckons two teenage boys ' Hey you two, get oot you hiv been in ther long enough !'.

In the Public Works Snooker League there was a surprise when the Harland and Wolfe team, the league leaders, were held to a draw by Rolls Royce at Hillington. The No.1 for H & W John Phillips won his frame and was still unbeaten for the season. In the Glasgow Individual events there was great interest between John Phillips and South African John Hubbard who played for Rangers. With players playing off handicap John Phillips was scratch and John Hubbard +7. Despite giving his Ibrox Park opponents 7 start, Johnny Phillips usually won.

Both players were good friends and both were to found playing on the snooker tables at the Imperial Club in Mitchell Street.

A few weeks after the Rolls Royce match, Harlands were fortunate to win at Albion Motors and remained top. The Mc Innes—Shaw Individual Shield saw three H & W
players in the second round The draw for matches to played at the Premier Rooms was:
J.Phillips ( H & W ) v J.Downie ( Cowlairs );  J.Hawthorn ( Cowlairs ) v A.Kinnear (H & W) ; J.Brown (H & W ) v A. Roberts ( Templetons)

## GLASGOW PUBLIC WORKS SNOOKER LEAGUE

| Team | Pl | W | L | D | F | A | Pts |
|------|----|----|----|----|----|----|-----|
| Harland & Wolfe | 14 | 12 | 1 | 1 | 61 | 23 | 25 |
| Knightswood | 14 | 10 | 2 | 2 | 57 | 27 | 22 |
| Cowlairs | 14 | 8 | 2 | 4 | 56 | 28 | 20 |
| Hydepark (Works) | 13 | 8 | 3 | 2 | 50 | 28 | 18 |
| Templeton's | 13 | 8 | 4 | 1 | 49 | 29 | 17 |
| Drysdale's | 14 | 7 | 5 | 2 | 44 | 40 | 16 |
| Roll's Royce | 14 | 5 | 6 | 3 | 45 | 39 | 13 |
| Albion Motors | 13 | 5 | 8 | 0 | 36 | 42 | 10 |
| Hydepark (Staff) | 13 | 2 | 10 | 1 | 25 | 53 | 5 |
| G.C.W.D. | 14 | 2 | 10 | 0 | 22 | 62 | 4 |

At 20 Craigton Road, Jimmy Welsh arrives home after his meeting in Bridgeton with Joan. Ruth is anxious to know the outcome although she pretends that she does not really care. Jimmy says ' Joan wants me to go back Ruth !'.  There was a long pause then Ruth said 'Well, ur ye going back ?'. Jimmy said ' No I told her things were too far gone for any return. However, she wants more money to keep William and Mary'. Ruth says. `That is fair enough Jimmy, it is not easy bringing up kids nowadays with the price of things. If you stopped drinking and gave less to the Mason's you would be a wealthy man'. Jimmy says ' I told you before Ruth I do not give that much to the Lodge. Besides much of it goes to good causes'.  Ruth says 'Jimmy, charity begins at home. It is time you showed more interest in Derek as well as supporting William and Mary. You do not see any poor publicans or the people at the top of the Mason's.'John is working mainly in London and living in a small hotel paid by the firm of John Sykes. He loves his job but misses Sandra. He constantly thinks about what he is going to tell her when he sees her. He travels back to Glasgow every fortnight for long weekends

John has already decided to close the Golspie Street pawnshop. He has told George that he has arranged a job at the pawnshop in Partick which will offer better wages. The notice has been placed in the window of the shop of pending closure.

Sandra arrives for a four day stay in the London hotel which is becoming a second home. John Sykes takes them both to view properties around the Gerrard's Cross area. The picture they look at is of 'Pantiles' a sizable house on the Amersham Road. The cost seems enormous but John Sykes says his company will buy the house and offer John and Sandra a mortgage at a very low interest rate. Within days the formalities are complete and the couple are heading for the London area to live. Sandra is over the moon. She says ' I will miss my family a lot but we can always go up now and again to see them'. John says. 'I will arrange for my parents to 'look after' our house on Mosspark Boulevard.    They will enjoy the extra space and my mother has always wanted a garden'.

John says ' Sandra I cannot think I have ever been happier. However, sometimes when I sit down and think about things I have a 'wee greet' thinking about the man that made so much of this possible'.  Sandra says ' I am sure Abe would want you to be as happy as you are'.

An elderly man went into the café on the corner of Neptune Street and Govan Road. He asked the owner for an empty glass lemonade bottle. On receipt he rushed out of the café quickly followed by the owner. The owner spotted him go further along Neptune Street to the Victoria pawnshop. There he smashed the window with the lemonade bottle and grabbed five watches. The pawnbroker and the café owner gave chase as he ran across open ground and doubled back down Neptune Street to Govan Road. He was eventually caught.

An agony aunt received a letter from a husband calling himself 'Henpecked'.

*' My wife is never happy unless she is nagging. She finds hundreds of things to nag about and although I ignore her, she gets worse ! I sometimes feel like walking out on her and leaving her to nag away her life alone'.*
*REPLY:*
*'Your habit of ignoring your wife gives her a feeling of power. The more silent you are the worse she will become. Give her a taste of her own medicine. She will soon come to her senses !. Women love to show their power even if it is by nagging'.*

There was a good scrap between around 100 boys at Clark Street, Kinning Park. They were watched by a number of girls who were cheering them on. The uproar drew two janitors from a nearby school as the fighting spread to several other streets.

The police arrived but the entire group had already disappeared.

Twenty two year old shipyard worker Johnny Phillips took a large support to the Bridgeton Working Men's Club. The occasion was the West of Scotland amateur snooker final. His opponent Peter Spence (Cambuslang) had previously won the title five times. Phillips started well and took the first four frames with much applause from the Govan support. Spence fought back and won three of the next four frames. However, in the ninth frame Spence missed a very potable black. It was fatal and Johnny Phillips stepped in to clinch the frame and the match by 6-3.

In the League title Harlands were being caught up and after drawing 3-3 with Cowlairs , the lead was down to just two points from Kinghtswood. However, Harlands stabilised the ship and went on to clinch the title a few weeks later. John Phillips went on to win the League Individual championship finishing the season unbeaten.

The Glasgow Individual Snooker Handicap Championship saw a lot of Rangers supporters cheer Johnny Hubbard (receiving 7 start) to a 3-0 win over John Phillips. The championship was played in a league format with each player playing his opponent in two matches of three frames. The two Imperial club players headed to Bridgeton Working Men's Club both on similar points totals. The Govan man lifted the title making amends for his earlier blemish to Hubbard.

The Harland and Wolff snooker team and John Phillips won all competitions they entered. The Team League and League Cup and three Individual titles.

A husband and wife went to the cinema with their young son. The husband and the son went off to get ice cream and almost immediately a man who was sitting in the row in front of the lady stepped over the seats and sat in her husbands seat. She told him the seats were taken at which point he became abusive. The husband returned and the interloper George Hart returned to his seat. When a seat became vacant at the opposite side of the wife from the husband Hart climbed over and occupied it. He became a nuisance and argumentative.   The Cinema manager and the Husband restrained him and took him to the Office where the police, on arrival, arrested him.

At Govan Police Court George Hart was fined £7 with an alternative of 30 days in prison by Fiscal Grindlay.

Ex Lord Provost of Glasgow Tom Kerr was provided with a dinner at the City Chambers on his 79 th birthday. The chairman William Carruthers welcomed all 40 guests and remembered every name. He gave a brief introduction and welcome to each guest.

At St.Mary's Church a talk was given to the youth fellowship. The minister said 'The talk this evening will be given by the chief local fire officer. A warm welcome is extended to all'.

187

Auld Jock and Fred decided it was time for a cigarette at their works in the Corporation Sewage Plant next to Stephens in Linthouse. Jock lit the fag and blew the smoke which was immediately whisked away down the River Clyde. It was a very windy day and on the Whiteinch bank opposite there was a fair bit of activity.

Jock says ' It looks as though we are just in time Fred; they are launching an oil tanker at Barclay Curle's'. Fred says ' I seen the name on the back of the stern was Hurricane; quite appropriate for todays conditions. Ah here she goes !'. The Hurricane was launched and slipped into the Clyde from the Barclay Curle launching platform.

Jock noticed something he was not happy with. He says 'Fred, I don't think the stern should be in that position. The angle looks wrong !'. Fred says ' Yes it is swinging round and coming over here fast Jock'. Jock says ' Right we're ooot o' here Fred' and they both ran off warning other worker. The Hurricane was heading towards a 30 foot high gantry and nothing seemed to be able to stop it. A huge crash was heard all over both sides of the river as the tanker careered into the gantry.

The Hurricane careered onwards towards Stephens Shipyard but fortunately came to rest just before it hit the first of the Stephens ships.

Ruth gets on well with all the neighbours at 20, Craigton Road. She enjoys their company and she blethers away with the other women in the close. Some of the other women ask about Derek and suggest he attends the Greenfield Club. The Club has an excellent reputation and very popular. Ruth says that Derek will join it when he is a bit older probably when he is 11.

The Greenfield Club had 3 age groups and met on Tuesday and Thursday evenings. Youngest age group (Play Centre 8 to 11) , Intermediate (11 to 15 ) Youth Club (15 and over).

The highlight of their year was about to take place at South Govan Town hall. A massed choir of 300 singers were scheduled to take part and all the backdrops were made and decorated by the various skill groups within the club. The props and backdrop were made by the woodwork section. The lassies made all the national costumes for the performance including Russian, Canadian and Danish outfits.

The Club, which was sponsored by the City Youth group and had over 300 active members, and held their activities at Greenfield School.

Four hundred miles south of Greenfield School John and Sandra were settled in to their new surroundings at the Pantiles in Gerrard's Cross. They were able to convey good news in the letters sent by Sandra to her mother Helen. A baby was on the way.

John made a trip to Glasgow on business and decided to walk down Golspie Street. He had arranged that the Pawnbrokers shop be converted into a tenement flat which was its original purpose many years before. The reddish sandstone bricks used during the conversion were already fading and looking grimy.

John looked across the road at the tenement and in his thoughts he seen Abe. The good times he re-called made him smile and the celebrations after some of the 'Projects' were completed he would never forget. He missed Abe.

The big evening arrived for the Greenfield Club. The leader Mrs E. Ferguson had things organised to the letter. Crowds came to the South Govan display from all over Govan. The stage was set with a huge wooden surround depicting a Television set. Many of the acts and songs came from both TV and Radio. The evening was a resounding success and much appreciated by the parents and relatives among the audience.

Jimmy Welsh still worked with John Henderson and spent a fair bit of time going to the yard and offices at Springburn. He enjoyed the trips out on the lorries and planning the setting up of the scaffolding. John still trusted Jimmy to ensure all the safety requirements were met. Henderson's prided themselves on having virtually no accidents.

Generally Jimmy and Ruth were more settled although Ruth was not happy when he came home occasionally drunk; but tolerated it. The single end was hardly the best place to live and in the winter months and with the dark coloured building there was a lack of light due to being a ground floor tenement flat with another block of tenements adjacent. Ruth felt that they needed something better. Across the road on Sunday's they could here the sound of the Mc Gregor Memorial congregation singing with gusto but they never attended. Ruth continued to work at Woolworth's and one day she seen two people enter the store that she recognised. It was Bernard and Junior. They walked past Ruth's counter looked at her and walked on much to Ruth's relief.

At 31, Daviot Street, Robbie continued to obtain employment as a labourer either at Stephens or at Fairfields. The conditions in the shipyards during the winter period were harsh for any of the shipyard workers especially on outside works. Snow had arrived and a white blanket descended over Govan. For the youngsters living in Drumoyne it was not at all bad news. Out came the sledges from years past and it was to the hill off the side of the Farm Lane Rise from Shieldhall Road.

The slopes provided hours of enjoyment for the Drumoyne kids. One feature that was built each year was a big mound in the middle of the slope. Around 4 or 5 would get on the biggest sledge; run up speed on the ice and as it went over the mound it was a great feeling to be in the air if only for a few seconds. Invariably everyone landed safely on the soft snow in front of the Shieldhall Road railings. A number of the parents were saying that everyone should make the best of it.

189

They had heard their was planning permission by the Scottish Special Housing Association to build on this land.

Derek made a few visits to Clydebank to see Uncle Jack and his Aunt Maggie. Maggie was a very popular lady with everyone she met. Small in stature but big in personality. Maggie had always lived in Clydebank and for a long period worked in Singers. During the second world war Clydebank had taken a terrible pounding from German bombs and a considerable amount of the town was flattened with a huge death toll of over 2,000.

Both families had suffered loss of houses. On Jack's side he had two Uncle's ; David and Bob; who were bombed out but survived. David's son Lawrence who was home at the time from the Royal Navy also survived. However Lawrence was later lost in action when his ship was bombed off the Island of Crete. This caused great anguish to the entire family at the time and for years afterwards. Maggie's family were also bombed out of their home and were evacuated to Helensburgh, Stirling , Kirkintilloch before returning to Clydebank. Many of the Clydebank population who experienced the bombing were never to return to the town after the war.

One Friday one of Derek's classmates pats him on the back. 'Well done Derek !'. Derek asks why 'You won the competition in the Govan Press did you not !'.

The Govan Press had a small competition for Under 12's. This involved two virtually identical photographs and you had to send in your entry with rings around the 5 differences. Derek says 'Yes I forgot about that'. His classmate said 'Good prize, two seats at the Lyceum'. Derek went over to see his mother at 20 Craigton Road after school. Ruth says ' Well done Derek !. Did you see the Govan Press ?'. Derek picked up the paper and it read 'Derek Wilson wins prize'. 'Well that is a surprise Maw, I did not think I would have had any chance of winning that prize'. 'Ruth says 'Well ther ye go son, ye never know yer luck !'. Derek says ' The only time I have not entered it in weeks and I win it !'. He continues ' Did you enter it for me Maw ?'. ' Ruth says ' Well I thought ye wid be happy Derek and two entries are better than one !'.

Ruth and her son go to the Lyceum. Both are well dressed and Derek has a tie on. The manager comes out to greet them both in the Foyer where Ruth hands him the winning tickets. The manager is all charm and after a pleasant talk for 5 minutes says. 'Come this way madam and Derek. It is a good film and you will have the best seats in the house'. The pair are taken by the manager to two reserved seats in the balcony front row in exactly the middle. Ruth says 'This is good Derek, we will have to try this competition more often !'.

The Lyceum Cinema was probably the best cinema in Govan and very popular.

Following on from the success of the show at South Govan Town Hall, the Greenfield Club receive many plaudits. A number of people from the organising committee for the Bellahouston Palace of Arts were present. The Greenfield Club are honoured to be invited to play a major part in a forthcoming concert. They were impressed by the Arts and Crafts section at the club and generally the very high standards provided throughout the Greenfield Club.

A feature of the Greenfield Club is that on either of the two week nights attendance all the Club members must participate as mandatory in Dancing and Swimming in the Greenfield School Pool. The Pool is usually packed on either of the two evenings and the changing cubicles piled high with clothing.

The Sunday People had an exclusive. It was called 'The Shadowland of Govan'. The investigation story suggested the public demanded answers to the following questions.

- 'Are Bingo Boys misfits or just gangsters ?'.
- 'Why are there more problem boys than problem girls ?'.
- 'What makes slum girls rebel ?'.
- 'How does a knife and razor gang get started ?'
- 'Is bad housing to blame for crime ?'.

There is speculation that West Drumoyne may be getting a Bookmakers as the betting laws in the country get relaxed. The likely location is a triangular piece of ground on Meiklewood Road between Cockburns factory and Andy's Café.

The small plot of land in question is popular with most of the children in West Drumoyne. It seems to offer up an abundance of berries every summer which are instantly edible and delicious. Andy and Peter who run Andy's Café and the Chip Shop next door continue to do a roaring trade. The day to avoid for the Fish Shop is a Friday as Catholic Families queue up in numbers for Fish; the Pope decreeing that Meat is forbidden.

The likely owner of the new bookmakers is Pat McShane. He has been operating a bookmakers operation out of the back of a car on Meiklewood Road adjacent to the swing park for many years. Pat lives in a semi detached house opposite the 50 pitches changing rooms. Derek is good friends with his son Raymie McShane who is an ardent St.Mirren supporter.

Throughout the UK there are strikes looming and the Shipbuilding Industry looks as if it will be affected. Most of the Unions planning on taking part in the Industrial Action have many members in the Shipyards. The wage claim by the Unions is 10%.

The Employers say they cannot afford it and the Government are getting involved in the form of the Minister of Labour, Mr.Iain McLeod. The talks break down and the Unions discuss whether to call an all out strike or effect a guerrilla type action around the shipyards.

Mr McLeod wants more talks to be held to avoid the strike and the employers issue statements to the National media.

The statement put forward by the Engineering and Allied Employers National Federation.

### ' THE STRIKE THAT HURTS EVERYBODY'

*THE REAL ISSUE IN THE ENGINEERING DISPUTE.*

*'This is not just a quarrel between the employers and their men about money. The real issue is this. Can we , in engineering, continue to earn our living ? All of us depend directly or indirectly on our customers overseas who buy the products of our skill. We know they won't pay more or wait longer for delivery than our foreign competitors who are eager to step in. We have come to a point where an increase in price results in lost orders. Any stopping or slowing down of production will inevitably mean late deliveries. Why throw away our trade with a strike ?  Why risk our livelihoods ?*

*We, the employers, deploring this strike , feel obliged to make this statement.*

### THE EMPLOYERS OFFERED TO PUT THE CASE IN THE HANDS OF AN INDEPENDENT ARBITRATOR.

The Strike started and feelings ran high around Govan. Around 150 men waited outside the gates at Fairfield's and jeered the apprentices and labourers, not part of the dispute, who entered the yard. A number of scuffles broke out.

The strikers assembled in the Elder Cinema building and the 800 present cheered loudly when the Union leaders confirmed they would press for the full 10% rise.

In London the National Federation of Postmasters met in London, they wanted more money. The Govan Road post office's post mistress was attacked twice in recent years and this was presented as an example of the dangers faced. In the first attack on the Govan Road postmistress six men entered the post office with knives. The post mistress with her assistant sent them packing by using clubs to beat them out the door. However she was disappointed by the extremely light sentencing given to people who attack post offices.

She went on to say 'I am nervous every time I see a Teddy Boy`. In the second attempted robbery Miss L.L.M. Heron and Mrs E. West her assistant were serving in the Govan Road post office one day. Two men entered and jumped over the counter grilles, Mrs West was struck and kicked on the head. Miss Heron was struck around the head and body and her clothing slashed. The ladies managed to set off the alarm bell which made the robbers run out the post office. The women gave chase and helped by some Govanites caught one of the robbers.

Both women were summoned to London where Mr.Marples the Postmaster General presented them with notecases and 15 guineas each.

The Trade Union were pressing for additional wages to reflect the dangers faced by post office staff.

Blackie the seven year old black cat who was resident in Govan Police station attacked Elizabeth Rankin the station turnkey when she arrived for work one day. She was badly clawed on the legs and received treatment for shock and the scratches. She said 'Blackie flew at me hissing and spitting'. A policemen caught Blackie and she was destroyed. The station had one of Blackie's four kitten's and this kitten was also destroyed. The policeman said ' We did it in case it had the same mad tendencies that Blackie had !'.

At 20 Craigton Road Ruth is talking to Jimmy before he catches the trolley bus on its way to the Govan Town Hall. There he is attending a Govandale Lodge Masonic meeting. He says 'We have a deputation from the Ibrox Lodge tonight Ruth !'. Ruth says 'I thought you were both from Govan Town Hall Lodges so how can you have a deputation from the same stable ?'.

Jimmy says ' Ruth, you do not understand, these are very important occasions ! Would you like to come to the Whist evening at the Neptune Lodge ? It is to raise funds for some very good charitable causes Ruth'. Ruth says 'I will come Jimmy so long as you keep your drink in moderation. Also, I will need a new dress if I am to be seen in such company, so we will go up to Glesga to John Lewis and C & A Modes. Aye and by the way I'll need ma her done tae !'.

Derek is looking forward to going to Govan High School now. Ruth has bought him a  black blazer and sewed the Govan High badge on. He has new trousers  and two pairs of Govan High socks with the red and black bands. In addition Ruth goes down to the Co-op store in Govan and buys him two white shirts and a red and black striped tie. Robbie gives him a good kaki army bag for the books he is going to get. The weather has been good and for the first time most Govanites watch the Olympic games on television. Britain does poorly and collects seemingly very few medals from the competitions in Rome.

The younger Govanites in West Drumoyne spend some time in Andy's Café listening to the jukebox.  The Eversley Brothers 'Cathy's Clown' was a very frequent choice . The last weeks at Drumoyne School are happy and Derek reflects how it would be good if things could stay as they are. Great classmates and friends; a great little school West Drumoyne and Govan were smashing places to live with always something to do. He thought back on a particularly nice man who attended most of the Govan Primary Schools. Mr.Scott would always be remembered . He came occasionally for the music lessons which were always good. Reverend Potts would usually come around during the religious periods for a short service and talk.

Jimmy Welsh and John Henderson have finished a meeting in Glasgow and decide to go to the Bridgeton Arms on the way back to the business premises. Richard the pub owner joins them in conversation. Jimmy says ' These strikes are terrible over in Govan. At the drop of a hat the Trade Unions call the workers out and the poor shipyard owners must be pulling their hair out '. John says ' I agree Jimmy. I do not think they know how hard it is to get business and more importantly how easy it is to lose it. We know that from our own experiences do we not Jimmy ?'.

Richard says. ' Difficult to argue pals. There are two sides to every story of course. The Unions are vilified in the media'. Jimmy says 'There are too many Communists agitating in the Yards and elsewhere. They want world revolution. We see how their people's workers paradise worked out in Hungary'. Richard says ' Well lets hope they sort it out and everybody gets back to work. I need the workers to survive and definitely workers wae a wee bit of money in their pocket'.

Mr.Belch a Director at Lithgows Shipyard in Port Glasgow says' It would be wrong to suggest that lack of steel was the only cause for frustration in the industry. On the labour front we have had a troubled time with petty demarcation disputes, overtime bans and unofficial strikes. It is a pity common sense does not prevail'.

A national negotiation is taking place in London to sort out the pay rises of most Clydeside Union members and the Employers. At local level there is another smaller dispute starting in Harland and Wolff with a smaller union. The Association of Supervisory Staffs and Technicians members are not happy. They have found out that after recent increases, the men they are supervising are getting more money than they are.
A strike is threatened.

Doctor J. Pearson assistant director of the Iron and Steel Research Association said in an annual statement.

' With the advent of Scientific and Technical civilisation, it is no longer true that the value of goods is the amount of work put into their making. The value is to be reckoned in the engineer's brain content.

The true creators of wealth these days are the engineers and technologists. Without them, workmanship no matter how good will not alone produce a desired product at an acceptable price.'

The reputation of Clydeside Shipbuilding remained high and with a good sales effort from the respective yards good orders for ships were being achieved.

John Robertson Brown (41) of Blackburn Street was in trouble. He had been caught stealing small lengths of brass from premises in 45, Scotland Street. He had a family of ten and was desperate for money. He was employed as a turner on the wage of £8 and 10 shillings a week. His wife was worried as he was the only breadwinner.

At Govan Police Court Baillie William Robertson delivered his verdict. 'For the sake of your wife and your family, forget about these wee bits of scrap in future'. Mr.Brown was admonished.

A six year old boy was knocked down by a lorry on Paisley Road West at Plantation. A few passers by picked him up and surprisingly he ran off saying 'I am going to the pictures'. The police arrived and went to the nearest cinema where the found the boy in the queue. He was suffering from shock and had a broken arm and taken to the Southern General Hospital. Both he and a woman had just alighted a tramcar when a lorry came up the inside and skidded. The woman was also taken to the Southern General Hospital with a leg injury.

Stephens Boys Club and a mixed team from the Pearce Institute were chosen to represent Glasgow. The event was a weekend drama course to be held at Dalguise. The oratory part of the competition was to be held at 2, Park Circus with Dr.J.Highet of Glasgow University as the judge.

In the City of Glasgow School's rowing event at Glasgow Green, Govan High's four were drawn on the south bank against Harlot's from Edinburgh in the heats.

Three young Govanites enjoyed a drink and they had a plan. Passing the Public House at 137 Neptune Street, Arthur Brennan (24), Charles Duncan (23) and Allan Russell (21) forced an entry to the pub one evening and gained access to the cellar. There they gained access to the liquor store and moved four crates of whiskey and 2,000 cigarettes to underneath the delivery hatch. As they raised the hatch to look out they spotted two policemen on the beat coming towards them. They lowered the hatch just in time.

The policemen walked past the premises but one of them noticed movement inside the pub. They opened the door and an initial search found nothing untoward.

However, they noticed a raincoat with water still dripping from it and the barman confirmed it was not there at closing time. The liquor store inspection soon found the items moved and a further search found the three robbers behind a services hatch. They were promptly arrested and all were drunk.

At Govan Sheriff Court all admitted the offence and said it was a drunken caper. Brennan was sent to Prison for 7 months, Duncan for 6 months and Russell for 9 months by Fiscal William Mc Nab.

At Bellahouston Park there was a large display by the Catholic Youth Service as part of Glasgow Youth week. 50 youth clubs took part and provided good entertainment with a good variety of events. These included Scottish and Irish country dancing, plays, operettas, choral singing, instrumental music, arts and crafts, physical training and netball.

A contribution was made by St.Francis Youth Club who provided the uniforms for the Pipe Bands. Nazereth House at Cardonald provided much of the choral items and demonstrations on Irish folk dancing.

Robert Reid (22) of Nethan Street was an apprentice plumber . He staggered into a public house in 59, Langlands Road and ordered a whiskey. The barman refused on the grounds he was drunk. Two policemen had followed Reid into the pub having seen him worse for wear. Reid grabbed a bottle of whiskey near the bar and moved out of the pub. The policemen ran after him and Reid threw the bottle,which was a display only item, at his pursuers. Fortunately he missed. At Govan Court Fiscal Mr.W.A.Grindlay fined Reid £2 for the theft of the bottle (valued at 3 pence) and £5 for the attempted assault on the policemen. He was given 21 days in which to pay.

Mr.Grindlay also fined Dock Labourer John Adair (30) £3 when he admitted stealing whiskey from Plantation Quay. Adair and a friend were spotted by two policemen and ran off and into a lavatory. The 'friend' managed to escape capture by smashing a bottle and threatening the policemen before running off. Adair said he found the whiskey in the lavatory and was going to hand it in.

The Glasgow Council elections saw Tom Kerr win the Fairfield ward easily well ahead of the Progressive, Communist and Scottish Nationalist. Labour also won the Govan seat with a big majority but the Progressives comfortably retained the Craigton ward. The political landscape was much the same.

At the Rob Roy Bar in Govan Road, John Gillespie and Frank Mulvenney meet with others to have a drink and reflect on the progress of the strikes. Frank has left the Communist Party in protest at the events a few years previously with the Hungarian uprising and the numbers of active Communist Party members in Govan has dwindled. John is still an active Labour Party member and supportive of the strike. However, the group of drinkers are not happy with the way things are going. John says ' I must say I think we will be lucky to get our demands. As Trade Unionists we should be united but we are not. This gives the Yards the advantage with their press backers to attack us as a rabble'. Frank says ' The problem is we have too many Unions and the Yard bosses simply play one off against the other. The Labour Party are a disgrace, instead of supporting the Unions they simply sit on the fence with mealy mouthed apologies to the Press bosses'. John says ' They should have defended us by saying that the delays to the ship launches were not simply down to strikes, for months we have been waiting for steel and countless other materials'. Frank says 'The Yard management are canny and have a big advantage. To win we need one union only representing each yard and better discipline on making agreements.'

John says ' You go to a meeting with the bosses and we all seem to have an understanding and basis of agreement on any issue. They refer it to the Directors who rarely give a response. Then we get these press statements which make them seem reasonable and us as troublemakers !'. Frank says ' Disunited we stand and divided we fall !'. All present said ' Aye that is right. Lets have another drink !'.

Shipwrights Association members stopped work at Alexander Stephen's Shipyard after a dispute with the Boilermakers Union. The dispute was who should carry out the works on Prefabrication. After 8 weeks the two unions finally had informal meetings at the Langlands Social Club in Nethan Street to try and resolve differences. The dispute meant that 250 other workers were paid off and a ship launch was delayed. It was hoped that sufficient agreement could be gained to enable the launch of the ship Chirripo.

The dispute rumbled on for weeks which ran into months before Sir Murray Stephen decided he had no option but to close the yard in the interim and lay 2,000 men off. The Lord Provost of Glasgow Mr.Hood offered to mediate in the dispute to sort things out.

Sir Murray Stephen and his directors produced a statement.
' The effects on the firm and their output are very serious. The equivalent of three months output on new ships has now been lost. It is difficult for anyone outside the industry to realise the effects which these delays have on our firm's clients. To have to explain to them that they must suffer because two unions claim one job and won't agree to any form of arbitration is unpleasant. Moreover, these disputes give the shipbuilding industry in Britain a bad name and rebound to its discredit.'

As the Stephens Shipyard was much quieter than normal another sound started up at Linthouse. It was the start of the building of the Clyde Tunnel joining Whiteinch at the opposite side of the River Clyde. The Main Contractor is Charles Brand (London) Ltd. and the cost of the project is estimated at £6,392,000. Hearing the noise were Mr. and Mrs. James Ogilvie who lived at 3, Drive Road, Linthouse. Mr Ogilvie was 83 and Mrs Ogilvie 82. They were a very popular couple devoted to one another and celebrating 60 years of marriage; their Diamond Wedding Anniversary.

The Govan Old age pensioners were taken on a day trip to Portobello. 450 Copland Road Primary schoolchildren were taken on a sail aboard the Maid of Cumbrae on their way to a day out at Millport.

John Campbell of the Govan Police force was a very fit man. He was walking along Gower Street when he saw two men trying to break in to the shop at 68, Gower Street, Ibrox. The men made a run for it on seeing the policeman. PC Campbell gradually gained on them and caught the first man James Mc Math (42). He moved quickly and handcuffed McMath around a lamp post. He then went in pursuit of the other man. After a long run he caught up with Bernard Regan (24) in Maxwell Drive and arrested him. McMath and Regan who both lived at 134, Kintra Street were each sent to prison for 60 days. Fiscal Mc Leod complimented Constable Campbell on his actions.

Patrick Condon was pushing his wheelbarrow during a hot day. He decided to stop at a pub and have a drink, or two. When he resumed his push of the wheelbarrow along the street a policeman noticed he was swaying about. Condon from 17, Neptune Street said he had 5 pints of beer and a whiskey but had only a few yards to go on his journey. He was fined £2 or 20 days in prison.

Andrew Hope (34) was walking along Govan Road with a girlfriend. Suddenly they were surrounded by five men who were singing football songs. They started shouting and swearing at the couple who tried to get away. Hope was caught knocked to the ground and the five proceeded to kick and punch him. Two policemen heard the commotion and arrived at the scene.

They gave chase after the five and caught two of the attackers. John Moore (20) of Castlemilk Drive and Angus Healey of Nethan Street were each fined £20 for the unprovoked attack by Fiscal W.Grindlay.

A downturn in orders saw 100 Foundry workers at Harland and Wolff, Govan, lose their jobs. The company said it would make efforts to find re-employment for as many workers as possible and that no apprentices would lose their jobs.

After a considerable number of strikes affecting most of the shipyards things slowly returned back to a small degree of normality. There was little or no trust existing between management and worker most of the time. Just a grudging acceptance that somehow they would have to work together to satisfy the delivery of ships on time as best they could. The one exception was the apprentices. Their wages were very low and they wanted more money. They launched a series of strikes and neither the shipyards or the unions knew how to resolve things. Eventually, a part bargain was struck whereby the apprentice, depending on age, would work to a scaled proportion in percentage to the skilled worker rate.

The River Clyde shipbuilding outlook was not looking as good as it should. Lithgow's at Port Glasgow remained the biggest and busiest yard but they had seen three sizable orders cancelled. John Brown's at Clydebank had a good period as did Scott's at Greenock. All three Govan yards struggled and inevitably W. Stephens started announcing permanent job losses. A new strike by shipwrights union and the platerer's union meant that the shipyard was forced to make 800 workers redundant. The Minister of Labour became involved and persuaded the company to withhold the employment notices pending further discussions.

Donald Forbes (23) sat with his head in his hands in Saughton Jail, Edinburgh. He was due to be hanged for the murder of a night watchman Allan Fisher at Granton. The jury at the trial found him guilty by a unanimous verdict but recommended mercy. Forbes looked up; this was going to be the happiest day in the remainder of his life set at 10 days. He was going to be married. Rita Mc Lean (22) had requested that she could marry her boyfriend before the execution. The appeal for marriage went to the highest authorities in Scotland and it was granted. A Glasgow property owner gave Rita £1,000 towards her costs for the rest of her life. The prison chaplain carried out the service after Forbes had been led from the condemned cell. The couple had a few minutes together before the condemned man was led away.

At 20, Craigton Road, Ruth has been following the story and is upset. She drinks tea and blows smoke to the ceiling from her cigarette. She says ' Jimmy, that is awful ! Poor wumin , she must really have loved him. They should stop the hanging !'. Jimmy says ' well, it is all very well but what about the poor watchman. He did not deserve to die Ruth . He is getting what he deserves. The lady concerned will soon get over it and return to her normal life. I do not think she will have any trouble getting another man having got the £1,000 !.'

A few days later Forbes was spared the death sentence and instead received life in prison.

# CHAPTER 20
# GOVAN HIGH

A man hands in his papers for the forthcoming General Election. He wants to contest the Glasgow Kelvingrove seat as the Independent Labour Party Candidate. Mr. William Park has been here before in a By Election. The Drumoyne school teacher knows he has no chance of winning but uses the election to forward his views on Banning the Bomb and Disarmament. The ILP has a popular candidate and Mr.Park hopes he can build on the 500 or so votes he got in the much publicised By Election. The Labour group are not happy, in a tight fight with the Unionists they feel they will need every vote they can get to retain the By Election gain.

Jimmy returns home from a meeting of the freemasons at Govan Town Hall. He tells Ruth that the brotherhood is expanding. He says 'Ruth we had a letter read out from the Grand Lodge. It came from the Earl of Eglinton and Winton, the Grand Master Mason of Scotland. Apparently, the Grand Lodge has now over 1,000 lodges under its jurisdiction'. Ruth says ' So how does that affect us Jimmy. You pay them too much and I am not convinced we get too much for it. John Henderson runs your company totally now and not you !! You get him all the contract's around here '.

Unemployed labourer James Hamilton needed some money. He had some skills with working on pipes and in particular gas pipes. He had the skills to remove gas meters and seal up the pipes afterwards as best he could. After a number of gas meter thefts around Govan the tenants began getting worried and became very vigilant. One day a man saw Hamilton walking down Helen Street with a bundle under his arm covered with a blanket. The man ran into his close from where Hamilton had come and smelled gas coming from his home. He followed the man who he spotted trying to open a gas meter. He called the police and James Hamilton was quickly arrested.

In Glagow Sheriff Court assistant Fiscal J.M.Hogg said that Hamilton had pleaded guilty to 8 offences of Gas Meter thefts plus other robberies. He said that although Hamilton tried to seal the pipes up as best he could a dangerous situation was left present.

James Hamilton (21) was sentenced to 9 months in prison.

The 1959 General Election saw Prime Minister Harold McMillan strong favourite to gain seats from Labour and increase the Conservative Party majority in the House of Commons. His slogan 'You have never had it so good !' was aimed at the folk who had a better standard of living than ever. It also gave an assurance that things would continue to improve. Much of the Govan populace had bought TV's and other goods on Hire Purchase. Around the UK most felt that the Conservatives had done a good job. However, around Govan, people were not quite so sure and their was an unease about the future.

At the Citizens Theatre there was a play for the Spring Season that caught the Govanites eyes. It was to be about the Burgh and called 'Gay landscape'. The story was about a Highland family who came to live in Govan. The author was George Munro and the play starred Iain Cuthbertson, Hilary Paterson, John McGregor supported by John Grieve, Irene Sunters and Edith McArthur. The critics gave the play top marks and George Munro received much acclaim. The performances were a complete sell out and everyone who saw it thoroughly enjoyed it. George Munro was said to have a fantastic knowledge of the Govanites and also the Gaels.

Throughout Scotland there was considerable unease amongst parents about their children being frequently subjected to Corporal punishment by the tawse. Some local councils wanted it banned. Dundee Education Committee decided to call for a ban and immediately came under fierce opposition in the form of the Scottish Schoolmasters Association. They sent a letter to the Secretary of State for Scotland Mr.John MacLay outlining their case for the retention of corporal punishment. The case implied that due to overcrowding in the schools with a high pupil/teacher ratio it would be impossible for the teacher to have control of his/her class. However, they were considering the position regarding using the tawse on infants.

The newspapers debated the subject but well respected columnist for the Evening Times, Meg Munro, felt that parents should respect the judgement of the modern teacher especially when they had to control classes of 40 or more.

The Glasgow Craigton seat at the general election was going to be close. Former Govan MP Jack Nixon Browne narrowly won his two previous election campaigns and had barely 200 votes majority to defend. Bruce Millan a 32 year accountant was again trying to unseat him. The country appeared to be thinking that the Conservatives would be likely to increase their majority. Labour had a lot of helpers canvassing, many diverted from the Govan seat which they felt they were on course to win easily.

Drumoyne was generally one of the quieter parts of Govan. However, they were to suffer the occasional bit of crime. One evening The Scottish Machine Tool Corporation (James Bennie and Sons Ltd) in Drumoyne Road was broken into and the safe blown open. The robbers managed to get £150 but missed another envelope which also contained £150. George Birrell the gateman discovered the break in on arriving at work after a weekend.

Two Govan 'Hooch' drinkers died in the Southern General Hospital on the same evening. 47 year old Andrew 'Muggie' McGhie collapsed in Blackburn Street, Plantation after being arrested for being drunk and incapable. He was a busker around Govan and Glasgow. 42 year old Hugh Boyle collapsed at home. The police were desperately trying to find the source of the 'Hooch'.

Andrew Hutton the Unionist Candidate for Govan faced an uphill task. Labour had a substantial majority and John Rankin looked like retaining the seat by a similar margin. Many of the Govan electorate had moved from Govan to the new estates on the outside of Glasgow and that gave Mr.Hutton a hope he could make inroads.

Jimmy and Ruth were split on politics. Jimmy was a strong Unionist and always voted for the Unionist Candidate. Ruth always voted Labour. Jimmy tried to persuade Ruth that Labour were not worth voting for. Ruth always said 'Labour are for the poor folk, the Unionists are for the rich. I am poor so I vote Labour !'.

A new School was built on Paisley Road West and it was impressive. Lourdes Roman Catholic School soon earned a good reputation and the pupils who attended were generally reasonably pleased to be getting their education there.

The school organised their first sports day at Nether Pollok and it was a big success. Other local schools were invited to inter school events and everyone had an enjoyable day.

The winners were:

Lourdes Boys champion: Anthony Morgan (Class 3A)

Lourdes Girls Champion: S.Ruddy (Class 2B)

Inter Schools Boys winners; Bellahouston Academy runner up; St.Augustines

Inter Schools Boys winners; Govan High; runners up; Bellahouston Academy

Primary Schools winner St.Constantine's; runners up Lourdes Primary

The Scottish Schools Athletic Association held the annual championships at Westerlands. R.N.Jardine of Govan High did well in the shot putting and threw a distance of over 49 feet.

Languages were taught in all of the Govan Secondary Schools. In an effort to keep the Gaelic Language alive the Scottish Education Authorities encouraged the learning of Gaelic in some schools. Bellahouston Academy took up the challenge. No fewer than 18 pupils spread between the first and sixth age groups achieved the highest award.

These were prizes awarded by the An Comunn Gaidhealach, Gaelic League of Scotland, Lewis and Harris Association and Skye Association.

As a result of Bellahouston Academy pupils doing well they were then able to participate in the Gaelic scene around Glasgow.

There was excitement at Fairfield Primary School when Margaret Leonard (11) was declared Govan Fair Queen. Margaret lived at 24, Elder Street, Govan. The attendants chosen were Ann Carnagle, Marjory Wright, Ann Muir and Carol Montgomery.

The 1959 General Election saw the Conservative and Unionist Party retain power with an increased majority. Most Political commentators felt it was a 'Landslide' victory.

At 31 Daviot Street Robbie is none too pleased with the results. He says to Derek 'bad results these for the ordinary working man'. At 20 Craigton Road Jimmy has gone to work happy on hearing the outcome of the election as Ruth prepares to go to work at Woolworth in Langlands Road. She feels miserable as she listens to the radio and reaches for the off button to switch off the speeches of triumph from the victors. The Conservatives had gained popularity with the slogan from Mr.McMillan 'You have never had it so good'. To many voters they compared the Labour austerity measures after the war with the new luxury goods that were entering their homes.

However, a crumb of comfort for Labour was that they gained rather than lost seats in Scotland and the Unionists failed to capture Glasgow. Govan was retained easily by Labour and Bruce Millan captured Craigton.

RESULTS:

**GLASGOW CRAIGTON:**
BRUCE MILLAN (Labour) 19,649   JACK NIXON-BROWNE (Unionistt) 19,047 Lab Maj 602

**GLASGOW GOVAN:**
JOHN RANKIN (Labour Co-op) 23,139 ANDREW HUTTON (Unionist) 13,319

G.McLENNAN (Communist) 1,869 Lab Maj. 9,820

Labour gained two seats in Glasgow and lost Kelvingrove At the end they held 10 of the 15 Glasgow seats with the Unionists holding the other five. Mr Park the Independent Labour Party from Drumoyne School increased his vote by around 50% to 740 votes.

**NATIONAL:**
CONSERVATIVE & UNIONIST PARTY 365 seats - 13,750,875 (49.4%)
LABOUR PARTY 258 seats—12,216,172 (43.8%)
LIBERAL PARTY 6 seats—1,640,760 (5.9%)

A great number of Govanites had enormous respect for Field Marshall Lord Montgomery; he was a national hero. Shortly before the general election he said 'Anyone that votes Labour is fit for the lunatic asylum'.
Immediately after the General election he withdrew his remark and apologised. Many Labour councils were unhappy because a sizable proportion of the men that had fought under him during the Second World war would have been Socialists.

The first day at Govan High arrives for Derek and virtually all of his class from Drumoyne. The weather is poor and heavy rain beats down on the pupils heading for the Langlands Road School. Derek has a new uniform and with the new arrivals is asked to stand outside in the courtyard of the reddish brick building. The other older pupils go straight in to the school.

At exactly 9 o'clock Mr.Greig comes out to read which class the new intake are to go to. The names are called out then 'Derek Wilson—Class 1B'. Class 1 B has Mr.Cuthbertson as form teacher on the upper floor of the school. Derek felt like a 'droont rat' as the rain which had gathered on his hair started running off down his collar and further down into his shirt.

' What a day said Mr.Cuthbertson and welcome to Govan Senior Secondary School'.

The name change of the school is a bit puzzling to most but everyone still thinks it is Govan High. Here is your timetable.

Every day seemed to have double sessions of Maths (Algebra, Geometry and Arithmetic), Miss Marshall will be your teacher. Every day will have double sessions of English (Language and Literature) several teachers names are read out.

Double French lessons (twice a week)—Miss Hoy.

Double Science lessons (Chemistry and Physics)- Mr.Maurice Hyman.

The other single lessons are read out and the much awaited music teacher.

Music—Mr.Mather. Someone at the back of the class whispered 'Gee Whiz'.

Sports, Art, History and Geography.

As the last announcement is made the bell rings and it is time to go to the playgrounds with the rest of the school. A return to Mr.Cuthbertson's class is made and the school rules and notices are read out.

In the afternoon the lessons start and the Derek's Khaki bag is soon starting to fill up with a multitude of books and notebooks. The last lesson of the day is single History with Miss Foxy Reynard. Derek initially thinks he has seen a giant bat; as the teacher wears a black cloak. Foxy is a largish lady and extremely intelligent.

During the course of the day the class caught sight of the headmaster a Mr.Hutchinson. He was an elderly man, seemingly aloof and rarely speaking to any pupil. His Deputy was a vicious Englishman called Mr. Bud Neil. When he took a class he would get the leather strap which was very think and stand it upright gripped in his hand. He would warn that any misbehaviour would not be tolerated.

At 20, Craigton Road, Jimmy is getting himself smartly dressed one Sunday evening. Ruth says 'It is unusual for you to be going to church on a Sunday night Jimmy ! I take it ye will be repentin' efter aw this drinking that ye dae'. Jimmy says 'It is rare I go to church Ruth but I could not really get out of this one. The Brotherhood are attending a church service at the MacGregor Memorial Church tonight !'.

Having adjusted his tie for one last time he sweeps back his dark wavy hair leaves the close and crosses the road to the Mac Gregor Memorial Church. Ruth smiles and closes the door behind him.

Four Freemason lodges are attending a divine service at the church. They are Lodges Corkerhill, Govandale, St.Columba and Ibrox. They have a large attendance.

The school lessons have started in earnest at Govan High and the music lessons are causing a lot of concern. They are held in the Dysart Street building and the teacher is Mr.Mather. Most felt before the music lessons that the reputation Mr.Mather had was probably over exaggerated. The one big plus Derek felt was that the lesson before was Arts which were held at the Ranch a good 10 minute walk away making the music lesson shorter than scheduled. One thing which most in the class were looking forward to was perhaps a chance to play a musical instruments. Unfortunately, the stock was low. It comprised only of a Tambourine (apparently donated by the local Salvation Army) with 2 sets of its metal jingles missing and two second hand triangles (apparently donated by the local boys brigade group). They were stored in a box behind   Mr.Mather's piano. The class was far too large for the seating capacity.

The two seated desks had three pupils and it was a squash. One day as the class entered the room they went to the desks and  there was a noise as the class settled. Then an almighty 'Whack'. Mr.Mather had produced his strap and slammed in on a desk adjacent to his piano. The wood varnish on   this desk was well worn and there was a slight groove where the music teacher had slammed down the tawse many times before. Mr.Mather said ' I do not expect such noise when you enter a class. You are here to learn music not to chatter; do I make myself clear ?'.

One girl said 'Yes Mr.Mather'.  Mr.Mather was a short man in his fifties, balding and with deep wrinkles on his forehead. Some previous pupils suggested he was in a Japanese Prisoner of war camp during the war. There was debate on whether that was on the British or Japanese side amongst the pupils. A few minutes into the lesson and Mr.Mather moved quickly across the classroom towards the desk where he kept his strap. He pointed and said 'You boy get out here !'.

A dozen mystified boy pupils tried to guess who he was pointing at before one lad who thought he was at the end of the finger stepped out. He was given three whacks with the strap in a particularly vicious fashion. He was made to put a towel over his wrists and hold his left hand under his right hand. After the first whack he was asked to change hands.  By instinct he tried to pull his hand away before the second whack and the towel fell on the floor.

This meant a fourth whack for allowing such a thing to happen. The boy was very red faced and in pain after the four whacks; after two on each hand had been concluded.

Of course the end of the lesson could not come soon enough for most and when the bell sounded there was great relief. Mr.Mather was a nasty vicious little man. He did like some of the class who had music inclinations. However, the vast majority did not enjoy his lessons in any shape or form.

At the British Oxygen Company's premises in Helen Street there was a loud explosion when a generator blew up. The firemen were quickly on the scene. When the firemen and the workers entered the Generator area there was a second much larger explosion. This was due to a build up of acetylene inside the generator. Six of the firemen and workmen were taken to the Royal Infirmary in Glasgow. Others who were not so badly hurt were taken to the Southern General before being allowed home.

The firemen injured were Station Officer W.Gills, Leading fireman A.Clubb, fireman P.Boyd, fireman J.O'Hagen, fireman W.Gilliland and leading fireman A.Campbell and fireman G.McFarlane. The workers injured were Joseph Patrick (49) Helen Street, Alex.Smith, Barloch Street, and Robert Brown.

The attendant in the cinema at 733 Govan Road noticed that one of the patrons, a youth, was staggering around in the aisles. The attendant approached the youth and asked him to leave. He immediately started to curse and swear and threatened to return with some of his friends to do the attendant over.

The police were called. At Govan Juvenile Court a 15 year old boy admitted the offence. Baillie James Bias said 'If we were in a room together and I had a strap I know what I would do to you. Unfortunately, we are not allowed'. The boy said he bought a bottle of wine from a licensed grocers on Govan Road.

He was put on probation for two years. It was conditional that he must be home by 10.00pm and must not drink. The boys grandfather said he could not control him.

James Hays (54) was working on repairing chimney stacks in Kellas Street Govan. Suddenly, he fell from the tenements into the back court. He was taken to the Southern General Hospital, bleeding from head wounds after his head hit a pile of bricks.

All interviewed said that the accident was a complete 'mystery'.

At Govan High as Class 1 B walked around the Main Building there always seemed to be a pungent smell. This came from the Science Lab and the Science Lessons of Mr. Maurice Hyman. The science teacher was a smallish man, bald and wore glasses. He had difficulty with speech and seemed to talk through his nose making his lessons difficult to understand.

With a large class, much of the time was spent standing in sizable groups around the experiment peering over shoulders to try and grasp what was going on. Derek found Chemistry a very hard subject to grasp. Remembering Atomic Numbers and Molecular Weights was difficult and the lessons were boring . The large science benches were pitted with years of acid burns and knife carvings. Derek was fascinated by a carving with wide grooves ' Big Tam; on top of; L; on top of; Mary

In the 'B' carving of 'Big Tam' was a blob of mercury which frequently split up. With a pencil the skill was to get all the bits of mercury into one big blob and from there move the blob around the groove. Mr Hyman was forgetful and an experiment would be started on one bench with a Bunsen burner boiling up a mixture of chemicals. He would move on to a different bench with another experiment while the class looked at the level of liquid in the first experiment getting lower and lower. Eventually, someone would say 'Mr. Hyman, that experiment over there looks like it is almost finished !'. The teacher would quickly move round to the bench. Too late ! A yellow smoke billows out of the top and the latest source of the Main Building's pungent aroma was started.

Mr. Maurice Hyman was none the less popular especially with the girls in the class. The girls all thought he was 'cute' . To all he was a thoroughly decent man teaching a very difficult subject to a sizable class with little or no materials. Whatever he did have to experiment with, he shared with the rest of the school by boiling it off. Despite having the appearance of a middle aged stereo-type he was remarkably fit. He once demonstrated a cart-wheel in the class and could touch the floor with the palms of his hands, legs absolutely straight, something no one else in the class could achieve. Derek often wondered what the Deputy Headmaster Bud Neil would have made of Mr. Hyman if he came in while he performed his fitness party pieces. The other part of Science was Physics and this was interesting. Derek always looked forward to this lesson.

The newsagents at 568, Govan Road had six schoolboy visitors. One ordered a bottle of lemonade and two of them went to the end of the counter. There they opened the bottle of lemonade and sipped it. The four other boys blocked the shop entrance by standing inside the door. Suddenly, one of the group went to the till forcing it open and taking a bundle of notes. All six ran out of the shop and headed towards Copland Road.

Several days later all six boys concerned were arrested. In Govan Juvenile Court one of the fathers pleaded that his son be spared a custodial sentence. 'Please, give my son another opportunity. I appeal to you sir in the name of God !'. The smartly dressed thirteen year old listened as Baillie Bias sentenced him to 14 days in a Remand Home. Two brothers aged 14 and 13 years were sentenced to 28 days in a Remand Home and two other 13 year olds were sentenced to 14 days each. Another boy who had not previously been in trouble was put on probation for one year. 207

Ruth sits at the table within their tenement flat at 20, Craigton Road. She is puffing on a cigarette and reading the In Memorium Columns in the Govan Press as ardently as ever. Jimmy is studying the horse racing runners and riders, pencil poised to write out his line. A ball crashes against the window. Ruth leaps up and opens the window. She says 'Away ye go; yell brek the windae !. Away wi ye !'.

She closes the window and asks Jimmy ' Are you going to Ibrox today ?' Jimmy says ' the season is over !'. Ruth replies 'Naw no that. Billy Graham giving a sermon; good man that !'. Jimmy says ' Not too sure !'. Ruth says ' You should go, you need redemption !'. Jimmy says ' What do you mean redemption ?'. Ruth continues ' Well for all that drinking ye dae for a start. The man above widnae approve of that '. Jimmy says ' Well what about you; you are not so perfect. Look at the way you swear at the boys when the ball hits the window'. Ruth says ' I do not swear at them the first or the second time. Only at the third time do I give them a blasting' . At that moment a ball smacked against the window and Ruth was up again opening the window and chasing the boys away. She closed the window and said to Jimmy ' That was number two !'.

Jimmy says ' If you come with me I will walk up to Ibrox and we will go and see it. You can buy tickets near the main entrance to get in. What religion is Billy Graham Ruth ?' Ruth replied 'Protestant !' Jimmy says ' Yes I know that Ruth, we would not be going to Ibrox to see the Pope !. What type of Protestant is he ?'. Ruth looks confused ' I do not rightly know Jimmy. We have a Church of Scotland so he must be Church of America !'.

Jimmy says ' I think I have heard him called Evangelical'.
The couple go to Ibrox and listen to the preachings of Billy Graham. The American had previously attended Scotland several years ago in an event held at the Kelvin Hall. A number of hymns were sang and the event passed off well.

During the day Govan has a large number of Religious groups all stopping and encouraging people in the street. Derek is visiting Govan and gets stopped by an American Mormon to talk about religion. After 5 minutes of persuasion Derek lets the Mormon know his parents are well into religion. 'Where do you all live ?' asks the Mormon. Derek replies '20, Craigton Road'.

As Jimmy and Ruth arrive home from Ibrox they meet with two Mormon's at the entrance of 20, Craigton Road. After a short discussion they enter the small tenement flat. Almost immediately the Mormon request that they all have solemn prayer to the Lord and all four are in prayer for around half an hour. Ruth makes them a cup of tea and eventually persuades them to leave on the pretext they must get ready to go out. Once gone Jimmy says ' Wait till I see Derek'.

Ruth says ' Well you keep saying you are religious but yea never go near the church Jimmy !'. Jimmy says ' Well after listening to Billy Graham I might just start going to the kirk'. Ruth says ' Aye right! The church is right across the road and you have been in it once. They have probably seen you stagger past enough times to know you are not one of them !'.

Five Govan youths decided they wanted a night at the dancing. The destination was the F & F Ballroom at 205 Dumbarton Road on the opposite side of the River Clyde.

On the way to the dancing they visited one or two public houses. While inside the Dance Hall they got into an argument and a general melee broke out. Chairs were thrown and chaos ensued before the five were apprehended and held in the managers office.

Andrew McGowan, (20) 14, Logie Street; Angus Healey (21) 74, Nethan Street; Robert Cockburn (20) 102, Blackstone Crescent; Cyril Gaffney, (18) 80,Nethan Street and Thomas Healey,(19) 74 Nethan Street.

Fiscal Robert Bord said the group were involved in a general melee bawling and shouting and causing alarm to other dancers. All five were fined £7 with an alternative of 60 days in prison.

An elderly lady, Miss Elizabeth Alexander, was in her shop at 451 Govan Road. Suddenly, four youths came into the shop. Two stood by the door while the other two went to the counter. One grabbed Miss Alexander and punched her on the face. The other went behind the counter and took a bundle of notes. The fourth youth ran off.

Miss Alexander was very small and stood on a box to sell her goods. She was taken in a police car on a tour of the area to see whether she could recognise the youths. Some time previously she had been attacked in similar fashion and £12 stolen from her.

Patrick Hoey (18) of 80, Kintra Street, was not happy when his mother suggested that a neighbour repaired their radiogram. He flew into a rage suggesting he could do the DIY on the radiogram himself. He picked up a pair of scissors and a tin plate and threw them at his mother. As his 12 year brother came in he kicked the kitchen door. The door hit his brother in the face and the police were called.

At Govan Police Court, Patrick's parents said he had a bad temper and was out of work. They were considering not allowing him back into the house. Baillie Robert McCutheon fined Hoey £3 which had to be paid immediately.

Skipper John Lockhart stepped off his Govan Ferry boat arriving at Wanlock Street. As he went to fasten the rope he heard a man begin to shout and swear at him because the ferry took too long from Meadowside. He then caught Mr.Lockhart by the tie and pulled him around the steps putting him in danger of falling into the River Clyde.

The police were called and the complainer was still bawling and shouting at the crew when they arrived. At Govan Police Court , Henry McKay(42) of 65, Cornwall Street, Kinning Park, admitted charges of breach of peace and assault. McKay said he had been on his way to work and had been shouting across the river for some time to get the ferry to cross. He was fined £5.

At Govan High, Class 1B was learning in English Literature Burn's 'Ode to a mouse' Derek thought it appropriate due to the number of mice which seemed to live in the Daviot Street tenement block where he lived. The first most famous verse.   Soon after arriving at Govan High most of the ex Drumoyne School pupils, including Derek, made a special effort to return to their old school. Mrs.Dewart had been an excellent teacher and had a spell of illness before the class had left for the last time.  Mrs Dewart was delighted to see that her old class had returned to thank her for the teaching and smiled broadly. She commented ' You all look so grown up now. How are you finding Govan High ?'. The answer from all was ' It's OK' and nothing else was added.


A landmark near the Govan High school was the Vogue Cinema. Many Govan children, including Derek, had attended the matinee's there over the years and with all Govanites the picture house was held with affection. A year previously there had been a fire at the cinema which caused considerable damage. The damage would have been worse had 59 year old Alex McBride the Caretaker at the Child Welfare Centre in Arklet Road not spotted the smoke coming from the building. The flooring and  50 seats in the stalls had been damaged. The cause was believed to have been someone throwing a cigarette on the floor. After some weeks the Vogue cinema was re-opened and performances re-started.


Jimmy Welsh arrives at the works yard of John Henderson. John says 'I have a job you will like Jimmy! St.Anthony's Chapel in Govan Road !!'.  Both John and Jimmy smile. Jimmy says ' You know me John a true professional !!'. John says 'I hoped and thought you would say that. Please carry out a survey and organise the project requirements.'  The scaffolding was required at the St.Anthony's Chapel in order to facilitate work on the Chapel roof. The scaffolding was 60 foot high. When Jimmy told Ruth about the project she laughed. ' I hope they don't ask you to confess otherwise ye'll be in ther fur a month !!'.   Jimmy says 'I have told John I will be professional. I went down there today and they are actually nice people. They showed me what they are doing around Govan looking out for the elderly and vulnerable'.

Ruth says 'Aye still widnae trust them. However, at 31 Daviot Street Robbie says the new neighbours opposite are Catholics and they seem nice enough'.

On a Saturday night James Duff from Greenfield Street got very drunk and decided to climb the scaffold at St.Anthony's Chapel to the very top. Once there he started to sing at the top of his voice. Many drinkers along Govan Road wondered where all the noise was coming from and looked up to see Duff singing. A sizable crowd gathered in apprehension as the painter by trade swayed backwards and forwards. Eventually, he was persuaded by the police to come down. He was asked in court why he climbed the scaffold. 'I did it for a bet' says Duff. 'Well you have lost your bet !. £3 pounds fine or 30 days in jail said Baillie James Will. Jimmy Welsh was in court and was relieved that no criticism was levied towards the scaffolding.

Ruth walks along Craigton Road with one of her neighbours. She is on her way to 'Housey– Housey' at the hall in 205 Crossloan Road. Ruth blethers away and they both hope that they can get a win. The evening is going well and the 190 present thoroughly enjoy the occasion. The Govan wumin blether away as only Govan wumin could. Suddenly the hall door bursts open and a squad of police officers burst in. Six of the organisers were arrested and taken down to the Govan Police Station for fingerprinting. The180 of those present were made to provide their names pending charges.

Ruth was furious when she arrived back at 20 Craigton Road. 'Jimmy, I hiv never seen anything like it !!. I wis sittin ther wi jist wan number tae get when in came the polis !'.

Jimmy says ' Well I have never heard of that before !. You will just have to do your gambling within the law Ruth !'. Jimmy smiled but Ruth did not and just stared at him.

At Govan Police Court Fiscal W.Grindlay outlined the case against the six accused. Mrs. Catherine Mc Minimee (36) of Moss Heights, Cardonald; Peter McGregor (50) of 31, Fairfield Street, Govan; Thomas Scott (33) of 10, Crossloan Road, Govan; George McMinimee (19) of 179, Queensland Drive, Cardonald; Duncan McIntosh (27) of 3, Elder Street, Govan; and John Hughes (27) of 38 Walkerburn Road, Cardonald.

Fiscal Grindlay said the raid was the first of its kind in Glasgow. When the Govan Hall opened it had about 120 people each paying 2 Shillings and 6 Pence for admission. Plain clothed police officers also attended and one of them won a prize of £5. On this occasion there were 12 games played and the prize money £26. On other occasions 200 and 300 people attended and prize money went up to £30.

Mrs.Mc Minimee said that they had applied for a license under the Lotteries Act to hold the Housey-Housey but the process seemed to take a long time. Each of the six were fined £10 or 30 days in jail.

Ruth and most of the Housey-Housey players were not happy. She awaited a letter from the Police telling her what was going to happen to her and the others. The Police let go several elderly people and also some younger players.

At Hawkhill School in Dundee the debate on corporal punishment for pupils was re-ignited. Four boy pupils were late for school and each was given one of the strap. One of the pupils Alan Smith told his father. His father decided he would have a word with the teacher and entered the playground to discuss the issue with the teacher Mr.Robbie.

Mr.Robbie advised Mr. Sydney Smith ; a garage hand; to take the issue up with the headmaster. Mr.Smith asked Mr.Robbie to take his spectacles off and when he refused he punched him twice on the head. Mr.Robbie was taken to hospital where they found that his nose had been fractured.

At Dundee Sheriff Court 37 year old Sydney Smith was jailed for 4 months. He said he thought his son had been unjustly punished as he had to take his 5 year old sister to school on the day in question. Mr.Smith was a former police officer.

A major row erupted at Bellshill Academy in Lanarkshire when two 14 year old girls refused to take the strap. They were backed by their parents. Georgina Wright and Jacqueline Baker were late getting into line for the afternoon session and spotted by a prefect. A teacher took them into a classroom and told them they were going to get the belt. They both refused and were taken to see the Rector. Again they refused to take the punishment and were sent home. The Rector wrote to both sets of parents. The girls contended that they did not hear the bell due to the noise. The parents backed the girls stance and the issue became a national news feature. The parents wanted a meeting with Rector Martin but he refused to meet them when they arrived at the school. They then contacted the local MP.

In Govan at Middlesex Street, Kinning Park four men decided that the argument they were having could not be resolved by conventional means. The four men (two on each side) stripped down to the waist for bare knuckle fighting. A large crowd gathered as they started swinging at their foes. When the police arrived a two of the fighters ran off. The remaining two continued to scrap and were arrested. At Govan Police Court Joseph McGealy (24) and David McGinty (38) were each fined £5 for breach of the peace.

At 712 Govan Road a crowd has gathered and some women have their hands clasped by the side of their faces. On the second floor John Mallon (52) has climbed out onto the ledge. He shouts 'I am gonnae jump !'. Below one of his pals shouts up 'John make sure ye hiv the 10 bob ye owe me in yer pockets !!'.

Behind Mallon efforts are being made by the police to break down the door which he has snibbed. Eventually the Fire Brigade were called and he was coaxed to go inside the tenement. At Govan Police Courts Fiscal W. Grindlay outlined that John Mallon was a known alcoholic. He was put on 12 months probation and sent to Alcoholics Annonymous for treatment.

At Battlefield Secondary School, 14 year old Jeanette Rooney has refused to take the strap. Jeanette slapped another girl on the bus journey to school. She was immediately expelled from the school when she refused to take the punishment from headmaster Mr.William Garland. After much media attention Jeanette agreed to go back to school and take the punishment but Mr.Rooney her father refused to let her.

The incident on the bus arose when Jeanette and her friend Susan McLaughlan tried to stop some other girls throwing nutshells at some of the passengers and other pupils. Susan also initially refused to take the strap. However after a few days she went back and got four of the belt.

Meanwhile at Bellshill Academy Rector Martin said that the pupils were told not to go near the wall where the girls were at the time the bell was rang. This was because they may not hear it. Both girls remained expelled and councillors and the local MP were involved trying to mediate.

A few days later at Battlefield Secondary School Mr. William Garland sent a letter to Mr.Rooney. He invited Jeanette to return to school. Mr.Rooney asked if Jeanette would be punished and the reply came back 'No, we will forget the whole matter. I am pleased it is all over'.

Govan had a visitor in the form of a runaway bullock. It ran down Govan Road pursued by police and helpers trying to catch it. No one knew where it came from and all efforts to catch it failed as it ran around the streets. Eventually it was cornered in Hoey Street and taken off to Paisley Market. Tuesday at Govan High and for Derek it means Art in the class of Mr.Speight. Derek is absolutely terrible at Art and quickly assumes the position of worst crayoning, painting and drawing. He thinks there is an art to art.

To make matters worse Mr.Speight has a habit of showing Derek's feeble effort against a spectacularly good effort by a classmate. Mr. Speight says ' If you look at this painting (Derek's) you can see how out of proportion the figures are. Now if you look at this one everything is just as it should be !'.

Mr. Speight has the reputation of being able to draw the strap the hardest in the whole of the school. On one occasion it was reputed he did have a mishap. He put the towel over a girls wrists. She is alleged to have tried to pull her hands out of the way as the strap came down. Somehow the force was then so great that it broke the girls wrist. Mr. Speight sent her packing off to the Southern General Hospital with one of her girl classmates. The one redeeming feature of the Art lesson was its location at the Ranch some ten minutes walk from the following lesson in Dysart Street. This was the Mr. Mather Music lesson. Hence an extra ten minutes could be 'skimmed off'. Mr.Mather usually said 'Whit kept ye lot !'.

Fairfield's Shipyard received a mammoth order for £3,500,000 for nine ferry boats for Turkey. On hearing the announcement many workers celebrated in the many Govan pubs.

At Bellshill Academy one of the two girls decides to go back to school and accept the punishment. Jacqueline Baker said she wanted to leave school with a clean record. Rector Martin gave Jacqueline one of the strap and Jacqueline said it did not hurt. Georgina White went to school and refused to take the strap. Once again she was sent home.

At the Vogue cinema the four women staff were a closely knit bunch. However, they had a good way of earning a little extra cash. The cashiers would issue tickets from the machine on some occasions. On other occasions they would refill the machine with old tickets and gain some cash after the counting up at the end of the evening. In total they defrauded the Vogue Cinema of £2 and 8 shillings over a period of time. They were caught by undercover police offcers. At Govan Police Court; Jean Kelly(21) of Fairfield Street, Joyce Morton(20) of Kingsland Drive, Patricia Daly(20) of Arthurlie Drive and Catherine O'Neil (32) were fined a total of £30.

At Hamilton Sheriff Court the parents of Georgina White are in dock. They are accused of refusing to let their girl go to school without a reasonable excuse. After the charges were read out they pleaded 'Not Guilty' and a date two months hence was set for the trial.

Two youths pushed over a motor bike on Govan Road. When the owner went to pick it up they were punched and kicked by the youths. At Govan Police Court, Raymond McGowan (19) and Thomas Watson (18) of Tormore Street, Drumoyne admitted the offences of breach of the peace and assault. McGowan was fined £10 or 60 days for each offence. Watson was fined £5 or 20 days for each offence.

The Govan Bowls Clubs gave out their annual awards.

**DRUMOYNE:** Champion R.Blair. Runner up  W.Copland
Presidents  J.Guthrie. Runner up G.Boyle
Junior Championship  D.Duncan  Runner up G.Douglas
Select pairs  J.Guthrie   W.Innes
Balloted pairs  R.Blair W.Copland


**LINTHOUSE:** Champion N.Hay  Runner up J.Woodsides
Presidents  J.Kinnear  Runner up G.Conkie
Vice Presidents  J.Wales, runner up G.Dunn
Club pairs  G.Milne  G.Smith
Select pairs  A.Hunter   A.Herald
Rink; P.Fleming, T.Steedman, T.Kinloch  N.Hay

The trial of Mr.White at Hamilton Sheriff Court in respect to 'no school' for his daughter Georgina was opened but immediately adjourned on legal points.

A few weeks later the trial resumed and Mr.White was found guilty. He was fined £1 but initially elected to go to prison on the issue. Judge Hay said 'You are being very stupid !' After several minutes Mr.George White said he would pay the fine.

At the Glasgow Education Committee meeting Councillor Dr. Daniel Docherty from Govan was representing one of his constituents on the basis that a girl had been excessively punished in one of the Govan schools. The Education Committee immediately put a block on naming the school and making it sub-judice for anyone to make any statement on the issue.

At 31 Daviot Street, Derek opened the door one Sunday to go out. Opposite just chapping the door was a Roman Catholic priest. Mrs. Mc Greskin opened the door and the priest said 'Hello Mrs.Mc Greskin, I noticed that Anne Marie was not at Mass this morning so I just popped round to make sure everything is all right'. Mrs. Mc Greskin said ' Anne Marie has a cold and will be at confession or mass next week'.

The Priest was very welcome into the world of the family and it was seen that he had a concern for one of the faithful. To Protestants like Derek and Robbie they felt it was an intrusion and the RC church keeping an eye on them. Robbie always thought that the RC people were good but had reservations on the teachings of the RC Church.

The McGreskin's were proving to be really good neighbours; always friendly and always helpful.

At a Govan Secondary School one pupil had enough. A 13 year old boy was asked to leave his seat in the Art Class but refused. After an altercation the boy swore at the teacher. He also gripped the teacher by the clothes near his throat and threatened to punch him. The boy was taken to the headmasters office. The art teacher said that the boy got the strap which he 'richly deserved'. On returning to the Art Class another altercation started between the two and the 13 year old boy threw a heavy vase, the object of class painting, at the teacher catching him a glancing blow to the head. The police were called.

At Govan Juvenile Court Baillie Gladys Dewar ordered the boy to be detained for 7 days pending reports. The school said that the boy was always disobedient and always threatening teachers and refusing to accept punishment. Baillie Gladys Dewar asked the boy if he knew right from wrong. He replied 'Yes'.

Ruth and Jimmy are on their way to the Wrestling at the Govan Town Hall. In the ring is the famous Zebra Kid, from the USA, unbeaten in 1,000 bouts. He is 6 feet tall and weighs between 22 and 23 stone. However, his run had just been ended by Louis Thez.

# GOVAN HIGH SCHOOL

MAGAZINE COMMITTEE
Standing: Tom Rae, Roy Ryder.
Sitting: Mrs. Methven, Jean Macaulay, Andrew Rennison (Editor).
Wilma Kerr, Miss Russell.

*PITLOCHRY EXCURSION*

Above—Barry Landman—
Excellent English Teacher

## At The Very Top

Dux of Govan High School, 17-years-old Jean D. Macaulay, took time off from her studies the other day to pose for the photographer. Full report and prizewinners who

received their awards in the Vogue Cinema, Langlands Road, yesterday, will appear in the "Press" next week.
—Plaza Photo

Myra Banks nee Soutar
1961 Dux award

Mr.Bud Neil—Deputy Head Master
The Fearsome Enforcer

The 1962 Govan High fire.

**photo 6**

# CHAPTER 21
## THE MAN BORN TO BE A SHIPYARD OWNER

Sir William Lithgow was a man with a shipbuilding yard pedigree. He received his baronet as a result of his fathers dedication and contribution to the shipbuilding industry on the River Clyde. Born in 1854 the original William Lithgow started as an apprentice draughtsman at Port Glasgow. Both his parents died before he was 17 and he was left £1,000 to be invested in shipbuilding. His father had been a seller of cotton and was wealthy. They built a shipyard in Port Glasgow and William Lithgow was the draughtsman and designer. Initially, most of the ships were iron, slow but steady for cargo transport across the oceans. Lithgow standardised much of the shipbuilding design reducing the costs. In 1890 the shipyard broke records by building no fewer than 34 ships totalling 70,000 tons in one year and received the Blue Riband award for maximum output.

William Lithgow married and moved to Drums in Langbank. He soon became known as a millionaire shipowner. In 1907 William Lithgow suffered serious health problems and died. His initial investment of £1,000 had been turned into £2,000,000.

After his death the shipyard was kept running by his close associates before James Lithgow and his brother, Henry, took over. James Lithgow was no less dynamic than his father and with the agreement of his brother, Henry, took on the public role. James Lithgow became Sir James Lithgow after the award of a baronet in 1925 for achievements to Shipbuilding. When Fairfields shipyard in Govan looked as though it might fail James Lithgow assumed a controlling interest. When James Lithgow died in 1952 his son William was too young to take on control. His wife controlled things until William was ready.

The Elder cinema closed down for a while which brought sadness to many Govanites. Although not enjoying the patronage it deserved most in Govan had a soft spot for the picture house. There was a pleasant surprise when it was announced that hopefully the pictures would return and be supported also by boxing promotions provided by Mr.Jim Docherty. Wrestling and Boxing promotions seemed to have great support in Govan, more than anywhere else where they seemed to fail.

At Govan High something which gave Derek and a lot of the Govan High pupils a lot of pleasure was the sweets bought at the small tuck shop store adjacent to the Dysart Street classes. The wine gums they sold had a unique taste for all the different flavours in the bag. All were fantastic especially the black gums. French was proving an interesting lesson. Miss Hoy was a very slight lady and was an excellent teacher. Although French would not be high on Derek's list of having success , the lessons he enjoyed.

Miss Hoy spoke the language  perfectly and the class learned an enormous amount of French words. Putting the words together into sentences was proving more difficult but knowing some words was a good start. One day Miss Hoy introduced a trainee French teacher. The name was difficult to pronounce so the shortened version of Monsieur  Lang,lang,pee was provided by the pupils. Monsieur Langlangpee was all sweetness and light when Miss Hoy was introducing him. After several weeks Miss Hoy decides to allow Monsieur Langlangpee to hold his first class by himself. Soon after his class starts he starts becoming frustrated that few in the class can pronounce French in the way he would like.

He then started throwing the board rubber at some of the boys he thought were not listening. Fortunately he was not provided with a strap.  One of the boys Iain Duncanson threw the rubber back and all hell broke out.  A brief 'skirmish' broke out and Duncanson invited Monsieur Langlangpee to a fight behind Dysart Street. Monsieur Langlangpee accepted but did not show up on the appointed day and time.  The French lessons under Miss Hoy went to script most weeks. Once a month Monsieur Langlangpee took the class which was always eventful especially his attempted teaching of Iain Duncanson. Invariably the teacher would lose his temper and start throwing insults to many in the class. Derek and many in the class felt he was a complete hothead and learned little in his lessons. After six months or so he went back to France with much relief amongst the pupils.

Sir William Lithgow had taken over the Chairmanship of Lithgow's Shipyard in Port Glasgow from his mother. He was keen and wanted to restore the yard to its former glory. He was concerned as he walked around the shipyard and saw empty berths where once there were sizable ships under construction.     Sir William decided action was needed and he wanted to lead from the front.  William Lithgow's yard was completely re-modernised with the latest technologies and construction techniques.

He put in some ideas of his own on design. Following the upgrade of the yard he assembled his sales force. They produced a film of the yard showing the techniques to be used. Also they showed the programme of works shown in the form of a bar chart. Sir William identified the big order placers in America and South America and with his sales force he was on his way to battle for orders.  The presentations were well received and some orders promised by very interested clients. Proposals and quotations would be submitted and Lithgow's were in with a real chance of winning some bids on price.

At Govan High it is a proud day for some pupils at the awards:
Jean McAuley was Dux winner; Runner up;  Alan O'Mara.
Intermediate Dux winner; Marjorie Smith
Junior Secondary Dux winner: Moira Donald  and Robert Lawrie.
Rotary Club prizes: Andrew Ronaldson and Edith Wilson.
Govan Burgh Band for music; Margaret Stewart.

Sir William Lithgow has just returned from his promotion tour of America and South America. The Shipbuilder was pleased with the way the tour had gone. He felt his presentation team had done him proud as they unveiled the features within the yard. The ships would be built on time and to budget. As he sat at his desk he opened a few letters which were not to his liking. Firstly, the Government had rejected his applications for funding. Secondly, on the basis that his yard was going to be more successful the new Scottish rating system would mean an extra £30,000 local tax would be charged to the yard. He got his secretary to demand an immediate meeting with the Scottish Ministers responsible; most especially Mr. McClay the Scottish Secretary.

Alexander Thomson arrived just in time to miss the last train from Govan Cross to Shields Road. He decided the best option was to walk through the tunnel in the pitch black to his one stop destination. The track had a high voltage line. When he arrived at Shields Road he was spotted at the station entrance by two policemen. In Govan Police Court, Thomson (33) was charged with disorderly conduct by walking on the track which had a live line. Baillie James Will said 'You are lucky to be here hale and hearty'. Thomson said 'We went out on Saturday night. I promised some friends that I would have their tea ready for when they got home'. Baillie Will said' Were you trying to be funny or smart ?'. Thomson replied 'Smart'. Baillie Will said ' If you had stumbled against the live rail would that have been smart ?'. Thomson said 'No. However, I did get home in time and had the tea ready !' Baillie Will fined Thomson who admitted being drunk £2.

There was a fight in the pub at 59 Langlands Road. The police were called but when they tried to arrest the 'fighters' they were attacked by some of the customers. Extra Policemen were summoned and five arrests were made. Watching proceedings was Mrs Herrity of 61 Langlands Road the mother of four of the men being charged. They were John (31), Hugh (28), Joseph (23) and James (21). The other man was Thomas Price (25). Baillie McKinlay told the Herrity's. 'Any mother would be proud to have four sons but not four sons like you '. All five were jailed for 60 days.

Lithgow's Shipyard sales force, buoyed by the interest they had generated in their trip to the Americas, made similar presentations around Europe. They were rewarded when they obtained two orders totalling £2,000,000. One was for an ore carrier for the Currie Line and the other was for a bulk cargo carrier from the Kristian Jegsens Redeiri based at Bergen in Norway. A few days previous they had received two similar sized orders from   Simonsen and Astrup based at Oslo in Norway. One order brought some satisfaction to Sir William Lithgow. It was the one from the Currie Line who had moved their shipbuilding to a German Yard away from Lithgow's. Another bit of good news was the return to work of the yard shipwrights when an 8 week strike by the Union's was resolved. The Lithgow's shipbuilding berths were beginning to fill up.

At Springburn, John Henderson owner of the Scaffolding company is unhappy with the proposed new rates system. He is going to appeal against a ground rateable value increase of around 50%. He talks about the situation with Jimmy Welsh his long time friend and effective project manager. John says 'I do not know how we are going to afford these increases Jimmy boy'. Jimmy says 'Well I suppose when a recession comes along the Government must look to get money in from where it can. However, the Labour Corporation in Glasgow is outrageous. John says 'The Labour group are blaming the central Government in Whitehall for the increases with reductions in grants'.

Jimmy returns home in the evening to 20, Craigton Road where Ruth sits in front of the fire. He is unhappy and says 'Ruth, I was speaking to John today and the work situation does not look so good. He is thinking of laying off a few of the men. I do not know if my job is safe while this recession lasts'. Ruth says ' I told ye not to vote for the Unionists !. ''You have never had it so good'' he said and you believed him ! I have not much, never had much and with you and your drinking never likely to have much'. Jimmy says 'I know Ruth. I will see if I can get a job in England. There are plenty of jobs down there'.

Sir William Lithgow has a plan. Following his successful sales efforts, helped by young enthusiastic Sales executives, he has plans in place to build a few yards in South America. The idea is bold but still in its infancy. However, his immediate concern is lowering the rateable value claim on the ground of his 'tail o' the bank' site. Going forward he thinks that the increase will add £15,000 to £30,000 cost to each vessel. He and the other shipyard owners are assembling their case for a rates re-evaluation to Mr.McClay and Lord Craigton for the Government.

A fog descends on Govan and the outlook in economic terms looks as bleak as the weather. A choking and arid taste is in everyone's throats as they wrap scarves around their mouths. A number of bad road accidents occur and the buses drive at a snails pace out of the Govan Cross bus stands, headlights dipped to pierce the gloom. Trains were badly delayed, no planes were flying out of Renfrew Airport and shipping was virtually at a standstill.

The Govan Housing stock was in a poor state around the Riverside part of the burgh with many slums. Glasgow Corporation were desperate to get new sites to build on but were hampered by Green Belt conditions preventing building. Baillie Gibson the sub convenor on the Glasgow Housing committee said 'Only 3 out of every 13 currently on the housing list of 130,000 will be re-housed in the next five years'.

The Clyde Tunnel was making progress but Govan was saddened with the news of the first major accident and deaths. Four large sandstone blocks fell and landed on top of the tunnel where a number of men were working including Owen Gallacher (42) of Thistle Street, Gorbals and Edward McNulty (22) of Buchan Street. Both were rushed to nearby Southern General Hospital but both died of their injuries.

The weather was bleak and extremely cold. The boys of Govan High Class 1B filed out of the school in two's and passed the Vogue Cinema, along Crossloan Road and on to Greenfield School. It was swimming lessons. On entering the swimming pool the early arrivals had the benefit of the cubicles inside the swimming hall. The other boys had to carry on to a set of cubicles around the back of the swimming hall nicknamed the 'Freezers'. On this particular day they could not have been given a more apt name. The water from the previous lessons on the floor had frozen over.

The skill was to try and move around on the wooden slatted boards and get back into the Swimming Pool Hall. The gentle noise of the pool pump could be heard alongside the boys chattering of teeth. On reaching the hall the boys were always ushered over to the far side of the pool from the cubicles and told to stand in a line. The reason was for Sports Master Mr.Mc Cracken to check the length of the toe nails before the boys entered the pool. He would say ' I am checking today for any Russian Wolfpeckers before you go in ! Those boys whose toenails are a bit long were given a large pair of rusting scissors and a bucket and told to go in a spare cubicle to trim accordingly. Fortunately, everyone had been forewarned so the scissors were never required.

Greenfield Pool was in essence too shallow for the High School pupils; it had been designed for very young swimmers of Primary School age. The deep end was no more than 4 feet deep and the shallow end barely 2 feet deep. The art of swimming was confined to teaching the doggy paddle which usually meant the pupils toes cracking against the bottom of the pool at the shallow end. However, for most the lessons provided a welcome escape from some very mundane days at the High School. Ruth is leaving Woolworth's after work one evening when she meets Jim Leslie. With his brother John they were in the same class at Govan High many years before. Ruth enquires about John and Jim tells her he is happy in England with Sandra. He also tells Ruth that he and his mother will once again be helping out the Kelvin Hall Circus. Ruth says that she has already booked tickets for an evening and will be present with Derek and Jimmy. Jim tells of some of the acts. The top act have just flown in from Chicago the 'windy city'. The famous American/Italian Bertolaccini family of acrobats. The Circus was still down at the far end of the Hall with the various rides in between. The dodgems were great fun with some lads seemingly intent on ramming every car in sight. The Circus was packed with spectators. The crack of the whip inside the tigers cage by the Master encouraging the animals up onto stools brought applause. The clowns made the kids laugh and a whole host of animals performed as never before. Ruth loved the entire afternoon with her 'man' and son.

During the latter months of the previous year Derek had joined the Greenfield Club. This club was based at Greenfield School and offered learning skills. In Govan High Class 1 B there was little in the way of craft skills as the class was classified as 'Academic'. The Greenfield Club offered training in woodwork and other good craft skills. The trainers were all good skilled people and Derek soon made a wooden boat with a mast. Following the woodwork lessons, swimming was popular in the Greenfield School Pool. However, after several weeks walking home in increasingly cold weather Derek had decided that he wished to play more football. His mother Ruth agreed and said it was a pity to leave a very popular, good and well run Club. Alexander Stephens invited many of the press, shipowners and engineering world to introduce their new diesel engine. It is the biggest diesel engine in Britain weighs 700 tons and is the size of a house. It was started up on supercharge. The engine was to be installed on the ship City of Melbourne scheduled to be launched from the Linthouse yard.

Patrick Harvie a 39 year year old boiler scaler was disappointed when he arrived home at 62 Whitefield Road, Govan. His wife had not arranged a party for their son so he spat in her dinner. His wife picked up the dinner and threw it on the fire. At this point he punched her, knocked her down and kicked her. After that he broke 62 panes of glass in their home. In Govan Police Court, Harvie said he was drunk and very disappointed that his wife had not arranged a birthday party for their son. Baillie Vallance sentenced Patrick Harvie to 60 days in prison.

The Govan High schooldays are becoming very mundane for Derek. However, one subject where he is doing well is Geography. Mr Mc Dermot the teacher is a small man by stature and a good teacher. The lessons are interesting and varied. At Maths Mr Cheyne is also good and Derek enjoys Geometry but not Algebra to the same degree. However, one slight diversion created interest for the pupils. Mr.Cheyne was an exceptional Chess player and he taught the class the basic moves of the game. Around once a month after school he would set up boards and pieces and play a simultaneous exhibition against around 20 pupils. Of course he would win them all. Derek got a few books out of the library on Chess and learned the basic openings. He selected the Ruy Lopez and the Scotch game (both Pawn to King 4 first moves) as white. As Black it was the Sicillian Defence or the Robatsch Defence. It was a game Derek enjoyed but could not spend as much time on it as he would like.

The other main Maths Teacher was Miss Benny Marshall. As well as providing the Maths lessons Benny also took the after school 'homework class'. The homework classes are essentially a class available for after school catch up. Tea is offered at 2 pence each cup but most of the pupils call it dishwater. Derek tends to use the homework class for catching up with doing usually 100 lines.

' I must concentrate on my lessons.

I must concentrate on my lessons.

I must concentrate on my lessons etc.

Derek is not at all happy at Govan High School and things are not getting any better.

At Govan Police Court a 16 year old boy is in dock accused of smashing windows in Neptune Street and Broomloan Road. He pleads guilty. With a friend, James McPherson of 138 Harmony Row who did not turn up at court, they also kicked in windows on a shop at 289, Summertown Road. At Neptune Street a bottle had been thrown through a families window and two plate glass windows at a shop at 159 Broomloan Road. The youths escaped through the back courts from the police but were later traced. Total damage was estimated at £99.

The 16 year old boy was sent to a Remand Home awaiting reports.

At Fairfields Shipyard the Boilermakers Society were in dispute with the Company. Fairfields quickly laid off other trades likely to be affected by the dispute. 100 members of the Boilermakers Society are involved and these include welders, caulkers, platers and burners. 150 other workers were laid off. 500 members of the Boilermakers Society scheduled a meeting at South Govan Town Hall. At the meeting the dispute moved to the over-reaction of Fairfield to suspend the 150 other trades as a reprisal and vindictive.

At Lithgow's the Shipwrights were threatening to go on strike in support of a wage claim. The news was met with dismay by the Lithgow's management. A spokesman said ' At a time like this when we are struggling for survival this is the worst thing that could happen'. A few days later Lithgows announced that the sales force had just received another order from overseas . The Jamaica Banana Products placed an order for £1,000,000 for a Banana Boat.

Derek has decided to join the 164th Boys Brigade based at St.Kierans Dean Park Parish Church on Copland Road. The decision was taken because of the friendship with classmates Ian Clark and Rab Warrender. Both were good footballers and could have easily got into the school teams. However, like many other boys in the age group they decided to play for the Boy's Brigade which they attended.

On a Friday evening Derek sets off from West Drumoyne and the bus journey ends at Govan Cross. He walks along Govan Road in the dark, running past the entry to the notorious Wine Alley, and on. He walks as far as Copland Road and a short walk takes him to the Church. Ian and Rab are there to welcome him and they proceed down the side of the church and up stairs at the rear to a small hall. There Derek is welcomed by the Captain Bill Caddy the leader and his two assistants Bill Taggert and Dan Thompson. Bill has the nickname of 'The Cancer Kid' due to his continuous smoking.

Both Bill and Dan now in their late 20's have been associated with the 164th BB since they were boys. Robert Waters is the senior Boy in the group and with Jim Parr they demonstrate the activities. Each week always starts with marching and formations. For the first few weeks Derek has only partial kit but soon has the full requirement. A small round hat, a white sash/belt clean smart black shoes and a shirt and tie. Ruth purchases most of the items and feels proud when she sees her son looking smart and tidy. She says to Derek ' Ye look a million dollars Derek, Ye'll be havin awe the lassies after yeh !'. From the outset Derek enjoys the BB and the activities in which they participate; signalling and morse code are particularly interesting.

Training for the Physical Exercises takes place on Wednesday evenings at Broomloan Road School's hall. Jumping the Horse with hand stands is frightening at first but soon he manages to master the leap. The last half of the evening session is taken up with football.

Around Govan there was a well known joke in respect to the Albion Dog Track, across the road from Ibrox Stadium. 'Is that dugs comin 'oot ?'. Naw it's the mugs that are comin 'oot, the dugs are still inside'.

In 1960 the Albion Dog Track closed its doors for the last time after dwindling attendances at its race meetings. Rangers were already using the centre of the track as their training ground and it was learned that they had purchased the ground from under the noses of Glasgow Corporation from the liquidated Glasgow Albion Racing Company. The Corporation wanted the ground for housing and it seemed likely that they would now have to purchase the defunct dog track from Rangers. Rangers claimed that they wished to remain at the Albion. The Corporation decided by a vote of 54 to 28 to start negotiations with Rangers for the Compulsory purchase of the Stadium.

Councillor J.C.Graham said that Rangers did not 'jump the gun' in purchasing the Albion. They are not that type of club. They are a credit to Glasgow'. Councillor William Campbell said it was strange that the Albion Company had been in liquidation for a year and the Corporation about to start a compulsory purchase that it suddenly changed hands.

Strikes still prevail along the River Clyde in the shipyards. The district delegate of the Boilermakers Society Mr. John Chalmers said that the problem was the lack of top quality management. Alfred Holt and company, the operators of the Blue Funnel line, placed orders at Fairfields for two cargo ships. However, they placed the remainder of the order for a further two similar cargo ships at yards in Holland.

Lord Aberconway at John Brown's Shipyard in Clydebank warned that difficult times were ahead for the River Clyde shipyards, even if his yard was to be successful in the bid for the new Queen liner. A few days later along the Clyde yards 500 workers were out on strike and another 500 laid off due to no work as a result of the strike.

Sir James Lithgow   Shipbuilder

Poor quality photo catches The Master of the Re-count. Jack Nixon Browne     Unionist Campaigning at the Moss Heights

LITHGOW'S SHIPYARD—
PORT GLASGOW 1950's

Sir William Lithgow
The man born to be a shipyard owner

Photo  4

# CHAPTER 22
## POWER TO THE GOVAN PEOPLE

John Gillespie and Frank Mulvenney meet at the Brechins Bar to have a drink and discuss the politics of the countless strikes on the River Clyde shipyards. Frank says ' The Government has got a credit squeeze on and we seem to be in a recession. They seem to have a set of rules for one group of people and a completely different set for the rest of us'. John says 'What is depressing me is the complete lack of anything from the Glasgow Labour MP's. They might as well be Tories. Little wonder that the turnouts at the Corporation elections are so low and likely to go down further'. Frank says 'You must take your hat off to the Govan Shipyard Union leaders. They have no support from anyone but they battle away for what they believe in regardless. The TUC should support them'. John says 'The Rating issue is the cause of many of the problems with a Labour dominated Corporation putting them up 50% or more. How can you ask some Govanites who live in a complete slum to pay the same as someone who has the means to own a private house. Where does the extra money come from to pay these rates come from when we have a pay freeze ?'. Frank says ' For the first time ever even the Shipyard owners are on our side on this one. Lithgow has the right idea !!' They both laughed and drank down quickly the first of their 'hauf and hauf' drinks.

Derek enjoyed the Broomloan Road school hall training with the 164th Boys Brigade. Discussions took place amongst the brigade about the presence of an individual called Bogo Logo at the football matches. Bill Caddy, Dan Thompson and Jimmy Taggart said it would be impossible to stop him attending matches at the 50 pitches.

However, they would make sure he was well monitored and chased if he became a nuisance. One of the brigade said Bogo had been involved in a fracas the previous weekend. A motorcyclist almost knocked him down when he stepped out into Govan Road. The motor cyclist stopped to see if he (Bogo) was alright. Bogo went over to him and told him to take his strapped helmet off . The cyclist refused so Bogo forcibly took the helmet off after a struggle. Once the helmet was off he hit the cyclist over the head with a bottle which smashed. He then helped the motor cyclist to put his helmet on with blood streaming down his face and told him to get down to the Southern General straight away. Derek had already seen Bogo at some of the matches and thought he must stay well clear of this individual at all costs. It was said his name was a shortened version of a Polish name which no Govanites could pronounce. Derek is given some bad news from some of the BB group. ' Bogo disnae like ye Derek, so I should watch out.' Derek says 'I have never spoken to him and do not really know him !!' The reply came 'It disnae matter just stay well out of his way if you see him. He is just pure mad !'.

A normal Friday evening saw learning of the morse code and signalling. On the way back to Govan Cross Derek sees Bogo walking down Govan Road in front of him. He decides to cross over to the other side and once level with Bogo runs. Bogo spots Derek and gives chase. Derek is the faster runner and is able to cross back over before the Plaza and looking behind notices that Bogo has given up the chase thankfully. For Now !!

The propaganda war on the shipbuilding industry continued with the Government announcing that the Shipyards were likely to be the odd men out in a new prosperous UK. They cited labour problems , high costs and reluctance to accept new ideas. The Shipbuilding industry on the River Clyde claimed that the report was several years out of date and a new young management team led by Sir William Lithgow had indeed invested heavily in modernisation.

They advised that some £25,000,000 had been spent ugrading the yards. The foreign competitors were well behind and using aged machinery and techniques to produce their ships. The River Clyde yards had brought in a young enthusiastic management team to push forward the Shipbuilding effort. However, the main danger still remained as poor labour relations with countless demarcation disputes affecting production.

Meetings took place all along the River Clyde shipyards and the employers offered a pay rise of 8 shillings and 6 pence more for semi skilled workers (7 shillings and 6 pence for the unskilled). In return they wanted more co-operation on how they could step up efficiency. The cost to the Shipyards was £5,000,000 per year. Ted Hill of the Boilermakers Society said 'If we can help in any way we will. However, it is up to the other trades as well'.

George Davidson (21) was a happy young man. The apprentice naval architect at Alexander Stephen's received a cheque from the Worshipful Company of Shipwright's. The award was presented by the Chairman of Alexander Stephens and gained for work in the yard and also achievements at Higher National Certificates at College. George said 'This has been a wonderful thrill. I have always been interested in ships since I was a wee boy'.

As Easter approached it was time for the Church service at the MacGregor Memorial. The Govan High classes went down Crossloan Road in twos and entered the Church which soon became almost full. The service lasted approximately one hour with the minister explaining the meaning of Easter and the resurrection of Christ. A series of class exams were due after the holiday and Derek was not at all confident of achieving decent marks in many subjects. Robbie was hanging in with a job as a labourer at Fairfields yard. Each morning Robbie prepared for his day at Fairfields shipyard. He had his usual metal container with two compartments at each end. Tea in one end, sugar in the other. He also had a small glass bottle full of milk.

225

Alexander Stephen's and Sons shipyard were in a state of shock. Following the Rate re-evaluation they anticipated a big increase in the rateable value of their site. However, what they did not visualise was an eight fold increase the rateable value of the site. The increase was from £5,625 to £46,000.

The increase at Fairfields Shipyard was from £13,359 per annum to £63,250 per annum. Both yards said they would appeal. The Greenock Chamber of Commerce were appealing to the Government on behalf of the tail o' the bank' shipyards.

At Govan High School the Sports Masters were enthusiastically organising the School Sports Day. The preliminary rounds to the Finals day were being held during lessons. For Derek it proved to be a complete washout in not reaching a single event semi final, let alone final. The long jump saw only a few of the pupils actually reach the sand pit as the jump line was a fair distance from the pit. For Derek the high jump saw the bar come down twice in the two allocated jumps. The running was better but in close finishes Derek was edged out. Not too many entered the few field events. The shot putt saw an extremely heavy ball thrown only a few feet.

So the big day arrived at Pirrie Park. Glorious sunshine on a Wednesday afternoon and the whole school in attendance. The only events left for the also rans to enter were the Long Distance events and the Pillow Fight. The Long distance race was over a mile and had a large field standing on the start line. The pistol fired and everyone just ran their hearts out. The Pillow Fight competition was a straight knock out. Two Boys sitting opposite one another on a greasy log with a pillow. The object was simple; Knock your opponent off before he knocks you off. Derek got a bye in the first round and managed to duck the pillow from the second boy before hitting him off the pole. The third round saw Derek's opponent make a huge swing only partially connected and unbalanced went crashing down onto the safety mat. Derek thought having reached the fourth round he may be in with a chance. However, a crashing blow to the chin soon had him spinning off the pole and the competition run had come to the end. Sports Day was good fun at the school and certainly broke up the tedium of many of the lessons. For Derek the exams had not gone well as he struggled in virtually all subjects. However, all the class marks were low in most subjects but that proved little consolation. The first year at Govan High School was drawing to a close.

The Govan Hall Wrestling evenings on Friday nights were popular and been a source of enjoyment for 3 or 4 years. However, they had a rival for the show when Wrestling started at the Kelvin Hall instigated by well known professional promoters. They managed to secure some top flight wrestlers including Billy Two Rivers (a Mohawk Indian) and tag wrestlers. The attendances soon began to build. With the competition the days of Govan Town Hall Wrestling were numbered.

The Clydeside Shipyard owners were seething at the rate increases and they went by deputation to see Lord Craigton at Edinburgh. Among those present were Mr.W.B.Johnstone Director of Alexander Stephens and Chairman of the Clydeside Shipbuilders Association. Sir William Lithgow. Sir Murray Stephen. Mr.John Brown. Mr.McClay (Barclay Curle).

The Scottish TUC threw their weight behind the Shipyard Owners in their objection to the new rating system. They released a statement 'It was their legislation which let loose the assessors to make their calculations without, seemingly, any thought or notion as to the significance as to what they were doing or of its consequences '.

Vice-Admiral J.Hughes-Hallett , Parliamentary Secretary, Ministry of Transport said 'These are very difficult times and rating responsibilities were as applicable to shipbuilding as any other industry. However, the weight of valuations now imposed were ill timed and ill conceived'.

The increased rents to most households and a pay pause brought the trade unions out onto the street. 100,000 workers came out on an official day of action along the River Clyde and on the Govan yards the strike was solid. A march of 1,500 went from Glasgow Green to Govan and on to Tinto Park home of Benburb Football Club. The march was led by the Caledonian Ladies Pipe Band and the marchers heard speeches from Dan MacGarvey (Boilermakers Society) and Jack Fergus (Amalgamated Engineering Union) and Cyril Bence (Dunbartonshire Labour MP).

Many at the march were disappointed that the local Govan Labour MP was not present to support the strike. They were dismayed the following day when Gerald Nabarro a Conservative MP accused the Govan Labour MP of snoring in the House of Commons during Question Time.

The Plaza was still a popular cinema serving up a diet of main film, B film, cartoon, Pearl and Dean adverts plus trailers for next weeks films. The small kiosk just outside the entry sold cigarettes, cigars, sweets, drinks and much more. Derek tried out a small bag of hot roasted salted peanuts a few times on previous visits and enjoyed them. One evening he decides to have a full bag of peanuts, scoffed the lot and felt unwell on the way home on the No.34 bus. A feature of the Plaza was the railway line which ran adjacent to the cinema. The train would come out of Harland and Wolfe at ten to five most days returning from delivering stock and materials. It would cross Govan Road and disappear down the track running towards Ibrox. Most in the yard were happy that they had work but behind the scenes the incoming order book was beginning to thin out. A new scheme to beat the TB illness in Scotland was launched. It was decided to carry out the experiments in Govan. The health officials said it was not because TB was higher in Govan, in fact it was lower. However, the Govan people have a 'remarkable community spirit' in helping. In the first hour over 100 people entered the Pearce Institute to receive the X Rays.

At Ibrox Park a sports meeting was taking place for the Glasgow Police. The crowd was poor compared to previous times. However, a sizable number went from Govan High to cheer the runners on in the various relay races. The school had some very good runners but were not expected to compete against the more 'elite' schools. However, they did well and in exciting finishes they were very narrowly beaten by Alan Glenn's and Bellahouston; being cheered on by many of the locals. In the sprints a newcomer from the Universities called Menzies Campbell was given a 2 yard start in the 100 yards and won by about 20 yards. Rangers won the 5-a-sides with a team that included Ritchie, Mc Lean, King, Penman.

The biggest cheer of the day did not go to a winner but to an old runner in a long distance race who finished about 2 laps behind the rest. The Ibrox sports days were always an interesting day out with a lot of interesting events.

The Glasgow Chamber of Commerce were downcast. At the monthly meetings of Directors Mr.Hope Collins said that Industry and Commerce would be driven away from Glasgow and new industries prevented from coming. Industry now finds itself with rate increases of anything between 100% and 600%. This means that cost increases to the customers will be between 2 and 10 %. We acknowledge that the present rating system was devised in the days of the horse drawn carriage.

Burnt Island Shipyard in Fife obtained a huge order from the Canadian Pacific Group after fierce competition from abroad. Burnt Island Shipyard was a vibrant go ahead yard and part of the order was given to Fairfields Govan to provide the diesel engines.

The tenants at West Drumoyne were in for a shock with a staggering increase in rents and rates. The increase was from £17 to £36 per annum a rise of over 100%. At 31 Daviot Street, West Drumoyne Robbie was unhappy and threatening not to pay the increase; a view shared by many tenants. At a time of a pay pause things were getting difficult.

The second Govan High year for Derek had started. The Class was 2B and the new Form teacher was Foxy Reynard. Foxy was a largish lady and well respected by most of the class.

Although History was her main subject the impression given was that she could teach most of the subjects well. When the need came she seemed to adapt to the English subjects when a teacher was unwell. The timetable was issued and to virtually everyone's dismay the Music teacher was Mr. Mather again.

John McClay the Scottish Secretary was not a popular man. However, despite widespread opposition to his Rents and Rates initiative he was sticking to his guns.

He says 'I have no intention of relaxing pressure on laggard authorities. Experience shows that the low rent tradition stamps an area as industrially and socially old fashioned so that new industry tends to hesitate before sinking new investment and new employment in such areas'. Mr.McClay said that those who could not afford the increases would be entitled to rebates. Across the political spectrum the rise in rates brought much dismay. Progressive Councillor Alexander Hart said the ratepayers would be appalled in his area. A report from the Scottish Home Department on the Scottish Economy highlighted that generally it was doing well. However, the unemployment was twice the UK average and the traditional industries such as mining and shipbuilding were in decline.

Jimmy goes in to the toilet at 20 Craigton Road single end to get changed. He comes out and says to Ruth 'What do you think Ruth ?'. Ruth looks up from her cup of tea and cigarette and says. 'Whit the hell is that Jimmy ?' Jimmy is standing just inside the main room of the single end in a string vest and a pair of Y Front underpants. Ruth laughs 'Wher did ye get the simmit ?'. Jimmy says 'Down at the Co-op in Govan. The salesman says the string summits are new in from Scandanavia and are selling like hot cakes !'. Ruth says ' Well that is probably because they are half price because there is nae material in them'. Jimmy says ' Ah but that is the clever part Ruth. Apparently the gaps trap warm air inside the clothes and it makes the body feel much warmer. The guy at the Co-op says it has been scientifically proven'. Ruth says 'Yer arse Jimmy. Whit are these pants ye have oan ?. They look like mens knickers'. Jimmy says ' They are the latest design in gentlemans underwear Ruth and they are called Y Fronts'. Ruth laughed and puffed on her cigarette. Jimmy continued. 'The Co-op man says that in summer you can wear the string simmit under a jacket instead of a shirt. In the same way it gives heat in the winter, it gives cooling in the summer !.

The Music lessons had re-started under Mr.Mather at Govan High. A new theme for Year 2 'Doh; Ray; Me; Fah; Lah; Tee; Doh. Followed by Doh;Tee; Lah; Fah; Me; Ray; Doh. It was tedious. Then the lessons moved to the musical instruments. Mr. Mather on the piano. The pupils in turn with the two triangles and the tambourine with the two missing symbols. 'Plink, plink, plink went the piano; tink tink went the triangles and bosh went the tambourine. Mr.Mather would leap from his seat ' What are you playing at boy !' as he scolded one of the triangle players. Mr. Mather continued 'You will have to come in much quicker than that !' The replay yielded the same miserable result. Mr Mather said to the errant nervous boy. 'You are just not paying attention to what you are told !. Come over here'. He produced his strap and placed a towel over the boys wrists after which he received one of the strap. Mr. Mather then said 'Right you lot are finished. Next volunteers please. Right you boy in the second row, Fiona at the back and you boy over there at the front'. Plink Plink, Plink , Tink Tink Bosh. And so it went on.

Robbers were busy at work in the Neptune Street Public House. They broke through the store wall of the pub and crawled along between the false ceiling and the roof. They dropped down and broke through just above the Lounge door. They removed glass to obtain entry into the offices and used explosives to gain entry to the safe. £400 was taken during the raid.

John Patrick Douglas a red leader was having trouble hearing the football results at 21, Golspie Street, Govan. He asked for silence a few times as his wife was struggling to keep the 18 month old baby quiet as the all important results came through. The baby had bronchitis and was crying and coughing. Douglas lost patience and pushed his wife against a window grabbed her by the throat and squeezed.

At Govan Police Court Douglas (33) was fined £3 for assault.

Govan High life continued with Derek continuing to struggle in most subjects. A very unusual event took place one afternoon in the English literature lesson. The regular teacher was away so a very attractive young lady took over the lesson. Derek was sitting in the front row middle and to the right in the corner desk; sitting alone was Iain Duncanson. As the lady walked backwards and forward past the front desks the smell of very alluring perfume came across to the boy pupils. She walked backwards and forwards commanding the attention of the whole class; especially most of the boys. She came down to Duncanson's desk turned round and slowly walked back along the front rows from where she had just come. Duncanson was fixed on her backside and the outline of her underwear under her skirt. At this point he discreetly undone the buttons on his trousers, reached inside his pants and pulled out his Lord John. The teacher turned around from the other end of the classroom heading towards Duncanson's desk. He stayed motionless as the young lady turned and started walking back in the opposite direction. Duncanson then started stroking his private part and it soon reached its maximum. His face was turning red. The teacher turned at the opposite end of the classroom and started walking back again completely unaware of what was going on. A few girls in the seats near Duncanson seen what was happening; their faces turned red but they remained quiet. As the teacher approached Duncanson he somehow managed to remain motionless and the routine started again as the teacher started her slow walk back in the opposite direction. Duncanson had to lift the desk in order to continue. As the teacher came back again a few minutes later the desk lid lowered and he became motionless again but with a very red face. The teacher asked him ' Are you feeling alright ?'. Duncanson replied ' Yes Ma-am'. The teacher continued with the lesson at which point there was a massive fountain of liquid from Duncanson's private part. He managed to direct the flow into his underpants and by the time the teacher had returned he was back to his normal self. Most in the class felt that Duncanson's underpants were probably so crusty that the would probably be destined for the breakers yard rather than the laundry.

230

Glasgow Corporation announced that some 3,500 houses were unfit for human habitation although still occupied. 2,000 of these houses were classified as dangerous. Many of the houses in question were in Govan and the situation was becoming dire.

At Govan High the new Maths Teacher Mr. Francis cuts a dashing figure with some of the girls in the class. 'Yes Mr.Francis, No Mr.Francis' they say. He always calls the girls by their Christian names ' Jean, Janet, Margaret etc.' To the boys it is the Surnames ' Mac Whinney, Mc Kenzie, Stewart etc'. Mr. Francis appears to be a well off man, always well dressed. Like many of the teachers it appears to be trendy to carry his strap over his shoulder, inside his jacket. That way he already has the instrument of punishment ready for when the pupil steps out in front of the class. Derek thinks he is a dreamboat as he spends lots of time gazing out of the window when the pupils are set lengthy sums. Miss Hoy is again teaching French and her French assistant (Monsieur Lang Lang Pea) has been given an occasional lesson to the class on his own. It appears he has had instruction in anger management and he is not the hot head he was previously.

Tommy Gillies a 16 year old Rangers fan was on his way home from a party and with a friend was singing 'Follow Follow' as they moved down Copland Road. Suddenly they were attacked and subjected to blows around the head. The ambulance arrived and Tommy was taken initially to the Southern General Hospital and then to the specialist hospital for head injuries Killearn Hospital. Tommy died soon after arrival.    Tommy Gillies of 1, Elphinstone Street was popular and the area were saddened that such a likeable young man could be murdered in such a way. Two suspects Hugh Moore and Alexander Kennedy were quickly arrested and charged with the murder. The funeral of Tommy Gillies saw 400 people turn up outside his house to see the hearse leave on its journey to Craigton Cemetery. Countless other people lined the route to the Cemetery to pay their respects. Ruth was worried and said to Derek 'You did not know the boy that got murdered Derek ?'. Derek replied 'Naw maw'. His mother says ' Be very careful down in that part of Govan son. It's not just the Wine Alley  but some of these other streets can be dangerous as well. Do not wear your Rangers scarf !'.

At Alexander Stephens Shipyard the apprentices have their own safe to hold money in. The company had put £400 in the safe to reimburse money borrowed by the 24 apprentices for a holiday organised by the yard in Spain. The thieves broke into the office where the safe was and manhandled out into a back yard. There they used crowbars to force it open and take the money. A spokesman for Stephens Shipyard said that the company would definitely not be asking the apprentices to refund the stolen money. Stephens would replenish the safe and the money inside at no cost to the apprentices. Stephens shipyard received an order for a ferry valued at £2 pounds from British Rail Cross Channel Ferries.

# CHAPTER 23
## MEETING WITH A MADMAN

At the Pearce Institute the basketball team is doing well. They sit at the top of the West of Scotland Basketball League nearing the end of the season. However the eventual winners are a foregone conclusion.    The USAF (United States Air Force)  have team of giants and are well versed in the skills of the game.      Basketball is popular in Govan and the main hall court is frequently used. Pearce Institute I  if not winning the top league can console themselves with the runners up prize and possible the second division title with Pearce Institute II topping the table. Govan Youth Club were mid table.

## WEST OF SCOTLAND BASKETBALL LEAGUE DIV.1

| Team | Pl | W | L | F | A | Pts |
|------|----|----|----|-----|-----|-----|
| Pearce Institute I | 13 | 11 | 2 | 701 | 514 | 11 |
| USAF Prestwick | 10 | 10 | 0 | 568 | 304 | 10 |
| IBM Greenock I | 11 | 6 | 5 | 450 | 457 | 6 |
| Elite | 8 | 5 | 3 | 350 | 147 | 5 |
| Glasgow University I | 12 | 4 | 8 | 491 | 542 | 4 |
| Kings Park I | 9 | 3 | 6 | 356 | 467 | 3 |
| Phoenix | 11 | 2 | 9 | 374 | 594 | 2 |
| Jordanhill College | 12 | 2 | 10 | 452 | 714 | 2 |

The teachers have had enough. Mr.Thomas Collins a teacher at Lourdes school is spokesman. He wants the Government to appoint a QC to question 6th form pupils about making a career in teaching. The present number of teachers to pupils ration throughout Scotland is unsustainable. Discussions are being held at the highest education authorities.

Harold McMillan the Prime Minister is to address the nation. To solve the economic problems there must be restraint on wages and also a cap on public expenditure. It is likely that a 'freeze' will be put on Roads, Schools and Housing expenditure. Robbie continued to have tenuous labouring work in the shipyards but often he would be laid off for weeks on end. At the same time there seemed to be a steady drift of people leaving Govan; going to housing schemes at Castlemilk, Nitshill and Pollokshaws. Within the shipyards many very skilled workers were being enticed to go and work in England and abroad; in particular Australia and Canada. Govan was losing a fair number of its population.

The 164th Boys Brigade in Copland Road provides great pleasure for Derek and the entire group. On Monday nights he attends a month long course on First Aid. Like clockwork every Friday the boys go up the stairway at the rear of the church to the small hall. The group line up and spend around 20 minutes marching in formation. Bill Caddy the leader has the complete respect of the Brigade and the Waters brothers are the senior Boys within the group. Being a relatively small Boys Brigade in terms of numbers has brought a good togetherness amongst the boys concerned.

One Friday evening Derek is walking along Govan Road towards the Bus Station at Govan Cross. He has his small hat and white sash on and when he comes to the entrance to the Wine Alley he runs for a short distance. As he approaches the Subway Entrance a figure steps out in front of him and grabs his jacket. It is Bogo Logo. 'Got you at last' says Bogo. The two grapple but within a short time Derek is lying on the ground with Bogo having a knee on each of Derek's upper arms. He starts to land heavy punches to the head. Left fist , Right fist. Suddenly a group of people come out from the Subway and other people come the opposite direction. One burly man from the Subway grabs Bogo and says ' What the f**k are ye daein'. Bogo tries to punch the man only to receive an almighty knuckle flush on his jaw. Derek scrambled to his feet.    Bogo tried again to punch the burly man only to see it blocked and in reply the burly man delivers another crushing blow to Bogo's jaw.

A few other passers by move in and deliver kicks  and punches to Bogo and he was on the run towards the Wine Alley. The burly man turns to Derek' Are you aw right son ?'Derek still breathless says 'Yes Thank you. You probably saved my life !'. The Burly Man says ' It looks like you might have a keeker cumin up son. It looks nasty. Get that seen to when ye get hame'. Derek says to the small group ' Thank you' and virtually in unison the say 'Nae bother son'. Derek explained to Robbie and his mother how he got his black eye  and also the help he got outside the subway. Ruth says ' Govan folk are great like that. They evaluate in a few seconds who is the good guy and who is the bad guy. Then they smash the hell out of who they think the bad guy is !'.Monday morning arrived and Derek took his seat in class with a 'keeker'. Only his good friend classmate Shug Mc Whinney smiled. It was usual   that at least one of the boys in the class had a 'keeker' at any given moment in time but Shug thought it was hilarious that Derek had one. However fate was to take a hand. As Shug walked down the corridor in the Main Building one late afternoon he was barged by a boy going in the opposite direction. The two squared up and 'wham'. Shug had a 'keeker' as well.

When Derek saw Shug he laughed. It transpired that the guy he squared up to was the Welby Wilson the best fighter in the school. For a week or so the pair sat in the class together each with a 'keeker' each which amused some of the teachers.

233

Shipyard orders were greeted with much happiness in Govan and the pubs along Govan Road and the Govan Central area done a roaring trade. Alexander Stephens and Sons gained an order for a cargo motor ship weighing 10,000 tons for the Brocklebank Line valued at £1,000,000. This provided the yard with one years work. Stephens also secured a large order for a complete re-fit of the Cunard Liner Parthin.

Fairfields secured an order from the Admiralty for £7,000,000 for a guided missile destroyer. This provided the yard with four years work There were several launches: Harland and Wolff launched the 15,000 ton tanker British Queen for BP. Stephen's Linthouse launched the South African frigate President Steyn. Both were launched on the same day just 15 minutes apart.

Poor economic conditions continued and British Shipyards were struggling raising the capital quickly enough to build ships. A Sunderland shipyard lost a large order because it could not raise the capital required quick enough. On another occasion the same firm was to win a big order from a Norwegian firm because they managed to raise the money quickly from a bank and another financial institution.

The opening hours for Sunday Drinking changed and Pubs were not allowed to open. However to satisfy the tourist trade Hotels could open at restricted hours. Some clubs could also open. This opened the debate about Sunday's in a religious context. With not many hotels in Govan the decision was not popular with the many regular drinkers.

The Church of Scotland were bemoaning a drop in numbers involved with the Church, especially the young. Of the 860,000 children aged between 5 and 14 years just 297,000 attended Sunday School. Of 230,000 between 15 and 17 years of age just 72,000 attended Bible class.
So 65% of children had no active bond with their church is was reported.

At the Linthouse Tunnel there was a massive explosion and the roof was blown off by compressed air. The 30 men working in the tunnel blundered around in the dark mist before forming a chain and getting themselves to safety. The blast went 100 foot in the air and shattered nearby windows. The tunnel roof would require repair before work could continue.

Charlie Brown a Boiler scaler (32) and Josephine Monaghan his lady friend who both lived at 3, Rafford Street, Govan were not getting on well. Brown got drunk and when he arrived home he found that Josephine had snibbed the door. Brown cursed and swore and smashed the door down breaking two panes of glass. Josephine fled and called the police. Brown who had two previous convictions was jailed for 30 days. The fiscal said he woke the neighbourhood up. Brown said he was too drunk to remember.

Jimmy has not been visiting the Govan pubs as often as in previous times and his relationship with Ruth has improved. They are mostly happy together but do have the occasional flare up; usually during the periods when Jimmy is drinking. Jimmy has written off to England for three jobs which caught his eye. The Freemasons have codes that they build into their letter writing which identifies them to a fellow Freemason. He receives a reply asking for him to go to an interview. The reply letter has been signed by a fellow mason and comes from Taylors Stainless Metals in Slough, Buckinghamshire. The company have offered to pay his expenses from Scotland to attend the interview and have hired a small room in Caledonia House near Easton Station. Jimmy attends the interview and things go well. He has a good chance to shine as he has the credentials to undertake a Foreman's job in a factory. He knows also about the metals and has good knowledge on the supply chains. After the Interview Mr. Taylor the owner says how impressed he was with Jimmy as a candidate. He has other candidates to interview and will let all the candidates know the selection result as soon as possible. He gives Jimmy the money for the train fares plus an extra £5 for other 'incidental' expenses. Jimmy is impressed with the companies professionalism and hopes dearly he will get the job.

Jim 'Jazz' McHarg (32) of Middleston Street, Ibrox. was hitting the big time with his band the Scotsville Jazz Band. The Band were invited to appear at the Marqee , one of London's prime jazz venue's. He promised the Band would 'blow the roof off'.

The group comprised : Malcolm Higgins (trumpet), Andy Tully (clarinet), Mark Bradley (trombone), Tony Lang (banjo), Alex Adam (drums).

Following their performances in London they were invited to play at various venue's around the UK.

Derek had just taken his mid term Science exam and he found the questions tough. He did not manage to finish all the questions and waited in trepidation for the results a few weeks hence. He took the paper to 20 Craigton Road. Derek says ' Maw, did you tell me you were good at Science at school ?'. Ruth replies 'Aye Derek, Ah wis a good wee pupil at the Sciences'. Derek says ' Well you could not tell me the answers to some of these questions'. Ruth looked at the questions and says ' It would be wrong of me to give you the answers at the moment Derek; the teacher is the one who will be able to give the answers and the explanations. I know the answers but not the explanations !'. Derek says ' Thanks Maw !.

# GOVAN HIGH DECEMBER 1961 SCIENCE EXAM PAPER.
# SEE APPENDIX 1 AT REAR OF BOOK

Two policemen were having a quiet walk along the peaceful environs of Elder Street. Suddenly through an adjacent window came a figure amid a noise of breaking glass. There was lots of shouting and abuse all around. On the street was 18 year old James Gillespie who had just been involved in a fight with his step-father. His mother, 40 year old Margaret Garrett, went out to see to her son and got into an altercation with the policemen. The step father David Craig also came out and he too was involved with the policemen and started swearing and shouting.

At Govan Police Court W.Grindlay the Fiscal fined Craig and Margaret Garrett £3 each or 20 days in prison. Margaret said it was the first time that James had had a drink and all three were drunk.

At the Bridgeton Arms Jimmy Welsh had come in for a drink following a visit to his two children William and Mary. Richard Crozier the pub owner was outlining the Unionist's chances in the Glasgow Bridgeton seat in a forthcoming Parliamentary By Election. Although Bridgeton was near Celtic Park it was noted as being a strong Unionist area. However, Labour held the seat and with current difficult economic conditions Labour was expected to hold comfortably. Richard says 'James Bennett the Labour guy says his trump card is John McClay the Scottish Minister. With all the work disappearing they probably have a point Jimmy do you not think ?'.

Jimmy says 'Not at all. The reasons for the loss of work are varied. Many of the old industries are finished. It is all right Labour saying that we should keep on 20,000 miners. If there is no coal to mine there is no need to have miners. Typical Labour rubbish !'.

Richard says 'Malcolm Mc Neil the Unionist looks like a younger Harold McMillan. I will be voting for him but I do not hold out much hope'.

Govan High announced the results of the exams for the year. Two teachers marked them. The first result was the subject teachers marks. The second was an independent teacher/master (sometimes from another school) which gave the final figures:

Derek's results:

The pass mark was 40%   First mark Govan High; Second mark Independent
Arithmetic 46%  (+8%) = 54%  ;  Geography  54% (-1%) = 53%
English 53% ( +2%) = 55% ;  French 53% (+11%)  = 64%
Maths 49% (+14%) = 63%  ;  Science  32% (-2%)  = 30 %

Derek was totally dismayed by the results which left him in 37th place in a class of 39.

His mother said that he must do more home work. Derek said 'How did you do when you took these tests ?'.

Ruth says ' I was always up around the 90%'s Derek !'.

Unionist candidate Malcolm McNeil focussed his election campaign on housing, saying that the Labour run Glasgow Corporation had not taken up its allowance to enable more properties to be built for private rent. He managed to get the use of a grey pony called 'Lady' pulling a Hackney Carriage to take Unionist voters from their tenement homes to the polling booth.

A Scottish Nationalist candidate Iain McDonald entered the election with a plea to get one Nationalist MP in Westminster. ' The Nationalists would stop the drain of jobs to England. We would stop the takeover by the English of Scottish firms with a view to closing them down. A Scottish Government would guarantee a job for everyone in Scotland !'. Mr. McDonald held meetings outside many of the local factories.

The Independent Labour Party candidate George Stone (like William Park at Glasgow Kelvingrove) was well received wherever he went and the small party were popular. He says 'I am a Jimmy Maxton man and if Jimmy was alive today he would be telling you to vote for me'. However, Mr. Stone knew from the outset he was fighting the Nationalist Candidate for third place. His slogan was 'Kill the birds with one Stone !!'.

The Labour Candidate James Bennett kept up a strong campaign assisted by 30 helpers chapping doors all round Bridgeton. Bread and butter politics seemed to be pushing him towards victory.

RESULT:

On a poor turnout of 41.9 % Labour ran out easy winners as expected.

James Bennett—Labour 10,930

Malcolm McNeil—Unionist- 3,935

Iain McDonald—Scottish Nationalist— 3,549

George Stone—586

The result saw the Scot Nats almost beat the Unionists and the by election saw them for the first time as a credible force in Scottish politics.

The large loss of jobs saw Glaswegians leave the city to find work elsewhere. Jimmy Welsh waited patiently to see if his initial interview for the job at Slough would bear fruit. He was hoping he would be short-listed and get an invite to visit Slough for the final interview.

Christmas and New Year approach and the Kelvin Hall Circus arrives with some new sets of acts. Ringmaster is Alfred Delbosq and amongst the animals he will be introducing will be the Elephants Karia and Karla. Four year old Jimmy the Chimp and Bella a white Shetland pony who the families in the audiences will love. Jim Leslie and his mother Marie will once again be helping out behind the scenes.

Jim is a reserve Clown for the season.

At a private hospital on the side of Lake Zurich in Switzerland a man has just returned to have his final eye inspection after a successful operation a few weeks previous. It is John Leslie and he peers into the mirror in the very up market hospital. The Swiss eye surgeon is delighted with his work in returning the squinty eye to normal after a series of operations over a year long period. John is delighted that he will no longer have to even wear glasses. No longer will he have to take any taunts like 'Ya skelly eyed B**s*a*d if he had a disagreement in Govan Road. His wife Sandra has been staying at Hotel Schwanen ,by Lake Zurich, in a small town called Rapperswill for the period of John's operation. Once he leaves the clinic they decide to go on a cruise down the Lake from Rapperswill to Zurich. John says 'I feel like a different man Sandra. I am not afraid to look properly at people anymore. Pity I did not have my eyes done before the wedding !'. Sandra says ' Does not matter John I love you skelly eyes or not !'. They both laughed.

John says 'Sandra this reminds me of the 'Maid of the Loch' on Loch Lomond. We must take a trip on it sometime when we get back. Sandra I would like to visit Golspie Street in Govan. It has changed of course but the memories of one man in particular will always be with me'. Sandra says 'I agree John, Abe was quite a character; he certainly brought a lot to our lives'.

On a following Sunday a sizable number of boys from the various Boys Brigades around Govan assembled adjacent to the Govan High School on Langlands Road next to Elder Park. A small band headed the procession of Boys Brigade marchers as they marched in order through Govan and onto Govan Cross. There, a small group of well wishers greeted them and waved. At this point all the Boys Brigade groups split up and marched to their respective churches. For the 129th BB and the 164th BB the march continued along Govan Road and in no time the St.Kiarens Dean Park Parish Church on Copland Road was reached. The Boys Brigade went upstairs to join the Church service which was well attended.

Transport Minister Ernest Marples was requested to attend a meeting with the Scottish Socialist MP's. They were concerned about the knock on effects of the probable abandonment of Q3 project on Clydeside by the Cunard line. The Q3 project was for the building of the replacement ships to the Queen Mary and Queen Elizabeth.

In Denmark Mr.Lan of Lindo Yard, Odense Steel Shipyards advertised for shipyard workers from Scotland. The response was overwhelming. Almost immediately 60 men had booked up the local hotels and most had interviews planned for the various posts. Trades required were Platers, Riveters, Caulkers, Welders, Pipe-fitters and other engineers.

Rumours started circulating around Govan about Harland and Wolff possibly closing the Govan yards and consolidating within their Shipyard in Belfast, Northern Ireland.

The eagerly awaited results of the Clydeside yards for the year end 1961 were provided. Most people expected bad results and they were to be proved right. The Clydeside Yards had their worst year since 1948. In 1948 the tonnage out was 356,000 output tons. In 1961 it was even lower at 323,000 output tons. However, a few yards did well especially at the low end of the Clyde at Greenock and Port Glasgow. Lithgow's Kingston and East yards had output of 89,000 tons. The sales efforts of Sir William Lithgow and his sales team had borne fruit.

John Brown's had a poor year with 40,700 tons compared with 63,700 tons in 1960.

Harland and Wolfe produced 29,000 output tons and Fairfields 24,380 output tons.

Alexander Stephens produced 16,000 output tons.

At Govan Police Court there is a family squabble. James Rankin (36) a dock labourer has pleaded guilty to wife assault. His mother in law is in court and says 'Go easy on him, he is a good boy ! He gives her £12 a week. My daughter is to blame not James. She slaps his face at least once a month'. Rankin of 81 Golspie Street told Baillie Alexander Garrow ' I am sorry for what happened. I had too much to drink'.

Fiscal W.Grindlay says Rankin struck his wife on the face with his fist and he had three previous convictions'. James Rankin was fined £3.

Much was written on the notion of hen-pecked husbands in the newspapers. The sympathy generally went to the husband where the impression was that he was given a dog's life. The wife was perceived as being too bossy. However, the response from the female side of the population was that you would not get a hen-pecked husband if he was to do the masculine thing and shoulder some of the decision making. By allowing the wife to make the decisions the husband is then in his element. When the wrong decision is made by his wife he simply says 'Well dear it was your idea, now look at the mess you have got us in !'.

Stanley Valentine Stevens (39) was an aircraft controller. He went for a drink in Govan and got drunk. He boarded a bus and when it drove off he fell backwards and off the bus hitting his head on the ground. Two boys ran to help him and William Rae a tenant on Govan Road also tried to help. Stanley Stevens was helped to his feet but on trying to support himself by holding on to a lamp post fell over and cracked his head on the pavement. Stanley was taken to Southern General Hospital where it was thought he had minor injuries. The police took him to the police cells in Govan Police Station where he was to be charged with being drunk and disorderly. He died five hours later and it was then found he had a fractured skull.

The inquest tried to establish who if anyone was to blame for the death and a formal verdict was returned. It was left to Stanley Stevens relatives to undertake civil proceedings if they wished.

239

# CHAPTER 24
# HARLAND & WOLFF

Harland and Wolff were one of three sizable shipyards built along the upper parts of the River Clyde at Govan. The others were Fairfields and Alexander Stephens.

The main Harland and Wolff shipyard was based in Belfast and gained world fame by building the ill fated HMS Titanic. The giant luxury liner sank in 1912 on its maiden voyage across the Atlantic with a considerable loss of life.

The company was formed in Belfast by Edward James Harland and his assistant Gustav Wilheim Wolff in 1861. They bought a small shipyard on Queen's Island from their employer Robert Hickson. Wolfe had relatives who owned the Bibby Line and the first three ship orders came from this source. The pair were very innovative in their designs and they were well received by the shipping lines. The orders for ships came to the yards and the Shipyard increased in size. In the early part of the 20th Century the orders for ships was considerable and meant that the Belfast yards alone could not cope. Extra capacity was sought and Harland and Wolff yards were bought or built around the UK.

The first of these was in Govan. Others followed at Bootle, Liverpool, North Woolwich and Southampton. In Govan the Harland and Wolff brand name took over several shipyards that already existed. These were The London and Glasgow Engineering and Shipbuilding Company, Middleton's and Govan New shipyards. Also Mackie and Govan old shipyards which were owned by William Beardmore and Company. In addition Harland and Wolfe took over a nearby yard, A and J. Inglis.

When Edward Harland died in 1895 he was succeeded as Chairman by William James Pirrie and it was he who oversaw the purchases of the old yards and the creation of Harland and Wolff, Govan. When fully opened the Shipyard had 7 berths and was building mainly Tankers and Cargo ships. The Harland and Wolff shipyard held a prime position in Govan near Govan Cross and had a branch railway line directly into the factory. To reach the shipyard the small train had to cross Govan Road and was a popular sight, except for road traffic.

Thirty seven year old James Heron had two artificial legs and manoeuvred his way around Govan in a wheelchair. One evening he was coming home after visiting a pub and started cursing and swearing at passers by in Harmony Row, Govan. The police arrived and told him to go home. At this point he launched a torrent of abuse and was arrested. Heron of 16 Greenfield Street was carried into Govan Police Court by two police officers. He told Baillie Alexander Garrow that he was trying to forget that his mother had died. The Baillie asked him 'When did she die ?' . Heron replied 'About a year ago.' Heron was fined £7 or 30 days in jail having had two previous similar offences.

Down in the House of Parliament in London, Govan MP John Rankin is thirsting for revenge. He was accused by Tory MP Gerald Nabarro of sleeping and snoring in the House of Commons during a Question Time session. Rankin has prepared a list of awkward questions in order to put Nabarro on the back foot.

John Rankin catches the Speakers eye and launches his series of tricky questions. Nabarro listens intently and without expression. After some minutes of receiving the questions he stands up and replies 'I see he is awake today !!'. The whole chamber burst into laughter at the flamboyant Tory's (who sported a handlebar moustache) retort.

At Brechin's Bar near Govan Cross John Gillespie and Frank Mulvenney meet up with a number of others to survey the current affairs of the burgh. Frank, after a few drinks, is in full flow. He says' Did ye hear about Lord Percival Posonby ? . Ponce for short. Well he was at home and suddenly plunged into darkness. He was beat all ends up because he did not know how to change a bit of fuse wire'. John says 'Typical of these folk. Well what do we think of the Bridgeton result ? A Labour win which was expected but a good result for the Scottish Nationalist. When I was knocking the doors a lot of people were saying the Westminster brigade are out of touch with Scotland and quite a few said they were voting for the Nationalist. It is the best result they have ever had (11%) and quite a few think they may do well in the future'.

Frank says 'I think Labour were lucky the Nationalist was a farmer. If he had been one of us he would have done even better. However, you will never get a Scottish Nationalist victory in Govan, will yeah ?'.

John says ' I think the outlook is grim. Govan is a forgotten outpost to these folk down in Westminster. The only one who seems to have taken an interest is Lithgow. He and his sales team still have faith in the Shipbuilding Industry'. The Government is nasty and vindictive. They have cut the subsidy to Glasgow Corporation and as a consequence the rents and rates have gone up between 33 and 50%. Think about it !. The poorest people living in the Gorbals and Govan are living in the worst housing conditions within Western Europe and are being asked to pay such a staggering rise. Of course most cannot afford it which means they will be means tested to the last penny. Compare that to our City of London friends. For example under the Companies Act special dispensation means they can conceal their true profits. A leading stockbroker did some figures and Barclays Bank, for example, published a net profit of £5,458,000 for 1960. The real profit according to the researching stockbroker was £17,000,000. The same story with the Midland Bank. £4,500,000 declared when the real figure was over £16,000,000. Westminster bank declared £3,400,000 when the real figure was £9,300,000. Lloyds declared £4,600,000 when £13,600,000 was the real figure.' Frank says ' Unbelievable !. Nothing is likely to change with the present set of politicians'.

At 20 Craigton Road, Ruth is getting ready to go to work at Woolworth's. It is Ruth who is looking into the mirror; looking back she sees Bridget Bardot. For years she has followed every aspect on how Bridget Bardot dresses and tries to copy. Her friends have nicknamed her Bridget. The concentration of looking at the mirror is disturbed, it is a letter dropping through the box. Ruth goes quickly and sees a letter with a postmark Slough, Bucks. It is addressed to Jimmy Welsh. Ruth is excited and puts the letter on the mantelpiece. That evening Ruth waits for Jimmy to arrive home. He walks in and immediately Ruth points to the letter. Jimmy 'I have been nervous aboot this letter all day. I jist hope it is no a Dear John'. Jimmy says 'Lets find out'.

He opens the letter the news is good, he cannot conceal it. His application for a position at Taylors Stainless Metals in Slough has borne fruit. Ruth says 'Whit does it say Jimmy ?'. Jimmy says 'I have been offered the job even without a final interview !'. Ruth is excited and they embrace. Jimmy says 'I have to start with them in 6 weeks time and they will arrange digs for me. They have even agreed to pay half my boarding until I find somewhere permanent'.

One firm gave a comparison of having a factory in Scotland as opposed to one in Sheffield, England. William Beardmore stated that they would pay £110,000 less for fuel and power in Sheffield than Scotland. Scottish Industry was looking at getting its fuel from America which was much cheaper or re-locating plant to England. Urgent meetings were being sought with the Government Ministers.

A second strike day was organised by the Trade Unions in Glasgow. It was solid as more than 200,000 people gathered at Glasgow Green and marched to St.Andrew's Hall. Trade Union leaders made speeches which cheered the crowds and Government Minister Maudling was the brunt of the strikers wrath.

The son of the Prime Minister Mr.Maurice McMillan said most people putting money into shares had little or no idea what the purpose of the Stock Exchange was. When a sample were questioned the replies were ' Capital Gains, Tax Free Profits, Making Money or Just a Gamble'. Mr.McMillan said that many thought of the Stock Exchange as just a gambling casino.

Down in Acton London, Mr.Newton forbade his daughter from marrying a Scotsman. His daughter Marilyn decided to go her own way and married Glasgow man Bruce MacDonald.

Mr.Newton refused to attend the wedding claiming all Scots are really 'foreigners'. A year after the wedding Bruce had still not been allowed into Mr.Newton's house although he allowed his daughter a couple of visits. Asked why he disliked Scots he said ' They are ok in their own country. However, when they come down here they cause trouble and the place gets overcrowded. I think the same goes for the Welsh and the Irish !'.

242

Clydeside disputes were ongoing and the latest to join were the popular crew's of the tug boats. When asked who they were striking against they replied 'Everybody, including their own union. They wanted to deal directly with the Scottish TUC as they considered the National Union of Seamen ineffective.    The 150 strong tugboat men operated 22 tug boats up and down the River Clyde. The employers only recognised one union. A spokesman for the tugboat crews said 'We are only tugboat crews that are members of the National Union of Seamen and we have the worst wages and conditions of the lot !'.

The rumours and noises coming out of Harland and Wolff continued to be negative until the fateful day arrived for many Govan families. Harland and Wolff issued a statement saying that due to a shortage of orders the Clyde foundry was going on short time. 200 workers were put on a rota of work with one week on and one week off. The company advised that at present the yard was working only at 50% capacity.

Govan High and Bellahouston Academy rowers did well in the early season Schools Regatta at Glasgow Green.  The Govan High B crew in the Clinkers fours won Heat 3. Bellahouston A won Heat 9
In the Tub Fours Bellahouston A and B both won their respective Heats.
The conditions were poor with a blustery wind throughout the races.

Govan Town Hall was chosen to host the Amateur Boxing Association competition preliminaries.  The match was between Scotland and the Northern Counties. The winners were to box in the ABA London Finals evening. A top attraction was Olympic Gold medallist Dick McTaggart. The bouts were (Scotland names first)
Flyweight : R.Mallon v T.Barbour :  Bantamweight: A.Young v A Rudkin
Featherweight: J.McDermott v T.Halpin: Lightweight: D.McTaggart v K.Hawkins
Lightwelter: A.Forbes v P.Young: Welterweight: A.Robertson v B.McCaffrey
Light middleweight: R.Scott v B.Gale:  Middleweight: J.Fisher v A.Matthews
Heavyweight: A Thomson v R.Davis

As expected, there was big turnout from the Govan boxing fans. They almost had audience participation as the evening of boxing had a near riot. Brian Gale had disappointed most of the crowd with his rough/tough tactics and was heard swearing throughout the fight with Bertie Scott. Gale was warned by the    referee on a number of occasions and then landed a very low blow on Scott.    The referee immediately disqualified Gale. He abused the referee and in turn the crowd abused him. On leaving the ring a spectator gave him abuse and Gale punched him.

Within a few seconds there was a riot as it appeared the entire crowd made for Gale. His trainer and second also became involved and it was a full five minutes before order was restored by police and stewards.

# CHAPTER 25
# GOVAN HIGH FIRE

A sunny Tuesday arrived and the sun shone through the windows of the main building at Govan High. Form teacher Foxy Reynard, looking like a giant bat with her flowing black teaching robes, as usual read out an announcement saying how good the attendance records were for Govan High School. Very few days were 'plunked off' and the school had one of the best (if not the best) record of attendance in the whole of Glasgow. As the form lesson ended and the class headed for the Ranch and Art, there was the unmistakeable pungent smell and yellow haze from the Science Lab indicating Mr Hyman was preparing his lesson. The Art Lesson passed by and a pleasant walk back to Dysart Street and Music courtesy of Mr. Mather. Mr. Mather was in one of his more sanguine moods, usually a prelude to an outburst later on during the lesson. Everyone in the class was on guard. Mr.Mather moved over to the piano and started to play one of his favourite pieces of music.

In an instant his mind had moved from the school to the Royal Albert Hall. 'Plink, plink, plink' went the piano. Mr.Mather was transposed to London and the Hall was spellbound with his brilliant piano playing. The audience was transfixed by the extreme skill and quality of the music. An hour later the adoring audience started to give their unrestrained gratitude for the entertainment. Mather from Govan moved his eyes from the keyboard to the standing room only music lovers in the Gods at the top of the Royal Albert. The hands were in the air with applause. Mather from Govan found the required few seconds to take one hand off the keyboard and give a circular appreciation to this section of adoring fans. He resumed his brilliant piano playing and in a few minutes found a break where he could look at the top level seats in the hall. As he looked at them they rose from their seats in unrestrained appreciation for the keyboard magician's efforts. He gave another circular movement of the hands and the crowd were ecstatic. In time he moved down the other levels until only the stall were left. He finished his masterpiece; this was the conclusion. His eyes closed and opened level with the adoring audience. He looked out and what did he see. A lot of spotty faced Govan High pupils listening to 'plink, plink, plink.

Mr. Mather was rattled. His back side leaped off the seat; all ten fingers went down on the piano keyboard making a terrible noise. 'You boy; get out here !!' Mr.Mather bellowed and strutted over the classroom to get his strap and towel from his desk over at the far side of the room. Derek was relieved that the finger pointed well away and further back from where he was sitting. However, the relief was only temporary. As Mr. Mather came back it was evident he could not remember who he pointed to. He said ' I told you to get out here boy. Do not be insolent !!' Nobody moved. 'You boy, get out here'. Derek pointed to himself. ' Yes you, get out here !! bellowed Mr. Mather.

Derek trudged out to the floor in front of the class. 'You know what this is for do you not ?'. Derek said 'No sir'. Mr.Mather was livid ' Yes you do you insolent boy !' Mr. Mather bellowed. He continued 'Now it is three for what you did and three for being insolent'. Mr.Mather placed the towel over Derek's wrists. The strap went over Mr.Mather's shoulder and came down in a particularly vicious fashion. The pain of the whack took a few seconds to record and transmit to Derek's brain registering around a 70% threshold. Mr.Mather said 'Other hand'. The same vicious whack from the strap also registered around 70% in pain threshold on the second hand.

It was then back to the first hand. 'Whack' the slap resounded around the class and the pain threshold had already reached the maximum 100% on the hand to brain indicator. Within seconds the second hand had reached 100% pain. Of course like many pupils had said on previous occasions once 100% is reached the teacher can use the strap as often as they like the pain level will go no higher. This was true with the 5th application of the strap. Derek's face was as red as beetroot. This was not unusual. All pupils who received punishment had red faces and in particular girls. With the last whack Mr.Mather tried to 'skim' the towel off Derek's wrists. This would have allowed him a 'bonus' application of the strap. However, Derek saw his intention and manoeuvred his wrists to prevent the towel going down. 'Get back to your seat boy' bellowed Mr. Mather.

Derek was livid at the sheer unfairness of it. In previous times he may have cried with the intensity of the pain. Not this time. He was determined to show Mr.Mather sheer defiance and spent the remainder of the lesson glaring at the teacher. The bell went for lunch time and Derek was surrounded by fellow pupils saying how unfair Mr.Mather was and asking what could be done about the teacher. Derek said 'I will be speaking with my mother in a few minutes and we will discuss this'.

Derek walked along Crossloan Road past the Vogue and on to 20 Craigton Road. His mother Ruth knew instantly something was wrong.

Derek said ' Maw, I have received six of the strap from an absolute moron and I did not do anything. My hands are absolutely numb and the pain is terrible'. Ruth says ' Derek you must have done something, no teacher gives you six of the strap without you having done something'. Derek says ' This Music teacher is a madman maw. I have never had such a thrashing in all my time at school or anywhere else and it was for nothing maw. I feel like going back to Govan High and punching him' Ruth says 'Derek that will get you nowhere. In these situations you let things calm down; the pain will soon go and then you will be able to think rationally. When Jimmy comes back you can discuss it with him. If he feels the teacher is out of order he will take the appropriate action'. Derek says ' Maw, You know as well as I Jimmy, Robbie, Jack and the rest of you will believe the teacher. I am disgusted !'.

Ruth says ' Derek. He certainly hit you hard with the strap it looks as though you have welts coming up'. Derek says ' The pain is terrible maw although my hands are turning numb which means they should be all right later this afternoon. So you are not going to support me maw ?'. Ruth says ' Derek, I suggest you let things settle for a day or so and we will discuss it further'.

Derek says ' At this moment I absolutely hate that f\*\*cking school. I hope it burns down and wee Mather is in there'. Ruth says ' Derek do not say things like that and do not swear !'.

It is June 1962 and a sunny early evening at West Drumoyne. Derek was talking to Robert Margach and several friends in Tormore Street. Robert was popular and tended to be a  leader rather than a follower. He usually decided where the lads were going to go.  As things were discussed the group noticed a large number of people walking through the scheme mainly coming from Cardonald.  Robert shouted out. 'Wher is everywan gau'in ?'.  The reply came back' We are going to see the fire at the school. Someone told us Govan High is on fire !'.

At that point the exodus to the school was joined and a large number of people had already gathered at the top of the hill on Farm Lane overlooking the school. It was a bright sunny evening and an amazing sight. The entire school roof was ablaze and the school looked doomed to finish in ashes. One of Derek's class mates said 'You will be disappointed Derek. There thankfully has been no casualties and wee Mather has been accounted for'.
Black smoke went up into the sky and for the fire crew's a constant battle to keep the hoses going and bring the flames under control.  After several hours most dispersed and for the Govan High pupils it looked like two weeks extra holidays may be a bonus.

The Main Building at Govan High was a mess when the pupils returned to school on the Monday. The weather being bright meant that the class form teachers could hold their class in groups in the Dysart playground. Foxy Reynard the form teacher for class 2B gave the good news that most had been waiting for that there would be no more lessons for the term and everyone was now on holiday.

Derek walked down to see his mother at lunchtime at 20, Craigton Road and gave the news on the school. Ruth said ' Well it is good that no one was hurt. That is the main thing. Wonder what caused the fire !'. Derek said 'No one seems to know. One teacher said that the hot weather sunshine coupled with some glass on the roofs shining through onto old wooden benches  may have been the cause.

The Evening Times reported that the Fire Brigade had ruled out arson as the cause of the fire. The Main Building was beyond repair. Mr.Wiiliam Hutcheson the headmaster said he had his suspicions as to the cause of the fire but said he would keep his suspicions to himself.

Jimmy had started his new job in Slough and came home from England on a fortnightly basis. They decided to attend the 164th BB Display at the Pearce Institute. Derek had several roles in the display with easy tumbling and jumping roles on the gymnastics; and a member of one of the competing basketball teams. In addition he performed a group display on the climbing bars as well as a small signalling display. The evening saw many marching exercises which pleased the large attendance present. This was the last time Derek was to attend a 164th Boys Brigade function.

Linthouse was probably one of the noisiest places in the country during the summer as the Clyde Tunnel project continued with much drilling. The project was behind schedule and over budget. The original cost of £3million was now £6 million and the ongoing works seemed to last an eternity. The main dispute involving Glasgow Corporation and the Scottish Office was over the cost of the approach roads; surprisingly not catered for during the original budget.

After several years in the doldrums there were queue's appearing outside the Lyceum Cinema on Govan Road. One film in particular. Dr.No with Sean Connery as James Bond. The film was on constantly at the Govan cinema's and virtually always attracting good size audiences.

Derek was at 31, Daviot Street when a letter arrived from the Govan High school. The letters from the school were always on small sized bits of paper; usually short and to the point.

The news was confirmation that the Main Building at Govan High had been condemned. The new term would start at the recently vacated Bellahouston Academy on Paisley Road West. This required discussion and soon a number of the mums were discussing the implications. Firstly there would be no allowance given for the travel; apparently West Drumoyne was marginally inside the ring where fares could be claimed. About two-thirds of the pupils were heading for Bellahouston the remainder staying to continue at Dysart Street and the Ranch.

The implications of the Govan High fire were coming home to roost for pupils at from the West Drumoyne scheme. The journey would involve a bus to Govan Cross and the subway to Cessnock. Then a 5 minute walk to the 'new' school.

The organising committee are well advanced with their plans and they have the Stock Car Racing World Champion, Chuck Lloyd, in attendance. The White City in Govan is to stage a Stock Car Racing summer season. The organisers feel confident that the Govanites will support Stock Car Racing but they are not certain.

John Johnston of the Glasgow Trades Council gave a speech to the Scottish TUC outlining housing conditions in Glasgow. 'There are 30,000 people homeless in Glasgow and nearly one third of the houses in the city have no inside toilet. Three or four families have to share a toilet on a stair head. The Secretary of State for Scotland should visit these houses and houses like them. These houses belong in the last century.'

Seven teenagers were saving hard to enter the world of Stock Car Racing. Edward Campbell 14 years, Moss Heights was the chairman of the group. His fellow school mates at Penilee School, Roddy Cumming 15 years, Allistair McDougall 16 years, Gordon Wright 15 years, Alan Mair 15 years who attended Shawlands Academy and William Gaffney 14 years from Lourdes School. Apprentice Instrument maker Gordon Hamilton 16 years was the seventh man.

Between them they pooled their savings and raised £10. They bought a 1947 Morris 10 . Edward said 'The original colour was grey but we have re-painted it pink, white and black. We have removed the upholstery in case of fire. All seats, apart from the driver's, have come out and all glass has been removed. We are fitting four metal 'roll bars' over the roof in case the car overturns during the race. Special bumpers have been fitted front and back and we will install a safety harness for the driver. The drivers at Fridays White City meeting will be Gordon Hamilton and myself. In Stock Car Racing no driving license is required and if you are under 16 you require your parents permission. They were apprehensive at first but when I said I will be able to ride a motor cycle at 16 ,which is more dangerous than Stock car racing, they agreed and are coming to watch'.

A fair has arrived at Craigton Road and set up opposite the Destructors at the rear of Tinto Park. Margaret and Dorothy two 16 year old girls joined the numbers attending the fairground and had a hurl on the various rides. Dorothy talked to Margaret but was getting little response. Agnes had spotted 19 year old Adam Wilson who was working at the fair. Margaret said ' He is a smasher Dorothy, let's go and talk to him'. Dorothy says 'Aw right then'. Adam is in charge of the shooting gallery and stands amongst the many prizes at the side of the stall. Few prizes seem to be getting won as the mainly young Govanites pay their money, pick up the rifle and fir the three shots.

Margaret soon engages in conversation with Adam and Dorothy decides to go and join her other friends. The punters keep coming and Adam is busy loading and re-loading rifles.

Margaret is infatuated with Adam and they chat during the not too frequent breaks in the rifle shooting. She has never seen such a good looking boy and is desperate to find out more about him. She asks herself 'I wonder if he has a girlfriend ?'. At last there is a break in the punters and Adam comes over and he and Agnes are chatting. Adam thinks Margaret is lovely and he decides to show her how to fire the rifle. He shows her how to put the rifle onto her shoulder. Margaret feels his strong arms around her as she tries to concentrate on lining up the shot. She says 'Adam there does not seem to be very many good shots from Govan !'. Adam says 'There may not be many opticians in Govan. Well they should focus on squeezing the trigger properly. Come here Margaret, I will show you how to get a direct hit'. Margaret is once again in his arms and he squeezes her as they look down to the target. Adam says 'If you listen to me you will be the best shot in the whole of Govan !. Give me the rifle ! Right ! some of these rifles are as much as 20 degrees out so I have to correct them from time to time'. He adjusts the sights until it lines up exactly and Margaret is soon in his arms again.

They fire three shots gently pulling the trigger each time the target falls. Adam gives Margaret the large cuddly bear. He says 'That is the first prize I have handed out this week. Margaret I wish I wis that cuddly bear !'. Margaret says 'So do I Adam'. Adam says ' When I finish for the night can I walk you home. I hear Govan is not always the safest place in the world !'. Margaret says ' I live at Elder Park Street it is not too far.' Adam walks Margaret home and they have several embraces and kisses in a few of the closes before they reach Elder Park Street. Margaret says 'My Ma and Da always wait up for me so I better be going in'. Adam says 'Will ye be coming up to the fair tomorrow night Margaret ?'. Margaret says 'Of course, thank you for a smashing night'.

The air at the White City track has a smell of fuel. The third Friday night meeting has once again attracted a large crowd. It is a brilliant spectacle and the Govanites love it. The races see some stock cars completely disintegrate and this causes great amusement. Towards the end of the evenings they have a figure eight display where the stock cars cross in the middle of the arena and amazingly there is no collision. This meeting sees a record 65 stock cars take part and only two from England. Jack Lloyd the world champion and Chic Woodroffe who won the Glasgow Grand Prix the previous week at White City. The Scottish challenge comes from Chubby Ralph Forbes.

At the Govan Fair Procession there was a Naganisbi Kwai display by the Govan Judo Club on one of the floats. They advertised that there would be a Black Belt display at 801 Govan Road every Sunday evening.

At the Fairground on Graigton Road Margaret has become a permanent feature at the side of the Shooting Gallery. To Adam's surprise someone hit the target and a prize was given out. After the winner had gone he took the rifle away for 'adjustment'.

Margaret was in love as any young 16 year old girl could be. Adam chaperoned her back to Elder Park Street. In a few days Adam will be moving on with the Fairground. He says 'Margaret I do not think I am ever going to be separated from you. I love you so much'. Margaret says 'I am sure we will see one another again. If you tell me where you are going I will come and see you'.    Adam says 'Why do you not come with me Margaret?'. Margaret says

'What would my Ma and Da say if I went away ?' Adam says ' Look Margaret do you love me ?'. Margaret said 'Of course I do, awe the lassies think you a smashin lookin'. Adam says 'Margaret, first there was me and then there was you. We are made for one another; it is in the stars'. Margaret says 'If you are going away, how can we be together ?'. Adam says 'I have had a word with the Boss and he says that you cannot come with me as we are both single. However, if we were married we could travel together in a bigger caravan. Will you marry me Margaret ?, I love you so much'.

At the White City the attendances continue to get bigger. The organisers are finding different formats of competition every week and the evenings are spectacular and interesting. There latest venture for the forthcoming weeks is the formation of a League.  The six teams for the inaugural league are: Glasgow Tigers, Glasgow Giants, Edinburgh Monarch's, Armadale Devils, Lanarkshire Eagles and the Clyde Dynamo's.

The fourth Stock Car Racing event once again had a large attendance with a tri-angular team competition. Glasgow, Armadale and Paisley competing. Armadale who brought just 10 people to the first event had a full coach load of supporters.  The individual competition was for the 'Cock o' the North' Cup.

 Margaret and Adam are at the shooting gallery as Margaret weighs up Adam's marriage proposal. She says 'What about my ma and da ?'. Adam says 'This is about you and me Margaret !. This is true love and when true love comes along you must grab it !. This is Romeo and Juliet in the streets of Govan !!. Do we get married or no ?'. Margaret smiled and said 'Of course we do. I love you Adam'. Adam gave Margaret a big kiss and a hug. Adam says. 'Right no time to dwell. Lets get down to the Registry office now'. Margaret said 'I will ask Dorothy to be my witness. Adam says 'Jimmy over there has already agreed to be my witness if the need arose. Lets go !!'.

At the White City the large crowds have persuaded the organisers and the stadium management to run extra events before darkness in the evenings brings things to an end in late August. Peter 'Pepsi' Dent the winner of the Cock O'the North  Cup has decided to bring his own team 'Scudovia Vitesse' to the event.  The following week was the 'Scottish Championship' open only to Scottish drivers. The prize was presented by STV's Sport commentator Arthur Montford

Down at Govan Registry Office a hastily convened wedding took place and Adam Wilson and his wife Margaret gave their vows and signed the book. They were pronounced Man and Wife.

A 'hooch' party in Govan went badly wrong when five men were rushed to the Southern General Hospital. A score of men drank methyl alcohol at a party believing it to be white whiskey. Three men died James Collins (36) a labourer of 28, Wanlock Street, Alfred Blacker (18) of 12 Copland Road and Michael Farrell (23) of 35, Aboyne Street who was found dead later in his own home. Two others were seriously ill in hospital. George Gracie (49) of 1, Elphistone Street and Charles Gilmour (31) of 8, Burndyke Street. Both were said to be very ill but recovering.

The remainder of the 'hooch' drinkers were said to be fine because they had already drank a considerable amount of whisky before the hooch. Normal whisky nullified the effects of the 'hooch'. Ten were taken to the Southern General and given even more whiskey to assist in the recovery.

Two policemen were watching some crates of export whisky being loaded onto a ship. Docker Alexander McIntosh (45) raised his arm to the policemen. The policemen immediately realised the significance of the gesture and ran towards him. McIntosh ran but was soon caught.
At Govan Police Court McIntosh was fined £3 for stealing a 15 shilling bottle of whisky.

The latter meetings of the Stock Car season saw a ladies race and the maximum 80 stock car entries competing in the 'Champagne Derby'. The final meeting had a massive Fireworks display and virtually everyone present had a great evening. Stock car Racing had been taken to the heart of the Govan folk.

At Elder Park Street Mr and Mrs McCulloch are wondering where their daughter Margaret has gone. They spot Dorothy and ask 'Hiv ye seen Maggie Dorothy ?'. Dortothy replies 'Yes, I was at her wedding earlier on today !'. Both Mr and Mrs McCulloch said simultaneously 'Whit'.

At Andy's Café in Berryknowes Road the teenagers are gathering. The Juke Box blares and they await the number 34 bus for the journey to Paisley Road West and the Flamingo Dance Hall. Some years previously the hall was a cinema called the Westway. Now it was a thriving dance hall where many of Govan and surrounding towns went. The Flamingo was laying on busses from Renfrew, Paisley and Johnstone to get the dancers home after the late dances.

The dancing was performed to Bob Ronald and his music with Benny 'Mammy' Ward and Dawson 'Jazz' Clark.
Friday was late night and the admission was six shillings.

251

At 31 Daviot Street Robbie is out of work. The recession is bad and he visits the 'Broo' to see if any jobs have come in. The Recession has hit the UK fairly badly in most parts but very badly in Scotland. The Shipbuilding Industry has shrunk and yards are barely hanging on. In addition the support industries to the shipyards are also affected. The news comes as Dr.Beeching is taking a calculated review of the Railway network and plans to close unprofitable lines. The Trade Unions have drawn up the battle lines.

ASLEF, the Railways Union, is consulting its 1,400 branches and 57,000 members on what action should be taken. Ted Hill of the Boilermakers Society tabled a resolution 'deploring the closure of railway lines and railway workshops`. The National Union of Vehicle builderscondemned the Transport Commission's decision to cut back the railway and cited the impact it would have on the communities served.

Govan had generally a very skilled a dedicated workforce in the shipyards. The skilled men felt that their skills in all the various aspects of building a ship were completely under-estimated. They felt under valued hence a move away from Govan and Scotland was on the cards.

Canada and many other countries did value having skilled people on board. In Woodlands Terrace Glasgow, the Canadian Immigration office saw a steady stream of Clydeside workers. John Inglis and Co. of Toronto wanted Turners, Horizontal Borers, Planners and Draughtsmen. It was unlikely they would feel homesick, the company according to their recruiting man Mr.Hill aleady had 1,500 mainly Glasgow men.

The conditions were good; a 40 hour week. Time and a half for 8 hours as overtime and then double time. Good housing, education and a non contribution pension augmented by the Federal Government.

In Glasgow, Sheriff Court, a 19 year old mother of two sobs with a handkerchief dabbing at her nose. She was pleading for her husband not to be jailed. Sheriff Ball had jailed her husband Adam Wilson for two weeks awaiting reports. Isobel Masson Smith or Wilson was pleading that he should be given another chance so that they could patch things up. Adam Wilson had pleaded guilty to having a bigamist marriage with Margaret Mc Culloch of Elder Park Street. The second marriage came to an end when a determined Mr.and Mrs McCulloch tracked Wilson down and took his daughter back home.

Isobell said in court. 'Since Adam has come back he is a different person and adores our second child. We are waiting to get a new house. Please !'. Wilson was fined £30 with no jail sentence.

The Industrial Training Council reported that children leaving schools were having greater problems in finding jobs due to the recession. They appealed to the Employers to try and take on more young people.

Another hammer blow for the workers in the Scottish economy came when it was announced that 20,000 Scottish miners would be made redundant due to the closing of pits. Mr. Alex. Moffat of the Scottish TUC said ' The policy of the Tory Government in relation to Coal, Railways, Steel and Shipbuilding has created an economic situation as serious in my opinion as the 1920's.

Alexander Stephen and Sons at Linthouse, despite the economic downturn, continued to offer apprenticeships. The training was always considered one of the best and the company owner Murray Stephens was always interested and encouraging. Some of the successful 15 candidates were: Robert Marshall, 366, Langlands Road, Govan. Norman Scarlett, 87, Arbroath Avenue, Cardonald. William Wallace, 2, Marlow Terrace, Kinning Park. Charles Stewart, 15, Elder Street, Govan. James Leckie, 3, Langcroft Road, Govan. Angus Young, 65, Greenfield Street.

The Govan Bowls season was drawing to a close. The Glasgow Public Bowling League Section C saw Langlands finish unbeaten and winners.

## GLASGOW BOWLS LEAGUE SECTION C

| Team | Pl | W | L | D | F | A | Pts |
|------|----|----|----|----|----|----|-----|
| Langlands | 10 | 8 | 0 | 2 | 64 | 16 | 64 |
| Nelson | 10 | 4 | 2 | 4 | 44 | 36 | 44 |
| Elder Park | 10 | 4 | 4 | 2 | 40 | 40 | 40 |
| East End | 10 | 3 | 5 | 2 | 36 | 44 | 36 |
| Oatlands | 10 | 2 | 4 | 4 | 35 | 45 | 35 |
| Richmond | 10 | 1 | 7 | 2 | 21 | 59 | 21 |

Mrs Dalziel of Bellahouston battled her way through to the final of the West of Scotland ladies singles championships. The final was held at nearby Cardonald Bowling Club against Mrs.Fowler of Yoker. Mrs Dalziel was in top form and won 21-5 to lift the trophy.

At St.Columba Church's in Copland Road a huge fire started and quickly spread. A great effort from the Fire Brigade using 50 officers managed to contain the flames and the church was saved. Rev.T.Murchison said that part of the roof and one of the towers had extensive damage.

Buchanan Street Bus station was seeing large numbers of busses going to various parts of the UK and a lot to London. Glasgow folk were trying to find work where ever they could get it. Skilled and non skilled alike would prefer moving than spend a life on benefits. As well as Buchanan Street Bus station, Glasgow Central railway station saw many carriages packed by single men and often by entire families. The Exodus was on. For many the question was 'What lies ahead ?. A new life away frae yer ain folk'.

The Buchanan Street coaches to London had two stops, Locherbie on the Scotland—England border and St.Neots. The Train to London Euston nearly always stopped at Carlisle.

The Railway network being put in the hands of Dr.Beeching put apprehension into almost everyone except the Governing Party. The Transport Commission gave Dr.Beeching one goal , 'Make the railways pay'. Dr.Beeching identified that there were 2,750 trains running in Scotland of which only 750 were paying their way. His solution was to simply axe the 2,000 trains not paying their way. He completely ignored the fact that some communities in Scotland virtually depended on their railway network. Also, the General public paid for the railway system through their taxes and paid for tickets to travel. Union men associated with the railways gave reaction.

Mr.Bridges (Harrow) ' This is becoming an attack on the social condition of our people'.

Mr.Tallon (Preston) ' Branch lines were being closed in areas where the road services are inadequate. People will have to buy motor cars or bikes to get around'.

Mr.Boyle (Warwick) ' I think in ten years time Dr.Beeching will be known as a national disaster. He is doing something that cannot be undone. Hundreds of miles of transport system are going, never to return'.

In the local elections the Progressives lost two seats in Glasgow and Labour were now in control with 69 seats to 42. The turnouts were very low with just 37.5 % voting showing disillusionment that any of the political parties had solutions to the problems faced.

The new Scottish Secretary of State, Mr. Michael Noble, took up his new position by saying that no railway line in Scotland would be closed unless there is an adequate provision of an alternative service. 'Noble words' commented the Scottish Press. However, few believed that he would sway many minds in Westminster.

The unemployment figures in Scotland continued to rise and the milestone of 100,000 was reached and passed. It stood at 100,603 the highest figure since the Second World War.

Michael Noble had succeeded John McClay as Secretary of Stae of Scotland. McClay had been deposed in the Harold McMillan 'night of the long knives' when the Prime Minister replaced one third of his Ministers.

John McClay enjoyed shooting and with the pressures of office now gone he was able to spend more time shooting near his home at Kilmacolm, Renfrewshire. The former Secretary of State for Scotland was born into the wealthy family of Joseph Paton McClay, 1st Baron McClay. He was one of five sons and was educated at Winchester and Trinity College, Cambridge. He was a member of the victorious Cambridge rowing side which won the boat race in 1927 acting as the bowman. His politics were National Liberal-Scottish Unionist. To most observers there seemed little difference between the two parties and they often worked together. McClay was held in much disdain by many Scots. It seemed inconceivable that living at Kilmacolm, not too far from Govan or Greenock, he could not see the efforts put in by the skilled work forces in the Shipyards in producing good quality ships. Or could he not see the efforts put in by Sir William Lithgow in promoting his yard and Clyde side shipbuilding generally. In the case of Lithgow's, many people felt that piling on rating increases to a yard struggling to survive was a major distraction. The yards were spending too much time with McClay and being diverted from the serious business of gaining much needed orders. In addition McClay or his Government had little idea on how to help the industry. At a time when most countries were part subsidising shipbuilding to help them be competitive, McClay was posted missing. Of course he had unpopular decisions to make ordered by the Government. However, his lack of interest and support at such a vital time was at least partly contributory to the rapid decline in Clydeside Industries. He was made a Companion of Honour and later a Viscount.

The Clyde Tunnel was progressing but costing much more than expected. The original cost was £3,216,000. The new revised cost was £6,392,000 almost double. An inquiry put the cost increase down to poor liaison between Glasgow Corporation and the Scottish Office. Also, division in Planning responsibilities was cited.

The Rangers Sports meetings were once popular. However, the attendances were steadily dropping every year and although good by Athletic meeting standards, were low compared to previous years.

The 100 yards handicap saw a Govan success as Conrad LaPointe of Bellahouston Harriers won in the Final. P.Ritchie also of Bellahouston Harriers finished second in the 100 yards Youth Final. J.Murdoch of Bellahouston came third in the Final of the 120 yards invitation. Crawford Fairbrother won the high jump which pleased the crowd. In the 220yards invitation W.M.Campbell was cheered home to a narrow win over two good quality English runners. The 5 a side football saw a Rangers team do well with Govan player Ronnie McKinnon managing to score a goal. Rangers team was Ritchie, McKinnon, Greig, Henderson and Willoughby. They beat Queen's Park 3-2 then Hibernian 3-1. Celtic lost to Third Lanark in the 1st Round.

A TRAM CAR PASSES THE PLAZA CINEMA. A SMALL ENGINE IS WAITING TO DELIVER MATERIALS TO THE HARLAND AND WOLFF SHIPYARD AT THE OTHER SIDE OF THE ROAD.

WHITE CITY (HOME OF STOCK CAR RACING)

CLOWNS
TWIN BROTHERS JIM AND JOHN LESLIE IN BOOK.

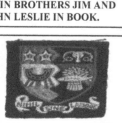

GOVAN HIGH SCHOOL BADGE

BACK COURTS IN CENTRAL GOVAN. SIMILAR TO BACKCOURTS BEHIND 20, CRAIGTON ROAD IN THE PERIOD.

Photo 3

# CHAPTER 26
## GOVAN HIGH— BELLA

The first day at Bellahouston Academy for the Govan High pupils proved to be a disappointment. The building was old and dull , the desks were the left overs from the Bellahouston Academy days and the scheduled demolition of the site was to be delayed until the new Govan High School was built. This of course meant that all the Govan High pupils would see out their last days at the school at Bellahouston. The proper Bellahouston Academy had moved in to a brand new school and this coupled with the very modern Lourdes school made some of the Govan High parents feel the poor relations.

On the first day it was apparent that Mr. Bud Neil was to have a more prominent role. He was the Deputy Head master, an Englishman, always very well dressed and a very strict disciplinarian. On the first day he came to the 3B class in which Derek was to be taught. He produced his new issue regulation strap for the year term. It was light brown and very thick with four tawses at one end. He was able to hold the strap vertically in one hand. He warned that despite the extra travel, lateness would not be tolerated. Each latecomer would be dealt with by a punishment of one of the strap.

Apart from the music teacher Mr.Mather it was difficult to come across a more nasty individual. The fortunate part of the new term was that a few subjects could be dropped and Music was the first go from the list provided to Derek. With the catering facilities already stripped out of Bellahouston Academy, dinners were provided at a church hall around five minutes walk from the school. Virtually the entire class had the meals as the time was limited to get home and back in the lunch hour. Within a few weeks most of the pupils were a bit down and missing the old Langlands Road site badly. Derek went to his mother Ruth and said 'Its no the same maw !'.

One morning Derek went to the bus stop at the junction of Shieldhall Road and Moss Road. A large queue was there to take pupils to St.Gerrards and Govan High as well as people to work. The buses arrived packed and few were able to board. Eventually Derek got on a bus and arrived at Govan Cross. Time was pressing on and it would be touch and go whether he would get to school on time. Derek was sweating and anxious the subway would soon arrive. To much relief he was able to get on the first train. As Cessnock he ran at full speed ; crossing Paisley Road West to the school.

As he entered the deserted playground a figure appeared from around the corner. It was Bud Neil. 'Go to my office' he said. When Derek arrived outside the office around a dozen other pupils were standing in line. Around ten minutes later and a few more late comers added to the queue; Mr.Neil returned.

One by one he took each pupil into his office and they got one of the strap. He would be visiting his mother that evening to discuss this particular problem of the transport and the over zealous punishments dished out by Bud Neil and his new strap. On the way home Derek called into his mother and discussed the problem. They came to the conclusion that walking to school was the only option.If pupils were down in the dumps at Govan High Bella, then the teachers also had a gripe. Dr. H.S.McKintosh the city director of Education estimated that there were 1,300 teachers short in Glasgow. He estimated that if Glasgow was to be staffed at the same pupil/teacher ratio as Aberdeen that would be the figure. Dr.McKintosh said married women teachers returning to help out was a great help. Also that pupils staying on a t school in higher numbers bade well for the future. He said. 'Better use is being made of the nations most precious asset, the potential abilities of its children'.

At Butlins Holiday camp, Ayr, 16 year old June Davy of 9, Queensland Drive, Cardonald won the Princess of the week competition. This enabled her to progress to the Regional Finals in Manchester.

The Boys Brigade numbers showed a decline in Britain by 2,801 to 87,802. The number of Life boys increased and the overall numbers throughout the world increased by around 5,000. The Govan Boys Brigade groups seemed to have relatively small numbers (around 20) but always regular in attendance.

The pupils or the teachers were not too happy at Govan High Bella and behind the scenes an angry set of parents were making their views known. Angry meetings took place on the issue of transport to Govan High Bella. When the pupils attended the Langlands Road school they were mostly within walking distance. This enabled them to reach the school easily and also in most cases return home at lunch time for their mid day snacks. The parents felt that the bus and subway costs should be met by Glasgow Corporation. The argument the Corporation put forward was that most pupils were within the regulation two miles from Govan High Bella. To some pupils at the east end of Govan the Bella school was as near as the Govan High school. However, to most it was farther and to Derek and his school chums in West Drumoyne the farthest away possible. The two mile limit seemed unfair. The Govan High Bella parents were unhappy and told the school they would be hearing again from them. A truce was agreed for now.

At Bellahouston Park, Bertram Mills Circus arrived. Franco Carroll fell off the horses when riding them around the ring but amazingly recovered before being trampled. Giant Teddy Bears were taken around the ring by Joan. Then there was Bela Roucka's jungle fantasy of tigers, panthers, leopards and puma's. Hire wire acts and all the usual fun of a circus was on display. Wrestling returned to Govan Town Hall as a 'one off' and again proved popular. The bill had world Champion Randolph Turpin against Rocky Bennett; Danny Flynn v M.Robson; Billy Graham v F.Woolley and Abduhl the Turk v Ray Webster.

The Kelvin Hall had become the new centre for wrestling with most of the better wrestlers taking part.

The Glasgow Corporation officials probably did not what hit them in the Govan High Bella dispute. The parents wanted the Corporation to put on or subsidise transport for their children.

The dispute took an unexpected twist when it was announced that St.Gerrard's School had just had £200,000 worth of Venetian Blinds fitted. That cost had risen to £381,000. To the Govan High parents it was the final straw. Around West Drumoyne the St.Gerrard's children pulled the legs of the Govan High pupils by saying how good the new Venetian Blinds were.

It was announced that three 20 storey blocks of flats were to be built on the site of the old Albion greyhound track. The flats would provide 285 houses and house around 900 people. The cost was estimated at £1,300,000 and the height would be 202 feet. No one would be able to see the matches from their vantage point due the position of the Ibrox Main Stand. All houses were to have balconies, central heating and internal toilets. On top of each block there was to be a roofed drying area. Hot water heating was by gas.

Govan Town Hall was to host amateur boxing. However, it was to be probably the last time. A fire during an amateur boxing evening at St.Andrew's Hall in Glasgow brought a re-action from Glasgow Corporation. They decided that after the Govan Boxing show; amateur boxing would not be allowed in Corporation Halls. The Western area Amateur Boxing Championships produced three knock outs in five minutes which cheered the Govan Boxing fraternity. Coal worker Andy Wyper knocked out his quarter final opponent Joe Land (Holyrood) in I minute 40 seconds. His semi final opponent David Walker lasted 1 minute 32 seconds. The final with Jim Jordan lasted one minute precisely the referee intervening.

Throughout the evening there were plenty of knock outs and the brother of professional Chic Calderwood, Tom Calderwood won the light heavyweight crown. The last evening of boxing at Govan Town Hall was greeted with some sadness. Perhaps it was fitting that the Corporation's last boxing evening was held in Govan whose populace were good supporters of the sport.

In the political world the Unionists were struggling badly and when a By Election came along at Glasgow Woodside most felt a Labour gain was on the cards.

The result was: Neil Carnmichael (Labour) - 8,303 ;
Norman Glen (Conservative) - 6,936 ; Jack House (Liberal) - 5,000
A.Niven (SNP) - 2,562 ; Guy Aldred (Ind.Socialist) - 134;
Robert Valler (Socialist GB) - 83.

Labour were jubilant at capturing another 'safe' Tory seat. However, the party with the most satisfaction was the SNP who were getting respectable and growing support.

The Govan High Bella dispute rumbled on. Nearly 200 pupils had a day off in what became known as the 'free hurl' dispute. Some children went to school and Headmaster William Hutcheson claimed the strike was 'Not as bad as expected'. The parents claimed that if 200 could be organised to strike at one days notice the rest would follow.

Mrs Jean Wilkie kept her two boys at home for the strike. She says 'It is costing me seven shillings and six pence for each boy to send them to school'. The parents then organised a petition signed by Govanites to the Secretary of State for Scotland to do something. They were unhappy with the poor support they got from their local politicians on the issue. Most pupils were hoping that another strike could be arranged perhaps of one weeks duration.

New Scottish Secretary of State Michael Noble had found his feet. He was threatening mainly Labour dominated councils with a cut in their grant if they did not increase the rents on their properties. The political arguments continued. Glasgow Corporation under Labour control were poor with their house building targets getting achieved. They put forward a housing proposal which involved new towns and furbishment of the inner city including Govan.

Michael Noble carried on with the poor relationship with the teachers who were increasingly feeling under-valued. Within Glasgow the classes were overcrowded badly and the teachers had a scheme to alleviate the problem. They had introduced a £100 incentive payment to teachers about to retire to keep them teaching. Mr.Noble scrapped the payment and felt the wrath of the teachers.

The question of 'Non Graduate' teachers was introduced and there was little agreement between the teachers. Some were for some against. However it was agreed that many Non Graduate women teachers were doing a very fine job and most of the Glasgow population had been taught by 'Non Graduate' teachers. Mr. Noble did gain some agreement from all sides with his proposals for slum clearance. One obstacle had been 'green field' sites which he was trying to get reviewed.

At Ibrox Park a quality Athletics meeting was arranged under the floodlights. Athletes from England, Scotland and Finland competed in the various competitions. Menzies Campbell was the main Scottish hope in the quarter mile but he came up short against a strong field. In a cold evening there was a poor crowd and in the junior event Hugh Barrow of Scotland just failed to overhaul Mike Jefferson of Sale Harriers in the mile.

The Finnish Pole Vaulter held the crowd in suspense as he tried to beat his own world record. Pentii Nikula just failed.

At 20, Craigton Road Ruth reads that Bridgitte Bardot has filed for divorce against her husband Jacques Charrier. The grounds were that he gave her a serious insult. Ruth sighed as she blew out smoke from her cigarette. 'Hmm' she said.

The TUC statements did not bode well for the Shipbuilding Industry. The 3,000,000 Engineering and Shipyard workers wanted a 7% rise and a 40 hour week. The claim was rejected by the employers. Mr.Harold Poole, President said 'At the same time they are giving £83 million pounds to the Surtax brigade they ask everyone else to accept wage restraint. If the present Government was paid by results they would have been in the workhouse !'.

Little Jimmy Little of Cornwall Street, Govan had his first wee 'swally'. He went to some waste ground and found an almost full bottle of wine. The 8 year old then challenged his pals to a fight before he was carried home unconscious. He was taken to Southern General Hospital to have his stomach pumped out. His mother Mrs. Margaret Little said 'While he was drunk he kept saying it was lovely mummy'. The ambulance took us down to the Southern General Hospital and on the way back he was still drunk. A taxi driver saw our predicament , offered us a lift home and refused to take the fare. The first thing this morning he said he has never been so hungry and wanted a piece. He had lemonade and we have agreed that is as strong as it will get !'.

Mr.John Rannie Shipyard Director of John Brown's forecast that a number of Shipyards would close down. At a Rotarians Meeting he said ' We are in a phase where the world's capacity to build ships is twice the tonnage demand. He said Britain still had the biggest Mercantile fleet and the normal continuous replacement should give full continued employment.

The industry is not full of decrepit old men basking in the glory of the past. Nor are they filled with 'Reds' who just enjoy troublemaking. Our men are grand, they could not be better'. The Rotarians asked him about demarcation disputes. He said 'On demarcation disputes 'We should get sense of perceptive here. Since 1953 John Browns have not lost a single day to demarcation disputes. Taking the entire Clydeside yards the total number of days lost to strikes is a quarter of one per cent. He continued that the Clydeside yards had spent £36 million in modernisation'.

The forecasts during the recession made grim reading for the Shipbuilding industry. However, there were some yards continuing to operate at virtually full capacity. These were Lithgow's , Greenock Dockyard, Fairfields and Stephens in Govan Connell's at Scotstoun.

The news for Harland and Wolff in Govan was grim and when news circulated in Belfast that they were closing the Govan yard many Govanites were accepting the inevitable. As well as Harlands, A and J Ingles was to close as well as Ship repairers Hendersons at Partick. Govan was to lose one of its three mainstay Shipyards.

Harland and Wolff in Belfast surprisingly denied the closure of the Govan yard. However, the workers were not convinced. Ingles had no ships on the berths and Harlands had one with another in for fitting out. 50 berths around the 22 shipyards on the River Clyde were empty.

Despite the continuing recession, W.Stephen's at Linthouse made a profit of £160,000 down from £366,000 the previous year. The company were battling hard for orders and received a welcome boost from the Admiralty with a £4,500,000 order for a Frigate.

They received a boost from the trade unions who agreed a no strike deal in return for certain concessions. The company welcomed it but could not guarantee jobs due to the economic conditions.

Govan was changing and to a lot of people not necessarily for the better. All hopes of saving the Harland and Wolfe Shipyard disappeared and when it closed there was a feeling of foreboding throughout Govan. In West Drumoyne there were a number of 'midnight flits' . Families who could no longer afford to pay the rent moved out during the night to destinations unknown.

Derek was not at all happy walking the couple of miles each way to Bellahouston each day but it was to have a few compensations. Rangers Football Club had moved quickly to purchase the closed down Albion dog racing track and use it as their training ground. As Derek walked to school he would often see the players come out from Ibrox, where they changed, and walk across the road to the training. So the walk did bring a small bit of compensation to see the fans favourite players.

In West Drumoyne Pat Mc Shane`s new bookmakers shop was to be joined by a new pub ' The Lochinvar'. Pat Mc Shane himself moved with his family to the Moss Heights. His son Raymie Mc Shane was a close friend of Derek's and attended Lourdes School.

Robbie was struggling with being out of work. Derek received some money from his mother to help with costs. In desperation he wrote to the British Army Hardship fund and was surprised to receive a payment of £2 and 10 shillings. A few very cold autumn days brought a very acrid tasting smog. This meant most Govanites wore a scarf over their mouths which became filthy after a few days.

The warm summer seemed a long way off. Derek had given up the 164th BB which he regretted. The group had brought much happiness and enjoyment. However, by the time Derek arrived home on Friday evenings from school he did not feel like making the virtual return trip to Copland Road. For the first time in his life his thoughts turned to when he would be 15 and leaving school.

What sort of job would be on offer? The notion that most Govan High School and St.Gerrards School boy pupils were being educated to become shipyard workers was demolished with the problems besetting the yards.

Derek came home from school one day and talked to Robbie about the problems faced. Robbie was bitter with the Government for not providing support to the yards. ' The Tories are only for the Lairds; they are not interested in the working class'. The pair decided that as they could not afford to go to the pictures that particular week they would have a game of shove ha'penny on the Living Room table.

After the game Derek said ' When Maw had difficult problems to solve she used to get out a bit of blank paper and write down two columns. One is good things and the other is bad things. So I have come up with my list'.

*Bad Things:*

- *We have nae money.*
- *Govan High Bella is too far away.*
- *I am a dunce at Govan High and unhappy.*
- *We cannae watch Rangers every match.*
- *The Bens are hopeless this season.*
- *Some of new people on the scheme are roughnecks and the scheme seems to be going to pot.*
- *I will miss my maw when she goes to England. You do not realise how much she means to you until she will be nae longer there.*

*Good Things:*

- *Uncle Jack and Aunt Maggie and of course Uncle Robbie.*
  *My pals and classmates.*

*Robbie* said; 'The key for me is to get a job. Until I get one all I can do is send begging letters to the Army.

Derek said 'On the money issue I am quite lucky. Maw gives me a bit.

With Govan High I will focus on the lessons where I am likely to do better and put the minimum effort into Chemistry etc. I would like an apprenticeship of some description. I enjoy Physics but seem to get poor marks.

I would like to follow in Grandad Boab's trade working with Instruments. When in the labs at Govan High I enjoy Instruments and testing temperatures and that sort of thing.

A week later Robbie got a job in Fairfields as a labourer. One of his friends had tipped him off that the position was coming up and he seized it with both hands.

In Slough Jimmy Welsh was still in lodgings. Getting somewhere to live was proving difficult both for him and his employers who were helping. Ruth was becoming unhappy with the lack of progress.

Although it was November it felt like mid winter. The walks for Derek along Shieldhall Road were bitterly cold.

The Trade Union movement were under constant attack from the media and the Conservative Party MP's. Paul Williams the Tory MP for South Sunderland called the Unions the 'wicked men' at work in Britain. He said ' The real tragedy of the situation is that many decent people are led astray into wild and unofficial strikes often on flimsy pretexts or false reports'. Mr.Williams advocated legislation to prevent the type of strikes that were happening.

Jimmy came home to 20, Craigton Road for extended stays He spent most time with Ruth and as always visited the two children from his marriage. On his way back he visited the Bridgeton Arms to see Richard the Pub owner. Richard said' Times are becoming hard around here now Jimmy !'. Jimmy said 'There is plenty of work where I am but a chronic shortage of accommodation. However, I do not have a lot of sympathy with the troublemakers in the yards. They were told what the strikes would do and they are now seeing the yards close'.

Richard said ' Och Jimmy it is not all down to the shipyard workers . We have a bad recession up here !'. Jimmy says 'If something is uneconomic there is nothing that can be done. If the coalmine has no coal then it has to close. If there is no demand for steel then it has to close. If the railways are uneconomic then steps must be taken. Finally, if no one wants to buy our ships then we cannot have men standing about while the rest of pay their benefits. I was in the same situation with John Henderson not knowing whether I had a job or not. I took the bull by the horns and moved to England which I have done several times in the past when work was scarce'.

Richard says 'You are a hard man Jimmy !!'. They both laughed.

In the Govan High School magazine a pupil had a go in verse at the teachers.

Teachers:
'Tis useless rubbish that they teach,
There useless folk themselves,
Like china ornaments are they,
Just fit for the mantelshelves !'.

Sir William Lithgow continued his high profile  sales efforts to get Shipping orders for his Yards. Approaching Christmas he received a welcome boost. They won two orders for Tankers worth £5,000,000 to give a welcome boost to the 'tail o' the bank' economy.

A giant wooden gate had been assembled at Fairfields shipyard. The gate was as large as a house and weighed 500 ton. It's destination was Greenock where it was to be fitted to the new Dry Dock. In previous times questions were asked how the structure would fit between the Govan tenements on its road journey to Greenock. The answer soon became apparent.

A crowd gathered at the Govan yard and it had already been decided that no formal launching ceremony for the large gate was to be performed. So the call went out. 'Right in she goes'. The tug boats were to tow the 150 foot wide gate down to Greenock for fitting.

A bitterly cold day saw the tug boats sail down the River Clyde with the giant structure. The bow waves were high on each of the tugs as they worked the cargo downstream. The tugboat men were very popular with Govan folk. They were in a seemingly permanent dispute. However, whatever the cause and the rights and wrongs the Clydeside public usually felt the tugboat men were right even if on occasions they may not have been.

The structure passed by Renfrew where the Simons-Lobnitz shipyard was already condemned to close. The workers were on strike in an effort to protect the jobs. However, most accepted that the jobs had gone and the discussions centred around the possibility of some jobs going to the Govan Shipyards.

A deputation was be sent to the Prime Minister including the Scottish TUC in an effort to have a review on the 1,500 job losses. It was one of the bleakest winters in more ways than one for Renfrew. Stephen's at Linthouse were able to absorb just 20 of the shipyard workers and appealed to the Government to provide more Naval shipping contracts.

The end year figures showed the sales effort of Sir William Lithgow keep them at the top of the Shipyard output league.

The figures were: Total Launching output 400,000 tons

Lithgow's— 66,000 tons output;  Fairfields, Govan—56,300 tons output; Stephens, Linthouse—48,100 tons output; Connell's, Scotstoun—34,100 tons output;

Blythswood—28,900 tons output; Greenock Dockyard—27,100 tons output; Scott's Greenock—25,800 ton output;

Harland & Wolff now closing and fitting out their last ship—21,000 tons output ;

Barclay Curle at Whiteinch had completely re-modernised the yard—9,900 ton output.

Denny Dumbarton—7160 tons output; Simons Lobnitz—6,000 ton output.

A phone rings at the offices of Taylors Stainless Metals in Buckinghan Avenue Slough. The receptionist answers and it is Ruth who asks to speak to Jimmy Welsh. Jimmy walks up the stairs to the works offices and picks up the phone. 'Hello'. Ruth says 'Jimmy I have some news !! I am pregnant !' The phone goes silent for a few seconds while Jimmy gathers his thoughts. He says 'Ruth I am over the moon !! I cannot wait to see you this weekend when I come up. I also have some good news. I have at last been provided with a rented flat not too far from where I work. I move in in a couple of weeks'. Soon the following weekend comes round and Jimmy and Ruth spend most of the time together.

The single end tenement flat would not be missed as the noise from the back courts with children playing and loud music from open windows was often annoying. Jimmy decided to go to the Bridgeton Arms and see old friend Richard Crozier. Both were of ardent Conservative and Unionist persuasion. Richard says ' Did you hear about the Govan Tunnel Jimmy ?'. Jimmy replied ' Yes, What do expect from a Socialist administration !. They build the tunnel and forget to put the roads joining to it. These comedians think they should be running the country !'. Richard and Jimmy laughed.

Geoffrey Rippon the Minister for Public Building and Works commissioned a review to establish whether ailing Shipyards could usefully manufacture components for the house building Industry. The report was to concentrate on the North East and Clydeside yards. The Government had a record tax haul of £3,636 million pounds. The Government were reported to be looking into a 'Ships for Oil' deal with cold war foes USSR. The deal if successful would save up to 1,000 Clyde shipyard jobs. The Scottish TUC welcomed the initiative . However, the politics of the situation and the trust in the Russians honouring their side of the bargain was expressed. The Prime Minister Harold McMillan listened to the arguments and said the possibilities would be investigated. The Russians wanted dredgers and fish factory ships.

Unemployment figures released saw a huge increase in people out of work. In Scotland it had now risen to over 136,000 with a sizable number from Clydeside. Out of the gloom Alexander Stephens secured an order for a giant dredger worth £2.8 million. The order was from the State Tin and Mining Enterprises in Indonesia. Lithgow's also secured two sizable orders for two tankers worth £5 million.

'The rental charges on housing should be greatly increased'. The members of the Glasgow Property Owners and Factors Association announced. Mr. Mason the spokesman said the rents had been kept too low under the 1957 Rent act and a revision was long overdue. He said the upkeep of the housing was becoming very high due to ongoing vandalism.
Govan Town Hall was chosen to host the Judo Black Belt Open championship of Scotland.

Jimmy Welsh was making more frequent trips to Scotland while Ruth went through her pregnancy. He met with his former wife Joan and they agreed finally on a divorce opening the way for his marriage to Ruth. His life with Joan and his son William and daughter Mary was all but over.

Ruth was over the moon and a simple marriage ceremony was arranged. A few days later her brother Jack and his wife Maggie helped clear out 20 Craigton Road and took Jimmy and Ruth in Jack's car to Glasgow Central railway station. A large van took the furniture away for disposal it being in poor condition and Ruth sent only a few large packages to their new home. Jack, Maggie and Derek bought platform tickets and waved them off. The train initially pulled away very slowly as the steam started moving the pistons. The carriages picked up speed and Ruth was waving out the lowered window. She called 'See you soon Derek !'. The train was gone.

Derek now lived with his Uncle Robbie and times were becoming hard in Govan. However, life at Govan High Bella as it become known was slowly improving. A sad aspect was that most pupils left the school to try and get work as soon as they became 15 years old. Derek was sorry to see a few of the ex Drumoyne School classmates leave having been in their company since he was 5 years old. Govan itself was a bit deflated with the closure of Harland and Wolff. For years they had been used to seeing the small train coming out the gate and crossing the road near the Plaza cinema and go up the track towards Ibrox. Now that was gone and the yard was virtually silent.

A number of Derek's friends had girlfriends and he was at the age where the lassies were becoming more interesting. A few girls at school caught Derek's eye but he was too shy to make any sort of approach. His friends seemed to have the right chat up lines whereas Derek felt tongue tied at the second sentence. Still as his mother had told him ' Focus on the schoolwork. The lassies can wait till later !'. Ruth wanted Derek to continue at Govan High and get good grades in the exams when he was 16 years old. Derek always wrote back and gave the news on Govan. Uncle Jack sent down the Scottish papers including the Govan Press in order that Ruth could catch up on the Bereavements column.

Govan was becoming one of the hotbed places in Scotland for basketball and the Pearce Institute had a strong side. They were put forward as the representative's of the West of Scotland for the annual match against the East of Scotland and won by 4 points. Govan Youth Club were storming away in their league beating Westside by 132 points to 18. The team had already amassed an amazing total of 1,009 points in 15 matches.

A new team to start was Stephens who were coached by former Pearce player Jimmy Petrie. The Stephens under 16's entered a tournament. They did well as it was their first outing but the competition was won by Penilee. This was the 'Lee's second successive win of the 'Pearce Trophy'.

Most Saturday's Derek went to the letterbox in anticipation of receiving a letter from Ruth his mother. Ruth was homesick already but being at home looking after baby Graeme meant she was always fairly busy. She always asked after many of the people in West Drumoyne and Govan. The neighbours at 31 Daviot Street and in particular Nan Sillers plus her mother. Ruth had an amazing number of friends. Virtually the whole scheme seemed to know she had gone to England to live and when they saw Derek they always asked to be reminded to his mother.

At 84, Meiklewood Road in West Drumoyne they have problems. 75 year old Elizabeth Grogan is lying in the back court in her nightclothes. Her daughter Bessie sporting a black eye has called the police. Both have been attacked by Thomas Easton 49 year old husband of Bessie after an argument between the married couple. At Govan Police Court Baillie Joseph Vallance said if you had a previous conviction you would have been sent to 30 days in jail. That is how I feel about attacks on women. Thomas Easton was fined £10. Prior to the Court appearance both Bessie and her mother Elizabeth wrote to the police requesting the charges be dropped.

Robbie encouraged Derek to go the Boys and Girls exhibition at the Kelvin Hall. The exhibition was opened by the popular Lord Provost Mrs. Jean Roberts. The opening ceremony was followed by the releasing of 100 multi coloured balloons which set off into the sky. A special disc was attached to each balloon and if returned to the Kelvin Hall the 5 shillings would be provided to the finder. Attendances at the exhibition were high and the most popular attraction was a simulated parachute jump from the top of the hall. Many interesting stalls catering for all the tastes of youngsters were on display. However, one stall caught Derek's eye. The Electricity Board stall was one of the larger and well lit. The stall staff were pleased to speak to all comers and offered good prizes to be gained by entering their quiz. This was a plan of a house and good positions for plugs , lights and switches had to be added. Derek spent around an hour on the stand and at the conclusion decided to take even more interest in electrics. On the following days at Govan High he was able to put together basic circuit wiring and was able at long last to ask sensible questions rather than barbled utterances of guesses.

At Glasgow Central Police DI Roy Fletcher is preparing to leave after a long and apparently successful career. He was not going to be out of work for too long as he would be accepting a Consultant role to the Security firm Glasgow Secure. Along Paisley Road West two budding entrepreneurs Junior and Bernie have at last started spending the monies and gains they have accumulated. They have spotted an area of land which they feel they could lease. They have enough money to provide a stock of second hand cars; a fast growing need in Glasgow. Junior says 'Bernie it will seem strange to be in a well respected profession like 2nd hand cars !!'.

# CHAPTER 27
# OH DR.BEECHING !!

Govan High had a number of good teachers. However, to Derek one teacher was head and shoulders above the rest. He was not totally popular with all pupils but no teacher at Govan High ever was.

Derek was suddenly starting to enjoy a few lessons at Govan High. One teacher in particular, Mr.Barry Landman, was firing his imagination. Mr.Landman taught English Literature. He had never given anyone the strap in his entire teaching career it was said. The first books 'Lost in the Highlands' and 'The Tay Bridge disaster' Derek read ardently and was able to answer all the questions asked on the books without hesitation. Mr. Landman explained the meaning of the books read. One particular book about an everyday man Mr.Potter and his family was dull and very slow moving; a fact brought up by the entire class.

Mr. Landman said ' Living in Govan , life is fast moving for you all. Something, good or bad, always seems to be happening. This book brings you back to what life is like for most people. They live a normal life where they go out to work; come home to the family and participate in a genteel  existence'. To many in the class they could identify with what he said. Fights between two drunks coming out of a pub on Govan Road was not uncommon. Huge migration of workers to and from shipyards along Govan Road. A huge population of over 100,000 packed into a relatively small area with poor housing a key issue. For the first time in his life Derek  thought 'Things were probably better elsewhere'.

Winter time at Govan High Bella was miserable. The lighting was on but the illumination was non existent. Cold weather made snow inevitable and a deep layer covered the footpaths all the way from home to school and back again. On the second day of snow Derek and several others struggled through the snow. Unfortunately, the conditions were such that he and a number of others were around 10 minutes late.

The entrance to the school was at the Cessnock end of the school on Paisley Road West . Derek was in a group and was relieved to see that Mr.Neil was not around. As the small group approached the door out stepped Mr.Bud Neil and told the group to go round the building to his office. As the group waited in the corridor to visit Mr.Neil one at a time a number complained how unfair the situation was. The queue moved down. A few boys came out wringing and blowing their hand from the one whack of the strap.

The girls came out and made no comment. As a tall girl entered the room before Derek  the door did not close properly and swung ajar. Derek heard Mr. Neil say ' Now Fiona, you know you must get here on time; there is no excuse for lateness. I will not punish you this time but beware !'

Derek thought perhaps he may be excused the strap. Fiona left and it was Derek's turn to face Bud Neil. No words were spoken apart from 'Hold out your hand'. With the cold weather the pain from the strap seemed to register almost at maximum level on the pain levels. Clearly Bud Neil was using his new issue strap to the maximum effect.

If the whack from the strap produced unwanted heat and pain the same could not be said for the heating system at Govan High Bella. The whole school always seemed to be cold. As the pupils looked out the windows they could see the snow drifting downwards to the ground. The playground was like an ice rink. Derek and many of the other pupils did not look forward to the return trips home. Once home Derek would quickly get the fire alight and even the gas fires in the two bedrooms were lit to provide additional heat. Robbie said when he came home ' It is hellish in the yards during this cauld weather'.

A Mossend steelworker James McCluskey was not happy. He wanted to see the Rector of the Bellshill Academy School. His son Jim (12) had received some punishment at school getting a minimum of 'ten o' the best' of the strap. His son had fainted in the corridor afterwards and had to be treated in the ambulance room. Jim had been caught reading a newspaper during a science lesson. Mr.McCluskey took his son to Bellshill Police Station and lodged a complaint against the school. Mr.Martin the School Rector said the teacher has been spoken to. 'He says he only gave three. The pupil drew his hand away on possibly three other occasions'.
The police agreed to investigate the complaint.

Mr.Michael Noble the Scottish Secretary brought a smile to the teachers at Govan High and throughout Scotland. Having felt undervalued despite handling large classes the teachers were to get a 7% pay rise. In addition Glasgow teachers were to get an extra £1 per week acknowledging the circumstances of overcrowded classes. Some of the Governments huge tax haul was being spent on the teachers.

At Govan High Derek was staring to enjoy and take interest in more of the lessons. Mr.Mc Donald the Physics teacher was relatively young and a former pupil of Govan High. Most of the lassies in the class thought he was 'dashing and dishy' with his blond curly locks. He introduced electricity into the Science lessons which Derek enjoyed. He had previously touched on the subject under Mr.Boyd at the Langlands Road school. Technical Drawing under Mr.Cleland was interesting and the lessons were well organised. Mr.Cleland was a stickler for accuracy and would not sign any work on drawings until it was perfect. However, the English Literature lessons under Mr.Barry Landman were exceptional and Derek was getting good marks.   If interest in Physics improved for Derek then Chemistry knowledge seemed to be going backwards. An exam result of 20% left Derek bottom of the class in the subject. The teacher Mr. Meechan was able and held the respect of the whole class.

The Clydeside Shipyards received a boost when two of the biggest unions agreed that there would be no more demarcation disputes. The Boilermakers Society and the Shipwrights Association said that they would not tolerate 'who does what' disputes. The two unions had a combined membership of 120,000 of which 12,000 were working on Clydeside.

All of Scotland were stunned when the long awaited Railways report was issued. No fewer than 51 Railway services were to be withdrawn and a staggering total of 435 stations were to be closed. Dr. Beeching's report brought widespread dismay around the UK especially to the 70,000 staff who were to lose their jobs. Glasgow was to lose two of its four main terminus stations; Buchanan Street and St.Enoch's. The latter station was an institution in Glasgow and had railway architecture second to none.

Dr.Beeching when questioned said 'If this is going to be done it should be done quickly'. Dr.Beeching was asked to assess the profitability of a rail network and report accordingly. He was not asked to consider that huge swathes of communities relied on their railway network. The railways were nationalised and the general public paid a huge amount in taxes towards the railway system. In addition they paid more money on the train tickets.

The principle was that the profitable lines would offset the losses of the less profitable branch lines. Dr.Beeching's financial plan suggested that the Railways would be in profit by 1970. Transport Minister Mr.Marples had a vested interest in that he was the owner of a road building company. In the same way he had assigned Dr.Beeching to review the railways he looked to expanding the road network and also had talks with the Coach Operators. Dr.Beeching was rapidly becoming the most unpopular figure in public life.

Predictions from Sociologists suggested that Scotland's population will decline greatly over the next 20 years. Mr.Leslie Ginsberg of Birmingham School of planning. He says that all industry will be gone and it will be a bleak 'no man's land'. A theory was that people in the North of England and Scotland were moving not just for economic reasons but because of weather conditions which were becoming harsh.

The cold weather brought the queue's back to the cinema's in Govan. Several war films were shown including the Bridge on the River Kwai and the Longest day. The Lyceum, Plaza and Vogue pulled out all the stops by providing good B films, trailers and Loony Tunes cartoons.

Derek reached age 15 in February and officially could leave school. However, he decided on his mothers advice to stay on at Govan High until at least the summer holidays and see what transpires; if anything. The weather was terrible from early December 1962 to late February 1963 with snow and ice being on the ground throughout. Record low temperatures were experienced and, apart from 1947, it was the coldest winter for a century. Early March at last saw a thaw and the Govan populace were able to get out more.

At 33, Logie Street there is a fire in a tenement block. Two floors above the fire stricken flat a family is desperate to escape as dense smoke pours through their tenement flat. 27 year Agnes Malloy is hysterical and tries to jump out of the window. Her husband David also 27 years manages to catch her and restrain her. Things are getting worse by the minute but they can hear the sound of the fire brigade. The three children Jacqueline (4) , David (2) and baby James are in fear. The firemen arrive and the ladder is put up the building. The entire family are brought down with baby James unconscious with the smoke inhalation. All are taken to the Southern General Hospital where they quickly recover.

On the top floor Mr.and Mrs James Pollock escape through a sky light onto the roof where they clung on to the chiment stack until rescued.

The Govan Press announces some good news. The Stock Car racing is to continue at the White City for another year. The events from the previous season drew big crowds and the Govan track was rewarded with some bigger races. They were to stage heats for the world championship, the European championship and also the Scottish championship. A popular race for lady drivers was to be arranged and known as the 'Champagne Derby'.

The Flamingo Dance Hall on Paisley Road West danced to Bob Ronald and his music. During Easter they had a special dance event with novelty dances and spot prizes.

Mr.Atkinson the President of the Associated Society of Locomotive Engineers and Firemen slammed the Dr.Beeching Railways plan. He says 'Around the UK , 2363 stations are to close as well as 271 branch lines. £30 million pounds worth of short haul freight traffic should be cut away was made without any consideration of the service to the people or the country but purely on a basis of profitability. It appeared to be economics gone mad. It is like saying that city stores and other shops, to give a service to the people, could close down between 10.00 and 12.30 plus 2.00pm to 5.00pm because most people were at work and the cost of keeping the building going was higher than the actual income from the business during those slack periods.'

Mrs.Ella Beeching the wife of Dr.Beeching was looking forward to her visit to Govan. She had been invited to launch the 7,000 ton passenger ferry Avalon from the Alexander Stephens and sons shipyard at Linthouse. However a 3 week dispute with the electricians caused a postponement.

Then Alexander and Stephens and Sons wrote to all concerned including Mrs. Beeching saying that the invitations had to be withdrawn 'with regret'. They said that after discussions with the British Rail Board the Avalon was now to be launched without ceremony.

On the day of the launch there was another ship being launched at Fairfields yard. It was the Cargo Liner Lancashire. Both ship orders were worth £1 million pounds each.

Govan High Bella wanted entries for the Sports day which had event heats held at Pirrie Park on Langlands Road. The Sports Masters were somewhat surprised to find that virtually everyone had entered every event in order to have half a day away from the Paisley Road West buildings. Every sports event was packed with entrants with the slowest boy runner in the school entering the 100 yards sprint and the weakest girl entering the shot putt despite scarcely being able to pick it up.

One positive was that the school meals which were served up at a nearby church hall adjacent to Bellahouston Park. The cooks were even able to provide special meals for a few diabetic pupils. A very able and helpful bunch of ladies. Derek saw out the school until summer while decisions were pending.

The noise of the Clyde Tunnel building subsided and at long last the Queen arrived to carry out the formal opening. A large crowd gathered for the historic event with the tunnel joining Govan to Whiteinch. A particular interest to many of the school pupils around Govan was a race through the pedestrian tunnel to see who would be the first unofficially to arrive out at the other side of the river. The attendant opened the door and a rush went down the stairway to the tunnel. For Derek the race was on once he arrived at the bottom of the stairs. As a 15 year old he was on the older age group status. The first bit was easy passing 7 and 8 year olds to the mid point or the lowest point of the river. The next bit was the hardest bit running uphill to Whiteinch. Eventually the race was won but not by Derek. However, great fun was had by all who joined the race; an impromptu bit of enjoyment.

The building of the Tunnel caused a number of houses to be flattened and of course more people leaving Govan.

Ruth came up for a few days from England leaving a friend and Jimmy looking after baby Graeme. She went round to see all her old friends and have a 'blether'. It was as if she had never been away.
Ruth told of the different things in England. ' I went into the butchers and said ' A pound of sausages please. The butcher gave me links. I said I asked fur sausages not links. He seemed confused'. Ruth continued ' He said that was what he considered as sausages!. Also the water is rubbish. You cannot get a lather from it unlike here and also their rolls are not so good. But apart from that most things are good'.

A few days later Derek joined his Uncle Jack and Aunt Maggie in taking Ruth to Glasgow Central Station as she departed for London Euston. From the visit Derek had the impression that his mother was sufficiently happy in England and would not be returning to Govan.

At a time when the people of Govan thought they were not getting total support from the Government bad news came from Japan. The prices they were quoting were in the view of British Shipbuilders 'Suicidal'. To get market share they were heavily subsidised by the Japan Government. Mr. John Brown of John Brown's Shipyard said that Sweden were following suit. He added that 'The British Shipyards outlook was grim. We would like British companies to place orders on the British yards. The Clyde Shipbuilders are not asking for subsidies from the Government. However, a help with the considerable costs of research would be welcome.' John Brown also felt that the Government should encourage a 'Scrap and Build' scheme. This involves the replacement of a Naval ship to be scrapped with an updated replacement.

The better weather made the walking to Govan High based at the old Bellahouston Academy a bit more palatable. The three Destructors in Craigton Road always seemed to be busy incinerating the waste from Govan. A walk past Ibrox Stadium would often result in seeing the Rangers stars of the day walking across to the Albion where they trained. Derek thought he would say 'Good morning' to the players as he walked past them. All would reply in some form or other 'Good morning son' Hello pal' or simply 'Good morning'. The only exception seemed to be John Greig who kept himself to himself; always business like and ignoring the ' Good Morning'. However, Derek felt it did not matter as he was becoming one of Rangers best players.

The Clyde Tunnel had been opened by the Queen to a chorus of cheers. However, two months later the good people of Linthouse were less than happy. Maggie Smith from Skipness Drive had taken an appeal to the Glasgow Valuation Appeal Committee Chairman Marcus Robinson and his fellow members. Maggie said 'The noise from the lorries at night is keeping me awake. These lorries are struggling tae get up the slope and they didnae hiv any suppressors fitted tae their electrics makin ma TV fuzzy '!.

The shipyards diversification ideas got short shrift from the Labour controlled Glasgow Corporation. Leader Mr. Peter Meldrum felt that the money should be spent on making permanent homes rather than a return to the prefabricated houses days.

The Stock Car Racing season re-started at the White City with the 'Rock and Roll Derby'. 60 cars competed and there were invitation by public speed events. The following week there were again 60 cars and they took part in The Grande Prix De Smash'. All the top Stock Racing Drivers took part.

The Clyde Shipbuilders were unhappy when they heard that the Japanese Shipyards were awarded the order for s ship from a London firm. Union leader Mr.Ted Hill said it was 'un British to place orders with Japan yards'. In the House of Commons Mr.William Whitelaw, Parliamentary Secretary to the Minister of Labour, said 'It is a fact that orders are being placed in other parts of the world, but this was something that had to be faced.

Off the leafy streets in Dumbreck there is a panic as a fire has caught hold. At 4,Melfort Avenue , Mrs Rhoda Rose wakes her daughter and carries her to safety. She then wraps her head in towels and re-enters the house and immediately goes to the first floor. She opens the window and throws out her furs and best clothes. With blazing wood coming from the rafters and noise from breaking glass the next door neighbour the Rev. Robert Eastman of St.Mary's Church, Govan rushed to the scene. He went into the building and led Mrs Rose out.

Summer arrived at Govan High Bella and many of the class were about to leave for the last time. The feeling was that a number would probably have stayed on to the fourth year had the school remained at Langlands Road nearer to where they lived. However, the role suggested that around half the class only would start the fourth term. After an exchange of letters with his mother Derek decided to stay on for some more months if he could not get employment. The search for a job proved futile with a number of better qualified pupils competing for the very few apprenticeships on offer in Govan. Derek tried virtually every firm in Helen Street where a sizable number of small firms traded. The usual response was ' Ye better come back when the gaffer is in ! 'There are nae jobs here son !' 'Write in and get on the waiting list for interviews'. The omens were that a move to England was on the cards before the year was out.

In response to intense lobbying the Government acted and set up a fund of £30 million to British Shipowners. This could be used if they placed orders on British Shipyards and the rate of interest was 5% the Bank rate. John Brown welcomed the initiative but asked if not more Government vessel orders could be placed. At the Scottish Liberals annual conference held at Gourock they said the £30 million fund was 'only tinkering at the edges'. Mr. Campbell Barclay, prospective Liberal candidate for Greenock, said the Government should introduce a scrappage subsidy to a British Ship Owner provided they bought the replacement vessel from British Shipyards. He went on to say 'Clearly a boost to the shipbuilding industry would spark off a chain reaction of prosperity in steel, engineering and all other associated industries'.

At Lambhill Street the boys of Kinning Park Secondary School were getting excited. They were off on a 10 day trip on the Eun Mara studying Navigation and all aspects of seamanship. The trip would take them to Gareloch and navigation teacher Mr.Jack Elder had a full programme of interesting subjects to explore.

At the White City the Scottish preliminary heats for the World Stock Car Racing Championship were being held with 60 cars entering. Also in the show there was an attempt by an e-type Jaguar and a Lotus Elite to beat the speed record around 2 laps set by William Jack in an Austin Mini. The record time was 56.2 seconds. Music was provided by the Red Hackle Pipe Band.

# CHAPTER 28
# FAREWELL GOVAN

At Heburn near Newcastle Don Lipton discusses the Clydeside situation. Both father James and son Don had served apprenticeships at Fairfields in Govan. James says to his son ' Well at least Fairfields and Stephens are still going so there is still hope for Govan. It is absolute madness to allow engineering companies like these to disappear. They are everything that is good about Great Britain. Large construction projects are taken on and the labour force is hired to carry out the work. In the case of the Shipyards we have sizeable construction projects from a fixed base with a highly skilled workforce in place to carry out the work. There are an extensive number of trades involved and all work is to ensure that motto Clydeside built means something.

They have their disputes of course; you have professional agitators within the Trade Union on one side and several nasty reactionary types of bosses on the other. However, most Clydesiders in the yards work hard, often in sub standard conditions with the weather to produce a continuously good product. The yards are the greatest training ground in the world; they produce good people as well as good ships. I never regretted my time in the Govan yards, it stood me in good stead to be in positions to work on Large projects around the world. Second only to the Geordies the Clydesiders are fantastic people'. His son Don says ' I will never regret my time in the yards and I enjoyed the company. Right from the first week they seemed to take me under their wing. Every Friday night we got 'blootered' in one of the multitude of Govan pubs. The training was first class. Not just the technical aspects but the general togetherness of each project. The feeling I have alas is that somewhere it has been decreed that the country does not wish to subsidise shipbuilding'. It must somehow stand on its own two feet against competition from abroad where Governments help this important industry with support to help them compete.

On the River Clyde at Glasgow Green the Glasgow University Western Regatta is underway. In the Schools event Govan High are in heat two against Crookston Castle. Both crews gave their all but Govan High finished second on a close finish. A few weeks later the Annual Schools Regatta has a record entry of 85 crews. Bellahouston Academy got to the Final of the 4 oared Coronation Challenge Cup. In the final they lost by one length to Hillhead High School. Derek is preparing to go south and Robbie has just lost his labourers job at Fairfields. He too will be travelling to England to try and get work. The day before the scheduled coach from Buchanan Street departs Derek takes a last look around Govan taking in the landmarks around Govan Road. He catches the bus into Glasgow in order to treat himself to watching a newly released picture. The film is called 'The Birds' by Alfred Hitchcock and all the audience thoroughly enjoy it.

The better weather made the walking to Govan High based at the old Bellahouston Academy a bit more palatable. The three Destructors in Craigton Road always seemed to be busy incinerating the waste from Govan. A walk past Ibrox Stadium would often result in seeing the Rangers stars of the day walking across to the Albion where they trained. Derek thought he would say 'Good morning' to the players as he walked past them. All would reply in some form or other 'Good morning son' Hello pal' or simply 'Good morning'. The only exception seemed to be John Greig who kept himself to himself; always business like and ignoring the ' Good Morning'. However, Derek felt it did not matter as he was becoming one of Rangers best players.

The Clyde Tunnel had been opened by the Queen to a chorus of cheers. However, two months later the good people of Linthouse were less than happy. Maggie Smith from Skipness Drive had taken an appeal to the Glasgow Valuation Appeal Committee Chairman Marcus Robinson and his fellow members. Maggie said 'The noise from the lorries at night is keeping me awake. These lorries are struggling tae get up the slope and they didnae hiv any suppressors fitted tae their electrics makin ma TV fuzzy '!.

The shipyards diversification ideas got short shrift from the Labour controlled Glasgow Corporation. Leader Mr. Peter Meldrum felt that the money should be spent on making permanent homes rather than a return to the prefabricated houses days.

The Stock Car Racing season re-started at the White City with the 'Rock and Roll Derby'. 60 cars competed and there were invitation by public speed events.The following week there were again 60 cars and they took part in The Grande Prix De Smash'. All the top Stock Racing Drivers took part.

The Clyde Shipbuilders were unhappy when they heard that the Japanese Shipyards were awarded the order for s ship from a London firm. Union leader Mr.Ted Hill said it was 'un British to place orders with Japan yards'. In the House of Commons Mr.William Whitelaw, Parliamentary Secretary to the Minister of Labour, said 'It is a fact that orders are being placed in other parts of the world, but this was something that had to be faced.

Miss Christina McKenzie the matron of the Elder Cottage Hospital was chosen to crown the Govan Fair Queen Maria Palta. The Govan Fair was extremely popular again with the Govan folk turning out in numbers to keep the long tradition going.

Three young men boarded a bus on Govan Road. Daniel Peline (20), Francis Osborne (20) and John Best (19) did not have any money. 52 year old Edward Donaghy the conductor asked for the fare. Almost immediately the three beat him up. He was punched and kicked as he lay on the floor of the bus.

Fiscal James Robertson asked Peline why he had beaten the conductor up. He replied 'Because we did not have any money'. The Fiscal said 'If you had no money you should not have boarded the bus'.

All three who had previous convictions pleaded guilty to breach of the peace and assault. The sentence was deferred awaiting reports.

Nine year old Colin Campbell of 48 Dumbreck Road was playing near railings. He tried to lever himself up when his hand slipped and became impaled on the rail. His father Dr. Douglas Campbell was quickly on the scene and using a hacksaw cut through the spike. The ambulance arrived and Colin was off to the Southern General Hospital. On arrival Colin had the spike removed from his hand.

Derek waited with expectation for a letter from his mother in the tenement flat at 31 Daviot Street, his home since he was born. This hopefully would confirm to him that it was in order to go to England and start a new life. The letter arrived and Ruth had put cash in the envelope for the coach fare. Derek had already made arrangements for Billy the budgie to have a new home across the landing with the McGreskin family. The budgie was a good age and still as chirpie and sociable as ever. As beautiful a creature as you would ever wish to see and going to a good home.

On the Monday Derek walked to Govan High School (Bellahouston) and told them he would be leaving on the Friday. Mr.McDermott the form teacher who was the regular Geography teacher asked Derek to stay behind at the end of the last Geography lesson. He said ' It is a shame you are leaving in some ways as you would almost certainly pass the Geography Exam at the end of the term and gain the Certificate. However, I wish you well and hope you have every happiness in the future' They shook hands. Derek left with the best wishes of all the Govan High teachers as he handed back his reference books. The last teacher was Mr. Barry Landman. Derek said to Mr.Landman if he could have a word with him at the end of the lesson. Derek said ' Thank you for all that you have done. I think you are a smashin teacher and I have learned a lot from you'. The pair shook hands and Derek left Govan High for the last time.

As when he first went to Govan High the day was very wet. He looked back at the temporary Govan High School at Bellahouston for the last time.

At the Vogue in Govan there is a Grand re-opening. The home of Bingola is being opened by Billy Raymond (Star of TV's Spot the Tune) and Charlie Simm (Star of TV's One o'clock Gang). The Caledonia Girl Pipers will also be in attendance.

It is a Friday in November 1963 and Derek and Robbie after saying their farewells to the neighbours in 31 Daviot Street are at Buchanan Street station. A large number of coaches are in line for the through the night trip to London Victoria Bus Station. The rain is non stop as Derek and Robbie take their seats. The rain runs down the outside of the windows virtually vertically. As the coach departs the rain droplets become horizontal. Derek reflects on his 'Time in Govan'. Certainly a very fractured family upbringing. However, this had left no real disadvantages. A good Primary School at Drumoyne and a reasonable education at Govan High. The whole area seemed to be 'fitba' daft and certainly living in Govan allowed watching Scotlands best team locally.

However, football is interesting for all levels of players teams from Boys Brigade to European Cup level. The team Derek will miss most is certainly Benburb Football Club. The team represented everything that is good about Govan. They are non sectarian and never ask a player about religion. They battle against immense odds competing for support against a Rangers club that is getting financially stronger and more ambitious. The Govan people turn up to the Bens big matches but the support for the run of the mill matches is on the wane. Derek is determined to be a Bens supporter for the rest of his life. As Uncles Robbie and Jack often said. 'You should support a team like the Bens as often when they are not so good as when they are successful'. They need your support as does the other Govan junior club St. Anthony's'. Both these clubs always seem to attract good people to run their clubs and they put enormous effort in'. Robbie and Jack with were extremely kind uncles.

The bus is heading down towards Locherbie which is the first of two stops. The other is St. Neots at the lower end of the A1. Derek reflects on what to expect when he reaches Slough in Buckinghamshire. He hopes for something with electrics involved and the opportunity of getting an apprenticeship. Above all else he is looking forward to seeing his mother Ruth and his baby brother Graeme. Ruth is a typical Govan lady, absolutely down to earth and kind. She is sociable and surely deserved better out of life. Jimmy Welsh is an amiable rogue; always popular but with a drink problem. Things are likely to be interesting. Robbie plans to get digs soon and to get a job. The coaches arrive at Lockerbie. The only café open after 11.00 is the one available for the coach travellers. The coach drivers, two from each coach, get preferential service as could be expected. Soon the Café owner is waving the large number of coaches off. The fourth coach with Derek and Robbie in it goes downhill to the bend in the road in Lockerbie's main street and is out of site from the café owner. A new life is about to start in England and a time in Govan is over.

## EXTRACT FROM THE EVENING TIMES APRIL 1962

When Glasgow took over Govan in 1912 the lamentations were loud and long. *Partick* people protested about their village being swallowed by Glasgow`s capacious maw but the Govanites felt it even more. After all, had a Russian Imperial duke not described Govan once as the `centre of intelligence in Europe`? Some Govan people even suggested that Govan was older than Glasgow, so the take over should have been on the other foot, so to speak.

Govanites still consider themselves different from Glaswegians. They don`t like the way that Glasgow has carved up Govan into different wards so that Govan Town Hall is actually in Kinning Park now and south Govan Town Hall (known still as the `new` Town Hall) is in Fairfield. And they don`t like the way that Glasgow is taking down buildings and moving good Govan people to such outposts as Pollock and Nitshill. Such famous places as Hoey Street and Harmony Row are taking on a forlorn look as the houses are demolished. Yes, one day there will be new houses there but will there be Govanites to occupy them? When you go round Govan today you see the notices proliferating protest meetings— not about disarmament but about housing in Govan.

## GREAT OCCASION

Glasgow Corporation have done one thing for Govan, though. The only Health and Welfare Department outside the George Square area is the one in Govan Town Hall. It`s a very busy place indeed but it has no vestiges left of the glory that was Govan. Govan independence is still upheld, however, by the Govan Weavers` Society and the local newspaper the `Govan Press`. The Weavers, an ancient body, don`t have any weavers among the nowadays—just as there isn`t a tailor, so far as I know, in the Incorporation of Tailors of Rutherglen.

But they keep to their traditions and have their supper of white wine and boiled eggs on the first Friday in June, the night of old Govan Fair. It`s a great occasion and you need a pretty good digestion for it. The boiled eggs are in bowls on the table and there are sandwiches for weavers who don`t fancy eggs. At one time salmon from the Clyde at Govan was served but the last time a salmon got up the Clyde as far as Govan was about 1895. Incidentally, the white wine isn`t white wine; it`s a Govan euphemism for whisky!

The Govan Weavers have their meeting at the Pearce Institute then march across to Miller`s Restaurant carrying their ram`s head and the spear which is said to have been wielded at Bannockburn. But I should put that in the past tense. Miller`s Restaurant has been taken over by a firm of brewers and is a restaurant no more. So now the Govan Weavers are like Partick Business Club—force to wander abroad.

# GOVAN HIGH 1961 SCIENCE EXAM

**Question 1:** Draw a diagram of a typical flower and label the six main parts of the flower. Which part of the flower may eventually develop into a new plant.

**Question 2:** Describe, very briefly, the process whereby a flower produces a seed

What are the four main methods of fruit and seed dispersal ?

Give one example (brief description or sketch) of each of these four methods of dispersal.

**Question 3:** Describe fully what happens when Iron rusts.

What is the composition of air ?.

Describe, briefly, an experiment to prove the composition of air.

**Question 4:** Describe, briefly, what happens in each case when each of the following substances is heated in air.

A)      Mercuric Oxide.  B) Magnesium  C) Manganese Dioxide D) Sulpher E)      Carbon F) Potassium Chlorate

All of these six chemical reactions can be put into one or other of two groups. Name the two groups and write each reaction under its correct group.

**Question 5:** Give an account (with sketch) of the reaction between sodium and water. Name the two substances produced by the reaction. How did you make a test on each of these two products ?. What does the sodium and water reaction prove about the composition of water ?.

**Question 6:** Write equations, first in words, then in chemical symbols, for the following reactions:

A)      Sodium and water      B) Calcium and water      C) Potassium and water.

**Question 7:** Describe with diagram, an experiment to break down water using an electric current.

Name on the diagram, the substance formed and indicate the relative amounts of each.

What deductions can be made about water from this experiment ?.

What test was applied to each product ?.

**Question 8:** Write down, in the form of word equations, three general chemical reactions which produce salts.

Describe, in full, how to make some solid copper sulphate.

**Question 9:** Complete each of the following word equations and below each write the full chemical equation.

Zinc + hydrochloric acid =

Magnesium + sulphuric acid =

Calcium + sulphuric acid  =

**APPENDIX 1.1**

Question 10: Draw a diagram of the apparatus used for the action of magnesium on steam.

Write a word equation for this reaction.

What other metal would react in a similar way ?.

Question 11: Make a diagram of an apparatus used to generate and collect hydrogen.

What happened to copper oxide when it was heated in hydrogen ?.

What vapour was produced ?.

How was this vapour identified ?.

Question 12: Define Pressure, Density, Force, Weight.

A rectangular block of stone measures 40cm long by 20cm broad by 15cm high and has a density of of 2,5 gm per cc.

What is its volume ?.

What is its weight ?.

What pressure will it exert when placed on its

A)    smallest face ?

B)    Its largest face ?

If a wall 1.5 metres high is built of these blocks, what pressure will be exerted on the ground under the wall ?.

Question 13: Draw an apparatus which would demonstrate that, at any selected point in a liquid the pressure depends on the depth.

Draw a diagram of an experiement which shows in what direction the pressure in a liquid acts.

Question 14: Calculate the pressure on a bathysphere which is at a depth of 4,000 feet in the ocean (The density of the water is 64 lbs per cub.ft.)

If the bathysphere has a glass window with an area of 2 square feet, what is the total force, in tons, pressing inwards on the window.

Question 15:  Draw an apparatus which can be used to measure of gas.

Describe how this apparatus is used.

How would you show that air exerts a pressure

A)    Upwards ?

B)    Downwards ?

C)    Sideways ?


Time 80 minutes allowed


**APPENDIX 1.2**

# A TIME IN GOVAN FOOTBALL

# CONTENTS PAGE

**A TIME IN GOVAN – FOOTBALL**

CHAPTER 1    THE KICK OFF
CHAPTER 2    THE HOBBLERS (1950-51)
CHAPTER 3    A STORM FRAE DOON THE WATTER (1951-52)
CHAPTER 4    A SEASON TO REMEMBER  (1952-53)
CHAPTER 5    BENBURB TARGET THE LEAGUE  (1953-54)
CHAPTER 6    TOMMY & SCOT ARRIVE  (1954-55)
CHAPTER 7    GOVAN SUCCESS AT ALL LEVELS  (1955-56)
CHAPTER 8    DELIGHT FOR THE GREEN AND WHITE (1956-57)
CHAPTER 9    SWEDEN HERE WE COME   (1957-58)
CHAPTER 10   WE WILL FOLLOW ON  (1958-59)
CHAPTER 11   CUP FINALS AND THE CUP FINAL (1959-60)
CHAPTER 12   HUMILIATION AND BULLETS (1960-61)
CHAPTER 13   UP WI' THE BUNNETS O' BONNIE DUNDEE  (1961-62)
CHAPTER 14   POOR AULD BENBURB  (1962-63)
CHAPTER 15   THE FINAL WHISTLE  (early 1963-64)

# A TIME IN GOVAN—FOOTBALL CHAPTER 1
## THE KICK OFF

The three main football teams in Govan are Rangers (of course) St.Anthony's and Benburb. The origins of the latter club are often sought. As well as a football connection in that the author's family were mostly Benburb football club supporters. The family had a deceased mother/grandmother who hailed from the village. The story of the clubs origins go back beyond the official club formation date to almost 250 years before and a famous battle in Northern Ireland.

THE BATTLES OF BENBURB :  Benburb is a town in South Tyrone, Northern Ireland and also is the name of a Junior football club in Scotland. Junior Football is effectively Non League Football as it would be known in England. Benburb Football Club play at Tinto Park and in 1951 are attracting huge crowds. The origins of the club ; as far as most supporters are aware of ; is that a group of workers from the town of Benburb went to work in the nearby Govan shipyards and then formed a team which has continued ever since. The assumption is only barely correct and 'the Bens' must be one of the few clubs where their name is derived from a battle. A précis of research is given below.

The Battle of Benburb was in 1646 and saw a decisive pitched battle victory for the Irish Confederate army under Owen Roe O'Neill. The Scottish Covenanters Army under Robert Monro was supported by the British settlers leader Robert Stewart from Londonderry. The Covenanters had landed in Northern Ireland 4 years previously with the objective of protecting the British settlers present after the 'Plantation of Ulster'. The Irish Confederates wanted to recover the Settlements for Ireland and restore Ireland totally to the Catholic faith.  A vested interest, the Roman Catholic Church envoy to Ireland, had shortly before the battle given weaponry to O'Neill. Monro was an able leader but rarely had the opportunity to test his well equipped army against the Irish Confederates on an open field. Monro was determined to catch a band of Confederates on the day of the battle and mounted a 15 mile chase after a band that was spotted. In early evening the chase ended with a 5,000 eager well armed  and motivated army in front of Monro with the formidable O'Neill at its head. Behind Monro he had a good army of 6,000 but very weary after trudging 15 miles to reach this confrontation. O'Neill managed to outflank Monro's army and trapped them up against the elbow of a river.

It finished in a rout with Monro losing between 2,000 and 3,000 killed or captures with O'Neill sustaining just 300 or so casualties. This proved to be the only notable victory by the Irish armies and of course attained a status with them. Over 200 years later in the late 1800's a group of Irishmen were forming a football team in the Govanhill area of Glasgow. Although essentially a team formed by Irish immigrants the club was non sectarian and membership was open to anyone.

1

They were Irish immigrants, proud of their roots and decided to call the team Benburb after the battle. The club were vying for the Irish community support but were them selves in a Battle in this context from another emerging team called Celtic. Benburb attracted good support and reached the final of the Scottish Junior Cup losing 3-1 to Burnbank Swifts in 1890. The team played in green jerseys displaying their Irish heritage and they appeared to have a reasonable degree of wealth. In the 1890's they took over the former Scottish League side Thistle's ground near Shawfield Stadium alongside the River Clyde. A few years later the ground was acquired by the City of Glasgow and the club were forced to seek a suspension from league matches for a year or so.

Benburb re-formed as a new football club in 1900 with Secretary Alex Parks and a few survivors of the previous club. The club found a new home with the acquisition of another former Scottish League club's ground; that of Linthouse. The ground was called Govandale and it was situated between Govan Road and the River Clyde roughly quarter a mile west of Govan Cross. A number of players; committee men and helpers from the former Elder Park club joined and the club were up and running again. Over the years the committee member content changed reflecting a predominantly typical Govan mix from the Shipyard working followers being mainly Protestant. At this time the club changed its colours from green to blue to reflect this. However Benburb has the distinction of being completely non sectarian throughout its history and has had good support from the predominantly Christian Protestant and Roman Catholic religions in Govan.

1951 and the start of the second half of the century saw mixed fortunes for the three Govan clubs. Rangers were floundering in the league around 7th place while St. Anthony's were in the lower half of the Central League. However for Benburb things were going well and they sat at the stop of the league They had enormous support from the Govan populace for a Junior side and gates were usually recorded in thousands. Star performers were goalkeeper Alex Forsyth and Midfield/Winger Dunky Rae. The new year brought some tough away cup fixtures and the supporters were hoping that the team could hang on to the first place in the league and perhaps land a cup.

The author's grandad Boab is a Queens Park follower. He does not go to many matches as he did in previous times but always looked for the Spiders results. Queens Park were an amateur side competing in a Professional Scottish League. They played their matches at Hampden Park a ground that could comfortably hold over 100,000 spectators. However the Queens crowds hovered around the 5,000 mark in the 2nd Division and few expected the club to challenge for honours until they changed from their all amateur policy. They had a very good second ground next to Hampden Park known as Lesser Hampden Park. Occasionally Boab watched the Bens.

# CENTRAL LEAGUE (January 1951)

| Team | Pl | W | L | D | F | A | Pts |
|------|-----|-----|-----|-----|-----|-----|-----|
| BENBURB | 20 | 14 | 2 | 4 | 58 | 17 | 32 |
| CAMBUSLANG RANGERS | 21 | 13 | 3 | 5 | 58 | 20 | 31 |
| KILSYTH RANGERS | 16 | 10 | 2 | 4 | 43 | 18 | 24 |
| SHETTLESTON | 20 | 9 | 5 | 6 | 43 | 30 | 24 |
| MARYHILL | 16 | 10 | 4 | 2 | 45 | 23 | 22 |
| PORT GLASGOW | 20 | 8 | 6 | 6 | 46 | 33 | 22 |
| POLLOK | 19 | 9 | 7 | 3 | 55 | 44 | 21 |
| GLENCAIRN | 17 | 7 | 4 | 6 | 33 | 25 | 20 |
| ST.ANTHONY'S | 17 | 7 | 7 | 3 | 32 | 34 | 17 |
| ARTHURLIE | 16 | 7 | 7 | 2 | 34 | 36 | 16 |
| BLANTYRE CELTIC | 15 | 7 | 6 | 2 | 35 | 40 | 16 |
| BAILLESTON | 19 | 5 | 10 | 4 | 35 | 44 | 14 |
| VALE OF CLYDE | 21 | 3 | 11 | 7 | 20 | 55 | 13 |
| MARYHILL HARP | 20 | 3 | 14 | 3 | 26 | 64 | 9 |
| PERTHSHIRE | 19 | 3 | 14 | 2 | 33 | 65 | 8 |
| VALE OF LEVEN | 17 | 3 | 13 | 1 | 21 | 53 | 7 |

Rangers were not having a good season by their normal standards. However they still had their inspirational captain in former Benburb full back Jock 'Tiger' Shaw. Also they had an enormous support and around 100,000 were tempted to an attractive Scottish Cup match at Ibrox Park. The opponents were top of the league Hibernian. Many spectators were turned away when the gates were closed 10 minutes before the kick off
RANGERS: Brown, Young, Shaw, Mc Coll, Woodburn, Cox, Waddell, Thornton, Simpson, Rae and Paton.
HIBERNIAN: Young, Govan, Ogilvie, Buchanan, Patterson, Gallacher, Smith, Johnstone, Reilly, Turnball and Ormond.
The tension and expectation before the match was enormous and the spectators were not to be disappointed. Rangers started well and after just 4 minutes Simpson gave them the lead after a scramble in the Hibs penalty box. Hibernian took control of the game and after a number of near misses equalised just before half time. Smith played a good pass to Ormond and the wingers accurate cross was smashed in by the advancing Smith,

3

The action remained constant in the second half. Rangers started the second half well and it was no surprise when they regained the lead. Paton crossed and Simpson again was on the mark to fire home from close range. Hibs responded by putting the pressure on and Rangers looked like scoring many times on the counter attack. Play raged from end to end and it was impossible to predict the next team to score. Fifteen minutes from the end Willie Ormond scampered down the line and crossed for Eddie Turnball to crash home a fearsome drive to equalise. With just three minutes left Willie Ormond received a quick free kick and his cross found Bobby Johnstone who controlled and fired home the winner.

A fantastic match by all who watched was the verdict.

RESULT: RANGERS 2  HIBERNIAN 3

At Govan Court on the Monday following the match two brothers appeared in dock. Archibald (30) and James Collins (26) of 32 Fairfields Street, Govan were accused of disorderly conduct. Archibald said it was the first Rangers match he had ever attended. ' There were people bawling and shouting all aroon me with around 5 minutes to go'. James said. 'People were throwing bottles from the Govan North stand onto the track. A wisnae dae'in anything !'. Superintendant Boss said both were under the influence of drink. The Baillie said ' You boys certainly distinguished yourselves. You are fined £1 each !'.

Benburb entered March still heading the league table with Cambuslang Rangers hot on their heels. The Bens play was usually described as 'solid' as they tended to battle out results. Dunky Rae usually added the little spark of invention that won most matches. A typical win was gained against Vale of Clyde at Tinto Park where two unopposed second half goals kept the 'chookie hens' a 2-0 win.

BENBURB: Forsyth, Ferguson, Cameron, Bambridge, Kyle, McIntosh, Rae, Thompson, Allan, Wilson and Muir.

VALE OF CLYDE: Hutcheson, Milligan, Watret, Dinning, Gwinne, Shields, Leishman, Deans, Mc Clymont and Reid.

RESULT:  BENBURB 2 VALE OF CLYDE 0

Although a poor match the Tinto faithful went home happy they were still top of the league.

**PLANTATION PARK  (THE PLOTS)**

**TINTO PARK  (BENBURB FOOTBALL CLUB)**

# CHAPTER 2
## HOBBLERS (1950-51)

Benburb were preparing a charge to try and gain a 1950-51 Central League title. However they were chased by Cambuslang Rangers who were edging ever closer on points. One department where the Bens were strong was goalkeeping. The experienced and great Benburb favourite big Alex Forsyth was being given a run for his place by a young up and coming Stewart Mitchell. Both worked tirelessly together and Alex's advice was sought repeatedly on when to play Stewart in goal.

Big Alex. had no hesitation in declaring the young 'apprentice' ready for action and during the run in both keepers working together was helping keep the Bens charge on track. Alex. Forsyth was in goal for a match against Dunipace.

BENBURB: Forsyth, Westwater, Cairns, Smith, Morton, Weir, Rae, Logie, Currie, Mullen and Ayre.

DUNIPACE: Finlay, McIntyre, Gardiner, Grant, Holleron, Heggie, Peebles, Vandermotten, Kerr, Ferguson and McDonald.

The Bens attacked non stop from the start but had to wait until mid way through the half for a goal to arrive when Smith shot home. Westwater converted a penalty shortly after before prolific scorer Logie added a third. In the second half the Bens could afford the luxury of a missed Westwater penalty before Ayre added a fourth. The third penalty of the match went to the 'pace and Kerr scored.

RESULT: BENBURB 4 DUNIPACE 1

Benburb Football Club had a celebration when their plans for a stand at the Drumoyne side of the ground were approved. This would be welcome for their support who would always be in the dry during the winter months.

In senior football Hibernian seemed unstoppable in their quest for the Scottish League title. They had also reached the semi final of the Scottish Cup and were paired with Motherwell at Tynecastle in the semi final.

HIBERNIAN: Younger, Govan, Ogilvie, Buchanan, Patterson, Combe, Smith, Johnstone, Reilly, Turnball and Ormond.

MOTHERWELL: Johnston, Kilmarnock, Higgins, McLoed, Paton, Redpath, Humphries, Forrest, Kelly, Watson and Aikenhead.

The match was a sell out. Motherwell stunned the large Hibernian support with a first minute goal. Aitkenhead crossed and Kelly headed in. On quarter of an hour things got worse for the Hibs when Ogilview was carried of with his leg broken in two places. Hibs were to play the rest of the match with ten players. Hibernian defended for most of the first half but Reilly equalised approaching half time. However the 'well regained the lead on the stroke of half time again Kelly being the scorer.

5

The second half was every bit as exciting as the first with play raging from end to end. Mc Leod extended the 'well lead before the ten men of Hibs replied with another Reilly goal. Despite a heroic effort the Hibs just could not equalise and Motherwell were through to play Celtic in the final.

RESULT HIBERNIAN 2 MOTHERWELL 3

The Final at Hampden Park attracted a huge crowd and a John McPhail goal (13 minutes) took the Scottish Cup to Parkhead much to the delight of Celtic. The match was touched by tragedy as a train carrying fans to the match crashed and two people were killed. The warm day and huge crowd of 134,000 contributed to two further deaths with fans in poor health collapsing and dying.

A number of the more enthusiastic Govanites travelled to London and Wembley Stadium. Scotland had a strong side and they were expected to do well.

ENGLAND: Williams, Ramsey, Eckersley, Johnston, Froggatt, Wright, Matthews, Mannion, Mortenson, Hassell and Finney

SCOTLAND: Cowen, Young, Cox, Evans, Woodburn, Redpath, Waddell, Johnstone, Reilly, Steel and Liddell.

The match was just 13 minutes old when Wilf Mannion and Billy Liddell collided head on. Both were lying on the ground. Liddell recovered but Mannion left the field concussed leaving England a man short.

Scotland attacked most of the time but were stunned when Hassell gave England the lead on the half hour with a good volley. However Scotland replied soon after when Bobby Johnstone danced through the England defence to equalise. The second half saw a spirited England side give Scotland a real run for their money and in particular winger Tom Finney. However Lawrie Reilly scored to put Scotland in front and Billy Liddell with a cut head from his clash with Mannion scored to put the match out of England's reach. Tom Finney however was not for giving up and reduced the deficit. Scotland held on.

RESULT: ENGLAND 2 SCOTLAND 3

At local level Govan High played Whitehill in a Schools Cup Final at Firhill. Many senior club scouts were present and in particular to see two Govan High players Billy Crawford and Tony Johnstone. Govan school players were also were well represented in the Glasgow Schools match v Lanarkshire. F.O'Hare and F.Whyte from St.Gerrards with J.Hume from Govan High played for the Glasgow Schools team.

Benburb continued to hold a small lead in points in their quest to win the Central League title. The key match came towards the end of the season. The main challengers were Cambuslang Rangers who trailed by just two points but with a better goal average. When the sides met at Tinto Park the question with the Bens team selection was who should play in goal. With the agreement and recommendation Alex. Forsyth who had been a Benburb stalwart recommended Stewart Mitchell his prodigy.

6

BENBURB: Mitchell, Ferguson, Cameron, Benbridge , Kyle, Montgomery, Allen, Thomson, Downs, McColl and Newman
CAMBUSLANG RANGERS: Gordon, Bell, Lumsden, Kidd, Martin, Ford, Newman, Chalmers, Logan, Mooney and Gowrie.

A large crowd attended the match and they were not to be disappointed as the sides battled out a 2-2 draw. Stewart Mitchell had some important saves for the Bens and his selection proved to be justified. Benburb were heading for a Central League title. As an additional bonus to the club inside right Thomson had been selected to play for the Central League Representative team.

In the Glasgow Charity Cup Rangers match with Celtic at Hampden Park saw several lightning strikes and torrential rain. However the match was able to progress and goals from Thornton and Findlay had the 'gers two up at half time. Celtic reduced the deficit through Charlie Tully but Rangers were through to the semi final. Third Lanark proved tough opponents at Cathkin Park and the game finished 1-1. The toss of the coin saw Rangers in the Final. Partick Thistle were the better team in the Glasgow Charity Cup Final but Rangers triumphed 2-1 to lift the Cup.

Govan High Schools football team set a record with no fewer than three of the age groups winning their respective leagues and progressing to the league 'deciders'. Two Govan High sides turned out at Cathkin Park. At Under 14 the opponents were St.Mungo and at Under 15 they played Shawlands Academy. It was the first time in 47 years that a school had achieved such a feat. Celtic Park hosted the annual Roman Catholic schoolboys match. This featured a select of the 4 best Catholic schools in Glasgow. St.Mungo's and St.Gerrards played against St.Aloysius and Holyrood. In the former team no fewer than six St.Gerrards players were selected. T.Cameron, G.Wylie, C.Docherty, R.Ferrier, F.Whyte and F.O'Hare.

At Govan Cross a number of pensioners with their bunnets on are debating the fitba'. Among them is Boab Wilson who is smoking his pipe.The group were discussing the season. Bert McGurn says ' The Rangers were rubbish! It looked like they would finish in their lowest ever position for the most part. Big Willie Woodbine (Woodburn) saved them most of the time.Bill White says ' I watched the Bens for the most part. They have a great set up and I enjoy the matches. If they carry on the way they are going they are going to get bigger crowds than Rangers. Great news aboot the Covered Enclosure.I am surprised that they raised such a sum of money through the half time sheet going around. The design of the cover looks as though they will have a stand better than most senior league teams. I just wonder where the money came from !'. Scott McKenzie says 'I feel a wee bit for the Ants. They produce so many good young players. Bobby Evans is a real star with Celtic and Scotland.

Some say Bobby turned up for the Ants without his comb and they loaned it to him. Others say they gave Bobby a spare pair of bootlaces when he was worried aboot them breaking. It was amusing the way the priests at Parkhead stood up in the front stand rows for Bobby and applauded when he ran out. Playing for the Ants they thought he was a Catholic. When they found out he was a Proddy they now keep still in their seats. The Ants have a lot of very good youngsters and they are worth watching. It is a shame the Catholic's do not give them more of a chance. Their crowds should be much bigger'.

Alan Crosby says 'I think something should be done about substitutes. If a player gets injured they should be allowed to put in a replacement. I am sorry to say it but I think the England result might have been different if Mannion had stayed on. Also the Hibs might have beat Motherwell had the guy not broken his leg'. Apparently they have tried it out on the Continent'.

Bert McGurn says: 'Ye couldnae have it Alan. You know what would happen. Some Italian team would want to put on a substitute for an injured player. The injured guy widnae really be injured and they would then have a fresh player while the honest team wid be playin wae whit they hid'.

Boab Wilson puffing on his pipe says ' I am disappointed with Queens. They should have done better in that league. However fingers crossed they will be back next season challenging to go back up. Good to see the Govan Schools teams doing well. St.Gerrards have some great wee players. Govan High have been brilliant. There is a saying that the wee Music teacher is helping with the coaching at the moment. Someone told me that if they do not do what they are told on the pitch they get the strap. If they get beat they get two of the strap each at the match. I do not believe that for one minute. It just cannot be true. Can it ?'.

With the success of Benburb plus the Govan High and St.Gerrards school teams the season was greatly extended towards mid summer. St.Anthony's also were having some late season joy.

Such was the strength of the Govan High school teams that two were invited to take part in the Pollok Juniors invitation tournament for schools. Centre Forward McCargo played at Hampden Park for the Glasgow Schools in the annual match against Bradford which the Glasgow side won 3-2.

GLASGOW: T.McBride (St.Alloysius), R.Bruce (Holyrood), G.Savage ( St.Mungo's) J.Blair (Eastbank), J.Clark (Victoria Drive), D.McLean (Rutherglen), A Ballantyne (John Street), J.Woods (Shawlands), M.Mc Cargo (Govan High), I Walker (Queens Park) and G.Mackie (Whitehill).
J.Woods scored a hat trick for the winners.

As champions of their league Benburb had a play off match to decide the Central League champions against Duntocher Hibs at Shawfield. A tight match was expected and a scoreless draw was the outcome with both goalkeepers the stars for their respective teams

BENBURB:Forsyth, Ferguson, Cameron, Bainbridge, Kyle, Montgomery, Allen, Thomson, Downs, Wilson and Gilmour

DUNTOCHER HIBS: McLaren, Stirling, Shaw, Bone, McIlroy, Maxwell, Smellie, McGill , Gallacher, Ryden and Murphy.

The replay four days later; again at Shawfield ; saw a lot more incident. Virtually all of it was around the Bens goal where Alex. Forsyth was again proving to be the hero. For his trouble he took a heavy knock on the thigh which greatly hampered his movement. This greatly contributed to the winning goal when he was unable to reach a lob due to his injury and the ball dropped into the net. Duntocher were the better side and deserved their victory. Not to be undaunted Benburb had another two cup finals still to play for. In the Kirkwood Shield they played Vale of Leven at Tinto Park.

BENBURB: Forsyth, Ferguson, Cameron, Bainbridge, Kyle, Montgomery, Allen, Rae, Downes, Wilson and Muir.

VALE OF LEVEN: Jackson, R.McNichol, Reason, Greig , Taylor, Gailey, J.McNichol, Smith, Feeney, Baxter and Mayberry.

A high scoring game saw a hat trick from Feeney help Vale to a half time lead of 3-2 with Downes scoring the Bens goals. The Bens equalised in the second half. The replay a few days later saw Vale of Leven comfortable winners at Millburn Park.

St.Anthony's young team battled through to the final of the popular Erskine Cup competition. They did not have too far to travel for the final with Tinto Park being the venue and Renfrew the opponents.

ST.ANTHONY'S: Harvey, Dorian, Coogan, Turnball, O'Donnell, Cloucherty, Gallacher, Goldie, Martin, Mullen and McKenna

RENFREW: Walkinshaw, Nibloe , Goodfellow, Moore, Docherty , Gemmell, Young, McIntyre, Scanlon, Williamson and McGuire.

The Ants were well on top for most of the first half. The pressure eventually told they got the decisive breakthroughs in the second half to win 2-1 and lift the Cup bringing joy to their followers .The Bens were hoping that it would be third time lucky when they took the field at Southcroft Park, Rutherglen against Ashfield. The match was the Final of the Glasgow Charity Cup. The game was shrouded in great sadness for the Benburb club following the death of John Mc Vicar long time stalwart at the club earlier in the week.

BENBURB: Forsyth, Ferguson, Swan, Bainbridge, Kyle, Montgomery, Hawson, Rae, Downes, Wilson and Muir.

ASHFIELD: Robb, Wilson, Conroy, Martin, Cassidy, Mc Phail, Graham, Divers, Mc Cartney, Boyd and Scott.

Ashfield wasted no time in getting on top and quickly raced into a two goal lead which they held until half time. In the second half Fred Downes halved the deficit and the same player equalised for the Bens. Extra time saw Ashfield score two unopposed goals and lift the trophy.

## CHAPTER 3
## A STORM FRAE DOON THE WATTER (1951-52)

The 1951-52 season saw Rangers start the season well in a League Cup group that contained East Fife, Aberdeen and Queen of the South. The Ibrox club progressed with relative ease into the quarter final and got drawn against Dunfermline. The first leg saw Rangers outplayed and the Pars were desparately unlucky not to secure a bigger margin of the victory than the one goal scored. The second leg was a very close match and Rangers finally triumphed 3-1. Dunfermline got what looked like a good goal disallowed in this match.

Celtic did not have it their own way in the League Cup group. In the last match at Cappielow in Greenock they went 2-0 behind to Morton. This enabled the home side to draw level on points with Celtic and very close on the goal difference formula. There was considerable crowd trouble at the match with many Celtic fans feeling they were heading out of the Cup. However the score remained unchanged and it was Celtic who qualified by the narrowest of goal difference margins.

Celtic easily won the quarter final match and were drawn to play their old firm rivals at Hampden Park in the semi final. The match was predicted to be close but in the event it was very one sided. Rangers scored two quick goals through Thornton and Johnson. Findlay added a third in the second half to send the Ibrox club through to the final against a strong Dundee side. Dundee were not going to be easy opponents having demolished Motherwell 5-1 at Ibrox in the semi final.

Over 92,000 turned up at Hampden Park for the Final.

DUNDEE: Brown, Follon, Cowan, Gallacher, Cowie, Boyd, Toner , Patillo, Flavell, Steel, Christie.

RANGERS: Brown, Young, Little, Mc Coll, Woodburn, Cox, Waddell, Findlay, Thornton, Johnson and Rutherford

Dundee played a good brand of football against Rangers who had the more 'direct' approach. However Willie Findlay scored the only goal of the first half to give the 'gers the lead. Bobby Flavell equalised straight after half time and the Taysiders were well on top. Johnny Patillo gave them the lead and seemingly on their way to lifting the cup. Three minutes from time Willie Thornton equalised for Rangers and a replay looked on the cards.

However,virtually from the kick off, Dundee pressed and were rewarded when Alfie Boyd netted the winner to take Cup to Dundee.

RESULT: DUNDEE 3  RANGERS  2

Benburb were looking forward to the new season. The previous season had seen a team comprised of mainly lower level players win the league and reach three cup finals.

The Benburb squad for the new season looked reasonably strong.
Goalkeepers : Alexander Forsyth;  Stewart Mitchell (Army); Douglas Johnstone
Backs: Charles Ferguson
Half Backs: Joseph Newbigging; Alexander McAllister (Penilee Moorpark); William McConnachie (Kilbirnie Ladeside); William Montgomery; Forwards; Duncan Rae; Fred Downes; James McCready (Penilee United) ;Alex. McConnachie (Ardeer) Alex Donnachie ( County Victoria)
St.Anthony's had a young side and signed O'Grady from St.Constantine's Boys Guild.

Benburb started the season with a trip across the city to play Dennistoun Waverley overlooked by the high tenements.. The Haghill Park black ash pitch was bone dry and with a fair wind blew up some dust which Alex Forsyth had to contend with in the first half. The Waverley scored early but the Bens gradually came into the game and Dunky Rae equalised. In the second half with wind advantage the Bens ran riot and secured an easy 6-1 win. However the season did not prove to be as good as the previous year and indifferent form saw the Bens in mid table. A 6-2 home defeat to Ashfield highlighted many weaknesses in the team.

It was with some relief to the Benburb club that they got a home draw in the Scottish Junior Cup against Dunoon Athletic for the first round. 'The Doon the Watter' team were joint bottom of the Western League.
BENBURB:Johnstone, Ferguson, Lumsden,  Newbigging, McConnachie, Montgomery, Craig, Rae, McCready, McAllister, McDonald
DUNOON ATHLETIC: Laurie, Fleming, Smith, Armstrong, Young, Barr, McEwan, Muir, McAlpine, McGoldrick and McKechan.

Benburb were soon on the attack and after 10 minutes were gifted a goal with a defensive lapse which was snapped up by Craig. McCreary doubled the Bens advantage but Muir pulled a goal back for Dunoon before half time. In the second half play raged from end to end but it was the visitors who equalised. Mc Goldrick stunned a large Benburb support by scoring near the end to give his side a famous victory. The Bens protested, as all good self respecting Junior clubs do in such circumstances, that McGoldrick was not signed. However a few days later the protest was quietly dropped as the Bens came to terms with the fact the were 'oot'.

Dunoon Athletic had pulled off a shock result and were rewarded with an away match against Larkhall Thistle who were top of the Lanarkshire League. A good crowd was guaranteed and duly delivered. The small Dunoon support watched their team provide heroic defence and hold out for a scoreless draw.

The replay saw a large contingent from Larkhall make the trip to Dunoon.

The Athletic proved that the result in the first match was no fluke with a battling display throughout and they achieved a 1-1 draw. The third match was played on neutral ground at Saracen Park home of Ashfield.

DUNOON ATHLETIC: Laurie, Fleming, Smith, Muir, Young, Armstrong, Mc Ewan, Sarrisin, Winning, McGoldrick and Woods.

LARKHALL THISTLE: Calder , Clark, McIntosh, Young, Rogan, Black, Mc Innes, Meek, Milne, Shanks and King.

Dunoon sat at the bottom of the Western League; Larkhall at the top of the Lanarkshire League. The Thistle were expected to finally see off their battling opponents and a large crowd assembled. Dunoon were paying no respect to league positions and centre forward Jimmy Winning was proving a handful as the seasiders dominated the first half. Calder in the Larkhall goal was busy throughout and pulled off several good saves. The second half saw play even up an exciting match saw play swing from end to end. The tie was decided mid way through the second half when Jimmy Winning followed up a fierce drive which was only partly saved by Calder to touch home. The seasiders held on for a famous win amid much excitement amongst their followers.

RESULT: DUNOON ATHLETIC 1 LARKHALL THISTLE 0

The draw for the next round saw the Athletic drawn at home to Pollok. The Glasgow club had scored 9 goals in the previous round and were having a good season. Special trains were laid on as well as a fleet of coaches from the Newlandsfield Park club as they headed to Gourock and on to Dunoon. The home club had created a lot of interest in their town and the Dunoon Sports Ground had a large crowd present.

DUNOON ATHLETIC: Laurie, Sharp, Smith, Muir, Young, Armstrong, Mc Ewan, Whitelaw, Winning, McGoldrick and Wood

POLLOK: McLellan, Swan, Duffy, Peat, Crawford, Gorgie, Ferguson, Cairns, Best, Patterson and Woods

A large crowd saw the Lok mostly on top in the first half. Prolific goalscorer Best opened their account mid way through the first half and Patterson added a second. It looked all up for the seasiders but they had several chances to reduce the deficit. On the stroke of half time Whitelaw reduced the deficit. Dunoon attacked non stop in the second period and equalised to force a replay at Newlandsfield. Result: Dunoon Athletic 2 Pollok 2

Dunoon Athletic took their biggest ever travelling support to the replay. The cup run and the performance of their team against the giants of Junior football had excited the town and 500 fans made the trip 'up the watter' to Glasgow.

POLLOK Mc Lelland, Swan, Duffy, Peat, Crawford, Forgie, Ferguson, Perrins, Best, Paterson and Wood

DUNOON ATHLETIC  Laurie, Sharp, Smith, Muir, Young, Armstrong, Mc Ewan, Whitelaw, Winning, Mc Goldrick and Wood

The contrast in venue's was stark. The Dunoon Athletic ground was the largest in Scottish Junior football with a capacity of 50,000. The large venue capacity was never tested with football but huge crowds were present for the Annual Kyle and Bute Highland games. The ground from a playing aspect was large and spacious and on grass. The Pollok ground was very tight and the surface black ash. One end of the ground was bordered by the River Cart and the fans were almost on top of the players standing on railway sleepers.

Pollok were out of the block s quickly and Laurie produced a save in the first minute. However, on 3 minutes Best gave the Lok the lead. Dunoon responded and roared on by their 500 fans peppered the Pollok goal. Jimmy Winning thought he had scored with a fierce drive but Mc Lelland brought off a fantastic save. The second half proved to be every bit as exciting as the first. Dunnon continued where they had left off in the first half and were rewarded when Wood equalised on 50 minutes. Play swung from end to end as each side strove to get the decisive goal. Midway through the half Pollok were awarded a penalty and Crawford scored. Perrin quickly added a third for the Lok. However the seasiders refused to give up and Mc Ewan reduced the deficit.

Try as they did the Athletic could not find the equaliser and Pollok progressed. The star man for Dunoon throughout the six Scottish Junior Cup matches was centre half Maurice Young.

Pollok scored freely throughout the Scottish Cup run (scoring 31 goals) with centre forward Best proving he was the best at finding the net. In the quarter final of the Scottish Junior Cup in front of a packed crowd Best was to score two more. However it was not enough for Pollok to win through as their opponents Camelon scored four times for a 4-2 win.

Pollok Cup Run : 1st Round bye.
2nd Round Whitletts Vics 2 Pollok 2 Replay Pollok 9 Whitletts Vics 2
3rd Round Dunoon Athletic 2 Pollok 2 Replay Pollok 3 Dunoon Athletic 2
4th Round Pollok 10 RAF Dalcross 0
5th Round Pollok 3 Dundee Elmwood 0

Matchday's at Tinto Park was heralded by the flagpole above the clubhouse. A union jack has been raised confirming a fixture is taking place. The music plays over the tannoy; the one record in the Bens music library. 'Oh the River Clyde the wonderful Clyde; the name always thrills me ........' ; when the song comes to the end the needle is put back to the beginning and it starts all over again.

Benburb attract good crowds to Tinto Park numbering on some occasions many thousands. However with the ground capacity at over 20,000 , Tinto Park always looks to have spaces in particular the top end of the ground. Tinto Park was built in the 1930's by volunteer labour from the Govan Workforce during the great depression. The quality of the ground could be seen by the excellent spacing of the track around the ground.

Also the curved terrace at the top end is a work of art which must have taken days to construct. The lower end of the ground which had a pronounced slope had the clubhouse. Behind the lower goal a smaller terrace was usually well populated and invariably saw unsuspecting goalies go bowling into the net. The theory went that if the Bens, who always chose to shoot uphill in the first half if they won the toss for ends, were not more than two down they had a chance of winning.

Benburb Football Club had their zenith years in the 1930's. Older Benburb followers continually recollect the years when Talisman legend Teddy Swift was at the Bens. They re-call that he was a natural leader and guided the Bens to two Scottish Junior Cup triumphs. In the first in 1934 Benburb beat Bridgeton Waverley 3-1 at Ibrox. In the second in 1936 they beat Yoker Athletic 1-0 after a replay at Hampden Park.

Teddy Swift was a manager at a local Govan wood yard Wykes. There he was relatively well waged and had his money supplemented by the Bens who had good attendances. Swift was a formidable defender and could have signed for countless senior clubs. However he chose to play at the Bens. He was always immaculately turned out with his boots spotless and the leather dubbined; his hair immaculately combed and always looked very confident with an aura about him.

In addition to the two Scottish Cup triumphs he also led Benburb to a third Final which turned out to be an excellent match. A record crowd as at that time for a Scottish Junior Cup Final turned up at Celtic Park, Parkhead, and saw the Bens take on Cambuslang Rangers. Benburb led 2-1 before Teddy Swift got injured. In the pre substitute days he had to hobble on the wing. Despite this Benburb gave a very good account of themselves and narrowly lost an exciting final by 3-2.

Benburb had a very good support and took supporters in numbers to away matches. The supporters buses left from Greenfield Street in Govan near Elder Park. 'Wingie' the one armed bens supporter was a first class singer and if you were fortunate enough to be on his coach you had some good entertainment. Many stories emerged from the Bens supporters on their travels. They would invariably offer the opposing fans a bet 'How much dae want to bet your team against the Bens ?' Many recalled the days when they took special trains around Scotland.

Also they recalled the day when a number of Bens Supporters coaches arrived to play at a tiny mining village. The streets were so narrow that the coach had to park right up against the house doors on one side to let the supporters out at the other. Effectively the residents remained blocked in for a substantial period while the coaches shunted backwards and forward .

14

Tinto Park hosted all sorts of matches in the 1950's. As well as Benburb football club they hosted many local league finals and charity matches including the annual Police v Clergy fixture. The ground had 16 entrance gates including two for the boys/o.a.p/unwaged. They went all along the front of the ground facing on to Shieldhall Road. On the east side of the ground was Craigton Road and on the other side of the road there were three massive Destructers to destroy the Govan rubbish.

The Destructers looked like an eyesore to most people although they of course provided a vital service. Behind the top goal was the site of Benburb's former ground 'Old Tinto Park'. This ground had a basic football pitch and took a direct hit from a German bomber in the second world war. During the summer months the ground had a fair on it for several weeks each year which was popular with the Govanites. On the west side of the ground is the Drumoyne Bowls Club which was also popular.

The Benburb Club at this time is very popular in the Govan community. Black and White posters are placed in many of the shop windows advertising the fixtures. The team is picked by committee and the team play in one of the two Scottish Central League's. There is a plethora of Cup competitions but the main ones are the Scottish Junior Cup, the West of Scotland Cup, the Central League Cup and the Glasgow Cup. The main local rival were the St.Anthony's club who played a few hundred yards away towards Ibrox Park at Moore Park.

Benburb Football Club history was something to be proud of. However following the success of the 1950-51 season the Bens were some way off the pace in the pursuit of league success. The shock early exit in the 'Scottish' had not been balanced by a challenge in the league. However as the season wore on form picked up and a few good cup runs were being constructed.A cornerstone of the Benburb team in season 1951-52 was once again goalkeeper Alex Forsyth. He brought the best out of all the younger players in the side. This fact did not pass unnoticed at nearby Ibrox park and the Bens keeper was signed with the purpose of playing for the Rangers third team and encouraging the younger players.

The popular Benburb goalkeeper was granted a Testimonial match at Tinto Park when he played for a central League select side against Rangers.

BENBURB: Forsyth, Hay, Lumsden, Mc Kechnie, Montgomery, Hogg, White, Mc Creadie, Rae, Mc Millan and Newman

DUNTOCHER HIBS: Brodie, Caldwell, Dearie, Bone Docherty, Singleton, White, Brown, Foster, Wilson and Murphy.

Benburb continued to close up on the leaders when they defeated Duntocher Hibs helped by two goals from consistent performer Dunky Rae.

# CENTRAL LEAGUE DIVISION A

| TEAM | PL | W | L | D | F | A | PTS |
|---|---|---|---|---|---|---|---|
| PETERSHILL | 22 | 17 | 3 | 2 | 60 | 22 | 36 |
| CAMBUSLANG RAN. | 22 | 15 | 4 | 3 | 62 | 34 | 33 |
| ASHFIELD | 21 | 14 | 5 | 2 | 69 | 41 | 30 |
| MARYHILL | 22 | 10 | 5 | 7 | 47 | 29 | 27 |
| BENBURB | 22 | 10 | 8 | 4 | 51 | 36 | 24 |
| DENNISTOUN WAV | 25 | 10 | 10 | 5 | 49 | 66 | 25 |
| SHAWFIELD | 24 | 11 | 11 | 2 | 49 | 47 | 24 |
| ARTHURLIE | 21 | 9 | 8 | 4 | 53 | 44 | 22 |
| RENFREW | 24 | 10 | 12 | 2 | 55 | 59 | 22 |
| KILSYTH RANGERS | 26 | 7 | 11 | 8 | 47 | 57 | 22 |
| DUNTOCHER HIBS | 23 | 9 | 11 | 3 | 57 | 71 | 21 |
| CLYDEBANK | 23 | 8 | 12 | 3 | 50 | 59 | 19 |
| PORT GLASGOW | 24 | 6 | 12 | 6 | 51 | 59 | 18 |
| STRATHCLYDE | 23 | 6 | 13 | 4 | 35 | 60 | 16 |
| GLENCAIRN | 22 | 4 | 13 | 5 | 33 | 52 | 13 |
| POLLOK | 19 | 4 | 11 | 4 | 32 | 52 | 12 |

The Scottish Football World was centre of attention with a couple of court cases during season 1951-52. The first followed the Near Year match between Celtic and Rangers at Parkhead. Charlie Tully scored a magnificent goal for Celtic. However the Celts were already four goals down and it was no more than a consolation.

Towards the end of the match bottles rained down from the Celtic terraces and the Glasgow Magistrates set up an enquiry into the trouble. In subsequent weeks the Celtic supporters flew the flag of Eire at matches and some other clubs in the league wanted the flag banned.

The Magistrates were left to decide the outcome. After taking advice from the Scottish Football Association Referee's Association, the Eire flag was banned at Celtic matches.

A second trial involved allegations of bribery at St.Mirren matches. The accused was a baker Joseph Mc Cudden. One of the players involved was Willie Telfer the clubs centre half. Mc Cudden had asked to meet Telfer and the St. Mirren centre half agreed. Mc Cudden asked if a player was to throw a match how could he achieve it. Willie Telfer thought hard about it and suggested a short back pass or a foul in the penalty box would be the most obvious. Mc Cudden offered Telfer £200 to lose a match for St.Mirren. Willie Telfer declined the offer. In the witness box it became apparent that the lawyer for    Telfer had instructed him to avoid answering questions which may incriminate him.

The result was that Telfer spoke in a low voice throughout his questioning and gave vague answers. `Aye that could be right; I  cannae remember aboot that; Naw that was wrong but ah it could be right'. The judge repeatedly asked him to speak up and if he understood the questions. Telfer replied he did. The Prosecution appeared to be making some headway when suddenly there was a noise as Willie Telfer fell to the floor of the witness box well after feinting. The court had to be adjourned. Approaching the final line of questioning after the trial re-started the prosecution asserted that Telfer could have influenced the result of the St.Mirren v Queen of the South match. Telfer replied ' Well if I did I done a pretty poor job of it. 'The match was scoreless!!' Telfer left the court cleared of any wrong doing. McCudden faced a heavy jail  sentence but after an appeal of clemency he was sentenced to just 8 months in prison.

The Scottish A Division was building up to have a close finish. Rangers after a poor start to the campaign started to make ground on the leaders and  just after the half way stage  had closed up to fourth place. Hibernian led and were making a big effort to retain their championship. Hearts were close behind . East Fife helped by the goals of  Charlie 'Legs' Fleming were holding third place.East Fife had beaten Rangers on an ice bound pitch just after the New Year.

EAST FIFE: Curran, Weir, S.Stewart, Whyte, Finlay, Mc Lellan, J.Stewart, Fleming, Gardiner, Bonthorne and Duncan.

RANGERS: Brown, Young, Little, Mc Coll, Woodburn, Prentice, Mc Culloch, Paton, Thornton, Cox and Liddell.

The match was described as a 'pantomime on ice' as both sides slipped and slithered throughout. East Fife took the lead with a fluke goal when several Rangers defenders fell over trying to clear a Jackie Stewart cross; the ball eventually hitting George Young and into the net. Rangers soon equalised when Willie Thornton headed in a free kick cross from Mc Coll. The second half saw East Fife score a similar goal through Bonthorne who headed in a free kick cross from Weir. Try as they may Rangers could not conjure up an equaliser.

RESULT: EAST FIFE  2 RANGERS 1

# SCOTTISH LEAGUE DIVISION A 1951-52

| TEAM | PL | W | L | D | F | A | PTS |
|------|----|----|----|----|----|----|-----|
| HIBERNIAN | 20 | 13 | 3 | 4 | 65 | 21 | 30 |
| HEART OF MIDLOTHIAN | 20 | 12 | 4 | 4 | 54 | 31 | 28 |
| EAST FIFE | 21 | 12 | 6 | 3 | 49 | 37 | 27 |
| RANGERS | 17 | 9 | 4 | 4 | 35 | 18 | 22 |
| DUNDEE | 18 | 8 | 6 | 4 | 36 | 33 | 20 |
| ABERDEEN | 19 | 7 | 7 | 5 | 41 | 39 | 19 |
| PARTICK THISTLE | 19 | 7 | 7 | 5 | 29 | 34 | 19 |
| QUEEN OF THE SOUTH | 19 | 6 | 7 | 6 | 30 | 33 | 18 |
| RAITH ROVERS | 19 | 7 | 8 | 4 | 28 | 32 | 18 |
| ST.MIRREN | 16 | 6 | 8 | 4 | 27 | 33 | 16 |
| CELTIC | 17 | 5 | 7 | 5 | 26 | 34 | 15 |
| MORTON | 19 | 6 | 10 | 3 | 32 | 27 | 15 |
| MOTHERWELL | 16 | 5 | 7 | 4 | 26 | 31 | 14 |
| AIRDRIE | 18 | 6 | 10 | 2 | 32 | 46 | 14 |
| THIRD LANARK | 19 | 4 | 11 | 4 | 28 | 40 | 12 |
| STIRLING ALBION | 19 | 4 | 12 | 3 | 20 | 59 | 11 |

Rangers recovered and staged a late comeback in a mid week match at Tynecastle. They trailed 2-0 before Findlay scored two late goals to keep their title chances alive. Another mid week afternoon fixture saw a complaint from the Glasgow Chamber of Commerce and many local companies. Rangers drew 1-1 against Hibernian in front of a crowd of 60,000 at Ibrox Park. It was observed that a number of Removal Lorries were ferrying fans up from Govan, some with around 50 people in the back.

The Scottish Cup saw Rangers receive a bye in the first round. Highland League Elgin City visited Ibrox Park in the 2nd Round and the Gers won easily 6-1. The 3rd Round saw a trip to Gayfield Park, Arbroath and Rangers proved too strong winning 2-0 against the gallant 'red lichties'. The quarter finals gave Rangers a home match against Motherwell and a tight match finished even at 1-1. The replay saw Rangers take the lead but Motherwell responded with two goals and progressed to the semi final. Rangers were to visit Fir Park again on the following Saturday and again the same result was recorded damaging the 'Gers title chances.

England came north for the annual Home International match. Demand for tickets was huge and a capacity crowd of 134,000 provided the Hampden roar. Scotland however did not have a good record against the 'Auld enemy at Hampden Park since the war and in fact it was 1937 when the dark blues of Scotland last tasted success in this home fixture.

SCOTLAND: Brown, Young, Mc Naught, Scoular, Woodburn, Redpath, Smith, Johnstone, Reilly, McMillan and Liddell

ENGLAND: Merrick, Ramsey, Garrett, Wright, Froggatt, Dickinson, Finney, Broadis, Lofthouse, Pearson and Rowley

Scotland started on the attack but were rocked when England scored with their first attack on 2 minutes. Stanley Pearson finished off some good work by Nat Lofthouse. The Scots tried to get back into the game but Stanley Pearson scored again in the last minute of the first half from a Broadis pass. The best player on the pitch acknowledged by everyone in the ground was the 'Preston Plumber' Tom Finney the winger from Preston North End.

England continued to be on top for most of the second half until Lawrie Reilly pulled a goal back for the Scots ten minutes from the end finishing off great work from Billy Liddell.

RESULT: SCOTLAND 1 ENGLAND 2

The Scottish Cup Final saw another huge demand for tickets. Motherwell required three matches to see off Heart of Midlothian. Dundee, their opponents, beat Third Lanark 2-0 in the other semi final. The Hi Hi had beaten Celtic after a replay and extra time in an early round.

DUNDEE: Henderson, Follon, Cowan, Gallacher, Cowie , Boyd, Hill, Patillo, Flavell, Steel and Christie.

MOTHERWELL: Johnstone, Kilmarnock, Shaw, Cox, Paton, Redpath, Sloan, Humphries, Kelly, Watson and Aitkenhead.

A capacity crowd of 134,000 saw Dundee have very much the better of the first half in their search for a Cup double. However try as they did they could not break the dead lock and half time arrived scoreless. Soon after the break the first goal arrived from Watson who took a pass from Gallacher and scored for the 'well. Almost immediately it was two as a strong shot from Redpath took a deflection to deceive Henderson. Dundee strove hard to respond but near the end two further goals for Motherwell from Humphries and Kelly produced a very flattering scoreline. Having missed out the previous season in the final Motherwell were Scottish Cup winners.

RESULT: DUNDEE 0 MOTHERWELL 4

Rangers closed up on Hibernian to produce a close finish to the Scottish A Division and moved into second place. Queen of the South opened the door for Rangers when Thomson scored four times against Hibernian in a 5-2 demolition at Palmerston Park, Dumfries.

However the same player showed he did not really care who he scored against when he netted both Quuen of the South goals against Rangers in a 2-2 draw. Rangers fell just short of the title which again went to Easter Road. Jock 'Tiger' Shaw was in the twilight of his Ibrox career. However he proved to be a true professional and inspirational to all the players at Ibrox. In the new year 'Old Firm' match at Parkhead he was easily 'man of the match'. It was only after Shaw left the field near the end of the match that Charlie Tully was able to score a consolation goal for the Celts.

After he recovered from the injury Jock played for the reserves without complaint and inspired them to a number of good wins. Rangers reached the 2nd XI Cup Final and Shaw inspired them to a 0-0 draw at Aberdeen in the first leg. In the return the Ibrox side won 1-0 to lift the trophy with Shaw receiving many of the plaudits. An article in the Evening Times by Billy Steel gave an insight to the former Benburb player Shaw's motivational qualities.

## ARTICLE BY BILLY STEEL:

### JOCK SHAW WITH AN EXAMPLE TO ALL

*'I remember Jock Shaw at the team talk before Wembley in 1947 giving the boys an idea of what to expect from the 'Auld Enemy' the following day. We were at Sonning on Thames, a quaint little village, a few miles from Reading enjoying the country air and toning up for the Saturday. The learned one of the press and radio had written us off as a bad investment and England were going to trounce us heavily. At least so we were told by the prophets of the sporting world. The result was a draw one goal each. Jock Shaw, captain of the Scottish team, was anything but pleased that anyone write off eleven Scots without anything but a battle and his words were brief but to the point. 'We have to get out and get cracking from the start'.*

*In the team there were several new faces to international football and having your debut at Wembley is a baptism of fire, like get flung in at the deep end. Right from the start our boys got cracking and it was later that day that learned that our skipper had rallied the team to give their all.*

### A BIG HEART

*This, however, is nothing he keeps exclusively for Scotland as all Rangers fans know and watching him play I often wonder how much a big heart is worth to a player or club. During his many years of outstanding service to Rangers I am sure football fans would put his greatest asset as his enthusiasm for the game.*

*Watching him play always reminds me of the boys at school having a wee game before the bell rings and anxious to get as much football in as short a time as possible*

## SHINING EXAMPLE:

*Not only is this a grand thing for Jock Shaw, it is also a shining example to his colleagues and the proper approach to the game which he obviously enjoys so much. The man the fans affectionately call 'Tiger' has had some great tussles in his time with Deleany, Smith and Matthews and many more and I am sure he enjoyed them all. Well that is Jock Shaw and to any young player who wants to play he should follow Jock's example. Go out and enjoy your game, play your hardest and best at all times. Never give up until the final whistle; no matter what the score. That's Jock '.*

Govan football remained successful as the locals played with enthusiasm and relish.

In the Govan Courts a box was called for as two boys appeared in front of Baillie Mc Crossan. One boy was 9 years and the other 6 years old. The younger one had difficulty seeing the bench. Both were accused of playing football in the street. They had no defence and admitted the offence. Baillie Mc Crossan asked 'How much do you boys get as pocket money ?'. The older boy said 'I get one shilling per week sir'. The Baillie carried on looking at the six year old 'And you ?'. The six year old said 'A tanner sir'

Mc Crossan said 'Right You are fined One shilling to the 9 year old and you six pence'to the six year old. He continued 'Let it be recorded that these arte the lowest fines imposed in a Govan Court in over 100 years'.

Benburb continued with a policy of attracting good players from Juvenile football and progressing them. This was despite the fact that they had good gates and could attract more seasoned and experienced players. John Bainbridge moved to Queens Park, Anderson to Partick Thistle, Mike Gallacher to Bolton Wanderers. 'Cheerful Charlie Ferguson moved to Heart of Midlothian and the Bens fans missed him when he went.

The season saw Benburb finish in fifth place and the club reached three semi finals. In the West of Scotland Cup they progressed to the semi final at the expense of Cleland, Maryhill Harp, Coltness United, Annbank United and Neilston. The latter two opponents drew large crowds to Tinto Park and Neilston protested after their defeat to the Bens. This delayed the semi final at Shawfield Stadium for a few weeks before Benburb were allowed to face Irvine Victoria. Despite huge support the Bens were disappointing and lost 2-1.

The Central League Cup semi final saw Benburb 2-0 up at half time against Kilsyth Rangers at Saracen Park, the home of Ashfield. Kilsyth fought back to equal the scores and in the replay they triumphed over a tiring Bens outfit. Bens threw in the obligatory protest that Kilsyth's Skinner was a ringer but the protest was over ruled.

The last of the the three semi finals was against Ashfield in the Glasgow Charity Cup but the Bens were well beaten.

St.Anthony's young side improved throughout the season. They reached the Final of the Erskine Cup. However off the pitch they lost an influential backer Jimmy Bell as Vice President. Jimmy was the owner of the White City Stadium.

The two central Govan Secondary Schools continued to do well and picked up countless accolades throughout the season. Among the success stories.

- J.Armour of St.Gerrards was selected for the under 15 Glasgow Schools team and played in the 6-1 triumph over Edinburgh Schools at Tynecastle Park.
- No fewer than 4 Govan players played for Glasgow Schools against London Schools. At Upton Park. W.Graham and S.Mc Quorqodale from Govan High; J.Fleming of St.Gerrards and G.Montgomery of Bellahouston Academy. All the Glasgow players were outstanding as they swept aside a strong London side by 2-0.
- In the selection for best Roman Catholic playing schools St.Gerrards had five players in a St.Mungo's/St.Gerrards select to play a prestigious match at Celtic Park against St.Alosius and Holyrood. A. Docherty, F.O'Hare, J.Fleming, T.Eager, and C.Docherty.
- Govan High won the 1st Division League decider with a 1-0 win over St.Mungo's at Cathkin Park.
- St.Gerrards won the Intermediate Shield with a win over St.Mungo's at Celtic Park.

The list seemed endless.

The Scottish Schools Presentation evening at Hampden Park saw Mr. Bob Kelly the Celtic Chairman help present the trophies. Also present for the evening were invited guests from the Govan Schools; Mr Blair from Govan High and Mr.Coneghan of St.Gerrards.

The first speech came from Mr.Jackie Gardiner of Queens Park the hosts. In presenting the QP Shield to Govan High he said.

' My advice to you boys is to put your career first. Think about when you are in your 30's and your playing career is coming to an end. I recommend the Queens Park motto and it is a good motto !. Play the game for the sake of the game'.

Mr.Blair the Govan High Headmaster was invited to give a short speech. He said. '

If you cannot play the game for the fun of the game then for any sake give it up !. It would be better for your own sakes and that of Scottish football if you joined Queens Park.

I hate any game which is over commercialised'.

22

Bob Kelly the Celtic chairman then presented the trophies to the two St.Gerrard school sides. He did not agree with the previous two speeches. He said. 'The standard of football has never been higher in the schools. I cannot agree with some of the things said about the professional footballer. For the level headed boy, professional football offers big inducements if he works at the game and reaches the heights'.

St.Gerrards headmaster Mr.Coneghan said ' I hope the day will come when we have manly behaviour on the pitch matched by manly behaviour on the terraces !. That is the aim of our school in guiding our pupils in that direction'.

# CHAPTER 4
## A SEASON TO REMEMBER 1952—53

Benburb announced their squad for the forthcoming season. Not surprisingly most of the previous season's squad was retained.

BENBURB SQUAD:

Goalkeepers:  A.Forysth; A Mc Lelland

Full Backs:  A.Lumsden; S.Hay

Half Backs: J. Mc Kechnie, D.Livingstone, D.Ford (Cambuslang Rangers), A. Crossan (Fauldhouse United).

Forwards: D.Rae; R.Young; J.Smillie; J.White; J.Montgomerie (Rutherglen Glencairn); J.Feeney (Vale of Leven) ; W.Maxwell (Barrhead South); E.Smith (Pollok);

Thomas McKay ( re-instatement  from Bury)

Player retained but not signed: William Montgomery (open to transfer)

Match Secretary: Alexander McVicar, Skipness Drive, Glasgow SW1

The signing of midfielder Eric Smith was put on hold. Pollok claimed that the player had already signed for them. Bens showed that he had signed for the club and the matter was handed over to the Scottish Junior Football Association to sort out. After a few days Benburb got the good news that he would be playing his football at Tinto Park.

The Bens first league match was away to Vale of Leven and after trailing 2-0 at half they eventually lost 3-1

Rangers kicked off their fixtures in a tough League Cup group that contained Hearts, Motherwell and Aberdeen. In a tight group Rangers looked out of the running but two wins over Hearts and Motherwell in their last two games saw them top the section.

The quarter final saw a 2 legged match with Third Lanark. The first at Ibrox Park saw a dull 0-0 draw. The second game played in midweek saw Rangers win 2-0 and progress to a semi final with Kilmarnock.

Benburb slowly began to find their feet in the League and a comfortable win over Rob Roy showed much promise. The Bens had a trialist centre forward called Newman,

BENBURB: Forsyth, Lumsden, Fitzsimmons, Mc Kechnie, Crossan, Ford, Rae, Smith Newman, Young and Montgomery.

ROB ROY: Harvey, Carbin, Ventre,  Sim, Cowie, Mackie, Kerr, Thomson, Bryans, Gray and Patrick.

Benburb scored three unopposed first half goals through Newman, Montgomery and an own goal. The Rabs grabbed a consolation goal in the second half leaving the Bens 3-1 winners.

In the Scottish Junior Cup Benburb were drawn away to Nithsdale and returned home with a comprehensive 6-1 win. St.Anthony's also progressed at the expense of Motherwell Juniors.

Two friends William Crawford (22) and Duncan Gilmour (24) went to Ibrox Park to see a Rangers match following a wedding celebration. They got into an argument over boxing and soon came to blows. The crowd found more entertainment in the fighting than the match. At Govan Police Court Baillie Johnstone fined them each £5. In court both said they were great pals really and were worst for wear for drink at the time.

Rangers travelled to Celtic Park for the first Old Firm match of the season. The Hoops scored two quick goals from Walsh and Rollo. Liddell replied for Rangers 18 minutes from the end but try as they did to level the points stayed at Parkhead.

In the League Cup semi finals most forecast that Rangers and Hibernian would be contesting the Final. However Kilmarnock and Dundee had other idea's.

At Hampden Park a late Jack goal gave Kilmarnock a narrow 1-0 win over Rangers.

In the other semi final at Tynecastle Park, Hibernian took a first half lead through Reilly. In the second half Steele equalised for Dundee and Bobby Flavell scored the winner 10 minutes from time to book the Dens Park club a Final at Hampden Park courtesy of a 2-1 win.

The Final teams were:

DUNDEE :R.Henderson, Follon, Frew, Zeising, Boyd, Cowie, Tonar, A.Henderson, Flavell, Steel and Christie

KILMARNOCK: Niven, Collins, Hood, Russell, Tyne, Middlemas, Henaughan, Harvey, Mays, Jack and Murray.

A crowd of 51,000 saw Kilmarnock on top for most of the opening half. However Dundee came more into the picture in the second half and two goals from Bobby Flavell took the League Cup to Tayside.

In the Glasgow Amateur League most of the Govan sides were in Division B. Gower Thistle had made a good start and led from Kinning Park. Elder Park, who many years previously in 1900 had provided members to help form Benburb at Govandale, were in mid table.

In the second round of the Scottish Junior Cup Benburb faced Lanarkshire League side Douglasdale. Essentially a village side Douglasdale produced many fine players over the years and were expected to provide the Bens with a tough match. A tough game it was but Benburb managed to win through with two unopposed goals.

St.Anthony's also had a tough draw away to Irvine Victoria. The Vics led 1-0 at half time and ran out easy winners with four unopposed goals at full time.

# GLASGOW AMATEUR LEAGUE—DIVISION B

| Team | Pl | W | L | D | F | A | Pts |
|------|----|----|----|----|----|----|----|
| GOWER THISTLE | 6 | 5 | 0 | 1 | 29 | 6 | 11 |
| KINNING PARK | 6 | 4 | 1 | 1 | 19 | 13 | 9 |
| CLEANSING | 6 | 3 | 3 | 0 | 20 | 15 | 6 |
| ELDER | 5 | 2 | 1 | 2 | 20 | 15 | 6 |
| HOUSTON PARK | 5 | 2 | 2 | 1 | 9 | 15 | 5 |
| FAIRFIELDS S I S | 6 | 2 | 3 | 1 | 13 | 28 | 5 |
| FAIRFIELDS ATHLETIC | 5 | 1 | 2 | 2 | 14 | 10 | 4 |
| RENFREW STEVEDORES | 5 | 1 | 2 | 2 | 9 | 17 | 4 |
| C.S.F. | 5 | 0 | 3 | 2 | 11 | 17 | 2 |
| ABBOTSHAUGH | 5 | 1 | 4 | 0 | 10 | 18 | 2 |

At Ibrox a key league game saw high flying Hibernian as visitors.
RANGERS: Niven, Young, Little, McColl, Woodburn, Cox, Mc Culloch,
Grierson, Simpson, Prentice and Liddell.
HIBERNIAN: Younger, Govan, Howie, Gallagher, Patterson, Combe, Smith,
Johnstone, Reilly, Turnball and Ormond.

Hibernian were the best side in the first half but missed a number of chances.
Rangers weathered early pressure and scored when Grierson beat Younger to a
Liddell cross and headed home. Lawrie Reilly equalised nine minutes later
when he dribbled past Rangers defenders and fired home. Rangers were the
better team in the second half and pushed forward to get a winner. They came
close on a number of occasions, one shot stiking the post.

However it was the Edinburgh side who took the points when Eddie Turnball
cracked a shot from just outside the box into the net. Rangers already had a lot
of ground to make up in the League.

Scotland opened their International season with a trip to Cardiff. A 65,000
all ticket crowd were at the match including 6,500 from Scotland. Wales totally
dominated the match in the first half and deservedly went ahead through Ford.
However in virtually Scotland's first attack on the half hour Brown converted a
long throw with a low shot. The second half proved to be a similar pattern and
Wales went close with a shot that crashed off the crossbar. Scotland broke
straight down the other end and a Billy Steele cross was headed home by Billy
Liddell to give Scotland a fortunate 2-1 win.

In the Scottish Juvenile Cup, Drumoyne Athletic had a tough draw. Their opponents were Dennistoun Juveniles away at Haghill Park. Dennistoun were the prime force in Juvenile football and a special reception had been held for them to celebrate them winning the top league and virtually every cup going. In the current season they had played 6 matches won 6 matches and scored 52 goals. Drumoyne Athletic played their home matches at Pirie Park. Pirie Park had a mix of grass and ash pitches. The secretary of the Athletic always asked the opposition circumspectly on arrival whether they played on ash or grass pitches. If the reply was ash they played on grass and vice versa. Drumoyne were unable to get into any of the South Glasgow Leagues but were fortunate to get a place in a Partick based Juvenile League. Some of the Drumoyne residents wished them well for their trip to Dennistoun but few went as they did not expect anything other than a thrashing. When they returned from the match they were asked 'Whit wis the score ?' 'We won' the Drumoyne players said and we have a Govan derby against Harmony Row in the next round!

In the West of Scotland Secondary Juvenile Cup 1st Round draw paired Rancel at home against Vale Emmett. Rancel were an interesting club. The name is derived from the first three letters of Rangers and the first three letters of Celtic. The team had a mixture of supporters from both the old firm clubs and they played away in perfect harmony together.

In league fixtures scheduled, Drumoyne Athletic were scheduled to play Anniesland United at Pirie Park in the North West Secondary League. A spin off team from the original Benburb called Anderston Benburb played away at Market Star.

Benburb had started their league campaign slowly despite having a strong squad. However after a heavy 4-1 defeat at runaway league leaders Ashfield they hit form against St.Roch's with an 8-3 scoreline after leading 4-1 at half time. Man of the match was Dunky Rae. The match was a prelude for a massive Scottish Junior Cup tie against Lugar Boswell Thistle. The Ayrshire side brought a large support to Tinto Park and a very big attendance was present.

Benburb scored an early goal from Dunky Rae but the 'Jaggy Bunnets' equalised before half time. Both teams scored again in the second half but neither could force a winner. The replay saw a large support travel down to Ayrshire. A special train was chartered as well as a fleet of coaches. On Greenfield Street the Bens supporters boarded the coaches; most surprisingly confident in front of a tough tie.

LUGAR BOSWELL THISTLE: Hall, Stirling, Love, Donnelly, Baird, Kelly, Turnball, Hamilton, Dick, Leslie and Black
BENBURB: Forsyth, Hay, Fitzsimmons, Mc Kechnie, Crossan, Ford, Rae, Smith, Campbell, Young and Montgomery.

27

The Jaggy Bunnets attacked from the start and missed a host of chances. They were made to pay when Dunky Rae scored on 22nd minutes. Lugar battered the Benburb goal and hit the post with a shot. Alex Forsyth pulled off a series of stunning saves.

In the second half Benburb survived early pressure before they added two more goals bringing huge roars from the Govan support. Benburb had progressed 3-0 and were drawn to play Bo'ness United at Tinto Park in the fourth round.

RESULT: LUGAR BOSWELL THISTLE 0  BENBURB 3

At Lesser Hampden Park trials were taking place for the Glasgow Schools team for the forthcoming match with London at Crystal Palace's Selhurst Park ground. There was a mix up and 12 of the 44 players on trial were found to be over age. The Govan schools were well represented and Armour of St.Gerrards scored freely.

The Govan schools players were:

A Team : Masson (Bellahouston Academy), Neville (Govan High), Duncan (Bellahouston Academy).

B Team : Hayes (Govan High), Catterson (St.Gerrards), Armour (St.Gerrards), Tennant (Govan High)

C Team : Mc Fee (Govan High) and Mc Guire (St.Gerrards)

Approaching the half way stage the Scottish League saw Hibernian, Heart of Midlothian and East Fife were the challengers for the title. Rangers were starting to find some form and won an exciting match at Shawfield Stadium against Clyde.

CLYDE: Wilson, Lindsey, Haddock, Campbell, Keogh, Long, Galletey, Baird, Buchanan, Robertson and Ring.

RANGERS: Niven, Young, Little, Mc Coll, Woodburn, Cox, Waddell, Grierson, Simpson, Prentice and Hubbard.

Galletly scored after two minutes for Clyde with a header but this was quickly cancelled out by a header from Billy Simpson a few minutes later. Prentice gave Rangers a lead when he dribbled along the bye line and scored from an acute angle. Clyde equalised on 30 minutes when Buchanan headed in a Robertson free kick and just a few minutes later the Bully Wee support were in raptures as Galletly headed them into the lead.

However Rangers equalised when Willie Waddell went on a mazy run and blasted the ball high into the net past Wilson. On the stroke of half time Derek Grierson gave Rangers the lead and both teams left the field with applause from the 30,000 crowd.

The second half saw Rangers in the ascendancy and they made the game safe with two goals from Billy Simpson. Buchanan pulled a late goal beck for a game Clyde side.

RESULT CLYDE 4  RANGERS 6

Bill Struth the Rangers manager was a man of vision as well as being a good and well respected football manager. He had good communication skills at all levels and at one time was on the Benburb Football Club committee helping them with their efforts. He had health problems but this did nothing to diminish his drive and enthusiasm for football. One of his passions was for floodlight football to be introduced in Scotland. He had lights installed at Ibrox Park and brought everyone who was interested along to show them off. He suggested the Glasgow Cup matches could be played under lights in order to restore interest in the flagging competition. He showcased schoolboy matches to show what the lights could provide. He met initially with widespread opposition but slowly and surely with floodlights becoming more popular south of the border in England his support increased. As a manager he was strict and it was a club rule that players wore collars and tie's on match days. If the Rangers were top dogs in Govan. Berryknowes Rovers from Cardonald were celebrating a five match unbeaten run. They were confident they would beat Glencairn Juveniles in the forthcoming Glasgow Juvenile Cup match at Penilee. In the Glasgow Amateur League Gower Thistle had built up an 8 point lead over Fairfield Athletic.

Over Falkirk way there was a huge demand for coach seats from the Bo'ness United fans for the forthcoming trip to Tinto Park for the match with Benburb. The club had already filled up spaces for 65 coaches. They enquired on the size of Tinto Park having being involved in chaotic scenes at Haghill Park Dennistoun when fans were scaling the walls to get in. The Benburb club told them the ground can easily hold 20,000 spectators and probably 30,000. There will be plenty of room for all who come. Equally in Govan the excitement mounted ahead of the match; Govan was gripped with Junior Cup fever.

Around Glasgow there was a thriving Churches Football League. However Govan had no successful sides in the top divisions. The only success in Churches football leagues came from St.Mary's Parish at Govan Cross in the Youth section where the team was top.

It is a week before the Benburb and Bo'ness United match. Bens won 4-0 at home against Bridgeton Waverley. However a few of the Bens committee were not present; they were spying on Bo'ness who had lost just one league match and were progressing in virtually all of the Cup competitions. The match against Benburb was dubbed 'tie of the round'. Bo'ness United won 7-0 against Grange and centre forward Alec Grieve scored five of the goals. The Bens committee members said 'He will not scoring so easy against Benburb !. We have our plans '.

The Annual New Year football match at Barlinnie Prison ended with much excitement as three of the prisoners escaped. The search was on for David Middleton, John Mac Adam and John Murney. One of the three was subsequently re-captured in Govan.

New Years Day arrived at Ibrox Park with the Old Firm match against Celtic. 80,000 turned up to see if Rangers could get themselves into the League title race. A Billy Simpson goal for Rangers following a mistake by the Celtic keeper decided the match in the 'gers favour.

Huge crowds were arriving at Tinto Park fully one hour before the kick off against Bo'ness United. Among them on time was Tom Kerr the Lord Provost of Glasgow and former member of the Benburb football club committee. Willie Ormond of Hibernian signed autographs having come to the match to cheer on Bo'ness and his brother Gilbert. 20,000 were present as the teams came out a ground record for Tinto Park.

BENBURB: Forsyth, Hay, Lumsden, Mc Kechnie, Crossan, Ford, Rae, Smith, Mc Allister, Young and Fitzsimmons.

BO'NESS UNITED: Ronald, Mitchell, Keaman, Simpson, Mc Blain, Patterson, McAra, Donaldson, Grieve, Ross and Ormond.

The visitors started well in a fog shrouded ground and Ormond passed up an early chance. Bo'ness were reduced to 10 players when Grieve fell down onto the hard pitch awkwardly. Bens went on the offensive with Rae giving his full back some anxious moments. Efforts to get Grieve back on the pitch failed and the East of Scotland side had to play with just 10 players. Grieve was found to have a pulled muscle.

Despite this Bo'ness had the bulk of the play and Alex Forsyth pulled off two great saves from Ross. Approaching half time Dunky Rae went scampering down the wing leaving his markers chasing. From his accurate cross Bob Fitzsimmons netted and sent himself into Govan folklore. Benburb got well on top in the second half but the visitors defence were solid. The danger to a Benburb win rapidly became the descending fog. A few times the referee stopped play to gauge how far he could see. Just when it seemed the game would be abandoned suddenly the fog lifted and the Bens were able to hang on without too many scares. Benburb were now into the 5th Round of the Scottish Junior Cup. The draw however could hardly have been less favourable. Away to favourites Ashfield.

The Glasgow Schools team to take on London was announced; containing three Govan players. Right winger G.Duncan (Bellahouston) , John Armour (St.Gerrards) with J.McCall (Bellahouston) as travelling reserve.

Also receiving recognition from Govan with representative honours was Dunky Rae of Benburb. Selected for Scottish Juniors against Northern Ireland. Ronnie Cook the Bens President was delighted. In an interview Ronnie said he played for Stephens Amateurs as a goalkeeper. He felt the best Benburb player he had seen was Willie Russell who went on to fame with Airdrie and Preston North End. Other players he mentioned who went on to great things from Benburb were George Johnstone, Tommy Divers and Frank Dunlop (all Aberdeen). Also, Gavin Malloch of Derby County.

St.Mary's continued to be in a strong position in the Churches League Youth section lying in second place but with games in hand.

## GLASGOW CHURCHES LEAGUE—YOUTH SECTION

| TEAM | Pl | W | L | D | F | A | Pts |
|------|----|----|----|----|----|----|-----|
| ST.Rollox C.O.S | 16 | 11 | 4 | 1 | 58 | 21 | 23 |
| St.Mary's Parish | 13 | 9 | 1 | 3 | 53 | 20 | 21 |
| Cowlairs Parish | 13 | 10 | 2 | 1 | 50 | 20 | 21 |
| St.Mary's C.O.S | 15 | 8 | 2 | 5 | 40 | 28 | 21 |
| Gordon Park C.O.S | 16 | 8 | 5 | 3 | 55 | 34 | 19 |
| Dalmarnock Cong. | 14 | 8 | 3 | 3 | 41 | 26 | 19 |
| Bargeddie Parish | 14 | 6 | 5 | 3 | 33 | 29 | 15 |
| Temple C.O.S | 14 | 5 | 7 | 2 | 38 | 31 | 12 |
| Barrhead Arthurlie | 14 | 5 | 7 | 2 | 47 | 50 | 12 |
| Kilbowie Christian | 13 | 4 | 7 | 2 | 17 | 30 | 10 |
| Kenure Park N.O | 12 | 3 | 9 | 0 | 23 | 39 | 6 |
| St.James C.O.S | 15 | 0 | 12 | 3 | 23 | 79 | 3 |
| Gairbraid Y.C | 15 | 1 | 14 | 0 | 14 | 84 | 2 |

Rangers started their Scottish Cup campaign with an easy 4-0 win at Ibrox over Arbroath. Goals from Mc Culloch and Prentice in the first half followed by a Billy Simpson goal late on seen off the 'Red Lichties'. The reward was a trip to Dundee in the second round.

St.Anthony's were having a poor season. However they had a good nucleus of support and a coach was run to all away matches; usually from the Pearce Institute. The Ants Jimmy Mc Lean formed a Social Club and a snack bar was opened for spectators at Moore Park for matches. The team were anchored next to bottom of league for most of the season.

A huge support from Govan was on its way over to Possilpark to see if Benburb could upset the odds and beat Scottish Junior Cup favourites Ashfield. Ashfield were a formidable side especially at their home ground Saracen Park a greyhound track. In their ranks they had a Govan man . Tommy Douglas was a free scoring left winger.  Many senior clubs were worried about their attendances being affected as Saracen Park would be almost full with over 20,000 spectators. The previous record was 11,500

ASHFIELD: Robb, Mc Gowan, Ferrier, Mc Phail, Cassidy, Mitchell, Graham, Divers, Black, Mc Carthy and Douglas

BENBURB: Forsyth, Hay, Lumsden, Mc Kechnie, Crossan, Ford, Rae, Smith, Mc Allister, Miller and Wilson

The kick off was delayed in order to let the many fans in and even after 15 minutes play supporters were still coming into the ground. Douglas was dangerous for Ashfield and Dunky Rae was to the fore for the Bens. Play raged from end to end in a thrilling cup tie. Every time the Bens attacked a huge roar went up from the Govanites. Both sides had chances but half time arrived with no score.

In the second half Ashfield had a player off injured and the Bens piled forward to capitalise on the 'field's misfortune. However, an Ashfield attack saw a long shot from Mc Phail deceive Alex Forsyth. A minute later the Benburb goalie pulled off a wonder save from Douglas as the 10 men from 'field had their tails up. Soon after Mc Carthy added a second for Ashfield but very quickly Miller reduced the arrears for the Bens. Ashfield returned to full strength and Black sealed the win in an exciting Cup tie by scoring a third.

RESULT: ASHFIELD 3 BENBURB 1

In the Scottish League Rangers were a long way behind but good form was seeing them creep up the league into third place and start to put pressure on the top clubs Hibernian and East Fife.

Rangers progressed into the 3rd Round of the Scottish Cup at the expense of Dundee. The match at Dens Park was scoreless at half time. However Rangers scored on the hour through South African winger Johnny Hubbard and a minute later Derek Grierson added a second to secure a 2-0 win. The reward was an Old Firm match against Celtic and Rangers applied to have a capacity limit of 95,000 for the match.

Benburb winger Dunky Rae was in the Scotland Juniors side against Northern Ireland. At Firhill Park. He scored two goals for Scotland in a 5-1 win in front of a 10,000 crowd and was then selected to play against Wales at Tynecastle Park. The team won 3-2 but Dunky by his own standards had a quieter game and was left out of the following match in Dublin against the Republic of Ireland.

Dunky felt that on the wing he had no service whatsoever against Wales. A sizable number of senior clubs made enquiries about signing Dunky Rae but none bore fruit. Dunky was an electric welder from Cardonald and an ardent Rangers supporter.

Rangers were granted a capacity of 95,000 for the visit of Celtic in the Scottish Cup 3rd Round. The gate receipts topped £7,000.

RANGERS: Niven, Young, Little, Mc Coll, Woodburn, Cox, Paton, Grierson, Simpson, Prentice and Hubbard.
CELTIC: Hunter, Haughney, Meechan, Evans, Stein, Mc Phail, Collins, Fernie, Mc Grory, Walsh and Tully.
  Rangers started well and Prentice scrambled in the opening goal after 11 minutes sending the blue hordes into raptures. Celtic fought back and came close on several occasions to equalising. In the second half play swung from end to end before Grierson sealed the win 3 minutes from time running on to a Hubbard pass and firing past Hunter. Rangers had progressed and had given themselves the chance of an unlikely League and Cup double.

*SNIPPETS:*
* The Glasgow Schools oldest age group team had some Govan representatives in the annual match against the Rest of Scotland at Stenhousemuir. A. Reid (Govan) left back; F.O'Hare (St.Gerrards) left midfield—team captain; G.Montgomery (Bellahouston) inside right.
D.Mac Farlane (Govan) was the reserve.
* The Glasgow Boys Guild side selected Rooney of St.Constantines in the right wing position for their match against Coatbridge.
* Berryknowes Rovers from Cardonald held Glencairn in the West of Scotland Juvenile Cup. The replay at Rutherglen saw the Glens win through 3-1.
* Brown from Drumoyne Athletic was selected to play for the Scottish Secondary Juvenile's side against the Scottish Schools FA side at Easter Road.
* To celebrate the Coronation of Queen Elizabeth a schools competition was organised. In the first round Harmony Row played Abbotsford at Tinto Park.
* The Glasgow Schools team to play the annual match against Bradford was: Wright (St.Mungo's), Mc Kay (Woodside), Mc Instrie (Kings Park), Mc Kechnie (Shawlands), Kane (St.Mungo's), Mc Call (Bellahouston), Cochrane (Govan), Montgomery (Bellahouston), Irvine (Eastbank), Dixon (Queens Park), Armour (St.Gerrards)   Reserve: Taggart (St.Mungo's)
The match was played at Hampden Park and won by Glasgow 3-0 with Irvine, Mc Kechnie and Dixon scoring.

  Derek has his first glimpses and experiences of football. At nearby Tinto Park he usually played with his friends playing hide and seek among the saplings at the rear of the large terraces. It is the Drumoyne Primary School playground and for the first time Derek is about to take part in a football game. It is a Monday and Eddie Moan and George McCleary are picking their teams. The class has started playing games at playtimes and lunch time. The teams picked last the week and then the same exercise starts again the following week. Eddie and George decide who has first pick in a split second by 'paper, rock and scissors'.Eddie put his hand behind his back and came out with his hand in a fist (a rock); George came out with his hands flat (paper) so he won as paper can wrap a rock.

The boys pick the best players first and after they reach five each they get advice on who is the best of the remainder. 'Pick him, Pick him' they shout excitedly. The third last is Donny Gibson and the last pick is Derek both now in Eddie's team. At their age the positional aspects of the game are easy; the best players go to the front of the team to score the goals; the not so goods at the back. The goals are a jacket at each end placed opposite the iron railings dividing the Drumoyne school playground. Eddie says to Donny and Derek 'You are the full backs and you stawn here at the back'. So Derek has his first game of football.

Benburb's inside right Eric Smith is in demand and it is Celtic who gain his signature. Former Benburb hero Teddy Swift who led the club to three Scottish Junior Cup triumphs is a scout for the Parkhead club. Good news for the Bens is that Eric will continue to play at Tinto Park for a further year to gain more experience.

Benburb supporters are pleased that the club continues to pick up players from lower levels, in particular Govan players, and develop them. Willie Currie from St. Constantine's Boys Guild is a hot property at centre forward and impressing all at Tinto Park. The Bens had started the season indifferently but steadily climbed the league and had of course a good Junior Cup run. St.Anthony's struggled throughout and finished the season one off the bottom.

Govan player Tommy Douglas continues the season in sparkling form and helps run Clydebank ragged with a 6-1 win in the next round of the Scottish Junior Cup at Saracen Park. The crowd was well over 20,000. However it was not Asfield who lifted the Scottish Junior Cup. They were well beaten in the semi finals at Ibrox on a Saturday evening match. Vale of Leven marched on into the Final with a 3-0 win.

Scotland took a large support to Wembley for the annual match against 'the Auld Enemy'.

ENGLAND: Merrick, Ramsey, Smith, Wright, Barrass, Dickinson, Finney, Broadis, Lofthouse, R.Froggatt, and J.Froggatt

SCOTLAND: Farm, Young, Cox, Docherty, Brennan, Cowie, Wright, Johnstone, Reilly, Steel and Liddell

England started the better but Lawrie Reilly was unlucky with a fierce shot which Merrick tipped onto the bar. On 18 minutes England deservedly took the lead when Broadis scored after a pass from the impressive Tom Finney. Scotland rallied well and put the England goal under a lot of pressure.

At times it seemed they must score but England held on to reach half time in the lead. Scotland continued where they left off in the second half and Lawrie Reilly soon had them level converting a rebound after a good save by Merrick. Fifteen minutes later it was the England fans who were cheering as Broadis again scored from a pass by Tom Finney.

Sammy Cox who was struggling with an injury prior to half time was carried off and Scotland had to play the remainder of the match with 10 men. Broadis almost completed his hat trick when he headed against the crossbar from a corner. Scotland finished strongly and forced 3 quick corners near the end. The last one from Liddell hits a post. Just when it seemed that their efforts would be in vain, Lawrie Reilly forced home an equaliser to send the travelling Scots home happy.

RESULT: ENGLAND 2 SCOTLAND 2

Rangers arrived at Hampden Park to meet Heart of Midlothian in the semi finals of the Scottish Cup. In front of 116,000 Wardhaugh scored for Hearts on 11 minutes converting a pass from former 'ger Rutherford. Derek Grierson went on a mazy run and scored to equalise for the Rangers approaching half time. In the second half each side had their chances but it was Prentice who scored; converting a pass from Hubbard. Rangers were on their way to the Final. At the match Archie Marshall got excited on the east terracing. He became abusive waved his hands around and challenged the fans around to a fight. When the police asked him to stop he became abusive to them also. At Govan Police Court Marshall was fined £2 by Baillie Thomas Blackwater. The Baillie said 'I can understand you getting excited at a football match but we take a dim view of this'. The Scottish Cup Final day duly arrived with Rangers taking on Aberdeen at Hampden Park. To get to the Finals the teams paths were

RANGERS 1st Round Arbroath (h) 4-0 2nd Round Dundee (a) 2-0
3rd Round Morton (a) 4-1; 4th Round Celtic (h) 2-0
Semi Final Hearts 2-1
ABERDEEN 1st Round bye; 2nd Round Aberdeen 2 St.Mirren 0
3rd Round Aberdeen 5; Motherwell 5; 3rd Round Replay Motherwell 1; Aberdeen 6
4th Round Hibernian 1; Aberdeen 1; 4th Round Replay Aberdeen 2 Hibernian 0
Semi Final Aberdeen 1; Third Lanark 1; Semi Final Replay Aberdeen 2, Third Lanark 1

Almost 130,000 spectators attended the match.
RANGERS: Niven, Young, Little, Mc Coll, Stanners, Pryde, Waddell, Grierson, Paton, Prentice and Hubbard.
ABERDEEN: Martin, Mitchell, Shaw, Harris, Young, Allister,Roger, Yorston, Buckley,
Hamilton and Hather

Rangers opened the scoring on 8 minutes through Prentice who converted a cross from Hubbard from a tight angle. Aberdeen fought back and laid siege to the Rangers goal. After half an hour George Niven the Rangers goalie was taken off with a badly cut ear.

George Young took over in goal and the 10 men of Rangers battled to keep the attacking Dons out. The Ibrox men survived until half time when Niven returned to huge cheers.

The second half continued in the same vein with Aberdeen piling on the pressure. They were rewarded ten minutes from the end when Yorston headed home and the Cup Final ended in a draw.

In the replay Rangers had the returning from suspension Willie Woodburn and Billy Simpson replacing Stanners and Prentice.

Aberdeen dominated the first half but were unable to score. Billy Simpson scored for Rangers on 40 minutes giving his side an undeserved lead. The second half saw a stronger performance from Rangers but they were unable to add to their lead. The final whistle saw mass celebrations from most of the 113,000 crowd. Rangers had won the first part of a possible double.

The next few weeks saw Rangers win games in hand and close the gap on Hibernian as well as overhauling East Fife. A win at Ibrox Park over Dundee meant they needed a point at Dumfries against Queen of the South. This was achieved with a nervy 1-1 draw and secured Rangers a League and Cup double.

The draw for the opening round of the Coronation Cup was made. The Cup was competed for by the four best English and Scottish sides and played entirely in Scotland.

1st Round: Rangers v Manchester United; Tottenham v Hibernian
Celtic v Arsenal; Aberdeen v Newcastle United

Celtic were always a good cup side and playing effectively at home in Glasgow gave their followers a belief that they could do well. They had after all won a similar Empire Exhibition prestigious Cup in 1938. In their opening match at Hampden Park against Arsenal they attacked non stop throughout the entire 90 minutes. The best player on the park was ex St.Anthony's Bobby Evans who was inspirational with his effort. Ex Pollok midfielder Bobby Collins scored the only goal of the match direct from a corner. A one armed referee from London officiated the match.

Hibernian and Tottenham Hotspur drew 1-1 at Ibrox Park (Smith for Hibs and Walters for Spurs). In the replay Lawrie Reilly scored both Hibs goals, the second in the last minute, to enable the Easter Road club to progress and meet Newcastle United.

Rangers had injury problems for the Hampden Park match against Manchester United. Benburb youngster Hunter Mc Millan was drafted in at centre forward and had a first class game. He opened the scoring for Rangers in the first half. Manchester United improved and progressed by scoring twice through Pearson and Rowley to gain a 2-1 win. In the last match Newcastle United easily brushed aside Aberdeen 4-0 at Ibrox Park. Milburn, White, Hannah and Young (own goal) were the goal scorer's

The first semi final at Ibrox Park saw Hibernian easily dispose of Newcastle United with three unopposed goals. Turnball and Reilly in the first half. Johnstone scored again for the Hibs in the second half. McClellan scored for the Geordies.

In the second semi final  Celtic won through 2-1 against Manchester United Rowley scored for Manchester United but goals from Bertie Peacock and Neil Mochan secured the Celtic win

The competition had some good attendances especially the old firm and Celtic had provided a lot of the excitement to the occasion. Hibernian would not be easy opponents.

CELTIC: Bonnar Haughney, Rollo, Evans, Stein, Mc Phail, Collins, Walsh, Mochan, Peacock and Fernie

HIBERNIAN: Younger, Govan, Patterson, Buchanan, Cowie, Combe, Smith, Turnball, Reilly, Turnball and Ormond.

Both sides had spells in the game when they were on top. Neil Mochan opened the scoring for Celtic after 15 minutes. Hibernian gradually applied more and more pressure to the Celtic goal but just could not get the breakthrough with goalie Bonnar outstanding. Three minutes from the end Walsh scored a second for Celtic in a rare attack and the cup was on its way to Parkhead.

Celtic had won a prestigious trophy in front of 117,000 spectators and could call themselves the Unofficial champions of Britain.

As the junior leagues entered the home straight Benburb had moved upwards to a mid table position well down on the previous first place during the previous season but higher than the early season positions. A few players went senior over the season including Bobby Gilmour who made his debut for Queen of the South at Left wing.

Dunky Rae received further recognition by being selected to play for the Central League side. He was watched by countless senior sides, had offers but declined them all and indicated he preferred Benburb.

Young St.Anthony's goalkeeper Chalmers Mc Millan attracted a lot of senior football club interest. Despite being low in the league all at the club went on a trip to Oban where they received a warm welcome for their match against an Oban District Select.

*SNIPPETS:*

* The Boy's Brigade Football League's around Govan tended to provide decisive results. Often teams would lose by double figure scores only to rebound and win by a similar margin the following week. An influence on the results was the call of School teams on the players of the Boys Brigade. A Boys Brigade match between the Glasgow Batallion and the Aberdeen Batallion at Haghill Park saw Miller from the 129th on Copland Road play inside left.

- Also collecting representative honours was Brown of Drumoyne Athletic playing for Scotland Juvenile's against Newcastle United Nursery at Cappielow Park, Greenock.
- In the West of Scotland Amateur League Babcock and Wilcox had finished their fixtures and sat 2 points ahead of Govan who had two games in hand. Stephens with six games in hand also had a chance. In the Primary Schools League Championship semi finals a lot of parents and friends went along to Tinto Park to see Greenfield take on Penilee.
- The annual Schools match at Hampden Park between Glasgow and Bradford saw several Govan players in the team. J.McCall (Bellahouston), C.Cochrane (Govan High), G.Montgomery (Bellahouston) and J.Armour (St.Gerrards)
  Three unopposed second half goals saw Glasgow triumph 3-0.
- At the Schools Under 14 level Govan players were selected for the Glasgow Schools side against Lanarkshire. G.Mc Cracken (Govan High), J. Kane and G.O'Hara (St.Gerrards).

### WEST OF SCOTLAND AMATEUR LEAGUE

| Team | Pl | W | L | D | F | A | Pts |
|------|----|----|----|----|----|----|----|
| Babcock and Wilcox | 30 | 22 | 6 | 2 | 111 | 48 | 46 |
| Govan | 28 | 21 | 5 | 2 | 101 | 44 | 44 |
| Wester Rossland | 25 | 18 | 5 | 2 | 82 | 43 | 38 |
| Killermont | 26 | 16 | 4 | 6 | 107 | 45 | 38 |
| Stephens | 24 | 16 | 5 | 3 | 73 | 41 | 35 |

- In the Primary Schools League Championship semi finals a lot of parents and friends went along to Tinto Park to see Greenfield take on Penilee.

At the Schools Under 14 level Govan players were selected for the Glasgow Schools side against Lanarkshire. G.Mc Cracken (Govan High), J. Kane and G.O'Hara (St.Gerrards).

Benburb progressed to the Erskine Cup Final where they met Shawfield. Bens secured the Cup in the first half building a 3-0 lead through goals from Dunky Rae and Bob Fitzsimmons (2). The Bens had a trophy to show for a hard working and eventful season.

The Schools Football Presentation Evening was memorable for St.Gerrards School in Govan. Their teams won the three key age group trophies at age groups 2, 3 and 4.

It was the first time one school had scooped the pool and the first school to win three age groups since 1932. The Shields were re-presented by Celtic's Bob Kelly Chairman and President. Mr Coneghan the school headmaster gave a speech and was obviously delighted by the success of the school.

On the other side of Glasgow the Anderson Benburb did not fare so well finishing second from bottom.

In the Summer Hospitals League the Southern General's title hopes had faded.

| Team | Pl | W | L | D | F | A | Pts |
|---|---|---|---|---|---|---|---|
| Assessors Dept | 9 | 7 | 1 | 1 | 42 | 24 | 15 |
| Gas Maintenance | 8 | 6 | 0 | 2 | 42 | 15 | 14 |
| Mitchell Library | 10 | 6 | 3 | 1 | 33 | 29 | 13 |
| Collector's Department | 7 | 5 | 0 | 2 | 34 | 16 | 12 |
| Office of Works | 9 | 4 | 3 | 2 | 34 | 34 | 10 |
| Barlinnie O.C. | 9 | 3 | 4 | 2 | 25 | 24 | 8 |
| Transport U.O. | 7 | 0 | 2 | 5 | 22 | 28 | 5 |
| Royal Infirmary | 10 | 1 | 6 | 3 | 29 | 41 | 5 |
| Crookston | 7 | 2 | 5 | 0 | 16 | 33 | 4 |
| Southern General Hospital | 10 | 0 | 10 | 0 | 14 | 47 | 0 |

John Dick was a member of the armed forces and based at Colchester. He was over six foot tall and an inside forward who hailed from Cardonald. West Ham Manager Ted Fenton signed him quickly as a professional footballer saying 'You will be hearing more of this player !'

Benburb Centre half Alex Mc Allister had the choice of three possible moves to Senior football. The former Govan High schoolboy had an offer from Stirling Albion and more trials with Rangers, the team he supported. However he elected to travel north and signed for Aberdeen.

A Govan man in the Ashfield side set the records tumbling. Tommy Douglas scored no fewer than 44 goals for the Saracen Park side in a hugely successful season for the club.

Tommy was on his way to Stirling Albion to try his luck in Senior Football.

## CENTRAL LEAGUE

| Team | Pl | W | L | D | F | A | Pts |
|---|---|---|---|---|---|---|---|
| Ashfield | 27 | 21 | 1 | 5 | 90 | 29 | 47 |
| Bailleston | 29 | 18 | 6 | 5 | 78 | 41 | 41 |
| Vale of Leven | 29 | 15 | 8 | 6 | 61 | 54 | 36 |
| Petershill | 28 | 15 | 9 | 4 | 66 | 52 | 34 |
| Blantyre Celtic | 30 | 13 | 10 | 7 | 44 | 65 | 33 |
| St.Roch's | 28 | 14 | 11 | 3 | 71 | 68 | 31 |
| Shawfield | 29 | 12 | 12 | 5 | 54 | 64 | 29 |
| Maryhill | 29 | 9 | 12 | 8 | 61 | 66 | 26 |
| Benburb | 29 | 11 | 14 | 4 | 68 | 78 | 26 |
| Bridgeton Waverley | 30 | 9 | 14 | 7 | 53 | 68 | 25 |
| Cambuslang Rangers | 28 | 10 | 14 | 4 | 54 | 52 | 24 |
| Kirkintilloch Rob Roy | 30 | 9 | 15 | 6 | 65 | 75 | 24 |
| Bellshill Athletic | 28 | 10 | 16 | 2 | 58 | 74 | 22 |
| Arthurlie | 29 | 8 | 15 | 6 | 62 | 73 | 22 |
| Blantyre Vics. | 27 | 9 | 15 | 3 | 51 | 70 | 21 |
| Renfrew | 29 | 7 | 18 | 4 | 47 | 51 | 18 |

Ashfield were strong favourites for the Scottish Junior Cup and played in front of an enormous number of supporters. It is estimated that the club were watched by over 100,000 spectators during the season where they won a large number of Cups as well as the League.

The Scottish Junior Cup was competed for by the Ashfield conqueror's Vale of Leven and Annbank United from the Ayrshire League.

VALE OF LEVEN: Mc Kenzie, Gilmour, Mc Nichol, Moran, Buchanan, Gailey,
Mayberry, Mc Keever, Cassidy, Moffat and Borland.

ANNBANK UNITED: Neeson, Davidson, Hunter, Anderson, Livingstone, Caggie, Paton, Price, Gray, Steele and Balfour.

In front of 56,000 Vale started well but were quickly on the backfoot as Annbank dominated proceedings. The Ayrshire side should have been well ahead by half time but for some resolute defending by the Vale. Vale of Leven were not showing the same form that had disposed of Ashfield.

The second half went very much the same as the first with Vale defending. However, in a rare excursion into the Annbank half Cassidy (who scored the 3 goals against Ashfield ) beat his defender and scored with a good shot. Try as they did Annbank could not retrieve the goal and the Cup was on its way to Alexandria.

RESULT: VALE OF LEVEN 1 ANNBANK UNITED 0

## SCOTTISH LEAGUE DIVISION A

| Team | Pl | W | L | D | F | A | Pts |
|------|----|----|----|----|----|----|-----|
| Hibernian | 29 | 18 | 6 | 5 | 89 | 50 | 41 |
| Rangers | 28 | 17 | 5 | 6 | 76 | 37 | 40 |
| East Fife | 29 | 16 | 6 | 7 | 70 | 44 | 39 |
| Clyde | 30 | 13 | 13 | 4 | 78 | 78 | 30 |
| St.Mirren | 30 | 11 | 11 | 8 | 52 | 58 | 30 |
| Dundee | 29 | 9 | 9 | 11 | 43 | 34 | 29 |
| Celtic | 30 | 11 | 12 | 7 | 51 | 54 | 29 |
| Partick Thistle | 30 | 10 | 11 | 9 | 55 | 63 | 29 |
| Hearts | 29 | 11 | 12 | 6 | 55 | 48 | 28 |
| Queen of the South | 29 | 10 | 12 | 7 | 42 | 60 | 27 |
| Aberdeen | 30 | 11 | 14 | 5 | 64 | 68 | 27 |
| Raith Rovers | 29 | 9 | 12 | 8 | 46 | 49 | 26 |
| Falkirk | 30 | 11 | 15 | 4 | 53 | 63 | 26 |
| Motherwell | 30 | 10 | 15 | 5 | 57 | 80 | 25 |
| Airdrieonians | 29 | 9 | 14 | 6 | 49 | 73 | 24 |
| Third Lanark | 29 | 8 | 17 | 4 | 50 | 73 | 20 |

*CLOSE FINISH AT THE TOP: RANGERS WON TITLE WITH LAST MATCH DRAW AT DUMFRIES AGAINST QUEEN OF THE SOUTH. MOTHERWELL AND THIRD LANARK WERE RELEGATED.*

# CHAPTER 5
# BENBURB TARGET THE LEAGUE (1953-54)

The Benburb squad for season 1953-54 was announced:

Goalkeepers : Alex. Forsyth, Stewart Mitchell

Full Backs ; Robert Fitzsimmons

Half backs: J.Mc Kechnie, Andrew Crossan, Alexander Mc Allister, George Ford, Peter Morton, George Kilday (Partick Avondale)

Forwards; Duncan Rae, Thomas Ball (Army), Robert Young, Hugh Currie, George Mc Arthur (Eastbank FP's), George Logie (Blantyre Vics), William Notman (Darvel) , William Miller.

Benburb had assembled a strong squad. Although goalkeeper Stewart Mitchell was signed it was likely he would be soon signing for a top English League club. Both West Ham United and Newcastle United were keen on his signature and it was to Tyneside he went. Similarly Alex McAllister was on the verge of leaving the Bens for Aberdeen. However he did play in an early season 'Govan derby' match against St.Anthony's won by Benburb 6-1.

As well as a strong squad on the pitch Benburb also strengthened off the pitch. Bob Millen the Ashfield assistant trainer joined the Bens. Benburb Treasurer David Mc Cracken returned to the club after the Summer Cricket season but with a bruised ankle from a knock by the cricket ball.

St.Anthony's started the season badly with the crushing defeat against the Bens. However the club felt they had a strong side that once gelled would be a match for anyone. James Mc Lean the club President and a number of enthusiastic followers gave the clubhouse a complete upgrade including a new referee's room at Moore Park.

St.Anthony's squad:

Goalkeepers; Henry O'Grady, John Higgins, Charles Mc Millen

Full Backs: Hugh Kelly (Dennistoun Waverley), James Smith (Blantyre Celtic), William Graham. William Dolan

Half backs: Peter Turnball (Oban), Thomas Craig, Serge Innocenti , James Cloherty,

Forwards: John Mc Ardle, John Farrell ( St.Theresa's Boys Guild), John Elliott, James Mc Nair ( Blantyre Celtic), Robert Mc Intyre.

Retained Player : George O'Donnell.

Rangers were in the same Section as Raith Rovers, Hamilton Accies and Heart of Midlothian for the Scottish League Cup. They opened the season with a 4-0 win at Kirkcaldy against Raith Rovers. And this set the tone of the group with the Ibrox club winning through to the quarter finals easily. Rangers beat Ayr United 4-2 at Ibrox Park in the 1st Leg of the League Cup. However they were given a scare in the 2nd leg as the 'Honest men' came close to overcoming the deficit winning 3-2. Rangers progressed 5-4 on aggregate.

The first Old Firm match of the season at Ibrox Park saw considerable crowd trouble. Bottles were thrown; banners and flags displayed and mounted police called to quell the trouble a half hour before the kick off.

An exciting game saw Paton give Rangers the lead in the first half but Duncan quickly equalised for Celtic. Despite chances at both end in the rain an exciting match finished all square.

It was announced that the forthcoming British Championship matches would act as a qualifier for 1954 World Cup. The top two would qualify for the competition to be held in Switzerland.

Benburb started their league campaign well and were amongst the early leaders in the opening months. Their Scottish Junior Cup opponents were Kilbirnie Ladeside from Ayrshire and certain to be a tough nut to crack.

BENBURB: Mitchell, Westwater, Fitzsimmons, Kildare, Crossan, Morton, Rae, Smith, Currie, Notman and Miller.

KILBIRNIE LADESIDE: Mc Farlane, Clark, Ryan, Gray, Pearson, Hodgson, Mc Kinnon, Ashe, Craig, Johnstone and Mc Intosh.

A large crowd including a big support up from Ayrshire saw a typical hard fought Junior Cup tie. Craig gave Kilbirnie the lead just before half time with a super shot from 20 yards. The crowd roared on the Bens in the second half and Dunky Rae scored to pull them level. It was all Benburb but they just could not score with Mac farlane producing many fine saves.

SCORE: BENBURB 1 KILBIRNIE LADESIDE 1

This was to be Stewart Mitchell's farewell game for Benburb and he was on the train to Newcastle United. Alex Forsyth, who had acted as virtually a personal coach to Stewart over several years, returned to the Bens goal for the replay.

For the replay Benburb had Weir in for Morton and Logie returning from injury replacing Currie. A considerable number of Benburb supporters made the trip to Kilbirnie with coaches parked all down Greenfield Street laid on for them. Alex Forsyth had a few good saves in the first half but was beaten by a good drive from Craig. In the second half the Bens peppered the Ladeside goal but could not get the all important equaliser.

RESULT: KILBIRNIE LADESIDE 1 BENBURB 0

Ashfield were expected to do well in the Scottish Junior Cup. Although they had lost a few key players to the Senior ranks they had been replaced by talented players. A trip to play St.Anthony's at Moore Park seemed a formality; a 2nd Round appearance expected. A slightly built youngster Billy Craig played inside right for the Ants and dominated proceedings. He opened the scoring and set up two goals for John Elliot before half time. Elliot completed his hat trick early in the second half to the stunned disbelief of the 'field. Ashfield pulled back two goals but were unable to make any further impression leaving the Ants to savour the shock of the round.

Like any good self respecting Junior side which has surprisingly been knocked out of the Scottish Junior Cup; Ashfied lodged a protest but this was rightly thrown out by the SJFA.

In the second round a first half header from Stewart for the Ants at Moore proved decisive as St.Anthony's beat Cleland 1-0.

Rangers bid to get to the Scottish League Cup Final led them to a semi final match against Glasgow rivals Partick Thistle.

RANGERS: Niven, Young, Little, Mc Coll, Woodburn, Cox, Waddell, Grierson, Paton, Prentice and Hubbard.

PARTICK THISTLE: Ledgerwood, Mc Gowan, Gibb, Crawford, Davidson, Kerr, Mc Kenzie, Howitt, Sharp, Wright and Walker

A crowd of 48,000 turned up expecting a probable Rangers win. Partick Thistle held Rangers at bay comfortably until the 34 th minute and then shook the 'gers by taking the lead. A McKenzie shot crashed off the post but Wright was on hand to get in another shot which went into the net off the post. On half time the Jags made it two when Niven was in trouble with a ball which hit the crossbar. Howitt won the battle of strength for the ball and forced it into the goal. An exciting second half ensued but Partick Thistle held on to meet East Fife in the Final of the Scottish League Cup.

RESULT: RANGERS 0 PARTICK THISTLE 2

In the League Rangers had once again made a slow start and were not far off the bottom of the pile. Long time Manager Bill Struth was not in the best of health and rumours suggested that the present league campaign might be his last.

St.Anthony's success in the Scottish Junior Cup saw a great increase in interest and for a league game at Port Glasgow four double decker busloads of supporters left the Pearce Institute.

Two players who were making a huge impact at Moore Park were youngster Billy Craig who was hotly trailed by Celtic. Also in the St.Anthony's ranks was former Dunoon Juniors centre half Maurice Young who was outstanding in the Ants defence. The pivot who was a plumber by trade did much work for the Ants in their clubhouse. He helped the Ants to a win in the Glasgow Cup over Benburb and had senior club Dunfermiline Athletic chasing for his signature.

The Scottish League Cup Final between East Fife and Partick Thistle was predicted to draw a very low crowd. However on the day a healthy 38,500 turned up to support the teams.

PARTICK THISTLE: Ledgerwood Mc Gowan, Gibb, Crawford, Davidson, Kerr, Mc Kenzie, Howitt, Sharp, Wright and Walker

EAST FIFE: Curran, Emery, Stewart (S), Christie, Finlay, Mc Lennan, Stewart (J), Fleming, Bonthorne, Gardiner and Matthew.

44

East Fife got off to the perfect start when Gardiner tried a shot from a tight angle which somehow found the net after 3 minutes. On 9 minutes it was 2-0 as Charlie 'Legs' Fleming had a shot blocked and followed up on the rebound to force the ball over the line. Play raged from end to end but half time arrived with no further score.

The Jags resumed on the front foot and Walker converted a hard driven cross on 48 minutes to reduce the arrears. Mc Kenzie scored a fine individual goal on 74 minutes to bring the scores level and put the Final in the balance. Christie won the cup for the Fifers when 3 minutes from the end he blasted home a shot from the edge of the box.

RESULT: PARTICK THISTLE 2 EAST FIFE 3

The scorer of the East Fife second goal Charlie Fleming was rapidly becoming the most feared striker in the league. Charlie was signed by manager Scot Symon from Blairhall Colliery Juniors in 1946. He scored frequently and after passing the 133 games for East Fife milestone he had scored no fewer than 139 goals. His goals had propelled East Fife into title contenders for the top Scottish Division and also frequent visitors to the latter rounds of the Cups.

Charlie Fleming was drafted in to play against Northern Ireland in Belfast; a double header match for both the British Championship and the World Cup qualifier.

NORTHERN IRELAND: Smyth (Distillery), Cunningham (St.Mirren), Mc Michael (Newcastle), Blanchflower (Aston Villa), McCabe (Leeds), Clough (Glenavon), Bingham (Sunderland), McIlroy (Burnley), Simpson (Rangers), Tully (Celtic) and Lockhart (Aston Villa)

SCOTLAND: Farm (Blackpool) , Young (Rangers), Cox (Rangers), Evans (Celtic), Brennan ( Newcastle), Cowie (Dundee), Waddell (Rangers), Fleming (East Fife),McPhail (Celtic), Watson (Huddersfield) and Henderson (Portsmouth)

The first half saw Scotland play poorly; Northern Ireland with Charlie Tully prominent were in control and unlucky not to be ahead.

The second half was one minute old when Charlie Fleming got his first chance. Mc Phail and an Irish defender challenged for a ball in the box. The ball came out to Fleming on the edge of the box and he hit a ferocious shot which Smyth did not see until the ball was in the net. On 69 minutes the East Fife forward scored his second. Waddell went on a fine run down the right wing and his cross found Fleming who shot; Smyth produced a fine stop but Fleming following up scored. Lockhart quickly pulled back a goal for the Irish from a penalty but the game was made safe for the Scots when Henderson scored in the dying minutes.

RESULT: NORTHERN IRELAND 1 SCOTLAND 3

With England easily beating Wales, Scotland required a win over Wales or England to qualify for the World Cup.

The match with Wales was one of the most exciting games between the two nations ever. Scotland without Charlie Fleming led 2-0 at half time through goals from Brown and Johnstone. Wales reduced the arrears through John Charles before Lawrie Reilly appeared to make the game safe for the Scots with a third goal. However Allchurch reduced the arrears and John Charles scored a fine individual goal to give the Wales team a draw. Scotland were not quite through to the World Cup Finals.

Benburb were operating a Juvenile team as well as a Junior team. Despite the early exit in the Scottish Junior Cup they were blazing a trail at the top of the league and good crowds were turning up for the home matches at Tinto Park.

In the City and Suburban League Division 2 the Govan Randolph team at the 50 pitches were doing well and led the division. Avon Villa who played at Plantation Park were having a good run in the West of Scotland Juvenile Cup.

## CITY AND SUBURBAN LEAGUE—DIVISION 2

| Team | Pl | W | L | D | F | A | Pts |
|---|---|---|---|---|---|---|---|
| Govan Randolph | 11 | 9 | 2 | 0 | 39 | 20 | 18 |
| Cowglen United | 11 | 8 | 3 | 0 | 32 | 19 | 16 |
| Good Shepherds | 8 | 7 | 1 | 0 | 39 | 9 | 14 |
| Knightswood Athletic | 10 | 6 | 2 | 2 | 28 | 20 | 14 |
| Mavisbank | 10 | 5 | 2 | 3 | 22 | 21 | 13 |
| Civic Star | 11 | 5 | 4 | 2 | 33 | 37 | 12 |
| Whitefield Hearts | 13 | 5 | 6 | 2 | 33 | 35 | 12 |
| Scotstoun Vics | 11 | 5 | 5 | 1 | 31 | 28 | 11 |
| Doncaster Vics. | 12 | 5 | 6 | 1 | 17 | 35 | 11 |
| Dale Athletic | 13 | 4 | 8 | 1 | 13 | 30 | 9 |
| Fraser's Athletic | 9 | 2 | 7 | 0 | 17 | 40 | 4 |
| Ladywell | 15 | 0 | 15 | 0 | 2 | 70 | 0 |

The St.Anthony's club were on the move. Twenty two busloads of supporters lined up at Govan Cross for the trip to Dalry Thistle in the Third Round of the Scottish Junior Cup. Hopes were high but the opponents down in Ayrshire; Dalry Thistle were a strong side.

DALRY THISTLE: Wright, Brannan, Gilchrist, Docherty, Hill, Mc Carthy,Gibson, T.Murray, Walker, Maxwell and H.Murray.

St.ANTHONY'S: Higgins, Kelly, Graham, Turnball, Young, Innocenti, McArdle, Craig, Elliott, Bryceland and Mc Nair

The travelling support had plenty to cheer on in the opening stages and Mc Ardle gave the Ants an early lead. For the most part the play was very even. However an unexpected turn of events sent the tie in the favour of Dalry Thistle. On 30 minutes Dalry were awarded a penalty which they converted. However almost immediately the Ants goalkeeper Higgins was taken off with a badly cut knee. The Thistle scored on half time from a rebound from a shot which hit the post. St.Anthony's almost got level a few times early in the second half but the handicap of playing without a recognised goalkeeper proved too much. They conceded goals at regular intervals and lost heavily.

RESULT: DALRY THISTLE 8 ST.ANTHONY'S 1

Benburb Juveniles were not having a great season. However this meant plenty of practice for goalie Andrew Barnes who was the son of former Benburb secretary Willie Barnes. His performances were putting him on the fringes of a place in the Scottish Youth International cup.

The Schools football league's saw St.Gerrards still challenging for the honours with Bellahouston Academy doing well in a few of the age groups. Govan High were finding it difficult to stay with the leaders at most age group levels. A particular problem for most schools was that pupils left at age 15. John Street were unbeaten at Christmas and top of the league.

Once a school player left for work he was no longer eligible to play for the school. Hence John Street had a sizable number of their team leave throughout the season and did not win a match between Christmas and the end of the season.

Bill Struth the Rangers manager was keen to showcase the potential of Floodlight football in front of a doubting Scottish Football Association. He arranged a match at Ibrox Park for the School teams. The match was between Glasgow and the West of Scotland teams: The trial match at Nether Pollok for the Glasgow team contained several from Govan:

A team: W.Wright (St.Mungo's), I.MacKay (Woodside), G.Smith (Victoria Drive), R.MacKechnie (Shawlands), H.Kane (St.Mungo's), J.Anderson (Woodside), G.Duncan (Bellahouston), G.Montgomery (Bellahouston), G.Taggert (St.Mungo's), E.Mac Donald (Victoria Drive), R.Seaton (Eastwood), J.Tennant (Govan), J.Armour (St.Gerrards).

B team: C.Christie (Albert), R.Masson (Bellahouston), F.Mc Gregor (St.Mungo's), J.Mac Guire (St.Gerrard's), R.Ramage (Whitehill), R.Elder (Albert), S.Grimshaw (Queens Park), D.Stevenson (Eastwood), R.Struthers (Camphill), L.Dixon (Queen's Park), J.Catterson (St.Gerrards), J.Farrell (St.Mungo's) , J.Hamill (Camphill), J.Currie (Govan High).

***SNIPPETS:***

- The Glasgow Corporation Youth League team had Govan player J.Greig at right half in the representative side.
- In the Nicholson Cup St.Gerrards were drawn home to Possil in the Second Round. In the Mc Neill Cup St.Gerrards were drawn at home to Petershill and Govan High were drawn away to the City Public in the Second Round.
- Former Govan High Schoolboy Davie Mathers was included in the Partick Thistle team for their match with Rangers.
- Benburb Juveniles beat St.Mungo 3-0 in a Second Round Replay in the Glasgow Cup.
- In the Renfrewshire League the big Govan derby between Avon Villa and Benburb Juveniles took place at Bellahouston Park and finished level 2-2. Also Govan Britannia played Park United at the 50 Pitches in the same league.
- Dunky Rae and Andy Crossan of Benburb were attracting the attention of senior clubs. Dunky was chased by Arbroath while Andy was being tracked by St.Johnstone. Both were happy to stay at the Bens. Dunky Rae lost his place in the Scottish Junior team to a Bo'ness youngster called Alex Scott. Scott was being trailed to come to Govan by Rangers.
- The Glasgow Schools team to play Edinburgh was chosen and had a few Govan players. Colin McCallum (Bellahouston) centre half; Peter Kane (St.Gerrards) inside left and J.Keenan (Govan High) reserve .
- The Boys Brigade League's were producing very few draws and some high scores. Only one game out of 50 ended in a draw after the fifth/ sixth round of matches. The 237th scored 38 goals in five matches for the loss of 10 despite losing two matches. The 243rd won three out of six matches but with a record of 42 goals for and 16 against.

1954 duly arrived with Rangers struggling in the league. A late surge; like the two previous season's would surely not put them in the frame for a title challenge. Any hopes of the challenge were quickly dispelled by their  fiercest rivals Celtic at Parkhead. Neil Mochan scored the only goal of the match which the buoys dominated throughout and only stout defending by the 'gers kept the margin to one.

With Rangers in the lower part of the league things were going from bad to worse. A number of their fans were injured when a Supporters bus on its way back from Kirkaldy crashed injuring several people on board. Driver Tommy Mc Clure was fined £2 with his license endorsed for careless driving.

# RENFREWSHIRE JUVENILE LEAGUE

| Team | Pl | W | L | D | F | A | Pts |
|---|---|---|---|---|---|---|---|
| Port Glasgow Parkfield | 6 | 4 | 1 | 1 | 15 | 11 | 9 |
| Carnwadric Bluebell | 5 | 4 | 0 | 1 | 31 | 5 | 9 |
| Craigielea Star | 4 | 4 | 0 | 0 | 16 | 4 | 8 |
| Avon Villa | 4 | 2 | 0 | 2 | 8 | 17 | 4 |
| Park United | 3 | 1 | 1 | 1 | 12 | 7 | 3 |
| Benburb Juveniles | 4 | 1 | 1 | 2 | 8 | 19 | 3 |
| Tradeston Holmlea | 4 | 0 | 2 | 2 | 8 | 10 | 2 |
| Royal Star | 2 | 0 | 1 | 1 | 4 | 13 | 1 |
| Penilee Athletic | 3 | 0 | 3 | 0 | 6 | 13 | 0 |
| Govan Britannia | 3 | 0 | 3 | 0 | 5 | 12 | 0 |

# CENTRAL LEAGUE—B

| Team | Pl | W | L | D | F | A | Pts |
|---|---|---|---|---|---|---|---|
| Benburb | 16 | 11 | 2 | 3 | 53 | 26 | 25 |
| Blantyre Vics | 15 | 9 | 5 | 1 | 39 | 29 | 19 |
| Rob Roy | 16 | 7 | 4 | 5 | 44 | 36 | 19 |
| St.Anthony's | 15 | 7 | 4 | 4 | 32 | 26 | 18 |
| Renfrew | 16 | 5 | 4 | 7 | 42 | 36 | 17 |
| Port Glasgow | 15 | 7 | 5 | 3 | 42 | 44 | 17 |
| Bellshill Athletic | 14 | 7 | 5 | 2 | 36 | 37 | 16 |
| Vale of Clyde | 14 | 5 | 5 | 4 | 36 | 30 | 14 |
| Pollok | 14 | 4 | 4 | 6 | 28 | 30 | 14 |
| Maryhill | 11 | 5 | 4 | 2 | 27 | 25 | 12 |
| Dunipace | 13 | 5 | 6 | 2 | 33 | 42 | 12 |
| Arthurlie | 16 | 5 | 9 | 2 | 28 | 35 | 12 |
| Bridgeton Waverley | 13 | 4 | 6 | 3 | 27 | 34 | 11 |
| Dennistoun Waverley | 15 | 5 | 9 | 1 | 38 | 45 | 11 |
| Maryhill Harp | 16 | 4 | 9 | 3 | 29 | 44 | 11 |
| Yoker Athletic | 15 | 2 | 11 | 2 | 30 | 45 | 6 |

Benburb continued to lead the division into the new year but a charge was emerging from Blantyre Vics. A win for the Bens over Rob Roy in front of a large crowd at Tinto Park kept them on course for the title.

BENBURB: Forsyth; Westwater, Mc Allister, Fitzsimmons, Crossan, Weir, Rae, Smith, Currie, Logie and Millar.

ROB ROY: Darroch, A. Campbell, Sloan, Blakeley, Kitson, Doyle, J.Campbell, Smith, Bryans, Chalmers and Steventon.

Logie opened the scoring for the Bens but weak defending allowed Rob Roy an equaliser. Miller restored the Benburb lead before half time and another unopposed goal for the bens secured a 3-1 win.

St.Anthony's goalkeeper John Higgins was available for more matches this being allowed by the RAF. Ants Secretary Francis Mc Inally was pleased with the level of support for the Govan side and the challenge for the league title.

- In the City Amateur League the Govan Randolph dropped to second place behind the Good Shepherd's.
- Gibbons from Harmony Row went for a trial to get in the Glasgow Welfare League side.
- The wumin of West Drumoyne were up in arms. A number of their boys aged 8 to 14 were up in court for playing football on Meiklewood Road. They descended down to Govan Police Courts. 'Ther no allowed tae play on the 50 pitches or the swing park !' Judge Cuthbertson said ' OK I will take a lenient view this time but do not let me see them in front of me again !'
- Govan High team members: Brown; Breigham; Mc Cracken; Currie; Hayes; Scott; Auld; Mitchell; Crawford (captain) ; Tennant; Dennis.
- Reg Walker of Benburb was picked for the RAF team against the Army. Reg was stationed in Egypt.

In the First Round of the Scottish Cup, Rangers were drawn at home to Queen's Park. The Spiders held the 'gers at bay until early in the second half when Willie Waddell scored. Gardiner's headed a second three minutes from the end to enable Rangers to progress with a 2-0 margin.

The Second Round saw a visit from Kilmarnock to Ibrox Park. The visitors shocked the 'gers with a goal in the first half from Murray. Rangers improved after the break and two quick goals from Grierson and Gardiner turned the tie around. However the Killie battled back and Henaughan equalised to secure a replay.

The following Wednesday at kick off time saw 1,000 still outside the ground trying to get in. Rangers struck early when Killie keeper was at fault in allowing a cross to reach Paton who scored in six minutes. Brown was again at fault with Rangers second goal when his punch from a cross hit Mc Culloch and rolled over the line.

Paton scored again for Rangers in the second half with a shot that eluded Jimmy Brown with Jack replying for Killie. Rangers progressed by a 3-1 margin in a match where the Rugby Park ground record was broken. Over 33,000 crammed in with many on the track watching and many more outside unable to gain entry.

Third Lanark's Cathkin Park was to host Rangers 3rd Round tie and a near ground record were watching. The Hi Hi pushed Rangers all the way but neither side was able to break the deadlock. 0-0 it finished. The replay at Ibrox was a complete contrast. A sparse crowd (15,000) turned out in a snow bound mid week day with much of the terracing dangerous. If goals were hard to come by in the first match they were plentiful in the replay which finished 4-4.

The Second Replay was at Ibrox Park with Rangers winning the toss for venue. A Monday afternoon fixture was again poorly attended compared to a weekend match.

RANGERS: Niven , Caldow, Little, Mc Coll, Young, Cox, Mc Culloch, Paton, Simpson, Prentice and Liddell

THIRD LANARK:  Robertson, Balunas, Murray, Kennedy, Forsyth, Muir, Barclay, Docherty, Kerr, Dick and Mc Loed

Thirds took the lead on the quarter hour through Kerr after a bad mis kick by Young. Simpson was floored in the box as Rangers sought the equaliser and Eric Caldow scored from the spot. The second half saw Rangers take command and goals from Paton and Prentice saw them through despite a late goal from the Hi Hi. Rangers winning 3-2.

The 4th Round (Quarter Final stage) saw Berwick Rangers arrive at Ibrox after a great Scottish Cup run. They had knocked out East Stirlingshire 7-0 ; Ayr United  5-1 and Dundee 3-0 all at home.

However, Rangers had little trouble disposing of the gallant Berwick side. The 'Gers scored two unopposed goals in each half to progress with a 4-0 margin. A semi final place in the Scottish Cup beckoned. Perhaps the season may not be so bad after all. * Down in the east end of London a Govan lad was making an impact John Dick had scored 11 goals for West Ham United and was being tipped as a Scotland International.

- Junior side Douglas Water Thistle had a 'hot property ' young centre forward called Douglas Baillie who was scoring freely. Rangers and Motherwell were showing considerable interest.
- Billy Mullen who was impressive with Benburb transferred to Partick Thistle.
- In the Scottish Juniors a side from the North Juniors was making good progress in the Scottish Junior Cup. In anticipation of a large crowd their home match with much fancied Petershill was moved to Pittodrie Park.

- The large local support helped Sunnybank to a win. In the Sixth round they beat Broxburn to reach the semi final. This was the best achievement by a North Region side for many years.
- John Burns of St.Gerrards, a full back, was selected for the Scotland Schools side to play against England at Wembley Stadium.

## GLASGOW CORPORATION YOUTH CLUBS LEAGUE

| Team | Pl | W | L | D | F | A | Pts |
|---|---|---|---|---|---|---|---|
| Ibrox Youth Club | 10 | 9 | 1 | 0 | 38 | 12 | 18 |
| Carnwadric Youth Club | 9 | 6 | 1 | 2 | 36 | 9 | 14 |
| Greenfield Youth Club | 7 | 5 | 1 | 1 | 23 | 11 | 11 |
| Heather Street Youth Club | 9 | 4 | 3 | 2 | 18 | 18 | 10 |
| St.Gerrards Former Pupils | 6 | 3 | 1 | 2 | 21 | 12 | 8 |
| Hinshelwood and Pollok YC | 10 | 3 | 7 | 0 | 7 | 24 | 6 |
| Queen's Park JFP | 8 | 2 | 5 | 1 | 7 | 22 | 5 |
| St.Anthony's FP | 8 | 2 | 6 | 0 | 13 | 31 | 4 |
| Holyrood JFP | 9 | 0 | 9 | 0 | 4 | 28 | 0 |

Benburb were continuing to set the pace at the top of the Central League. However their lead was gradually getting cut down by a fast finishing Blantyre Victoria side. A trip to Newlandsfield to play Pollok saw the Bens arrive with a huge support all hopeful the Bens could avoid defeat.

POLLOK: Coutts, Newman, Geary, Lynch, Bowie, Gibson, Clark, Russell Evans,Perrins and Bruce.

BENBURB: Forsyth, Westwater, Cairns, Morton, Crossan, Weir, Rae, Smith, Currie, Logie and Miller.

Pollok pressed the Bens from the start and Alex Forsyth brought off some smart saves. All against the run of play Currie gave the Bens the lead approaching half time. Almost immediately Forsyth picked up a bad leg injury and was helped off the field. Currie donned the goalkeepers jersey and the Bens held out until half time.

The second half saw the ten men of Benburb more than hold their own and mid way through the half Eric Smith increased the lead. In a frantic finish to the match both sides scored once and the Bens picked up two important points.

RESULT:  POLLOK 1; BENBURB 3

Rangers were hoping for another second half of the season revival. A trip to face East Fife and Charlie Fleming looked a must win match if this was to be achieved.

EAST FIFE: Curran, Emery, S.Stewart, Christie, Finlay, Mc Lennan, J.Stewart, Fleming, Gardiner, Bonthorne and Matthews.

RANGERS: Brown, Young, Little, Mc Coll, Woodburn, Cox, Waddell Grierson, Gardiner, Thornton and Mc Culloch

East Fife started well and were well on top throughout the first half. Fleming caused them endless problems and the 'Gers defence were hard pushed to keep the Fifers out.

Against the run of play Grierson gave Rangers the lead on half time. The second half saw much the same pattern and East Fife swarmed around Rangers goal. On 55 minutes Charlie Fleming managed to get on the end of a cross to equalise. Four minutes later Fleming was at it again when he headed home a Mc Lennan cross. Rangers rallied but were unable to trouble a resolute East Fife defence.

Result : EAST FIFE 2; RANGERS 1

St.Gerrards had a powerful side and were more than a match for any school team.

The squad comprised of A.Mc Gill, C.Neville, T.Mulholland, J.Armour, E.Gallagher, M.Conner, G.O'Hara, A.Boyd, F.Fox, J.Mc Guire (captain), P.Catterson, J.Mc Bride.

Peter Catterson and Joe McBride were very frequent scorers for the St.Gerrard's side.

Govan High were providing good players to senior football.

The latest was Billy Crawford who was doing well at Partick Thistle. His brother was captain of the Govan High team. The Scottish Cup quarter Finals kept the two Govan sides apart with both at home. Govan High faced St.Mungo while St. Gerrards were against Kings Park. The Schools Football Association reported that they had no record of a boy ever being sent off in a match for a long time.

Bellahouston Academy not to be outdone by their fellow Govan Schools were also doing well in a few of the age groups. The most famous player produced by Bella was Davie Meiklejohn who made his name a few hundred yards along the road at Ibrox Park with Rangers.

Benburb continued to set the pace in the Central League. However Blantyre Victoria were having a remarkable run of form and the gap at the top narrowed slowly. St.Anthony's also were in contention and keeping pace with Blantyre Vics.

The Bens had an important match against Dunipace in front of another good crowd. A win would keep the pressure on their rivals.

BENBURB: Forsyth, Westwater, Cairns, Smith Morten, Weir, Rae, Logie, Currie, Mullen and Ayre.
DUNIPACE: Findlay, Mc Intyre, Gardiner, Grant, Holleron, Heggie, Peebles, Vandermotten, Kerr, Ferguson and Mc Donald

Benburb were on top from the start but it took until mid way through the first half before Eric Smith fired home a shot from the edge of the box following a corner. Soon after Westwater blasted home a penalty for the Bens and Logie added a third before half time.

Westwater missed a penalty before Ayre added a fourth for the Bens, Kerr replied for Dunipace near the end.
RESULT: BENBURB 4 DUNIPACE 1

In the Amateur International Scotland travelled down to England with a fair sprinkling of Queens Park players.
Weir (Queens Park), Harnett (Queens Park), T.Stewart (Bishop Auckland), Cramer (Queens Park), Valentine ( Queens Park), Hastie (Queens Park, Callaghan (St.Mungo's), J.Ward (Queens Park) , M.Murray (Queens Park) , Mc Quarrie ( Billingham), W.Omand (Queens Park)
In front of a poor crowd; Lewis gave England the lead which they held until half time. After the break Scotland improved and two goals each from Mc Quarrie and Junior Omand gave the Scots a thumping 4-1 win.
RESULT: ENGLAND 1 SCOTLAND 4

Rangers stuttering season led them to a semi final against Aberdeen at Hampden Park. A huge crowd turned up but for the Ibrox side it was a miserable afternoon. 111,000 saw the Dons on top from start to finish. O'Neil scored three , Leggat Buckley and Allister from a penalty saw Aberdeen, who led 2-0 at half time, very easy winners by 6 goals to nil.

The Scotland v England International was brought forward to enable preparation for the forthcoming World Cup. Providing Scotland could avoid a heavy defeat they were certain to qualify.

SCOTLAND: Farm, Haughney, Cox, Evans, Brennan, Aitken, Mc Kenzie, Johnstone, Henderson, Brown and Ormond.

ENGLAND: Merrick, Staniforth, Byrne, Wright, Clarke, Dickinson, Finney, Broadis, Allen, Nicholls and Mullen.

The 134,000 all ticket crowd did not have long to cheer a Scotland goal when Brown forced the ball in after 7 minutes. On the quarter hour Broadis equalised for England before half time. England, with Tom Finney prominent, were well on top in the second half and goals from Nicholls, Allen and Mullen put them out of sight. Willie Ormand scored a last minute goal to make the score slightly more respectable. Both countries were on their way to Switzerland for the World Cup Finals.

RESULT: SCOTLAND 2 ENGLAND 4

At Tinto Park work started on the Bens new pitch length cover.

The Scottish Cup Final saw the conquerors of Rangers, Aberdeen, take on Celtic.

To reach the Final Celtic had the following path 1st Round—bye.
2nd Round Falkirk 1 Celtic 2; 3rd Round Stirling Alb 3; Celtic 4
4th Round Hamilton 1 Celtic 2; Semi Final Motherwell 2 Celtic 2
Semi Final Replay Celtic 3 Motherwell 1
Aberdeen's path 1st Round—bye.
2nd Round Duns 0 Aberdeen 8; 3rd Round Hibernian 1 Aberdeen 3
4th Round Aberdeen 3 Hearts 0; Semi Final Rangers 0 Aberdeen 6

ABERDEEN: Martin, Mitchell, Caldwell, Alister, Young, Glen, Legget, Hamilton, Buckley, Clunie and Hather

CELTIC: Bonnar, Haughney, Meechan, Evans, Stein, Peacock, Higgins, Fernie, Fallon, Tully and Mochan.

130,000 spectators turned up to see what was an eagerly awaited Cup Final.

The first half of the match saw little in the way of action. However after six minutes of the second half Neil Mochan gave Celtic the lead. Pat Buckley quickly equalised for Aberdeen.

However it was to be Celtic's day when Sean Fallon netted the winner a quarter of an hour from the end. It was to be a memorable season for the Parkhead side as they also won the league. Rangers improved gradually and finished in fifth place.

RESULT CELTIC 2 ABERDEEN 1

In the Scottish Junior Cup the shock team from the North Juniors Aberdeen Sunnybank had a semi final date at Pittodrie against Bailleston. Bailleston took a big support north and after going behind early on fought back to go 2-1 up. However the Aberdeen side were level before half time and went on to win 4-2.

The Scottish Junior Cup Final at Hampden Park saw Aberdeen Sunnybank take on Lochee Harp. If it was rare for a team from the North to get to the final; usually dominated by teams from the Central belt of Scotland it was also rare to have a team from Dundee getting to the final hurdle. One of the poorest crowds at a Junior Cup Finals for many years, under 23,000 , witnessed an engrossing match.

LOCHEE HARP: Mc Mahon, Jack, Pacione, Fox, Logan, Mc Cann,Cord, Duncan, Craig, Blythe and Cochrane

ABERDEEN SUNNYBANK: J.Stephen, Harper, Murray, Simpson, Scott, Garden, Chalmers, Yeoman, Cruikshank, Ingram and W.Stephen

On the quarter hour mark Duncan gave the Harp the lead. This was pegged back within seven minutes when W.Stephen headed home. Before half time winger Chalmers gave the Aberdeen side the lead. The second half saw play move from end to end but no further goals were scored. The Cup had been won by one of the rank outsiders.

RESULT: LOCHEE HARP 1 ABERDEEN SUNNYBANK 2

John Burns of St.Gerrards school was selected for the Scotland Schoolboys team to play at Wembley against England. An enthusiastic crowd of 90,000 mostly cheering the English on. At half time things looked promising for the Scots as they went in scoreless despite facing a strong wind. In the second half England were mostly defending but managed to break away and score the only goal of the match.

ENGLAND SCHOOLBOYS 1 SCOTLAND SCHOOLBOYS 0

Hampden Park saw a lot of Govan visitors as the eagerly awaited Scottish Secondary Schools Shield Final took place. The two Central Govan schools St.Gerrards and Govan High played much good football. St.Gerrards led 2– 0 at half time with goals from O'Conner and Joe Mc Bride. Peter Catterson scored two more goals for St.Gerrads in the second half and despite a fair bit of attacking Govan High were on the end of an emphatic 4-0 loss.

RESULT: ST.GERRARD'S 4 GOVAN HIGH 0

The Central League title was now down to two teams both on equal points with five matches to play. Benburb led on goal average only. However their challengers for the title Blantyre Victoria were averaging five goals per match during the run in and things were beginning to look ominous for the Chookie Hens.

However a Currie goal at Tinto Park gave Benburb a 1-0 win over Renfrew and it was four match hurdles to overcome to win the league.

Blantyre Vics also won and scored 11 goals in their next two matches to become the highest goal scorers in the entire Central League. However the Bens still maintained a marginal lead on goal average after beating St.Anthony's at Moore Park in the run in.

Blantyre Vics at last slipped up giving Benburb the chance to win the title with a home match against Pollok. However, the large Bens support were to be disappointed as the Lok won 5-3 in an exciting game. Blantyre Vics travelled to Maryhill knowing that only a point would leave them with only Rob Roy to beat at home to claim the title. At Lochburn Park everything was on course as the teams were locked at 1-1 with Vics well on top. However an injury reduced them to 10 men and in the very last minutes the 'Hill scored the winner. This left Blantyre Vics with a home match against Rob Roy and an eight goal margin required to win the title. Blantyre won 3-1 but the league title had been won by Benburb.

Govan High continued to produce many good players. Davie Mathers and Willie Crawford were doing well at Partick Thistle. Goalkeeper Ken Brodie of Duntocher Hibs was capped as a Scottish Junior International against Wales and Eire.

Bellahouston Academy had a good season and won a league decider 3-1 against Dumbarton St.Patrick's at Lesser Hampden Park. George Duncan their right winger was much sought after by several clubs as well as being capped by the Scottish Youth team. Bellahouston had the pleasure of walking out at Celtic Park to play against a well supported St.Mungo's in the Final of an age group Secondary Schools Final.

'Bella' like Govan High and St.Gerards were producing some very good and talented players. At Shawfield Juniors Roseberry Park ground the much fancied Eastbank faced up against Govan High in the semi final of the Glasgow Cup. Govan High fought hard all the way and the match ended in a draw.

Govan provided a number of players for the Annual Regional matches. G.O'Hara (St.Gerrards), G.Mc Cracken ( Govan High) and R.Burns (Govan High) were all in the squad.

Glasgow Schools went down to Bradford Park Avenue's ground to play the Annual Inter City match and once again the Govan schools were represented in a team that won 4-1.GLASGOW: Thomson (Whitehill, Rice (St.Mungo), Keddie ( Woodside) , Anderson (Woodside), Mc Grory (Knightswood), Mc Quire (St.Gerrards), Miller (St.Mungo) , Dixon ( Queens Park), Buchanan ( Eastwood) , Seaton ( Eastwood) and Duncan ( Bellahouston)

In the annual match between Glasgow and London from Govan only Joe Mc Bride from St.Gerrards played. Glasgow had a very good record against the Londoners with a 20 wins to 9 wins in the series of matches. The games were often close and the Hampden Park match saw a poor match in front of a very poor crowd end 0-0.

57

In the City and Suburban Amateur League, Govan Randolph finished their season in a mid table position. They either won or they lost; no draws. Ladywell did not have one of their better season's. The Good Shepherd's guided the rest of the flock home.

## CITY AND SUBURBAN AMATEUR LEAGUE  DIV. 2

| Team | Pl | W | L | D | F | A | Pts |
|------|----|----|----|----|----|----|----|
| Good Shepherds | 20 | 17 | 2 | 1 | 66 | 20 | 35 |
| Cowglen United | 21 | 16 | 4 | 1 | 53 | 32 | 33 |
| Civic Star | 21 | 14 | 5 | 2 | 65 | 53 | 30 |
| Whitefield Hearts | 22 | 13 | 7 | 2 | 54 | 51 | 28 |
| Mavisbank | 19 | 10 | 4 | 5 | 36 | 56 | 25 |
| Scotstoun Vics | 22 | 10 | 11 | 1 | 40 | 53 | 21 |
| Govan Randolph | 22 | 10 | 12 | 0 | 43 | 42 | 20 |
| Doncaster Vics | 21 | 7 | 10 | 4 | 31 | 65 | 18 |
| Fraser's Athletic | 22 | 7 | 12 | 3 | 32 | 67 | 17 |
| Knightswood Ath. | 22 | 6 | 13 | 3 | 38 | 49 | 15 |
| Dale Athletic | 22 | 6 | 14 | 2 | 26 | 47 | 14 |
| Ladywell | 22 | 0 | 22 | 0 | 22 | 77 | 0 |

St. Anthony's had a very good season. Throughout they gave the young taleneted players of Govan a chance and it paid off with a remarkable third place finish. The oldest player in the squad was 25 year old Maurice Young. He rarely ever played a bad game and his talents were being eyed not too far away down Shieldhall Road.

The Ants in turn were trying to entice St.Gerrard  School players John Burns and prolific goalscorer Peter Catterson to Moore Park.  Former St.Anthony's player Bobby Evans was selected to be part of the Scotland World Cup squad for Switzerland. Evans had left 10 years previous to go to Celtic Park. Many Govanites continually recalled how they had a connection with Bobby. 'Bobby was flappin one day when he coulnae find his comb. I lent him mine and we have been pals ever since !'.

Benburb, after a punishing set of matches, won the league title by virtually crawling over the line with Blantyre Vics and St.Anthony's closing fast. The League Decider at Shawfield was against Kilsyth Rangers who had all but swept all before them  during the course of the season.

# CENTRAL LEAGUE—DIVISION B

| Team | Pl | W | L | D | F | A | Pts |
|---|---|---|---|---|---|---|---|
| Benburb | 30 | 21 | 5 | 4 | 94 | 47 | 46 |
| Blantyre Vics. | 30 | 22 | 6 | 2 | 102 | 53 | 46 |
| St.Anthony's | 30 | 17 | 6 | 7 | 69 | 52 | 41 |
| Port Glasgow | 30 | 13 | 10 | 7 | 80 | 76 | 33 |
| Renfrew | 30 | 11 | 11 | 8 | 76 | 65 | 30 |
| Rob Roy | 30 | 11 | 11 | 8 | 78 | 76 | 30 |
| Bridgeton Waverley | 30 | 12 | 12 | 6 | 74 | 78 | 30 |
| Pollok | 28 | 9 | 8 | 11 | 50 | 63 | 29 |
| Maryhill | 28 | 11 | 11 | 6 | 59 | 55 | 28 |
| Maryhill Harp | 29 | 9 | 13 | 7 | 55 | 74 | 25 |
| Vale of Clyde | 30 | 9 | 14 | 7 | 61 | 72 | 25 |
| Dunipace | 29 | 11 | 16 | 2 | 76 | 89 | 24 |
| Arthurlie | 29 | 9 | 15 | 5 | 51 | 61 | 23 |
| Bellshill Athletic | 30 | 9 | 16 | 5 | 56 | 62 | 23 |
| Dennistoun Waverley | 29 | 7 | 17 | 5 | 51 | 76 | 19 |
| Yoker Athletic | 28 | 6 | 16 | 6 | 57 | 86 | 18 |

The Westwater brothers were in opposition to one another. Tennant a youth International from Govan High was on the left wing for the Bens and Eric Smith was playing his last game for Benburb before his move to Celtic.
KILSYTH RANGERS: Lowe, Westwater, Sherry, O'Brien, Holmes, Glover, Mc Farlane, Rankin, Querry, Patterson and Mulhall.
BENBURB: Forsyth, Westwater, Cairns, Tracey, Crossan, Ford, Rae, Smith, Logie, Patterson and Tennant.
The match was very one sided from almost the beginning. Kilsyth took a stranglehold from the start and Rankin fired them into an early lead. The crowd of over 15,000 saw the 'Gers increase their lead when Querry headed in a flicked on corner. Rankin scored with a scorching shot and the same player added a fourth just on half time following up a shot which came off the post. Benburb had a good spell at the start of the second half cheered on by a big Govan support but further goals from Patterson and Querry saw a very heavy defeat for the Bens.
RESULT: KILSYTH RANGERS 6 BENBURB 0

The Bens also reached the Final of the Kirkwood Shield but lost out to Vale of Leven after a replay. Despite the late season setbacks it was a good season for the Tinto Park side and their large number of followers.

Veteran goalkeeper Alex Forsyth was a very popular member of the Bens team. He joined the Benburb club in 1938 and provided great service to the club. Rangers occasionally called on his services to help out with training new keepers. Alex. was the mentor of Stewart Mitchell who worked in the Co-op at Shieldhall. Stewart was making great progress with Newcastle United.

## SCOTTISH LEAGUE DIVISION A

| Team | Pl | W | L | D | F | A | Pts |
|------|----|----|----|----|----|----|-----|
| Celtic | 29 | 19 | 7 | 3 | 71 | 29 | 41 |
| Hearts | 30 | 16 | 8 | 6 | 70 | 45 | 38 |
| Partick Thistle | 30 | 17 | 12 | 1 | 76 | 54 | 35 |
| Clyde | 30 | 15 | 11 | 4 | 64 | 67 | 34 |
| East Fife | 30 | 13 | 9 | 8 | 55 | 45 | 34 |
| Dundee | 30 | 14 | 10 | 6 | 46 | 47 | 34 |
| Hibernian | 29 | 15 | 11 | 3 | 70 | 49 | 33 |
| Rangers | 29 | 13 | 9 | 7 | 54 | 33 | 33 |
| Aberdeen | 30 | 15 | 12 | 3 | 66 | 51 | 33 |
| Queen of the South | 30 | 14 | 12 | 4 | 72 | 58 | 32 |
| St.Mirren | 30 | 12 | 14 | 4 | 44 | 54 | 28 |
| Raith Rovers | 30 | 10 | 14 | 6 | 56 | 60 | 26 |
| Falkirk | 30 | 9 | 14 | 7 | 47 | 61 | 25 |
| Stirling Albion | 30 | 10 | 16 | 4 | 39 | 61 | 24 |
| Airdieonians | 30 | 5 | 20 | 5 | 41 | 93 | 15 |
| Hamilton Accies | 29 | 4 | 22 | 3 | 29 | 95 | 11 |

Drumoyne School had a football team but it was only in the final years that they played in the much coveted 'Govan Cup' a small competition between all the schools in Govan. Drumoyne School usually did well in the competition but it was acknowledged that St.Saviours from Govan centre usually started as favourites.

Scotland had qualified for the World Cup Finals in Switzerland. They were in a tough group of four. The competition had sixteen teams divided into four groups of four. Each group had two seeded teams and two un-seeded teams. The two seeded teams ( Austria and Uruguay) played the two un-seeded teams (Scotland and Czechoslavakia) and the group winners and runners up progressed.

Scotland opened against Austria in Zurich. Austria proved to be a very physical side and Scotland battled hard against them. The Austrians scored a solitary goal in the first half through Probst which proved to be the winner. The referee seemed lenient with many of the Austrian challenges. Scotland felt they had a good claim for a penalty when Neil Mochan was barged off the ball in the penalty box. The referee blew for foul play in favour of the Scots but awarded an indirect free kick. Scotland were rightly proud of the teams effort.

The second match proved a completely different story.

URUGUAY: Maspolli; Santamaria; Martinez; Andrade; Varela; Abbadie; Miguez; Schiaffino; Borges;Cruz and Ambrois

SCOTLAND: Fred Martin; Willie Cunningham; John Aird; Tommy Docherty; Jimmy Davidson; Doug Cowie; John Mc Kenzie; Allan Brown; Neil Mochan; Willie Fernie; Willie Ormond.

Substitutes: Bobby Evans; George Hamilton; John Anderson; Robert Johnstone; Jackie Henderson; Davie Mathers; Alex Wilson; Jimmy Binning; Bobby Combe; Ernie Copland; Ian Mc Millan

Coach; Andy Beattie

Uruguay were a class above Scotland and dominated from the first whistle. The South Americans were comfortable when in control of the ball; the Scots hurried and guilty of many misplaced passes or clearances.

Scotland held out for 17 minutes before Carlos Borges scored the opener for Uruguay. On the half hour the lead was doubled when winger Oscar Miguez was on the mark. Scotland held on until half time keeping Uruguay out.

The second half was barely two minutes old when any hope Scotland may have had ended when Carlos Borges scored his second. From this point until the end of the match was a torrid time for Scotland and Uruguay added goals at regular intervals through

Julio Abaddie (54 minutes); Carlos Borges (57 minutes); Oscar Miguez (83 minutes) and Julio Abaddie (85 minutes).

Some good saves from Fred Martin kept the score below double figures.

Scotland were generous in defeat praising the excellent play of the Uruguayans. The sweltering heat in which the match was played was considered a factor. Two players with Govan connections made the squad. Bobby Evans from Celtic and formerly St.Anthony's. Davie Mather from Partick Thistle and formerly Govan High School.

After the dust had settled many Govanites and Scots in general were mystified why the two top scorer's in Scotland had not been picked. The player who scored the two goals against Northern Ireland in his only International match (which effectively earned Scotland their place in the Finals) did not reach the squad. Charlie Fleming was the top goal scorer in Scotland with no fewer than 35 goals for East Fife. Close behind him was Jimmy Wardhaugh of Hearts with 34 goals. Neil Mochan of Celtic who had a good season was selected but his haul of 25 goals was some way behind the aforementioned.

# WORLD CUP 1954
## GROUP A
BRAZIL 5 MEXICO 0
YUGOSLAVIA 1 FRANCE 0
BRAZIL 1 YUGOSLAVIA 1

| Team | Pl | W | L | D | F | A | Pts |
|------|----|----|----|----|----|----|-----|
| BRAZIL | 2 | 1 | 0 | 1 | 6 | 1 | 3 |
| YUGOSLAVIA | 2 | 1 | 0 | 1 | 2 | 1 | 3 |
| FRANCE | 2 | 1 | 1 | 0 | 3 | 3 | 2 |
| MEXICO | 2 | 0 | 2 | 0 | 2 | 8 | 0 |

## GROUP B
WEST GERMANY 4 TURKEY 1
HUNGARY 9 SOUTH KOREA 0
HUNGARY 8 WEST GERMANY 3
TURKEY 7 SOUTH KOREA 0
PLAY OFF: WEST GERMANY 7 TURKEY 2

| Team | Pl | W | L | D | F | A | Pts |
|------|----|----|----|----|----|----|-----|
| HUNGARY | 2 | 2 | 0 | 0 | 17 | 3 | 4 |
| WEST GERMANY | 2 | 1 | 1 | 0 | 7 | 9 | 2 |
| TURKEY | 2 | 1 | 1 | 0 | 8 | 4 | 2 |
| SOUTH KOREA | 2 | 0 | 2 | 0 | 0 | 16 | 0 |

# GROUP C

URUGUAY 2 CZECHOSLAVAKIA 0
AUSTRIA 1 SCOTLAND 0
URUGUAY 7 SCOTLAND 0
AUSTRIA 5 CZECHOSLAVAKIA 0

| Team | Pl | W | L | D | F | A | Pts |
|------|----|----|----|----|----|----|-----|
| URUGUAY | 2 | 2 | 0 | 0 | 9 | 0 | 4 |
| AUSTRIA | 2 | 2 | 0 | 0 | 6 | 0 | 4 |
| CZECHOSLAVAKIA | 2 | 0 | 2 | 0 | 0 | 7 | 0 |
| SCOTLAND | 2 | 0 | 2 | 0 | 0 | 8 | 0 |

# GROUP D

SWITZERLAND 2 ITALY 1
ENGLAND 4 BELGIUM 4 aet
ITALY 4 BELGIUM 1
ENGLAND 2 SWITZERLAND 0
PLAY OFF: SWITZERLAND 4 ITALY 1

| Team | Pl | W | L | D | F | A | Pts |
|------|----|----|----|----|----|----|-----|
| ENGLAND | 2 | 1 | 0 | 1 | 6 | 4 | 3 |
| SWITZERLAND | 2 | 1 | 1 | 0 | 2 | 3 | 2 |
| ITALY | 2 | 1 | 1 | 0 | 5 | 3 | 2 |
| BELGIUM | 2 | 0 | 1 | 1 | 5 | 8 | 1 |

# QUARTER FINALS

## AUSTRIA 7 SWITZERLAND 5

Switzerland were 3 up in the first 20 minutes but Austria fought back to lead at half time after an amazing first half. Austria held on to progress to the semi finals

## URUGUAY 4 ENGLAND 2

Uruguay went ahead through Borges after 5 minutes before Nat Lofthouse equalised for England on the quarter hour . Varela restored the South Americans lead five minutes before half time. Schiaffino increased the Uruguay lead shortly after half time before Tom Finney gave England hope on 67 minutes with a goal. However 10 minutes later Ambrois sealed the win for Uruguay.

YUGOSLAVIA 0 WEST GERMANY 2
BRAZIL 2 HUNGARY 4

## SEMI FINALS
WEST GERMANY 6 AUSTRIA 1
URUGUAY 2 HUNGARY 4  after extra time

## FINAL
**HUNGARY:** GROSICS; BUZANSZKY; LORAN; LANTOS; BOZSIK;
ZAKANIAS; HIDEGKUTI; CZIBOR: KOCSIS: PUSKAS; TOTH
**WEST GERMANY:** TUREK; POSIPAL: KOHLMEYER; ECKEL;
LIEBRICH;  MAI; MORLOCK; F.WALTER; RAHN; O.WALTER;
SCHAFER
Referee : William Ling (England)

Hungary started as strong favourites to win the match and scored twice in the first ten minutes through Puskas and Czibor. However they relaxed slightly and the Germans were level by the 20 minute mark with goals from Morlock and Rahn.  Hungary were the better side but could not score and Helmut Rahn scored the winner for West Germany six minutes from the end.
RESULT:  HUNGARY 2 WEST GERMANY 3

The season drew to an end with many Benburb supporters  wishing former favourite Teddy Swift was still in their defence. Teddy had a position in football as Celtic's scout and was recommending Duntocher goalkeeper Dick Beattie to be brought to Celtic Park.

64

# CHAPTER 6
## TOMMY AND SCOT ARRIVE

Scot Symon was appointed Rangers manager in succession to Bill Struth. Symon was previously manager at East Fife and Preston North End. He was not a universally popular selection with the 'Gers fans and there were early indications that he would take time to win over the Ibrox fans. A League Cup section defeat against Clyde brought a chorus of boos and jeers around the ground.

Benburb supporters were quite excited that the re-instatement from senior football was a Govan man. Tommy Douglas, who faced the Bens in the Saracen Park Scottish Junior Cup match two seasons prior, tried a season at Stirling Albion but was unable to make the breakthrough to regular first team football.

With the consistant popular talent Dunky Rae on one wing and the goal scoring prowess of Tommy Douglas on the other the Bens would probably have considerable firepower. However a lot of emphasis would fall on how the defence shaped up.

The Benburb squad was:

Goalkeepers: A.Forsyth, R.Mac Kay (Riverside FP)

Backs: J.Westwater, J.Patterson, J.Cavins, R.Walker

Half Backs: P.Treacy, A.Crossan, P.Ford, J.Dougan (Strathclyde)

Forwards: D.Rae, A.Patterson, H.Currie, G.Logie, W.Mullin, D.Mitchell (Dalry Thistle) , T.Douglas ( Stirling Albion)

St.Anthony's also were busy signing players. They signed a considerable number of young very talented players from around the Govan area. At centre half they had the ultra dependable Maurice Young easily the oldest player in the squad at 25 years old. The young Ants team were keen to get started.

The St.Anthony's squad was:

Goalkeepers: J.Higgins, M.Mc Colgan

Backs: J.Clocherty,

Half Backs: J.Mooney, M.Young, J.Rodgers, R.White, W.Burns.

Forwards: W.Craig, J.Colrain, J.Quigley, J.Best, H.Bryceland, J.Stewart, J.Phillips, E.Andrews.

The Ants were delighted at the capture of local starlet Johnny Quigley and were optimistic of signing John Burns the Scotland schoolboy International.

During the summer months efforts were being made to complete some of the Youth Leagues. Many teams were divided on Religious grounds. The Protestant Boys Brigade Leagues, having fewer teams in each league, managed to finish the fixtures on schedule. However the Roman Catholic Boys Guild teams in bigger leagues struggled badly and games were being played on summer evenings at the 50 pitches and other grounds.

The St.Vincent League was split into three sections:
St.Constantine's had a good season in section A. They won 12 of their 24 matches and drew 4 with 8 losses. 66 goals for 61 against and the 28 points gained a 5th place finish.

Central Govan Schools St.Saviour's and St.Anthony's struggled badly to raise reasonably strong teams due to calls from stronger sides elsewhere and both trailed in near the bottom of Section C.

St.Mary's of Duntocher the winners of Section A beat St.Theresa's of Possilpark; the play off winner with Good Shepherds (Section C winner) 4-2 in the Final.

Both Benburb and Rangers were having large covers built. At Ibrox a huge pitch long cover was built to enable their fans to be kept dry while watching the 'Gers. Benburb also went for a pitch length cover and the season started with the Bens cover being built.

St.Anthony's duly signed John Burns and their young team played some excellent football. After four matches they led the league with maximum points including victory over local rivals Benburb. However young promising players always attract much interest amongst senior clubs. The performances of Johnny Quigley were closely monitored by English club Ipswich Town. The 100% St.Anthony's run came to an end when they drew away at Blantyre Celtic. A backs to the wall performance saw goalkeeper Mick Mc Colgan play on after a collision with a broken arm. Despite the agony he pulled off a string of fantastic saves.

Rangers Scottish League Cup campaign gradually improved and they qualified from the section that included Clyde, Partick Thistle and Stirling Albion. The two leg quarter final saw a narrow 2-1 defeat at Motherwell. At Ibrox Rangers were unable to pull the single goal deficit back and were eliminated with a 1-1 draw.

George Dick (38) was in a hurry to enter Ibrox Stadium. He lifted his 12 year old son over the turnstile and the Stewards objected. They pointed out that there was a separate turnstile for the boys. Dick started to shout and swear and challenged one of the Stewards to a fight. The police were called and George Dick was arrested. At Govan Police Court Dick was fined £1 by Fiscal W.Grindlay. He said 'I intended to pay for my son and offered the Steward 2 shillings. I am afraid I lost my head'.

The Central League sections had been distributed (whether intentionally or not) to list all the strongest sides in Section A. Powerful clubs like Ashfield and Kilsyth Rangers were not finding the going as easy as they might have expected. Benburb had a terrible start to the season losing 4-1 at Renfrew. They always looked like scoring but on the other hand were conceding an abundance of soft goals.

# CENTRAL LEAGUE—SECTION A

| Team | Pl | W | L | D | F | A | Pts |
|------|-----|----|----|----|----|----|-----|
| Bailleston | 9 | 7 | 1 | 1 | 22 | 11 | 15 |
| St.Anthony's | 9 | 6 | 2 | 1 | 17 | 15 | 13 |
| Cambuslang Rangers | 8 | 4 | 1 | 3 | 20 | 10 | 11 |
| Duntocher Hibs | 9 | 4 | 2 | 3 | 19 | 10 | 11 |
| Pollok | 9 | 5 | 3 | 1 | 22 | 18 | 11 |
| Renfrew | 9 | 4 | 3 | 2 | 18 | 12 | 10 |
| Ashfield | 9 | 5 | 4 | 0 | 21 | 17 | 10 |
| Clydebank | 8 | 4 | 4 | 2 | 17 | 19 | 10 |
| Vale of Leven | 9 | 2 | 2 | 5 | 14 | 12 | 9 |
| Kilsyth Rangers | 9 | 4 | 4 | 1 | 18 | 14 | 9 |
| Rob Roy | 9 | 4 | 4 | 1 | 24 | 25 | 9 |
| Blantyre Vics. | 9 | 3 | 4 | 2 | 18 | 15 | 8 |
| Port Glasgow | 9 | 3 | 4 | 2 | 22 | 23 | 8 |
| Benburb | 9 | 1 | 6 | 2 | 15 | 23 | 4 |
| Blantyre Celtic | 9 | 1 | 7 | 1 | 11 | 24 | 3 |
| Maryhill | 8 | 0 | 7 | 1 | 7 | 27 | 1 |

Rangers start had been disappointing and it was to get worse. Rangers were coasting to a 2-0 win in the Scottish League Cup against Stirling Albion with one minute left. Willie Woodburn the Rangers centre half was ordered off. A few weeks later the Scottish Football referee's decided that their patience with Woodburn had run out and he was suspended 'Sine Die'. The 34 year old was a physical player of that there was no doubt but the sentence was disproportionate and ended the career of someone who was probably still Scotland's best centre half. Most around the Govan football fraternity were stunned.
Could there ever have been a harsher way to treat a footballer?.

The first Old Firm derby saw Rangers visit Parkhead with Stanners at centre half as replacement for Willie Woodburn. Rangers were poor and fortunate to reach half time with the score at 0-0. In the second half Walsh scored a good goal for Celtic and Higgins secured a 2-0 win with a goal in the last minute. Scot Symon was already a man with problems as Rangers manager.

Benburb had a poor start to the season. They led with three Bain goals at Clydebank well into the second half in a league match but somehow lost three goals in the latter part of the match to draw 3-3.However one of the biggest matches to be held at Tinto Park saw the opening of the club's new Covered Enclosure. It was well populated as the teams came out for a Scottish Junior Cup 1st Round match with Shotts Bon Accord. The Govan populace had turned out in huge numbers to support the Bens despite their poor form at the start to the season. It was the first match to be held in front of the enclosure and for many it was possibly the best.

BENBURB: Forsyth, Westwater, Cairns, Patterson, Carden, Ford, Rae, Logie Bain, Mitchell and Douglas

SHOTTS BON ACCORD: Mc Dougall, Duncan, Wilson, Roberts, Love, Nelson, Mc Loed , Smith, Mc Menamin, Mc Farlane and Mc Bain.

Shotts started the better but Bens took the lead on 12 minutes through Geordie Logie whose shot found the net through many Shotts defenders. On 35 minutes the game had to be delayed when Benburb's goalkeeper received a bad injury in a goalmouth melee. Alex. Forsyth was taken straight to Southern General Hospital. 'C'Mon the 10 men' roared the Bens faithful'. However on the stroke of half time after continuous pressure Shotts Bon Accord were awarded a penalty. Nelson converted the penalty past Logie the stand in Benburb keeper. The second half saw an onslaught from the Lanarkshire side and the small Geordie Logie was kept busy. From a rare attack the Bens were awarded a free kick near the penalty box. Westwater smashed in a fierce shot which hit the crossbar; Bain following up ran the ball into the net to the joy of the home support. A minute later Tommy Douglas cut in and fired home a third goal for the Bens. A huge number of challenges went in from the sides as the Bens strove to hold onto their lead. Shotts scored very late on but Benburb emerged victorious from a bruising cup tie that provided non-stop excitement to the spectators. RESULT: BENBURB 3 SHOTTS BON ACCORD 2

St.Anthony's also had a tough draw away to Bailleston in the 1st Round. Maurice Young scored from a penalty early on but the home side quickly equalised and went on to score three more before half time. In the second half they added another and the Ants had lost 5-1.

In the Renfrewshire Juvenile League the Govan sides were squaring up to put in their league and cup challenges. Avon Villa had been knocking on the door for a while and were expecting to do well. Benburb Juveniles, Govan Brittania and Tradeston Holmlea were hoping for the best. Three early season fixtures took place at the black ash pitches affectionately known as the 'Plots' (Plantation Park).  Avon Villa v Craigielea Star at Plantation Park Benburb Juveniles v Govan Britannia at Bellahouston Park  Tradeston Holmlea v Butters Juveniles at Plantation Park

An ongoing problem for both Benburb and St.Anthony's was having a consistant team. Several of the players were in the Armed Forces and were not always available. The Ants were always a better side when Johnny Quigley played after he got released from his barracks in Colchester. Bens reluctantly released Reg Walker, who lived in Howatt Street Govan, the player was often overseas for long spells .

Benburb had several big matches on the horizon. The first of these was a Scottish Junior Cup 2nd Round match against Petershill. Petershill had one of the biggest supports in Junior football and a crowd in excess of 11,000 turned up to see if the Bens could repeat their heroics of the previous round against Shotts Bon Accord.

BENBURB: Johnstone, Westwater, Ford, Patterson, Carden, Mc Allister, Rae, Logie, Bain, Tracey and Douglas.

PETERSHILL: White, Mac Farlane, Mc Nab, Robb, Kyle, Mc Kenzie, Stewart, Hunter, Gallagher, Mc Iver and Devlin.

The game took an early pattern which carried on throughout the match. Petershill had most of the play but Bens were dangerous when they broke away through wingers Rae and Douglas. Bens goalkeeper Davie Johnstone brought off smart saves from Stewart, Hunter and Gallagher before the Bens took the lead on half time. Bain fired in a fierce shot which the Peasies defence could not clear and Tommy Douglas made no mistake from close in. The second half was much the same pattern. Bain put the Bens two up before Gallagher headed home for the Peasies to reduce the leeway. The same player hit a rocket shot in to equalise. However the Bens steadied the ship and Westwater put them back in front. The Bens added a fourth near the end to claim another famous Junior Cup match win in an exciting match.

RESULT: BENBURB 4 PETERSHILL 2

The draw for the next round paired the Bens with Ashfield at Tinto Park. A huge crowd assembled and the kick off was delayed. The Bens were being asked to again play against a high ranking side to make progress.

BENBURB: Forsyth, Westwater, Ford, Paterson, Carden, Mitchell, Rae, Logie, Bain, Tracey and Douglas

ASHFIELD: Robb, Ralston, Houston, Rice, Cassidy, Clinton, Graham, Mc Carthy, Dawson, Innes and Mac Guire

Bens started brightly but on the quarter hour mark a bad mistake by Carden allowed Billy Dawson a free run in on goal. The 'field man made no mistake lashing a fierce shot past Forsyth in the Bens goal. Before the Bens could recover, Innes dribbled his way through the Bens defence before sending a crisp shot into the net. Bens recovered and stormed back roared on by the vast bulk of the crowd. Tracey sent in a fierce drive which Robb did well to parry but Tommy Douglas was on hand to score. .

The Bens were well on top and Tommy Douglas mesmerised the Ashfield defence before crossing for Logie to equalise. It was a rip roaring cup tie with everyone getting their money's worth. Benburb were brilliant in attack but not so good in defence. Approaching half time Dunky Rae forced a corner. The delivery was excellent and Patterson headed the Bens into the lead.

The second half continued very much in the same action packed way of the first. However both defences were tighter and not so many chances created. Benburb had a great chance to increase the lead when Bain was brought down in the penalty box. Westwater stepped up and hammered the penalty against the crossbar. Near the end Ashfield forced a throw in near the corner flag. It was flicked on and there was Billy Dawson to force in the equaliser.

RESULT: BENBURB 3 ASHFIELD 3

For the replay the following week Benburb introduced a new goalkeeper Jeff Lamont. However he had big game jitters and gave away an early goal with a misplaced kick, allowing Billy Dawson to score. The goalkeepers indecision was apparent throughout the first half and Ashfield had added two more goals to send the Bens out of the Scottish Junior Cup.

Despite the defeat Benburb were proving great entertainers in virtually every match they played and won 7-6 at Blantyre Victoria after trailing 4-2 at half time.

The Scottish League Cup Semi Finals paired Hearts with Airdrie and East Fife with Motherwell who had knocked out Rangers in the quarter finals.

East Fife scored early on in front of a poor crowd at Hampden Park through Gardiner. Motherwell equalised before half time through a Kilmarnock free kick on the edge of the box. In the second half Bain got the winner for the 'well with a header.

Airdrie scored in the first minute through Price but goals from Wardhaugh and Urquart had Hearts ahead at half time. In the second half the Edinburgh side scored two more through Wardhaugh and Bauld to cement a place in the Final against Motherwell.

With Rangers form still erratic many of the older supporters were yearning for the present players to emulate the attitude of players from the past.

Was it not former Benburb player and Ibrox legend Jock 'Tiger' Shaw on seeing some younger Rangers players shaking before a big match. 'You should see them other guys in the away changing room. Let them do all the shaking !'

St.Anthony's were being called the young Celtic. Four of their talented young players were on the books of Celtic. Ian Whyte (wing half), Billy Craig (inside or outside right), Hugh Bryceland (outside left) and John Colrain (inside left). Like Benburb, the Ants were always good for scoring goals. Alas for both the Govan clubs in this particular season they were becoming prone to letting goals in also.

70

Glasgow Cup 1st Round.

ST.ANTHONY'S ; Flynn, Chuckley, Clocherty, Whyte, Young, Burns, Craig, Murphy, Maher, Colrain and Bryceland.

PERTHSHIRE: Davidson, Walker, Smith, McIntyre, Bunting, Mitchell, Gallacher, Murphy, McIntosh, Donnachie and Mc Clure

Ants scored after 2 minutes through Craig who scored after the goalie parried. However the Shire equalised a minute later through Gallacher. In the second half, after 65 minutes, Mc Clure scored for the visitors but the Ants drew level through Maher. The same player gave St.Anthony's the lead but a late goal from Gallacher meant the match ended level with a replay required.

RESULT: ST.ANTHONY'S 3 PERTHSHIRE 3

The Scottish League Cup Final saw Hearts bring a big support through from Edinburgh amongst the 56,000 crowd. The Edinburgh side were trying to capture their first major prize for around 48 years and the betting was in their favour.

HEART OF MIDLOTHIAN: Duff, Parker, McKenzie, McKay, Glidden, Cumming, Souness, Conn, Bauld, Wardhaugh and Urquart.

MOTHERWELL: Weir, Kilmarnock, Mc Seveney, Cox, Paton, Redpath, Hunter, Aitken, Bain, Humphries and Williams.

Willie Bauld gave Hearts an early lead when he converted a cross from Souness with a header. Bauld scored again on 16 minutes when after taking a pass from Conn side-stepped the defender and lashed into the net. Motherwell responded well and put Hearts under a lot of pressure and several near misses deserved better reward. However Humphries was brought down in the box and Redpath reduced the arrears. On the stroke of half time Wardhaugh increased the Hearts lead from another Souness cross.

The second half was exciting with play swinging from end to end. Willie Bauld completed his hat trick with 3 minutes left before Bain hit a second for the 'well'.

RESULT: HEARTS 4 MOTHERWELL 2

Christmas Day 1954 arrived. A Christmas present in the form of a league match between the two Govan Old Firm rivals Benburb and St. Anthony's was scheduled for Tinto Park. Both had been in recent good form and both sides knew how to score goals.

BENBURB: Forsyth, Westwater, Cairns, Patterson, Carden, Ford, Bain, Logie, Martin, Tracey and Douglas

ST.ANTHONY'S: Mc Colgan, Young, Checkley, Mooney, Friel, Clougherty, Craig, Colrain, Murphy, White and Phillips

Benurb drew first blood when they scored an early goal. Logie converted Bain's cross.

St.Anthony's soon responded when Clougherty equalised with a rocket shot. Ants went ahead when they were awarded a penalty and Maurice Young scored. Minutes later it was 3-1 when John Colrain fastened onto a ball from Craig and scored easily. On the stroke of half time Tracey reduced the arrears for the Bens, when put through by Tommy Douglas.

The second half was every bit as exciting as the first. Benurb scored two quick goals. Tracey scored after a good passing move before Tommy Douglas scored from a free kick on the edge of the box putting the Bens ahead. However, the Ants were not finished and scored two late goals to secure victory.

RESULT: BENBURB 4 ST.ANTHONY'S 5

In the annual Glasgow v Edinburgh Schools match at Cathkin Park the bigger Edinburgh side won easily. After leading 5-1 at half time they added one more to win 6-1.

The Glasgow officials reflected that in the past the Glasgow side had some good players including Davie Mather of Govan High and George Duncan of Bellahouston Academy. A Govan player who did not go through the schools teams was Clyde's Harry Haddock who attended St.Gerrards. He was considered 'too wee' at the time.

St.Gerrards progressed in the Scottish Intermediate Cup beating St.Modan's of Stirling 4-1. However, in the secondary competition St.Gerrard's went down 3-1 at Airdrie Academy.

Bellahouston Academy were having their best season ever at football. However, in cup competitions they were having very tight matches and winning through only after replays. They had a backlog of fixtures. St.Gerrards continued to do well but not as well as in previous years.

Govan High teams were having a poor season and a few of the teams had steady heavy defeats. However, the Intermediate team was finding a late burst of form and started to challenge for honours.

Aberdeen were beginning to look like all the way winners of the League. Rangers were in second place but playing inconsistently. The likely challengers looked like Celtic or Hearts.

Bill Struth the former Rangers manager was still actively involved at the club. He was scouting for players and he had unearthed a couple of possible prospects. One was Maxwell Murray, a Scottish Amateur International playing for Queen's Park. The other was a young Scottish Junior International playing for Bo'ness United who were having a good run in the Scottish Junior Cup. The player was Alex Scott a winger who studied the art of the game. His hero was England Internationalist Stanley Matthew and he hoped to reach similar heights.

# SCOTTISH LEAGUE—DIVISION A

| Team | PL | W | L | D | F | A | PTS |
|------|----|----|----|----|----|----|-----|
| Aberdeen | 19 | 16 | 3 | 0 | 45 | 14 | 32 |
| Rangers | 18 | 12 | 4 | 2 | 50 | 21 | 26 |
| Celtic | 18 | 10 | 2 | 6 | 51 | 26 | 26 |
| St.Mirren | 18 | 10 | 3 | 5 | 42 | 29 | 25 |
| Hearts | 16 | 11 | 3 | 2 | 52 | 26 | 24 |
| Clyde | 19 | 7 | 5 | 7 | 42 | 33 | 21 |
| Hibernian | 19 | 10 | 8 | 1 | 39 | 38 | 21 |
| Falkirk | 18 | 8 | 7 | 3 | 32 | 29 | 19 |
| Partick Thistle | 19 | 7 | 7 | 5 | 40 | 45 | 19 |
| Dundee | 19 | 8 | 11 | 0 | 29 | 36 | 16 |
| Queen of the South | 18 | 6 | 11 | 1 | 26 | 41 | 13 |
| Motherwell | 16 | 5 | 9 | 2 | 25 | 36 | 12 |
| Kilmarnock | 18 | 4 | 10 | 4 | 29 | 42 | 12 |
| Raith Rovers | 19 | 5 | 12 | 2 | 31 | 40 | 12 |
| East Fife | 17 | 4 | 11 | 2 | 25 | 44 | 10 |
| Stirling Albion | 19 | 0 | 17 | 2 | 19 | 77 | 2 |

Concern was expressed at the behaviour of Rangers supporters at away matches. Following the game at Dumfries against Queen of the South a number of 'Gers fans went to the Forrester's Arms Public House. Initially everything was friendly and jovial.

However, as the evening wore on the songs became very anti Catholic and the barmen received complaints from the regular drinkers. After several warnings two of the regulars, Mr. Maxwell and Mr. Mitchell, suggested the police be called. This was overheard by a group of Rangers fans and the two regulars were attacked. Bottles and glasses were used on the pair and Mr.Mitchell received a broken jaw. Mr Maxwell was chased out of the pub and tripped. One of the fans jumped and stamped on his back. Fortunately for Mr.Maxwell the police arrived and arrested 5 Rangers supporters involved.In Dumfries Court, John Thomas (30) of Hoey Street admitted three similar previous offences and was sentenced by the Fiscal to three months imprisonment. James Mc Doanld of 48, Harmony Row was sent to prison for 30 days .William Mc Gregor Mc Kenzie (27) of 21 Robert Street, William Willis (26) of 59, Harmony Row and Robert Whyte of 2, Hoey Street were each fined £8 or 30 days imprisonment.

Shawfield Stadium was keen to have matches played under the floodlights.. They obtained permission to stage a match between the Scotland Under 23 side and the England Under 23 side. Scotland were not too hopeful; the team did not look strong and there seemed to be a general dearth of young talent in Scottish football. England on the other hand had a powerful side and they had demolished a strong Italy Under 23 side recently.

From 31 Daviot Street, West Drumoyne, Grandad Boab and his son's Robbie and Jack wanted to see a match under floodlights. All were wrapped up warm against a cold damp evening. They were hoping Scotland would do well. In the first minute England were down to ten men when Ayre had to be taken to hospital with a dislocated elbow. Substitutes were allowed and England brought on Anderson some minutes later.

England opened the scoring following a quick free kick between Haynes and Blunstone. Scotland flickered a bit and had one or two efforts to warm up the home support in the big crowd. The half time whistle arrived but the second period saw the Scottish defence overwhelmed. Duncan Edwards scored three and with Ayteo and Haynes gave the home players non stop problems. The post was struck; the crossbar was struck. Goalkeeper Duff was heroic. The end score was Scotland 0 England 6 Scotland were best served by Walsh and Caldow. Grandad Boab was enthused with the English side and, in particular, stand in Centre Forward Duncan Edwards. ' Whit a pity he was not born in Scotland'. Robbie said 'What a pity Scottish 'fitba' is in such a bad way !'.
RESULT: SCOTLAND U 23 0 ENGLAND U 23 6

Rangers title challenge was beginning to fade and Aberdeen looked set to capture their first Scottish League title. Paddy Buckley was a prolific goal scorer for them and the defence gave little away. The Scottish Cup seemed to be the Ibrox club's best chance of silverware.Rangers got a bye to the 5th Round and then got a home draw with Dundee.The match ended in stalemate and the scoreless draw meant a replay at Dens Park. Another tight match was served up with few incidents like the first game. Ten minutes from the end, Gallacher the Dundee defender headed into his own net from a deft Mc Culloch cross. Rangers playing in red held on and progressed to the 6th Round.

## THE ROAD TO HAMPDEN 'We are in the Cup'

*Frae Inverness's royal seat, to where the Tweed and North Sea meet;*
*Auld Scotia's fitba' clubs compete, this January day;*
*Fans, five, ten, twenty thousand strong, With fervour cheer their teams along,*
*Hoping to sing the victory song,*
*On Hampden's way see there the Rangers hopes are bright, With power*
*precision Ibrox might; Yet how these doughty Queens will fight.*
*And Fifers worthy of their name, will seek to lead their club to fame.*
*Wi warlike fans and swirlin breeze, Cauld snow an chills the players knees;*
*Clubs making some last minute switch, the cries the same tho puir or rich.*

The reward for Rangers` win at Dundee could hardly have been tougher with a trip to Aberdeen. The cup tie took place in snow and several fans were hurt when a crush barrier collapsed.

ABERDEEN: Martin, Mitchell, Smith, Allster, Young, Glen, Hamilton, Yorston, Buckley, Wishart and Hather.

RANGERS: Niven, Little, Cox, Mc Coll, Young, Rae, Mc Culloch, Paton, Miller, Neillands and Hubbard.

Aberdeen started the brighter and in seven minutes took the lead through Hather; the winger running on to a through ball from the impressive Buckley. Rangers quickly equalised when Neillands lashed in a shot after 11 minutes. The remainder of the first half was cagey on the snow bound pitch. In the second half it was the Dons who scored the winner after 51 minutes. Wishart headed home Hamilton's accurate cross. Rangers tried to level but the Dons held on for a deserved win.

Rangers had a reasonable season near the top of the league. Scot Symon was already building a side for the following season. Bill Struth was constantly at grounds looking at players and always a welcome visitor wherever he went. On the other side of the Old Firm Benburb legend Teddy Swift was doing the same exercise for Celtic.

The Scottish Schools FA oldest age group managed to obtain the use of Celtic Park for the annual match against England. Three Govan players looked likely to make the team George Duncan, Ian Cumming (goalkeeper) and Bruce Carter ( all Bellahouston Academy).

Kilsyth Rangers were having a good season leading the league and progressing to the semi finals of the Scottish Junior Cup. To win the league they had to lock horns with the two Govan sides. In the match earlier in the season Benburb celebrated a 7-3 win at Tinto Park. At Duncansfield the Bens were 2-0 down early in the second half. They then scored four unopposed goals to win 4-2 and thus complete the double over their in form league opponents. Benburb proved that they could score goals but, all to often the defence also conceded a few.In the run in Kilsyth Rangers visited Moore Park. The Ants played well without Johnny Quigley but were undone by error's from goalkeeper Lee. Kelly of the Rangers took advantage twice and the Ants trailed two nil at half time. In the second half the visitors scored another unopposed goal and their drive to the championship was still on.

In the South Eastern Juvenile Cup the draw for the first two rounds was made with much Govan interest:

1st Round:  Tradeston Holmlea v League Hearts;  Finnieston Hearts v Govan Brittania

2nd Round Avon Villa v Carnwadric Bluebell , Park United v Finnieston Hearts or Govan Brittania, Tradeston Holmlea or League Herats v Partick United.  Benburb v Butters.

- Govan Juvenile Courts was noisy. In front of Baillie Jasmina Anderson were 11 boys plus their probation officers. The Baillie said she had a complete football team in front of her. They were charged with playing football on a Sunday and making too much noise. One mother said 'They have nae wher else tae play and they didnae even go wi ther fitba boots on'. Jasmina Anderson said it was impossible to tell the boys not to play football. They were all admonished and told to play quieter so as not to disturb the residents.

- In the Schools Intermediate Cup competition semi finals, St.Gerrards made short work of Falkirk winning 8-2. In an effort to entice the Glasgow Rugby playing schools into playing football; Queen's Park made Lesser Hampden Park available and provided excellent coaching.

- The trials for the Glasgow Schools team to play against London assembled at Lesser Hampden Park and there was plenty of Govan interest amongst the contenders for forward places. G.Mulholland (St.Gerrards), F.Burns (St.Gerrards), R.Burns (Govan High) and I.Lochead (St.Gerrards)

- In the West of Scotland Amateur League Govan Amateurs chances of the title had gone although they had a good season finishing in the top half of the league's top division. In the second division Stephens and Craigton Athletic were trying to avoid relegation.

- In the Renfrewshire Juvenile League Avon Villa crashed 6-1 away to Cardwadric Bluebells. Govan Brittania could not make the home advantage at the 50 pitches count as they lost 4-0 to Renfrew Athletic. Tradeston Holmlea did make 50 pitches home advantage count with a 2-1 success over Park United.

Rangers Willie Woodburn made his second appeal against his 'Suspended sine die' sentence from the Scottish FA. He had a lot of support from the Rangers supporters who felt he was harshly dealt with. Woodburn had openly apologised and showed remorse for the incident against Stirling Albion. The Rangers club wrote a plea to the Scottish FA. The chances looked favourable initially. However the SFA referred the case to the Referee's Committee. As a majority of the Referee's Committee made the original decision to ban Woodburn and therefore were always unlikely to overturn the verdict. The appeal from Willie Woodburn was rejected.

Aberdeen were closing in on their first 1st Division title win. A win at Shawfield against Clyde would secure the flag. A tense match saw a penalty from Glen decide the issue and the title was on its way to Pittodrie.

# WEST OF SCOTLAND AMATEUR LEAGUE DIVISION 2

| Team | Pl | W | L | D | F | A | Pts |
|------|----|----|----|----|----|----|-----|
| Laidlaw | 20 | 12 | 3 | 5 | 72 | 43 | 29 |
| Barclay Curie | 17 | 10 | 3 | 4 | 46 | 26 | 24 |
| Lambhill | 13 | 10 | 1 | 2 | 54 | 22 | 22 |
| Budhill | 20 | 9 | 7 | 4 | 56 | 56 | 22 |
| Houston and Crosslee | 16 | 8 | 5 | 3 | 52 | 40 | 19 |
| Scott's Strollers | 21 | 7 | 9 | 5 | 50 | 51 | 19 |
| Mac Farlane Lang | 19 | 8 | 9 | 2 | 56 | 70 | 18 |
| Morriston YMCA | 18 | 7 | 10 | 1 | 30 | 37 | 17 |
| India of Inchinnan | 16 | 5 | 8 | 3 | 29 | 35 | 13 |
| Stephen's | 18 | 6 | 11 | 1 | 40 | 58 | 13 |
| Craigton Athletic | 16 | 4 | 9 | 3 | 45 | 50 | 11 |
| Glenpatrick | 18 | 1 | 12 | 5 | 41 | 95 | 7 |

Scotland Amateurs were represented by no fewer than nine Queen's Park players for the International against England at Hampden Park. A crowd of 5,500 saw Rae from Third Lanark give Scotland the lead but goals from Flanagan (Walthamstow Avenue) and Darey (Wimbledon) had England ahead at half time. Max Murray missed a sitter for Scotland before he crossed for Ward to equalise. England looked to have won the match when Crampsey the Scottish goalkeeper misjudged a corner allowing Flanagan to score his second. However a late rally saw a headed own goal from Cresswell (Bishops Aukland) give Scotland a draw.

RESULT SCOTLAND 3 ENGLAND 3

The Scotland v England Under 18's School's International took place at Celtic Park, Parkhead. On the morning of the match both sets of players went to the City Chambers to meet Glasgow Lord Provost Tom Kerr, himself a football enthusiast. Mr Kerr attended the match.

SCOTLAND: Thomson (Whitehill), Mc Kay (Woodside), Mc Gregor (St.Mungo's), Mc Guire (St.Gerrards), Gallacher (Greenock High), Hart (Eastbank), Duncan (Bellahouston), Dixon (Queen's Park), Carter (Bellahouston), Orr (Woodside) and Wright (Douglas Ewart).

ENGLAND: Skelton (North Manchester), Ballantyne (Quarrybank), Costello (Malvern College), Clish ( Houghton), Marnham (Malvern College), Walsh (Ealing), Neil (North Portsmouth), Tate (Leicester Gateway), Randle (Wolverhampton), Booth (Heanor) and Peel (Beades School, North Manchester).

Referee C.Faultless (Glasgow) did not make a mistake!

Scotland did most of the pressing but it was England who scored two goals in the first half through Randle and Walsh. Scotland pressed strongly in the second half and Orr scrambled in a goal. However it was not to be and England held on.

RESULT: SCOTLAND 1 ENGLAND 2

With the end of the season approaching two Govan sides were struggling in Juvenile football. Govan Randolph accumulated a number of fines and were ordered to pay up. They refused and were thrown out of the league. Govan Britania were struggling with injuries and getting replacement players. They announced they would quit at the end of the season. Popular Linesman Robert Brady of Elder had one altercation too many and was fined 10 shillings and warned as to his future conduct.

Rangers had a prestige friendly under the lights at Ibrox Park against Racing Club of Paris. The French side was packed with members of the France football team. Goals from former Benburb player Hunter Mc Millan (2), Billy Simpson (2) and Johnny Hubbard gave the Rangers an impressive 5-1 win.

## CATHOLIC SCHOOLS UNDER 12 LEAGUE

| Team | Pl | W | L | D | F | A | Pts |
|---|---|---|---|---|---|---|---|
| St.Margaret's | 11 | 9 | 1 | 1 | 57 | 10 | 19 |
| St.Saviour's | 9 | 7 | 1 | 1 | 25 | 5 | 15 |
| St.Peter's | 10 | 5 | 2 | 3 | 23 | 16 | 13 |
| St.Contantine's | 9 | 3 | 4 | 2 | 21 | 10 | 8 |
| St.Conval's | 6 | 4 | 2 | 0 | 17 | 13 | 8 |
| St.George's | 9 | 2 | 3 | 4 | 20 | 21 | 8 |
| St.Anthony's | 9 | 4 | 5 | 0 | 19 | 27 | 8 |
| St.Robert's | 7 | 3 | 3 | 1 | 7 | 14 | 7 |
| Lourdes | 8 | 3 | 4 | 1 | 20 | 33 | 7 |
| St.Paul's | 8 | 2 | 5 | 1 | 8 | 19 | 5 |
| St.Bonaventure's | 7 | 1 | 5 | 1 | 12 | 32 | 3 |
| St.Monica's | 11 | 0 | 8 | 3 | 15 | 40 | 3 |

Former Benburb, Rangers and Scotland full back Jock Tiger'Shaw believed in carrying out all the repairs to the car himself. When he was repairing his car at his home at Main Street, Glenboig, someone from within his house shouted that George Young was on TV. Suddenly while he was watching the TV someone shouted into his house that his car had caught fire. When Coatbridge Fire Brigade arrived Jock's car was already a burned out shell.

## CENTRAL LEAGUE

| Team | Pl | W | L | D | F | A | Pts |
|------|----|----|----|----|----|----|----|
| Ashfield | 25 | 17 | 4 | 4 | 76 | 32 | 38 |
| Renfrew | 26 | 15 | 3 | 8 | 75 | 40 | 38 |
| Duntocher Hibs | 24 | 14 | 2 | 8 | 70 | 29 | 36 |
| Bailleston | 24 | 12 | 6 | 6 | 59 | 37 | 30 |
| Kilsyth Rangers | 24 | 14 | 8 | 2 | 65 | 47 | 30 |
| Benburb | 24 | 12 | 6 | 6 | 72 | 69 | 30 |
| Clydebank | 28 | 11 | 10 | 7 | 56 | 59 | 29 |
| St.Anthony's | 25 | 12 | 11 | 2 | 49 | 58 | 26 |
| Cambuslang Rangers | 22 | 9 | 8 | 5 | 55 | 59 | 23 |
| Vale of Leven | 24 | 6 | 9 | 9 | 50 | 42 | 21 |
| Rob Roy | 28 | 9 | 16 | 3 | 50 | 98 | 21 |
| Pollok | 27 | 8 | 15 | 4 | 53 | 76 | 20 |
| Blantyre Vics | 21 | 8 | 10 | 3 | 52 | 48 | 19 |
| Port Glasgow | 25 | 6 | 19 | 6 | 51 | 77 | 18 |
| Maryhill | 25 | 4 | 16 | 5 | 42 | 76 | 13 |
| Blantyre Celtic | 23 | 2 | 15 | 6 | 32 | 74 | 10 |

The Scottish Cup Final day duly arrived. Clyde were again the underdogs this time against Celtic whose support swelled the crowd above 106,000 by kick off.

CLYDE: Hewkins, Murphy, Haddock, Granville, Anderson, Laing, Divers, Robertson, Hill, Brown and Ring
CELTIC: Bonnar, Haughney, Meechan, Evans, Stein, Peacock, Collins, Fernie, Mc Phail, Walsh and Tully

Clyde, with former St.Gerrards pupil Harry Haddock, proved to be stuffy opponents as they did against Aberdeen and kept Celtic at bay reasonably comfortably for most of the first half. Robertson had the ball in the Celtic net during a rare Clyde attack but the goal was ruled out. Approaching half time Walsh was put through by Fernie and scored with a low shot.

In the second half Clyde were pinned back for long periods but still posed the occasional threat to Celtic. Towards the end, with Celtic fans holding their green and white scarves aloft, Clyde pushed forward in a desperate attempt to get the equaliser. With 3 minutes to go they forced a corner. Archie Robertson delivered and the ball went straight over the hands of Bonnar and into the net. The Clyde team and support went wild. They had earned a replay.

The following Wednesday the teams met again at Hampden Park and 68.000 was the crowd. Clyde again proved to be tight in defence. Tommy Ring scored in the first half. Celtic piled on the pressure but could not break Clyde down and the cup was on its way to Shawfield.

Benburb continued to score heavily until the end of the season. A second half comeback at Alexandria saw them rattle in five goals.
VALE OF LEVEN: McDade, Gilmour, Muir, Anderson, Todd, Galley, Mayberry, McColl, Cassidy, McDonald and Ross
BENBURB: Forsyth, Westwater, Cairns, Patterson, White, Mitchell, Drummond, McKeown, Bain, Brown and Douglas
Muir scored from a free kick 25 yards from goal to give the Vale the lead which they held until half time. The second half saw Bain and Brown each score a brace of goals as the Bens ran out easy 5-2 winners.

Two of the Govan sides in the Renfrewshire Juvenile League were doing well. Park United and Avon Villa who both played mainly at Plantation Park were near the top of the league. Tradeston Holmlea who played mainly at the 50 pitches also done well but Benburb Juveniles and Govan Brittania struggled somewhat throughout.

The under 15 Schools International between Scotland and Wales took place at Somerset Park, Ayr and many youngsters with their parents turned up to cheer the home side on. There was much interest in the Scotland centre forward Joe Baker who was scoring freely. R.Burns of Govan High was on the left wing.
SCOTLAND: J.Mc Donald (Dundee), J.McGregor (Larbert), D.Leiper (Wishaw), W.Stevenson (Edinburgh), W.Cook (Galston), J.Mc Nab (St.Moden's High), W.Little (Dumfries), S.Reid (Wishaw), J.Baker (Motherwell), J.Hunter (Airdrie), and R.Burns (Govan High).
WALES: R.Twigg (Barry), G.Palmer (Cardiff), B.Jones (Swansea), F.Collins (Merthyr), B.Goode (Merthyr), M.Edwards (Wrexham), J.Thomas (Swansea). C.Evans ( Tedegar), F.Thomas (Swansea), A.Lovell (Swansea) and B.Perry (Aberdare).

Scotland attacked from the off and Sammy Reid converted a through pass from Joe Baker. The lead lasted just one minute as Evans scored a similar goal for Wales.

Hunter restored the Scotland lead on the half hour and Joe Baker thundered in a good shot to give Scotland a 3-1 half time lead. Sammy Reid converted a penalty early in the second half before Frank Thomas reduced the lead with a long shot (goal of the game). The last goal of the match a minute later was scored by R.Burns, of Govan High, who was overjoyed and celebrated with gusto.

RESULT: SCOTLAND 5 WALES 2

## RENFREW SHIRE JUVENILE LEAGUE

| Team | Pl | W | L | D | F | A | Pts |
|------|----|----|----|----|----|----|-----|
| Carnwadric Bluebell | 16 | 12 | 2 | 2 | 49 | 26 | 26 |
| Park United | 16 | 11 | 2 | 3 | 37 | 19 | 25 |
| Avon Villa | 16 | 12 | 3 | 1 | 53 | 27 | 25 |
| Port Glasgow Parkfield | 14 | 9 | 2 | 3 | 32 | 18 | 21 |
| Tradeston Holmlea | 14 | 9 | 3 | 2 | 28 | 22 | 20 |
| Renfrew Athletic | 17 | 10 | 7 | 0 | 58 | 37 | 20 |
| Butters Juveniles | 18 | 7 | 8 | 3 | 26 | 40 | 17 |
| Craiglea Star | 18 | 6 | 9 | 3 | 43 | 47 | 15 |
| Benburb Juveniles | 15 | 4 | 9 | 2 | 23 | 46 | 10 |
| Govan Brittania | 20 | 2 | 17 | 1 | 18 | 46 | 5 |
| Carnwadric Star | 20 | 0 | 20 | 0 | 3 | 52 | 0 |

Govan High were not in contention for any of the School's Football honours, the school's football prowess being in a `lull` state. However, the other two Govan Secondary School's were holding the Burgh flag aloft with pride.

At the older age group these two fierce rivals came head to head at Hampden Park in the Semi Final of the Secondary Shield.

A tense closely fought match finished scoreless. However Bellahouston were declared winners on the better corner count by 13 to 7.

In the annual Glasgow v Bradford match the same two schools had representation.  J.Mulholland of St.Gerrard's played right half; and W.Mc Lean played left half.

Glasgow were easy 3-0 winners with goals from Horn (Holyrood), Sim (King's Park) and Hilley (Queen's Park).

In a lower age group team centre forward W. Murray from Govan High was amongst many scorer's as Scotland routed Ireland 9-0 at Broomfield Park, Airdrie.

The Final School positions saw a strong showing by Bellahouston Academy but they were ultimately unable to capture the two championships they were after. In the older age group they lost in the final play off to Greenock High. In the youngest age group Bellahouston were the most consistent side. However on reaching the final play off against St.Mungo's Celtic Football Club offered Celtic Park for the match. The Govan side were overawed by the occasion and lost 5-0.

In Juvenile Football Avon Villa who continued to play most of their matches at Plantation Park were having a good season and with success in the various Cups were likely to be playing well into the summer. They were usually represented by the following team.

Avon Villa: Mc Gennitry, Shields, Craig, Linsay, Murray, Stewart, Brown, Pirie, Bradshaw, Coyle and Miller.

Rangers were not for giving up on the Willie Woodburn Suspended 'Sine Die' situation and gained a small crum of comfort from the SFA. Willie Woodburn would never be allowed to play but could take up a manager or trainers position.  A few English lower division clubs were soon in contact with the former Rangers player.

St.Constantine's were having a very good season. They reached the Final of the Johnston Cup.

At Petershill Park they faced favourites Dennistoun.

ST.CONSTANTINE'S: Mc Gonnigle, M.Barrett, Mc Connell, Greig, Cavanagh, Hilliss, Kerr, Fox, Bell, Farmer and T.Barrett.

The Saints found the early going tough and in no time were three goals behind. However they fought back and goals from Hilliss and Farmer reduced the arrears to one goal at half time.  St.Constantine had the better of the second half and got a deserved equaliser to force a replay.

RESULT: DENNISTOUN 3 ST.CONSTANTINE'S 3

St.Constantine's were pleased with the selection of Moore Park for the replay; virtually a home fixture and the guarantee of good support from the Govan folk.

The Saints went ahead with much excitement but in the second half Dennistoun drew level and the Cup was shared.

Rangers under new manager Scot Symon had made progress finishing third. They had set a target to improve for the next season.

# SCOTTISH LEAGUE    DIVISION A

| Team | Pl | W | L | D | F | A | Pts |
|---|---|---|---|---|---|---|---|
| Aberdeen | 30 | 24 | 5 | 1 | 73 | 26 | 49 |
| Celtic | 30 | 19 | 3 | 8 | 76 | 37 | 46 |
| Rangers | 30 | 19 | 8 | 3 | 67 | 33 | 41 |
| Hearts | 30 | 16 | 7 | 7 | 74 | 45 | 39 |
| Hibernian | 30 | 15 | 11 | 4 | 64 | 54 | 34 |
| St.Mirren | 30 | 12 | 10 | 8 | 55 | 54 | 32 |
| Clyde | 30 | 11 | 10 | 9 | 59 | 60 | 31 |
| Dundee | 30 | 13 | 13 | 4 | 48 | 48 | 30 |
| Partick Thistle | 30 | 11 | 12 | 7 | 49 | 61 | 29 |
| Kilmarnock | 30 | 10 | 14 | 6 | 46 | 58 | 26 |
| Falkirk | 30 | 8 | 14 | 8 | 42 | 53 | 24 |
| East Fife | 30 | 9 | 15 | 6 | 51 | 62 | 24 |
| Queen of the South | 30 | 9 | 15 | 6 | 38 | 57 | 24 |
| Raith Rovers | 30 | 10 | 17 | 3 | 49 | 57 | 23 |
| Motherwell | 30 | 9 | 17 | 4 | 42 | 62 | 22 |
| Stirling Albion | 30 | 2 | 26 | 2 | 29 | 105 | 6 |

The Scottish Junior Cup Final brought together Kilsyth Rangers and Duntocher Hibs. Duntocher Hibs had Celtic bound goalkeeper Dick Beattie in the team.

In the semi finals at Parkhead 30,000 saw the 'Hibs beat favourites Ashfield 4-0.

Kilsyth also had a Celtic connection with left back Dennis Mochan, brother of Neil, who was a key player at Celtic Park.

A big crowd of almost 65,000 watched the match at Hampden Park.

KILSYTH RANGERS: Low, Westwater, Mochan, O'Brien, Moles, Glover, McFarlane, Gallacher, Querrie, Forrest and Kelly

DUNTOCHER HIBS: Beattie, Pirrie, Cleland, O'Donnell, Falconer, Scott, Callaghan, Whalen, Mc Ewan, Mc Dowell and Kemp.

The big crowd saw very little action throughout the 90 minutes; the nearest to a goal was a shot from Hibs Callaghan which hit the post.

The replay on the following Wednesday attracted a crowd in excess of 40.000.

In the first half it was all Hibs and it was a big surprise when Alex Querrie scored on a rare Kilsyth break. However Tim Whalen rounded off continued pressure from Duntocher to take the sides in level at half time.

If the first half was all Duntocher the second belonged to Kilsyth who dominated throughout. Alex Querrie added three more goals to his single in the first half and finished a Cup Final scorer of four goals. For Dick Beattie a Hibs hero throughout the cup run it was a bad night. He gave away two of Querrie's goals and seven minutes from the end got carried off and taken to hospital.

The Kilsyth Rangers team bus arrived home with the players aloft displaying the cup in an evening of wild celebration for the town.

RESULT: KILSYTH RANGERS 4 DUNTOCHER HIBS 1

Scotland supporters headed south in large numbers for the annual British Championship match against the 'auld enemy'.

ENGLAND: Williams (Wolves), Meadows (Man.City), Byrne (Man.Utd), Armstrong (Chelsea), Wright (Wolves), Edwards (Man Utd), Matthews (Blackpool), Revie (Man.City), Lofthouse (Bolton Wanderers), Wilshaw (Wolves) and Blunstone (Chelsea)

SCOTLAND: Martin (Aberdeen), Cunningham (Preston N.E), Haddock (Clyde),Docherty (Preston N.E), Davidson (Partick Th.), Cummings (Hearts), McKenzie (Partick Th.) ,Johnstone (Man City),Reilly (Hibernian),McMillan (Airdrie) and Ring (Clyde)

It did not take England long to get on top and a mistake from Fred Martin in goal gifted Wiltshaw an early goal. Nat Lofthouse was soon on the scoresheet as he went through a few weak challenges to fire home England's second.

Lawrie Reilly finished off a good passing move to bring Scotland back with a hope of preserving their unbeaten record at Wembley dating back to 1934.

However a few minutes later another error from Fred Martin in failing to gather a cross presented Revie with an easy chance. England added a fourth by half time through Nat Lofthouse.

The second half was much the same pattern and Wiltshaw scored three more to bring his tally to four. Scotland pegged away and Tommy Docherty scored a consolation goal from a free kick.

SCORE: ENGLAND 7 SCOTLAND 2

# CHAPTER 7
## GOVAN SUCCESS AT ALL LEVELS

The pre season player movements provided a big shock for the Bens supporters. Great favourites Dunky Rae and Tommy Douglas departed to Clydebank and Kilsyth Rangers respectively. The shock was partly compensated with a good signing from St.Anthony's in the form of Maurice Young. Also Davie Drummond a class forward re-signed. John Baxter a good young midfielder signed from Gordon Park YC.

BENBURB SQUAD:

Goalkeepers: Thomas Stewart (Gordon Park YC); Thomas Marshall (Clydebank)

Backs: William Gray (Cambuslang Rangers); William Sutherland (Stephens Juv.)

Half Backs: John Wilson (Port Glasgow Rangers), John Mc Alpine (Stephens Juv.)

James Little (Eaglesham Amateurs), Maurice Young (St.Anthony's). John Baxter (Gordon Park YC)

Forwards: Richard Gibb (Gordon Park YC), Murdoch Mc Nichol (Gordon Park YC)

Peter Treacy, James Flanagan (PO Telephones), Thomas Mc Geown, David Drummond, A Gregal (Campsite Black Watch), William Bain

Alex. Mc Vicar of the Benburb football club got a life membership honour of the Central League committee.

At St.Anthony's Celtic were taking an interest in big John Colrain. However the Moore Park club were pleased that the Celts allowed the bustling centre forward to stay with the Ants in the interim. Also at the Ants was the classy attacking inside forward Johnny Quigley, a great favourite.

An early season league match saw the Ants travel to Newlandsfield.
POLLOK:Mc Dade, Gow, Glass, Lynch, Mc Feat, Stewart, Hamill, Cameron, Mateer, Mc Coquerdale, Fraser,
ST.ANTHONY'S: Lee, Langam, Tullie, Harkins, Burnett, Hughes, Travers, Doyle, Kelly, Quigley and Phillips.

The Ants were on the top from the start and after just 5 minutes Johnny Quigley did some ball juggling just outside the box before scoring with a great shot. On the half hour good play from Quigley and Kelly set up winger Phillips and he scored the Ants second. Quigley added a third and St.Anthony's were on their way to an easy win.
RESULT: POLLOK 0 ST.ANTHONY'S 3

Tradeston Holmlea who often played their fixtures on pitch 12 at the 50 pitches were not happy. An incident at the Maryhill Juniors Tourney saw their Secretary charged and immediately banned from football 'Sine Die'. They appealed but were then fined another £5.

Another Govan side Park United who usually played at Plantation Park (the Plots) were under investigation for playing 'ringers' (ineligible players).

The Renfrewshire Juvenile League was disbanded and all the teams were put in the City of Glasgow and District Juvenile League.

Rangers and Celtic were drawn in the same Scottish League Cup group. The first match between the sides was postponed. When the sides finally met at Ibrox they had each gathered maximum points from the other two sides in the section; Queen of the South and Falkirk and stood on six points each.

Rangers had former Benburb player Mc Millan at Inside left. Celtic also had a former Benburb player Eric Smith at Inside left and former Ants player Bobby Evans at right half.

RANGERS: Niven, Caldow, Little, Mc Coll, Young, Baird, Scott, Simpson, Murray, Mc Millan and Hubbard.

CELTIC: Bonnar, Haughney, Fallon, Evans, Stein, Peacock, Collins, Fernie, Mochan, Smith and Mc Phail

70,000 passionate supporters saw Celtic take early charge of the match. On 17 minutes they got their reward when Mochan outjumped Young and knocked on to Mc Phail who outmuscled Caldow and scored with a fierce shot. Eric Smith extended the Celtic lead when he finished off a slick left wing move by converting Mochan's pass. Rangers fans had something to cheer about when Fallon put into his own net when trying to clear a free kick making it 2-1 to Celtic. However before half time Eric Smith scored the goal of the game. Taking a pass he beat Sammy Baird before firing a fierce shot from distance which was almost saved by Niven.

In the second half Celtic went further ahead when Eric Smith set up Neil Mochan who scored with ease. Celtic played out the remaining minutes in control of the match and surely the section.

RESULT : RANGERS 1 CELTIC 4

The teams were to meet again 4 days later. Celtic required a draw only to progress and Rangers required a big win to have any chance. The bookies odds gave Rangers no chance.

For the Parkhead match Rangers played Sammy Baird at inside left and the team were urged to get an early goal to have any chance of progress. Celtic fans were in full song but were silenced early in the match when Sammy Baird scored an excellent goal and Rangers continued to attack. Approaching half time the Gods turned unfavourably to Celtic when Jock Stein picked up an injury and hobbled out the game on the left wing.

Alex.Scott had an excellent match. He and Max Murray hit the posts and Billy Simpson and Max Murray increased the Rangers lead to three. Sammy Baird added a fourth and Rangers had a narrow goal average lead with one game to play.

RESULT:  CELTIC 0 RANGERS 4

The final matches saw Rangers score six (6-1) at Ibrox against Queen of the South and they were through to the Quarter Finals.

In addition they made a reasonable start to the League campaign and looked to be contenders for the title.

Trouble with supporters of the Old Firm flared during the Group stages of the League Cup.

Mc Phail of Celtic claimed someone through a rock at him. The Rangers fans said it was only a tennis ball.

The match between Falkirk and Celtic saw a stormy affair with bottles thrown from the crowd.

Police introduced a permit scheme to the followers of the Old Firm clubs for the Supporters club travel.

Former St.Gerrards school centre forward Peter Catterson, under persuasion from former St.Anthony's player and now Kilmarnock manager Malky Mc Donnald, joined Kilmarnock Juveniles.

The young striker showed his goal scoring prowess by netting on his debut against Airdrie. In his first four matches he had scored three goals. Then at Easter Road he scored an early goal against the Hibs. The Edinburgh side fought back and led 2-1 before Peter Catterson missed a sitter and Killie lost 2-1. Soon afterwards Catterson was in the reserves having scored 4 goals in 5 games. In the reserve side he continued his goal scoring exploits. Surely a re-call would come.

Park United finally won a Cup when they lifted the West of Scotland Juvenile Final held over from the previous season. In the Final over 2 legs they beat Salts Athletic in the first leg at Brandon Park, Bellshill by 2-1. A big crowd turned up for the second leg at Haghill Park and United scored a 3-2 victory, winning 5-3 on aggregate. This was added to when they won the Maryhill Tourney played over the summer months.

Both Benburb and St.Anthony's made respectable starts to the new season after the initial fixtures.

The Scottish Junior Cup saw Benburb with a home tie with Lanarkshire club Thorniewood United.

BENBURB: Stewart, Young, Cairns, McAlpine, Nicholson, Treacy, Gibb, Mc Geown, Bain, Gregal and Moffatt.

THORNIEWOOD UNITED: Mc Farlane, Hogg, Ure, Robertson, Kennedy, Moffat, Miller, Runciman, Coyne, Haves and Deleany

Bens attacked non stop in the first half missing chances to take the lead against a stodgy defence. The second half saw Thorniewood take charge and run out 4-2 winners; a defeat which deflated the Govan faithful.

RESULT: BENBURB 2 THORNIEWOOD UNITED 4

# CENTRAL LEAGUE DIVISION A

| Team | Pl | W | L | D | F | A | Pts |
|------|----|----|----|----|----|----|-----|
| Shettleston | 10 | 6 | 1 | 3 | 20 | 11 | 15 |
| Blantyre Vics. | 10 | 6 | 2 | 2 | 28 | 16 | 14 |
| Petershill | 10 | 5 | 1 | 4 | 33 | 18 | 14 |
| Kilsyth Rangers | 10 | 5 | 3 | 2 | 20 | 14 | 12 |
| Benburb | 10 | 5 | 3 | 2 | 15 | 15 | 12 |
| Ashfield | 9 | 3 | 1 | 5 | 22 | 14 | 11 |
| Duntocher Hibs | 9 | 3 | 1 | 5 | 20 | 17 | 11 |
| Cambuslang Rangers | 11 | 5 | 5 | 1 | 25 | 25 | 11 |
| Renfrew | 9 | 3 | 3 | 3 | 20 | 19 | 9 |
| Shawfield | 10 | 3 | 4 | 3 | 19 | 22 | 9 |
| Bailleston | 10 | 3 | 5 | 2 | 16 | 25 | 8 |
| St.Roch's | 9 | 2 | 4 | 3 | 18 | 21 | 7 |
| Bridgeton Waverley | 9 | 3 | 6 | 0 | 21 | 27 | 6 |
| Strathclyde | 9 | 2 | 5 | 2 | 11 | 19 | 6 |
| Glencairn | 10 | 2 | 6 | 2 | 15 | 25 | 6 |
| Vale of Clyde | 9 | 0 | 6 | 3 | 9 | 24 | 3 |

The defeat against Thorniewood was felt badly by the Benburb committee and the club members. Shortly after the Scottish Junior Cup exit long serving Alex McVicar was deposed as match secretary and replaced by Robert Mc Grath. A vote was taken on the rest of the Committee and they were all asked to stand down. A new committee was elected. Not too long afterwards the Benburb Juvenile side was pulled out of the Juvenile City and District League.

St. Anthony's progressed in the Scottish Junior Cup with an easy win over Douglasdale.
Two quick goals from Tullie put the Ants in charge and although Carr pulled one back for the 'Dale`, Johnny Quigley added a third for St. Anthony's before half time. The Ants added another after half time for an easy win.
RESULT: DOUGLASDALE 1 ST.ANTHONY'S 4

In a league match St.Anthony's trailed Maryhill by 3-0 before a remarkable comeback saw Johnny Quigley and Phillips inspire a great 4-3 win.

A former St.Anthony's player seemed destined for the top level of football with Celtic very interested in his progress. Unfortunately, things did not work out for Tommy Philbin. He dropped down into Juvenile grade of football with Park United and found a new lease of life. The very competitive Maryhill Juniors competition was secured when United won a replay. He scored one of the goals in the replayed final against Cadwadric Bluebell and was man of the match. Outside right Gibbons and centre half Alex Brown, who played with a sticking plaster over one eye, were also top performers.

Davie Mc Cracken the Benburb took up the position of the West of Scotland FA Vice President.

## SCOTTISH LEAGUE CUP SECTION 4

| Team | Pl | W | L | D | F | A | Pts |
|------|----|----|----|----|----|----|-----|
| Rangers | 6 | 5 | 1 | 0 | 22 | 8 | 10 |
| Celtic | 6 | 4 | 1 | 1 | 16 | 9 | 9 |
| Falkirk | 6 | 2 | 3 | 1 | 12 | 15 | 5 |
| Queen of the South | 6 | 0 | 6 | 0 | 3 | 21 | 0 |

Rangers having progressed from the League Cup section faced Hamilton Academicals in the Quarter Finals. The Accies gave a good account of themselves in the first leg and lost narrowly 2-1. However, the return match at Ibrox Stadium saw Rangers win by 8 unopposed goals and get through on aggregate by 10 goals to 1.

The semi final draw paired Rangers with Aberdeen at Hampden Park.
In the other semi final, Motherwell played St.Mirren at Ibrox Park.
Gemmell gave St. Mirren the lead after they had been on top for most of the first half. However, a short back pass from Willie Telfer gave Mc Seveney an equaliser and Sloan gave the Fir Park side the lead before half time. Saints fought hard to get the equaliser but their efforts seemed in vain. However, 5 minutes from the end Gemmell got the equaliser following a free kick. In the first half of extra time after one minute Gemmell scored for the Buddies. The 'well' battled hard and Mc Seveney got the equaliser to ensure a replay.
RESULT:  MOTHERWELL 3 ST.MIRREN  3

The replay took place at Parkhead in front of 22,000 spectators.
Saints took the lead in 17 minutes through Laird and a second half goal from Brown secured the tie for the Buddies with a 2-0 scoreline.

At Hampden Park, Aberdeen continued their good recent record over Rangers in the first half. 90,000 saw Aberdeen retain the football much better and they scored an early goal through Graham Leggat. On the half hour Wishart extended the Dons lead with a spectacular shot high into the net from the edge of the box after beating Young.

Rangers responded in the second half with Johnny Hubbard pulling a goal back on 52 minutes with a shot from a tight angle. A few minutes later things looked bleak for the Dons as Graham Leggat was carried off on a stretcher. Rangers piled forward with non stop attack. Mc Coll had a shot come back off the crossbar and Jimmy Miller had a shot come back off the post.

Despite the pressure Aberdeen held on and went through to the Final to meet St.Mirren.

RESULT:  ABERDEEN 2 RANGERS 1

At the 50 Pitches a new team was making an impression. Sligo Celtic were formed with a few members with the Irish connection. They had a very young side and they were enjoying their football. The coach was Paddy Cahill the former St. Anthony's and Scottish Junior International. Several of the players were already attracting the attention of senior clubs and Peter Carlie spent a month at Plymouth Argyle on trial.

Govan Amateurs competed in the top West of Scotland League Division 1 and the early season saw them in the lower half of the league table.

## WEST OF SCOTLAND  AMATEUR LEAGUE

| Team | Pl | W | L | D | F | A | Pts |
|------|----|---|---|---|---|---|-----|
| Babcock and Wilcox | 7 | 5 | 1 | 1 | 27 | 11 | 11 |
| Killermont | 4 | 3 | 0 | 1 | 12 | 4 | 7 |
| Mossvale YMCA | 3 | 3 | 0 | 0 | 7 | 2 | 6 |
| Rhu | 4 | 3 | 1 | 0 | 11 | 5 | 6 |
| Lambhill | 4 | 3 | 1 | 0 | 10 | 8 | 6 |
| Mearns | 4 | 2 | 2 | 0 | 18 | 12 | 4 |
| Laidlaw | 5 | 2 | 3 | 0 | 13 | 15 | 4 |
| Bearsden | 5 | 2 | 3 | 0 | 13 | 20 | 4 |
| Govan | 6 | 2 | 4 | 0 | 9 | 16 | 4 |
| Albion Motors | 4 | 1 | 3 | 0 | 7 | 10 | 2 |
| Villafield | 5 | 1 | 4 | 0 | 11 | 20 | 2 |
| Wester Rossland | 5 | 0 | 5 | 0 | 8 | 23 | 0 |

# GLASGOW AMATEUR LEAGUE DIVISION A

| Team | Pl | W | L | D | F | A | Pts |
|---|---|---|---|---|---|---|---|
| Sligo Celtic | 9 | 8 | 0 | 1 | 39 | 15 | 17 |
| Panmure Thistle | 8 | 6 | 1 | 1 | 35 | 21 | 13 |
| Norwood | 7 | 5 | 2 | 0 | 20 | 12 | 10 |
| Blythswood Strollers | 8 | 3 | 3 | 2 | 19 | 15 | 8 |
| Olivetti | 8 | 2 | 2 | 4 | 17 | 13 | 8 |
| Houston Park | 8 | 3 | 3 | 2 | 17 | 10 | 8 |
| Kinning Park | 10 | 3 | 6 | 1 | 24 | 29 | 7 |
| Claremont | 7 | 3 | 3 | 1 | 20 | 19 | 7 |
| Cleansing | 9 | 3 | 5 | 1 | 22 | 34 | 7 |
| Millerston | 8 | 3 | 4 | 1 | 17 | 28 | 7 |
| Fider | 9 | 1 | 6 | 2 | 15 | 31 | 4 |
| Shieldhall Vics | 7 | 1 | 6 | 0 | 12 | 30 | 2 |

St.Anthony's were given a home tie against Lanarkshire league outfit Lesmahagow in the 2nd Round of the Scottish Junior Cup.
St.ANTHONY'S:Flynn, Langan, O'Hare, Harkins, Murphy, Clocherty, Travers, Kelly, Tullie, Quigley and Phillips
LESMAHAGOW: Mc Beth, Matthews, Todd, Turner, Dunbar, Anderson, Menzies, Hunter, Neil, Thomm and Halcrow.
A decent crowd saw a close match and the 'Gow were unfortunate when they had Anderson carried off injured after half an hour. With ten men the 'Gow gave as good as they got and scored a second half solitary goal winner.
RESULT: St.ANTHONY'S 0 LESMAHAGOW 1
Two weeks later the Ants had another home cup match this time a Central League Cup tie against Benburb in a Govan derby.
St.ANTHONY'S: Lee, Langan, O'Hare, Harkins, Murphy, Clocherty, Travers, Kelly, Hughes, Quigley and Phillips
BENBURB: Marshall, Young, Cairns, Wilson, Nicholson, Tracey, Gibb, Mc Alpine, Bain, Gregal and Mc Geown
Both teams had chances in the early match play but it was Travers who opened the scoring for the Ants with an excellent shot on 25 minutes. Bens attacked and were unlucky not to equalise when Lee made a fortunate save with his foot.

Just before half time the Ants were awarded a penalty. O'Hare stepped up but Marshall made a great stop and the Bens cleared.

In the second half Benburb went all out for the equaliser and were quickly rewarded when Mc Alpine headed past Lee. Bain put the Bens ahead and the Tinto Park side held out to progress into the next round.

RESULT: St. ANTHONY'S 1 BENBURB 2

John Quigley the St.Anthony's inside left who rarely played a bad game was in demand by senior clubs. Both Stirling Albion and Celtic wanted him to turn out in trial matches. A number of English clubs were also monitoring his progress. In a league match against Port Glasgow Quigley and Phillips both scored a brace as the Ants ran riot with a 6-1 triumph at Moore Park.

Floodlight football was becoming more popular and Clyde were proud of the floodlights at Shawfield. They played Manchester United in a friendly under the lights at Shawfield and won 1-0.

The Scottish League Cup Final was contested by St.Mirren and Aberdeen at Hampden Park.

ABERDEEN: Martin, Mitchell, Caldwell, Wilson, Clunie, Glen, Leggat, Yorston, Buckley, Wishart and Hather.

ST.MIRREN: Lornie, Lapsley, Mallan, Neilson, Telfer, Holmes, Rodger, Laird, Brown, Gemmell and Callan

The first half saw much bright play from both sides but no breakthrough was forthcoming. However, within two minutes at the start of the second a Hather cross bounced of a back tracking Buddies full back and the Dons were one up. Saints piled on the pressure to get back into the game and were rewarded when Holmes headed home a free kick from Lapsley.

Play went from end to end as both sides sought the winner. It duly arrived when Graham Leggat saw Lornie off his line and lofted a high shot over his head into the net. The cup was on its way north to the delight of the travelling Aberdonians in the crowd of 44,000.

RESULT: ABERDEEN 2 ST.MIRREN 1


Rangers made a very popular signing when a South African centre forward arrived. Don Kitchenbrand was an immediate hit with the Ibrox fans. He scored goals and wherever Rangers played the ground attendance records were in danger of being broken. The Ibrox side were playing with confidence and, after a slow start, were in the leading sides challenging for the league title.

A crunch game came in the New Years Day Old Firm fixture at Parkhead.The match was decided when Billy Simpson rose to flick on a Brown kick out. Don Kitchenbrand was on it very quickly and lobbed the ball over the advancing Dick Beattie and into the net. Rangers held on comfortably to the lead and were in a good position for the second half of the season.

RESULT: CELTIC 0 RANGERS 1

Copland Rangers trained at Ibrox Park and played their home fixtures mostly at Bellahouston Park or the 50 pitches. The 'Rangers' competed in the Glasgow Secondary League and pulled off a good 3-1 win over Dennistoun Juveniles. Copland Rangers also ran an Under age team who competed in the Glasgow Under age League.

Govan teams were having generally good results. Tradeston Holmlea who played at the 50 pitches pulled off several surprise results. These included a 4-1 success at Plantation Park in the league over strong going Park United.

A Plantation Park 'derby' match between Park United and Avon Villa drew a big crowd for a Scottish Cup match. Park started as favourites but it was the Villa who progressed with a 4-2 win.

## SCOTTISH LEAGUE DIVISION A

| Team | Pl | W | L | D | F | A | Pts |
|---|---|---|---|---|---|---|---|
| Rangers | 19 | 12 | 1 | 6 | 49 | 16 | 30 |
| Hearts | 21 | 13 | 4 | 4 | 63 | 26 | 30 |
| Hibernian | 21 | 13 | 5 | 3 | 56 | 33 | 29 |
| Celtic | 21 | 11 | 5 | 5 | 39 | 22 | 27 |
| Aberdeen | 19 | 10 | 3 | 6 | 50 | 27 | 26 |
| Queen of the South | 22 | 11 | 8 | 3 | 48 | 29 | 35 |
| Falkirk | 21 | 9 | 8 | 4 | 42 | 35 | 22 |
| Aidrieonians | 22 | 8 | 9 | 5 | 52 | 64 | 21 |
| Dundee | 21 | 8 | 9 | 4 | 36 | 39 | 20 |
| Kilmarnock | 22 | 7 | 9 | 6 | 35 | 32 | 20 |
| Motherwell | 19 | 6 | 7 | 6 | 30 | 37 | 18 |
| Raith Rovers | 20 | 6 | 8 | 6 | 29 | 42 | 18 |
| St. Mirren | 17 | 6 | 6 | 5 | 34 | 34 | 17 |
| East Fife | 22 | 6 | 11 | 5 | 37 | 44 | 17 |
| Dunfermiline | 20 | 6 | 10 | 4 | 22 | 45 | 16 |
| Partick Thistle | 19 | 4 | 11 | 4 | 23 | 41 | 12 |
| Clyde | 21 | 4 | 13 | 4 | 24 | 47 | 12 |
| Stirling Albion | 21 | 2 | 15 | 4 | 13 | 56 | 8 |

For the first time in the season Rangers had hit the front and with games in hand plus good form the Championship appeared to be in their grasp.

Down at Paisley Road Toll there was a stir. Park United appealed against the result with Avon Villa. They claimed that the Villa had played a Junior level player. The appeal, upheld, Avon Villa were thrown out of the competition.

## GLASGOW FP LEAGUE—DIVISION 1

| Team | Pl | W | D | L | F | A | Pts |
|---|---|---|---|---|---|---|---|
| Govan High | 15 | 9 | 4 | 2 | 48 | 21 | 22 |
| Vale of Leven | 13 | 10 | 1 | 2 | 39 | 21 | 21 |
| Eastbank | 14 | 10 | 1 | 3 | 46 | 20 | 21 |
| John Street | 14 | 8 | 2 | 4 | 45 | 24 | 18 |
| Queen's Park | 13 | 6 | 2 | 5 | 36 | 34 | 14 |
| Whitehill | 16 | 6 | 2 | 8 | 32 | 35 | 14 |
| St.Mungo's | 15 | 5 | 1 | 9 | 24 | 31 | 11 |
| St.Patrick's | 16 | 5 | 3 | 8 | 20 | 28 | 13 |
| King's Park | 12 | 5 | 2 | 5 | 28 | 25 | 12 |
| Woodside | 15 | 3 | 3 | 9 | 27 | 55 | 9 |
| Dalziel | 13 | 3 | 2 | 8 | 18 | 38 | 8 |
| Clydebank | 12 | 1 | 3 | 8 | 19 | 40 | 5 |

Govan High former pupils had assembled a strong side for the season having narrowly avoided relegation in the prior season. A powerful Vale of Leven side seemed destined to challenge the 'High' for the title.

At 31, Daviot Street, West Drumoyne Grandfather Boab and his grandson Derek were sitting at the table. They were writing on cardboard cards the details of a forthcoming Old Age pensioners trip. Boab was on the Committee and took his duties seriously. He looked at the Sunday newspaper in front of him with great satisfaction. He lit his pipe and for the second time read the match report of a Queens Park match and looked fondly at the League table. The Spiders looked like they were on their way back to the top of the Scottish league Division B and possibly promotion.

BERWICK RANGERS: Mc Laren, Wilkie, Runciman, Paterson, Thom, Campbell, Redpath, Lawrence, Watt, Arnott and Morton.

QUEEN'S PARK: F.Crampsey, J.Savage, W.Hastie, R.Cromer, J.Valentine, J.Robb, W.Hopper, R.Mc Cann, C.Church,J.Ward and D.Orr

D. Orr deputising for the injured Junior Omand opened the scoring on 16 minutes. C. Church added a second before half time following in after a shot struck the crossbar. The Queen's held on comfortably in the second half .

RESULT: BERWICK RANGERS 0 QUEEN'S PARK  2

# SCOTTISH LEAGUE—DIVISION B

| Team | Pl | W | L | D | F | A | Pts |
|---|---|---|---|---|---|---|---|
| Queen's Park | 15 | 11 | 1 | 3 | 30 | 10 | 25 |
| Ayr United | 15 | 10 | 4 | 1 | 37 | 25 | 21 |
| Cowdenbeath | 16 | 9 | 5 | 2 | 42 | 36 | 20 |
| Stenhousemuir | 16 | 8 | 5 | 3 | 43 | 32 | 19 |
| Dumbarton | 11 | 8 | 2 | 1 | 28 | 18 | 17 |
| Brechin City | 13 | 7 | 3 | 3 | 23 | 20 | 17 |
| St.Johnstone | 12 | 7 | 3 | 2 | 33 | 16 | 16 |
| Dundee United | 15 | 3 | 3 | 9 | 34 | 35 | 15 |
| Stranraer | 14 | 6 | 6 | 2 | 31 | 34 | 14 |
| Morton | 13 | 5 | 5 | 3 | 25 | 19 | 13 |
| Hamilton Accies | 14 | 6 | 7 | 1 | 37 | 32 | 13 |
| East Stirling | 14 | 4 | 5 | 5 | 37 | 40 | 13 |
| Albion Rovers | 14 | 4 | 6 | 4 | 28 | 31 | 12 |
| Arbroath | 15 | 5 | 8 | 2 | 28 | 31 | 12 |
| Forfar Athletic | 15 | 3 | 8 | 4 | 19 | 31 | 10 |
| Alloa Athletic | 14 | 3 | 8 | 3 | 22 | 31 | 9 |
| Berwick Rangers | 14 | 3 | 8 | 3 | 22 | 39 | 9 |
| Third Lanark | 15 | 4 | 10 | 1 | 23 | 35 | 9 |
| Montrose | 15 | 2 | 11 | 2 | 17 | 53 | 6 |

Rangers supporters were relatively well behaved on most of their travels. However on the odd occasion they had problems. A trip to Dumfries saw a 2-1 defeat at the hands of Queen of the South. Bottles and stones rained down from the terraces. The Dumfries police force were well prepared and swooped straight into the crowd and arrested 8 troublemakers.

Gates at Scottish League football matches was starting to drop from high levels. After four months (end November) the crowds had dropped by 76,000 spectators.

Poor quality matches and television were cited as possible reasons.

After a few season's with limited success, the Govan High School teams were beginning to stir. In the Scottish Secondary Shield 2nd Round the previous season's champions Greenock came a cropper against Govan High at Pirrie Park losing by 5-1.

In the Intermediate Shield St.Gerrard's came unstuck losing 4-1 at home to Cumnock Academy. Bellahouston were one of the favourites. However, they made an early exit after a trip to Edinburgh losing 3-2 to Holy Cross.

Bellahouston were a good league side and led the oldest age group with 11 points after 6 games. They were followed by Queen's Park—9 points and St.Mungo's—8 points.

St.Gerrard's were in contention in the second oldest age group following a win over St.Ninian's put them a point ahead of Shettleston.

Govan High were doing well in the youngest age group. They led the division jointly with City Public; each school with 14 points.

In the trial games for the Glasgow team at Nether Pollok the following Govan players challenged for places in the Under 15 team to play Edinburgh. Whitelaw– Bellahouston (left back); Murray– Govan High (centre forward); Logan—Bellahouston (inside left) and Shiels—St.Gerrard's (right half).

## GLASGOW BOYS CLUB LEAGUE

| Team | Pl | W | L | D | F | A | Pts |
|---|---|---|---|---|---|---|---|
| Harmony Row | 8 | 8 | 0 | 0 | 41 | 11 | 16 |
| St.Mary's | 8 | 6 | 1 | 1 | 30 | 18 | 13 |
| Bridgeton Cross | 8 | 5 | 2 | 1 | 32 | 18 | 11 |
| Saracen N.E. | 8 | 4 | 4 | 0 | 26 | 17 | 8 |
| University Sett. | 8 | 3 | 4 | 1 | 26 | 34 | 7 |
| Giffnock North | 7 | 3 | 4 | 0 | 14 | 11 | 6 |
| Church House | 6 | 2 | 3 | 1 | 19 | 17 | 5 |
| St.Francis | 7 | 1 | 5 | 1 | 15 | 29 | 3 |
| Pearce Institute | 6 | 1 | 5 | 0 | 6 | 32 | 2 |
| Rotten Row Boys Club | 6 | 0 | 5 | 1 | 10 | 32 | 1 |

Harmony Row were setting the pace in the Boy's Club League.

Rangers were eying a possible double. However their first match in the Scottish Cup provided them with a tough home draw against Aberdeen. The Dons held a good record against the 'Gers in recent matches.

An exciting first half saw chances at both ends. However half way through the half Alex. Scott gave the 'Gers the lead. The second half saw the pitch condition deteriorate and Rangers were to take advantage on 75 minutes when Fred Martin, the Aberdeen custodian, lost the grasp of the slippery ball and Don Kitchenbrand scored. With ten minutes to go Graham Legget fired a fine goal but despite a lot of Dons pressure Rangers held on.

RESULT: RANGERS 2 ABERDEEN 1

The 6th Round saw Rangers with another tough match at Dundee. Dundee were slightly the better side. However, the match was decided just before half time. A long ball looked to be heading out of play for a Dundee goal kick. Alex Scott was after it refusing to give up. He caught the ball, set himself and delivered a perfect cross for Don Kitchebrand to head high into the net.

RESULT: DUNDEE 0 RANGERS 1

The 7th round draw was again unkind to Rangers with a difficult away match against Heart of Midlothian at Tynecastle Park.

HEARTS: Duff, Kirk, Mc Kenzie, Mac Kay, Glidden, Cumming, Young, Conn, Bauld, Wardhaugh and Crawford.

RANGERS: Niven, Shearer, Little, Mc Coll, Young, Rae, Scott, Simpson, Kitchenbrand, Baird and Hubbard

The match was every bit as close as expected for the first half hour; the best effort a shot from Baird pushed round the post by Duff. On 36 minutes Tynecastle went wild with excitement when Young crossed for Crawford to score, the ball just crossing the line before George Young cleared. On half time Willie Bauld latched onto a Conn pass and scored easily.

In the second half Rangers fought hard to get back into the match but Hearts added a third when Conn scored following an overhead kick shot from Dave Mac Kay. Willie Bauld completed Rangers misery with a fourth near the end.

RESULT: HEART OF MIDLOTHIAN 4 RANGERS 0

Copland Rangers were a popular club around the west side of Ibrox Park. In the Secondary League they were in contention for honours in an extremely tight league. St.Constantine's led the way from Rancel who lost a young promising midfield player called Pat Crerand to junior club Duntocher Hibs.

The Glasgow Schools under 15 side prepared for their match with Edinburgh Schools with a practice match against a strong St.Gerrards under 16 side.

ST.GERRARD'S: T.Ross, F.Dorris, F. Harvey, J.Shiels, R.Mc Geown, J.Mc Inally, F.Herron, A.Bradley, I.Lochhead, E.Mowen and J.Cunningham

Two Govan High players and one Bellahouston player made the Glasgow squad. Rankine left half (Govan); Murray centre forward (Govan); Whitelaw left back (Bellahouston).

The Glasgow team travelled to Tynecastle Park and after going behind hit back to lead 2-1 at half time. In the second half the Edinburgh boys lost heart and Glasgow stormed on to an impressive 6-2 win with Murray amongst the goals.

## GLASGOW SECONDARY LEAGUE

| Team | Pl | W | L | D | F | A | Pts |
|---|---|---|---|---|---|---|---|
| St.Constantine's | 9 | 6 | 2 | 1 | 39 | 25 | 13 |
| Rancel | 11 | 6 | 4 | 1 | 25 | 18 | 13 |
| Corkerhill | 7 | 5 | 1 | 1 | 25 | 15 | 11 |
| Copland Rangers | 9 | 5 | 3 | 1 | 22 | 18 | 11 |
| Tollcross Clydeside | 8 | 5 | 3 | 0 | 22 | 15 | 10 |
| Regent Star | 9 | 4 | 3 | 2 | 25 | 20 | 10 |
| Dennistoun Juvs. | 8 | 4 | 3 | 1 | 27 | 25 | 9 |
| Quarrybrae Athletic | 5 | 3 | 0 | 2 | 16 | 8 | 8 |
| Letham Thistle | 8 | 3 | 3 | 2 | 28 | 23 | 8 |
| Shettleston Juvs. | 6 | 3 | 2 | 1 | 14 | 10 | 7 |
| Rutherglen Waverley | 9 | 3 | 5 | 1 | 24 | 23 | 7 |
| Pollok Hawthorn | 10 | 3 | 6 | 1 | 19 | 27 | 7 |
| Dennistoun Hearts | 7 | 2 | 5 | 0 | 14 | 15 | 4 |
| Penilee YC | 7 | 1 | 6 | 0 | 7 | 30 | 2 |
| Penilee Thistle | 9 | 1 | 8 | 0 | 13 | 39 | 2 |

Benburb were having a solid if unspectacular season. Several of the Bens players were attracting senior attention. Ginger haired goalie George Marshall was sought after by Clyde and Stirling Albion had right half John Wilson and inside left Tony Gregal at Annfield Park for trials. An impressive young performer on the few games he played was John Baxter a midfield player. John was in the Army and postings meant he did not figure too much. Donnie Nicholson, the Benburb centre half, was a consistent performer
BENBURB: Marshall, Young, Cairns, Wilson, Nicholson, Watson, Mc Cormack, Smith, Bain, Gregal, Fitzsimmons.
PETERSHILL: White, Mc Farlane, Scobbie, Turnball, Clydesdale, Mc Nab, Blakely,Young, Stewart, Docherty and Adams
Blakely opened the scoring mid way through the first half. Bain quickly equalised. RESULT: BENBURB 1 PETERSHILL 1

# CENTRAL LEAGUE  DIVISION A

| Team | Pl | W | L | D | F | A | Pts |
|---|---|---|---|---|---|---|---|
| Kilsyth Rangers | 21 | 15 | 4 | 2 | 53 | 25 | 32 |
| Petershill | 20 | 13 | 2 | 5 | 62 | 27 | 31 |
| Ashfield | 20 | 12 | 2 | 6 | 61 | 29 | 30 |
| Bridgeton Waverley | 22 | 12 | 7 | 3 | 66 | 50 | 27 |
| Benburb | 23 | 11 | 8 | 4 | 47 | 41 | 26 |
| Shettleston | 20 | 11 | 6 | 3 | 40 | 29 | 25 |
| Duntocher Hibs | 21 | 7 | 7 | 7 | 46 | 45 | 21 |
| Blantyre Vics | 23 | 9 | 11 | 3 | 55 | 56 | 21 |
| Baillieston | 21 | 9 | 10 | 2 | 45 | 47 | 20 |
| Renfrew | 18 | 8 | 7 | 3 | 40 | 42 | 19 |
| Shawfield | 20 | 6 | 7 | 7 | 36 | 42 | 19 |
| St.Roch's | 21 | 5 | 8 | 8 | 46 | 52 | 18 |
| Cambuslang Rangers | 22 | 6 | 13 | 3 | 39 | 56 | 15 |
| Glencairn | 23 | 6 | 15 | 2 | 39 | 62 | 14 |
| Strathclyde | 20 | 5 | 12 | 3 | 23 | 48 | 13 |
| Vale of Clyde | 21 | 0 | 16 | 5 | 27 | 74 | 5 |

The Scottish Cup Semi Finals saw Celtic paired with Clyde and Heart of Midlothian playing Raith Rovers.

At Hampden Park Celtic wasted no time in going ahead against Clyde when after 2 minutes Sharkey pounced on a poor back pass from Keogh to score. The afternoon got worse for Keogh when after 19 minutes he brought down Fernie in the penalty area and Haughney scored the Celts second. A minute later Mc Phail replied for Clyde. Play raged from end to end and Clyde came close on many occasions.

However, Celtic held on to reach the Final.

RESULT: CELTIC 2 CLYDE 1

In the other Semi Final at Easter Road, Edinburgh a huge crowd turned up expecting an easy Hearts win. However Raith Rovers gave a good account of themselves and in Willie Mc Naught they had the best player on the park. He kept a check on Willie Bauld the prolific Hearts goalscorer. The match finished scoreless and a replay was required.

The replay, also at Easter Road, saw Wardhaugh give the Hearts the lead from a free kick on the edge of the penalty box. Raith were effectively reduced to 10 men when Mc Lure the left back was injured. In the second half Wardhaugh added a second and Crawford headed the third to seal the cup final place.

RESULT: RAITH ROVERS 0 HEART OF MIDLOTHIAN 3

- The Catholic Association Schools team for their third round tie at Port Glasgow had one Govan boy in the team called Smith.
- Park United travelled north in the Scottish Juvenile Cup to play Inverurie North Street. The coach was joyous on the way back following a sparkling 4-1 win.
- Sligo Celtic continued to lead the Glasgow Amateur League by two points but second placed Panmure Thistle had two games in hand.
- In the Former Pupils league Govan continued to set the pace with Vale of Leven close behind.
- In the top league in England, Cardonald player John Dick scored a hat trick for West Ham United against Tottenham Hotspur

At 31, Daviot Street, West Drumoyne pensioner Boab, a life long Queen's Park supporter, smoked his pipe with more contentment. Queen's had just knocked Motherwell out of the Scottish Cup and gates for the Spiders had risen sharply; on one occasion 17,000 for a league match.

Against Montrose they led by a Church goal at half time. However in the second half they went to town scoring freely and winning 7-1. Devine and Omand both added two each with Mc Cann and Reid getting the others.

In the oldest age group School trials a number of players from Govan went to Nether Pollok for the Selection Trials.

These included: J.Mulholland (St.Gerrards fullback), G.Mulholland (St.Gerrards midfielder), Mc Donald (Govan High goalkeeper), Elliot (Bellahouston midfielder), Ferguson (Bellahouston winger) plus Mc Eachan (St.Gerrards).

In the Scottish Schools 4th Round of the Oldest age group Bellahouston and St.Gerrards had powerful sides and were paired together. The first match was close and ended in a draw. The replay was also very close but Bella emerged the victors with a 3-2 margin.

In the younger age groups Govan High were once again beginning to produce good players. Division 4 group saw them clinch the title with a 2-1 win over City Public Schools.

The Govan High team was:
Birney, Bickerstaff, Donnachie, Hendry, Robertson, Mc Kendrick, Mc Kay, Whitelaw, Littleson, Ferguson and Mc Alpine.

Bellahouston Academy were doing well in the Scottish Secondary Shield and reached the semi final to play Airdrie. The Bellahouston team which won 2-0 and progressed to play Dumfries Academy was: Cumming, Whitelaw, Mc Lean, Beattie, Mc Callum, Mc Lean, Ferguson, Elliot, Thompson, Kay and Mc Cosh.

The next oldest age group from Bellahouston Academy were represented by: D.Kerr, J.Murray, J.Smith, E.Aird, N.Campbell, J.Young, J.Shanks, A.Attwood, J.Tait, B.Thomson, and J.Logan

St.Anthony's announced that they would run a Juvenile League knock out competition throughout the summer months at Moore Park.

In the second half of the season St.Anthony's played a strong Parkhead side at Moore Park in the Central League.

ST.ANTHONY'S: Mc Ginlay, Langan, O'Hare, Harkins, Conner, Clocherty, Travers, Kelly, Brown, Quigley and Phillips.

PARKHEAD: Hill, Barrie, Little, Mc Millan, Kellechan, Anderson, Gallacher, Rae, Best, Reilly and Brandon

St.Anthony's scored an early goal through Brown but an unfortunate own goal from O'Hare soon squared things up. The Ants went in at half time in the lead when Johnny Quigley scored an opportunist goal. In the second half Quigley and Phillips scored again for the Ants and despite a late fight back by Parkhead the Ants picked up the points.

RESULT: ST. ANTHONY'S 4  PARKHEAD  3

After the humiliation at Wembley in 1955 when Scotland lost 7-2 to the 'Auld Enemy' revenge was in the air. Hampden Park was full to the capacity and a keen tussle was expected. Scotland picked a team with just two Anglo-Scots.

SCOTLAND: Younger (Hibernian), Parker (Falkirk), Hewie (Charlton), Evans (Celtic), Young (Rangers), Glen (Aberdeen), Leggatt (Aberdeen), Johnstone (Manchester City), Reilly (Hibernian), Mc Millan (Airdrie) and Smith (Hibernian)

ENGLAND: Matthews (Coventry), Hall (Birmingham City), Byrne (Manchester United), Dickinson (Portsmouth), Wright (Wolverhampton Wanderers), Edwards (Manchester United), Finney (Preston North End), Taylor (Manchester United), Lothouse (Bolton Wanderers), Haynes (Fulham) and Perry (Blackpool)

England started nervously and took 5 minutes to get a semblance of control. The first chance fell to Johnny Haynes but George Younger made a sparkling save. Scotland had a slight edge throughout the opening half which was exciting but were unable to get the breakthrough.

The second half saw Scotland continue having the edge but a poor pass by Hewie gave Taylor a chance. Again Younger came to Scotland's rescue and pulled off a good save. On 60 minutes Hewie raced down the left wing and crossed a high ball. Graham Legget waited for it to drop before hitting a shot that went past Matthews and into the net. The Hampden roar went up, Scotland were ahead. Almost immediately Younger pulled off another good save from a Taylor header.

England pressed for the equaliser but the Scotland defence held firm. With the clock ticking down to 90 minutes a left wing move from England saw the cross come to Johnny Haynes. His shot hit the post and flew into the net for the equaliser. Scotland were stunned.

RESULT: SCOTLAND 1  ENGLAND 1

Park United from Plantation Park were having a great run in the Scottish Juvenile Cup. However their luck ran out with the Semi Final draw. They were paired with Burnbank Swifts who had recently extended an amazing unbeaten run to 35 games.

Avon Villa also from Plantation Park were also playing well and making progress in a few of the cup competitions. However they were the victims of a surprise defeat at Plantation Park to the Partick Dolphins by 4-2.

Jock Tiger Shaw (Former Benburb and Rangers full back) was a proud coach of Bailleston when David Wilson their forward signed the forms for Rangers.

For the Scottish Cup Final, Hampden Park was a sea of Maroon for the Hearts and Green and White for Celtic. Celtic had three former Govan Junior players in their line up. Bobby Evans and Billy Craig from St.Anthony's. The third was Eric Smith from Benburb.

CELTIC: Beattie, Meechan, Fallon, Smith, Evans, Peacock, Craig, Haughney, Mochan, Fernie and Tully.

HEART OF MIDLOTHIAN: Duff, Kirk, Mc Kenzie, Mc Kay, Glidden, Cumming, Young, Conn, Bauld, Wardhaugh and Crawford.

A strong wind made life difficult for both teams. Hearts had the edge early on and on 19 minutes Crawford latched on to a mistake by Bobby Evans and fired a shot at goal. Beattie elected to try and catch the ball but it slipped from his fingers high into the net. The second half again saw Hearts holding a slight advantage and Crawford increased the lead on 48 minutes after good work by Conn and Bauld. Haughney reduced the arrears when he shoulder barged Duff going for a high ball. The keeper dropped the ball and the Celtic forward put the ball in the net. Ten minutes from the end Conn added a third for the more accomplished  Hearts side and the Scottish Cup was on its way to Edinburgh. The crowd (almost 133,000) for the match was enormous and not far short of the record Hampden Scottish Cup Final attendance.

RESULT: CELTIC 1  HEART OF MIDLOTHIAN  3

After the Hearts celebrations had died down they took stock of their league challenge. Rangers had gained a point at Hibernian. Max Murray had given the Gers the lead but Turnball and Reilly had put the Hibs ahead by half time. Sammy Baird equalised on the hour mark and Rangers held on. With Hearts losing points in their games in hand the title was quickly confirmed as Rangers.

Over the past seasons Rangers had found their best form in the second half of the season. They had almost overhauled teams that had big point advantages. This season they had hit the front just after the New Year and the points gap between themselves and nearest challengers, Hearts, just got wider.

Scot Symon had delivered his first title to Rangers as manager. In addition to the league flag, Rangers could now participate in the European Cup as Champions of Scotland.

In the schools league's a harsh winter put many of the matches behind schedule. Each of the 4 age groups had three sections with a play off at the end of the season between the section winners to decide the champions

The oldest age group (Division 1)saw Bellahouston Academy and St. Gerrards won their respective sections Both schools then won their respective semi finals; Bella edging out Holyrood by 1-0. Efforts were made to get the game played at Ibrox but Rangers had already started re-seeding the pitch. In the final some excellent quality football was played, as could be expected, with two Govan Schools participating and Bellahouston won 2-0.

In Division 4 the youngest age group Govan High were winners of one of the Sections. In the semi final decider they faced Eastbank and made no mistake winning 4-0. In the Final they met a big powerful St.Patrick's team from Dumbarton. The game was close and well into the second half it was scoreless. St.Pat's scored and three quick goals near the end gave them a flattering 4-0 win.

The Govan High team was:-

J.Birney, J.Bickerstaff, W.Barratt, T.Hendry, D.Robertson, C.Mc Kendrick, R.Donnachie, D.Whitelaw, N.Littleson, A.Ferguson and A.Forbes

The squad for Glasgow schools was chosen and two Govan players were listed.

Goalkeeper: J.Mc Rae(Hyndland),

Backs: Mc Daid ( Clydebank), Sharp (Knightswood),

Half Backs: Alexander (Crookston Castle), Muldoon (St.Mungo's), Wilson (Knightswood), Harrison (Eastbank), Mc Kendrick (Govan High),

Forwards: Cunningham (Queen's Park), Webb ( Crookston Castle), Mc Adam (St. Mungo's), Tyrell (City Public), Ferguson ( Govan High), Clark ( Riverside), Mullen (St.Mungo's)

In the Bradford v Glasgow match just one Govan player was selected . Mulholland of St.Gerrard's played inside right and helped his side to an easy 4-1 at Bradford Park Avenue's ground.

103

In the Scottish Junior Cup favourites Petershill had a tough match at Shawfield against Whitletts Victoria. The Ayrshire side were level 2-2 at half time but the Peasies scored the winning goal 4 minutes from the end. Lugar Boswell Thistle won the semi final clash with Broxburn Athletic.

With both clubs having good support a big crowd of over 64,000 attended.

PETERSHILL : G.White, Mc Farlane, Scobie, Turnball, Clydesdale, L White, Stewart, Young, Hogg, Docherty and Burns.

LUGAR BOSWELL THISTLE: Fraser, Love, Cathie, Mc Ewan, Baird, Donnelly, Bingham, Collins, Sharp, Neil and Wilkie.

The Jaggy Bunnets were up at them, roared on by their support and forced a corner in the opening minute. For the first 20 minutes the Peasies goal was under siege but held out. After 25 minutes the Springburn showed how to score .A Burns cross was touched in at the back post by Stewart.

The Ayrshire side should have equalised shortly after the goal A long shot from Young on 36 minutes put Petershill two up. On the stroke of half time Hogg headed in a corner and put the Peasies out of sight.

Hogg added a fourth for Petershill in the second half before Lugar gave their support something to cheer with a consolation goal.

RESULT: PETERSHILL 4 LUGAR BOSWELL THISTLE 1

# WEST OF SCOTLAND AMATEUR LEAGUE DIVISION 1

| Team | Pl | W | L | D | F | A | Pts |
|------|----|----|----|----|----|----|-----|
| Mossvale YMCA | 17 | 12 | 4 | 1 | 45 | 25 | 25 |
| Govan Amateurs | 16 | 10 | 3 | 3 | 34 | 19 | 23 |
| Babcock and Wilcox | 17 | 10 | 4 | 3 | 52 | 38 | 23 |
| Rhu | 18 | 9 | 6 | 3 | 42 | 37 | 21 |
| Mearns Amateurs | 13 | 9 | 3 | 1 | 55 | 25 | 19 |
| Bearsden | 18 | 8 | 8 | 2 | 52 | 50 | 18 |
| Albion Motors | 17 | 8 | 8 | 1 | 48 | 39 | 17 |
| Killermont | 13 | 6 | 3 | 4 | 30 | 22 | 16 |
| Laidlaw | 19 | 5 | 14 | 0 | 41 | 70 | 10 |
| Villafield | 19 | 3 | 14 | 2 | 33 | 56 | 8 |
| Wester Rossland | 17 | 1 | 14 | 2 | 16 | 67 | 4 |

In the First Division of the West of Scotland Amateur League Govan Amateurs were having a good season. With just two games to go they were in contention for the title.

Park United stood in the way of a long unbeaten run by Burnbank Swifts in the Scottish Juvenile Cup semi final. The United played an excellent game and drew the first match. The replay at Douglas Park, Hamilton saw the Swifts edge through.

St.Constantine's had a good season and progressed to the West of Scotland Juvenile FA Lady Darling Cup Semi Final. This competition had a huge entry and the Saints saw off Milton Battlefield by 5-0. In the Final they lost out to Livingston United.
A creditable effort by the Saints.

Both Benburb and St.Anthony's reached Cup Finals at the end of the season. The Ants did not have to travel too far for their Final; played at Tinto Park against Dennistoun Waverley. The Ants lifted the North Eastern Cup winning a tight match by 3-2 after extra time with John Quigley amongst the goals. The team was:
ST.ANTHONY'S : McGinlay, Langan, O'Hare, Harkin, Scott, Clocherty, Kelly, Travers, Currie, Quigley and Phillips.

Benburb had a tough assignment against Ashfield in the Glasgow Charity Cup at Petershill Park. The 'field led 1-0 at half time and scored two more unopposed goals in the second half for a 3-0 win.

Govan High Former Pupils had a good season and led the Division 1 for virtually the entire season. However, they were hauled back by Vale of Leven FP who managed to win the title by one point.

## GLASGOW FP LEAGUE DIVISION 1

| Team | Pl | W | L | D | F | A | Pts |
|---|---|---|---|---|---|---|---|
| Vale of Leven | 22 | 15 | 4 | 3 | 66 | 34 | 33 |
| Govan High | 22 | 13 | 3 | 6 | 69 | 38 | 32 |
| Eastbank | 22 | 15 | 6 | 1 | 66 | 33 | 31 |
| John Street | 22 | 11 | 6 | 5 | 63 | 29 | 27 |
| St.Mungo's | 22 | 12 | 8 | 2 | 54 | 44 | 26 |
| King's Park | 22 | 8 | 9 | 5 | 47 | 42 | 21 |
| St.Patrick's | 22 | 7 | 11 | 4 | 28 | 41 | 18 |
| Queen's Park | 22 | 7 | 11 | 4 | 50 | 67 | 18 |
| Whitehill | 22 | 6 | 12 | 4 | 41 | 57 | 16 |
| Woodside | 22 | 6 | 12 | 4 | 40 | 71 | 16 |
| Dalziel | 22 | 1 | 16 | 1 | 26 | 71 | 9 |

# CHAPTER 8
# DELIGHT FOR THE GREEN AND WHITE (1956-57)

Benburb announced their squad early for the forthcoming season.
BENBURB:
Goalkeeper: A.Smith (Holy Cross Boys Guild)
Backs: A Rutherford.
Half Backs: R.Fitzsimmons, D.Nicholson, R.Treacy, A.Gregal, A.David
(Milanda Amateurs)
Forwards: W.Syme, J.Mc Alpine, A.Trotter (Strathclyde), R.Ferrier
(St.Constantine), T.Douglas (Kilsyth Rangers), J.Mc Cormack, J.Watson.

The Bens fans were happy to see favourite Tommy Douglas back from
Kilsyth Rangers. Bob Fitzsimmons should be available to play in more matches
following his spell as part of the armed forces.

A player who would not be returning to Benburb after his armed forces spell
was the impressive John Baxter. John was a physical training instructor with
the Highland Light Infantry based at Aldershot. As a consequence he was
unable to play too many games for the Bens. However Hibernian noted his
potential and he was signed up for the Easter Road club. David Mac Craken the
Benburb club secretary was very much in a minority with his views on re-
instatements of senior class players into the juniors.

He said to Newspapers: ' I am definitely opposed to re-instatements. I don't
think ex seniors are good for the junior game and much prefer the system of
recruiting young amateurs and juveniles. If the re-instatement door was closed
many junior players would think twice about stepping up if they knew there
was no way back.

Two other players were leaving the Army for good. They were Davie
Mathers and Willie Crawford who left Glencorse Barracks in Edinburgh. Both
were team mates in the Govan High school football team some years previous
and were now to join Partick Thistle as professional footballers.

Rangers and Celtic were again drawn in the same section of the Scottish
League Cup. A midweek match saw Celtic gain a narrow but deserved 2-1 win
at Parkhead putting them two points clear of Rangers. The other two teams in
the group, East Fife and Aberdeen, were struggling.

The decisive game at Ibrox saw the gates closed with 500 people outside the
ground. The crowd inside was 85,000 anticipating an exciting match; they were
to be disappointed. It was a poor match which was scoreless and leaving Celtic
in the pole position to qualify. A big Celtic support went to Methil in Fife and
the Buoys duly qualified with a 1-0 win. The Juvenile Competitions (players
under age 21) finished their Summer programme of competitions.
St.Constantine's had double success winning the Juvenile Summer Cup and
also the Mc Neilage Cup.

Mosspark Amateurs made a slow start to their league campaign in the Scottish Amateur League Under 16's against some very strong opposition in a very small league.

Left winger Muir from the Govan Force was selected for the Glasgow Police Team.

## SCOTTISH AMATEUR LEAGUE UNDER 16's

| Team | Pl | W | L | D | F | A | Pts |
|------|----|----|----|----|----|----|-----|
| Drumchapel Amateurs | 3 | 3 | 0 | 0 | 18 | 6 | 6 |
| Drumchapel | 3 | 2 | 1 | 0 | 21 | 9 | 4 |
| Letham Thistle | 2 | 1 | 1 | 0 | 12 | 4 | 2 |
| Giffnock North | 1 | 0 | 1 | 0 | 1 | 9 | 0 |
| Mosspark Amateurs | 3 | 0 | 3 | 0 | 1 | 48 | 0 |

The first Govan 'Old Firm' derby between St.Anthony's and Benburb took place at Moore Park in a league encounter.

ST.ANTHONY'S : McGinlay, Buchanan, O'Hare, Campbell, Scott, Clougherty, Scally, Travers, Cowie, Quigley and Crum.

BENBURB: Reynolds, Rutherford, Cairns, McCormack, Nicholson, Ferrier, Syme, Mc Alpine, Newman, Gregal and Douglas

Benburb totally dominated the first half and led by three clear goals at the break. Newman a trialist headed in the opener and two penalty kicks from Tommy Douglas saw the Bens with a big advantage at half time.

St.Anthony's came out for the second half a different team and slowly but surely gained the upper hand. They pulled two goals back and the Bens were left hanging on as the final whistle sounded.

RESULT: ST.ANTHONY'S 2 BENBURB 3

Benburb generally made a promising start to the season in the league with a good 4-2 win over a strong Petershill side at Tinto Park. Also they travelled to Helenslea Park and came from 3-1 down to win 4-3 against Parkhead.

St.Anthony's had a number of very close matches where they were narrowly beaten by the odd goal. The Gods were not smiling on the Moore Park club as they slipped towards the bottom of the league.

In the West of Scotland Amateur League Govan Amateurs went top, although the chasing pack had games in hand.

# WEST OF SCOTLAND AMATEUR LEAGUE

| Team | Pl | W | L | D | F | A | Pts |
|------|----|----|----|----|----|----|----|
| Govan Amateurs | 7 | 4 | 1 | 2 | 17 | 13 | 10 |
| Albion Motors | 5 | 4 | 1 | 0 | 12 | 3 | 8 |
| Killermont | 5 | 3 | 0 | 2 | 11 | 5 | 8 |
| Mearns Amateurs | 6 | 3 | 1 | 2 | 13 | 9 | 8 |
| Babcock and Wilcox | 6 | 3 | 2 | 1 | 13 | 6 | 7 |
| Bearsden | 6 | 2 | 2 | 2 | 10 | 12 | 6 |
| Villafield | 4 | 2 | 1 | 1 | 17 | 7 | 5 |
| Glasgow Transport | 5 | 2 | 2 | 1 | 17 | 16 | 5 |
| Rhu | 6 | 2 | 3 | 1 | 13 | 15 | 5 |
| Mitanda | 6 | 2 | 4 | 0 | 12 | 14 | 4 |
| Mossvale YMCA | 4 | 0 | 4 | 0 | 2 | 11 | 0 |
| Laidlaw | 6 | 0 | 6 | 0 | 9 | 35 | 0 |

The Rangers Football club were saddened by the death of Bill Struth their former manager. He had been 33 years at Ibrox and had much respect throughout Scottish Football. He was a man who showed great interest in aspects outside Rangers. Bill Struth served on the Benburb Football Club committee in the 2nd World War years.

The Rangers manager had considerable success and was always looking at ways of encouraging progressive change. For example when the introduction of floodlights became an issue he installed them at Ibrox Park and put on Schools Represenative matches. He invited all and sundry to see the quality of the lighting and the benefits for the future of football.

Bill Struth was an Edinburgh man and his childhood House overlooked Tyncastle Park; home of Heart of Midlothian. He moved over to the west of Scotland by becoming the trainer to Clyde. He soon had Clyde as the fittest team in Scotland. He was a stickler for cleanliness and scrubbed the dressing room floor at Shawfield twice a week. He gave every player who played for him his personal attention and although strict he was very popular. Bill Struth was much sought after in 1914 and in particular by Rangers who wanted his methods of training adopted at Ibrox.

He moved to Ibrox after several abortive attempts by Rangers to recruit him. He was very popular again and his methods of training were even more intense and thought out than when he was at Clyde.

William Wilton, Rangers manager, died when he fell off a yacht at Gourock and it was Bill Struth that Rangers turned to as their next manager. In his time he insisted on quality and instilling into players what an honour it should be to play for the club. Under Struth Rangers became the dominant football club in Scotland.

He helped oversee the building of the main stand and insisted on high qualities of craftsmanship.

After having his leg amputated, ill health dogged his latter years.

The match immediately following the death of Bill Struth was an 'Old Firm' league game against old rivals Celtic at Celtic Park. The Rangers players required little motivation for the fixture following the sad times they had experienced.

At Celtic Park every flag in the ground was at half mast and the players observed a 30 second silence in memory of Bill Struth.

CELTIC: Beattie, Haughney, Fallon, Evans, Jack, Peacock, Higgins, Collins, McPhail, Fernie and Mochan.

RANGERS: Niven, Shearer, Little, Mc Coll, Young, Logie, Scott, Grierson, Murray, Baird and Hubbard.

53,000 sun drenched spectators were packed into Parkhead. Celtic started fast but Rangers almost took the lead when a Sammy Baird shot hit the crossbar.

The opening goal was not long delayed when Johnny Little went down the line and crossed for Max Murray to head in at the far post on 30 minutes.

In the second half Rangers were on top and Alex. Scott secured the win on 70 minutes when Grierson sent a through pass through the middle and Scott raced on to score easily.

RESULT: CELTIC  0 RANGERS 2

Scottish football got a recruit from the Ayrshire juniors. He was an Insurance representative and worked his way up to be a grade 1 referee. Tom Wharton immediately set two records when he refereed his match at the top level at Love Street Paisley.

Weighing in at 16 stone he was the heaviest referee ever in Scottish top level Football and at 6 feet 3 inches he was the tallest.

The St.Mirren fans immediately dubbed him 'Tiny Wharton'.

The Scottish Junior Cup 1st Round draw saw both the Govan sides drawn away. St.Anthony's looked to have the more difficult tie at Forth Wanderers. However after a good performance they came through to the second round courtesy of a 2-1 win.

Benburb travelled to Lanarkshire side Douglasdale. Defensive frailties proved to be the Bens undoing and by half time they trailed 3-0. A good response in the second half was not enough to retrieve the situation and a 4-1 score line sent the large Govan support home disappointed.

St.Anthony's league form had been poor but they showed what they were capable of with a win at Moore Park over the strong Kilsyth Rangers side. Brogan headed home a Quigley cross to give them a 1-0 win.

In the Scottish Junior Cup 2nd Round the Ants were given a very tough draw with a tie away at Ayrshire side Cumnock. Poor league form meant St.Anthony's were all but bottom of the league.

In the first half the Ants were under siege for long periods but held on to ensure they went in at half time scoreless. The second half was much more even ant the teams scored one goal each. A creditable result for the Ants and a good crowd could be expected for the replay.

A week later the teams met at Moore Park.

ST.ANTHONY'S: Mc Ginlay, Langan, O'Hare, Godfrey, Scott, Clocherty, Travers, Quigley, Gallacher, Neish and Brogan.

CUMNOCK: Schofield, Mc Culloch, Mc Kenna, Mooty, Kelly, Alexander, Kennedy, Sherry, Strachan, Munn and Whiteside.

Johnny Quigley was the Ants trump card in the early exchanges and scored an early goal to the delight of the Ants support. However, within three minutes Strachan headed an equaliser for the Nock. The Ants pushed the Ayrshire men back, piling on the pressure before Gallacher put them ahead right on half time.

John Quigley added a third goal for the Ants before Strachan scored again near the end to set up an exciting finish. However, St.Anthony's held on prompting a mini invasion from their younger followers to progress to the 3rd Round.

RESULT: ST.ANTHONY'S 3 CUMNOCK 2

The Schools Football season started with Bellahouston (the holders) being held 1-1 by Holyrood at the older age group. In the middle (third level) there were big wins for St.Gerrards and Govan High. In the youngest age group Govan High had an emphatic win to start the season.

Govan High centre forward Murray was scoring freely in a team line up which was usually:

K.Brown, T.Dearie, W.Christie, G.Wood, A.Hunter, G.Reid, I.Burt, J.Bowie, W.Murray, D.Stephen and W.Collin

At the oldest age group St. Mungo's were soon setting all sorts of records by scoring heavily and had a clean goals against column. Govan High punctured that record by scoring the first goal against them but the Saints came back and won 4-1. The Under 15's trials for the annual match against Edinburgh saw just two Govan School players attend the trials.: midfielder A. Ferguson of Govan High and forward McInally of St.Gerrard's.

With a slight decline in interest with religions, the Churches League lost one Division. There were no apparent Govan based Churches operating in the League's.

In the Glasgow Welfare League Youth section it was Stephen's Youth Club which were setting the pace at the top.

## GLASGOW WELFARE LEAGUE - YOUTH SECTION

| Team | Pl | W | D | L | F | A | Pts |
|------|----|----|----|----|----|----|-----|
| Stephens Youth Club | 8 | 7 | 0 | 1 | 40 | 14 | 14 |
| S.C.W.S. Youth Club | 8 | 5 | 0 | 3 | 27 | 19 | 10 |
| Letham Thistle A | 5 | 4 | 1 | 0 | 24 | 9 | 9 |
| St.Margaret's Youth Club | 8 | 4 | 0 | 4 | 27 | 29 | 8 |
| Dennistoun Juveniles A | 10 | 3 | 1 | 6 | 11 | 27 | 7 |
| Ruchazie Hearts | 6 | 3 | 1 | 2 | 12 | 15 | 7 |
| John Brown's Youth Club | 7 | 3 | 0 | 4 | 28 | 23 | 6 |
| Templeton Youth Club | 8 | 2 | 0 | 6 | 16 | 45 | 4 |
| Larkfield Thistle | 5 | 1 | 1 | 3 | 7 | 10 | 3 |
| Ruchill Thistle | 3 | 0 | 0 | 3 | 1 | 31 | 0 |

In the Scottish League Cup Quarter Finals Celtic travelled to Dunfermiline for the second leg. They lost 3-0 but having won 6-0 in the first game at Parkhead they were through to the semi finals. Partick Thistle had to fight hard against Cowdenbeath in both matches but eventually got through with a 2-1 score line in both matches; 4-2 on aggregate.

In the semi finals Celtic were mostly on top against Clyde at Hampden Park and two goals from Billy Mc Phail ; one in each half; secured a 2-0 win.
At Ibrox Park a poor match between Partick Thistle and Dundee saw the teams level and scoreless at 90 minutes. Extra Time was required but no goals were scored. The replay at Ibrox Park saw a better match and Partick Thistle inspired by Hagan and McKenzie won through 3-2.

The Scottish League Cup Final was an all Glasgow affair with Celtic strong favourites.
CELTIC: Beattie, Haughney, Fallon, Evans, Jack, Peacock, Walsh, Collins McPhail, Tully and Fernie.
PARTICK THISTLE: Ledgerwood, Kerr, Gibb, Collins, Davidson, Mathers, Mc kenzie, Smith, Hogan, Wright and Ewing.

Celtic were on top for most of the first half and Ledgerwood could only watch as a shot from Bobby Collins flew past him and crashed off the crossbar. If the Jags thought they had luck then all was about to change. Centre half Davidson got a bad head injury and played the remainder of the game in attack. Smith went down injured and hobbled around on the wing, virtually useless.

111

Thistle were down to 10 men before half time. In the second half it was wave after wave of Celtic attack but the Jags held firm taking the game to extra time. Again in extra time the Jags thwarted Celtic and earned a replay in front of around 59,000 spectators.

RESULT CELTIC 0 PARTICK THISTLE 0

The replay saw Celtic quickly on top and Bobby Collins opened their account. The Jags were never in the hunt and Billy Mc Phail added two more unopposed goals to bring delight to the green and white support.

RESULT: PARTICK THISTLE 0 CELTIC 3

Rangers were in the European Cup for the first time and drawn against French side Nice. The first leg at Ibrox developed into a brawl as the almost 60,000 crowd vented their anger on the French side. Every challenge appeared to be cynical and Alex Scott and Johnny Hubbard were the main targets. To make matters worse Nice took the lead in the first half through Faivre.

Rangers attacked virtually non stop and were rewarded when Max Murray equalised. In the second half Max Murray got down the wing and crossed for Billy Simpson to head home. Rangers should and could have won by more but a very difficult 2nd Leg was on the horizon.

The 2nd Leg match was played on a pitch full of water after a torrential downpour.

NICE: Colonna; Bonvie; Martinez, Ferry, Gonzales, Nuremburg, Fox, Ujlaki, Ruben—Bravo, Muro and Faivre.

RANGERS: Niven, Shearer, Caldow, Mc Coll, Young, Logie, Scott, Simpson, Murray, Baird and Hubbard

Johnny Hubbard had an early chance and fired in a good shot which unfortunately got stopped by the ground water. Nice were a very physical side but Rangers were holding them and on 40 minutes the 'Gers took the lead. Max Murray was brought down inside the penalty area and Johnny Hubbard scored from the spot to give Rangers a half time lead.

The second half saw Nice pile on the pressure and were rewarded with two goals in a minute around the hour mark. Firstly Ruben—Bravo scored after a good run down the middle and Fox equalised with a volley. Rangers had their backs to the wall but an inspired game from George Niven in goal meant a 2-1 score line but the chance of progressing if they could win the play off.

RESULT: NICE 2 RANGERS 1 Aggregate 3-3

For the third match Rangers were without George Young. Another rough house game saw the French Club through by 3-1. The Rangers goal came via an own goal from a Nice defender.

Two Govan Junior players were selected for the Glasgow team to face the Ayrshire Juniors at Rugby Park. Johnny Quigley from the Ants and Donnie Nicholson from the Bens.

In Juvenile Football the Govan teams made the news. Park United went to Rutherglen and beat Glencairn Juveniles the holders in the West of Scotland Cup by 3-1. The Park United supporters at Plantation Park were always raucous and after a number of complaints they were finally fined £1 for the behaviour of some of their support against Port Glasgow Parkfield.

Two Avon Villa players got lost trying to find the ground of Shettleston Violet. The team played with 9 men and won 4-2 against all odds. Frank Anderson of Avon Villa was suspended as he did not submit a defence for being sent off against Glencairn.

In the delayed City and District League Championship decider from the previous season Avon Villa beat Ferndale Athletic 2-1 to lift the Cup. Manager Archie Lindsay was delighted to take the Alex. (Sandy) Carmichael Trophy back to Plantation Park.

Copland Rangers were doing well and Rangers kindly provided them with the use of Ibrox Park to enable training for their big Scottish Juvenile Cup match against Letham Thistle at Pirrie Park. A number of senior scouts were running the rule over the Govan sides players.Goalkeeper Lunney was being watched by Manchester United. Hutchison the right half was being tracked by Accrington Stanley and Queen's Park were interested in inside forward Edminston.

Park United were hoping for a good run to the latter stages of the Scottish Juvenile Cup. The were given a long trip to Aberdeen and the Old Meldrum team. The Plantation Park side built up a 3-1 lead but in the second half they fell away and lost 4-3.

St.Anthony's had a tough but reasonably local Scottish Junior Cup 4th Round tie at Renfrew. A large crowd was present for St.Anthony's short trip to Renfrew.

RENFREW: Brackenbridge, Cavanagh, Harkinson, Mc Intosh, Sherry, Scollan, Cuthbertson, Divers, Stevenson, Clydesdale and Cuthbert
ST.ANTHONY'S: McGinlay , Langan, O'Hare, Conner, Scott, Clocherty, Gallacher, Travers, Sheerin, Quigley and Brogan

The game started with a bang when Renfrew scored a quick goal. McGinlay's punch was not far enough and Divers who had a short spell at Benburb and was on Celtic's books rammed home. The Ants were undismayed, came back strongly and John Quigley scored to pull them level. Play raged from end to end with both sides looking like scoring with every attack. Cuthbertson put the 'frew ahead and Langan scored a spectacular own goal to give the home side a two goal cushion. However approaching half time Sheerin and then John Quigley had the Ants level at 3-3.

The second half saw St.Anthony's have most of the play and only smart saves from Brackenbridge kept 'frew in the cup.

RESULT: RENFREW 3 ST.ANTHONY'S 3

A crowd of 6,500 packed in to Moore Park for the replay.
Unlike the first match the defences were for the most very much on top.
St.Anthony's were awarded a penalty in the first half when Quigley was
brought down. Unfortunately for the green and white hoops Clocherty smashed
the ball over the bar.

RESULT: ST.ANTHONY'S 0 RENFREW 0

The second replay was played at Keanie Park home of Johnstone Burgh.
St.Anthony's again took a large support through to Johnstone. They were
rewarded early in the game when Gallacher converted a left wing cross. The
Ants continued to press and Sheerin burst through to put them 2-0 up. Renfrew
replied right on half time through Cuthbertson. The second half saw the Ants
continue to have the edge and they deservedly progressed into the next round.

RESULT: RENFREW 1 ST.ANTHONY'S 2

The New Years Day Old Firm match duly arrived. Rangers were off to their
usual very slow start in their League Championship quest. However they had
good form prior to Christmas and moved within range of leaders Heart of
Midlothian and second placed Motherwell. The match itself saw Rangers gain
a comfortable 2-0 win with goals from Max Murray and Billy Simpson.

However there were a number of arrests inside the ground due to an
unexpected source of trouble. A stray Orange balloon danced along the turf in
the wind from the Rangers end. It skipped and danced to the half way line. As it
lined up to head towards the Celtic net a huge roar went up from the Copland
Road end. The balloon veered off and big roar came up from the Broomloan
Road end. The balloon again changed direction and was now heading towards
the Celtic goal.

A fan rushed from the Broomloan Road terrace to try and stop it but was
promptly arrested by the police force and marched away. The balloon was now
heading straight for the net helped along by a huge roar from the Rangers end
when one Celtic fan made one final dash to save honour and succeeded in
puncturing the balloon right on the goal line just as he was grabbed by the
police force. There were a number of bottle and tumbler throwing incidents and
many arrests.

Benburb were having a good if not spectacular season. Despite the early
Scottish Cup exit, league form had been good and they were looking to make
progress in the West of Scotland Cup. Former player Dunky Rae was not so
regular in the Clydebank team after his wife delivered twins. Clydebank were
making progress in the Scottish Junior Cup. In the 4th Round they were drawn
to play at Roseberry Park against Shawfield. The match drew Shawfield's
biggest crowd for years and the home team took the lead helped by their young
star inside forward Frank Mc Lintock. Two late goals sent the large Bankies
support wild and into the next round. Mc Lintock was signed by Leicester City
immediately after the match.

The Bens had some bad luck in their West of Scotland Cup match against fancied Rob Roy. Leading 2-1 and on top the match was abandoned due to poor conditions. The second attempt at settling the tie brought a good crowd to Tinto Park.

BENBURB: Smith, Rutherford, Cairns, Mc Cormack, Nicholson, Young, Bain, Mc Alpine, Gavin, Forrest and Douglas

ROB ROY: Boyd, Barclay, Kerr, Orr, Calder, Cairney, Duncan, Mc Bride, Friel, Wood and Mc Nab

The Rabs had former Bellahouston Academy player George Duncan, on his way to signing for Rangers, playing on the wing. He got very little scope from the experienced Gordon Cairns.

Bens took the lead on 3 minutes when big centre forward Willie Gavin headed home. Two minutes later it was two when Gavin burst through the middle to blast in an unstoppable shot. Willie Gavin turned provider when he set up John Mc Alpine for the Bens third and Forest made it four before half time with a rasping drive.

Play became rough and Tommy Douglas was carried off. Bain was also helped off with an injury and George Duncan got free for the only time in the match to reduce the arrears for Rob Roy. Both Douglas and Bain tried to resume but both had to leave the match; Tommy Douglas on a stretcher. The nine men battled on and when Bain surprisingly re-appeared the Bens added a fifth on full time through Willie Gavin.

RESULT: BENBURB 5 ROB ROY 1

The most popular teams in all of the Glasgow area football played in the YMCA Senior League. Deaf Athletic made many friends with their attitude and sportsmanship. They celebrated every goal they scored as if it was a Cup Final goal.

In the 2nd Round of the Scottish Secondary Schools Shield, Govan High went down at Pirrie Park 2-1 to Bathgate St.Mary's. Bellahouston, the holders, went out 3-0 to Bathgate Academy. St. Gerrard's were left to keep the Govan flag flying after a comprehensive 8-2 win over Hamilton Academy.

The final pool of under 15 players arrived for trials at Nether Pollok. Just one Govan player, Alex Ferguson of Govan High, made it through the trials for the match against Edinburgh. The match at Cathkin Park saw Glasgow easy winners by 3-0 with midfielder Ferguson doing well.

Govan High were doing well at the above age group and represented by: Hendry, Bickerstaff, Barratt, McDonald, Robertson, Ferguson, Littleson, Whitelaw, Turnball, Mc Lean and Forbes.

# YMCA SENIOR LEAGUE

| Team | Pl | W | L | D | F | A | Pts |
|------|----|----|----|----|----|----|----|
| Kilsyth | 11 | 10 | 0 | 1 | 52 | 9 | 21 |
| Cathcart | 11 | 9 | 1 | 1 | 53 | 17 | 19 |
| Croftfoot | 13 | 9 | 3 | 1 | 29 | 24 | 19 |
| Tollcross | 12 | 8 | 4 | 0 | 37 | 28 | 16 |
| Parkhead | 11 | 4 | 2 | 3 | 41 | 21 | 15 |
| Giffnock | 12 | 7 | 4 | 1 | 34 | 28 | 15 |
| Lairds | 10 | 7 | 3 | 0 | 30 | 22 | 14 |
| 30th BB | 11 | 5 | 5 | 1 | 28 | 28 | 11 |
| Garngad | 12 | 4 | 7 | 1 | 18 | 42 | 9 |
| 108th BB | 11 | 3 | 6 | 2 | 29 | 30 | 8 |
| St. Thomas's | 11 | 4 | 7 | 0 | 35 | 41 | 8 |
| Somerville | 13 | 2 | 8 | 3 | 31 | 42 | 7 |
| Eastern | 12 | 3 | 8 | 1 | 28 | 38 | 7 |
| Chrymon | 11 | 2 | 8 | 1 | 18 | 25 | 5 |
| Deaf Athletic | 13 | 0 | 13 | 0 | 8 | 78 | 0 |

St.Anthony's were drawn away at Annbank United from Ayrshire in the 5th Round of the Scottish Junior Cup. The Ants support for the match was going to be considerable. Many coaches would be meeting outside Ibrox Stadium to ferry the Ants support down to Ayrshire.

In addition a special train had been chartered to leave from Ibrox Station to the match. Interest in the Ants had never been higher for many years. The St.Anthony's danger man was John Quigley and his form in the match would probably decide the outcome.

In another Scottish Junior Cup match there was Benburb interest with Jock 'Tiger' Shaw the Bailleston trainer on one side and Dunky Rae the Clydebank winger with the opposition.

In the Glasgow Secondary Juvenile League, Copland Rangers were mounting a challenege at the top end of the league. St.Constantine's were mid table and Penilee Thistle who played their home games at the 50 pitches near the bottom.

Rangers could not have had a much tougher draw in their first Scottish Cup outing. They were away to Heart of Midlothian who topped the Scottish League and walloped the Ibrox side in the same competition the year before.

HEART OF MIDLOTHIAN: Brown, Parker, Kirk, Mackay, Glidden, Cumming, Young, Conn, Bauld, Wardhaugh and Crawford

RANGERS: Niven, Shearer, Caldow, Mc Coll, Young, Davis, Scott, Simpson, Murray, Baird and Hubbard

Young missed an early chance for Hearts when clean through. A few minutes later Max Murray was floored in the penalty box and John Hubbard scored from the penalty. A minute later Rangers doubled their advantage when Max Murray got through and fired home. Hearts were rocking and Alex. Scott scored a third after an error by goalkeeper Brown.

The second half saw Hearts try to recover lost ground but Rangers defence held firm. Ten minutes from the end Billy Simpson scored a fourth and Rangers were through to the next round.

RESULT; HEARTS 0 RANGERS 4

In the league Rangers edged closer to Hearts and with games in hand could catch them up. An exciting finish to the League programme seemed certain. Willie Woodburn was keeping up his appeals against his 'Suspended Sine Die' sentence from the SFA. He was allowed to appeal every six months and with Rangers backing him all the way he re-launched an appeal each time the previous appeal was turned down. It was a war of attrition and big Willie was determined to reclaim his honour.

In Schools football at the oldest age group trials were held to select a team to represent Glasgow. Some Govan Players were in contention.
Brown—full back (Govan High) Quinn—half back (St.Gerrard's) Lochhead—forward (St.Gerrard's).

At the Intermediate level Shield competitions Govan High were drawn at home to St.Mungo at Pirrie Park. Two of the stars in the win over Edinburgh were in direct opposition. Ferguson (Govan High) and Mac Adam (St.Mungo). In Juvenile Football (under 21) Copland Rangers players continued to train in Rangers car park at Ibrox. A number of their players were attracting the attention of Junior clubs. These included goalscorer Tom Hutchieson; Mc Laren (centre half); Thomson (left half back); Edmiston (centre forward) and Clark (inside right).

The green and white supporters of St.Anthony's descended on Annbank for the big Scottish Junior Cup match. New Pebble Park was packed to the rafters. The home team started well and the travelling support had little to cheer about during the first half. Wilson gave Annbank the lead when his shot beat Mc Ginley the ball slipping through his fingers. The Ants came back into the match in the second period and Sheerin headed home the equaliser from a corner. The Ants held on for a replay at Moore Park.

ST.ANTHONY'S: McGinley, Langan, O'Hare, Conner, Scott, Clocherty, Gallacher, Travers, Sheerin, Quigley and Brogan.

ANNBANK UNITED: Mackie, Reynolds, Hunter, Pollock, Mc Lean, Winship, Taylor, Hanlon, Gilmour, Blackwood and Wilson.

There were long queue's outside the Moore Park ground as the match started. Play was for the most part very even. John Quigley was at the centre of most things good for the Ants. St.Anthony's took the lead on 39 minutes when Travers thumped the ball into the roof of the net after Mackie blocked a shot.

The second half was much the same pattern and near the end McGinley produced two good saves. The Ants held on and their younger supporters again rushed on the field at the end of the match. St.Anthony's were now in the quarter finals of the Scottish Junior Cup.

RESULT: ST.ANTHONY'S 1 ANNBANK UNITED 0

Rangers had another very tough draw in the Scottish Cup this time against their old firm rivals Celtic.

CELTIC: Beattie, Haughney, Fallon, Evans, Jack, Peacock, Higgins, Fernie, McPhail, Mochan and Collins

RANGERS: Niven, Shearer, Caldow, Mc Coll, Davis, Baird, Scott, Simpson, Murray, Morrison and Hubbard.

Bobby Morrison made a dream debut start for Rangers when he converted a through pass from Simpson on 7 minutes. Within three minutes Celtic were level when Billy Mc Phail finished off a good move by shooting into the roof of the net. Rangers responded and Alex. Scott sent in a free kick cross for Billy Simpson to rise high and head home. The green and white hoops were not behind for long and Higgins converted a right wing cross.

The second half saw Rangers looking the more likely to score and the Celtic goal had many escapes. With a quarter of an hour to go, however, Bobby Collins sent the green and white supporters wild when he converted a flicked on corner. Five minutes later the Rangers support were heading for the exits when Mc Phail and Fernie passed the ball through the Rangers defence for Willie Fernie to convert.

Rangers looked finished but a rash challenge by Jack on Johnny Hubbard gave Rangers a penalty chance. Hubbard took the kick himself and converted. With time running out Rangers pushed everything forward and a mistake by Jack let in Max Murray for the equaliser.

RESULT: CELTIC 4 RANGERS 4

The replay at Ibrox Park saw Celtic dominate from start to finish and won through with two unopposed goals. The midweek match played in freezing conditions attracted a crowd of 88,000. With Rangers exit from the 'Scottish' they were able to focus on the league campaign. Slowly but surely they were pulling up on the leading clubs and a tight finish was on the cards.

# SCOTTISH LEAGUE DIVISION 1

| Team | Pl | W | L | D | F | A | Pts |
|---|---|---|---|---|---|---|---|
| Heart of Midlothian | 25 | 18 | 3 | 4 | 64 | 38 | 40 |
| Raith Rovers | 25 | 13 | 5 | 7 | 70 | 40 | 33 |
| Rangers | 22 | 15 | 5 | 2 | 58 | 32 | 32 |
| Motherwell | 23 | 14 | 5 | 4 | 58 | 36 | 32 |
| Kilmarnock | 25 | 11 | 5 | 9 | 44 | 28 | 31 |
| Aberdeen | 34 | 13 | 10 | 1 | 61 | 45 | 27 |
| Celtic | 22 | 10 | 7 | 5 | 42 | 30 | 25 |
| Dundee | 23 | 11 | 9 | 3 | 43 | 39 | 25 |
| Hibernian | 25 | 7 | 10 | 8 | 46 | 45 | 22 |
| Dunfermiline | 23 | 8 | 11 | 4 | 40 | 50 | 20 |
| Partick Thistle | 23 | 7 | 10 | 6 | 29 | 36 | 20 |
| Queen's Park | 24 | 7 | 12 | 5 | 36 | 42 | 19 |
| East Fife | 25 | 7 | 13 | 5 | 46 | 63 | 19 |
| Queen of the South | 23 | 8 | 13 | 2 | 40 | 68 | 18 |
| Airdrie | 23 | 7 | 12 | 4 | 52 | 66 | 18 |
| St.Mirren | 25 | 7 | 14 | 4 | 37 | 56 | 18 |
| Falkirk | 25 | 5 | 14 | 6 | 33 | 57 | 16 |
| Ayr United | 25 | 6 | 16 | 3 | 36 | 64 | 15 |

In the Glasgow Amateur League Cup the Cleansing Department did not have too far to travel. They had reached the semi final against Dalglish United and the match was at Tinto Park across the road from the depot. The Cleansing had a good season in 1954 when they cleaned up the medals by winning the Glasgow Amateur League Cup. Since that year their form had been rubbish.

For the match at Tinto Park they were without their two key players. Centre half Jimmy Duncan and Centre forward George Morrison.

CLEANSING DEPARTMENT: Cameron, R.Moir, J.Moir, Craig, Duncan, McQuade, McInnes, McDonald, Parks, Spiers and Stirling.

Dalglish had the edge in the first half and went in a goal up. The Cleansing came back in the second half and scored two goals. However Dalglish also scored two more goals and went through to the final.

RESULT: CLEANSING DEPARTMENT 2  DALGLISH 3

St.Anthony's again took good support with them for their Scottish Junior Cup 6th Round tie at Kilsyth. The ground was packed for what promised to be a close match.

KILSYTH RANGERS: Lowe, Mc Andrew, Mochan, Duncanson, Sievewright, Mc Lure, Bryans, Mc Gregor, Querrie, Borella and Campbell

ST. ANTHONY'S: McGinlay, Langan, O'Hare, Conner, Scott, Cloucherty, Gallacher, Travers, Sheerin, Quigley and Brogan

Kilsyth started strongly but the Ants held firm and chances came at both ends. Ten minutes from the break a fierce shot from Bryans was palmed away by McGinley but in the resulting scramble Romeo Borella gave Rangers the lead. A few minutes later Johnny Quigley was taken off injured.

Quigley was back for the second half and St.Anthony's pressed to get the equaliser. In a breakaway Querrie hit the crossbar for Kilsyth. Ants had some good efforts but none found the net and they exited the Cup after a grand effort.

RESULT: KILSYTH RANGERS 1 ST.ANTHONY'S 0

With Jock 'Tiger' Shaw as trainer to Bailleston excitement was mounting with the club's Scottish Junior Cup run. They had a 6th Round tie at Newtongrange against Loanhead Mayflower. The Bailleston folk filled 25 coach loads of supporters for the match in which the Glasgow club started as favourites.

However, it was the underdogs who took a first half lead through Wardrop. Drysdale pulled Bailleston level but a late goal from the home side saw them progress to the semi finals.

In the Glasgow Catholic Primary School's League three Govan school's were to the fore. St.Saviours were setting a hot pace at the top.

## GLASGOW ROMAN CATHOLIC PRIMARY SCHOOL LEAGUE

| Team | Pl | W | L | D | F | A | Pts |
|---|---|---|---|---|---|---|---|
| St.Saviour's | 12 | 12 | 0 | 0 | 54 | 8 | 24 |
| St.Constantine's | 11 | 9 | 1 | 1 | 64 | 11 | 19 |
| Lourdes | 11 | 6 | 3 | 2 | 47 | 18 | 14 |
| St.Margaret's | 11 | 7 | 4 | 0 | 24 | 23 | 14 |
| St.George's | 10 | 6 | 4 | 0 | 44 | 21 | 12 |
| St.Robert's | 11 | 5 | 5 | 1 | 43 | 18 | 11 |
| St.Monica's | 13 | 3 | 8 | 2 | 16 | 47 | 8 |
| St.Anthony's | 9 | 0 | 3 | 6 | 4 | 45 | 6 |
| Damshot | 11 | 1 | 8 | 2 | 8 | 58 | 4 |
| St.Conval's | 12 | 0 | 11 | 1 | 11 | 72 | 1 |

After a trial match at Ibrox Park under the floodlights a few Govan players were chosen to represent Glasgow Schools on a trip to Stamford Bridge to play London Schools. Andrew Whitelaw (Bellahouston) - left back, William Murray (Govan High—centre forward, James Shields (St.Gerrard's) - reserve

The match was exciting with London on top in the first half and deservedly leading 1-0. However the Glasgow team came back strongly and equalised through W.Raey of Kings Park and thus earned a well deserved 1-1 draw.

For the Under 14 Glasgow Select team the only Govan player selected was Kane, a half back from St.Gerrard's.

In the older age group School's football St.Gerrard's were strong and won the league division C. However in the semi finals despite starting favourites the Govan side lost out 2-1. No Govan side reached the League decider finals.

In the Scottish Intermediate Cup age group Govan High battled through to the semi finals to meet West Calder at the ground of Stenhousemuir. Despite a great effort the Edinburgh area side progressed to the final courtesy of a 2-1 win.

Celtic Park was the venue for the Scotland v England under 18's match. Scotland were on top for most of the first half which remained scoreless. However Scotland got the breakthrough early in the second half and went on the win by three unopposed goals.

The Glasgow Schools under 15 team to make the long trip to Sutherland was: Ian Mc Rae (Hyndland), Colin Meldrum (City Public), Robert Sharp (Knightswood), Robert Wilson (Knightswood), George Harrison (Eastbank), Alexander Ferguson (Govan High), George Mc Dermid ( Rutherglen), George Boardman (Albert), Robert O'Neil (Strathbungo), John Cunningham (Queen's Park), Tom Sturgeon (Rutherglen)
And Grant Mc Gregor (Shawlands) reserve to travel.

The annual match against the Auld Enemy took place at Wembley.
ENGLAND: Hodgkinson (Sheffield Utd), Hall (Birmingham), Byrne (Manchester Utd), Clayton (Blackburn Rovers), Wright (Wolves), Edwards (Manchester Utd), Matthews (Blackpool), Thompson (Preston North End), Finney (Preston North End), Kevan (West Bromish Albion) and Grainger (Sunderland).
SCOTLAND: Younger (Liverpool), Caldow (Rangers), Hewie (Charlton Athletic), Mc Coll (Rangers), Young (Rangers), Docherty (Preston North End), Collins (Celtic), Fernie (Celtic), Reilly (Hibernian), Mudie (Blackpool) and Ring (Clyde)

The match was barely two minutes old when Tommy Ring scored for Scotland. He picked up a rare miss control from Stanley Matthews and beat several England defenders before drawing and firing past Hodgkinson. The tartan bunnits were aloft.

121

England responded with much attacking but several smart saves from Tommy Younger kept the Scots ahead at half time.

Early in the second half Scotland had the ball in the net again but a foul by Reilly on the goalkeeper saw the effort chalked off. Tommy Docherty was putting in some tough tackles and was booed every time he was involved in play. On 64 minutes England equalised when Derek Kevan headed in a Grainger cross. Scotland piled on the pressure in search for the winner and Mudie and Mc Coll came very close with good shots.

With just six minutes to go it was England that got the winning goal. Scotland were unable to deal with some Stanley Matthews trickery on the edge of the box. The ball ran loose and Duncan Edwards smashed a shot from the edge of the box off the post and into the net. Scotland should have equalised when Tommy Ring crossed for Willie Fernie just a few yards out to head over an empty net.

RESULT: ENGLAND 2 SCOTLAND 1

The Juvenile League side Copland Rangers saw a number of their players watched by Junior Clubs. In particular Tom Hutchieson the wing half back. Other players were Willie Edmiston the outside right, James Mc Keachie the inside right and Bruce Mc Kinven the centre half.

The Scottish Cup semi finals saw Celtic paired with Kilmarnock and Falkirk against Raith Rovers.

At Hampden Park, in front of 80,000, Kilmarnock took a first half lead with a goal on 35 minutes. Harvey went down the wing and crossed for Mays to head home in grand style. The second half saw Celtic pile on the pressure for the equaliser. Jimmy Brown in the Killie goal was inspired but a corner 7 minutes from the end for Celtic saw Higgins head home.

The replay saw Kilmarnock win 3-1 with Mays again proving to be the Ayrshire hero with two goals.

At Tynecastle Park 48,000 spectators turned up to see an exciting match between Raith Rovers and Falkirk. On the quarter hour former Rangers player Derek Grierson headed home to put the Bairns ahead. At the half hour Raith equalised when Copland slammed home a long pass. Before half time the Fife side took the lead through Mc Ewan and they were unlucky not to increase their lead; prevented by a great save from Slater.

The second half started with a Falkirk equaliser when Leigh deflected a cross into his own net. Play raged from end to end with both sides trying for the winner but none was forthcoming and a draw was a fair result to a game of first class entertainment.

The replay again drew a big crowd. Falkirk opened with non stop attack against Raith Rovers and were rewarded when Doug Moran scored after 20 minutes. The game evened up but chances were scarce and the Bairns held on to their advantage to progress to the Scottish Cup Final.

Rangers and Heart of Midlothian were well clear of others in the race for the Scottish League title. They met at Tynecastle Park in a match which was forecast as being the match which may decide the title. Rangers were just two points behind Hearts but with two games in hand. Rangers had the superior goal average.

HEART OF MIDLOTHIAN: Marshall, Kirk, McKenzie, Parker, Milne, McKay, Wardhaugh, Conn, Bauld, Young and Crawford.

RANGERS: Niven, Shearer, Caldow, Mc Coll, Young, Davis, Scott, Simpson, Murray, Baird and Hubbard.

Hearts totally dominated the opening exchanges and the Rangers goal had some narrow escapes. Niven was inspired in the Rangers goal and pulled off some smart saves.

In a rare sortie up field on 35 minutes, Alex Scott beat his full back and went to the bye line before delivering to Billy Simpson to head Rangers in front.

Rangers had more of the play in the second half and Niven came to the rescue in the last few minutes with a good save from Conn. Rangers were in pole position for the league title and with it a place in the recently introduced European Cup.

RESULT: HEARTS 0 RANGERS 1

A few weeks later the 'Gers travelled to Hampden Park for a midweek fixture against Queen's Park. The match saw Rangers defence struggle to cope with an inspired Queen's Park front line.

In the first few minutes Junior Omand of Queens Park was brought down in the penalty box and a penalty awarded. Cromar stepped up but shot wide. On 13 minutes of constant Spiders pressure, Herd shot the Hampden side ahead after a goalmouth scramble. Five minutes later it was two when Devine headed in a Heron corner. Three minutes later and former Queens Parker Max Murray headed in a corner from Hubbard to reduce the leeway.

The 40,000 crowd were on their toes and enjoying a thrill a minute. Herd and Mc Ewan waltzed through the Rangers defence leaving Devine to smash in Queen's third goal. Herd sent a good pass down the touchline a minute later and Devine picked it up unchallenged to run in and beat Niven to make it 4-1. Rangers needed a reply before half time and Johnny Hubbard scored on 40 minutes.

On the stroke of half time the same player cut the deficit to one goal after good work by Baird.

Queen's goalkeeper Crampsey sustained an injury and it was backs to the wall for the Spiders. They held out until the 60th minute when Max Murray scored from good play from Baird. Rangers were well on top but had to wait until the 78th minute when Billy Simpson scored. Alex Scott added a sixth near full time.

RESULT: QUEEN'S PARK 4 RANGERS 6

After four appeals Willie Woodburn of Rangers finally got his 'Sine Die' ban lifted. It had been a long haul for the former Scotland pivot but finally after excellent support from the club and its thousands of supporters a semblance of justice was served up.

Thousands of Rangers supporters travelled to Dumfries to see if the Ibrox club could lift the League Championship against Queen of the South. The first half was tight but a Johnny Hubbard penalty gave Rangers the lead after 15 minutes. Max Murray added two more goals in the second half and the league flag was destined for Ibrox with a 3-0 win.

The Scottish Cup Final drew a crowd of around 81,000 to Hampden Park to watch Kilmarnock and Falkirk.

FALKIRK: Slater, Parker, Rae, Wright, Irvine, Prentice, Murray, Grierson, Merchant, Moran and O'Hara

KILMARNOCK: Brown, Collins, J. Stewart, R. Stewart, Toner, McKay, Mays, Harvey, Curlett, Black and Burns

Kilmarnock played the better football but Falkirk had the best early chance when Grierson headed across the goal to Merchant who headed badly over the bar. Falkirk went ahead when Merchant was pulled down by Toner. John Prentice stepped up and scored with a shot into the corner. Right on the stroke of half time Killie drew level when Black crossed for Curlett to score from six yards.

The second half produced a lot of tension but few chances. Curlett almost won the match for Killie with a shot which came back off the post.

RESULT : FALKIRK 1 KILMARNOCK 1

The replay was again at Hampden Park and 80,000 turned up for the match. Falkirk were slightly the better team throughout and Jimmy Brown in the Killie goal was the busier keeper. Merchant gave Falkirk the lead mid way through the first half. Curlett provided a 78th minute equaliser and the game went to extra time.

In the first half of extra time Dougie Moran fired in the winner for the Bairns and the Cup was on its way to Falkirk.

RESULT: KILMARNOCK 1 FALKIRK 2 (after extra time 1-1)

In the Scottish Junior Cup little Loanhead Mayflower took their place in the semi finals. They had tough opponents at Celtic Park in Kilsyth Rangers. Loanhead had a couple of early chances but fluffed them. Kilsyth showed them how to score when Alex. Querrie went through the middle and scored with the wee rangers first shot. Before half time Alex. Robertson and Bryans had added further goals. Loanhead had most of the play in the second half but Kilsyth held on comfortably.

RESULT: KILSYTH RANGERS 3 LOANHEAD MAYFLOWER 0

In the other Semi Final Duntocher Hibs were hot favourites to win against Banks o'Dee from Aberdeen. The match was played at Muirton Park, Perth in front of 10,000 spectators. The Aberdeen side were on top for most of the first half but had to wait until the 35th minute to score when Ewan took advantage of a defensive lapse.

A minute later Mc Kenzie added a second. Right on half time the Hibs were given some hope when Currie headed a goal. In the second half the Hibs were unable to equalise and Lornie secured the final place for Banks O'Dee with a quarter of an hour left.

RESULT: BANKS O'DEE 3 DUNTOCHER HIBS 1

Park United and Avon Villa were fierce rivals in the Juvenile City and District League. They both shared Plantation Park and knew a lot about each other. Avon Villa were none to pleased when their rivals reported them for playing no fewer than four 'ringers' in their matches. Avon Villa were fined and had other penalties imposed.

Govan Amateurs had a great season and were within touching distance of winning the West of Scotland Amateur League

## WEST OF SCOTLAND AMATEUR LEAGUE—DIVISION 1

| Team | Pl | W | L | D | F | A | Pts |
|------|----|----|----|----|----|----|-----|
| Govan Amateurs | 20 | 13 | 4 | 3 | 59 | 37 | 29 |
| Babcock and Willcox | 20 | 11 | 5 | 4 | 56 | 23 | 26 |
| Killermoat | 20 | 11 | 5 | 4 | 50 | 25 | 26 |
| Mearns Amateurs | 18 | 11 | 4 | 3 | 47 | 24 | 25 |
| Albion Motors | 19 | 11 | 6 | 2 | 47 | 37 | 24 |
| Bearsden | 20 | 9 | 7 | 4 | 46 | 39 | 22 |
| Glasgow Transport | 20 | 8 | 9 | 3 | 52 | 57 | 19 |
| Milanda | 18 | 6 | 7 | 5 | 46 | 41 | 17 |
| Rhu | 20 | 5 | 7 | 4 | 42 | 60 | 14 |
| Laidlaw | 20 | 3 | 14 | 3 | 35 | 79 | 9 |
| Mossvale YMCA | 19 | 1 | 17 | 1 | 25 | 63 | 3 |

After years in the doldrums the Govan Police football team had some success. At Moore Park, Govan they had a chance to win the Glasgow Police Cup against Central Division. The Govan team was :
Simkins, Guthrie, Mc Millan, Jackson, Miller, Neil, Mc Arthur, Spence, Harrison, Mc Lachlan and Muir.

Govan won the cup with a 2-1 win; their first success for many years. The smallest player on the park Mc Lachlan crossed for Spence to head the first goal. The second goal was an exact repeat of the first. The Police spectators were well behaved and there were no arrests reported.

RESULT: GOVAN POLICE 2 CENTRAL DIVISION 1

The Scottish Junior Cup Final at Hampden Park saw Kilsyth strong favourites to lift the trophy. A rain deluge before the match made life difficult for spectators and players .

KILSYTH RANGERS: Lowe, McAndrew, Mochan, Robertson, Duncanson, McClure, Bryans, Liddell, Querrie, McGregor and Borella

BANKS O'DEE: Ogston, Fowler, Robertson, Warrender, Studd, Fraser, Ewan, Walker, Anderson, McKenzie and Lornie

Banks O'Dee took the game to Kilsyth Rangers in the opening half with the 'wee Rangers' very subdued. Towards half time the 'Dee' launched a fierce spell of pressure on the Kilsyth goal but the Central League side held firm.

The second half continued with the same pattern until the inevitable goal came from the northern side. A fierce shot was parried but Walker controlled the rebound and fired in the opening goal.

Kilsyth rallied but could not get the better of a well organised defence.

RESULT : KILSYTH RANGERS 0 BANKS O'DEE 1

There was to be disappointment for John Quigley of St.Anthony's. After a fantastic season with the Ants he was released from his provisional signing forms by Celtic. He immediately looked for a higher profile team and favourites to sign him were Ashfield. However a number of senior clubs wanted to run the rule over him in the months ahead.

Maurice Young the Benburb centre half had countless head injuries as most Junior football centre halves seemed to receive. On one occasion he received two black eyes for his troubles.

Each of the three Govan Schools had players in the Glasgow Schools team to meet Bradford Schools at Hampden Park.

GLASGOW: J.Cruickshank ( Queen's Park), S.Lynch (St.Mungo), A.Whitelaw (Bellahouston), J.Connelly (Holyrood), A.Summers (Hyndland), A.Turpe (Whitehill), H.Samson (John Street), A.Bradley (St.Gerrard's), W.Murray (Govan High), W.Raey (Kings Park) and W.Dunn (Shawlands)

Connelly opened the Glasgow account after just two minutes when his long shot sailed over the Bradford keeper and into the net. On eight minutes Murray of Govan High finished off a good move with a tap in. Bradford reduced the arrears just after half time when Hill scored.

However Raey and Dunn added further scores for Glasgow to secure a comprehensive win.

RESULT: GLASGOW 4 BRADFORD 1

# CENTRAL LEAGUE—DIVISION A

| Team | Pl | W | L | D | F | A | Pts |
|---|---|---|---|---|---|---|---|
| Duntocher Hibs | 26 | 21 | 2 | 3 | 84 | 33 | 45 |
| Kilsyth Rangers | 27 | 20 | 2 | 5 | 79 | 29 | 45 |
| Petershill | 29 | 17 | 7 | 5 | 79 | 43 | 39 |
| Shettleston | 30 | 13 | 8 | 9 | 65 | 50 | 35 |
| Maryhill | 28 | 14 | 10 | 4 | 84 | 68 | 32 |
| Ashfield | 26 | 13 | 8 | 5 | 62 | 44 | 31 |
| Clydebank | 29 | 13 | 11 | 5 | 61 | 31 | 31 |
| Rob Roy | 29 | 12 | 12 | 5 | 77 | 64 | 29 |
| Bailleston | 29 | 11 | 11 | 6 | 64 | 55 | 28 |
| Blantyre Celtic | 30 | 10 | 13 | 7 | 51 | 62 | 27 |
| Parkhead | 29 | 9 | 12 | 8 | 55 | 57 | 26 |
| Benburb | 28 | 9 | 14 | 5 | 47 | 68 | 23 |
| St.Anthony's | 28 | 6 | 18 | 4 | 33 | 64 | 16 |
| Renfrew | 29 | 5 | 18 | 6 | 47 | 78 | 16 |
| Dunipace | 29 | 6 | 19 | 4 | 47 | 95 | 16 |
| Arthurlie | 29 | 5 | 19 | 5 | 48 | 94 | 15 |

St.Anthony's spent most of the season in the wooden spoon position in the league. They pulled up towards the end of the season and could reflect on an excellent Scottish Junior Cup run.

Benburb had a poor season despite the odd good win. They did reach the final of the Erskine Hospital Cup with a 1-0 win over Pollok. Impressive displays from Mike Jackson in midfield and Tommy Douglas on the wing paved the way with Gavin getting the goal in the first half.
Bens lost the Final.

In the annual match at Parkhead between the top Catholic schools the St.Gerrard's players selected were J.McNally, J.Quinn, I.Lochead, J.Bradley and E.Mowen

**THE FIFTY PITCHES (CARDONALD PARK)**

**MOORE PARK (SAINT ANTHONY'S FOOTBALL CLUB)**

Photo 9

# CHAPTER 9
## SWEDEN HERE WE COME ! (1957-58)

The qualification group for Sweden 1958 saw Scotland in a 3 team section with Spain and Switzerland. Spain were clear favourites but Scotland were thrown a chink of light when Switzerland forced a 2-2 draw in Madrid. If Scotland could beat Spain in their first match they would have a good chance of qualification by beating the unpredictable Swiss in the other matches.

The opening Scotland match saw George Young playing his last match for his country at centre half before retirement. The Spaniards were expected to exploit the big centre half for pace.

SCOTLAND: Younger; Caldow; Hewie; McColl; Young; Docherty; Smith; Collins; Mudie; Baird and Ring

SPAIN: Ramallets; Olivella; Campanal; Garay; Vergas; Zarraga; Miguel; Kubala; Di Stefano; Suarez and Gento

Scotland were inspired by a great captain playing his last home match and attacked for most of the opening period. On 22 minutes a cross was headed against the crossbar and Jackie Mudie scrambled home the loose ball. Spain responded and on 30 minutes Kubala scored an equaliser after a good through ball. The Spaniards were guilty of some cynical fouls and the German referee spotted one in the penalty box on 39th minute. A penalty for Scotland. John Hewie stepped up and hit a poor shot but somehow it eluded the Spanish goalie and the Scots were ahead.

In the second half Spain drew level when Suarez finished of a good move which included some brilliant play from Di Stefano. Scotland were desperate for the win and helped by constant lack of discipline from the Spain team. Scotland regained the lead on 70 minutes when Mudie shot with precision from the edge of the box into the corner of the Spanish net. Hampden roared their approval and the roar went up again nine minutes later when Mudie finished off a good move to complete his hat trick.

RESULT: SCOTLAND 4 SPAIN 2

Scotland travelled to Switzerland buoyed by the victory over Spain. The Swiss took a 13 th minute lead through R.Vonlanthen but after sustained pressure Jackie Mudie equalised on 33 minutes. In the second half Tommy Ring secured the points for Scotland with a 71st minute winner.

The Scots now knew that a home win over the Swiss at Hampden would secure them a place in the World Cup Finals in Sweden.

At Tinto Park there was a surprise close season announcement that Tommy Douglas had been released. He had been bothered by niggling injuries, in particular knee problems. Tommy soon found a new club when Petershill signed him. However, he would have to fight for his place with John Phillips of St.Anthony's also moving to Petershill Park.

The Benburb squad was announced:
Goalkeepers: Andrew Smith; John Kelly (Corkerhill Juveniles)
Full Backs; Gordon Cairns; Maurice Young
Half Backs: Donald Nicholson; Ronald Fitzsimmons (Weirs Recreation);
Kenneth Mac Kay (Port Glasgow Rangers); Jim Mac Cormack; John Thomson
(Ashfield Juveniles)
Forwards: John Mc Alpine; Kenneth Brooks: Anthony Gregal; Michael
Jackson; William Mc Lean; David Drummond
Before the season started Celtic scout and former Benburb legend Teddy
Swift had put a word in the right place and Mike Jackson was on his way to
Celtic Park turning down a move to Manchester United.

Former Benburb, Rangers and Scotland full back Jock 'Tiger' Shaw was
leading Bailleston to success. However after playing in the Lanarkshire Cup
Final against Lesmahagow he was unhappy that the presentation took place in
the boardroom at Douglas Park, Hamilton. Jock felt the Cup should have been
presented on the pitch. Jock was a hard task master at Bailleston in keeping his
players at peak fitness. He often told them about the time he played two games
in one day for Benburb at Cathkin Park. He thoroughly enjoyed the experience.

Park United were attracting good crowds to the tenement surrounded football
pitches at Plantation Park. They were top of the League by just two points from
Cadwadric Bluebell with just two games to go. They met at Plantation Park
and the Bluebell won 4-2 and went on to win the title. However, within a few
days the teams met again at Plantation Park in the semi final of the Glasgow
Cup and this time, inspired by left winger Colin Mc Gilp, the United won 4-1.

In the Dennistoun Waverley tournament at Haghill Park, two of the Govan
Juvenile teams were drawn together with Park United playing Avon Villa;
United winning 5-1.
PARK UNITED: Buchan, Mullins, Gibbons; McIntosh, McAllister, Philbin,
Elliot, Jones, Kearney, Fitzsimmons and Mc Gilp
AVON VILLA: McGennity, Craig, Mooney, McClymonts, Williamson,
Anderson, Nolan, Mc Keshie, Mitchell, Cassidy and Wallace.

At 31 Daviot Street in West Drumoyne Derek was preparing for his first ever
football match. He had been attending the 281st Lifeboys and was invited to
play against another Lifeboy team from Cathcart at the 50 pitches. The first
problem for Derek was getting a pair of football boots. He told his mother who
produced a pair of second hand boots a few days before the match. Derek said '
Maw they look a bit big for me !'. .
Ruth his mother replied 'Nae bother son, all you do is put paper inside the
boots at the toe's'. The boots were leather and had a very big hard toe section
with a strap across the mid section.The ankles were protected with the boot
going above the heel. The laces were tied around the bottom of the boot and
around the ankle section which had a loop.

The Saturday for the match duly arrived and Derek was a bit disconcerted that the 281 were playing in white shirts and black shorts; 'England's' colours. The other side were in dark blue with white shorts 'Scotland's' colours and the players were already saying 'We are Scotland and you are England !'.

The game was a disaster for Derek who played atrociously at left back being given the run around by a tricky winger. The 281st lost 8 goals to 2. With not too many football games thereafter for the 281st Lifeboys, Derek dropped out the lifeboy group; the other activities not being enough to sustain his interest.

The Drumoyne School had a football team at the older age groups. Derek went to all the practice matches but was never good enough to get into the teams. However he watched the team and encouraged his school pals in all their games. Mr. Park was the teacher who organised the team and tended to keep the same players for every match. The Primary School Govan Cup was always keenly contested. Derek watched an older age group from Drumoyne School play     St.Constantine's at Pirrie Park in the Final one year. Two goals from Tiny Duncan had Drumoyne 2-1 ahead at half time but a good St. Constantine side came back and won the cup 3-2 in front of a good excited crowd.

The team to beat most season's in the Govan Cup for Primary Schools was St. Saviours from Central Govan who seemed to produce a procession of good players. The Govan Schools approached St.Anthony's Football Club about holding the Primary Schools Finals at Moore Park and they readily agreed. The ground was to prove a popular venue for the schools teams which reached the finals in subsequent years.

At the 50 pitches the layout of some of the pitches was, to say the least, 'unfortunate'; at least for many of the goalkeepers who played there. A number of the pitches were 'back to back' with the goalposts from one pitch being directly behind the goalposts of the next pitch along. Hence a goalkeeper as well as keeping his eye on the play on his pitch in front of him had to keep an eye on what was coming behind; there being no nets.

Often they would be hit with the ball from the pitch behind, distracting them and allowing their opponents a goal. A few instances saw goalkeepers struck on the head with the heavy bladder ball from behind and felled. If a goal was scored the goalie had often a 40 yard trek to retrieve the ball. St.Anthony's main officials for the forthcoming season were President Alan Kernochan, Match Secretary, John Smith  and Tom Mooney who lived at the Moss Heights.

A player to arrive at Moore Park was Alec Crawford who scored a good goal in a pre season friendly against Saltcoats Vics. Crawford previously played for Ruchazie Hearts where he was a regular scorer.

The St.Anthony's summer Juvenile Tournament was a success and the Final was between Letham Thistle and Penilee at Moore Park. Sean Fallon and Bertie Peacock of Celtic were invited to present the trophies.

Former St.Gerrard's footballer Pater Catterson transferred from Kilmarnock, where he had few first team games, to Third Lanark.

With the new season about to start, the Juvenile (under 21) teams were still catching up on the previous seasons fixtures. During the summer evenings at Plantation Park large crowds were drawn to watch the matches; especially Park United and Avon Villa.

Park United reached two finals. They lost 3-1 to Alder United (Dunbartonshire) in the Glasgow Juvenile Cup but won 4-2 against Ashfield Juveniles to capture the West of Scotland Cup. The United team were also in other cups amid a large backlog of fixtures.

The Clyde Navigation Trust were having an excellent season. The Trust team were usually employed keeping the River Clyde clear for the shipping. The Trust had reached the semi Final of the Scottish Welfare Cup as well as winning the Glasgow Welfare league. They had also reached the semi final of the Rangers Cup. John Docherty had scored over 60 goals for the team and Jimmy Thomson was averaging two goals per match. Ex Queen's Park Bob Mc Kirdy and experienced centre half Alex Mc Intyre were key players.

The Govan Police team hoped to make it a double after reaching the league decider against Southern. Mc Dermid and a Neil penalty had the Govan side level at 2-2 until the last minute. Then Southern were awarded a penalty which they converted and won 3-2.

Benburb's David Mc Cracken was elected as President of the West of Scotland Junior Football Association. He was a popular choice and with a good business acumen and drive. The prospects for the Juniors seemed good.

Team building at Benburb was dealt a blow before a ball was kicked for the new season. Classy midfielder Mike Jackson was in demand from both Manchester United and Celtic and it was to Parkhead that Jackson went to provide his signature for senior football. Mike had been training with Celtic and reserve team manager Jock Stein was greatly impressed. He said ' Watch that boy making a hit as a senior. He has the ability to reach the top'. Stein was keen to develop the talents of the young Mike Jackson.

Benburb signed Govan High's Robert Burns who played on the left wing. He was a Scotland schoolboy international and a keen Benburb supporter. His family had a long tradition of involvement with the club.

The Hospital League was played during the summer months. The Southern General Hospital were relegated during the previous season but were making a determined effort to gain promotion.

131

# GLASGOW AND DISTRICT HOSPITAL LEAGUE

| Team | Pl | W | L | D | F | A | Pts |
|------|----|----|----|----|----|----|----|
| Southern General Hospital | 14 | 12 | 2 | 0 | 63 | 25 | 24 |
| Ruchill | 11 | 9 | 2 | 0 | 51 | 16 | 18 |
| C.Hotel | 13 | 8 | 4 | 1 | 49 | 32 | 17 |
| Waterlows | 11 | 7 | 2 | 2 | 43 | 24 | 16 |
| Coathill | 12 | 7 | 3 | 2 | 37 | 28 | 10 |
| Bus Works | 10 | 2 | 6 | 2 | 19 | 30 | 6 |
| Govan F.S. | 12 | 2 | 8 | 2 | 31 | 46 | 6 |
| Assessors | 11 | 1 | 9 | 2 | 25 | 54 | 4 |
| S.E.A. | 12 | 1 | 12 | 1 | 21 | 62 | 3 |

Rangers were in a group which contained Partick Thistle, Raith Rovers and St.Mirren.

Rangers were expected to win the section. However, in the end they were left hanging on during the last match at Kirkcaldy against Raith Rovers. Raith won 4-3 and had Rangers on the rack for much of the match. With the retirement of George Young at the centre of the 'Gers' defence a huge void had to be filled. Rangers turned to John Valentine of Queen's Park to replace Young. There was much criticism of Scot Symon's decision from much of the Rangers support. Valentine had an excellent season with Queen's Park in the top league.

However, he did not commit himself to full time professional football preferring to be part time. He continued to live in the North East Scotland area and carried on with a sales rep job. The Ibrox faithful felt the day would come when he would be 'found out'.

| League Cup Section 2 | Pl | W | L | D | F | A | Pts |
|------|----|----|----|----|----|----|----|
| Rangers | 6 | 4 | 2 | 0 | 18 | 10 | 8 |
| Raith Rovers | 6 | 4 | 2 | 0 | 16 | 10 | 8 |
| St.Mirren | 6 | 3 | 3 | 0 | 5 | 14 | 6 |
| Partick Thistle | 6 | 1 | 5 | 0 | 4 | 9 | 2 |

Rangers were drawn against Kilmarnock in the quarter finals. In the first match Killie won 2-1. The second match was a tense affair. Rangers had young Moles at centre half for John Valentine. Rangers support were unhappy that Don Kitchenbrand had been left out of the side. The Ibrox side went ahead with a Johnny Hubbard penalty but Killie were level before half time when Black headed in. Rangers attacked non stop in the second half but were thwarted by some stout defending by the Ayrshire men as the clock ticked down. A quarter of an hour from the end Alex Scott scored to bring the sides level. In the final few minutes Jimmy Brown in the Killie goal spilled a high cross and Billy Simpson scored to send Rangers through and please most of the 60,000 crowd.

Celtic all but secured a semi final place with a thumping 6-1 Parkhead win over Third Lanark. The return match at Cathkin Park saw Peter Catterson (former St.Gerrard's) make his Thirds debut. He was involved in most of the Thirds` better moments but this failed to prevent a 3-0 Celtic win and a 9-1 aggregate success.

Rangers met Brechin City in the semi final at Hampden Park. A gallant effort was not enough from Brechin and the Ibrox side won easily with four unopposed goals from Harry Melrose (2) , Shearer (pen) and a Patterson own goal.

The other semi final at Ibrox Park was an all Glasgow affair with Celtic taking on Clyde. Celtic went 2-0 ahead in the first half with goals from Wilson and the impressive Billy McPhail. Keogh scored for Clyde before half time and in the second period Innes equalised with a deflected shot. Celtic soon regained the lead when Bobby Collins ran through the Clyde defence to score and Eric Smith finished off a good hoops passing bout. Celtic were in the final and a date with destiny with their Old Firm rivals Rangers.

Rangers were playing in the European Cup for the second time. A visit from St. Etienne was keenly anticipated and 85,000 turned up for the first leg at Ibrox Park.

Ongoing injuries to John Valentine saw Harold David play at centre half.
RANGERS: Niven, Shearer, Caldow, McColl, Davis, Baird, Scott, Simpson, Kitchenbrand, Murray and Hubbard
ST.ETIENNE: Abbes, M.Tylinski, R,Tylinski, Wicart, Domingo, Baptiste-Bordas, N'Jo-Lea, Mekhloufi, Ferrier, Goujon and Lefevre

Like Nice during the previous year, the French side were extremely physical and made few friends with the Ibrox fans with some of the tackles. On 14 minutes they stunned the Ibrox crowd when Mekloufi opened the scoring. Rangers responded with all out attack and the physical presence of Don Kitchenbrand was reaping rewards for the 'Gers. It was Kitchenbrand who brought Rangers level on 19 minutes with a good header.

St.Etienne held on until half time despite intense Rangers pressure. Rangers got the breakthrough early in the second half through Alex Scott at which point St.Ettiene discipline went out of the window. A few minutes after the Scott goal one of the Tylinski brothers got his marching orders by the referee for a cynical foul.

Rangers attacked non stop thereafter and should have scored many times. The only goal they got came on 83 minutes from Billy Simpson.

RESULT: RANGERS 3 ST.ETIENNE 1

John Valentine returned for the second match at St. Etienne playing centre half. Ferrier gave the French side the lead and that is how it stayed until half time. Davie Wilson scored an equaliser on 61 minutes to stun the French support. Despite a late second goal for St. Etienne, Rangers held on to progress to the next round.

Benburb signed Ronnie McKinnon a promising young inside left from the Govan Methodists team. The Bens got off to a good start in the league and were four goals up at half time during a trip to Renfrew. Coyne (2), Gregal and Syme being the scorer's.

A big support came up from Ayrshire for the West of Scotland Cup match against Auchinleck Talbot.

BENBURB: Kelly, Young, Cairns, Thomson, Nicholson, Fitzsimmons, Syme, McLean, Stevenson, Gregal and Taylor

AUCHINLECK TALBOT: Candish, Ritchie, Boyd, Currie, Luggie, Gibson, McAffer, Rae, McDowell, Cunliffe and Duff

Bens were on top throughout the match. Young scored from the penalty spot midway through the first half and Stevenson added a second before the break. In the second half the Bens ran riot with Stevenson scoring two more to complete his hat trick. Thomson and Gregal added two more late strikes. The Ayrshire club pegged away and were rewarded with a consolation goal.

RESULT: BENBURB 6 AUCHINLECK TALBOT 1

Govan Amateurs gained an early season 1-1 away draw at Laidlaw. The team was:

Salisbury Tinley, Ferguson, Crichton, A. McKie, Galloway, Hetherington, Montgomery, Clark, W. McKie and Cuthbertson

Peter Kane the St. Constantine's centre forward signed for Petershill Juniors. Almost immediately he became a fans favourite as he scored on a regular basis for the Peasies. During an early season match against Blantyre Victoria he scored five goals including a cheeky back healer.

The Scottish Junior Cup saw both the Govan sides drawn away.
St.Anthony's travelled to Stonehouse Violet and a stormy game ensued. The home side won 3-1 helped by a very disputed penalty. Ants fan Patrick Blair was so incensed that he ran on the pitch and punched the referee. Two days later at Hamilton Sheriff Court he was fined £7 with the option of 30 days in prison.

Benburb travelled down to South Ayrshire for a meeting with Kello Rovers. The large Bens support saw the Rovers take the lead through Craig mid way through the second half. In the second half Benburb piled on the pressure and got a deserved equaliser to force a replay.

The replay at Tinto Park saw an easy win for the Bens in front of their own Govan support. Tony Gregal gave them a first half lead and in the second half they added four more unopposed goals with Stevenson and Syme getting on the score sheet.

Benburb's reward for the win over Kello Rovers was a tricky trip to Douglasdale; the club which had scored four past the Bens to knock them out during the previous season.

Benburb took good support to Lanarkshire with each of the three larger local shipyards advertising the match well and filling at least one coach each with their workers. Benburb were determined lightning was not going to strike twice. The first half saw Benburb on top at Crabtree Park but somehow the 'dale' held out. However, intense pressure in the second half brought the goal from the Bens and they were in the next round.

Rangers and Celtic met in the Scottish League Cup Final at Hampden Park.
CELTIC: Beattie, Donnelly, Fallon, Fernie, Evans, Peacock, Tully, Collins, Mc Phail, Wilson and Mochan
RANGERS: Niven, Shearer, Caldow, McColl, Valentine, Davis, Scott, Simpson, Murray, Baird and Hubbard

In the first few minutes a fiercely driven cross from Neil Mochan hit Valentine on the head and sent him reeling. After recovering, Celtic were foraging towards the Rangers goal virtually non stop. A 30 yard free kick from Collins crashed off the crossbar with Niven beaten. Rangers survived until half way through the first half when Wilson scored following a well placed corner from Charlie Tully.

George Niven was working overtime in the Rangers goal pulling off several brave saves. However, on the stroke of half time Neil Mochan dribbled past Bobby Shearer and from a tight angle scored a second for Celtic.

The second half continued along the same pattern and it soon became evident that Rangers were to be on the wrong end of a hammering. Max Murray was moved to the left wing hobbling with his leg heavily strapped.

Rangers, despite a re-shuffled attack, took the game to Celtic in the early stages of the second half but had a let off when Niven produced an excellent stop from Collins when all seemed lost. However Collins was soon provider to Celtic's third goal on 53 minutes when he crossed from the right. John Valentine went up to head but missed the ball and Billy Mc Phail headed in for number three.

Rangers got on the score sheet when they had a bit of luck. A long ball looked as though it was going out for a goal kick. Alex. Scott had not given up the chase. The ball struck the corner post and rebounded into play. Scott fed Mc Coll who crossed for Billy Simpson to head a Rangers goal. For ten minutes Rangers battled to retrieve the Final.

However a Celtic goal on 68 minutes ended all hopes. A Neil Mochan corner saw Billy Mc Phail rise completely unchallenged to head in number four. The Celtic fans were in joyous mood, it was now a case of how many they would score. Mochan added a fifth with a first time shot. Mc Phail scored from close range after Rangers defence failed to clear and Willie Fernie added the seventh just before the full time whistle from the penalty spot.

RESULT: CELTIC 7 RANGERS 1

There were a number of arrests made and 10 Rangers fans appeared in front of Glasgow Magistrates for causing trouble after Celtic scored the fourth goal. They were detained for four days. A 16 year old appeared in Govan Juvenile Court and he was detained for 4 days in a remand home.

At Pirrie Park the older Govan High age group had a resounding 7-0 win over Rutherglen Academy. The team was Barron, Bickerstaff, Wood, Jardine, Crichton, Reid, Bowie, Mc Lean, Murray, Callen and Burt.
In the same division both Bellahouston and St.Gerrard's were trying to restore fortunes;

Bellahouston regular team: Kennedy, Simpson, Whitelaw, Miller, Beattie , Phillip, Mc Callum, Thompson, Tait, Browning and Melvin

St.Gerrards regular team: Haddock, O'Donnell, Mc Nally, Gallacher, Mc Combs, Hagan, Herron, Bradley, McBeth, Haughey and McGee

Govan High pulled off a surprise result when they beat the League title holders St.Mungo's and the race at the top was close.

The School's Association expressed concern regarding over enthusiastic parents at matches. Two matches involving Govan teams were cited. A match between St.Gerrard's at Eastbank won 4-3 by the Govan School. Also, Bellahouston Academy v Govan High won 2-1 by Govan High. The Schools football association expected the matches to be played in a gentlemanly spirit.

In the 3rd Round of the Scottish Junior Cup another big crowd were drawn to Tinto Park. A fair number came from Provanmill to support their team St.Roch's.

An exciting match saw the sides level at half time with Tony Gregal scoring for the Bens and Rooney replying for the Candy. The second half saw both sides find the net once each and it was a replay at Provanmill Park.

Widespread predictions were that the visit of Benburb for the replay would see the ground record broken.

ST.ROCH'S: Melklam, Gallacher, Dolan, McClafferty, Wallace, McInally, Duff, Sinclair, McMillan, McNeil and Hales

BENBURB: Kelly, Young, Cairns, McCormack, Nicholson, MacKay, Alexander, Mc Alpine, Stevenson, Gregal and Syme.

At the start the Govan support gave a huge roar for the Bens. It paid off as in the first attack Jim Mac Cormack set up Stevenson for the opening goal. Play went from end to end in a typical Junior Cup tie fashion and St.Roch's drew level before half time. Kelly could only palm a high cross out to the wing. A return cross left Hales with the chance to equalise.

In the second half the Bens had a slight edge on chances created and from a crossfield pass Alexander became the Bens hero when he scored from close range. Benburb held on and moved into the fourth round.

RESULT: ST.ROCH'S 1 BENBURB 2

Tony Gregal who gave many good performances for Benburb signed provisionally for St. Mirren. The 4th round draw saw Benburb drawn away to Clydebank. The interest in the match was considerable and television highlights were to be shown during a ten minute slot on the evening following the match. Bens were negotiating with the Army to get their three players in uniform (Jim Mc Cormack; Jack Taylor and Billy Syme) available for the trip to Kilbowie Park.

At Dunterlie Park young Govan player Ronnie Mc Kinnon made his debut for Benburb in the 3-0 reverse to Arthurlie.

Former Bens player Tommy Douglas was recovering from the removal of a cartilage in his knee during an injury hit spell at Petershill.

In the Glasgow Schools league's the Govan challenge was coming from Govan High at the oldest age group and St.Gerrard's in the next age group down. New school Lourdes were doing well at the youngest age group. However at the oldest age group Govan High lost in the Scottish Schools Shield at Coatbridge High by 4-1.

In the Govan Primary Schools League the latest results were:
Hillington 3 Elder Park 6; Greenfield 8 Fairfield 0; Hill's Trust 0 Lorne Street 4.

# GLASGOW SECONDARY JUVENILE LEAGUE DIV.A

| Team | Pl | W | L | D | F | A | Pts |
|------|----|----|----|----|----|----|-----|
| St.Constantines | 9 | 5 | 1 | 3 | 25 | 14 | 13 |
| Pollok Hawthorn | 6 | 4 | 0 | 2 | 25 | 8 | 10 |
| Rutherglen Waverley | 6 | 4 | 0 | 2 | 23 | 15 | 10 |
| Govan Methodists | 9 | 4 | 3 | 2 | 27 | 22 | 10 |
| Cowglen | 8 | 4 | 4 | 0 | 22 | 14 | 8 |
| Butters | 7 | 4 | 3 | 0 | 21 | 35 | 8 |
| Copland Rangers | 5 | 3 | 1 | 1 | 22 | 15 | 7 |
| Regent Star | 6 | 3 | 2 | 1 | 19 | 15 | 7 |
| Corkerhill | 5 | 2 | 1 | 2 | 11 | 7 | 6 |
| Stonelaw | 8 | 2 | 5 | 1 | 26 | 23 | 5 |
| Rancel | 5 | 0 | 5 | 0 | 5 | 15 | 0 |
| Drumchapel Thistle | 8 | 0 | 8 | 0 | 15 | 45 | 0 |

The aftermath of the Celtic 7-1 triumph over Rangers resulted in chants of 'seven-seven-seven' at most Celtic matches. Also 'What is the time ? Seven past Niven !'

*A Rhyme sent in to the Evening Times.*

*So mighty 'Gers have fallen from grace. Gosh !, What a blow to the human race.*
*Oh wad some power the giftie gie them. Tae skelp Celts when next they see them.*
*This really was a great debacle. And some will want Symon to sack all.*
*But dear Rabbie would have had a line. To comfort him at this sad time.*
*Always play the game as best ye can. Never forgettin yer brither man.*
*He has got to win some of the time. Not always to be beaten at full time.*
*This sad tale might go on forever. But then I am not a Burns or Reiver.*
*Let it be said I'm a Thirds supporter. And hope this week they'll play a snorter.*

Thos Craig, 24, Quadrant Road, Glasgow, S3

Rangers 2nd Round tie against Milan proved to be very one sided in the Italians favour. At Ibrox Park in the first leg they gained a 4-1 lead with Max Murray getting the Rangers goal. The second leg was a formality and Milan won through 2-1 on the night and 6-2 on aggregate.

Impressive performer for Rangers was new centre half Willie Telfer from St.Mirren.

Brechin City were a patient club. After their League Cup semi final against Rangers at Hampden Park they wrote polite letters to the Scottish Football Association requesting their share of the gate money. With no response they went public and eventually their share of the gate was provided. At the same time Celtic were complaining they never received their share of the gate money from their Ibrox Park semi final. Eventually it was paid with Rangers saying an admin delay had held up things.

Govan Amateurs and Stephens led their respective divisions in the West of Scotland Amateur League.

Former Benburb favourite Dunky Rae returned to football after a spell out helping his wife with twins. However the spell did not last long and he was released by his club Clydebank.

Benburb were having a reasonable season and had some good performers. Sam Stevenson was a regular goalscorer. Maurice Young and Gordon Cairns were reliable full backs. Donnie Nicholson was a solid centre half and John Mac Kay was a useful mid field player. They were looking forward to the big upcoming match against Clydebank in the Scottish Junior Cup.

Benburb had a huge support travel over to Kilbowie Park. The Bens fans were confident of victory.

CLYDEBANK: Devlin, Miller, E.McCreadie, Mills, Crawford, Elliot, J.McCready, Mc Guigan, McLaughlin, Frickleton and Davies.

BENBURB: Smith, Young, Cairns, McCormack, Nicholson, McKay, Syme, Drummond, Stevenson, Gregal and Taylor.

In a foggy day both sides struggled to break down the opposing defence. Syme had a headed chance for the Bens but headed straight at Devlin. Near half time the bankies took the lead when J.Mc Creadie crossed for Mc Laughlin to head into the net.

The second half saw Benburb do a lot of attacking, force a lot of corners and miss several chances but they were unable to get the equaliser. As in the first half ,with just three minutes remaining, the Bankies scored an identical goal. J. McCreadie crossed and McLaughlin headed into the net. The Bens were out despite having most of the game.

RESULT: CLYDEBANK 2 BENBURB  0

Scotland had two attempts offered to them to reach the World Cup Finals. A win over Spain or Switzerland would secure the place.

The first chance in Madrid saw Scotland lose heavily. Matoes (11) and Kabula (33) scored for the Spaniards in the first half. Basora (60 and 87) added two more and a Smith goal was not enough to prevent a 4-1 reverse.

A second and final chance awaited Scotland with the last match against Switzerland at Hampden Park.

SCOTLAND: Younger, Parker, Caldow, Fernie, Evans, Docherty, Scott, Collins, Mudie, Robertson and Ring

SWITZERLAND: Parlier, Kernan, Morf, Grobety, Koch, Schnelter, Chlesa, Ballaman, Meler, Vonlanden and Riva

Scotland started nervously and the crowd became impatient. However Scotland took the lead on the half hour when Tommy Docherty won a tackle in midfield and put a pass through for Archie Robertson to draw the keeper and score with a low shot. The Swiss responded with a goal soon after. Docherty having set up the Scotland goal helped the Swiss with a poor cross field ball. Riva was the beneficiary and ran through to smash the ball beyond Tommy Younger.

Just on half time Jackie Mudie headed against the crossbar.

Scotland came out for the second half with all guns blazing and on 52 minutes Willie Fernie beat three defenders before crossing for Jackie Mudie to convert. The crowd were relieved. On 70 minutes Scotland had a huge slice of luck when a through ball found Alex. Scott well offside. However the whistle was not blown and the linesman's flag not raised. Scott ran on and put the ball in the net as the Swiss defenders stood appealing. Vonlanden scored for Switzerland on 80 minutes setting up a tense finish. Scotland hung on and were in the World Cup Finals.

| Qualifying Group 9 | Pl | W | L | D | F | A | Pts |
|---|---|---|---|---|---|---|---|
| Scotland | 4 | 3 | 1 | 0 | 12 | 9 | 6 |
| Spain | 4 | 2 | 1 | 1 | 12 | 8 | 5 |
| Switzerland | 4 | 0 | 3 | 1 | 6 | 11 | 1 |

Northern Ireland pulled off a major surprise when they defeated much fancied Italy at Windsor Park, Belfast by 2-1. Mc Ilroy and Cush got the Irish goals.

All four home countries had qualified for the 1958 World Cup Finals. It was announced that a great number of games would be televised.

Rangers trip to Celtic Park for the New Years day fixture was eagerly awaited. Rangers were thirsting for revenge after the 7-1 mauling by Celtic in the Scottish League Cup Final. However, the sides had several changes for different reasons. Celtic had half their normal side out through injury and big John Colrain the former St.Anthony's player was at centre forward. Rangers form after the Scottish League Cup Final had been poor until a few weeks before the match.

New younger players were brought in with Ralph Brand and Davie Wilson on the wings. Alex.Scott played at centre forward for the injured Max Murray.

A frozen pitch made life difficult for the players. Sean Fallon had difficulty against Brand from the outset and it was Alex. Scott who gave Rangers the victory with the only goal of the match. Hearts seemed to have an unassailable lead in the league.

## SCOTTISH LEAGUE DIVISION 1

| Team | Pl | W | L | D | F | A | Pts |
|------|----|----|----|----|----|----|-----|
| Hearts | 20 | 17 | 1 | 2 | 77 | 19 | 36 |
| Clyde | 18 | 12 | 5 | 1 | 50 | 31 | 25 |
| Rangers | 16 | 10 | 3 | 3 | 42 | 24 | 23 |
| Hibernian | 20 | 11 | 8 | 1 | 40 | 30 | 23 |
| Raith Rovers | 20 | 9 | 6 | 5 | 38 | 26 | 23 |
| Celtic | 17 | 9 | 4 | 4 | 36 | 20 | 22 |
| Aberdeen | 19 | 10 | 8 | 1 | 44 | 36 | 21 |
| Kilmarnock | 19 | 9 | 8 | 2 | 35 | 35 | 20 |
| Partick Thistle | 20 | 9 | 9 | 2 | 44 | 51 | 20 |
| Third Lanark | 19 | 9 | 9 | 1 | 45 | 45 | 19 |
| Falkirk | 20 | 7 | 8 | 5 | 41 | 52 | 19 |
| Motherwell | 18 | 7 | 9 | 2 | 36 | 40 | 16 |
| St.Mirren | 20 | 7 | 11 | 2 | 38 | 41 | 16 |
| Queen of the South | 21 | 6 | 11 | 4 | 31 | 46 | 16 |
| Airdrie | 20 | 7 | 13 | 0 | 35 | 61 | 14 |
| Dundee | 20 | 6 | 12 | 2 | 25 | 48 | 14 |
| East Fife | 20 | 5 | 12 | 3 | 29 | 57 | 13 |
| Queen's Park | 19 | 3 | 16 | 0 | 24 | 59 | 6 |

Park United were faltering with their form in the Juvenile world. First they got knocked out of the West of Scotland Cup at Plantation Park 4-1 by Shettleston Violet. Then they lost 6-3 at Shotts Victoria amid a rumpus. Tommy Philbin was sent off 6 minutes from the end and after a row the match was abandoned.

A happier occasion for Park United was the visit to Miss Barrier's tea rooms in Glasgow to be presented with the West of Scotland Juvenile Cup from the previous season.

Copland Rangers players were in constant demand with virtually all of the team being invited to Junior Clubs for trials. These included:
Right back Albert McKenna; Right half Tom Hutchison; Inside right Charles McPherson; Centre Forward James Hazelton; Inside left James Williamson and outside left Donald McAskill

The side also had the distinction of being the first Juvenile side to play under floodlights. Partick Thistle invited them to play their Collins Cup tie against L. Pieters at Firhill.

At Shieldhall Stephens beat Arbecco 3-2 in the Amateur League. The team was:
STEPHEN'S : Frew, McIntosh, McConnell, Carroll, Hillhouse, Connelly, McManus, Hackett, Kennedy, Thomson and Allen.

In the Former Pupils league's Govan High were having a decent season lying fourth in the First Division. In the Second Division Bellahouston Academy were top by one point from Vale of Leven B while St.Gerrard's were third seven points behind.

Former Benburb, Rangers and Scotland full back Jock 'Tiger' Shaw was none to happy with referee Mr. Kelly when he called the fixture off. As trainer of Bailleston he and an army of helpers cleared snow from the Station Park pitch for the match against Douglas Water Thistle. Jock not to be outdone played a practice game on the pitch.

There were countless tributes to the retired Rangers and Scotland centre half George Young. An inspiration on the pitch and a gentleman off the pitch. This letter was sent to the Evening Times from John Penman.
*' I am an 11 year old and being a victim of polio I went into Falkirk Infirmary a year ago having an operation on my foot and leg. The school janitor promised that if I was home when Rangers played Hearts at Tynecastle he would take me in to the match.*
*I was taken to the match on crutches and we stood at the gates of Tynecastle until the Rangers bus came in. I saw big Geordie and shyly asked him for his autograph. He patted me on the head and said '' Yes my son''. He took the book and got all the other players to sign it to.*
*It is a memory I will always treasure'.*

In the Juniors Central League Cup, Benburb lost out to Strathclyde at Tinto Park by a score of 2-0. Former Govan Methodists Juvenile player Ronnie Mc Kinnon was playing in his favoured inside right slot.

Avon Villa crashed out of the Scottish Juvenile Cup losing in the last sixteen to Hunting Tower.

Former St.Gerrards' centre forward Ian Lochead was playing for a number of different teams. These included Drumchapel Amateurs, Glasgow Schools and Scotland Schools. In addition he was being tempted by Renfrew Juniors and also from a distance by Celtic. A player who also was playing games for Drumchapel Amateurs was Bobby Burns a former Govan High and Schoolboy International

In the Scottish Amateur Cup match between Govan Amateurs and Troqueer, tempers flared. Govan Amateurs felt the referee was terrible and asked the Association to appoint a new referee for the replay after the sides drew 2-2. The Association refused and the same referee was in position at Dumfries for the replay.

The 'Doonhammers' team had not lost a home match for several years in all competitions and the Govan cause looked hopeless. However, a major upset took place as Govan Amateurs smashed the Troqueer record, winning 5-0.

In a small Scottish League Mosspark were the winners of the Scottish under 16 League. Each team played their opponents 4 times each.

## SCOTTISH AMATER LEAGUE UNDER 16

| Team | Pl | W | L | D | F | A | Pts |
|---|---|---|---|---|---|---|---|
| Mosspark | 11 | 9 | 2 | 0 | 70 | 14 | 18 |
| Giffnock North | 10 | 5 | 4 | 1 | 15 | 27 | 11 |
| Drumchapel | 9 | 4 | 3 | 2 | 40 | 13 | 10 |
| Stephens | 10 | 0 | 9 | 1 | 7 | 90 | 1 |

There was a major surprise when the Catholic Primary Schools team was selected. Not one Govan player made the squad despite more than useful players within the St.Anthony's, St.Saviour's and St.Constantine's teams.

The Govan Primary School League produced some emphatic wins. Hills Trust 0 Elder Park 8; Lorne Street 1 Elder Park 5; Hills Trust 2 Fairfield 3; Greenfield 1 Hillington 1; Fairfield 1 Lorne Street 3; Greenfield 3 Bellahouston 2; Elder Park 0 Gowanbank 3

With Hearts almost out of sight and heading for the Scottish Division 1 title Rangers were hoping for a good Scottish Cup run. In their 1st Round match they were drawn away to Cowdenbeath and attracted just under 17,000 spectators. Cowdenbeath sent their support wild when Gilfillan scored an early goal which they held on to until half time. The second half saw Rangers pressure and they were rewarded with three unopposed goals from Billy Simpson followed by a brace by Max Murray.

Rangers then travelled to Station Park, Forfar and scored freely. John Hubbard opened the scoring on 8 minutes and two goals in a minute from Ralph Brand and Max Murray ended the game as a contest mid way through the first half. Billy Simpson added a fourth on half time. The second half was much the same and the 'Gers kept the scoreboard ticking over. Murray, Simpson and Ian McColl took the tally to seven just after the hour. Brand and Murray added two more before the biggest cheer of the afternoon went to Craig of the Loons who headed a consolation goal.

For the third round in a row Rangers were given an away tie against 2nd Division opposition. However, with Dunfermline in the promotion race a tricky tie was predicted.McWilliams opened the scoring for the Pars. However, Rangers responded with goals from Max Murray and Ralph Brand. The second half was very even and scoreless leaving the 'Gers progressing into the quarter final stage.

The quarter final's saw Rangers away again this time to Queen of the South at Dumfries. Max Murray gave Rangers an early lead and on 20 minutes Billy Simpson headed home the second. Black reduced the arrears after some pressure and Jim Patterson brought the house down with an equaliser on the stroke of half time. In the second half Rangers regained the lead when former Bellahouston Academy schoolboy John Duncan went on a run down the wing and crossed for Jimmy Miller to convert. The Doon hammers equalised after Sammy Baird handled a cross in the penalty box giving a penalty to the home side. Billy Ritchie pulled off a great save from Patterson but while Rangers celebrated Black crossed in the loose ball and Jim Patterson scored. Rangers got the winner when a long run from the half way line by Max Murray saw him sweep the ball into the net and Rangers were in the semi finals. With Max Murray appearing more often in the side the scope for big South African centre forward Don Basil Kichenbrand were limited. Kichenbrand was popular with the Rangers supporters and when Murray was announced as playing at Ibrox Park ahead of Kichenbrand many supporters booed. Like John Valentine Max Murray was a part time player and the 'Gers support wanted more commitment especially after the 7-1 humiliation from Celtic. Kich was an automatic choice for the side until the previous close season. Then he suffered appendicitis and was waylaid for a lengthy period. After scoring 27 goals for Rangers he transferred to Sunderland where he scored goals soon after his arrival.

St.Anthony's were not having a good season. Goal scorer Alec Crawford had missed a number of matches with the team. The Ants had injury problems and this resulted in Crawford playing several different positions including left back. However, as the injuries subsided, Alec Crawford was restored to his favoured centre forward position for the visit of high flying Johnstone Burgh. The Ants produced a top class performance and Alec Crawford was amongst the goals as they trounced the Burgh 5-2 at Moore Park.

Benburb were having a good season but without challenging for the league title. A highlight was a 10-3 win over Dennistoun Waverley at Tinto Park.

In the Scottish Junior Cup Jock 'Tiger' Shaw the Bailleston trainer was pleased to see his side reach the semi final of the Scottish Junior Cup. They beat Yoker 3-1 at home in the quarter final. Clydebank who knocked Benburb out were two goals up at Shotts in the first half. Then they had Miller sent off and Shotts equalised in the second half.

At Kilbowie Park in the replay Shotts won 4-2.

Stephen's entered the home straight in the Glasgow Welfare League looking to bring the title back to Govan. St. Saviours also harboured hopes.

## GLASGOW WELFARE YOUTH LEAGUE

| Team | Pl | W | D | L | F | A | Pts |
|---|---|---|---|---|---|---|---|
| Stephen's | 15 | 12 | 2 | 1 | 86 | 25 | 26 |
| St.Margaret's | 14 | 11 | 1 | 2 | 92 | 21 | 23 |
| Dennistoun Juv.A. | 15 | 9 | 2 | 4 | 51 | 11 | 20 |
| St.Saviour's | 11 | 8 | 2 | 1 | 47 | 18 | 18 |
| Brown's YC | 13 | 7 | 1 | 5 | 43 | 16 | 15 |
| Shanks | 15 | 7 | 1 | 7 | 57 | 58 | 15 |
| Regent Star A | 15 | 7 | 0 | 8 | 48 | 44 | 14 |
| Templeton YC | 15 | 5 | 0 | 10 | 36 | 79 | 10 |
| Post Office YC | 11 | 4 | 1 | 6 | 28 | 49 | 9 |
| Elmbank BC | 8 | 2 | 0 | 6 | 20 | 42 | 4 |
| Rolls Royce Apps. | 12 | 1 | 0 | 11 | 17 | 82 | 2 |
| South Shawlands | 12 | 0 | 0 | 12 | 12 | 79 | 0 |

In the West of Scotland Amateur League top division Govan Amateurs held a narrow lead of one point from Rhu with a few games left. In the second division Stephen's also held a narrow lead from several clubs.

Former St. Gerrard's school player Joe McBride was making a hit at Kilmarnock and scoring on a frequent basis.

St.Gerrard's had a League decider against Camphill.

ST.GERRARDS'S: Hughes, Wright, McMillan, Mc Phee, Dignon, McHenry, Neary, McDermott, Millerick, Okney, and Kelly

CAMPHILL: More, Quinn, Harkness, Henderson, Thompson, Tannahill, Struthers, Blackwood, Ainslie, Sproul and Bowie

St.Gerrard's got off to a poor start in a very rough match. Struthers gave Camphill an early lead. Then Millerick missed a penalty for the Govan school. On half time McDermott scrambled in an equaliser for St.Gerrards.

St.Gerrard's were well on top in the second half but from a breakaway Blackwood gave Camphill the lead. The Saints continued piling on the pressure and were rewarded when Neary scored. However from the re-start Camphill forced a corner from which Sproul scored. St.Gerrard's were awarded a second penalty and Millerick made no mistake.

RESULT: ST.GERRARD'S 3 CAMPHILL 3

Trials for the Glasgow School's team and also the Scotland Schools team for a match against England at Champion Hill Dulwich were held. The trials contained two Govan High players (W. Murray and A. Ferguson); one Bellahouston player (A. Whitelaw) and one St.Gerrard's player (P.McDonald). England won a close match 4-3.

In the Glasgow v London match at Hampden Park, Glasgow took an early lead from Peter Mc Donald (St.Gerrard's) . However London hit back and ran out easy 4-1 winners. Alex Ferguson (Govan High) had a penalty saved at 1-3. In the Bradford v Glasgow match Murray from Govan High scored the goal for Glasgow early on. However, Bradford battled back and equalised, the match ending 1-1.

Govan were having some success in the School's competitions.

Bellahouston reached the final of the Senior Shield against Dalziel High. The sides met at Hampden Park in front of a number of excited school supporters. McCallum of Bellahouston burst through the Dalziel defence and scored with a 25 yard shot on 20 minutes. This proved to be the winning goal, Bellahouston winning 1-0. St.Gerrard's reached the play off's in the League Decider's at the oldest age group. In the semi final the match against Whitehill was played at Lesser Hampden Park. Extra time was needed before St.Gerrard's got the winner and won 2-1. In the Final they played Holyrood at Hampden Park and a good match ended 2-2  The replay at Cathkin Park proved to be another exciting match and ended 3-3. The 2nd Replay was at Firhill Park.

St.Gerrard's led 2-1 until the last few minutes. A Holyrood free kick on the edge of the box crashed against the crossbar. St.Gerrard's went down the other end and were awarded a penalty which was converted. This gave St. Gerrard's the First Division Shield for the first time.

At the youngest school's age group Lourdes were the League Champions. Former St. Gerrard's player Peter Catterson was released by Third Lanark and signed for Junior side Duntocher Hibs.

The Old Firm were concerned about overcrowding on the away team terraces.

- At Green Street, Bridgeton the entire management and virtually all the players of both Clyde and Celtic attended the funeral of nine year old James Ryan who was killed when a wall collapsed at Shawfield. The street was packed with mourners as the hearse drove out towards the cemetery.

- At Palmerston Park, Dumfries a number of spectators were injured at the Queen of the South match against Rangers. A smashed crush barrier caused many men, women and children to be crushed and they were taken onto the pitch surround. Eventually the whole pitch side was full of spectators as the game carried on.

Govan Amateurs were the victim of a shock result against Scottish Cables (Renfrew) in the West of Scotland Amateur Cup. Like any good self respecting Govan side that is victim of a shock result they lodged a protest suggesting Eddie McLean, for the winners, was a professional.

Glasgow schoolboys beat Lanarkshire at Broomfield Park, Airdrie by 2-0. Both goals were scored by Govan High players, A. Ferguson after 2 minutes and W. Murray with a late strike.

In the Amateur International at Wembley, England got off to a good start when Hamm scored after 15 minutes. Scotland who had no fewer than seven Queen's Park players in the side equalised through winger Orr. Orr who was a spider scored again soon after to give the Scots the lead before Bradley equalised against the run of play before half time. In the second half Scotland were on top for the most part and Orr completed his hat trick to give Scotland a 3-2 win. Due to the meagre attendance at the match the series was discontinued.

In the Scottish Juvenile Consolation Cup Tadeston Holmlea were having a good run. In one of the latter rounds they welcomed Fife team Townhill to the 50 Pitches. The Consolation Cup was for clubs knocked out in the early rounds of the Scottish Juvenile Cup.

The Scottish Cup semi finals saw Rangers come face to face with Hibernian who included former Benburb player John Baxter. The first match ended 2-2 in front of 76,000 spectators. The second match in front of 75,000 saw Hibernian gain a two goal lead well into the second half. The goals came from a Turnball penalty and Fraser. Sammy Baird converted a Rangers penalty near the end. Then controversy in the last minute when a high ball from Mc Coll came into the penalty box. Hibs goalkeeper Leslie appeared to spill it after a challenge from Ralph Brand and Max Murray forced the ball over the line in the ensuing scramble. Referee Davidson awarded the goal.

The Hibs players asked the referee to consult with his linesman and to the disbelief of the Rangers support the goal was disallowed. The arguments raged long after the match but Hibernian were in the Final.

At Celtic Park Johnny Coyle scored twice in the first half to put Clyde in control over Motherwell. Coyle added a third soon after half time. The last half hour saw a Motherwell revival and a goal from Pat Quinn was reward for considerable pressure. Ian St. John reduced the arrears further and in a dramatic finish Motherwell hit the crossbar. However Clyde held on to play Hibernian in the Final.

Scotland were hoping for a good performance and victory over England in their match at Hampden Park.

SCOTLAND: Brown, Parker, Haddock, McColl, Evans, Docherty, Murray, Forrest, Herd, Mudie and Ewing

ENGLAND: Hopkinson, Howe, Langley, Slater, Wright, Clayton, Finney, Douglas, Kevan, Haynes and Charlton.

128,000 spectators soon provided the Hampden roar. For the first twenty minutes the sides were even. However a goal from Bryan Douglas on 22 minutes seemed to take a lot of heart out of Scotland and Bobby Evans and Bill Brown were saving the side from a cricket score. Derek Kevan added a second on 35 minutes and the Scots were relieved to reach half time with just the two goal deficit.

In the second half former St.Anthony player Bobby Evans quickly became man of the match with an unbelievable number of last ditch tackles and blocks. However, he was unable to prevent a Bobby Charlton, playing his first full England match, score in the 65th minute. Derek Kevan scored his second goal of the match ten minutes later.

Evans and Brown continued their excellent form until the end of the match in a one sided affair. The Scottish football fans feared the worst for the forthcoming World Cup.

RESULT: SCOTLAND 0 ENGLAND 4

St.Anthony's provided sad news with the announcement that Bob Cuthill passed away. Bob had been with the Ants for 36 years. In his time he helped to develop many top quality players including Bobby Evans (Celtic), Charlie Watkins (Rangers), Malky Mc Donald (Brentford manager) and Billy Craig (Third Lanark).

Benburb or St.Anthony's did not have any players selected for the Central League side to play against the Irish B side in Belfast. However, Celtic were still finding the Junior world a treasure trove for good players. From the Central League side they signed Pat Crerand who had an outstanding season with Duntocher Hibs and Billy McNeil from Blantyre Victoria.

The Scottish Junior Cup semi finals saw former Benburb and Rangers player Jock ' Tiger' Shaw the Bailleston trainer take his side to Falkirk for a semi final with Pumpherston. Bailleston had a blow early in the match when after six minutes Jim Tennant was carried off with concussion and taken to Falkirk Infirmary. This left his side to play the rest of the match with ten players. Craven gave Pumph. the lead but Bailleston fought back and on the hour mark Jimmy Ross scored an equaliser.

After some pressure Pumph. regained the lead through Whyte. However Bailleston urged on by Jock Shaw and a fair chunk of the 10,000 crowd kept on trying for the equaliser. They were rewarded in the last minute when they were awarded a penalty. Captain Adam Ross converted and a replay was fixed for Celtic Park.

In the replay Bailleston started as strong favourites having most of the support. Jimmy Ross gave them an early lead. However, Berry equalised for Pumph before half time and it was the same player who scored the winner in the second half to secure a 2-1 win and a place at Hampden Park.

The other semi final saw two of the favourites clash at Firhill Park. There were long queues of spectators as the teams kicked off. Irvine Meadow, whose support was large, were the better team in the first half and Duncan Barr put them into a deserved lead on 18 minutes.

The second half saw a turn round as Shotts went all out for the equaliser. On 76 minutes it duly arrived with a Cruikshank header. Tragedy struck the Meadow in the last minute when Gray scored an own goal to send Shotts through to the Final by a score of 2-1 in front of a crowd of over 20,000.

Benburb were excited with the form of their new goalkeeper John Gallacher. Gallacher was signed from St. Bonaventure Boys Guild team. He was selected to play for the Glasgow Boys Guild team which won against the Manchester Boys Guild team at Celtic Park.

Not such good news for the Bens was the ongoing ankle problems encountered by Bob Fitzsimmons. 'Fitzy' was a legend at the Bens after scoring the winner against Bo'ness United during a Scottish Junior Cup match at Tinto Park.

Former St.Anthony's player Johnny Quigley was doing well at English Division 1 side Nottingham Forest and as well as providing good consistent performances was a regular goal scorer.

Frank Haffey who lived in Copland Road, Govan had a career that started with Campsie B.W. and then Maryhill Harp Juniors. His excellent form saw him sign for Celtic.

In the Glasgow Amateur League Sligo Celtic who played their home matches during the season at the 50 pitches were putting in a challenge for the title. Cleansing on the other hand were struggling and in danger of finishing up in the dustbin of relegation.

# GLASGOW AMATEUR LEAGUE DIVIDION A

| Team | Pl | W | L | D | F | A | Pts |
|---|---|---|---|---|---|---|---|
| Sligo Celtic | 14 | 9 | 2 | 3 | 44 | 21` | 21 |
| Whitelaw United | 12 | 9 | 1 | 2 | 33 | 13 | 20 |
| Alley's | 12 | 7 | 3 | 2 | 41 | 34 | 16 |
| Shieldhall Vics. | 13 | 6 | 3 | 4 | 33 | 32 | 16 |
| Cameron Thistle | 14 | 5 | 5 | 4 | 41 | 28 | 14 |
| Norwood | 11 | 4 | 4 | 3 | 24 | 18 | 11 |
| Kinning Park | 14 | 4 | 7 | 3 | 30 | 46 | 11 |
| Dalglish United | 10 | 5 | 5 | 0 | 33 | 24 | 10 |
| Pollok Star | 15 | 2 | 8 | 5 | 29 | 42 | 9 |
| Crowie | 9 | 3 | 6 | 0 | 16 | 38 | 6 |
| Cleansing | 14 | 2 | 12 | 0 | 25 | 53 | 4 |

Govan Amateurs were having a good season and reached the semi finals of the West of Scotland Cup against Eaglesham which was scheduled to be played at Lesser Hampden Park. Key players for Govan were Alfie Ferguson in defence and Davie Mitchell and Ian Davidson were the inside forwards. Top scorer was medical student Ian Clarke.

Stephens did well to reach the Final of the Glasgow Welfare Youth Cup Final. However, when they arrived for the Final match against St.Margaret's at Crookston they found the ground locked up. Both sides plus the respective spectators waited outside until the grounds man arrived with five minutes to kick off. While the teams changed, the groundsman and spectators assembled the goalposts and put out the flags.

Stephens led at various times in an exciting match but it was St.Margaret's who ultimately won the cup with a 4-3 scoreline. The nets and corner posts were left for the grounds man to take care off.

Both Benburb and St.Anthony's had good seasons finishing in the top half of the table. Off the pitch at the Bens long time (30 years) treasurer John Dickie was presented with an inscribed wallet for services to Benburb Football Club. The McVicar family had a long tradition at the Bens on the committee's over the years. Most of the committee were deposed several years before. However unity returned to Tinto Park and Alex. Mc Vicar took over as match secretary at the club.

The Scottish Cup Final saw Hibernian and Clyde play at Hampden Park in front of a crowd in the region of 100,000.
HIBERNIAN: Leslie, Grant McLelland, Turnball, Plenderleith, Baxter, Fraser, Aitken, Baker, Preston and Ormond
CLYDE: McCulloch, Murphy, Haddock, Walters, Finley, Clinton, Herd, Currie, Coyle, Robertson and Ring
The match was very even for the most part. Clyde, with Govan player Harry Haddock in the team, got the bits of fortune that were required to win the Cup. On the half hour Coyle fired in a shot which took a big deflection off former Benburb player John Baxter and flew into the net.
In the second half Hibs pressed hard for the equaliser but good work from 'keeper Mc Culloch and the Clyde defence held them out. The Edinburgh side were effectively playing with ten men due to an injury to Aitken who was a passenger.
RESULT: HIBERNIAN  0  CLYDE 1

## CENTRAL LEAGUE

| Team | Pl | W | L | D | F | A | Pts |
|---|---|---|---|---|---|---|---|
| Parkhead | 32 | 25 | 4 | 3 | 92 | 37 | 53 |
| Johnstone Burgh | 32 | 23 | 4 | 5 | 91 | 55 | 51 |
| Rob Roy | 32 | 18 | 11 | 3 | 103 | 77 | 39 |
| St.Anthony's | 32 | 17 | 10 | 5 | 82 | 72 | 39 |
| Pollok | 32 | 16 | 12 | 4 | 79 | 72 | 36 |
| Vale of Leven | 32 | 13 | 10 | 9 | 91 | 73 | 35 |
| Shawfield | 32 | 13 | 10 | 9 | 61 | 59 | 35 |
| Benburb | 32 | 14 | 13 | 5 | 79 | 74 | 33 |
| Perthshire | 32 | 14 | 13 | 5 | 80 | 77 | 33 |
| Arthurlie | 32 | 14 | 14 | 4 | 70 | 77 | 32 |
| Port Glasgow | 32 | 12 | 15 | 5 | 62 | 68 | 29 |
| Dunipace | 32 | 11 | 16 | 5 | 65 | 84 | 27 |
| Renfrew | 32 | 10 | 20 | 2 | 65 | 94 | 22 |
| Strathclyde | 32 | 8 | 19 | 5 | 53 | 77 | 21 |
| Bridgeton Waverley | 32 | 7 | 18 | 7 | 63 | 92 | 21 |
| Dennistoun Waverley | 32 | 6 | 19 | 7 | 47 | 90 | 19 |
| Blantyre Celtic | 32 | 6 | 19 | 7 | 47 | 91 | 19 |

The Scottish Junior Cup Final saw Shotts Bon Accord very strong favourites against East of Scotland side Pumpherston at Hampden Park

PUMPHERSTON: Bennett, Mole, Murphy, Farmer, Halpin, Johnstone White, McKay, Craven, Young and berry.

SHOTTS BON ACCORD: Boag, Graham, Clark, Dundas, Hadcroft, Craig, Cruikshank, Garvie, Black, Wales and Sneddon.

The 'stones' were slightly the better side in the first half but without producing many efforts on goal. Halpin at the back for Pumph was the tallest player in Junior football at 6 foot and 4 inches was having a quiet time for the most part. However the big centre halfgave away a free kick. The ball was floated in and during the ensuing scramble Black opened the scoring for the Bon Accord.

The game opened up and Shotts managed to scramble a ball off the line. At the other end Craig had a shot come back off the post and Halpin in desperation hit a ball over his own crossbar to safety.

In the second half Shotts had the edge and were unlucky when a Garvie headed 'goal' was ruled out for offside. Pumph battled to the end and Young had a shot crash off the crossbar. Black added a second goal for Shotts a few minutes from the end of a good Junior Cup Final in front of 33,000 spectators. The stones gave an excellent account of themselves.

RESULT: SHOTTS BON ACCORD 2 PUMPHERSTON 0

An all Govan Cup Final took place between Mc Neil's and Cecil Star at Moore Park. McNeil's had already won the City and Suburban League Division 1 title and duly completed a double.

In the Glasgow Former Pupils League Bellahouston FP won Division 2 and gained promotion. St. Gerrard's also had a good season and finished third.

In a friendly match Harmony Row welcomed visitors from Rothsey. Both sides enjoyed the occasion with the 'Row' winning 9-2 at Bellahouston Park. A return match was played a few weeks later at Rothsey with Harmony Row winning again by 3-2.

HARMONY ROW: Patterson, Kirk, McWilliams, Driver, Carson, Kean, Johnstone, Riddell, Blackie, McCarthy and Crawford.

In the Final of the Boys Guild Challenge Cup St. Saviours did well to hold St. Catherine's to a draw. The replay took place at Provanmill Park.

ST.SAVIOURS: Reilly, Greenan, McKenzie, Monoghan, Neary, Hollowood, Mitchell, Mc Inally, Cassidy and Herron

St.Saviours took an early lead through McInally with a lob over the 'keepers head. However, St.Catherine's came storming back and McInally equalised before half time.

In the second half Mills and Orr scored for St. Catherine's and these two unopposed goals won them the cup.

RESULT: ST.SAVIOURS 1 ST.CATHERINE'S 3

Tradeston Holmlea won the popular Dennistoun Waverley tournament beating Parkhead Juveniles 4-1 in the Final in front of a good crowd.

TRADESTON HOLMLEA: Munro, Craig, Harvey, Forbes, Bryce, McAuley, Duncan, Whitelaw, McClure, Smith and Blair.

Drummond gave Parkhead an early lead but Whitelaw quickly equalised from the penalty spot. McClure put Tadeston in front after a mix up in the Parkhead defence and the same player added a third before half time. McClure completed his hat trick in the second half and the trophy went back to the side that often played at the 50 pitches.

RESULT: PARKHEAD JUVENILES 1 TRADESTON HOLMLEA 4

## 1958 WORLD CUP FINALS

Scotland travelled to Sweden for the World Cup Finals. Even the most eternal optimist didn't give the team much chance but they hoped there would be a shock result in their favour somewhere along the line.

The World Cup starts and most Scots are none to happy. The World Cup schedule is that all the matches are played simultaneously. The Television is to show England v Russia instead of Scotland's match against Yugoslavia. However, the Scotland match is to be broadcast on the Radio live. Most Govan families have the football on the television live but the sound turned down to listen to Scotland.

The airwaves appeared to be jammed and trying to get a reception from Sweden was proving difficult with the signal coming and going. The match on the television was England v Russia. England were 2 goals down at one stage but Derek Kevan and a late Tom Finney penalty secured a draw. The surprise of the night was Wales courtesy of a John Charles goal drawing 1-1 with Hungary. However, not far behind was Northern Ireland who also secured a good result beating Czechoslavakia 1-0 thanks to a Cush goal.

Scotland had a tough match against Yugoslavia who had beaten England 5-0 not so long before the finals. Scotland went behind early on and the whole of Scotland were constantly re-adjusting the radio's to try and hear the match. Half Time arrived with no further score. Early in the second half the radio said 'It's Scotland on the attack; their through and' ————zzzzzzzz the radio signal had gone. A number of people put their heads out of the tenement windows to find out what had happened by calling out to neighbours.

The signal came back and an excited commentator was describing the goal scored by Jimmy Murray of Heart of Midlothian. There was considerable noise in the back courts of the tenements with all the windows open, it being summer. 'C'mon Scotland' The radio continued to be faint but eventually it was established Scotland drew 1-1, a really good result.

The second match up saw Scotland take on Paraguay. However, with just 2 channels BBC and ITV for television the selected single match was England v Brazil. England did well to hold the Brazilians to a scoreless draw. Wales led through Ivor Allchurch but a late Mexico goal meant they had to settle for a 1-1 draw. Northern Ireland scored through Peter McParland but were well beaten by Argentina 3-1.

Scotland having drawn with Yugoslavia should surely beat Paraguay who had lost their opening game 7-3 to France. Most in Scotland were confident that coach Dawson Walker and his team would get the 2 points which would take them near to qualifying.

Dawson Walker had been appointed coach when manager designate for the team Matt Busby failed to recover from his injuries sustained in the Munich air crash. The first half was not broadcast at all in Scotland due to technical difficulties with the radio signals. Despite constant adjustment of the radio knob nothing could be heard. However a strong signal was heard just as half time was blown and a jaw dropping score line.

Paraguay 2 Scotland 1, Jackie Mudie had scored for Scotland to equalise but the South Americans had scored right on half time. In the second half Scotland had a considerable number of chances but missed them. Paraguay added a third before Bobby Collins of Celtic reduced the arrears. It was all too late and Scotland were as good as out after such a disappointing result.

Scotland knew nothing but a win was required against France but trailed by 2-0 at half time. Rud Fontaine scored one of the French goals and he went on to set a World Cup record of 13 goals for the competition. Scotland played well in the second half and Sammy Baird of Rangers pulled a goal back . However, try as they may they could not equalise and were out. The radio signals being so poor for this match, most Scots had the game switched off at half time.

The final group match saw England v Austria as the featured match on the television. For the third match in a row England drew with Johnny Haynes and Derek Kevan scoring in a 2-2 draw. This meant that England would have a play off with Russia which was lost 1-0. Wales were proving to be the surprise package of the World Cup and held the hosts Sweden to a scoreless draw.

This meant Wales had to play Hungary in a play off and Medwin and Allchurch scored to give Wales a remarkable 2-1 win. Northern Ireland pushed the holders West Germany all the way and two goals from Peter McParland of Aston Villa secured a 2-2 draw. This meant they had to play Czechoslovakia again.

The Czech's scored first but McParland equalised to take the game to extra time. The same player netted the winner in extra time to take his team through.

Wales put up a fantastic effort against Brazil but lost out when a 17 year old
Pele scored the only goal of the match. Northern Ireland were absolutely
drained following their play off exertions which went to extra time and lost
heavily 4-0 to France.
Brazil played top quality football throughout and beat the hosts Sweden in the
Final by 5-2 in Stockholm.
The highlights of the Scotland games were usually shown on television the
following evenings after the 3 matches.

| Group 1 | Pl | W | D | L | F | A | Pts |
|---|---|---|---|---|---|---|---|
| West Germany | 3 | 1 | 2 | 0 | 7 | 5 | 4 |
| Northern Ireland | 3 | 1 | 1 | 1 | 4 | 5 | 3 |
| Czechoslavakia | 3 | 1 | 1 | 1 | 8 | 4 | 3 |
| Argentina | 3 | 1 | 0 | 2 | 5 | 10 | 2 |

Play Off Northern Ireland 2 Czechoslovakia 1 after extra time

| Group 2 | Pl | W | D | L | F | A | Pts |
|---|---|---|---|---|---|---|---|
| France | 3 | 2 | 0 | 1 | 11 | 7 | 4 |
| Yugoslavia | 3 | 1 | 2 | 0 | 7 | 6 | 4 |
| Paraguay | 3 | 1 | 1 | 1 | 9 | 12 | 3 |
| Scotland | 3 | 0 | 1 | 2 | 4 | 6 | 1 |

| Group 3 | Pl | W | D | L | F | A | Pts |
|---|---|---|---|---|---|---|---|
| Sweden | 3 | 2 | 1 | 0 | 5 | 1 | 5 |
| Wales | 3 | 0 | 3 | 0 | 2 | 2 | 3 |
| Hungary | 3 | 1 | 1 | 1 | 6 | 3 | 3 |
| Mexico | 3 | 0 | 1 | 2 | 1 | 8 | 1 |

Play Off:    Wales 2 Hungary 1

| Group 4 | Pl | W | D | L | F | A | Pts |
|---|---|---|---|---|---|---|---|
| Brazil | 3 | 2 | 1 | 0 | 5 | 0 | 5 |
| USSR | 3 | 1 | 1 | 1 | 4 | 4 | 3 |
| England | 3 | 0 | 3 | 0 | 4 | 4 | 3 |
| Austria | 3 | 0 | 1 | 2 | 2 | 7 | 1 |

Play Off: USSR 1 England 0

## QUARTER FINALS
West Germany 1 Yugoslavia 0    Sweden 2 USSR 0
France 4 Northern Ireland 0    Brazil 1 Wales 0
## SEMI FINALS
West Germany 1 Sweden 3    France 2 Brazil 5
## 3rd/4th PLACE
West Germany 3 France 6
## FINAL
Sweden 2 Brazil 5

**SCOTLAND SQUAD:** Tommy Younger (Liverpool); Tommy Docherty (Preston NE)
Alex.Parker (Everton); Eric Caldow (Rangers); John Hewie (Charlton Ath); Harry Haddock (Clyde); Ian McColl (Rangers); Eddie Turnball (Hibernian) Bobby Evans (Celtic);Doug Cowie (Dundee); Dave McKay (Hearts);Bill Brown (Dundee) Sammy Baird (Rangers); Graham Leggat (Aberdeen); Alex. Scott (Rangers); Jim Murray (Hearts); Jackie Mudie (Blackpool); John Coyle (Clyde); Bobby Collins (Celtic) Archie Robertson (Clyde); Stewart Imlach (Notts.Forest); Willie Fernie (Celtic)

## CATHOLIC SCHOOLS UNDER 14—SECTION B

| Team | Pl | W | L | D | F | A | Pts |
|---|---|---|---|---|---|---|---|
| St.Pauls Whiteinch | 8 | 5 | 3 | 0 | 20 | 18 | 10 |
| Our Lady and St.Marks | 8 | 4 | 3 | 1 | 26 | 16 | 9 |
| St.Bernard's | 8 | 4 | 3 | 1 | 20 | 19 | 9 |
| St.Anthony's | 9 | 4 | 5 | 0 | 24 | 28 | 8 |
| Our Holy Redeemers | 5 | 3 | 2 | 0 | 11 | 7 | 6 |
| St.Cuthbert's | 5 | 2 | 3 | 0 | 11 | 14 | 4 |
| St.Peter's | 7 | 2 | 5 | 0 | 5 | 20 | 4 |

# CHAPTER 10
## WE WILL FOLLOW ON (1958-59)

At 31 Daviot Street, West Drumoyne, Derek is listening in on a discussion taking place between his mother Ruth and his Uncle Robbie. Robbie has kindly offered to take Derek to a number of Rangers matches during the forthcoming season. Ruth has absolute confidence that Robbie will ensure that Derek is well looked after at the matches.

The feeling was that matches at Ibrox Park would be very safe, away matches should be ok. Derek is over the moon and already wears his red, white and blue scarf. Ruth says I have spoken to Jimmy and he says he will also take Derek to some of the matches when he is not working or elsewhere. So from being occasional Rangers matches it was to be regular Rangers matches home and away. At the end of the conversation both Ruth and Robbie repeat a lecture they have given many times. Ruth says ' You must support Rangers for football reasons and do not get into trouble'. Robbie says ' Rangers are a football club not anything else. Just go to enjoy the matches'.

Benburb announced some signings for the forthcoming season. Most were favourites with the Bens support. However, the poor previous season meant that the Bens support wanted something a bit better. There had been a marked drop in the crowds as the team struggled at the lower end of the League table. Re-signed Maurice Young, Gordon Cairns, Davie Drummond, Bob Blair, Kenny McKay and John McAlpine. Late season trialist goalkeeper Johnnie Gallacher signed and another newcomer Benburb paid a fee to St.Constantine's for, stylish midfielder Benny Murphy who very quickly became a favourite of the Bens supporters.

Bobby Burns who was a Drumoyne and Govan High player was a popular signing on the left wing. Bobby played for Scotland Schoolboys at Wembley and his family had a long tradition with Benburb. His late grandfather and his father were both former Presidents of the club.

Dunky Rae (former Benburb favourite) who was on the Clydebank transfer list surprisingly attracted no offers. Another ex Benburb favourite Tommy Douglas moved to Dalry Thistle from Petershill. His time at the 'Peasies' was blighted with a number of injuries.

Released were John Cresswell who played with the Mc Kinnon twins in the Govan Methodist Church team. Billy Syme who missed many games due to his army postings.

Both the Mc Kinnon brothers were set fair for a resumption in Junior football. Ronnie went to Dunipace after being released by Benburb and very quickly was signed on provisional forms for Rangers. It was planned that he would play one season at Dunipace before moving back to play in Govan at Ibrox Park. Donnie was attracting interest from Glencairn.

Benburb had an early season match at Tinto Park against Vale of Leven

BENBURB: Gallacher, Cairns, Wilson, Gibson, Young, Murphy, Strang, McIlmoyle, Lickerish, McLoed and Drummond

VALE OF LEVEN: Greenshields, Bellingham, Ormiston, Gemslin, Galley, Douglas, Gibb, O'Donnell, Reid, Hoggan and Logie

Benburb were well on top at the start of the match but were stunned when Reid headed in a Logie cross. Constant pressure followed from the Bens and Davie Drummond showed good skill to level 10 minutes later. On half time Lickerish headed home a corner from Davie Drummond.

In the second half Vale came into the game and on 60 minutes a 35 yard shot flew over Gallacher for the equaliser. Both sides went all out for the winner which went the way of the Bens sending the Govan support home happy.

RESULT: BENBURB 3 VALE OF LEVEN 2

St.Anthony's appointed Robert Lockhart from Govan Juveniles as their trainer.

Derek and Robbie were at Rangers opening match against Hearts which started well for the Ibrox Park team who were three goals up at half time. The second half was scoreless and Rangers were off to a winning start. However, Rangers came a cropper at Kirkcaldy when they crashed 2-1 to Raith Rovers and a home draw a few days later against Third Lanark gave the momentum and lead to Hearts.

| Team | Pl | W | L | D | F | A | Pts |
|------|----|----|----|----|----|----|-----|
| Hearts | 6 | 5 | 1 | 0 | 16 | 10 | 10 |
| Rangers | 6 | 3 | 2 | 1 | 16 | 7 | 7 |
| Raith Rovers | 6 | 2 | 4 | 0 | 10 | 18 | 4 |
| Third Lanark | 6 | 1 | 4 | 1 | 11 | 18 | 3 |

Hearts beat Rangers at Tynecastle and despite winning their last two matches Rangers were out.

Harmony Row Youth Club had a tradition of inviting one of the old firm players to present the annual player awards. A break in tradition saw Harry Haddock of Clyde present the prizes and a very popular choice the Govan man was.

The City and Suburban Juvenile League started and an early season match between fierce Plantation Park rivals Avon Villa and Park United ended in a 1 -1 draw.

Rangers travelled across Glasgow for the first league 'Old Firm' match of the season. Derek had already visited Parkhead once before when Rangers beat Celtic 2-1 in a Glasgow Cup match courtesy of a late Jimmy Miller goal. However, the tensions were extremely high as the teams came out on a very wet day.

CELTIC: Beattie, McKay, Mochan, Fernie, McNeil, Peacock, Smith, Tully, Conway, Collins and Auld

RANGERS: Niven, Shearer, Caldow, Mc Coll, Telfer, Davis, Scott, Brand, Murray, Wilson and Hubbard.

A Tricolour was displayed at the Rangers end but was immediately set on fire. The intensity of the match meant that nobody really noticed the heavy rain. Big Harold Davis seemed to relish the conditions and he tackled fiercely in midfield. Celtic had playing a new class centre half in Billy Mc Neil who seldom put a foot wrong.

Celtic were the better team in the first half and took the lead on the 26th minute. Berty Peacock floated in a free kick. Eric Smith passed the ball to his left and the oncoming Bobby Collins scored with a well placed shot past Niven. The Celtic end was a sea of green, white and yellow. A few minutes before half time Davie Wilson went down in the penalty area and a spot kick was awarded. The tension rose to high levels but the coolest man in the house was Johnny Hubbard who converted.

The second half saw Rangers get a grip. However, a breakaway saw Eric Smith looking an ocean offside bearing down on the Rangers goal. The former Benburb player carried on and scored easily. The referee was surrounded by irate Rangers players. Referee Harvey consulted the linesman and disallowed the goal saying Smith had handled the ball. The Celtic players surrounded the referee. Again he went over to the linesman. The tension mounted all over Celtic Park. He then pointed to the centre spot and the goal stood. It took an eternity for the kick off. Rangers were like wounded animals and laid siege to the Celtic goal. They were soon level. Alex. Scott got through on the right wing; his fierce drive was partially saved by Dick Beattie. However, Ralph Brand was on the spot to tap home and the blue hordes were joyous.

RESULT : CELTIC 2 RANGERS 2

There had been a lot of crowd trouble at the match but that paled into insignificance with what was to follow. As Rangers supporters marched down London Road singing in celebration of a hard fought draw, a number of Celtic supporters managed to get onto the railway bridge above London Road. They rained bottles down onto the Rangers supporters below. Many were badly hurt. A police group got on the railway line and chased the bottle throwers who ran in the opposite direction. A sizable group of Rangers fans also made chase at the lower level hoping to catch the culprits when they came off the railway track and no doubt hand them over to the police!

In the Scottish League Cup the semi finals were played for the first time under floodlights. Partick Thistle and Celtic locked horns at Ibrox Park and things looked bleak for the Jags when goalkeeper Tommy Ledgerwood was carried off with an arm injury in the 47th minute. He returned 20 minutes later with his arm strapped and played on the right wing. He surprised Celtic with his pace and trickery and sent over some good crosses.

Against all odds McParland scored with a header for Partick and a few minutes later Mc Kenzie waltzed through the Celtic defence to score number two. The Jags held on and won the match 2-1 to progress to the final.

Hearts met Kilmarnock at Easter Road and were well on top for most of the match. Thomson scored a first half goal for Hearts with a long shot. Crawford and a Willie Bauld header extended the Hearts lead to 3-0 and sent most of the 41,500 crowd home happy.

Benburb set out on the Scottish Junior Cup trail with a trip to Shawfield at Roseberry Park. The ground is not too far from the 'original Benburb ' ground of 1898 at Polmadie. Benburb took a good support to the match and after a scoreless first half it was the Bens who scored the sole score winner and progressed to the second round.

St.Anthony's went 'Doon the watter' and secured an easy 4-0 win over Dunoon Athletic.

Govan Primary League Results : Bellahouston 6 Hill's Trust 0, Elder park 3 Copland Road 1, Greenfield 6 Lorne Street 1, Hillington 1 Drumoyne 10, Drumoyne 5 Bellahouston 5, Copland Road 0 Greenfield 6.

In the oldest age group Bellahouston Academy made a strong start with a 7-1 win over Shawlands. The team was:

BELLAHOUSTON ACADEMY:  Blair, Smith, Whitelaw, McLean, Anderson, Logan, Thomson, Browning, Tait, Roxburgh and Melvin

In the Scottish School Shield competitions the early rounds saw the Govan schools in exciting matches. St. Gerrards match with John Street saw three penalties saved in a 1-1 draw. The team was:

ST.GERRARD'S: J.McLaghlan, R.Smyth, W.Coyle, S.Herbert, J.Egan, W.Campbell, J.Berry, J.Bradbury, R.Wilson, J.Brennan and G.Scauler.

The Govan High v Bellahouston match was fiercely contested. Bella went 2-0 up only for the 'High' to fight back to level the score at half time. The Bella again went ahead by two goals to 4-2 only to see the High come back again and equalise; the match finishing 4-4.

The Intermediate and younger Govan High teams all did well. In the Intermediate Shield Govan won 8-3 over Shawlands and in the two youngest age groups a 9-1 win was recorded against Larkhall and a 5-0 win over Strathbungo.

MOTHERWELL: H.Weir, Mulvenney, Stewart, Aitkin, Martin, McCann, A.Weir, Reid, St.John, Quinn and Hunter
RANGERS: Niven, Shearer, Caldow, Davis, Telfer, Stevenson, Scott, McMillan, Simpson, Brand and Hubbard

Rangers attacked non stop at the start and after Simpson had gone close twice Brand gave Rangers the lead when he blasted home a pass from Mc Millan. Joyous stuff for the Rangers players but no joy for the spectators. Behind both goals the spectators were tumbling down and all the weight was on those at the front. The crowd was overspilling onto the park. Derek and countless others were pinned against the wall unable to move and enormous weight pressing from behind. The situation was desperate; the crush was in danger of draining the life from many spectators. Fortunately, the police and ambulance service were aware of the problem and as the crowd force sprang back for a split second each person trapped behind the wall was lifted out. There were too many people on the track surrounding the pitch that a procession took place to take all misplaced spectators behind the main stand. In Derek's case ,like many others, it was the treatment room to recover.

The match raged on a fantastic contest. Motherwell came back and equalised on 35 minutes. Quinn was sent through by St.John and he shot past Niven. Just on half time Ian St.John gave Motherwell the lead when he turned quickly on a cross from Reid to fire in a good goal. Rangers came out for the second half all guns blazing and the pressure told when Johnny Hubbard fired home a pass from McMillan on the edge of the box. Both sides had chances to win the match and Motherwell finished with ten men when debutant Stewart was taken off.

RESULT: MOTHERWELL 2 RANGERS 2

Many Rangers supporters at the match were very unhappy including Robbie. Clearly the entry gates should have been closed probably an hour before kick off when the ground was all but full. Robbie like a number of Rangers supporters vowed that it would be a very long time before they would attend a match at Fir Park if ever. The sheer greed of Motherwell Football Club had put the lives of ordinary supporters in danger. Derek vowed that he would never go to Fir Park for the rest of his life. But for the efforts of the Police, Stewards and Ambulance people who were alert to the situation, lives would definitely have been lost in a foggy day at Motherwell.

When Queen's Park heard about a match between Harmony Row Boys Club and Bradford St. Clare's they kindly offered Lesser Hampden Park as the venue. This was appreciated by both clubs and an enjoyable occasion was had by both clubs.

The Govan side won 3-0 with goals from Davie McDonald, Tommy Hendry and Davie McKenzie.

163

Rangers home game with Hearts looked as though it could go a long way to deciding where the winners flag would go. Rangers won easily with five unopposed goals from Max Murray (3) and Ralph Brand (2) all before half time. The Rangers second goal was memorable as left winger Andy Matthew picked the ball up on his own penalty area ran all the way down the left wing amid huge cheers and his goal bound shot was deflected in by Max Murray. The school's football season was in full swing. In the Scottish School's Shield. Bellahouston the holders had a tough draw. Away to much fancied St.Mungo's they lost 2-0.

A local derby was thrown up when Govan High played St.Gerrard's at Pirrie Park. St.Gerrard's won an exciting match of fluctuating fortunes by 6-4.

In the Govan Primary League results were : Bellahouston 10 Lorne Street 0; Greenfield 9 Hill's Trust 0; Hillington 4 Copland Road 2; Bellahouston 7 Elder Park 1; Greenfield 7 Hillington 0; Hill's Trust 1 Copland Road 8; Hillington 1 Bellahouston 8; Elder Park 4 Greenfield 1; Drumoyne 7 Hill's Trust 4; Copland Road 2 Lorne Street 1; Bellahouston 3 Greenfield 3; Hillington 2 Elder Park 0; Hill's Trust 1 Lorne Street 3; Drumoyne 8 Copland Road 1.

The Glasgow representative teams did not have too many Govan players involved.Walker of Govan High was included in the oldest age group squad. Craig from St.Gerrard's was in the under 16 year olds.

Walker was in the Glasgow Secondary Schools side which ran riot against the Glasgow RC Schools side. He was amongst the scorer's with Willoughby and Forrest in a 7-2 scoreline.

Govan Juveniles were producing good players. Ronnie Cheyne was being tempted by Petershill and Alex Wilkie the goalkeeper was trailed by Bailleston.

1959 dawned and the weather was abysmal. For Robbie and Derek it was off to Ibrox for the Old Firm New Year's day match. Due to previous trouble there was a crowd restriction. The rain sheeted down and the strong freezing cold wind cut through the spectators like a knife. Robbie and Derek stood as near to the Main stand as possible at the Copland Road end to try and shield from the elements but with no success. Only one flag for each side appeared on the terraces whether official or unofficial. The Celtic fans roared 7! 7! 7 ! Reminding the Gers supporters of a League Cup Final score. The referee was called Jack Mowat and he must have had thoughts of abandoning the match several times as the pitch became ever more waterlogged. Bertie Peacock gave Celtic a lead which was cancelled out by Andy Matthew. The match was decided by two penalties. Eric Caldow tucked his away. At the other end Celtic were awarded a penalty. Bertie Auld and the referee tried to find the penalty spot in the sea of mud. The Celtic player took the kick after a long delay and smashed it against the underside of the crossbar leaving Rangers 2-1 winners. At the end both sets of fans were immediately on the way home to thaw out. It was difficult to imagine a worse set of conditions for a football match.

The following day Rangers were at Firhill to play Partick Thistle and Robbie and Derek were inside as the gates were closed long before the kick off with a capacity crowd inside. Unlike Motherwell they placed the safety of spectators before profit. Firhill had high walls behind the goals where small disabled cars were parked.

The Jags scored a goal in each half through George Smith (who apparently was a Rangers fan) to secure a 2-0 win.

It was announced that the gates for Scottish League matches had risen sharply with a number of sides in the title race.

At Tinto Park two distinguished guests arrived to watch Benburb play Shawfield. Mrs Nixon-Browne, the wife of the Under Secretary of State for Scotland, joined her husband to watch the match. Mr. Jack Nixon Browne had previously been the Unionist MP for Govan. After boundary changes he moved to the Craigton seat and won a narrow vote against Bruce Millan (Labour) at the previous General Election.

Mrs Nixon-Browne was very popular at the Benburb Club. She always commented that every time she came to watch the Bens they won. The match against Shawfield continued her winning run.

Down in South London at Sandy Lane Tooting, there was Govan interest in the English FA Cup match between Tooting and Mitchum and First Division Nottingham Forest. Forest had five Scotsmen in their regular side including John Quigley the former St. Anthony's player. Most predicted an easy win for Nottingham Forest against the part time amateurs. However, the match was played on a bone hard frosty pitch and the Toots roared on by a 14,000 crowd were fired up. After Tooting hit the bar in the early play a mix up in the Forest defence allowed Tooting a simple run in goal to the delight of the South Londoners. A long shot from 35 yards beat the Forest goalie and a major upset was on the cards. Tooting held on until half time and the ears of the nation were hearing the unbelievable news.

Forest had a few early scares in the second half before a fortunate own goal in their favour allowed them a route back. Later in the second half the referee sounded his whistle and to the disbelief of the crowd Forest were awarded a penalty. This was converted and a replay at Nottingham was secured. Forest made no mistake in the replay in front of 42,000 spectators with a 3-0 win. The next round saw Grimsby Town (who had shocked Manchester City in the previous round) beaten by 4-1.

A 1-1 home draw against Birmingham City in Round 5 meant a potentially difficult replay at St. Andrews. However,the Forest hit top form and won 5-0. Forest had a home draw against Bolton Wanderers in the 6th Round and came through a tight match 2-1 to progress to the semi finals. John Quigley had moved from Moore Park to one step away from Wembley.

John Quigley got recognition for his fine form when selected for a Scotland team in a practice match against the Scottish League. However, the match scheduled at Ibrox Park was postponed due to poor weather.

In Govan both Benburb and St.Anthony's were having very poor seasons. The Ants were bottom of the league and Benburb were also on the slide and certain to occupy a very low league position.

## CENTRAL LEAGUE

| Team | Pl | W | L | D | F | A | Pts |
|---|---|---|---|---|---|---|---|
| Johnstone Burgh | 22 | 16 | 4 | 2 | 68 | 27 | 34 |
| Pollok | 21 | 14 | 2 | 5 | 69 | 39 | 33 |
| Glencairn | 22 | 12 | 3 | 7 | 52 | 32 | 31 |
| Cambuslang Rangers | 20 | 12 | 5 | 3 | 59 | 42 | 27 |
| Shettleston | 22 | 11 | 7 | 4 | 63 | 40 | 26 |
| Shawfield | 19 | 11 | 5 | 3 | 44 | 28 | 25 |
| Rob Roy | 22 | 11 | 8 | 3 | 61 | 60 | 25 |
| Duntocher Hibs | 19 | 8 | 7 | 4 | 40 | 41 | 20 |
| St.Roch's | 20 | 9 | 9 | 2 | 44 | 44 | 20 |
| Vale of Leven | 23 | 7 | 10 | 6 | 46 | 63 | 20 |
| Bailleston | 19 | 8 | 10 | 1 | 41 | 42 | 17 |
| Parkhead | 21 | 6 | 12 | 3 | 38 | 48 | 15 |
| Benburb | 31 | 5 | 13 | 3 | 30 | 52 | 13 |
| Blantyre Vics | 18 | 4 | 13 | 1 | 31 | 64 | 9 |
| Clydebank | 22 | 4 | 17 | 1 | 39 | 70 | 9 |
| St.Anthony's | 21 | 2 | 15 | 4 | 19 | 54 | 8 |

Benburb mourned the death of long time supporter Adam Kenneth. Adam had supported the Bens for 60 years right back to the days when they played at Helen Street.

Duntocher Hibs released former St.Gerrard's Scottish Youth player Peter Catterson. Peter trained with the Bens in the interim pending finding a new club.

Robbie and Derek continued to follow the fortunes of Rangers. A bitterly cold day sees them travel to Love Street, Paisley to take on St.Mirren. Although bitterly cold the match is played in brilliant sunshine and Rangers right winger Alex Scott steals the show with an exhibition of brilliant wing play. Andy Matthew gave Rangers the lead followed by a good goal from Alex. Scott. In the second half Max Murray increased the 'Gers lead before Gemmell scored for the Buddies. Despite a good spell of pressure from the Love Street team Rangers held on to win 3-1.

Love Street was a comfortable ground for a spectator and was oval shaped. A good stand at one side of the ground faced over to a decent sized cover at the opposite side.

Govan Primary School League Results: Hill's Trust 0 Bellahouston 9; Drumoyne 5 Elder Park 1; Bellahouston 4 Copland Road 0; Elder Park 0 Bellahouston 9; Hillington 0 Greenfield 10; Drumoyne 3 Lorne Street 0; Bellahouston 12 Hillington 1: Hill's Trust 0 Drumoyne 5; Greenfield 2 Bellahouston 7; Copland Road 2 Drumoyne 2; Lorne Street 3 Hill's Trust 1; Glasgow League Shield : Toryglen 8 Copland Road 0; Mount Florida 4 Hill's Trust 0; John Maxwell 2 Greenfield 3;

In the City and Suburban Juvenile League (Under 21), Govan Star were suspended awaiting payment of dues to the League. Park United were on a great run of form being unbeaten in 19 matches and into the 5th Round of the Scottish Juvenile Cup.In the Corporation Youth League the Govan sides were doing well. Ibrox Youth Club led the way with St.Anthony's second.

## GLASGOW CORPORATION YOUTH LEAGUE

| Team | Pl | W | L | D | F | A | Pts |
|---|---|---|---|---|---|---|---|
| Ibrox YC | 12 | 12 | 0 | 0 | 64 | 12 | 24 |
| St.Anthony's FP | 12 | 10 | 1 | 1 | 58 | 14 | 21 |
| Heather Street YC | 13 | 9 | 2 | 2 | 69 | 19 | 20 |
| Gowanbank YC | 11 | 9 | 2 | 0 | 60 | 13 | 18 |
| St.Gerrard's FP | 12 | 8 | 3 | 1 | 66 | 29 | 17 |
| Sandwood YC | 15 | 5 | 6 | 4 | 38 | 61 | 14 |
| Castleton FP | 14 | 4 | 9 | 1 | 33 | 75 | 9 |
| Carwadric YC | 12 | 4 | 8 | 0 | 18 | 49 | 8 |
| Queen's Park JFP | 11 | 3 | 7 | 1 | 25 | 31 | 7 |
| Holyrood JFP | 9 | 2 | 5 | 2 | 18 | 31 | 6 |
| Lambhill Street FP | 12 | 1 | 11 | 0 | 14 | 75 | 2 |
| Honchilwood YC | 13 | 0 | 13 | 0 | 2 | 56 | 0 |

The Rangers Scottish Cup quest took them to Station Park, Forfar for the 1st Round. Max Murray gave Rangers an early lead but an Eric Caldow own goal levelled things up. The Loons gave a very good account of themselves in front of a crowd numbering 9,800.Forfar could have been ahead by half time and left the field to rapturous applause. Rangers slowly got on top in the second half and goals from Jimmy Miller and Alex Scott secured the Ibrox side a 3-1 win.

Next up were Hearts and Andy Matthew gave Rangers the lead. Jim Murray equalised for Hearts and before half time Kirk put the ball into his own net to give Rangers the lead. Another Kirk mistake saw Matthew score Rangers third. Johnny Hamilton scored for Hearts on the full time whistle. Rangers were through courtesy of a 3-2 score line.

The 3rd Round and Celtic have been drawn at home to Rangers. Celtic had not beaten Rangers at Parkhead for over 50 years in the Scottish Cup and Rangers were in good form while Celtic results were indifferent. Many people in Govan had mixed feelings about the match. Derek's uncles Robbie and Jack liked the three ex Benburb players in the Celtic team; Eric Smith, John Divers and Mike Jackson. They also liked and respected greatly former St.Anthony's player Bobby Evans. They were also aware big Frank Haffey lived in Copland Road. Young Ian Lochead from St.Gerrard's was in the team at centre forward due to injuries. Robbie says 'I hope the ex Govan boys play brilliantly but Rangers sneak home 2-1 !'. Jack says 'I hope Celtic win; these guys are all good players and three ex Bens players will cause Rangers plenty of problems. Evans is the best player Scotland has had for years. This match will not be as easy for Rangers as predicted !'

CELTIC: Haffey, McKay, Mochan, Smith, Evans, Peacock, McVittie, Jackson, Lochhead, Wilson and Divers.

RANGERS: Niven, Shearer, Caldow, Davis, Telfer, Stevenson, Scott, McMillan, Murray, Wilson and Matthew.

Due to the terrible problems at the previous Parkhead Old Firm match the crowd has been restricted to 30,000. No flags of any description have been allowed. The teams take the field with huge gaps on the terracing; very unusual for an 'Old Firm' match. Rangers wasted no time in attacking and a couple of surging runs by Alex Scott caused mayhem in the Celtic goalmouth in the early stages. However, the Celts weathered the storm and then started to dominate the game with all the 'Govan' players playing well. On half time it was former Bens player Johnny Divers who gave Celtic a deserved lead after a mistake in the Rangers defence. The second half saw the green and white hoops continue to be on top and it was no surprise when after a good run by Lochead , McVittie increased the lead. Rangers finished strongly and Max Murray pulled a goal back in the last minute but it was too little, too late for the Ibrox side. Celtic were deserved winners helped in no small way by the 'Govan' connection. RESULT: GOVAN (CELTIC) 2 RANGERS 1

Nottingham Forest met Aston Villa in the semi final of the English FA Cup. A tense match saw defences on top for the most part. The first half ended scoreless. In the second half the same pattern continued until near the end Forest started to attack more frequently. With a few minutes left John Quigley found himself free inside the penalty box and smashed a low shot into the net. The goal proved to be the winner and it meant that Govan would have an interest in the FA Cup Final at Wembley.

In the Scottish FA Cup semi finals Celtic matched up against St. Mirren at Hampden Park. Third Lanark played Aberdeen at Ibrox Park in the other semi final. At Ibrox Park Third Lanark gave their fans something to cheer in the first few minutes. Aberdeen failed to clear their lines in the penalty box and Dick waltzed in to put the Hi Hi into the lead in front of 28,000 spectators. After quarter of an hour of almost constant Warriers attacks Aberdeen scored with their first shot at goal. Norrie Davidson blasted a shot from 20 yards high into the net. The remainder of the match saw end to end play with the Thirds having a slight edge. Despite a few near misses from the Glasgow club the score remained 1-1 and a replay was required.

At Hampden Park Celtic were favourites but St.Mirren were expected to push them all the way. The Celtic support in the crowd of 74,000 turned the ground into a sea of green and white and they raised several tri-colours. The early part of the match saw an onslaught from St.Mirren and Frank Haffey pulled off several smart saves. St.Mirren got their reward for attacking play when Miller, who hailed from Copland Road Govan, cut in from the right and smashed a fierce shot past Frank Haffey. Miller added a second on the half hour from a breakaway trundling the ball into the net when through. Before half time the Buddies had added a third when Gerry Baker was clean through with the Celtic defence claiming offside. The Saints striker scored easily and the tie was already beyond Celtic. Celtic attacked for most of the second half but a late Tommy Bryceland goal put the icing on the cake for the Buddies who were in the final.

The Aberdeen v Third Lanark replay at Ibrox Park saw Norrie Davidson of the Dons score the only goal of the match on 35 minutes. A good Aberdeen defence in the second half saw Martin relatively untroubled and his team through with the single unopposed goal.

Benburb were making good progress in the Central League Cup despite poor league form. A fourth round tie saw them at Clydebank. Brodie and Benny Murphy were two of the scorer's as the Bens ran out 3-1 winners.

From 31 Daviot Street Derek and his uncle Robbie boarded the Rangers supporters bus to see the match at Falkirk. Rangers are just edging ahead in the race for the title and predictions are for a win at Falkirk. Brockville Park at Falkirk had a Boys section and Derek entered under the watchful eye of George Walker son of the bus organiser.

169

FALKIRK: Slater, Richmond, Rae, Price Prentice, McMillan, Murray, Wright, White, Moran and Oliver.

RANGERS: Niven, Shearer, Caldow, David, Telfer, Stevenson, Scott, McMillan, Murray, Brand and Wilson.

The boys enclosure was a good idea in theory. Unfortunately, a group of Falkirk thugs aged in late teens had got in and started taking discreet punches at any boy with a Rangers scarf on. Derek received a few blows in the first five minutes. Some of the older boys started grouping against the thugs and several scraps were taking place.

The game was exciting. Falkirk needed points to avoid relegation; Rangers needed points to try and win the title. The difference was Falkirk had a world class player at centre forward in John White.

Falkirk took an early lead when Wright fired in a shot from the edge of the box. Niven got a hand to it but could only watch as the ball trundled into the net to the delight of the home fans (1-0). In the boys section the Rangers support were getting considerable abuse from the thugs. Falkirk were well on top and the Bairns support were in delight again on the quarter hour when Dougie Moran finished off a good run by Wright (2-0). John White the Falkirk centre forward was at the heart of every Falkirk attack. Rangers went for a quick reply and Max Murray converted a Davie Wilson cross soon after. (2-1). Wright restored the Bairns two goal lead when he ran through on a long clearance unchallenged and scored easily (3-1). Rangers responded five minutes later with a repeat of their first goal; Wilson crossed and Max Murray scored from close in (3-2). Falkirk again restored the two goal margin when John White gained possession of the ball in the penalty box, worked a bit of space and slammed the ball into the net past Niven (4-2). At half time there was additional entertainment in the boys enclosure in the form of several scraps and lots of insults.

The second half was every bit as exciting as the first. Rangers soon reduced the deficit when Richmond brought down Davie Wilson in the penalty box. Eric Caldow scored and Rangers were going all out for the equaliser. (4-3). A few wminutes later it was all level as Ralph Brand and Alex Scott broke through the middle. Scott passed to Brand who scored easily.(4-4). Rangers tails were up but at the other end John White was a constant threat. Rangers went into the lead when Ian Mc Millan headed in a cross(4-5).

However, Falkirk were not finished and the final part of the match saw them attacking non stop. A cross came over George Niven collected the ball in the air only for Dougie Moran to shoulder barge him. The ball and keeper finished up in the net. A pause and the referee awarded the goal much to the dismay of the Rangers support. As the full time whistle blew the Falkirk thugs were gone very quickly.

RESULT: FALKIRK  5  RANGERS    5

As the supporters bus headed for Glasgow, Robbie said the Falkirk support were not much better in the other parts of the ground. He says ' Well we can add Falkirk to Motherwell as two grounds we will never visit again`.

In the Juvenile League old rivals Park United and Avon Villa were top of the league. Both were drawing good numbers of spectators to the black ash Plantation Park pitches. Not included were the ones who leaned out of their tenement windows to see the action.

## CITY AND DISTRICT JUVENILE LEAGUE

| Team | Pl | W | L | D | F | A | Pts |
|------|----|----|----|----|----|----|-----|
| Park United | 13 | 8 | 0 | 5 | 46 | 17 | 21 |
| Avon Villa | 13 | 9 | 3 | 1 | 41 | 20 | 19 |
| Cadwadric Bluebell | 15 | 9 | 6 | 0 | 57 | 39 | 18 |
| Ferndale | 15 | 6 | 7 | 2 | 34 | 28 | 14 |
| League Hearts | 8 | 6 | 1 | 1 | 22 | 13 | 13 |
| Olivetti | 11 | 6 | 4 | 1 | 35 | 22 | 13 |
| Shettleston Vics. | 12 | 5 | 4 | 3 | 27 | 26 | 13 |
| Tradeston Holmlea | 13 | 3 | 6 | 4 | 33 | 35 | 10 |
| Glencairn Juveniles | 13 | 3 | 7 | 3 | 21 | 21 | 9 |
| Parkhead Juveniles | 15 | 3 | 10 | 2 | 22 | 26 | 8 |
| Arden Thistle | 16 | 2 | 12 | 2 | 26 | 64 | 6 |

Govan High were doing well in the Scottish Intermediate Shield. In the semi final they were drawn against Clydebank High; the match being played at Roseberry Park home of Shawfield Juniors. Govan won 2-1 and progressed to a Final against St.Mary's, Bathgate.

The match was to be played at Firhill Park and free tickets were issued to all the schools in Govan to go along and support the team. A fair number did but on the day of the match there was a torrential downpour and many thought the game would probably be off. The Partick Thistle ground staff performed a minor miracle and the game was on. St. Mary's went ahead before half time. In the second half Govan High equalised to the roars of the Govan folk. In a tense finish St. Mary's grabbed the winner to collect the Shield on a 2-1 score. All the crowd were housed in the Firhill Park main stand. The Govan support was at one end and the Bathgate school folk at the opposite.

The Scottish Junior Cup saw a strong challenge coming from Irvine Meadow. In the semi finals they travelled to Firhill to play Lanarkshire League side Carluke Rovers. A crowd in excess of 25,000 saw diminutive Meadow winger 'Hookey' Walker give his side the perfect start with a goal in the first minute. Meadow were on top for most of the first half and increased the lead shortly before half time when Carroll scored from the penalty spot. Carluke improved after half time and Rodger reduced the deficit. However, the Rovers were unable to get the equaliser and Meadow were in the Final.

In the second semi final 128 busloads of supporters left Johnstone to cheer on the Burgh in the match against Shettleston at Celtic Park. A tense match saw Shettleston have a slight edge in the first half but they were unable to score. Johnstone were handicapped by head injuries to centre half Peachie Patterson and Benny Murney who collided. Blood streamed from Murney's head and he had to go off for periods during the rest of the match. The second half saw the Town press for the winner and it duly arrived courtesy of a goal from O'Brien. It was to be an Irvine Meadow v Shettleston Final.

Johnstone Burgh were on their way to the Central League title as a consolation. However in their matches against St.Anthony's who finished bottom they struggled. Alec Crawford helped the Ants to a 5-2 win at Moore Park. At Keanie Park the Burgh fans thought it was going to be a repeat when left winger Gormley scored twice for the Ants in the first half. However slowly but surely the Burgh fought back and levelled 2-2 to secure a draw.

Benny Murphy, Benburb's stylish midfielder, was much sought after by senior clubs and had several trial matches. He starred for Cowdenbeath in one fixture.

In the English FA Cup Final there was a Scottish flavour. Nottingham Forest had five Scots in their side including former St.Anthony's player John Quigley. The opponents Luton Town also had one in the team, Alan Brown.

LUTON TOWN: Baynham, McNally, Hawkes, Groves, Owen, Lacey, Bingham, Brown, Morton, Cummings and Gregory

NOTTINGHAM FOREST: Thomson, Whare, McDonald, Whitefoot, McKinley, Burkitt, Dwight, Quigley, Wilson, Gray and Imlach

The Forest seemed to have the match won inside the first half hour. Dwight opened the scoring when he got free down the middle and scored with a good shot on 10 minutes. After 15 minutes Wilson headed in a good cross from Imlach to make it two. However, Dwight sustained a terrible injury and was carried off leaving Forest with 10 men.

The second half saw Luton push forward and they got reward late in the game when Sid Owen scored. Forest held on to deservedly take the Cup and leave Johnny Quigley one very happy Govan man.

RESULT: LUTON TOWN 1 NOTTINGHAM FOREST 2

John Dick hailed from Cardonald. His football career had seen him go from Maryhill Juniors to Aberdeen. However, before his career at Aberdeen started he was drafted into the Army and based mainly at Colchester. It was here Ted Fenton, the West Ham United manager, saw the potential in the tall forward who scored many goals.

It was to John Dick that Scotland turned when Denis Law was declared unfit for the annual match against England. Having lost 4-0 at Hampden Park the previous year, optimism was hard to find in the Scottish camp as they stayed at their hotel on the River Thames at Sonning. The same hotel that Jock Tiger Shaw had inspired Scotland to a good result at Wembley some years before.

ENGLAND: Hopkinson (Bolton), Howe (West.Brom), Shaw Sheff.Utd), Clayton (Blackburn), Wright (Wolves), Flowers (Wolves) , Douglas Blackburn), Broadbent (Wolves), Charlton (Man.Utd.) , Haynes (Fulham) and Holden (Bolton).

SCOTLAND: Brown (Dundee), McKay (Celtic), Caldow (Rangers), Docherty (Arsenal), Evans (Celtic), McKay (Tottenham), Leggat (Fulham), Collins (Everton), Herd (Arsenal), Dick (West Ham) and Ormond (Hibernian)

England had all the possession in the early part of the match. Scotland had to thank Bill Brown in goal for a couple of good stops as the half wore on. Towards half time Scotland had an equal share of the game but few chances. The second half started with play even and few chances. England scored the winning goal on the hour when Bobby Charlton headed home a cross from Douglas.

RESULT: ENGLAND 1 SCOTLAND 0

The end of the football season was approaching rapidly and Rangers had a chance to wrap up the title with a trip to nearest rivals Heart of Midlothian. The Rangers fans were packed into the Gorgi Road End amongst a crowd of 25,000.

HEARTS: Marshall, Kirk, Lough, Thomson, Milne, Cumming, Blackwood Murray, Young, Rankin and Hamilton

RANGERS: Niven, Shearer, Provan, Davis, Telfer, Stevenson, Scott, McMillan, Murray, Millar and Wilson.

Hearts were the better team throughout and scored a goal in each half through Cumming and Rankin. After Hearts scored the second goal one of their fans very much worst for wear from drink was being escorted by 2 policemen and 3 Stewards including a lady. He waved his plain maroon scarf to the hordes of Rangers supporters behind the Gorgi Road goal. 'Away back tae Glasga ya mugs ye!` All of a sudden there was a cry from the back of the terrace 'Watch Out !'

Derek, who was standing at the front, saw a bottle which had been thrown from the back head towards the front terrace. As if in slow motion the bottle travelled past the spectators at the front. As the front fans looked up they could see the bottle spin, each time the neck was at the bottom some beer would drop out. Most were relieved initially to see it pass by and onwards towards the pitch. Then to everyone's horror it started dropping in amongst the pack escorting the drunk Hearts fan out. Amazingly it missed the policemen and the stewards  but landed flush on the head of the Hearts fan; an amazing piece of accuracy by the thrower.

The drunken Hearts fan was pole axed and lay motionless on the ground with lots of blood coming from his head. Within a few seconds around a dozen policemen appeared at the front of the terrace and looked up to try and gauge where the bottle had come.   A few seconds more after some pointing, the police went in and pulled out five completely innocent spectators and frogmarched them outside. The poor Hearts fan was removed  from the ground in a stretcher after being patched up.   RESULT:  HEARTS 2 RANGERS 0

| SCOTTISH LEAGUE DIV 1 | Pl | W | L | D | F | A | Pts |
|---|---|---|---|---|---|---|---|
| Rangers | 33 | 21 | 4 | 8 | 91 | 49 | 50 |
| Hearts | 32 | 20 | 6 | 6 | 87 | 47 | 46 |
| Motherwell | 33 | 17 | 8 | 8 | 78 | 50 | 42 |
| Dundee | 32 | 16 | 9 | 7 | 58 | 48 | 39 |
| Airdrieonians | 33 | 15 | 12 | 6 | 63 | 61 | 36 |
| Celtic | 33 | 13 | 12 | 9 | 68 | 52 | 34 |
| Partick Thistle | 33 | 14 | 13 | 6 | 58 | 56 | 34 |
| St.Mirren | 33 | 13 | 13 | 7 | 67 | 73 | 33 |
| Third Lanark | 32 | 11 | 11 | 10 | 73 | 75 | 32 |
| Hibernian | 33 | 13 | 14 | 6 | 68 | 69 | 32 |
| Kilmarnock | 32 | 11 | 13 | 8 | 50 | 50 | 30 |
| Clyde | 33 | 12 | 17 | 4 | 61 | 62 | 28 |
| Stirling Albion | 33 | 10 | 15 | 8 | 53 | 64 | 28 |
| Raith Rovers | 33 | 10 | 15 | 8 | 58 | 68 | 28 |
| Aberdeen | 32 | 11 | 16 | 5 | 59 | 61 | 27 |
| Falkirk | 33 | 10 | 17 | 6 | 56 | 77 | 26 |
| Dunfermiline | 32 | 9 | 16 | 7 | 56 | 84 | 25 |
| Queen of the South | 33 | 6 | 21 | 6 | 38 | 96 | 18 |

A large crowd assembled at Ibrox Park for the last match of the League season. Rangers needed a point to secure the league title. If they lost then a Hearts win at Celtic Park would take the title to Tynecastle. Rangers opponents Aberdeen brought down a good and noisy support scattered around the ground. The Dons needed a win to avoid relegation. Plenty of red and white scarves were in evidence but hugely outnumbered by an expectant home support.

RANGERS: Niven, Shearer, Caldow, Davis, Telfer, Stevenson, Scott, McMillan, Murray, Brand and Matthew.

ABERDEEN: Martin, Caldwell, Hogg, Brownlie, Clunie, Glen, Ewan, Davidson, Baird, Wishart and Hather.

Rangers were quick out of the traps and Ralph Brand gave them an early lead. However as the half wore on it was evident that Aberdeen were playing well and always looked likely to score. With just two minutes of the half remaining Norrie Davidson equalised for the Dons. The half time whistle went with the 'Gers slightly fortunate to be level. The news from Parkhead was that Heart of Midlothian were a goal up. As it stood Rangers would win the title by a single point. Early in the second half Norrie Davidson grabbed his second and Aberdeen looked certain to avoid the drop if they could hang on.

The crowd were booing the home side as they toiled to get the equaliser which would give them the title. Suddenly news filtered through that Berty Auld had equalised for Celtic against Hearts and right on time former Benburb player Eric Smith bulleted home a header to give Celtic a win and deliver the league title to Ibrox. Rangers were booed off the park despite winning the league. Another result from the matches played saw Dunfermiline beat Partick Thistle 10– 1.

John Walker the Govan High and Glasgow Rep. midfielder signed for Middlesborough. A number of Govan players featured in trials for the Glasgow Under 17's side. These included Goalkeeper Campbell (Govan High), Half Back: Strachan (Govan High), Half Back Gillespie (St.Gerrard's), Forward Queen (Lourdes), Forward Brown (Govan High).

In the semi final of the Cameronian Cup St.Gerrard's met St.Mungo's at Nether Pollok.

ST.GERRARD'S: Keevins, Craig, Haddock, Dignam, Donnelly, McMillan, McCartney, Boyd, Kelly, Haughey and Quinn

Brogan gave St.Mungo's a tenth minute lead but Kelly had the Govan School level by half time. With two minutes left Quinn scored a good goal for St.Gerrard's. However, Dougherty equalised for St.Mungo's with virtually the last kick of the game. In extra time St.Gerrard's tired and faded badly out of the game although Kelly did manage to score. However, St.Mungo's scored four times through Rossi (2), Heffron and Dougherty.

RESULT: ST.GERRARD'S 3 ST.MUNGO'S 6 after extra time

The Scottish Cup Final attracted a lot of attention. Once again there was no Old Firm interest and a good spectacle was anticipated. The Scottish daily Express added to the occasion by giving out soldiers hats with checks which were either black and white if you preferred St.Mirren or red and white if you wanted Aberdeen to win. The supporters of both clubs mixed freely and the atmosphere was friendly at kick off.

ABERDEEN: Martin, Caldwell, Hogg, Brownlie, Clunie, Glen, Ewen, Davidson, Baird, Wishart and Hather.

ST.MIRREN: Walker, Lapsley, Wilson, Neilson, McGugan, Leishman, Rodger, Bryceland, Baker, Gemmell and Miller

A huge crowd turned up for the match with 108,600 the official attendance. Play was even at the beginning as both teams tried to carve open a chance.Aberdeen had the misfortune to have injuries to two players in quick succession. Caldwell was struggling with a pulled muscle and went off for treatment and very soon afterwards Clunie came out of a challenge with Bryceland badly. After a lengthy delay Clunie resumed to loud cheers from the Dons fans and the neutrals. There were more cheers a few minutes later for Caldwell who came back on but playing on the left wing with Hather filling in at right back.

Two minutes before half time the Buddies took the lead when Baker picked out Miller; a good cross and Bryceland scored. On 63 minutes the Saints increased their lead when Baker went into the box and under a challenge from Clunie the ball broke loose and Govan man Miller prodded the loose ball into the net. On 75 minutes Gerry Baker made it three with a good shot from the edge of the box. On time Hugh Baird brought a good roar from almost everyone in the ground with a well deserved consolation goal for Aberdeen. The Glasgow Police announced that the match must have set some sort of record. A crowd of over 108,000 in a Glasgow football stadium and not a single arrest.

RESULT: ABERDEEN 1 ST.MIRREN 3

Rangers fans who booed the side off the pitch when they lost to Aberdeen were cheered when the team won 3-0 at Highbury against Arsenal.

The school's football season was drawing to a close.

Govan High lost out in the Intermediate age deciders to Colston by a score of 3 -1.

Govan Primary School results: Greenfield 3 Elder Park 0; Hillington 0 Hill's Trust 8; Croftfoot 1 Bellahouston 7;

The Glasgow under 14's team were doing well and had one Govan player involved; left winger J.Robertson from Lourdes. A comprehensive 8-1 win over Lanarkshire was achieved with centre forward Forrest scoring several goals.

Lourdes were well represented in the Under 13 Glasgow team with goalkeeper T.Conway; left half N.McGowan and winger J.Anderson. Lourdes managed to reach the Division 4 age group final. They met St.Mungo's at Moore Park. St.Mungo's with a strong wind at their back scored twice in the first half. Lourdes pounded away at the St.Mungo's goal in the second half but were unable to score.

The highlight of the season was the win of the Intermediate age group over England by 3-2. John Walker of Govan High was a key player in this match. Also at Moore Park the Govan Boys Brigade Finals were held. The Junior age group seen the 119th Coy take on the 168th Coy. At the older age group saw the 105th Coy play the 168th Coy.

Donnie Mc Kinnon the Glencairn centre half had an early end to the season when he fractured his arm in a match against St.Johnstone. Several senior clubs were interested in Donnie including Partick Thistle. Twin brother Ronnie was about to join Rangers on a full time basis.

Benburb's season was generally poor although they did better in the cup competitions. They had a good run in the Central League Cup reaching the semi finals . Facing them for a place in the final was Cambuslang Rangers. Petershill Park saw the Bens get off to a good start when Eddie Wilkie cut in from the left and fired home. The second half saw an improved 'wee gers' and they scored an equaliser to gain a replay. The replay took place again at Petershill Park. After 90 minutes with defences dominating the match was scoreless. Thirty extra minutes were played which was tense but no goals were scored.

The second replay took place at Newlandsfield Park.

The Bens team was Gallacher, Cameron Cairns, McIlmoyle, Young, McCulloch, Burns, Jackson, Murphy, Kiernan and Wilkie.

Benburb were the better side in the first half but could not get the key opening goal. The same pattern continued in the second half. Fifteen minutes from the end the Bens were awarded a penalty which John Cameron smashed into the net off the inside of the crossbar. Cambuslang who had been defending for most of the match piled on the pressure and scored twice before the final whistle, much to the delight of their travelling support.

RESULT: BENBURB 1 CAMBUSLANG RANGERS 2

Football and politics came together when Prime Minister Harold McMillan visited Ibrox Park and was introduced to the Rangers and Celtic teams prior to the Glasgow Charity Cup match. The crowd were respectful and applauded. The match was a 1-1 draw. Celtic won on the toss of a coin.

Brilliant sunshine greeted the teams as they took the field at Hampden Park in the Scottish Junior Cup Final. Irvine Meadow had a big support and Shettleston tempted out a good following from the east end of Glasgow. The crowd was recorded at 65,211. The danger men were predicted to be Meadow winger 'Hookie' Walker and Shettleston's George O'Brien who had been scoring freely all season.

Glasgow Lord Provost Myer Galpern was presented to the teams before the match. He was a keen football man and represented the Shettleston Ward in Glasgow. He was hoping for a Town victory

IRVINE MEADOW: Prentice, Hughes, Isaac, Dickie, Crawford, Carr, Carroll, Curran, Wark, Morrison and Walker

SHETTLESTON: Brown, Reid, Sim, Sinclair, Bell, Duncanson, Graham, Black, O'Brien, Wright and Quinn

Play was bright from the start and both goalkeepers pulled off smart saves in the opening minutes. However the next full length diving save was by Irvine Meadow's Hughes trying to keep out a Quinn header. Penalty !. George O'Brien stepped up but Prentice brought roars from the Ayrshire support with an excellent stop.

On 24 minutes Carroll of the Meadow was well clear behind the 'Town' defence with the whites claiming offside. Brown came out and dived at Carroll's feet and both players fell to the ground. A penalty said referee Gordon from Newport on Tay. Morrison stepped up and scored. A top class Junior match continued with much good attacking play but the score remained 1-0 to the Meadow at half time.

Shettleston started the second half looking for the equaliser and laid siege to the Meadow goal. Meadow respond and a Carroll shot hit Sim on the hand. The full back could do little about it and 'accidental' was expected decision. However referee Gordon pointed to the penalty spot. After a lot of protests Morrison rolled the ball into the net to extend Meadow's lead. Shettleston attacked non stop for the remainder of the match. Graham had a header cleared off the line with the 'Town' claiming the ball was over the line. Town continued to press and Provost Myers Galpern and his wife were on their feet as Sim scored a late goal.

RESULT: SHETTLESTON 1 IRVINE MEADOW 2

At Moore Park, St.Anthony's appointed Joe Conner as Match Secretary. Joe wasted no time in approaching former Ants player Jimmy Rice as coach. Jimmy had a spell at Manchester United in his career. St.Anthony's had finished the season with some good form despite being bottom. They were already predicting a good season with centre forward Alec Crawford being asked to be captain. The Ants signed four players from St.Constantine's Boys Guild team. Frank Mc Grillon (wing half); Francis Herron (outside right); Dailly (centre forward) and Alec Bradley (inside left).

**178**

# CITY AND DISTRICT JUVENILE LEAGUE

| Team | Pl | W | L | D | F | A | Pts |
|------|----|----|----|----|----|----|----|
| Avon Villa | 18 | 14 | 3 | 1 | 57 | 21 | 29 |
| Park United | 15 | 10 | 0 | 5 | 61 | 21 | 25 |
| League Hearts | 15 | 12 | 2 | 1 | 52 | 22 | 25 |
| ShettlestonViolet | 16 | 9 | 4 | 3 | 43 | 32 | 21 |
| Carnwadric Bluebell | 17 | 9 | 8 | 0 | 64 | 55 | 18 |
| Olivetti | 17 | 7 | 8 | 2 | 46 | 40 | 16 |
| Ferndale | 18 | 6 | 9 | 3 | 37 | 35 | 15 |
| Parkhead Juv. | 20 | 4 | 12 | 4 | 32 | 66 | 12 |
| Glencairn Juv. | 15 | 4 | 8 | 3 | 24 | 23 | 11 |
| Tradeston Holmlea | 19 | 3 | 12 | 4 | 39 | 74 | 10 |
| Arden Thistle | 18 | 2 | 14 | 2 | 27 | 82 | 6 |

The two Plantation Park sides continued to dominate the league but the strong League Hearts were finishing fast. Park United were playing virtually every night to make up fixtures as they were having good runs in the many cups and tournaments.

At Tinto Park the Fairfields Inter Department tournament final took place.

ELECTRICIANS: Hillhouse, McNab, Geary, Gallacher, Gibson, Hamilton, Kelly, Bennie, McNeil, Hunter and Carlin

JOINERS: McTurk, Mathie, Rollins, Barr, McKendrick, Spence, Kinnaird, McQueen, Hay, McKinnon and Wilson

After some electrifying runs down the wings the sparks went ahead when McNeil made a good connection with a cross. The Joiners put the shutters up for a while and screwed home an equaliser from Hay.

Some illuminating play in the second half gave the sparks the cup with two unopposed goals.

RESULT: ELECTRICIANS 3 JOINERS 1

Playing throughout the summer months Park United won three titles. They were;

Glasgow Cup, League Champions, North Eastern Cup. The regular team was: Denovan, McDonald, Wilson, Henderson, Devlin, Hays, Hamilton, Kearney, McKenzie, Robb and Porteous

Not to be completely outdone Avon Villa won two; Scottish Consolation Cup and the League Cup.

Three ex Benburb players in the same Celtic squad.
Eric Smith (left) John Divers (centre)
Mike Jackson (right)

Jock 'Tiger' Shaw  Benburb, Rangers and
Scotland

Jock 'Tiger' Shaw leads out Scotland at Wembley in
1947

Charlie 'Legs' or 'Cannonball'
Fleming East Fife and Scotland

George Young Rangers and
Scotland

Willie Woodburn  Rangers and Scotland

**Photo 10**

# CHAPTER 11
## CUP FINALS,CUP FINALS AND THE CUP FINAL (195960)

Robbie and Derek plan to carry on watching football throughout the forthcoming 1959-60 season. They look forward to visiting some new grounds including Easter Road, Muirfield Park home of St.Johnstome and Ayr United. Also, hopefully Benburb will get a good cup run and that will involve a few days out on the Bens supporters bus.

Rangers are in a tough League Cup group with Hibernian, Motherwell and Dundee. Robbie and Derek were in Edinburgh for the first football match of the season. The streets between the Edinburgh Waverley Station and the Easter Road ground of Hibernian were packed. The Hibs are playing host to Rangers in the Scottish League Cup Group match. Being the first match of the season a huge Orange Parade has followed Rangers to the match, a tradition from years past. It is a hot sunny day and with the large street side crowds it is proving difficult to get along the pavements. The spectacle is colourful and the bands enthusiastic and entertaining. Inside the ground there is a large crowd and most of the Rangers support including a sizable number of Orangemen are behind the down slope end goal. Hibernian still had several players from their golden era a few years previously and also included John Baxter a former Benburb player in their team.

HIBERNIAN:Wren, Grant, McLelland, Nicol, Plenderleith, Baxter, Scott, Fox, Baker, Gibson & Ormond.

RANGERS:Niven, Shearer, Caldow, Davis, Telfer, Stevenson, Scott, McMillan, Miller, Brand & Matthew

Rangers scored on 25 minutes through Ralph Brand but Hibs soon equalised when Ormond headed in a cross from Jim Scott, younger brother of Alex in the Rangers side.. However, the home side were having trouble with the pace and sharpness of Rangers Ralph Brand and he and Matthew gave the Gers a 3-1 interval lead. The huge travelling support were ultimately treated to a 6-1 win with Brand getting four Matthew and Miller a strike each.

On the following Wednesday, Rangers came back down to earth with a bump when they entertained Motherwell. The Fir Park side had a forward line which looked very small. However Motherwell deservedly beat Rangers on the evening by 2-1 and completed the same scoreline to win the group easily from Hibernian, Dundee and Rangers.

Meanwhile Benburb were assembling a very useful side after the disappointment of the previous seasons. They drew 3-3 at Tinto Park with Arthurlie.

BENBURB: Gallagher, Cameron, Hiddleston, Clark, Young, Mc Culloch, Mc Donald, Kelly, Murphy, McEwan & Ewing.

St. Anthony's made some good signings with new secretary Joe Connor pleased to retain the services of Alec Crawford.

The early part of the 1959/60 saw an unbelievable run of form by St. Anthony's. By mid September they were still unbeaten in the league. With Alec Crawford at centre forward they probably had the best player in the league and the diminutive Frank McGrillan ;signed from St. Constantine's was a class act. In September 1959 they were top of the league.

Alec Crawford was said to have hailed from one of Govan's 'better known' families and on ability should have been playing a few yards along the road at Ibrox. His one weakness was his temper and many of the centre halves who marked him were guilty of terrible challenges. Frank McGrillan was small in stature but had a heart the size of a lion. He battled tirelessly and most felt if he had been inches taller he would easily be playing senior football. Crawford was scoring freely and scored two goals in a win over Benburb. He took a head knock in that fixture but recovered to play in the next match against Arthurlie where again he scored two goals.

| Central League 'B' | Pl | W | L | D | F | A | Pts |
|---|---|---|---|---|---|---|---|
| St.Anthony's | 11 | 10 | 0 | 1 | 37 | 7 | 21 |
| Petershill | 12 | 9 | 2 | 1 | 34 | 10 | 19 |
| Port Glasgow | 12 | 9 | 2 | 1 | 33 | 17 | 19 |
| Bailleston | 10 | 8 | 1 | 1 | 35 | 19 | 17 |
| Clydebank | 10 | 6 | 2 | 2 | 34 | 11 | 14 |
| Blantyre Vics | 10 | 5 | 3 | 2 | 29 | 19 | 12 |
| Benburb | 11 | 5 | 4 | 2 | 22 | 18 | 12 |
| Arthurlie | 11 | 4 | 3 | 4 | 21 | 18 | 12 |
| Blantyre Celtic | 10 | 4 | 5 | 1 | 21 | 18 | 9 |
| Vale of Leven | 11 | 3 | 6 | 2 | 23 | 36 | 8 |
| Parkhead | 12 | 3 | 7 | 2 | 21 | 28 | 8 |
| Maryhill | 12 | 4 | 8 | 0 | 28 | 39 | 8 |
| Perthshire | 11 | 3 | 7 | 1 | 27 | 41 | 7 |
| Bridgeton Waverley | 11 | 3 | 7 | 1 | 12 | 31 | 7 |
| Vale of Clyde | 12 | 2 | 7 | 3 | 19 | 44 | 7 |
| Gourock | 11 | 2 | 9 | 0 | 16 | 29 | 4 |
| Strathclyde | 11 | 1 | 8 | 2 | 15 | 42 | 4 |

In the car park at the Copland Road end of Ibrox Park one Saturday morning there is a small football match going on. It is 7-a-side and it`s between boys aged 9 to 12 years of age. Each team is supplemented by an adult. On one side is Frank Haffey and his friend is on the opposite side to even it up. They play for around half an hour before Frank encourages the boys take a turn at trying to score a penalty against him. The boys enjoy his company and he teaches them small improvements in their play each time they have the session. Frank lives on Copland Road and had played a few seasons at Celtic and has had some sparkling performances. He is a pleasant character, full of life and well liked by most who know him.

Benburb were assembling a very useful side after the disappointment of the previous seasons. They drew 3-3 at Tinto Park with Arthurlie. They have retained the services of John Gallacher who has interested a host of senior clubs both in Scotland and England.

BENBURB: Gallagher, Cameron, Hiddleston, Clark, Young, McCulloch, McDonald, Kelly, Murphy, McEwan & Ewing.

Govan Amateurs were consistent. In four season's they had won the West of Scotland League twice and been runner's up twice. However, as well as collecting or being in contention for the trophies they had developed an excellent reputation for acts of sportsmanship throughout many seasons. Good players from Govan Amateurs who had recently left were Davie Mitchell who joined Aberdeen after only a few games with Renfrew. Also Ian Clark who joined Queen's Park.

Former St. Gerrard's and Scotland youth centre forward Peter Catterson having left Duntocher Hibs spent time training with Benburb. He got a good offer from Carluke Rovers and was soon on his way to the Lanarkshire club.

Peter Marshall was a Rangers fan with a love for horses. While he was waiting in the queue to enter the Rangers v Motherwell match he saw a policeman sitting on a horse. He went over to the horse put his arms around its neck and started kissing the animal. Other fans had great difficulty in getting him to let go. Eventually a few other policemen arrived and asked Marshall to go away. He challenged them all to a fight before he was arrested. At Govan Police Court Fiscal W.Grindlay said 'It is unusual for anyone to want to kiss a horse. He was drunk !' Peter Marshall was fined £1.

There was local derby at the fifty pitches. New club Cardonald locked horns with St.Constatine's in the Glasgow Secondary League.

The Glasgow Cup was competed for every season by the six Glasgow senior teams. At the end of the season the same teams competed for the Glasgow Charity Cup. In a match at Hampden Park Rangers overcame the hosts Queen's Park by 5-1 after being 4 goals up at half time. However the best player on view was a spider, Junior Omand, who delighted the 8,000 crowd with some great skill and scored a good goal.

182

Scottish Football was saddened by the sudden death of Davie Meiklejohn the manager of Partick Thistle. Davie had once been a pupil at Bellahouston Academy and had many great years playing for Rangers at Ibrox Park. Craigton Cemetery was packed with mourners including many from his former opponents including Jimmy McGrory of Celtic.

Rangers had a few important matches in a relatively short space of time. As well as an Old Firm derby they had two European Cup matches against Anderlecht from Belgium.

RANGERS: Niven, Shearer, Little, Davis, Telfer, Stevenson, Scott, Wilson, Miller, Baird and Matthew

CELTIC: Haffey, McNeil, Kennedy, MacKay, Evans, Peacock, McVittie, Jackson, Conway, Divers and Auld.

A 60,000 all ticket crowd saw Rangers take the initiative early in the match and Davie Wilson headed home a headed cross from Jimmy Miller. Former Benburb player Mike Jackson was Celtic's best player and left Willie Telfer a clean pair of heals and shot into the side netting. The game became very physical and Harold Davis went off for treatment after a challenge from Jackson. Davis soon returned and in a few minutes Jackson was receiving treatment after a challenge from Davis. The second half saw play even up before Jimmy Miller got free on the wing and crossed and Alex Scott headed into the net to the delight of the home support. Mike Jackson continued to be Celtic's best player and it was he who scored an excellent goal with a fierce drive from 20 yards that gave Niven no chance. Rangers stepped up the pace towards the end and Jimmy Miller scored a third.

RESULT: RANGERS 3 CELTIC 1

Rangers came out to huge cheers from an 80,000 crowd in their European Cup match with Anderlecht from Belgium. Within ten minutes Anderlecht were being booed from all quarters as they put in one cynical challenge after another. Rangers had scored two goals in the opening three minutes. Miller headed in a Scott cross and then Alex Scott drove a fierce drive across the goalie and into the far corner of the net. At this point Anderlecht players were kicking at anything that moved and the crowd did not like it.

After half time Andy Matthew added a third for Rangers before the Belgians stunned the crowd with two quick goals. Sammy Baird fired in a fourth for Rangers and it was the same player who converted a penalty to give Rangers a three goal cushion for the second leg. The second leg between the sides proved to be no quieter. Alex Scott was barged off the pitch into a barrier and received a bad head wound.

He returned after 10 minutes. Rangers kept their composure and won 2-0 with goals from Andy Matthew and a good goal from Ian McMillan. Rangers were into the 2nd Round and the next opponents were Red Star Bratislava.

Players with a Govan connection were doing well. Former Govan High player Alex Ferguson broke into the Queen's Park Strollers team and scored two in a 3-2 win over Morton Reserves. Former St.Gerrard's schoolboy Joe Mc Bride was a regular in the Kilmarnock first team and Harry Haddock another St.Gerrard's schoolboy was still captain at Clyde.

Heart of Midlothian were setting a fast pace at the top of the Scottish League and were aiming to reach the final of the Scottish League Cup. 27,500 spectators turned up at Easter Road to see Hearts make short work of a plucky Cowdenbeath side with a margin of 9 goals to 3.

Third Lanark reached the semi final and the supporters in the classes at Drumoyne School were allowed to stay up later than normal. The Hi Hi were at Ibrox Park for their semi final against Arbroath. The 'Red Lichties' brought a few thousand supporters with them and the entire crowd of 12,000 was housed in the Rangers enclosure and stand side of the ground. Arbroath gave a good account of themselves in the first half and held Thirds at 0-0. Early in the second half Joe Mc Innes gave Third Lanark the lead and further goals from Craig and Ian Hilley put them in the Scottish League Cup Final.

The Scottish League Cup Final saw Heart of Midlothian as overwhelming favourites against Third Lanark. The match gave the Hi Hi the opportunity to give their supporters a day out at Hampden Park. Their manager George Young was very popular and in Jocky Robertson they had the smallest goalkeeper in the league at just 5 foot and 5 inches tall.

THIRD LANARK: Robertson, Lewis, Brown, Reilly, McCallum, Cunningham, McInnes, Craig, D.Hilley, Gray and I.Hilley

HEARTS: Marshall, Kirk, Thomson, Bowman, Cumming, Higgins, Smith, Crawford, Young, Blackwood and Hamilton

The match got off to a sensational start when a long ball upfield saw Marshall misjudge the wind and he barely got his fingers to it at full stretch. Matt Gray followed it in and tapped it into the empty net. The Warriors fans were delighted , the Hearts players giving Gordon Marshall some black looks. Throughout the first half Hearts pushed forward but they found the Thirds defence stout with Jocky Robertson inspired. Half Time arrived with the Cathkin Park side still ahead.

In the second half the Hearts camped in the Thirds half of the pitch in a search of the equaliser and it duly arrived on 56 minutes. Johnny Hamilton sent in a great shot that hit the post and went in to bring the scores level. Within another few minutes Alex Young moved through the middle of the Hi Hi's defence and fired home. Thirds never gave up and put in a good finish.

However, Hearts were the better side and despite the best efforts of Jocky Robertson they were worthy winners.

RESULT: THIRD LANARK 1 HEARTS 2

The Scottish Junior Cup 1st Round draw gave both the Govan sides tough assignments. St.Anthony's had a home match against Rob Roy. Benburb could not believe their bad luck when they were drawn away to old adversaries Ashfield.

A crowd of 5,000 attended the match and John Armour the former St.Gerrard's schoolboy made his debut for the Ants.

ST.ANTHONY'S: Brown, Doyle, Duffy, Curran, Kelly, O'Neil, Mowan, Cuddihy, Crawford, McGrillan and Armour

ROB ROY: Craig, McFarlane, Cairns, Urquhart, Lindsey, Reid, Jennings, Rafferty, Smith, O'Donnell and Irving

The game was tense with little flowing football. Rob Roy got a stroke of luck when winger Jennings shot hit a stone on the pitch and deceived goalkeeper Brown to give the Kirkintilloch side the lead.

The Ants had all the play in the second half and hit the woodwork twice as well as having a goal disallowed. A few claims for penalties were turned down and the Rabs held on to the delight of their followers.

St.Anthony's also had a tough cup draw in the West of Scotland Cup away at Glenafton. The Glens built up a two goal lead but two goals from Alec Crawford forced a draw. Crawford scored 18 goals in the first 13 games for the Ants until the end of their 13 game unbeaten run against Bailleston.

Ashfield were playing their home matches at Dennistoun Waverley's Haghill Park ground due to works at Saracen Park. The small ground had a black ash surface and was overlooked by tenements. Two sizeable groups of supporters from the Bens and Ashfield arrived and a good atmosphere was created.

Benburb were very much the better side in the first half but had to wait until 5 minutes before the interval before Lindsey scored following a scramble in the goalmouth. If the Bens were the better side in the first half it was Ashfield after the break and the Bens goal was under siege for long periods. The 'field equalised forcing a replay.

The replay at Tinto Park a week later saw a similar pattern. However Ashfield took the lead against the run of play with a penalty. This was cancelled out when Jim Kelly headed home. The second half saw Ashfield on top with both sides scoring a goal apiece. Extra time failed to produce any more goals with the Bens hanging on towards the end. A third match was scheduled for Newlandsfield, the ground of Pollok.

Benburb had concerns about Johnny Gallacher in goal being able to play. He had suspected broken ribs. The Bens staff including former keeper Alex Forsyth worked overtime to get him available for the match.

ASHFIELD: Munro, Gibson, McNab, McLeod, Cassidy, McInnes, Thomson, Rooney, Logan, Hannaway and Cameron
BENBURB: Gallacher, Cameron, Hiddleston, McCulloch, Young, Murphy, Brown, Kelly, Brodie, Kiernan and Taylor

Ashfield made the brighter start and John Gallacher had to make a couple of smart stops. However the Bens soon started to get into the match and after having a blatent penalty claim turned down they took the lead. John Cameron managed to get down to the line and crossed for Jack Kiernan to head home much to the delight of the Govanites.

The second half saw the Bens contain Ashfield and look the more likely side to add to their lead. Then Mc Culloch took a bad head knock and was taken to hospital leaving the Bens with 20 minutes to hang on. Ashfield piled forward and Gallacher and Maurice Young were excellent in keeping Ashfield out.

RESULT : ASHFIELD 0 BENBURB 1

The Bens reward was a home match against the favourites for the Scottish Junior Cup, Johnstone Burgh. Senior clubs were after Benburb's stars in the matches against Ashfield. Benny Murphy had requests from Charlton Athletic to have him down to London for trials and Jim Kelly had offers from Celtic to go on trial.

Robert Lockhart was a hard working and co-operative football person. As well as being secretary of Govan Juveniles he helped out St.Anthony's with football injuries. Govan Juveniles were producing countless good players. The latest targets for Junior clubs were centre forward James McIntyre who had scored 11 goals in his previous three matches. Also Paul Brechin who was being trailed by Benburb.

Former Govan Juveniles players were twins Donnie and Ronnie Mc Kinnon who was on Rangers books. Donnie was centre half for Glencairn and obtained man of the match awards for some of his performances.

Alfie Woods was centre forward for Stephens Boys Club. He was probably the smallest player on the pitch as they took the field against Queen's Park (Victoria 11) in the Mitchell Shield semi final at Hogarth Park. However despite his size Alfie was a prolific goal scorer and in a rich vein of form with 8 goals in his previous 3 matches for the shipbuilders.

Schools Results: Govan Primary Schools League
Bellahouston 5 Sandwood 0; Drumoyne 7 Copland Road 0; Hillington 2 Greenfield 4;  Greenfield 3 Bellahouston 5; Copland Road 3 Hillington 1; Sandwood 2 Drumoyne 3;  Bellahouston 7 Copland Road 1; Hillington 0 Drumoyne 7; Greenfield 0 Sandwood 5;
Drumoyne 5 Bellahouston 1; Sandwood 7 Hillington 0; Copland Road 2 Greenfield 3;
Sandwood 3 Bellahouston 3; Greenfield 6 Hillington 1.

# WEST OF SCOTLAND AMATEUR LEAGUE 1st DIVISION

| Team | Pl | W | L | D | F | A | Pts |
|------|-----|-----|-----|-----|-----|-----|-----|
| Govan Amateurs | 8 | 8 | 0 | 0 | 18 | 10 | 16 |
| Westclox Amateurs | 8 | 6 | 1 | 1 | 24 | 15 | 13 |
| Milanda Amateurs | 9 | 5 | 2 | 2 | 28 | 22 | 12 |
| Bearsden Amateurs | 9 | 4 | 2 | 3 | 24 | 17 | 11 |
| Barr & Stroud | 8 | 4 | 2 | 2 | 17 | 16 | 10 |
| Mearns Amateurs | 9 | 5 | 4 | 0 | 21 | 20 | 10 |
| Barclay Curle | 8 | 3 | 3 | 2 | 23 | 23 | 8 |
| Glasgow Transport | 9 | 2 | 5 | 2 | 14 | 28 | 6 |
| Babcock and Wilcox | 8 | 1 | 5 | 2 | 19 | 22 | 4 |
| Stephens Amateurs | 7 | 1 | 6 | 0 | 8 | 16 | 2 |
| Killermont Amateurs | 7 | 1 | 6 | 0 | 10 | 26 | 2 |
| Rhu Amateurs | 8 | 1 | 7 | 0 | 10 | 28 | 2 |

The Glasgow Schools under 15 team trials contained several Govan schools players.

Campbell (Govan High) - Goalkeeper, Gillespie (St.Gerrard's) - Full Back, Brown (Govan High) - Forward, Robertson (Lourdes) - Forward

Govan High and St.Gerrard's came head to head in two important cup matches.

In the Cameronian Cup for the biggest Secondary Schools in Glasgow, Govan High won by the only goal scored (1-0). A week later it was St.Gerrard's who triumphed with the only goal scored (1-0). Govan High failed to progress further in the Cameronian Cup losing surprisingly to Hyndland by 4-0.

Lourdes were developing strong football teams and at one of the older age groups a regular team was; R.Christie, G.Borthwick, R.Holy, M.Harran, F.McCarron, J.Farrell, B.McNulty, G.Cassidy, A.Dignon, J.Donnelly, F.McAleer,

Park United who won 3 trophies during the 1958-59 season held a prize giving evening at the Neptune Masonic Lodge in Scotland Street. The Scottish Juvenile League President Mr.William Hendry made the presentations. Afterwards all present had a Supper and Dance evening.

Approaching mid season the big Plantation Park derby result was;

Park Utd. 1  Avon Villa 3

A large crowd descended on Tinto Park for the big Scottish Junior Cup tie between Benburb and Johnstone Burgh. Johnstone Burgh were top of their league and Benburb were in the top half of their Division. Coachloads of fans arrived from Johnstone keen to cheer their team to victory.

The defences remained on top for most of the afternoon with very few clear cut chances. Bens had most of the chances but failed to capitalise. Dan Mc Sorley scored with one of the few Burgh chances and that was enough to send his team through. Jim Hiddleston joined Benburb and played some games at left back. His father Jimmy Hiddleston had played for Benburb also before moving on to St.Johnstone.

Players with Govan connections continued to do well.

Former Govan High and Glasgow school representative player Alex.Ferguson made the breakthrough into the Queen's Park first team and scored the Spiders goal in a 1-1 draw at Forfar Athletic. Alec Crawford of St.Anthony's had a trial match for Morton reserves and scored a hat trick. Numerous senior clubs showed interest in the Ants top goal scorer. Ronnie Mc Kinnon was a regular player for the Rangers reserve side playing at right half. Former Benburb inside left Tony Gregal was breaking through into the St. Mirren first team.

Rangers had a tough match in the European Cup against Czechoslovakia side Red Star Bratislava. The first match at Ibrox Park was a high scoring and incident packed game. Ian Mc Millan put Rangers ahead in the 1st minute after a good pass from Alex Scott. The Czechs played excellent football and scored two good goals from Scherer and Dolinsev to lead approaching half time.

The Czechs had Matlak sent off very harshly after a strong challenge. Approaching half time Sammy Baird out muscled the Czech goalkeeper who dropped the ball for Alex Scott to score. The Czech goalie was carried off with a head wound. Scherer put the Czechs ahead mid way through the second half despite playing with 10 men. Rangers launched a final onslaught and a Davie Wilson goal pulled them level. In the last minute Jimmy Miller got a vital goal for Rangers to give them a narrow lead to take to Bratislava.

RESULT: RANGERS 4 RED STAR BRATISLAVA 3

A week later Rangers made the trip behind the Iron Curtain and an afternoon match in Bratislava. Rangers were on the back foot from the start and the defence was stretched on several occasions. However the first half ended goal less and the home fans whistled their displeasure at some of Rangers time wasting.

In the second half Rangers made good progress down the left on 75 minutes leaving Davie Wilson free. His cross was perfect and Alex.Scott scored with a header. The home side went mad and there were many scuffles. One scuffle saw Jimmy Miller sent off leaving Rangers with 10 men for the last 9 minutes. Tichy scored with 2 minutes to go but the Rangers held on for a good win.

RESULT: RED STAR BRATISLAVA 1 RANGERS 1 (AGGREGATE 4-5)

St.Anthony`s remained near the top of the league. However, the camp was not altogether happy and Secretary Joe Conner who had done much to produce a very strong side decided to resign and left the club. Billy Elliot the Ants trainer and former boxer also resigned. Centre forward and captain Alec Crawford was much sought after and spent a lot of weeks on trial with senior clubs including Celtic and Stirling Albion. As a consequence the Ants results started to slip slightly.

Approaching Christmas the two Govan rivals met at Moore Park in a league game. Benburb fielded a strong side.

ST.ANTHONY'S: Brown, Doyle, Duffy, Curran, Kelly, McEachan, Herron, McGrillan,Rose, Collins and Cuddihy

BENBURB: Forsyth, Cameron, Hiddleston, McCulloch, Young, Kiernan, Lindsey, Kelly, Taylor, Chalmers and Brown

The Ants were well in command in the opening stages of the match. McGrillan scored in the first minute and soon he headed home a Maurice Young clearance that had come off the post. Soon it was three when Rose was brought down in the penalty box and Kelly smashed home the spot kick. Benburb settled and Brown reduced the arrears. Bens piled forward and Chalmers reduced the arrears further but there was time before the interval for Rose to give the Ants a 4-2 lead. The second half proved equally as exciting and the Ants held on to ultimately win 5-4

RESULT : ST.ANTHONY'S 5 BENBURB 4

Hughie Gilkinson was a Govan man through and through. He had spent the last 21 years with just one club, Govan Amateurs. He was player, official and now trainer of the club. Govan Amateurs continued to receive ongoing admiration for their sportsmanship. When two players of the opposing team Dirrans collided, Hughie was straight on the pitch to treat the stricken players; the opposition having no trainer.

Govan won 4-1 in a replay with great play from Jimmy McLure, Dougie Wilkie, Alan Stoak and Jimmy Hetherington. The referee put in a special note to say the match was played in the best sportsmanship.

Paisley Benburb had a big Scottish Juvenile Cup tie. The rules stated the game had to be played on an enclosed ground. Benburb heard about it and immediately offered their namesakes use of the ground at no cost. The match was drawn 1-1 against Lothian United and a replay took place the following week at Whitburn.

In the various schools league's the half way stage of the season was reached. The Govan challenge was not as strong as previous seasons although a few schools were in contention.

At the oldest of 5 age groups St. Gerrard's sat fourth with an outside chance. At the 3rd age group Lourdes were still in contention. At the youngest age group Lourdes were having a decent season and Govan High were improving by the week.

Some crowds at the Scottish Juniors matches were very high and on many occasions higher than senior clubs gates. There were exceptions. Strathclyde's home league match against Blantyre Celtic attracted a crowd of nil. The once famous Strathies had fallen on bad times and their very existence was being threatened. The day in question was one of the worst for weather and many supporters may have thought the match at Springfield Park would be off. A few spectators turned up late and were admitted into the ground free as the gatekeeper could not be bothered to re-open the pay gate. The Springfield Park ground provided a bleak background being black ash and no cover for spectators. The few spectators present huddled around the changing block. Strathclyde were having a poor season and the wee Celtic were on a good run and still interested in the Scottish Junior Cup. It was backs to the wall for the Strathies in the first half but they held on until half time scoreless. In the second half the home side improved and gave their small hard working committee something to cheer about when Freddy Falconer netted the winner. Strathclyde paid the £12 'guarantee to Blantyre Celtic at the end of the match.

The Springfield Park ground was well kept up although sparse. Across the road was Celtic Park and several other Junior clubs were nearby. Celtic proved to be good neighbours and always willing to help out the Strathies whenever required. They played friendly matches, supplied almost brand new football's and training kit. A lot of other acts of kindness were forthcoming from the Parkhead club which went to keeping the Strathclyde club afloat.

Third Lanark played Rangers in a league match at Cathkin Park around the Christmas New Year period. The Ibrox side won 2-0 but their chances of catching the leaders Heart of Midlothian already looked remote. When Third Lanark played a home match their supporters shouted 'Hi Hi Hi' a tradition that went back to when the club was in its infancy. The club were formed as the 3rd Lanarkshire Rifle Volunteers and were a force in the formative years of Scottish football. Their ground Cathkin Park was said to have been the original 'Hampden Park'. Hampden Park was only a short distance away. It is said that when the footballers from the soldiers met up with their comrades in arms their greeting was 'Hi Hi Hi' and it stuck. They were sometimes given the nickname 'The Warriors' but most times 'the Hi Hi' was used. They had a very popular manager in George Young who had succeeded another popular manager Bob Shankly who had moved on to Dundee as manager. After the Third Lanark v Rangers match George Young exited the changing rooms at the corner of Cathkin Park and signed autographs for around half and hour and discussed virtually anything with both Thirds and Rangers supporters.

1960 arrived with the New Years Day Old firm derby at Parkhead. A very poor match was brought into life with a good Jimmy Miller goal in the second half which gave the Rangers the spoils with a 1-0 win. However, the win still left Rangers three points behind Hearts and Kilmarnock were the team in form and moving to just two points behind the Ibrox Club.

## SCOTTISH LEAGUE DIVISION 1

| Team | Pl | W | L | D | F | A | Pts |
|------|----|----|----|----|----|----|----|
| Hearts | 21 | 15 | 2 | 4 | 66 | 34 | 34 |
| Rangers | 21 | 15 | 5 | 1 | 57 | 21 | 31 |
| Kilmarnock | 21 | 14 | 6 | 1 | 37 | 31 | 29 |
| Dundee | 21 | 11 | 6 | 4 | 44 | 31 | 26 |
| Hibernian | 21 | 11 | 7 | 3 | 76 | 50 | 25 |
| Motherwell | 21 | 10 | 7 | 4 | 41 | 44 | 24 |
| Clyde | 21 | 9 | 6 | 6 | 40 | 38 | 24 |
| Raith Rovers | 21 | 10 | 9 | 2 | 40 | 34 | 22 |
| Airdrie | 21 | 9 | 10 | 2 | 33 | 49 | 20 |
| Partick Thistle | 21 | 9 | 10 | 2 | 33 | 53 | 20 |
| Ayr United | 21 | 8 | 10 | 3 | 44 | 50 | 19 |
| Celtic | 21 | 7 | 9 | 5 | 43 | 37 | 19 |
| St.Mirren | 20 | 8 | 11 | 1 | 50 | 46 | 17 |
| Aberdeen | 21 | 6 | 12 | 3 | 33 | 50 | 15 |
| Third Lanark | 20 | 7 | 13 | 0 | 40 | 51 | 14 |
| Dunfermline | 21 | 4 | 11 | 6 | 49 | 57 | 14 |
| Stirling Albion | 21 | 3 | 12 | 6 | 27 | 39 | 12 |
| Arbroath | 21 | 4 | 14 | 3 | 25 | 64 | 11 |

Former East Fife and Scotland player Charlie 'legs' Fleming had moved to England and Southern League Bath City. He was idolised by adoring fans at Twerton Park and scored on a regular basis. His nickname was now Charlie 'cannonball' Fleming. Charlie enjoyed his football and lifestyle at Bath and helped the City to pull off several notable giant killing exploits in the English FA Cup.

Benburb were starting to find some form and had an important match with Lesmahagow in the West of Scotland Cup looming up fast. However the club were rocked with the death of Davie McCracken. Davie was a former West of Scotland Junior Football Assoc. President and general secretary of Benburb Football Club for a considerable number of years. He was heavily involved in the erection of the large covered enclosure at Tinto Park.

On the playing side Watford were frequent visitors to Tinto Park to watch centre forward John Taylor who was a frequent goal scorer. Since his de-mob from the Army Taylor had scored 10 goals in 7 matches for the Bens. Benny Murphy a classy midfielder had been selected for the Central League team along with Alec Crawford of St.Anthony's.

The eagerly awaited match with Lesmahagow duly arrived with the Bens confident of winning against their Lanarkshire League opponents.
BENBURB: Forsyth, Cameron, Hiddleston, Kiernan, Young, Rees, Lindsey, Kelly, Taylor, Murphy and Brown
LESMAHAGOW: Mitchell, Matthews, Glennie, Hynd, W.Burns, Carlyle, T.Burns, McLaughlan, Jackson, Reid and Lowe

Gow started the better and the Bens had a blow in the opening minutes. Johnny Cameron over hit a back pass and Forysth had to dive at the opponents feet to retrieve the situation. Unfortunately, he was badly injured and had to leave the field. Hiddleston took over between the posts and the Bens played with ten men. After 10 minutes Ian Forsyth returned but badly hampered in his movements.

A few minutes later a cross came over and due to his injury he punched the ball into his own net. A few minutes later what should have been an easy save was spilled into the net by the stricken goalie. The Bens, now two down and a decision urged by the sizeable crowd, allowed Forsyth to leave the pitch and continue to play with 10 men.

The Bens started the second half urged on by the crowd and took the game to the visitors. They forced several corners and from one taken by Jim Kelly, John Taylor headed home. Against the run of play Mitchell scored for Lesmahagow. However the bens kept up the pressure and Jim Kelly reduced the arrears near the end. With just minutes to go the Bens were awrded a penalty and Jim Kelly blasted home to great cheers from the home support.
RESULT: BENBURB 3 LESMAHAGOW 3

Govan Amateurs continued to dominate the West of Scotland Amateur League Div.1. Manager Alfie Ferguson had good forwards in Jimmy McClure, Alfie Wilkie and Charlie Petrie.
Govan Juveniles continued to produce good players who attracted considerable interest from the Junior clubs. The team reached the semi final of the Johnstone Cup and had just won through to the 3rd round of the Glasgow Juvenile Cup.

In School's football Govan High were making good progress in the younger age group cup competitions appearing in two semi finals.
Primary School League results: Sandwood 8 Copeland Road 0; Drumoyne 3 Bellahouston 5; Sandwood 0 Hillington 0; Copeland Road 0 Greenfield 2; Sandwood 2 Greenfield 1; Bellahouston 2 Greenfield 3; Hillington 1 Bellahouston 8; Hillington 0 Copeland Road 1.
Southern Primary Shield: Sandwood 6 Croftwood 2; Victoria 1 Elder Park 0; Bellahouston 2 Sir John Maxwell 2; replay Sir John Maxwell 2 Bellahouston 2;
2nd replay Bellahouston 3 Sir John Maxwell 2; Toryglen 4 Hillington 0; Sandwood 3 Drumoyne 1; Bellahouston 1 Mc Gill 3
A very strong Glasgow schools side selected for the Scottish Schools Cup had three Govan players:
Campbell (Govan High), Gillespie (St.Gerrard's), Parkes (St.Mungo's), McArthur (Victoria Drive), McCraken (Shawlands), McLean (Holyrood), Robertson (Lourdes),Willoughby (Colston), Forrest (Onslow), Rollo (North Kelvinside) and Samson (John Street)
In the older age groups Bellahouston and St.Gerrard's were having good runs and were in contention to win their respective league's.
St.Anthony's seemed set to lose their best player in Alec Crawford. The centre forward had trials at several senior clubs and East Stirlingshire were keen to get the 23 year old on board before the forthcoming Scottish Cup match with Morton.
The 'shire had played 14 matches without a win. The paperwork was duly completed and the deal done. Crawford had left the Ants and with Frickleton from Clydebank he made his debut against Queen of the South at Firs Park. Queens went ahead early in the match but on the half hour after considerable 'Shire pressure Frickleton scored. A few minutes later Alec Crawford scored an excellent goal and the same player was on hand to score after a shot came off the crossbar. In the second half the Doon hammers came back strongly but East Stirlingshire held on for a narrow 4-3 win.
A week later it was Scottish Cup week and the 'shire were making a visit to Cappielow Park, Greenock to play Morton. Morton were on top for most of the match but the 'shire got the only goal of the match in the second half from Mc Innes and moved into the next round.

The Glasgow Secondary League had no fewer than 21 teams. A new club, the Drumoyne Strollers who played at the 50 pitches, started their fixtures late and had only played 8 matches until the end of January 1960. They had 1 win and 7 losses and were second bottom of the league above Cranhill who were pointless.

# GLASGOW AMATEUR LEAGUE - DIVISION A

| Team | Pl | W | L | D | F | A | Pts |
|---|---|---|---|---|---|---|---|
| Sligo Celtic | 11 | 8 | 3 | 0 | 35 | 18 | 16 |
| Cleansing Dept. | 14 | 7 | 5 | 2 | 36 | 43 | 16 |
| Dennistoun Hearts | 9 | 7 | 1 | 1 | 36 | 18 | 15 |
| Cameron Thistle | 9 | 5 | 0 | 4 | 30 | 15 | 14 |
| Gray Dunn | 11 | 6 | 3 | 2 | 38 | 31 | 14 |
| Clydeside United | 10 | 5 | 5 | 0 | 21 | 21 | 10 |
| Pollok Star | 10 | 5 | 5 | 0 | 26 | 21 | 10 |
| Norwood | 10 | 4 | 5 | 1 | 30 | 33 | 9 |
| Caruthers United | 9 | 2 | 5 | 2 | 14 | 27 | 6 |
| Alley's | 10 | 2 | 6 | 2 | 26 | 42 | 6 |
| Remington Shavers | 10 | 1 | 7 | 2 | 21 | 27 | 4 |
| Lynedoch Star | 11 | 2 | 9 | 0 | 18 | 32 | 2 |

There were two fifty pitches sides at the top of the Glasgow Amateur League. However they were coming under pressure from the pack behind. Sligo Celtic continued to play on the pitch at the corner of Fulbar Road and Shieldhall Road. The Cleansing were near the top but were looking for ways to brush up on their defence to sustain the challenge.

The top of the Juvenile League had a familiar look with both the Plantation Park pair Avon Villa and Park United well in contention.

## CITY AND DISTRICT LEAGUE

| Team | Pl | Pts |
|---|---|---|
| Avon Villa | 15 | 21 |
| Tradeston Holmlea | 14 | 16 |
| Park United | 11 | 16 |
| Carnwadric | 11 | 14 |
| Parkhead Hibs | 13 | 14 |
| League Hearts | 11 | 13 |

Scottish Amateurs were in trouble a few days before a match with Wales at Rugby Park, Kilmarnock. Queen's Park had a Scottish Cup match at Clyde which meant most of the players would not be available. Queen's however provided youngster Alex.Ferguson the former Govan High schoolboy to the team in midfield . He scored the opening goal and Scotland led 2-0 at one stage. However poor defence by Scotland saw the match end in a 3-3 draw.

The 1st round of the Scottish Cup saw Rangers play in England. Berwick Rangers faced the Ibrox side and gave a very good account of themselves. A 16,000 all ticket crowd. Davie Wilson opened the scoring for Rangers before Whitelaw sent the home support into ecstasy with an equaliser before half time. In the second half constant Rangers pressure told when Wilson scored his second on the hour mark. Two minutes from the end Davie Wilson completed his hat trick and Rangers were in Round 2.

Former Rangers player Derek Grierson returned to Ibrox for the 2nd Round of the Scottish Cup as his latest team Arbroath faced Rangers. The conditions were poor but Rangers scored two goals in the first ten minutes through Alex Scott and a Brown own goal. Arbroath conceded no more goals but Rangers progressed to the third round.

East Stirlingshire had Alec Crawford at centre forward in a snow covered Firs Park against non league Inverness Caledonian. The 'shire were two up at half time but had to settle for a draw as the highlanders fought back in the second half. The match at Inverness was much delayed due to snow. However, when it went ahead Alec Crawford was amongst the scorers as the 'shire built up a 3-0 half time lead. The Caley fought back and reduced the arrears but a late East Stirling goal secured a 4-1 win. East Stirlingshire now had a plum 3rd Round home match against Hibernian.

Inverness Caley sent a good luck message to the 'shire before the match at Firs Park. Two players with Govan connections were involved. Alec Crawford for East Stirling and John Baxter who had already achieved a remarkable career at Hibernian. Hibernian were the better team throughout. Baxter set up Fox for the opening goal on the half hour and Joe Baker added a second just before half time. Late in the match the same player scored a third and Hibs were through to the 4th round with a 3-0 scoreline.

Rangers also progressed to the 4th round with a comfortable 3-0 win at Ochilview Park against Stenhousemuir. Jimmy Miller gave Rangers a 12th minute lead. After half time Ian McMillan and Davie Wilson added the other goals. Benburb travelled down to Lesmahagow for the West of Scotland Cup. John Gallacher returned to be in goal and Jack Kiernan drew first blood for the Bens who went on to win through 2-1 with a good display. Bens had Benny Murphy and John Taylor picked for the Central League team.

| City and Suburban League | Pl | Pts |
|---|---|---|
| Avon Villa | 16 | 21 |
| Park United | 12 | 18 |
| Tradeston Holmlea | 14 | 16 |
| Carnwadric Blue. | 11 | 14 |
| Glencairn | 12 | 14 |

Park United were taking closer order with Avon Villa.

Scotland were producing a number of top class under 23 players. The match against England Under 23's who also had a strong side was eagerly awaited. The sides met at Ibrox Park under the floodlights in front of a crowd of 22,000. Scotland played well in the early stages and took the lead on 26 minutes. Denis Law challenged Marshall and the keeper spilled allowing Ian St. John a roll into the net. Alan Cousin had the crowd cheering again soon after when he went through the English defence to crash in a second. Denis Law was majestic and giving the England defence a torrid time. He was manhandled in the box by Maurice Setters and MacKay scored from the spot kick. Three nil for Scotland and the likelihood of many more to come thought the crowd.

However England were not lying down and they had a dangerous forward line who pulled a goal back. Ian St.John headed a fourth for a rampant Scotland in the second half but the English started finding their shooting boots. Jimmy Greaves scored a spectacular goal to make it 4-2 and a few minutes later scored with a fierce shot from an acute angle. A mistake from Adam Blacklaw in goal presented George Eatham an easy goal and a superb match finished honours even at 4-4.

There was a football game on Broomloan Road, Govan. Suddenly John McGiffen miscued with a clearance and the football landed on the roof slates of Cantell and Cochrane at 155, Broomloan Road. McGiffen went to retrieve the ball. Someone noticed that there was someone on the roof and called for the police. Ninety minutes later McGiffen put his head over the parapet and begged that he be rescued. He was wearing only a shirt and trousers, little protection against the evening cold. The Fire Brigade were called and raised a ladder to enable him to come down. Trembling with cold from exposure McGiffen was taken to the Southern General Hospital where he was thawed out. In the mean time the police found that McGiffen had a record and they put him behind bars for two days. Fiscal G.Boyd asked McGiffen why he had taken 90 minutes to show himself. McGiffen replied that he had seen the police arrive and thought he would stay out of sight as he believed he would be thought to be committing a crime. It was only when he became cold he realised he had to be rescued. In the meantime many of the boys who had been playing football in Broomloan Road came forward and confirmed that he had been playing football. Fiscal Boyd allowed McGiffen to leave after being admonished.

Benburb were making progress in the Cup competitions. The team were playing well and looking to reach the latter stages of the West of Scotland Cup, the Central League Cup and the Glasgow Cup. At Kirkintilloch they came from behind to beat Rob Roy 2-1 with midfielder Jim Kelly again amongst the goals. At Firs Park, Falkirk, two players with a Govan connection came face to face. Alec Crawford former St.Anthony's centre forward led the East Stirlingshire attack against Quenn's Park who had former Govan High player Alex Ferguson in the team. Alec Crawford scored the first 'shire goal in a 2-0 win.

In the European Cup 3rd Round Rangers went to Holland to meet Sparta Rotterdam. The 'Gers got off to a good start when Scott beat his full back went down the by line before crossing for Max Murray to score. Sammy Baird made it 2-0 mid way through the first half after a flick from Ian Mc Millan. George Niven was barged as he went for a high cross and spilled the ball for De-Fries to score. On 63 minutes Max Murray added a third for Rangers before De Fries scored for Sparta with two minutes left.

RESULT: SPARTA ROTTERDAM 2 RANGERS 3

The match at Ibrox Park saw over 82,500 spectators expecting Rangers to progress. A quarter of an hour before the start a large bird cage was walked around the Ibrox track and the crowd were respectful by being quiet as the bird in the cage was walked past. 'If I had known I wid av brought some Trill !' said one Rangers fan. Rangers attacked but could produce little in the way of shots. They were to pay because Van Ede scored ten minutes from the end to level the tie. The final whistle sounded and Rangers having been cheered onto the pitch were booed and jeered off at the end.

RESULT: RANGERS 0 SPARTA ROTTERDAM 1

The third match play off was to played at Highbury in London. In effect this was a home match for Rangers who had overwhelmingly the larger of the visiting supports in the 34,000 crowd. Sparta drew first blood on six minutes when Verhoeven headed in a corner. Rangers fought back on a very muddy pitch and the player (Verhoeven) who had put the Dutch team ahead sliced a free kick from Davie Wilson into his own net.

The second half saw Harold Davis take control of the muddy midfield and a fierce drive from Sammy Baird on the hour mark put Rangers ahead to the delight of the vast bulk of the crowd who were cheering everything Rangers did. Van Der Lee defelected an Ian McMillan cross into his own net for a second Sparta own goal. Bosselaar scored from a penalty near the end for the Dutch side but Rangers held on for a semi final tie with German side Eintracht Frankfurt. Rangers could now be playing a European Cup Final in Glasgow.

The Scottish Junior Cup was arousing a lot of interest. A quarter final match between Greenock and Johnstone Burgh saw 8,000 at the Ravenscraig Stadium and a drawn match. The replay at Keanie Park, Johnstone saw an all ticket 13,500 crowd. Johnstone went ahead by Dan McSorley. Jim McCartney equalised for Greenock before half time and the same player was on the mark again in the second half as the tail o'the bank side won 3-1. On the Monday after the match a number of supporters appeared in Paisley Sherriff Court. Hugh Clabby of 24, Clydeview Road, Greenock was fined £9 after an altercation with a   police officer. He admitted assaulting the police officer and spitting on him as well as breaching the peace. A number of other arrests were made at the match.

A match against Ardeer Thistle beckoned for Greenock in the semi final.

In the Quarter Finals of the Southern Primary School's Championships Drumoyne won at home 7-2 against Croftfoot.

Bellahouston Academy had a good run in the Cameronian Cup for the larger Secondary Schools in the Glasgow area. However in the semi final they bowed out to a good Holyrood side. Two Govan schools players made the trials for the match against England at Burnley. Roxburgh (Bellahouston) and Craig (St.Gerrard's).

Govan High got better throughout the season at the middle and younger age groups. One of the sides won through to the Final of the Castle Cup (under 15's) and a match against Kingsridge. After a close game the 'High' won 2-1 and brought the Cup back to Langlands Road. Surprisingly the selectors had no players from the Govan Schools in the Glasgow team at this age group.

The Govan High Intermediate team continued their good form and forced themselves into the league play off's. In the semi finals they lost out 4-2 to St.Mungo's. Lourdes however managed to win through to the Final which was played at Cathkin Park.

The Scotland under 15's team were strong and beat West Germany 2-1 at Ibrox Park. Jim Forrest and Alex.Willoughby were good performers with the former scoring two good goals.

SCOTLAND: Ewington (Broxburn), Parkes (St.Mungo's), Moncur (Broxburn), Watson (Airdrie), Markie (St.Mary's, Bathgate), Combe (Belleview Edinburgh), Moonie (Airdrie), Willoughby ( Colston), Forrest (Onslow), Graham (Bailleston), Mitchell (Falkirk)

Govan High won the Division 5 (youngest age group) play off's beating John Street 3-2 after being twice behind. The Drumoyne school team are strong with Bernie Quinn and George Mc Cleary who live in Tormore Street two of their better players. In the Govan Cup they get through the early rounds comfortably. In the semi final they are drawn against the usually strong St.Constantine's school at Pirrie Park. Drumoyne triumph 4-1 and head for the final at Moore Park, home of St. Anthony's.

The opponents are St.Saviours who always seemed to produce good footballers. Prior to the match the school get the children to make small banners and good luck messages. The match is close but an early goal for St.Saviours proves decisive and they hold on for a deserved 1-0 win and lift the Govan Primary Schools Cup.

Derek never played a match for Drumoyne School but was always very supportive of the team like several other boys. At Drumoyne School the years long ritual of playground football goes on. The picking of teams is decided by the same method of two boys putting their hands behind their back and produce a symbol of paper, scissor or stone. The last games are being played after years of untold fun and no little wearing out of shoes.

As spring approached in Govan the weather was good and a fest of football was in the offing. Benburb were still progressing in 3 cups and a quarter final match at Tinto Park beckoned against Ardeer Thistle. The match was played on a Friday evening and a large number of people were walking from West Drumoyne towards Tinto Park. There were also substantial numbers walking up Craigton Road from Govan. A huge fleet of coaches came up from Ayrshire bringing thousands of supporters and the Bens biggest crowd for a number of seasons assembled.

Derek and his pals were in the ground early behind the lower end goal which was totally packed a full quarter of an hour before kick off. The Bens committee were directing the incoming crowd down both sides of the ground and at kick off the top end terraces were unusually well populated. Ardeer Thistle were a big attraction. They were unbeaten for the entire season to the evening when the match was played. They had Tommy Duffy at centre forward who was on his way to setting a British goal scoring record of 97 goals. Huge cheers greeted the visitors as they took to the field and the Bens also received a good cheer as the experienced Maurice Young led out the Royal blue clad Benburb side. The match was non stop excitement from start to finish, incident packed and memorable for everyone who watched.

Bens started brightly and Jim Mc Donald on the right wing looked very dangerous with tricky dribbling runs. Benburb forced a series of early corners and cheered on by their faithful took the lead with a goal at the top end of the ground after intense pressure. A Mc Donald corner led to a scramble and Jim Kelly forced the ball in, provoking much celebration from the Govanites. Almost from the kick off the Ayrshire side responded and kicking down the slope laid siege to the Bens goal. Time and again they looked likely to score but John Gallagher the Bens goalie brought off a series of smart saves. The half time whistle arrived with a big ovation from the Bens support for their teams efforts.

Despite Benburb having the advantage of the slope it was the visitors who attacked non stop and the Bens defence were defending a series of free kicks and corners. Maurice Young, John Cameron and goalkeeper John Gallagher were outstanding in enabling the Bens to hold out. As the game approached the latter stages Benburb had a short spell of pressure and Jim Kelly took a pass from Jim Mc Donald ran through the inside right channel and smashed home the home sides second to a huge roar. Jim Kelly was a big ginger haired well built midfielder and to the Govan youngsters was known as 'Big Jum'. The match ended and the Bens went off as heroes having won against a first rate Ardeer Thistle side. The crowd was the largest Derek had ever seen at Tinto Park. As Derek walked back down Shieldhall Road his pal Donnie Mc Intosh said 'Awe Dear Thistle, well done the Bens. C'mon the Chookie Hens !'

RESULT: BENBURB 2 ARDEER THISTLE 0

The Drumoyne Strollers who played at the 50 pitches managed to keep themselves off the foot of the table. The playing record in the 21 team league was Played 11; Won 3; Lost 8; Draws 0, For 9 goals, Against 60 goals, Points 6. The team had closed up to being just 2 points behind Cardonald who played on the adjacent pitch. Drumoyne Strollers had a late season problem arising. They had 29 games left in two months to complete their fixtures.. At the top St.Contantine's looked favourites to take the Glasgow Secondary League with Govan in third place.

Hampden Park was the venue for several big matches over the period of a few months. As well as the Scottish Cup Final there was a Home International match between Scotland and England and a forthcoming European Cup Final. Frank Haffey the cheerful Govan goalie from Celtic gave a quip for him from trainer Dawson Walker before the match. At Turnberry to big Frank and the rest of the squad he said 'Right boys lets make this a Haffey and glorious day!' The match against the 'auld enemy' attracted 130,000 to Hampden Park most wanting a Scotland win. As usual there were 20,000 England supporters somewhere in the midst of passionate Scots who gave the sides a huge 'Hampden roar' as the teams entered the fray.

SCOTLAND: Haffey, Mc Kay, Caldow, Cumming, Evans, McCann, Leggat, Young, St.John, Law, Weir

ENGLAND: Springett, Armfield, Wilson, Clayton, Slater, Flowers, Connelly, Broadbent, Baker, Parry & Charlton.

Scotland had the better of the first half and Graham Leggat fired them into a deserved lead which brought a huge Hampden Park roar. England improved after the break but were held at bay by a few smart saves plus one lucky save from Govan goalie Frank Haffey. However there was little he could do when England were awarded a penalty and Bobby Charlton equalised. England had a chance to win the match when they were awarded a second penalty. Haffey pulled off a good save from the spot kick but the referee ordered a re-take. This time Bobby Charlton shot wide.

RESULT : SCOTLAND 1 ENGLAND 1

Scotland's Schoolboys were facing humiliation at Wembley at Wembley Stadium, trailing 5-0 to England after an hour. However a stirring fight back saw them score 3 goals near the end and went close on several other occasions. The score was England 5 Scotland 3.

The Govan Schools were not well represented in the Glasgow Representative sides. However Brady of Lourdes was selected at inside left for the Under 13's and Conway from the same school was selected in goal for the Under 14's.

In the Scottish Cup 4th Round Rangers had a home tie with in form and high scoring Hibernian who included John Baxter the former Benburb player returning to Govan.

The game was exciting from the outset with Hibernian a goal up in two minutes. Baker went down after a tackle from Patterson and Bobby Johnstone blasted home the penalty. The 'gers fought back and the game was evenly poised with each side launching good attacks. Three minutes before half time Sammy Baird converted a Davie Wilson corner to send the sides in level at half time. Davie Wilson gave Rangers the lead in the second half when he sent in a free kick which Muirhead in the Hibs goal misjudged. Hibs fought back and a few minutes later were level. McLeod scored with a spectacular shot into the roof of the net after a Grant free kick.

Rangers surged forward to get a winner and avoid a trip to Edinburgh for a replay. They were rewarded when Davie Wilson burst down the wing and his cross was blasted into the net by Jimmy Miller.

RESULT: RANGERS 3 HIBERNIAN 2

The semi finals saw an Old Firm match at Hampden Park. Rangers were clear favourites as Celtic had indifferent form all season. However the form book was turned upside down when Stevie Chalmers headed home a Colrain corner on 25 minutes. The goal signalled non stop pressure from Rangers but Celtic survived until half time. The second half saw much the same pattern and the pressure finally told when Jimmy Miller dived to head a cross from Davie Wilson into the net like a bullet. Non stop pressure from the Ibrox side followed but Celtic hung on with Frank Haffey inspirational.

RESULT: CELTIC 1 RANGERS 1 Crowd 80,000

Celtic played better during the first half of the replay. Davie Wilson gave Rangers a 27th lead. Neil Mochan brought Celtic level soon after and there was no further score in the first half. Rangers dominated the second half and Jimmy Miller who gave Bobby Evans a torrid time headed Rangers in the lead. Despite having Harold David hobbling around Rangers remained on top and increased the lead through Davie Wilson who headed in a Scott cross. Harold Davis was carried off but the 10 men scored a fourth against a poor Celtic side.

RESULT: RANGERS 4 CELTIC 1 Crowd 71,000

In the other semi final Kilmarnock had little difficulty disposing of Clyde with two first half goals. Andy Kerr scored on the half hour dribbling around the Clyde defence before shooting low past Mc Culloch. Billy Muir added a second a minute later with a similar goal. Try as they did Clyde never looked likely to force a replay.

RESULT: CLYDE 0 KILMARNOCK 2 Crowd 45,000

Rangers were having a good season and the climax was two important ties. In the European Cup they were faced by Eintracht Frankfurt in the semi final over two legs. The winner had a Hampden Park date with either Barcelona or Real Madrid. Rangers lost heavily in Frankfurt by 6-1 in the first leg. However a capacity 80,000 tickets were sold for the return leg at Ibrox. Eintracht wore a German version of the Arsenal kit with string tie ups on the shirt. They had a midfielder called Weilbacher who provided a bewildering array of bicycle kicks to show off his athleticism. Eintracht scored early and went on to score an easy win of 6-3 despite a good effort from the Ibrox club. The Germans left the field to a standing ovation from the entire Ibrox crowd.

The second tie which gave Rangers a chance of glory was a Scottish Cup Final against Kilmarnock at Hampden Park. Rangers unusually were the underdogs against a good Killie side as they took the field in front of 108,000 spectators.

RANGERS: Niven, Caldow, Little, McColl, Patterson, Stevenson, Scott, McMillan, Miller, Baird & Wilson

KILMARNOCK: Brown, Richmond, Watson, Beattie, Toner, Kennedy, Stewart, Mc Inally, Kerr, Black & Muir

The pivotal moment of the match came midway through the first half when a high ball went spinning up in the Killie box. It looked food and drink for Killie keeper Jimmy Brown. However Rangers centre forward Jimmy Miller managed to get great elevation in his challenge to the keeper and outjumped Brown to head home. The Rangers fans went wild, Killie were stunned and the Ibrox side went in at half time with the lead. Rangers scored a second goal when Jimmy Miller headed in a free kick from Billy Stevenson on 67 minutes.

RESULT: RANGERS 2 KILMARNOCK 0

On the way back to Govan the Rangers players passed many of their supporters on an open topped bus and shared the moment with each group. They slowed down the bus and showed the Scottish Cup off to great cheers from their supporters.

Back in Govan St.Anthony's hopes of a title disappeared with the departure of Alec Crawford to senior football. However they were to finish high up the league after one of their best seasons for a long time.

The Scottish Junior Cup semi finals threw up an eagerly awaited tie. Greenock faced Ardeer Thistle at Firhill Park. In the other semi final St.Andrew's faced Thornton Hibs at Starks Park, Kirkaldy. A crowd of 12,000 or so saw Smith give St.Andrew's the lead. The goal was cancelled out almost immediately when Campbell scored for the Hibs.

Hazzard of Thornton Hibs was carried off and soon after Joe Kenney their right back was badly injured and hobbled the remainder of the match on the left wing. Despite the numbers disadvantage Thornton battled all the way and held on for a 1-1 draw.

The replay was also an exciting match at the same venue. Carmichael gave St.Andrew's an early lead with a good shot and Keddie increased the advantage mid way through the first half. Tran for Thornton Hibs reduced the deficit near half time with a header.

Try as they could the Hibs could not find an equaliser and St.Andrerw's won out in the Fife derby to book a date at Hampden Park.

RESULT  ST.ANDREWS UNITED  2 THORTON HIBS  1

The Scottish Junior Cup semi final match at Firhill drew an amazing crowd of 29,000 to see Ardeer Thistle take on Greenock. A lot of interest was focussed on the Ardeer Thistle centre forward Tommy Duffy who seemed well on course to break the goalscoring record for semi professional football in the UK.   Tommy hailed from Renfrew. His best friends were John Anderson and Matt Gray and as schoolboys they practiced for hours with a 'tanner ba' perfecting their skills. John went senior with St. Mirren before moving on to Stoke City in England. Matt. Gray played Scottish League Division 1 football with Third Lanark.

Tommy went to Benburb but was released before going down to Ayrshire and start his goal scoring exploits.

ARDEER THISTLE: Bishop, Sweeney, Thomson, Hood, Andrews, Murray, Templeton, Brannon, Duffy, McLeod and Reilly

GREENOCK: McGinlay, Reilly, Hogg, Stewart, Buchanan, Brabender, Gibson, McCartney, McKellar, Samuel and Winter

Ardeer started the better and Hogg the Greenock right back sliced a clearance into his own net. The Thistle were two up on 21 minutes when Jim Reilly hit a fierce shot into the roof of the net. The third goal for Ardeer arrived soon after when a good passing move set McLeod free and he finished with a good shot.

The match was end to end and exciting. Murray of Ardeer was taken off with a bad leg injury and just before half time McKellar scored with a rocket shot for Greenock to give them hope in the second half.

Murray resumed hobbling on the wing. To make matters worse for the Thistle Brannon was taken off with a bad head injury (broken nose) leaving the team with nine players plus Murray on the wing. Almost immediately Stewart scored a second goal for Greenock. Brannon returned some minutes later. Near the end Bishop the Ardeer Thistle goalie made a hash of a long shot from Gibson and fumbled the ball into his own net.

RESULT: ARDEER THISTLE 3 GREENOCK 3

Ardeer Thistle felt the Gods were against them in the first match. The replay was decided in the second half when a Winter's shot for Greenock hit the underside of the bar and came out. The referee awarded a goal to most people's surprise. Jimmy Mc Cartney scored late on with a good shot.

RESULT: GREENOCK 2 ARDEER THISTLE 0

The reputation of Govan Amateurs for sportsmanship and helping clubs with problems was enhanced. At the start of the season Paisley side Mossvale YMCA appealed for help when their changing rooms were wrecked by vandals. A local headmaster and Govan Amateurs combined to provide the club with a complete set of strips to enable them to carry on. On the pitch under Alfie Ferguson the team won the West of Scotland Amateur League and also the League Cup.

Govan Juveniles continued to provide good players and Paul Brechin was impressing Benburb after several trial matches. Bob Mc Crindle was due to sign for Glenafton and goalkeeper Alex Wilkie was on trial with Queen's Park. Robert Lockhart the trainer helped out Greenock Juniors by getting Jim McCartney of Greenock Juniors fit after injuries while the tail o' the bank club were chasing the Scottish Junior Cup.

The Govan Juveniles team reached the final of the Johnstone Cup and went on to beat Ruchazie Hearts in the final.

Govan teams were appearing in cup finals and semi finals from Rangers in the Scottish Cup down to youth football. Harmony Row had an excellent season in the Glasgow YMCA boys league finishing as champions. They also reached the final of the League Cup with a match against Peel Glen at Keppoch Park.

Benburb were making progress through a number of cup competitions. They reached the final of the Glasgow Cup with a win over Pollok at Petershill Park. In the Central League Cup semi final, they had a tight match with Kilsyth Rangers at Shettleston. However mid way through the second half Jim McDonald scored for the Bens and a second cup final fixture was to be looked forward to. The West of Scotland Cup semi final saw Benburb return to Shettleston with a big following from Govan.

However, it was not to be the Bens night against Thorniewood United and they lost narrowly to the only goal scored.

The first of the Benburb cup finals was a Glasgow Cup Final at Celtic Park against Shettleston. All the crowd of around 3,000 were accommodated in the Main Stand and large Enclosure below. The remaining 3 sides of the ground were empty. Bens took the field to a good cheer from their Govan followers led by Maurice Young their captain.

BENBURB: Gallacher, Cameron, Fleming, Mc Culloch, Young , Rees, Lindsay, Kelly, Taylor, Brown and McDonald
SHETTLESTON: Brown, Reid, Murray, Sinclair, Shiels, Duncanson, Collins, Kelly, Mulholland, Black and Craven

The Bens must have feared it might not be their day in the opening few minutes. Maurice Young received a kick in the head and had to leave the field with blood pouring from a bad wound. The Bens re-organised and with 10 men held their own for a long while.

After some time a tannoy announcement went out asking for a doctor to report to the changing rooms immediately. Shettleston eventually got on top and East Stirling bound Jim Mulholland gave them the lead on 16 minutes. Bens 10 men were struggling and were relieved to see Maurice Young return with a huge white bandage around his head. The Town remained in the lead until half time.

Benburb started brightly in the second half but were deflated when the referee awarded Shettleston a penalty for hand ball from which Reid scored. Mulholland added a third and the Bens first cup chance was gone. For Shettleston it was the third Glasgow Cup success in a row.

RESULT: BENBURB 0 SHETTLESTON 3

On the following Wednesday Benburb took good support over to Shawfield for a Central League Cup Final with St. Roch's. Benny Murphy gave the Tinto Park side the lead but the Bens ran out of gas near the end when tiredness crept in. The 'Candy' scored three unopposed goals in the second half to secure the cup. Perhaps it would be truer to say two unopposed goals as Maurice Young's pass back to John Gallacher went over his head for the third goal. At the end of the match a lot of 'candy' fans jumped over the dog track fences to celebrate their cup win. The Bens fans were stunned to say the least.

A lot of talk amongst the Bens fans was the fixture schedule that saw them play a whole host of matches within a very short period. Just two days previously they had played a match against Petershill following on from the Glasgow Cup Final on the Saturday. However Benburb had completed one of their best ever seasons for many a year and gave their supporters great enjoyment throughout. Alex Mc Vicar had done a fantastic job with the team as manager and former goalkeeper Alex. Forsyth took a lot of credit with his role as trainer.

RESULT: ST.ROCH'S 3 BENBURB 1

Not to be outdone by the Bens St.Anthony's finished the season well under new boss Peter Madden. Pat McInally a signing from St.Roch's was scoring freely netting 10 goals in 7 matches.

The Ants reached the final of the Pompey Cup where they lost out to Ashfield at Lochburn Park, Maryhill.

Former Rangers player and penalty expert Johnny Hubbard was happy at his new club Bury in Lancashire. Johnny had a part time job coaching at local schools in the area. He still enjoyed snooker and on returning to Glasgow the South African was always warmly greeted by the Ibrox faithful.

Derek is sitting in Drumoyne School and is nervous. He is just about to ask his teacher Mrs. Dewart if he could have some time off in two days hence in order to go to the European Cup Final match at Hampden Park. Uncle Robbie has managed to get two tickets and would like to get into Hampden as early as possible.

The morning playtime bell sounds and Derek is quickly out of the seat. 'Mrs. Dewart can I have a word please'. Mrs. Dewart says 'What is it Derek?'. Derek says 'Mrs. Dewart, My uncle has managed to get me a ticket for the Cup Final on Wednesday . Is it possible I could leave the school an hour early to get to the match. The gates open at 5 o'clock and we would like to get in early'. Mrs Dewart says 'Derek. No problem at all. We will probably break for the afternoon at 2.00pm and go down to Pirrie Park as the weather is good. You go when you like after that'. Derek says 'Thank you Mrs. Dewart !'.

Mrs Dewart says ' My husband is a big football fan. He supports the Hi Hi's they play near Hampden Park at Cathkin Park'. Derek says ' I have been to Cathkin Park to see Third Lanark play Rangers'. Mrs.Dewart says 'I hope you enjoy the match with your uncle. Please tell me all about it on Thursday it should be good. Real Madrid are a fantastic team'.

Derek  is surprised that Mrs. Dewart knew so much about football as she never once talked about the sport in the years she took the class. However, the forthcoming match has Glasgow buzzing in anticipation as they are likely to see some of the World's finest players. The weather forecast is good and Derek and Uncle Robbie arrive at the Hampden Park gates at 5.00pm. The gates open and they head as planned for the 'Celtic' end of the stadium to the right of the Main Stand. A spot right at the front near the Main Stand is taken with a great view.

A long pre match programme of events was arranged to get the huge crowd in early  with the pipes and drums very popular. The Main Stand appeared to be mainly Real Madrid fans and the high South stand opposite was a sea of red and white from the German support. They added a lot to the spectacle with their horns. The weather was perfect sunshine and the match was surely the greatest that could ever have been played.

REAL MADRID: Dominguez, Marquitos, Pachin, Jose Maria Vidal,  Jose Santamaria, Jose Marie  Zarraga, Canario, Luis del Sol, Alfredo De Stefano, Ferenc Puskas, Francisco Gento.

EINTRACHT FRANKFURT: Egon Loy, Freidel Lutz, Hermann Hofer, Hans Weilbacher, Hans Walter Eigenbrodt, Dieter Stinka,  Richard Kress,  Dieter Lindner, Erwin Stein, Alfred Pfaff, Erich Meier.

Scottish referee Jack Mowett was in the middle.

The game was essentially Spain v Germany. Real Madrid had no fewer than 8 Spaniards in their line up. The manager Miguel Munoz was Spanish also. The only non Spaniards were Di Stefano and Puskas as well as the goalkeeper. Eintracht were entirely German and managed by a German, Paul Oswald

The crowd was claimed to be anything between 127,000 and 135,000. Being in the ground it appeared every bit as large a crowd as you had at the recently played match against England. An explanation given was that a number of Real Madrid fans were unable to obtain tickets for the main stand and did not want to stand in such a large crowd. The tickets were then re-offered to the Glaswegians who had of course no such reservations and were immediately snapped up.

The teams took the field to a huge roar and there was feeling around that what was about to follow was something special. The game started slightly cautiously but both teams always looked likely to score. The Germans took the game to Real Madrid more and more. The crowd were thrilled as they were at Ibrox a few weeks before by the athleticism of Eintracht captain Hans Weilbacher and his bicycle kicks. The breakthrough finally came on 18 minutes when Kress scored for Eintracht. This awoke the Spanish giants out of any complacency they may have had and two quick goals from Di Stefano on 27 and 30 minutes, after some suspect goalkeeping from the German custodian, changed the complexion of the final. Thrills continued until half time but the score was unchanged. Early in the second half on 46 minutes Ferenc Puskas was to score the first of his 4 goals and ended the tie as a contest. Eintracht attacked but looked vulnerable to breaks by an express winger Gento who raced down the Main stand side of the pitch setting up chances. On 56, 60 and 71 minutes Puskas blasted in fearsome shots to run the Real score to six.

However, Eintracht were not finished and a Stein score brought a huge cheer from the Hampden crowd on 71 minutes. Almost immediately Di Stefano completed his hat trick and 2 minutes later another huge roar greeted another goal from Stein. So 7-3 at the finish. Real collected the cup but no one left the ground for a considerable time afterwards as both teams took deserved applause.

No one ever wanted the occasion to finish and if football ever had an equivalent of an encore the crowd would have taken it. A never to be forgotten occasion for anyone fortunate enough to witness it. Could there ever be a better football match than this one? Both participating clubs were generous in their praise of the Glasgow fans and Real Madrid even suggested that many more Finals should be played in Glasgow.

The next day at Drumoyne School all the boys who went to match were excitedly telling of what they saw. It was something special. Surely the greatest football match of all time.

The Scottish Junior Cup saw Greenock take on St.Andrews United at Hampden Park. On entering the ground the Scottish Daily Express handed out hats to signify which team you supported. The vast majority plumped for the dark blue and white of Greenock. However a good support had come down from Fife and they also had a large contingent in the Main Stand.

GREENOCK: McGinlay, Reilly, Hogg, Stewart, Buchanan, Brabender, Gibson, McCartney, McKellar, Samuel and Winter

ST.ANDREWS UNITED; Lister, W.P.Penman, Hughes, Crookston, Davidson, Wills, Carmichael, Fraser, Smith, W.Penman and Borella

A crowd of 34,603 saw Greenock on the attack from the start. Lister in the St. Andrews goal had some smart saves before Greenock scored the opening goal in 25 minutes. McKellar moved the ball back and forth on the edge of the box before unleashing a fierce shot to give the tail o' the bank side the lead.

St.Andrews came more into the game as half time approached but Greenock held the lead at the break. In the second half St.Andrews forced the pace and Greenock were being pinned back. Former Kilsyth Rangers player Italian Romeo Borella pounced on some indecisive work by the Greenock defence and scored the equaliser on 56 minutes. A few minutes later the same player found himself in a good position in front of goal and made no mistake with a rasping drive. Penman scored a third goal for the Fife club and there was no way back for Greenock.

They battled to the end and a Winter shot hit the underside of the bar. The Scottish Junior Cup was heading to Fife for the first time since 1912-13.

RESULT: ST.ANDREWS UNITED 3 GREENOCK 1

The Scottish Junior Football world had seen some large crowds during season 1959-60. However some clubs started to struggle badly and there was great sadness when Shawfield Juniors announced that they were going to fold. A lot of persuasion was put to the club and former fans sent in cheques and money to keep them going. Shawfield were one of the main clubs in Junior Football for a very long time.

They were winners of the Scottish Junior Cup shortly after World War Two beating Bo'ness United 2-1 at Hampden Park. The club had a good ground at Roseberry Park and they were always willing to allow school matches to be played there. In addition they had produced some excellent young players, one of the last being Frank McLintock who went to Leicester City. Shawfield were certain that they could not carry on and a good club was lost. Another club to become defunct was Douglasdale who played Benburb twice in the 1950's Scottish Cup matches. The mines adjacent to the village closed down and the population moved away from the area. However, it was announced that the new town of East Kilbride might soon have a new team called East Kilbride Thistle. Also, Strathclyde announced that they would carry on. The club were victims of constant vandalism and the boiler was stolen.

Shawfield's last ever game was North Eastern Glasgow Cup Final against Shettleston. The Town were in a rich vein of form and won 3-1 having been 2-0 at the interval.

The Central League decider at Shawfield Stadium went to Bailleston, the team coached by former Benburb and Rangers star Jock 'Tiger' Shaw. They beat Shettleston 2-0.

Some Govan players on the move during the forthcoming close season.

John Cameron—Benburb to Clyde. John Gallacher—Benburb to Ayr United
Jim Kelly—Benburb to Ardeer Thistle. Jim McDonald –Benburb to Hibernian
John Taylor—Benburb to Watford.

Alex.Ferguson—Queen's Park to St.Johnstone

# GLASGOW SECONDARY JUVENILE LEAGUE

| Team | Pl | W | L | D | F | A | Pts |
|------|----|----|----|----|----|----|-----|
| St.Francis | 25 | 18 | 4 | 3 | 104 | 52 | 39 |
| Govan | 25 | 16 | 5 | 4 | 70 | 43 | 36 |
| St.Constantine's | 22 | 17 | 4 | 1 | 62 | 22 | 35 |
| Drumchapel Thistle | 20 | 13 | 2 | 5 | 82 | 39 | 31 |
| Pollok Hawthorn | 20 | 14 | 3 | 3 | 64 | 35 | 31 |
| Rancel | 20 | 14 | 4 | 2 | 52 | 32 | 30 |
| Dennistoun Hearts | 23 | 13 | 6 | 4 | 43 | 35 | 30 |
| St.Roch's | 17 | 12 | 2 | 3 | 32 | 22 | 27 |
| Stonelaw | 20 | 11 | 4 | 5 | 70 | 39 | 27 |
| Dennistoun Juveniles | 22 | 8 | 3 | 11 | 40 | 31 | 27 |
| Bailleston | 22 | 12 | 8 | 2 | 39 | 42 | 26 |
| Regent Star | 24 | 10 | 9 | 5 | 88 | 51 | 25 |
| Meadowpark | 21 | 11 | 10 | 0 | 44 | 53 | 22 |
| Rutherglen Waverley | 21 | 10 | 10 | 1 | 53 | 39 | 21 |
| Ruchazie Hearts | 19 | 8 | 9 | 2 | 45 | 46 | 18 |
| Corkerhill | 17 | 7 | 7 | 3 | 44 | 58 | 17 |
| Calfhall | 21 | 7 | 14 | 0 | 19 | 103 | 14 |
| Cranhill | 18 | 5 | 12 | 1 | 14 | 88 | 11 |
| Drumoyne Strollers | 17 | 5 | 12 | 0 | 11 | 68 | 10 |
| Cardonald | 23 | 4 | 18 | 1 | 38 | 84 | 9 |
| Butters | 17 | 3 | 11 | 3 | 24 | 60 | 9 |

In the North west Juvenile League the two shipyard teams never really got into contention for the title. Stephens finished mid table and Harlands finished in the lower half but well clear of the bottom.

The Central League saw both the Govan Junior sides finish well in the top half of the league. The Ants after a brilliant start and an indifferent mid season recovered well and finished fourth just two points behind the second placed Petershill. Benburb gained steadily on the Ants throughout the season after a slow start and eventually finished sixth just three points behind their Govan rivals.

In the Hospital League played in the Summer months the Southern General had made a complete recovery after their relegation and subsequent promotion to the top division.

They led in the early league table with maximum points.

## GLASGOW HOSPITAL LEAGUE

| Team | Pl | W | L | D | F | A | Pts |
|------|----|----|----|----|----|----|-----|
| Southern General | 8 | 8 | 0 | 0 | 41 | 10 | 16 |
| Royal Infirmary | 8 | 6 | 2 | 0 | 28 | 7 | 12 |
| Stobhill | 7 | 4 | 2 | 1 | 16 | 14 | 9 |
| Hairmyers | 8 | 4 | 3 | 1 | 20 | 18 | 9 |
| Evening Citizen | 8 | 4 | 4 | 0 | 26 | 28 | 8 |
| Evening Times | 6 | 3 | 3 | 0 | 17 | 16 | 6 |
| Coathill | 8 | 2 | 4 | 2 | 18 | 22 | 6 |
| Office of Works | 7 | 2 | 4 | 1 | 15 | 19 | 5 |
| Waterlow | 8 | 1 | 6 | 1 | 13 | 35 | 3 |
| Ruchall | 8 | 1 | 7 | 0 | 11 | 38 | 2 |

The Final of the Glasgow Welfare Cup was contested by two Govan teams in the youth section. Harmony Row YC played Stephens YC at Old Crookston Park.

There was a fire at Tinto Park and the Benburb Football Club pavilion was damaged.St. Anthony's immediately came to the help of the Bens offering anything they needed in order to carry on. The first matches of the Benburb new season would be played at Moore Park at no cost to the Bens.

Former Benburb and Aberdeen centre half Alex.McAllister enjoyed his golf and became good. He joined the Police force and got selected for the Lanarkshire Police golf team.

A MID 1950's BENBURB FOOTBALL CLUB TEAM.
THE PLAYER WITH THE DAZ WASHED SHORTS IS DUNKY RAE
SCOTTISH JUNIOR FOOTBALL INTERNATIONAL WINGER

| JOHN QUIGLEY ST.ANTHONY'S & NOTTINGHAM FOREST | RONNIE McKINNON BENBURB/DUNIPACE RANGERS & SCOTLAND | BOBBY EVANS ST.ANTHONY'S CELTIC & SCOTLAND |
|---|---|---|

LEFT:
SIR ALEX.FERGUSON
GOVAN HIGH SCHOOL
AND BENBURB
FOOTBALL
CLUB SUPPORTER

RIGHT:
FRANK HAFFEY
CELTIC & SCOTLAND

Photo 13

**REAL MADRID—EUROPEAN CUP WINNERS 1960**

**BILL STRUTH
RANGERS MANAGER**

**ALEC CRAWFORD
ST.ANTHONY'S & BENBURB**

**IBROX PARK
BILL STRUTH STAND ON LEFT.
THIS STAND IS PURE QUALITY
AND IBROX PARK IS ONE OF THE
BEST FOOTBALL GROUNDS IN
THE WORLD**

Photo 14

# CHAPTER 12
# HUMILIATION AND BULLETS (1960-61

The 1960-61 football season has started and all three of the larger Govan sides are doing well. St.Anthony's retained most of the good side they had during the previous season with Brown, the dependable goalie, supported by the fearsome pair at full backs Duffy and Doyle. Also, they had Mc Inally up front and the diminutive Frank McGrillan always a class act. Jack Kelly was appointed the new coach of the Ants.

ST.ANTHONY'S SQUAD:
Goalkeepers: A.Brown, J.Docherty (St.Vincents BC)
Full Backs: G.Doyle, P.Duffy, A.Cosker (St.Roch's)
Half backs: A.Bradley, J.Kelly, I.Phynn, E.Smith (St.Vincent's BC), L.Boland, A.McGeachan.
Forwards: E.Rose, F.McGrillan, P.McInally, P.Brogan, J.Scott, H.McNeil, J.Dastey (Possil Y.M.C.A.)

The Ants sat second in the league when they made the short trip to Tinto Park for the Govan 'Old Firm' derby without the injured Mc Grillan.

BENBURB: Munro, Trialist, Atwell, Brechin , Young, Murphy, Lindsey, Downie, Matthews, Mc Donald and Fleming
ST.ANTHONY'S: Brown, Doyle and Duffy, Physos, Kelly and J.Brogan, Mc Quillan, Rose, Mc Inally, T.Brogan and Smart.

The Ants started the better and took the lead on 5 minutes through Mc Quillan after the Bens defence got in a fankle. The Moore Park side were well on top throughout the match until the last 15 minutes when the Bens suddenly burst into life. However, the Ants hung on for a deserved win.

RESULT: BENBURB 0 ST.ANTHONY'S 1

The Greenfield Youth Club was a hive of many activities. The Club was popular and had a large membership. The football section had unearthed another strong player who was doing well in Junior Football. Ian Davidson was doing well in Pollok's team at outside left. He joined a long list of players from Greenfield's YC to make the grade. Others included Stewart Mitchell (Newcastle United), Stewart McCorquodale (Rangers), Billy Timmins (Bellshill Athletic), Gordon McCorquodale (Perthshire).

At Ibrox Park Rangers made two much publicised signings. Jim Baxter from Raith Rovers a midfielder and Doug Baillie a centre half from Airdrie. Baillie was a giant man and had previously been a centre forward at Junior club Douglas Water Thistle where he scored consistently.

Rangers had a league match at Parkhead. Amazingly this was the third meeting between the sides in the first few weeks of the season.. The previous two were Scottish League Cup games. The first at Ibrox saw Doug Baillie make his debut for Rangers. He was given an extremely uncomfortable afternoon by John 'Yogi' Hughes of Celtic and the Parkhead side were 3-2 winners.

The second match watched by 60,000 was at Parkhead and a section winner decider. Rangers trailed at half time by a single goal scored by Stevie Chalmers in the first two minutes. However in the second half goals from Harold Davis and Ralph Brand turned the game around and the 'Gers won the match and the section.

The third match was the first of the 'Old Firm' league games and took place in brilliant sunshine just one week later. Another very tight match was anticipated.

CELTIC: Fallon, McKay, Kennedy, Crerand, Kurilla, Peacock, Conway, Chalmers, Carroll, Divers and Hughes.

RANGERS: Ritchie, Shearer, Caldow, David, Patterson, Baxter, Scott, McMillan, Millar, Brand and Wilson.

Alex Scott scored for Rangers after two minutes and the Celtic defence were soon having a difficult afternoon. However they were unlucky when a Steve Chalmers shot hit the inside of a post and came out. In the second half Rangers asserted their advantage in midfield and Jimmy Miller scored a fine individual goal to put his side two up on 66 minutes. Twelve minutes from the end Ralph Brand ended a long spell of Rangers pressure by hooking home the third goal. Harold Davis bulleted in a header for Rangers fourth before Davie Wilson added a fifth with a shot into the roof of the net.

The Rangers fans wanted seven but in front of a deserted Celtic fans terrace Stevie Chalmers scored a good consolation goal.

RESULT: CELTIC 1 RANGERS 5

Derek is due to go for a trial at football to see if he can get into the Govan High football team. He asks Robbie ' I would like to start playing football on a more regular basis. I never played a game for Drumoyne School and my only game for the Lifeboys was terrible. Ultimately I would love to play for the Bens and I would never leave them '. Robbie replied ' The one you want to ask is your father Jimmy Welsh. He was a good player and I think played for Strathclyde when they were winning everything and also Ashfield before the War. I was never any good at football myself but when I was in the Army I was in the same Battalion as Tommy Docherty who was a great player for the Army.

The key to be being a good footballer is practice. Tommy practiced non stop; mostly on his own. He had a bladder and would hit it against a wall endlessly. He would practice volleys with both feet. He could hit a ball. He would practice trapping, chesting and heading '.

Derek went to 20 Craigton Road and when his mother Ruth went out for a 'wee blether' and a cigarette with the neighbours, he had a word with his father Jimmy. Jimmy says 'Derek , if you want to be a footballer you must be dedicated, that was my mistake. I was in to dancing, winching, drinking and spent a lot of time at work. I wish I played more football and less drinking. The first thing you must do is get in a team and play on a regular basis. Playing with your pals is good but it is not as good as the real thing. Do you think you are good enough to get in the Govan High team ?' Derek says 'I do not know. I imagine with such a large amount of boys it might be difficult to get in the team.' Jimmy replied ' Derek, you did not answer my question. Do you think you are good enough to play for Govan High at football ? Answer that question and take it from there'.

The day of the football team trials soon came around and Derek was in team B against team A. Team A seemed to have all the better players that Derek knew about. The Trainee Sports master asked for preferred positions of play. Derek said right half but finished up playing left back as no else wanted to play there. However, he is to play well and Team B beats Team A easily. The first match is against Lourdes a new school on Paisley Road West. There are two matches with both schools having such large numbers of players mostly very keen. Derek is told that unfortunately he is in the B team but is to be made captain. The player that Derek is to mark looks at least two years older and he gives him an uncomfortable match. High B lose just 4-3 and play well.

The Southern General Hospital won the Hospital League Division 1 easily and with matches to spare after the season finished in late August 1960. Govan players making early appearances for their new clubs made good impressions. Alex Ferguson former Govan High player scored against Falkirk for St.Johnstone who went 6-0 up at half time against Falkirk in a League Cup match, eventually winning 7-1.

Donnie Mc Kinnon was making a favourable impression at Partick Thistle in the reserve side at Centre half. The Jags noticed that Donnie had an added skill as a goalkeeper.

Benburb had a lot of team re-building after the previous successful season. However they made a reasonable start to the league campaign. St.Anthony's made a good start to the season and shared the lead of the Division with Cambuslang Rangers. In the West of Scotland Cup 1st Round both the Govan sides made an early exit. Benburb travelled to Lanark United and after trailing 0-1 at half time eventually went on to lose by four unopposed goals. St,Anthony's travelled to Bellshill Athletic and fell behind in the first half. Both sides scored one goal each in the second period meaning an exit for the Ants on a 2-1 scoreline.

Gourock are anchored at the bottom of the Central League and in poor run of form. In their last two matches they lose 14-3 to Bellshill Athletic and 9-0 to St.Roch's. After 7 matches they are pointless and conceded 44 goals.

A new club East Kilbride Thistle were gearing up to start playing during the following season 1961-62. A number of senior and junior clubs as well as individuals sent in donations to help them on their way. Among the donations was a £25 cheque from the Manchester United manager Matt Busby.

Rangers had a difficult League Cup quarter final tie against Dundee. In the 1st Leg a single goal on 51 minutes from Alex Scott decided the issue when he pounced on a short back pass from Ian Ure. The second leg was a thriller. Alan Gilzean had a penalty saved by Rangers Billy Ritchie and Davie Wilson scored for Rangers. Billy Smith, the Dundee right back, was injured and hobbled down the wing for the remainder of the match. Ian Mc Millan scored just before half time to increase the 'Gers lead to 2-0 and 3-0 on aggregate. The second half saw a remarkable comeback from the Dens Park club. Alan Cousin headed a goal to bring Dundee into the tie and the ground was in uproar when the same player headed a second goal. A few minutes later and Penman converted a penalty for the home side and the tie was level. However, Rangers responded and Ian McMillan put the Ibrox side level, ahead 4-3 on aggregate, with ten minutes to go. Ian Ure played a short back pass to his keeper a few minutes later and Ralph Brand pounced to seal Rangers place in the semi final courtesy of a 5-3 aggregate score.

Robbie and Derek were making an effort to visit more different grounds around Scotland following Rangers. A visit to Muirton Park in Perth saw them watch a St. Johnstone team take on an in form Rangers side.

ST.JOHNSTONE: Taylor, McFadyen, Lachlan, Walker, Little, McKinven, Newlands, Gould, Gardiner, Innes and McVittie

RANGERS: Ritchie, Shearer, Caldow, Davis, Patterson, Baxter, Scott, McMillan, Miller, Brand and Wilson

Rangers applied a lot of first half pressure. However it was the Saints who went in a goal up at half time through former Celtic player Matt. McVittie.

Things looked bad for the Ibrox side when Eric Caldow scored an own goal leaving the 'Gers with a lot to do. However, within a few minutes Rangers were level when first Brand headed home and then Miller nodded in the equaliser. The Saints who were part timers visibly tired towards the end and Rangers scored three more goals through Scott, McMillan and Brand. Muirton Park was one of the better venues in the league and with no trouble at the match the occasion was enjoyed by the spectators.

RESULT: ST.JOHNSTONE 2 RANGERS 5

The Scottish Junior Cup saw Benburb and St.Anthony's playing their respective 1st Round matches at home. St.Anthony's had a comfortable win over Troon with McInally, Brogan and McQuillan on the score sheet in a 3-0 win.

Benburb faced a tough match against Maryhill Harp. The Bens had an edge throughout the match but had to wait until the second half before Jim McIntyre scored the decisive goal for a 1-0 win. Soon after the elation had died down in the Tinto park dressing rooms when long serving manager Alex.McVicar announced that he was retiring from his position. The McVicar family had a long association at the club and the announcement came as a shock. Alex. was a fine centre forward in his time and won a Scottish Junior Cup winners medal in 1932 with Glasgow Perthshire. He scored the winning goal in a 2-1 win at Firhill Park over Kirkintilloch Rob Roy. In his time at Keppoch Park he scored over 130 goals. He would definitely be missed at the Bens.

Derek continued to strive to get into the Govan High football teams. He drove his friends to distraction with constant requests for games of headers and small sided games. With no one available he would practice volleying a tennis ball off a wall. Alas no place in the Govan High teams was forthcoming. Every week Derek would read the team selection on the notice board and he was reserve for the B team. This was a poor situation as it meant attendance for the matches and the travel involved if it was an away match on Saturday mornings. If fortunate enough to play it was worthwhile but to turn up at some seemingly far off school to watch matches often in poor weather was difficult.

The normal Govan High teachers often did not always attend the Saturday morning games in protest for their dispute and the teams were run by trainee teachers who had limited knowledge of the players. However, a few games were given in the first team when the regular left back was playing for Glasgow schools and occasionally a game in the second team. The last of those was a match on the ash parks at Holyrood school. The High were six goals behind at half time but a better second half left a score of 6-1 with Scott Mc Kenzie scoring.

A number of offers of Boys Brigade football came Derek's way and he joined the 164th BB in Copland Road.

Broomloan Road applied for entry in the Primary Schools Govan League. In the Cameronian Cup 1st Round Govan High won away at Woodside by 7-0. However in the 2nd Round they lost 3-0 at home to St.Mungo's.

In the Crookston Cup 1st Round St.Gerrard's won 7-0 at Pirrie Park against Our Lady's and Govan High won 6-0 over Hyndland at the same venue. In the 2nd Round St.Gerrard's lost at home 2-1 to John Street.

Govan Primary School results: Drumoyne 1 Pollokshields 2, Hillington 5 Greenfields 0

Players with a Govan connection continued generally to do well. John Baxter formerly with Benburb and after several season's at Hibernian was appointed club captain. John rarely missed a game for the Hibs and was always one of the teams strongest performers. However, John had the misfortune to sustain a broken jaw in a training ground accident and having recovered received serious injuries as a result of a bad car crash on the A8 in foggy conditions. Also in the car was Hibernian's other former Benburb player Jim McDonald who was unhurt. Jim (who was a former trainee butcher) was playing well in the Hibs reserve side but finding it impossible to break into the first team. The club indicated that they would likely see Jim breakthrough to the first team after a two year learning curve.

Davie Mathers former Govan High and Scotland squad player who had been working in Oxford and playing for Headington United returned to Partick Thistle and met up with former St.Gerrard's player Joe Mc Bride who was becoming a prolific goal scorer at the Jags. John Gallacher the former Benburb goalkeeper was breaking through into the Ayr United first team after some excellent performances in the reserves.

Very soon and by coincidence Christmas Eve arrives and Robbie and Derek are off to Ayr; the occasion is the Ayr United v Rangers League match. On paper a certainty for Rangers excepting they had to overcome a Govan connection. Former Benburb goalkeeper John Gallacher was between the sticks for Ayr United and was to play the game of his life. Someset Park was a good ground and although well packed most supporters were comfortable.

AYR UNITED:Gallacher, Burn, Thomson, Walker, McLean, Glen, McIntyre, Curlett, Price, Fulton and Mc Ghee

RANGERS: Niven, Shearer, Caldow, Davis, Patterson, Baxter, Scott, McMillan, Miller, Brand and Wilson.

Ayr started well in the first few minutes but were quickly pushed back. The match report is essentially about one man apart from the goal scorer. A few extracts:.

* On 19 minutes Rangers were awarded a penalty. Brand gave the ball all he had but Gallacher twisted in mid air and somehow got a hand to the shot and put it over the bar. The save of season of that there is no doubt by the young 'keeper. * The young keeper was soon to distinguish himself again with a neck or nothing dive at Ralph Brand's feet.
* On 28 minutes Peter Price went through the middle and placed a shot past George Niven. * In the second half Gallacher again brought the house down with a breathtaking save from Jimmy Miller.* Gallacher 'what a keeper' again thrilled the crowd with yet another breathtaking save this time from Ian Mc Millan.* The final whistle saw the Ayr fans run onto the field.

216

1961 arrived with the annual Old Firm match this time at Ibrox. Rangers must have felt they were going to be undone by another former Benburb player following on from the heroics of John Gallacher at Ayr. Johnny Divers had given Celtic a first half lead. Govan based goalie Frank Haffey always played well against Rangers despite the abuse he received from the Ibrox faithful. However goals from Ralph Brand and Davie Wilson turned the match in Rangers favour and a 2-1 win.

Uncle Robbie and Derek return home from a Benburb match at Tinto Park. Derek is a bit down in the mouth because the Bens played so badly. Robbie says ' Yes they were awful ! However, a good supporter sticks by his team through thick and thin. With the Bens it will come right sometime. They have good people involved at the club. I was talking to Mrs Cook who was doing the teas and pies today. She says her son will soon be playing for the Bens and he is a good player'. Derek says ' Lucky devil, I wish I could soon play for the Bens'. Robbie says. 'Have you decided who you are playing for yet Derek ?'. Derek says ' Yes the 164th BB, my first game is after the Rangers trip to Dundee. Two classmates Ian Clark and Rab Warrender are very friendly and I get on well with them. I stand with them when I go to Ibrox; two thirds way down aisle 13. They are based at Copland Road St.Kiarens Dean Park Parish Church. The complete uniform is 3 shillings and 6 pence which maw is already buying for me. Rangers have drawn Dundee in the Scottish Cup away. A large number of Rangers fans descend on Buchanan Street station for the journey North. The Football Special trains see the Rangers fans joined by St.Mirren supporters as they are playing Dundee United at the same time as Rangers play Dundee. It is a very sunny day although bitterly cold as the blue masses arrived at Dens Park. The St. Mirren supporters were almost latterly across the road at Tannadice Park.

DUNDEE: Liney, Hamilton, Cox, Ure, Smith, Stuart, Penman, Gilzean, Cousin, Wishart and Robertson
RANGERS: Niven, Shearer, Caldow, Davis, Patterson, Baxter, Scott, McMillan, Murray, Brand and Wilson.
Rangers played in red and Dundee in blue. Rangers started brightly and were soon ahead through Max Murray. Dundee struggled badly with the pace of Ralph Brand and he breezed through the home side to score two quick goals. Alex Scott added a fourth before half time. In the second half Cousins replied for Dundee but a late goal from Max Murray ensured Rangers were through. It was a happy train home as St.Mirren also won through with a single goal from Rab Stewart. Another result which raised a few eyebrows in the Cup was Hibernian 15 Peebles Rovers 1. Joe Baker scored nine.

217

The School's Football season continued with moderate success for the Govan School's.

* Bellahouston Academy were having a reasonable season with a few players in contention for representative honours. Among these was Andy Roxburgh. Other players to make the trials were Craig (St.Gerrard's), MacCarron and Donnelly (both Lourdes).

Bella were top of the league. However during a week of poor weather Govan High managed to get the Pirrie Park playable and held Bellahouston to a scoreless draw.

* At the under 15 level only Conway the Lourdes goalkeeper made the squad from the Govan schools.

* At the under 16 level centre half only Neilson from Bellahouston Academy made the squad from the Govan schools.

* A normal Bellahouston Academy line up was;
Young, Gulpan, Will, Blair, Nelson, Murray, Murray, Roxburgh, Robertson, Whitehead and Malloy.

* A normal St.Gerrard's line up at one of the younger age groups was;
Bunkworth, Clarke, Fox, Brennan, McLean, McLaughlin, Dearie, McPhee, McGild, Gorman and Paterson

* Govan Primary School Results; Greenfield 0 Hillington 3;Pollokshields 2 Drumoyne 4 Pollokshields 1 Sandwood 5; Greenfield 0 Drumoyne 5.

An interesting game at Ibrox Park saw Ronnie Mc Kinnon playing right half for Rangers reserves. In opposition was Donnie McKinnon for Partick Thistle reserves. Ronnie was the happier with Rangers winning 3-0. Also at Ibrox Park Rangers scored a 4-2 result in a friendly over Arsenal. Miller,Wilson and Brand had Rangers 3-0 at half time in front of 32,000. Herd pulled a goal back for the Gunners before Henderson added a fourth for Rangers with Arsenal replying late with a consolation.

Benburb were struggling and went to in form Greenock in the 1st round of the Pompey Cup. The tail o' the bank side won 8-0. Former Bens player Tony Gregal was finding it difficult to maintain a regular place in a strong St.Mirren side.

Tom McGregor who was secretary of the Erskine Hospital Cup competition and a Benburb stalwart was taken ill causing concern for all those at Tinto Park. Fortunately he soon recovered. Benburb match secretary Willie Brown made some decent signings to try and improve a poor season for the club. He signed Bobby King from Shettleston who immediately became a supporters favourite. Also two big strong policemen in the form of Hugh McMillan and Lindsay Harrison.

With funds running dry and gates falling the Bens turned to old player Jock 'Tiger'Shaw to help them out by arranging a friendly against the Rangers 3rd team who Jock managed.

When at Bailleston Jock produced good centre forwards in Davie Wilson and also Billy Stark who had scored a hat trick against the Bens in a 3-0 win. Now he was in charge of the Rangers youngsters, centre forward Forrest looked promising.

BENBURB: Kerr, Sharp, Atwell, King, Young, Rees, Breechin, Cahill, McIntyre, Buchanan and Fleming

RANGERS: Ritchie, Currie, Reid, Wood, Sutherland, Anderson, Watson, Young Forrest, Bowie and Evans

Forrest was quickly among the goals with two in the opening minutes. Rangers built up a 4-0 half time lead with further goals from Anderson and Bowie. The Ibrox side eased off in the second half running out 5-1 winners. A bit of good news for the Bens was the selection of Hugh McMillan for the Glasgow Police team. Benburb noticed that Goalkeeper Eddie Munro was very useful on the pitch during training sessions. He was given some matches at inside forward and played well retaining the position for a number of weeks during an injury crisis before going back in goal.

Showing even handedness Jock 'Tiger' Shaw offered to play St.Anthony's at Moore Park a few weeks later which was accepted. Ants signed Frank Doris a powerful centre half from St. Constantine's.

In the Juvenile League Avon Villa lead the Govan challenge. The team recorded an excellent 3-1 win in Fife against Kelty Rangers in the 4th Round of the Scottish Juvenile Cup. Much sought after centre half from Govan Juveniles Campbell Thompson was having trial matches for Benburb. Govan Juveniles continued to produce good players under a management team of five ex Govan High pupils. These included team manager John Wilson and trainer Richard Lockhart. The Govan Juveniles team had no fewer than 13 ex Govan High School players.

Richard Lockhart heard from one of his former team mates from Govan High, Dan Thompson, now Sports master of the 164th BB that they had little or no kit left. The very next day Richard turned up at Dan's door with the old Govan Juveniles kit of blue with a yellow band. Richard treated players for injury three nights a week from all parts of Govan and never turned anyone away. The Harmony Row Boys team were having a good season. A regular team line up was: Healy, Daniels, Halligan, A.Flanagan, Moodie, Yulle, Clarke, Rae, E.Flanagan, Carty and McKenzie

| Team (top positions) | Pl | W | L | D | Pts |
|---|---|---|---|---|---|
| League Hearts | 13 | 10 | 1 | 2 | 22 |
| Avon Villa | 9 | 6 | 2 | 1 | 13 |
| Arden Thistle | 8 | 5 | 1 | 2 | 12 |

For Derek the first match for the 164th BB could not come soon enough. Having stood on countless touchlines around Glasgow School Parks with the Govan High school teams the prospect of regular football was refreshing. The first match duly arrives and it is at the 50 pitches and against the 133rd BB. The teams enter the changing rooms a long green corrugated iron building with 18 doors. The rooms are dark and each team has one side of the room with eleven pegs down each side. There is no water, this is provided by a cast iron well where water is obtained by pressing a button. It is to pitch 12 that the teams head. There are no nets or corner flags and the lines look decidedly faded. For this home match Dan Thompson is the referee.

The whistle goes and the 164th in their new blue shirts with wide yellow band are on the defensive. They are used to it as they sit one place off the bottom of the league. The game could not have got off to a worse start for Derek. He passes the ball back to keeper Norrie Clark who is not expecting it in the first minute. 'Gee whiz thinks Derek !' The ball passes through the legs of the startled keeper and into the goal. The 164th fight back and score two quick goals themselves to lead 2-1.There is no more scoring in the first half but the 164th score another two goals in the second half and eventually win 4-2. Apart from the own goal, a good start thinks Derek. The players in the team make him feel welcome and he looks forward to the next match. The 164th better players were Jim Parr and Henry Ellis.

At the next BB meeting Dan Thompson announces the draw for the Govan Cup for Boys Brigade teams. The 164th have a match against the bottom team in the league and if they win they are at home to the 119th from Linthouse. All the regular boys who play say ' We should win the first match but the second is going to be difficult. The 119th have Naismith at centre forward. He plays for Glasgow Schools one year up from us and he scores lots of goals at Boys Brigade level.

Govan players or players with a sound Govan connection are having mixed fortunes. At East Stirlingshire Alec Crawford after a lengthy period out of the team returns at outside left in a Scottish Cup tie at Alloa. The 'shire led most of the match and were 4-2 ahead in the second half. However a late collapse saw Alloa Athletic through by 5-4. A few weeks later Alec Crawford was restored at centre forward for lowly 'shire in a league match at promotion chasing Stranraer. The former Ants man was a stand out, scored two goals and East Stirlingshire won 3-2.

John Baxter was captain of Hibernian and they were having a good run in the Inter cities fairs Cup. In the quarter final they were drawn against Barcelona and thanks to two goals from Joe Baker, Preston and McLeod drew 4-4 in Barcelona. Around 45 to 50 thousand spectators turned up for the second leg. Joe Baker gave Hibs a lead on 10 minutes.

Barcelona scored two goals before half time to lead 2-1. Hibs shooting down the Easter Road slope piled the pressure on and equalised when Preston converted a corner taken by Willie Ormond.

Hibs scented blood and the pressure on the Barcelona goal was intense. Two penalties were turned down for Hibs by the German referee. Finally it was third time lucky when McLeod was fouled inside the box and the referee pointed to the spot. Barcelona went mad and chased, harried, pushed and abused the referee. For 5 minutes the Hibs players watched what was going on, Baxter telling them to keep calm. Bobby Kinloch, who was to take the penalty kick, got fed up waiting and took the ball to the penalty spot and sat on it. The kick was taken after the Barcelona players were moved out for long enough. Bobby Kinloch stepped up and scored. Barcelona went mad and at the final whistle the referee needed a big police escort to the dressing room. The Barcelona players damaged the Hibs changing rooms before leaving and most in Edinburgh were glad to see the back of them.

A story which emerged after the match concerned John Baxter. The former Benburb player spotted a number of Clyde players who had come over to support the Hibs. In the long queues; John immediately went over and made arrangements for them to enter through the VIP gate. Hibernian and Clyde had a close relationship after the Scottish Cup Final a few years previously. Hibernian and Roma finished level over two legs in the semi finals. However, the Italian club won 6-0 in the play off. It could have been an all British Final as Birmingham City reached the Final losing out eventually to Roma. The first leg at St. Andrew's was a 2-2 draw. The return leg in Rome saw victory to Roma by 2-0 and 4-2 on aggregate.

Another ex Benburb player was playing in big matches. Stewart Mitchell the Newcastle United goalkeeper played in front of over 50,000 in an FA Cup quarter final at St.James's Park. Unfortunately, the day did not go entirely to plan as Russell of Sheffield United scored three unopposed first half goals. The Geordies fought back with a goal but the Sheffield club progressed with a 3-1 win.

Donnie McKinnon was making more appearances for the Partick Thistle first team and playing well.

In the Scottish Cup Rangers were drawn away to Motherwell. After previous near disasters the match was made all ticket. Motherwell were late in notifying the arrangements for the tickets and many supporters wrote to the club with cheques and cash. The club returned the money and said that the tickets would be on sale at Fir Park during a forthcoming weekday. When the game went ahead Rangers scored twice through Max Murray and Motherwell responded with a goal from Ian St. John. Jim Baxter was injured and played on the wing hobbling as best he could.

221

In an exciting finish Bert Mc Cann grabbed a late equaliser for the 'well. The replay at Ibrox Park saw McPhee give Motherwell an early lead. This was cancelled out quickly by a good shot from Davie Wilson. Ian Mc Millan put Rangers ahead. Near half time Motherwell were awarded a free kick on the edge of the penalty box. Pat Deleany took the kick and it thundered through the Rangers wall into the net.

2-2 at half time was a fair reflection of the play with Motherwell's small forward line playing some excellent passing football. The second half saw the quality of the 'well passing further improve and it was no surprise when Bobby Roberts put them ahead mid way through the second half. Soon after Ian St.John added a fourth and near the end Bobby Roberts added a fifth cementing a 5-2 win.

RESULT: RANGERS 2 MOTHERWELL 5

The Pearce Institute's prayers were answered as they won the Churches League Division 2. From early season only a miracle was going to stop them claiming the title.

| Team CHURCHES DIV 2 | Pl | W | L | D | F | A | Pts |
|---|---|---|---|---|---|---|---|
| Pearce Institute | 26 | 25 | 1 | 0 | 155 | 27 | 50 |
| Maryhill Y.M. | 26 | 21 | 4 | 1 | 101 | 38 | 43 |
| Chryston COS | 26 | 15 | 7 | 4 | 70 | 73 | 34 |
| St.Nicholas Parish | 26 | 16 | 10 | 0 | 90 | 67 | 32 |
| 200th BB ex members | 26 | 14 | 10 | 2 | 70 | 76 | 30 |
| Temple COS | 25 | 14 | 10 | 1 | 58 | 50 | 29 |
| Hillhead Baptist | 25 | 12 | 10 | 3 | 39 | 54 | 27 |
| Church House | 26 | 13 | 12 | 1 | 62 | 46 | 27 |
| Colston Milton | 26 | 11 | 11 | 4 | 61 | 62 | 26 |
| St.James YF | 26 | 9 | 16 | 1 | 42 | 89 | 19 |
| Martyrs Parish | 26 | 6 | 18 | 2 | 54 | 79 | 14 |
| Ruchazie Parish | 26 | 6 | 18 | 2 | 54 | 84 | 14 |
| Whitevale COS | 26 | 6 | 19 | 1 | 41 | 79 | 13 |
| Castlemilk YF | 26 | 1 | 23 | 2 | 33 | 106 | 4 |

Things were getting desperate for Govan side Arden Thistle in their Juvenile Cup tie at Bellahouston Park against Shettleston Violet. The Violet were leading 6-3 and got the benefit of a throw in from the referee. A Thistle player protested and having been previously cautioned was sent from the field of play by referee Currie from Balloch. Alex. Young an 18 year old Thistle player was disappointed and accused the referee of picking on the sent off player.

An argument ensued and Young kicked referee Currie in the groin. The referee was carried to the pavilion and Young refused to provide his name to the official. Eventually he was traced through the team lists. At Govan Police Courts Young was found guilty of assault and put on probation.

Towards the end of the season Queen's Park decided to thank Govan Juveniles. The Govan side had provided many promising players for trial matches that the Hampden Park club, as a thank you, sent a team down to the 50 pitches for a match. A good crowd was drawn to the touchlines at the sight of the famous spiders shirts.

The Scottish Football Association were responding to the needs of the country and imposing an austerity drive. For the match against England the players were to travel on the overnight sleeper on the Thursday night. One training session on the Friday and then to Wembley. The Scottish media were not impressed by the preparation.

Scotland headed to Wembley with many thousands of supporters there to cheer them on.

ENGLAND: Springett, Armfield, McNeil, Robson, Swan, Flowers, Douglas, Greaves, Smith, Haynes and Charlton.

SCOTLAND: Haffey, Shearer, Caldow, Mc Kay, Mc Neil, Mc Cann, Mc Leod, Law, St.John, Quinn and Wilson.

England were on top from the start and Bobby Robson gave them a 9th minute lead, Jimmy Greaves who was thriving on the service provided by Johnny Haynes doubled the advantage on 21 minutes and on 30 minutes the same player added a third. Scotland made a slight revival and most Scots thought they would surely do better in the second period.

HALF TIME: ENGLAND 3 SCOTLAND 0

Scotland came out with all guns blazing and Dave McKay had reduced the deficit just 3 minutes into the second half. Five minutes later Davie Wilson reduced the lead to just one goal and surely a famous win was on the cards. The dream lasted about two minutes. Bryan Douglas took a free kick just outside the area. The shot was not particularly well struck but somehow it eluded the wall and wrong footed Frank Haffey. The keeper partially stopped it but was unable to catch up with the ball as it entered the net. The Scottish team were stunned. Having got back to 2-3 and seemingly on top they had given away a terrible goal. However they pounded away at the England goal for the next quarter of an hour and with luck could have pulled another goal back. However on 73 minutes England's powerful centre forward Bobby Smith added the fifth and the game seemed over. Almost immediately however Pat Quinn had scored for Scotland and at 3-5 with quarter of an hour to go there was still some hope albeit slim. Scotland attacked but were badly exposed to the counterattacks and the master of the pass.

Johnny Haynes scored two quick goals on the 78th and 82nd minutes to bring up an astonishing score line. The Scots were routed and the noise coming out the many radio's was piling the anguish on as the commentators were joyous with England's performance. To complete the miserable afternoon Jimmy Greaves and Bobby Smith brought the tally to nine within another 3 minutes and Scotland were reduced to keeping the score below 10 which they just about managed.

FULL TIME: ENGLAND 9    SCOTLAND 3

The Scottish nation was stunned and in disbelief. The worst result ever in Scottish football; a proud football nation reduced to keeping the score within single figures. Those in Daviot Street listening to the game on the radio of the Rangers persuasion blamed keeper Haffey. Within hours of the result the Rangers fans had the reply to 'Seven past Niven' (a reference to the 7-1 Celtic League Cup Final win over Rangers in 1957) with 'Haffey past Nine'. The debate over the defeat seemed to go on for weeks and the Scottish Football fans wanted at least some explanation. The Benburb supporters were not happy that everybody seemed to be blaming the Govan goalkeeper Frank Haffey for the defeat.

True the big keeper was at fault for a couple of the goals but the rest of the team played no better. One thing which annoyed virtually all Scots was the way some of the team tried to sectionalise the blame in particular the forwards ' Well the attack scored three times; it was the defenders and goalie that let us down !'. Ian St. John who was never a favourite with Rangers, was criticised for such sentiments. Most felt it was a team game and all the players who played were responsible for the disaster. One feature was the capitulation near the end of the match when they had clearly given up; not a trait most Scots like.

The Scottish FA went into discussions to analyse the disaster. The team manager must be given more powers and the selection committee less was one outcome. However, most Scottish football fans were already looking forward to the match the following year. Surely with players like John White and Jim Baxter coming through, a win over the English would not be beyond them.The Scottish Cup semi final stage saw Airdrie take on Celtic at Hampden Park and Dunfermiline play St.Mirren at Tynecastle Park, Edinburgh.

Celtic had a huge advantage in the vocal stakes from the 72,600 crowd. Airdrie never got out of the starting blocks and were under constant pressure in the first half. On 18 minutes John 'Yogi' Hughes rose to head a Byrne cross in for first goal. Six minutes later the same player blasted home from close range after a Willie Fernie shot was blocked. On 35 minutes Stevie Chalmers ran on to a good through ball and scored easily. Almost on half time Willie Fernie waltzed through the Airdrie defence to score number four. The second half saw Airdrie defend well and create a few chances. However, it was Celtic who were deservedly in the final.

The second semi final saw St.Mirren play Dunfermiline at Tynecastle. Jock Stein had built a strong team with a good defence and the Fifers brought a good support. The game was tight and very few chances emerged. It finished stalemate 0-0. The gate was 32,000.

The replay, at the same venue, again saw a big support from Fife. The second game was every bit as tight. It got decided when Melrose took a shot which hit a Saints defender and crashed off the underside of the crossbar. The referee judged it crossed the line. Dunfermiline were in the final for the first time in their 76 year history against Celtic with a famous ex Celt in charge.

The European Cup Winners Cup 'Battle of Britain' soon came round as Rangers and Wolverhampton Wanderers came out to a rain drenched Ibrox Park in front of a full house 80,000 crowd.

The Ibrox match saw Rangers playing without two of their best players in Jimmy Miller and Ian McMillan (the wee Prime Minister). Doug Baillie was played at Centre Forward and Bobby Hume came in on the left wing for the injured players.

RANGERS: Ritchie, Shearer, Caldow, Davis, Patterson, Baxter, Scott, Wilson, Baillie, Brand and Hume.

WOLVERHAMPTON WANDERERS: Finlayson, Stuart, Showell, Clamp, Slater, Flowers, Deeley, Murray, Farmer, Mason and Durandt.

Derek was in the cover opposite the Main Stand sheltering from the elements. Wolves were favourites to win over the two legs. They were further boosted after 10 minutes when Harold Davis received a bad knock and was forced to play on the right wing. Davie Wilson dropped into midfield. Despite the setback Rangers played well and even Davis on the wing got mighty cheers from the crowd as he put in several fearsome challenges. The Ibrox side pressed for a goal and were duly rewarded approaching half time with a rasping drive from Alex Scott an erstwhile midfielder.

The roar was enormous with sheer joy breaking out around the ground for the goal and most thought that to take a one goal lead under the circumstances would be an achievement. Wolves came out for the second half and attacked. A shot hit the post as Rangers defence was put to the test. However, they weathered the storm and Ralph Brand extended the Rangers lead with eight minutes left. The Rangers fans were delirious and song after song cascaded down from the rain soaked crowd. A fantastic effort from 11 heroes.

RESULT: RANGERS 2 WOLVERHAMPTON WANDERERS 0

The second leg saw a massive support (up to 10,000) leave Glasgow heading for the West Midlands. They were confident the 'Gers would progress. Alex Scott was played at centre forward in the absence of the still injured Jimmy Miller. Davie Wilson played on the right wing and the 'Iron man' Harold Davis returned after injury.

Rangers were roared on every time they attacked and Alex Scott gave them the lead just before half time to spark off amazing celebrations on the terracings at Molyneaux . Wolves were by no means finished and only a succession of second half saves by Billy Ritchie kept them at bay before Peter Broadbent reduced the arrears. However, Rangers held on and had reached the final of a major European competition.

RESULT: WOLVERHAMPTON WAND. 1 RANGERS 1 (Aggregate 1-3)

The Scottish media were in a frenzy at the Rangers result and the achievement just a few days after the 9-3 Wembley debacle had lifted the spirits of most Scots.

At a very much lower level of football the 164th were preparing for the big Govan Cup match against the 119th. With light evenings, pitch 12 at the 50 Pitches was allocated for this match on a Thursday evening. Derek immediately identified one very unwelcome spectator. A nasty local half wit nicknamed Bogo Logo had turned up and had told everyone he wanted to speak to Derek before the match. As the teams kicked in before the match Bogo came near the pitch but was ushered away by Dan Thompson and Jim Taggart, the 164th BB leaders.

Eventually Bogo was allowed to say a few words to Derek. He said 'Derek, come over here I wulnae hurt yea ! Derek moved closer but was very wary. The BB Leaders watched closely. Derek said 'What dae ye want Bogo ?'. Bogo said ' Derek I want you to score three goals against these b**st*rds the night. If you don't you are f**cking deed, do I make myself clear ?' Derek found it hard to catch his breath when the statement was made but was relieved when Dan and Jimmy told Bogo to go over the other side of the pitch away from the 164th BB people at the match.

A good number of people had gathered for the match mostly friends of the 119th BB players. They had the best player at the age group in Govan called Naismith who was a regular in the Glasgow Schoolboys team in addition to Govan High School and the 119th BB. They were overwhelming favourites to win and by half time led by 5-1 with Naismith scoring three. The 164th were playing well enough and could have scored several more goals. In the second half 164th came back into the game helped by a strong wind at their backs and reduced the lead. However, Naismaith scored the 119th 's sixth and the match was over. The 164th plugged away and Derek scored with a good shot from the edge of the box. So 6-3 it finished and Bogo on the touchline was none too happy. 'I'll f**cking kill him !'.

Dan and Jim escorted Derek and the other 164th BB players back to the green corrugated iron changing rooms. Dan said to Jim ' How on earth is this man allowed to be walking the streets of Govan ?. He is totally mad!'

Scotland started their efforts to reach the World Cup Finals in Chile. They were in a group which included Eire and Czechoslavakia. The first two matches were against Eire followed by a trip to Czechoslavakia.

Scotland made short work of Eire at Hampden Park a result which was expected. Ralph Brand gave Scotland an early lead after good work by David Herd in the 14th minute.

The same player added a second on the 40th minute. The Irish improved after half time and the wingers Giles and Haverty gave the Scots full backs problems. On 52 minutes Haverty reduced the arrears. David Herd eased tensions among the 47,000 crowd with a 3rd Scotland goal six minutes later and the same player added a fourth five minutes from the end.

RESULT: SCOTLAND 4 EIRE 1

Scotland travelled to Dublin a few days later and took on Eire at Dalymount Park. In front of a good crowd Alec Young scored an early goal on 4 minutes for Scotland. On the quarter hour the same player added a second and Scotland were on course for maximum points. Four minutes from the end Ralph Brand added a third. The Irish were a poor side and were booed by their own fans for periods during the match.

RESULT: EIRE 0 SCOTLAND 3

A few more days and Scotland were in Bratislava and a 50,000 crowd cheering on a good side. Czechoslavakia were favourites to win the group and tipped to do well should they reach Chile. Pospichal gave the Czechs the lead after just six minutes when he raced from the centre circle unchallenged before shooting. The ball went under the body of Scottish goalkeeper Leslie who should have saved. No too long after Jim Baxter gave away a penalty with a blatant unforced hand ball in the penalty box. Kvasnak scored from the spot kick. Before half time the match was all over as a contest when Kadraba added a third goal. Pat Crerand and Kvasnak had a scrap on 55 minutes and both were sent off. Pospichal added a fourth goal five minutes from the end against an increasingly demoralised Scottish team. Scotland needed a win at Hampden Park in the Autumn to stay in the World Cup.

RESULT: CZECHOSLAVAKIA 4 SCOTLAND 0

Jim Cumming seemed to have a bright career as a goalkeeper. The former Bellahouston Academy keeper had representative honours at schoolboy and youth level. He signed for Queen's Park but the competition for the one goalkeeper position was fierce. Hence he went junior with Rob Roy where he helped the Kirkintilloch club win just about everything except the Scottish Junior Cup. However, a job as structural draughtsman meant he reverted back to amateur football with Clydesmill.

227

The Scottish Junior Cup was again well followed. A 4th Round tie when St.Roch's entertained Cambuslang Rangers. 6,500 turned up including Celtic manager Jimmy McGrory. The match had an 'old firm' feel and the black ash pitch made control of the ball difficult. The wee 'Gers built up a big 3 goal lead but two late goals from the Candy meant they were hanging on at the final whistle.

In the semi final they had another 'old firm' feel about their match against Dundee St.Joseph at Muirton Park, Perth.

The Joey's were cheered on by their followers and made a bright start. However, they were to see Cambuslang Rangers take the lead with an overhead kick on 13 minutes. Tees had the ball in the net again but was ruled offside. In the second half Tees tried a fierce shot from the edge of the box and the 'wee Gers' were in their comfort zone. Dastry added a third from the penalty spot to confirm a place in the final. However, the Dundee side never gave up and Reid had the 'Joey's' singing with a consolation goal. However, Cambuslang followers were to have the last cheers as Tees dived to head in number 4 and a fifth was scored just on time

RESULT: DUNDEE ST.JOSEPH'S 1 CAMBUSLANG RANGERS 5

Ashfield lined up against Dunbar United in the other Scottish Junior Cup semi final at Tynecastle Park, Edinburgh. On their passage to the semi final Ashfield overcame a stormy tie with Arthurlie in a match that was not concluded.

In the 5th Round tie a tight match was taking place at Dunterlie Park, Barrhead. The local side Arthurlie had a large support at the match against Ashfield and they were in a high state of excitement. With twenty minutes to go Ashfield were awarded a penalty. The kick was taken and the ball struck the post. The referee ordered a re-take as an Arthurlie player was in the area. The second kick was taken and scored. At this point the referee was attacked from both ends of the ground and he was moved to an adjacent fence for his protection from about 100 spectators.

He was, with the help of Arthurlie officials and a local policeman, smuggled into the changing rooms where he was locked in for his own protection. Several Arthurlie fans were subsequently arrested and three sent to jail for 60 days.The match abandoned with 20 minutes left was awarded to Ashfield.

In the Tynecastle Park match Dunbar were effectively at home and piling on the pressure to Ashfield from early in the match. The 'field were resolute and held on until half time. The second half started with Dunbar attacking and they were rewarded when Meikle burst through the middle and scored. However, after having worked hard throughout the match to get in front United gave away a gift goal a few minutes later. The defence were in confusion when Taylor stepped in and equalised. Minutes later a deflection put McCall of Ashfield in and he converted the chance.

Dunbar responded with all out attack and Meikle grabbed a second goal for United to bring matters level at 2-2.The same player completed his hat trick near the and Dunbar United were through to the final.

RESULT: DUNBAR UNITED 3 ASHFIELD 2

Rangers were homing in on a Scottish League Division 1 title. The Ibrox club were top for most of the season and Kilmarnock provided a consistent finish, reducing Rangers lead to just a few points. A last day of the season win over Ayr United, including former Bens goalkeeper Johnnie Gallacher, would give Rangers the title. Rangers were homing in on the Scottish League title.

RANGERS: Ritchie, Shearer, Caldow, Davis, Patterson, Baxter, Wilson, McMillan, Scott, Brand & Hume

AYR UNITED: Gallacher, Burn, G.McIntyre, W.McIntyre, Glen, Curlett, Fulton, Gibson, Christie, A Mc Intyre & Bradley.

With Ayr already doomed to relegation and Rangers requiring a win the motivation levels of the teams could hardly be different. Gallacher performed heroics again for Ayr but was still beaten seven times as Rangers claimed the title with a 7-3 win.

Rangers had raced into a four goal first half lead with two goals from Alex Scott and singles from Davie Wilson and Ralph Brand. Ayr replied on half time from W.McIntyre. The second half was much the same as the first with Alex Scott completing his hat trick with Davie Wilson and Ralph Brand adding their seconds. Fulton and Christie added two more for Ayr to make the score line more respectable.

So in glorious sunshine a strong Rangers side took the cheers from the fans for a good season. The European Cup Winners Cup Final was looming up fast.

A Charity match at Moore Park involving a Benburb/St.Anthony's select team against a Kinning Park Juvenile Select was played. The proceeds were to go to the parents of popular Avon Villa player Eric Bradley who died in Kenya. The parents wanted to raise money to bring his body back to Scotland.

The Scottish Cup Final saw Celtic as clear favourites to win over Dunfermline. However the Pars had a good manager in former Celt Jock Stein and their cup run was based around a good well organised defence.

An enormous crowd of 113,600 turned up on a very wet day including a good support from Fife. Whatever happened it seemed they were going to enjoy themselves.

DUNFERMLINE ATHLETIC: Connachen, Fraser, Cunningham, Mailer, Williamson, Miller, Peebles, Smith, Dickson, McLindon and Melrose

CELTIC: Haffey, McKay, Kennedy, Crerand, McNeil, Clark, Gallagher, Fernie, Hughes, Chalmers and Byrne

The match was exciting with Dunfermline having a good start followed by a spell of pressure from Celtic. There were several near things at both ends but no goals as half time approached. Down went Williamson the Dunfermline centre half. He was taken off for a spell with a leg injury and suddenly the Pars defence looked vulnerable. However they held out until half time. Williamson re-appeared for the second half with a leg bandaged. Both sides had chances and both goalkeepers were kept busy. A quarter of an hour from the end Williamson overstretched and was in agony. He left the field on a stretcher leaving his side to see through the remaining minutes for a replay chance.

The Pars held firm and a large cheer came from their support as Williamson bravely came back on for the last two minutes. The final whistle went with much celebration and approval from the Fifers in the crowd.

RESULT: DUNFERMLINE  0 CELTIC  0

The midweek replay again drew a large crowd of 88,000.
The second match was played in the rain again. Celtic were the better side but their hearts were broken by Pars goalkeeper Eddie Connachan who was in constant action and came to the rescue with a string of fantastic saves.  In the second half Dunfermline put together a few attacks and Davie Thomson headed them ahead from a George Peebles cross. The large Celtic support immediately knew it was not to be their day and the mindless ones sent in a barrage of bottles. Charlie Dickson scored again for the Pars and the Scottish Cup was on its way to Fife amid wild scenes at Hampden Park and also in Dunfermline when the team arrived home.

RESULT: CELTIC  0 DUNDERMLINE ATHLETIC  2

Govan Schools players were not represented as Scotland schoolboys beat England 3-2 at Sunderland. Glasgow travelled to play London at  Stamford Bridge.  Despite having two players injured during the match the Glasgow side pushed a strong London side all the way losing just 2-1.

The day of the European Cup Winners Cup dawned. Derek felt quite relieved that his father Jimmy Welsh had told him he had got a ticket for the match. So he was able to boast to his friends that he would be at the match. Virtually everyone in Govan of the blue persuasion wanted to be at Ibrox Park. Rangers were taking on the Italian giants Fiorentina in the first of 2 Legs.
Derek and his father arrived at Ibrox Park a half hour before kick off. The large queues shuffled forward towards the Broomloan Road gates. Derek asked Jimmy ' Can I have my ticket please ?' Jimmy replied ' I will give it in at the gate !' The queue moved ever nearer the gate. When Jimmy and Derek arrived at the turnstile Jimmy produced one ticket and tried to lift Derek over the top of the turnstile. Immediately the turnstile operator rushed round from his booth and with a helper pushed Derek back out. He said to Jimmy ' You have a ticket so you can go in.

He does not so he is 'oot'. You cannot lift him over turnstile for a match like this. Derek moved away from the outside of the turnstile. As he walked back through the crowds he was met by George who he recognised as the son of the Rangers Supporters Club secretary who he knew from the various trips on the bus. George says ' Derek, turn round and get on you hands and knees'. Derek complied. George says ' Now keep down and near my legs. When I present my ticket at the turnstile I will take a step back . You fill the gap and when the turnstile moves I will kick you in the backside and you must be like a bullet from a gun. Run like f**k; dae ye hear me ?. Derek says ' Yes, thanks George'. George says ' Do not worry, you will be in, I can assure you of that !'

As Derek moved closer to the turnstile his heart pounded hard, the suspense was unbearable. The biggest match in Rangers history and he might not see it. The next few minutes were important. As he looked left and right he suddenly realised he was not alone. It seemed like half of Govan kids were in the same position as he all crawling up to the gate amongst the legs. George says ' Right remember Derek; like a bullet.

Do not give them a chance to stop you'. George entered the turnstile booth and presented  his ticket. He stepped back as planned and Derek filled the gap. The turnstile moved round and Derek was off like a  bullet. A Gateman put his arm out but Derek ran round it and was in. He ran and was chased for a few yards. The Gateman turned to try and catch some other 'Bullet's' who seemed to be pouring through the turnstiles. As Derek ran on he felt an arm around his waist. He cursed his luck as he was stuck fast in the clutch of the arm. He looked up and it was Jimmy. He says ' Now where do want to stand Derek ?' They looked round and saw the amazing sight of the gate where they were supposed to ejecting the Bullets getting pushed open and hundred's of people pouring in.

Eventually with the help of many police and stewards the gate was closed. The crowd was enormous; probably over 90,000. Ibrox Park was a huge and comfortable ground  at 80,000. However, this crowd was well in excess of that figure. It was heaving with humanity. The Broomloan Road end of the ground was above capacity and some fans were filling up the stairway's to relieve pressure. A huge roar greeted the teams as they walked out onto the pitch; the tension mounted.

RANGERS: Ritchie, Shearer, Caldow, Davis, Patterson, Baxter, Wilson, McMillan, Scott, Brand and Hume.

FIORENTINA: Albertosi, Robotti, Gonfiantni, Castelletti, Orzan, Rimbaldo, Hamrin, Micheli, Petris, Da Costa, Milan

Fiorentina quickly subdued the crowds enthusiasm by endless passing across the back. However this paved the way for Luigi Milan to get on the end of a good passing spell and put the Italian club a goal up in 12 minutes.

Rangers missed a penalty chance when Eric Caldow failed to convert. After that they rarely looked like scoring and the first half ended with the score unaltered. The second half was much the same pattern as the first although the Italians showed they had a cynical side to their game with several deliberate body checks and trips. This did not go down at all well with the Ibrox faithful. The game was a disappointment and Rangers task in the Second Leg in Italy became even harder when Luigi Milan again scored on 88 minutes.

RESULT:   RANGERS 0 FIORENTINA 2

A massively subdued crowd left Ibrox and headed homewards.

The next day much of the talk at school and on the West Drumoyne estate was how many of the Govan kids had managed to get into Ibrox; legally or otherwise. It seemed that every Govan lad who wanted to see the match had got in one way or another. For seemingly the first time ever Rangers were unable to give the exact numbers who were in the ground. Eventually an official figure was given as 80,000. However, the 'unofficial' figure was estimated at 90,000 and some said 100,000 were in Ibrox.

The second leg should have been a formality for Fiorentina. However, Rangers played much better with the return of regular centre forward Jimmy Miller. His bustling style caused panic in the Italian defence throughout the match. Fiorentina took a 12 minute lead again through Luigi Milan who scored two in the first leg.

Rangers attacked non stop in the second half and were rewarded when Alex Scott reduced the deficit. Rangers had several other chances to reduce the gap further but were caught by a breakaway on 86 minutes when Swedish International Kurt Hamrin scored and secured the Cup for Fiorentina.

Rangers had completed an excellent season winning the Scottish League Cup, The League and reaching the Final of the inaugural European Cup Winners Cup. Within their ranks they had some quality players in Eric Caldow, Jim Baxter and Alex. Scott. The omens looked good for the following season.

St.Anthony's had a good season but Benburb had a poor season and slipped down into the lower half of the league. The one shining light was the consistent performances of the veteran centre half Maurice Young. A popular loyal player with the Bens supporters. A crowd of 40,000 turned up at Hampden Park for the Scottish Junior Cup Final. Cambuslang Rangers had a good season and started as favourites against their East of Scotland opponents Dunbar United.

DUNBAR UNITED: Gillespie, Bellamy, Dunn, Howieson, Rae, Brown, Craig, Rennie, Meikle, Traynor and Gorman

CAMBUSLANG RANGERS: Russell, Dawkins, Brown, Hosie, Dastey, Newlands, Friel, Thomson, Tees, Swan and Dickie

Dunfermline manager Jock Stein and Rangers manager Scot Symon were in attendance at the match.

After an even start Dunbar took the lead when Traynor pounced on a 'wee Gers' error and fired into the corner of the net. The East fans were making plenty of noise and their team were playing good football. Cambuslang forced a number of corners before a breakaway saw a hesitant defence allow Craig a free run and he fired home for the second goal. The 'wee Gers' responded when Dickie converted a Friel cross just before half time. The second half saw play swing from end to end providing the crowd with good entertainment. A quarter of an hour from the end Thomson equalised for Cambuslang Rangers. Both sides pressed for winner but the match ended in a draw. The game was rated one of the best Junior Finals.

RESULT: DUNBAR UNITED 2  CAMBUSLANG RANGERS  2A lot of Comment was made that the 40,000 crowd was lower than expected. The replay attracted 23,000 for a midweek match.

Unlike the first match which was open, the replay was a cagey affair with chances at a premium. The Scottish Junior Cup winners were decided in the last quarter of an hour. Meikle took a long pass and scored on 77 minutes to send the travelling East fans wild. Five minutes from the end Craig scored a second for Dunbar and they ran out worthy winners.

RESULT: CAMBUSLANG RANGERS 0 DUNBAR UNITED  2

A man stood in the court dock. His name was Andy Moffat and behind him was the entire committee of Dennistoun Waverley. The accused pleaded 'Guilty'. The crime was running 'Housey-Housey' at the Dennistoun Waverley club without license. The Waverley paid a small fine for their indiscretion. Andy Moffat was the most popular person in Scottish Junior Football.

He worked tirelessly for his beloved Waverley and was the only full time football manager in junior football. He helped organise a good summer competition for Glasgow Juvenile sides at Haghill Park. He was manager of the Dennistoun Waverley Junior team and also helped with the various Juvenile sides that played out of Haghill Park. He had helped with the building of a Social Club and also raised funds for a covered enclosure at black ash pitch at Haghill Road. An elderly man approaching 70 and still putting as much energy and enthusiasm into his many roles as someone half his age.

If a good juvenile grade player came on the scene Andy knew about him quickly and he would be enticing him for a 'trial' at the Waverley. He was generous. Many teams in danger of defaulting a match because of the lack of an enclosed ground. The offer was made by Andy and if the club had no funds he would give it free of charge. He knew Waverley were not big enough to survive against the bigger clubs in Scottish Junior Football but he made the best of what he had. He also helped with the local scouts and guides groups making available the ground in which they could build a hut.

When it came to handing out awards at the various juvenile league team and individual presentations Andy Moffat was always top of the list to present the trophies. He seemed to know every player in the Juvenile Leagues personally, always witty and pleasant. When his wife died he received countless letters of sadness. In all of Scottish Junior or Scottish Juvenile football there could hardly ever have been a popular figure.

## SCOTTISH LEAGUE DIVISION 1

| Team | Pl | W | L | D | F | A | Pts |
|------|----|----|----|----|----|----|------|
| Rangers | 33 | 22 | 6 | 5 | 81 | 43 | 49 |
| Kilmarnock | 32 | 19 | 5 | 8 | 69 | 42 | 46 |
| Third Lanark | 33 | 19 | 12 | 2 | 94 | 79 | 40 |
| Celtic | 32 | 15 | 9 | 8 | 61 | 41 | 38 |
| Motherwell | 33 | 15 | 11 | 7 | 68 | 55 | 37 |
| Hibernian | 33 | 15 | 14 | 4 | 65 | 63 | 34 |
| Aberdeen | 33 | 13 | 12 | 8 | 71 | 72 | 34 |
| Dundee | 33 | 13 | 14 | 6 | 60 | 51 | 32 |
| Partick Thistle | 33 | 13 | 14 | 6 | 58 | 65 | 32 |
| Dunfermline | 32 | 12 | 13 | 7 | 63 | 72 | 31 |
| Dundee United | 33 | 12 | 14 | 7 | 55 | 58 | 31 |
| Heart of Midlothian | 32 | 11 | 13 | 8 | 46 | 51 | 30 |
| Airdrieonians | 33 | 10 | 13 | 10 | 60 | 68 | 30 |
| St.Mirren | 33 | 11 | 15 | 7 | 53 | 57 | 29 |
| St.Johnstone | 33 | 9 | 15 | 9 | 44 | 62 | 27 |
| Raith Rovers | 33 | 10 | 16 | 7 | 45 | 64 | 27 |
| Ayr United | 33 | 5 | 16 | 12 | 48 | 74 | 22 |
| Clyde | 33 | 5 | 17 | 11 | 52 | 77 | 21 |

Players with Govan connections were having mixed fortunes as the season end approached. Former Govan High School player Alex Ferguson broke through into the St.Johnstone first team. In one of his first games he played in a match where Third Lanark went 3 goals up through Goodfellow, Hilley and McInnes. The Saints fought back to equalise through Newlands (2) and Walker only for the Hi Hi to secure the win with a late strike from Goodfellow.

234

Jim McDonald the former Benburb winger was a regular in the Hibernian reserves team throughout the entire season. However, he did not break through into the first team and was released at the end of the season.

Former St.Gerrard's player Joe McBride was a regular scorer for Partick Thistle and was the club's top league scorer with 14 goals.

At Juvenile level Burnbank Swifts were sweeping all before them and went on a remarkable record of being undefeated in 39 games. They had reached the Scottish Juvenile Cup Final and drew 2-2 against League Hearts at Petershill Park coming from two goals down at half time. On the run to the final they beat Avon Villa from Plantation Park by 3 goals to 1. However, it was Avon Villa who were to end the Swifts proud record with a win in the West of Scotland Juvenile Cup semi finals. Burnbank Swifts won the second game against League Hearts 3-2 at Somervell Park, Cambuslang.

Sligo Celtic who play at the 50 pitches battled through to the final of Glasgow Amateur Jubilee Shield at Croftfoot . Their opponents Whitevale Star had a good season and started favourites.

SLIGO CELTIC: Haggerty, Reilly, H.Boyle, C.Boyle, Hamilton, Coyle, McConnel, Murphy, Caddell, Finlay and Kilfeather

WHITEVALE STAR: Bradley, D.Nelson, Carroll, Crillie, Madden, Cron, Fleming, Horn, T.Nelson, Weaver and McMillan

The early part of the match saw a series of excellent saves from Haggerty keeping the Star at bay. Time and again he saved point blank efforts before the overdue goal came from McMillan for the Star. This sparked Sligo into action and Caddell managed to get on the end of a long cross to equalise. The second half was similar to the first and Jimmy Fleming set up Tommy Nelson for the winner.  RESULT: SLIGO CELTIC  1  WHITEVALE STAR  2

Govan Juveniles continued to provide good players to other clubs. However, they were pleased when Paul Brechin asked to leave Benburb and return to a former club. Govan Juveniles were providing good players to the Junior level including Jimmy Driver and John McCracken to Irvine Victoria.

In the Juvenile football world Avon Villa became the top Govan team winning three trophies in season 1960-61.They captured the West of Scotland Cup, the Dennistoun Waverley Tourney and the Springburn and District Cup. The Plantation Park club were assembling a good set of players for the following season.

Govan side McNeil's won the City and Suburban Amateur League First Division with just 5 defeats in 24 matches played. The record was;  Played 24, Won 19, Lost 5, Draws 0, Goals For 87, Goals Against 40, Points 38.

Cockburn's United from West Drumoyne had an even better record with just one defeat in 22 matches played.  The record in the Glasgow Amateur League C Division was;  Played 22, Won 17, Lost 1, Draws 4, Goals For 96. Goals Against 29,  Points 38.

## PARTICK THISTLE'S GOVAN LINK

**FIRHILL PARK**

**Season 1956-57**
(Back) Kerr, Gibb, W. Smith, Harvey, Davidson, Mathers
(Front) Thomson, Wright, G. Smith, Crawford, Ewing

**MATHERS AND CRAWFORD ex GOVAN HIGH**

**Season 1962-63**
(Back) Hogan, Brown, Niven, Harvey, McKinnon, Cunningham
(Front) Smith, Duffy, McBride, Whitelaw, McParland

**DONNIE McKINNON (GOVAN HIGH)
& JOE McBRIDE (ST.GERRARD'S)**

Photo 12

# CHAPTER 13
# UP WI' THE BUNNETS O' BONNIE DUNDEE (1961-62)

The Scottish Junior Football fraternity are a close knit group. When a team is likely to fold there is always a certain degree of sadness. With attendances dropping many of the clubs were in danger of folding. During the season Douglasdale in the Lanarkshire made a brave attempt at the start of the season to keep going. However, with the local mining pits closing the population was too small to support a team at Junior level.

Strathclyde, a famous old name in Junior Football, always seemed in danger but everyone was pleased when they stated they would continue.

During the season Stonehouse Violet closed down unexpectedly from the Lanarkshire League. Douglas Water Thistle were in trouble for the same reasons as Douglasdale with the population moving from the area due to Mining pits being closed.Derek picks up a copy of the Govan Press at McCutcheon's newsagents on Shieldhall Road. He immediately turns to the back page and cannot believe what he is reading. He reads the print for a second time. 'Benburb are likely to have two re-instatements from Senior football.

Alec Crawford from East Stirlingshire and Jim McDonald from Hibernian'. Two superb players and exciting times ahead for the Bens during the forthcoming season. Derek scans the squad list of players being signed over the next few weeks.

First signing Maurice Young who has reached the veteran stage is to be involved as player coach helping the young players. He was as popular as ever with the Bens support. Bob Millan returned as trainer and Bellahouston Harriers athletic coach Jack Gifford would look after the fitness. Jack was the Scottish three mile running champion.

Others signed were

- centre half's Campbell Thomson from Govan Juveniles who was highly rated. Boyd McPhee from Saltcoats Victoria.
- goalkeepers R.Kerr (re-signed), R.Suttle (Perthshire)
- full backs I.Atwell (re-signed), Tommy Hannon (Arden Thistle)
- mid field Bobby King (re-signed), Davie McCulloch (Paisley Benburb)
- forwards Jim McIntyre (re-signed), A.Clark (re-signed), C.Belford (Re-signed), Joe Parker (Glenwood YC), George Easton (Gowanbank YC)

Virtually all Benburb supporters could not wait for the season to start.
After a few games the Bens had an unwelcome incident. Thieves broke in to the Tinto Park clubhouse and stole musical equipment including a record player and the loudspeakers.

However, the Bens had a second set at the clubhouse and the announcement of the teams was unaffected. The theft was discovered by groundsman James Willis of 59, Harmony Row, and Joseph Rodgers of 176, Langlands Road who look after the players gear. The cost to the club was estimated to be £50. Peter Madden the secretary who done much to bring success to the Ants left the club at the end of the season due to time constraints.

St.Anthony's were pleased to monitor the progress of former players. Johnny Quigley had built himself a good career in England and the Ants were pleased that former player John Colrain although released by Celtic had done well at Clyde. Celtic had re-signed former Ants full back W.O'Neil for another season. Jack Kelly became player/coach at the Ants and looked forward to the challenges ahead.The diminutive Frank McGrillan re-signed giving the club a boost. Other players to re-sign were goalie Andy Brown and John Phinn, High Burke, Tom Brogan, John Kerr and Davie Thomson. Centre forward John Adams signed from Duntocher Hibs and the new match secretary was Dennis Donnelly of 6, Luath Street, Govan.

Derek indicates to Govan High, despite getting selected, that he does not want to play for the school team and instead re-joins the 164th BB team. The team is strengthened by a few players moving up from the 164th Life Boys notably Graham Smith a centre forward and Robert Moffat a winger. Most of the stronger players from the previous season are still within the age group. The season starts with a good win over the 56th.

The next match scheduled is a local derby against the 129th who are based very close to the 164th BB in Copland Road. Local derbies at any level of football are very eagerly anticipated and this one was predicted to be very close to call. The 129th had clearly the better players within their brigade. However three of their brigade played on a regular basis for the Govan High team. On the day of the match at the 50 pitches the 129th encountered a serious problem when their goalkeeper sustained a non football related injury when he fell on broken glass. His parents forbade him to play. On the way to the pitches it became very evident that none of the 129th players wanted to play in goal. The boy who was eventually persuaded to play in goal made it clear he would only play between the posts for two goals then he would revert to playing on the pitch.

From his first handling of the ball it was clear he was never a goalkeeper. The 164th quickly spotted the weakness and hit the ball towards the 129th goal at every opportunity. The first goal arrived when a hefty clearance saw the ball bounce just outside the area and over the stand in goalie for the opener. 164th Centre Forward Graham Smith took the opportunity to shoot on sight of goal and quickly added a second. This prompted a change of 'keeper and a very small winger took over the last line of defence role. Unfortunately, he was very small and even when jumping could go nowhere near the cross bar.

Two more Graham Smith shots and it was 4-0 and another new goalkeeper. The 129th had more of the attacking but the 164th were able to defend well. Towards half time another goal was added and the amazing score of 5-0 came up.

The second half was exactly the same and Graham Smith took his tally to 5 goals with the others shared around in a 10-0 romp. A very unforeseen score line which was much discussed throughout the next week amongst the Govan High pupils.

The Boys Brigade League was noted for big decisive wins for one side or another. Govan Boys Brigade teams played almost exclusively on three sets of pitches on Saturday mornings. The 50 pitches was the most used followed by Bellahouston Park which had better pitches. Plantation Park had the nickname of the 'plots' and the three black ash pitches was surrounded by high tenements. The pitches had no nets or corner flags and the lines were not altogether clear. It was to the 'plots' that the 164th BB football team went to play a 'Top of the Table' clash with the 131st BB. Both had 100% records and both had scored freely. The 131st had a good side captained by an extremely well built centre half who was determined that nothing should pass. They also had nippy, slick forwards.

No sooner had the match started when a young girl came to the side of the pitch and said 'Can you lot keep the noise doon, ma maw is trying to get the waen to sleep'. The 131st BB easily brushed aside the 164th and after leading 3-0 at half time went on to record a 12-0 win. If the 164th BB thought they were going to win the league then their hopes were dashed.

Rangers started the season in a Scottish League Cup group which included Third Lanark, Airdrieonians and Dundee. Many Rangers supporters did not make the trip to Cathkin Park for the opening match against Third Lanark. They calculated that the crowd would almost certainly be greatly in excess of the capacity and they would be right. 15 minutes before kick off with the ground heaving the gates were closed and around 5,000 supporters outside started to hiss and boo.

Some of the gates were forced open and fans poured in. After Rangers scored their goals in a 2-0 win hundreds of supporters who were sitting around the track ran onto the pitch. Six white police horses came on to get them off the pitch and they were moved to the other side of the touchline.

In the aftermath much of the blame was levelled at the supporters. However, many thought the match should have been all ticket.

Rangers progressed through the group stage with some comfort. In the European Cup they travelled to Monte Carlo to play Monaco. A 6,000 crowd were in attendance including a few hundred Rangers supporters.

Jim Baxter was on top form in Rangers mid field and it was he who fired Rangers ahead on 10 minutes. Mid way through the first half Baxter set up a Miller v Goalkeeper chance which the goalie parried only for Alex Scott to prod into an empty net. In the second half Rangers were very casual and Monaco reduced the arrears. A penalty to Monaco saw Ritchie save but the follow up was converted. Rangers responded and after some pressure Alex Scott scored the winner with a header from a Davie Wilson cross.

RESULT: MONACO 2 RANGERS 3

The second leg was not the formality that the 65,000 crowd expected. Hess scored early on levelling the tie. At half time Rangers were booed off the pitch with slow handclaps around the ground. However, shortly after half time Christie had scored twice and the speed of the handclaps went up three fold.

A mix up in the Monaco defence allowed Alex Scott a run in on goal and he made no mistake. Hess reduced the arrears near the end but Rangers were through to the next round.

RESULT: RANGERS 3 MONACO 2 (AGGREGATE 6-4)

The first 'old firm' league clash took place at Ibrox Park in front of 70,000 people. Jim Christie opened the scoring for Rangers but former Benburb player John Divers equalised before half time. Willie Fernie gave Celtic the lead in the second half but a late rally by Rangers saw Jim Baxter fire home an equaliser two minutes from the end.

However, the match was overshadowed by the deaths of two Rangers fans when a rail gave way on the exit from the ground. The two who died were Thomas Thomson (30) and George Nelson (22). The post mortem stated that they were suffocated and also Mr. Nelson had his back broken after coming down Passageway No. 13. At least 14 others were injured. One eye witness said it was like a stampede with the victims being swept along in the middle of it as the barrier collapsed.

Rangers progressed to the semi finals of the Scottish League Cup courtesy of two wins of 3-1 against East Fife. In the semi finals they were faced with St. Johnstone at Celtic Park. The other semi finals saw Heart of Midlothian square up to Stirling Albion at Easter Road.

41,000 saw St.Johnstone stun Rangers by taking command of the match and goals from Gardiner and Bell had them a deserved 2-0 lead at half time. The second half saw Rangers recover and Davie Wilson pulled one back. Eric Caldow equalised and the match went into extra time. Davie Wilson made himself the match hero when he headed the Ibrox side into the final.

In the Easter Road semi final things were quiet with few chances for either side. Just before half time Dyson fired the Albion ahead. Willie Bauld scored a good goal on 71 minutes and the match went into extra time. In extra time Wallace got the winner for Hearts.

Rangers were invited to play Eintracht Frankfurt, an occasion to celebrate the opening of the Hampden Park floodlights. An amazing crowd of 105,000 turned up for the match which saw the Germans once again beat Rangers, this time by 3-2. Rangers gifted Eintracht with two first half goals. They gifted another shortly after half time after being the better side to that point. Eventually the Rangers pressure paid off and Harold Davis headed two goals for Rangers who came close to levelling late on.

RESULT: EINTRACHT FRANKFURT 3 RANGERS 2

Down at Cheam School in Surrey there was a football talent emerging. The footballer had quickly moved through the football rankings in the school teams. He was soon in the first team. Then he was made centre forward and just a week later he was captain of the side. Football has always been his favourite game. In the first match with Prince Charles as captain they played a local prep school in an Under 13 match. Cheam did not do well but the result was lost in despatches. Scotland's big match day arrived and a win over the powerful Czecholslavakian team was essential. Most expected Scotland to do well. The match was played on a Tuesday afternoon at Hampden Park and followed intently all over Scotland on the radio. Scotland had a good team on paper, probably one of their strongest ever.

SCOTLAND: Brown, MacKay, Caldow, Crerand, McNeil, Baxter, Scott, White, St.John, Law and Wilson.

CZECHOSLAVAKIA: Schrof, Bomba, Popluhar, Novak, Bubernik, Masupust, Kavasnak, Pospichal, Scherer, Kadraba and Masek

Despite the afternoon kick off over 51,000 turned up to see the match. They were stunned on 6 minutes when Kvasnak gave the Czechs the lead with a fantastic shot in their first attack. Scotland piled forward in response and on 21 minutes Ian St.John equalised. Slowly but surely Scotland were getting on top of the Czech's with Denis Law playing his best game in a Scotland shirt. He had been heavily criticised after the 9-3 debacle against England. To the fans he was an idol and to see him getting 'stuck in' seemed to inspire the rest of the team. Scotland were first to every ball and probably felt they should have been ahead at half time.   Half Time: Scotland 1 Czechoslavakia 1

In true Scottish tradition the team made qualification harder by conceding a second goal to the Czech's soon after half time when Scherer scored. However, this signalled a massive onslaught from the Scots who could rarely have played better. Alex Scott was terrorising the Czech defence down the wingJim Baxter and Pat Crerand ruled the roost in midfield and Denis Law looked dangerous every time he had the ball played to him. The equaliser finally arrived on 62 minutes when Law swept home a cross. The same player brought the house down when he scored the winner seven minutes from the end.

RESULT SCOTLAND 3 CZECHOSLAVAKIA 2

Unless Eire could pull off a surprise then a play off between the two countries was on the cards.

Schools football resumed and the representative matches at under 15's saw just two Govan players involved, Naismith (full back) from Govan High easily the best player in his age group at the school. Also Brady (forward) from Lourdes. Other age groups (under 16's) saw Culpan and Malloy from Bellahouston plus McCormack of Govan High get invitations to go for trials for the matches against London and Bradford.

Culpan (Bellahouston) was also selected at under 18's along with Campbell (Govan High), Sheridan (Lourdes), MaCaryon (Lourdes), McNulty (Lourdes). A few months into the season and the Benburb support were getting restless. For one reason or another the team was not settled through injuries, suspensions or unavailability. When Alec Crawford was available then the team looked like they would score plenty of goals. However, in defence the Bens were conceding goals of the 'soft' variety and the results were hence always close. One result which was not close was the West of Scotland 1st Round tie at Irvine Meadow where the Bens lost 7-0. The Meadow winger 'Hookey' Walker was tormenter in chief and but for the heroics of the Bens keeper the score could have been doubled. On the Benburb supporters bus on the way to the match a one armed supporter known as 'wingie', who was an excellent singer, sang out 'We'll rook the Meadow'. On the way back the coach was quiet with most realising it was not going to be the season that was hoped for.

To Carronbank Dunipace the coach travelled. Bens an early goal down but did everything to pull level. In the last minute Jim McDonald popped up with the equaliser and a 1-1 draw.

Alec. Crawford was already a very popular addition to the Bens team whenever he played. In front of a big crowd for an evening match against Greenock he showed his worth to the Bens. Greenock were one of the best Junior sides in the league if not the country. The 'tail o the bank' side quickly went 2-0 up shooting downhill. Jim Mc Donald, the Bens tricky winger, pulled a goal back near half time. In the second half Greenock quickly scored a third to a huge roar from a big support they carried. However, the Bens came storming back and Alec. Crawford scored two excellent goals to gain the Bens a point and send a good Bens support home happy.

RESULT : BENBURB 3 GREENOCK 3 The following Saturday the Bens entertained Renfrew with Alec.Crawford was to the fore for his team.

BENBURB: Kerr, Mc Fee, Hansen, King, Mc Auley, Baxter, McIntyre, Fisher, Crawford, Kiernan and Mc Donald.

RENFREW: Connolly, Collins, McGrogan, Purdon, McDermid, Dickie, McShee, Dougan, Rundall, McAdam and Kinder

241

Alec Crawford gave the Bens a first half lead and was unlucky with two other efforts. The sports reporters called him the Spearhead of the Bens attacks. However despite his efforts the Bens finished up losing 3-2 after some diabolical defending. This included an own goal from Bobby King which was virtually the Frew's first effort. Both the other two visitors goals were utterly preventable. Bens need some new defenders to support the efforts of what looked like a free scoring forward line.

RESULT: BENBURB 2 RENFREW 3

A big match for the Bens was against Johnstone Burgh. Alec Crawford was not present but the Bens still had a strong side listed.

BENBURB: Kerr, Hannan, Atwell, King, McPhee, Kiernan, McDonald, Kennedy, Marshall, Scanlon and Murphy.

JOHNSTONE BURGH: Walker, Gallagher, Gow, Dick, Patterson, McFarlane, Henderson, Fraser, McDermid, Henry and Collins.

Phil Murphy gave the Bens an early lead when he headed in a Jim McDonald cross. On the half hour Collins equalised but Billy Marshall put the Bens ahead by half time. Bens looked as though they may hang on for a win but the Burgh equalised and gained a deserved share of the spoils.

RESULT: BENBURB 2 JOHNSTONE BURGH 2

St. Anthony's had mixed news. Generally the side were playing well and everyone at the Ants was pleased when Frank McGrillan was selected for the Central League side. Frank was small in stature and a few other smaller players were making an impression. James Johnstone at Blantyre Celtic and Joe Fascione of Rob Roy were having outstanding season's with their respective club's.

Children entered the Moore Park dressing rooms and used a bit of lighted paper to see their way around. Unfortunately, things went wrong with the lighted paper and soon the St.Anthony's clubhouse was in flames. Fortunately the kit and football boots were retrieved. Benburb stepped in and offered the freedom of the Tinto Park facilities to the Ants until the Moore Park Clubhouse was brought back to standard. Both sides were now playing at Tinto Park.

As the end of the year approaches Govan experiences some very cold weather. This is evident as Derek and the rest of his 164th BB team arrive at Plantation Park for an away league match against the 163rd BB. After getting changed into the 164th blue shirts with a wide yellow band the team heads of to Pitch 3 at the far end away from the changing rooms.

The black ash pitch is in terrible condition with several frozen puddles and a few bricks frozen solid into the ground around the half way line. The frost completely obliterated the lining around the pitch but both sides accepted a fair shout solution from the 163rd provided referee. The 164th won the first match between the teams easily earlier in the season but on their home patch at the Plots the 163rd BB got good results.

Graham Smith quickly scored twice for the 164th and a comedy own goal due to the conditions had the 164th 3-0 up at half time. The second half saw a fight back from the 163rd and with virtually the only three attempts they had they secured an unlikely draw. A disappointing day for Derek's team and the league championship was now gone. The 129th beat the leaders 131st and moved up into second place ahead of the 164th and the 281st.

The Scottish League Cup Final at Hampden Park saw Rangers face Heart of Midlothian.

HEART OF MIDLOTHIAN: Marshall, Kirk, Holt, Cumming, Polland, Higgins, Ferguson, Elliot, Wallace, Gordon and Hamilton
RANGERS: Ritchie, Shearer, Caldow, Davis, Patterson, Baxter, Scott, McMillan, Miller, Brand and Wilson

A crowd of 88,635 turned up to see Rangers start well and put on the pressure in the early stages. Hearts held out comfortably and a midfield struggle transpired. Rangers took the lead when Jimmy Miller sent in a long shot. Every Hearts defender expected it to be gathered by Marshall and Marshall thought a defender would clear it. The end result was the ball found the net.

The second half saw Hearts push forward for the equaliser and they were awarded a penalty after a tackle by Harold Davis on Gordon. Cumming scored from the spot kick and after extra time the tie required a replay. A supporter ran on the pitch near the end and punched referee Davidson.

RESULT: HEART OF MIDLOTHIAN 1 RANGERS 1 after extra time

The replay was much delayed partly because of the poor weather and it was nearing Christmas when 41,000 turned up at Hampden Park for the replay. Jimmy Miller scored an early goal on 7 minutes when he headed an Alex. Scott cross in. Norrie Davidson equalised for Hearts within one minute when he headed in a Cumming free kick. After an exciting passage of play Ralph Brand headed Rangers ahead on 15 minutes. Shortly afterwards Ian McMillan added a third following up to score after the ball struck the crossbar.

Rangers remained on top throughout the remainder of the match and lifted the Scottish League Cup for the 4th time.

RESULT: RANGERS 3 HEART OF MIDLOTHIAN 1

Willie Thornton was pleased with his young Partick Thistle side. 19 year old Donnie McKinnon (former Govan High) was playing well and 23 year old Joe McBride (former St.Gerrard's) was scoring on a regular basis. McBride scored a hat trick at Love Street in a 3-1 win against St.Mirren.

At Love Street when St.Mirren were playing Rangers the rain poured down. A supporter put up an umbrella and immediately the people behind him complained. Neil Quinn of Preston Street, Paisley was disappointed that his view of the match was obstructed and had an altercation with the man holding the umbrella.

At Paisley Sherriff Court Quinn said 'I took him out of the crowd in order to get a good whack at him'. Quinn (20) was fined £10 for fighting. Sherrif John Morrison said 'He was lucky not to get a jail sentence as he could have caused a riot !'. Dundee were leading the Scottish league and building up a lead over Rangers and Kilmarnock. At fog shrouded Ibrox Park they had a chance to display their credentials as    potential league champions.

RANGERS: Ritchie, Shearer, Caldow, Davis, Patterson, Baxter, Scott, McMillan, Christie, Brand and Wilson

DUNDEE: Liney, Hamilton, Cox, Seith, Ure, Wishart, Smith, Penman, Cousin, Gilzean and Robertson

The kick off was delayed to allow the late fog delayed supporters to get into the ground. Dundee hit the post in their first attack before Jim Christie had a great chance for Rangers. He was clean through, dribbled around the keeper then hit the ball past the post. For the remainder of the first half Dundee held the edge but the teams went in for their cup of tea scoreless.

Immediately after half time Penman crossed and Alan Gilzean headed past Ritchie. A few minutes later the same combination of Penman feeding in Alan Gilzean saw the Dundee forward flick past Ritchie for number two. Alan Gilzean completed his hat trick from a Gordon Smith corner.

Rangers came back strongly and applied pressure. Five minutes from the end before Ralph Brand reduced the arrears. However Dundee were to have the late joy when Alan Gilzean scored his fourth and Penman added a fifth.

RESULT: RANGERS 1 DUNDEE 5

Rangers faced East German side Vorwaerts in East Berlin in the second round of the European Cup. The first match in East Berlin saw Rangers win 2-1 with goals from Eric Caldow from the penalty spot and Ralph Brand. The East Germans had taken an early lead through Kohle.

The second leg was played in Malmo in Sweden due to political issue's. The first attempt at the match was abandoned by fog before half time with Rangers winning 1-0 through Willie Henderson. The second attempt was successful being played at 9.00am the following morning. The crowd was 65 at kick off but this built up to around 300 by half time. The score at half time was 0-0 but a spectacular own goal gave Rangers the lead. Noldner equalised for Vorwaerts but two goals from Ian McMillan put the match out of reach for the East Germans. Willie Henderson added a fourth securing a 4-1 win (6-2 on aggregate).    Players with Govan connections continued to do well.

Former Govan High player Alex Ferguson returned to Govan and Ibrox Park in particular. He was included in the St. Johnstone side to play against Rangers. In a bitterly cold day Rangers were 2-0 winners. Ronnie McKinnon made an appearance in the Rangers first team at right half.

Former Benburb full back John Cameron made the breakthrough into Clyde's first team and soon had regular games.

The Czech's duly beat the Irish twice and this set up a play off against Scotland.

The match was played in the Heysel Stadium in Brussels in front of a sparse crowd. Before the match the Scots were having lots of problems getting players released for the match from the various clubs. Also the team had sustained a number of injuries. There was no fewer than 5 changes from the Hampden Park match and the 12th player (reserve) was a goalkeeper Jim Herriot.

SCOTLAND: Connachan, Hamilton, Caldow, Crerand Ure, Baxter, Brand, White, St.John, Law and Robertson.

CZECHOSLAVAKIA: Srolf, Hledik, Tichy, Pluskal, Popluhar, Masopust, Pospichal, Scherer, Kvasnak, Kucera and Jellnek

Despite the changes Scotland played well throughout.. A free kick on 39 minutes was floated in by Jim Baxter and Ian St.John headed in at the back post to give Scotland the lead at half time. The Czechs played better in the second half but it was Scotland who were dominating play against a very physical side. Connachan was badly impeded on a cross ball and forced to concede a corner when a free kick should have been awarded. From the corner Hledik headed the equaliser.

Ian St.John restored Scotland's lead immediately when he converted a cross from Ralph Brand with 20 minutes to go. However the Czechs equalised again with just 8 minutes remaining when a shot from Scherer saw the ball hit the underside of the crossbar and come out. The referee judged the ball had crossed the line and the game went to extra time. In extra time a John White shot hit the post but immediately the Czechs scored through Pospichal and later Kvasnak added a fourth. Scotland were out of the World Cup.

RESULT: SCOTLAND 2 CZECHOSLAVAKIA 4 (after extra time)

Benburb were drawn away to Dundee North End in the 2nd Round of the Scottish Junior Cup. A sizable number of Benburb supporters assemble at the bottom end of Greenfield Street to board the two supporters buses. In previous times the Bens could count on a coach full of supporters from each of the three big shipyards in Govan. Today, however, they have, although still good support, less than they had before.

Derek and Robbie are there standing with the other probable travellers to Dundee. There is a conflab with the Supporters Club secretary. The day is freezing and the weather forecast predicts that the weather may well be even worse at Dundee. The game could be in doubt. Several of the supporters are worried that they could have a wasted day if they travel all the way to Dundee and the game is off.

The Supporters Secretary makes the offer. 'If you go to Dundee and the game is off there will be no refund ! We will make a tour of several landmarks on the way back and make a day out of it. That is the best we can offer. If you still definitely want to go please board the first bus. If you do not wish to go then please accept our apologies and we will see you at Tinto Park for next week's game'. Around 20 supporters departed leaving around 40 remaining. The Supporters Club Secretary says ' It is uneconomical to run the second bus. However, what we will do is take the additional Fans over on the second coach to Tinto Park and they can go with the team.

So two coaches set off from Govan on the long trek northwards to Dundee. Not long after the supporters coach was travelling it appeared that there was a problem with the coach heating. 'Wingie' the clubs most ardent supporter calls out to the driver. 'Kin ye turn up the heating driver, its f**cking cauld on this charabang'. The driver says ' The heating is on maximum' . Wingie replied 'Maximum!, Maximum!, even the polar bears wid be complaining aboot this. With the cold the inside windows were steaming up and it was impossible for the passengers to see out. However, by the time the coach reached Stirling heat suddenly appeared and a big cheer was given.

'Wingie' was a one armed keen Bens fan. The story was he had his arm blown off during the war although no one was really sure. However, one thing was certain he had an excellent singing voice and a good way of getting all the coach involved. As the coach was initially cold he started with 'I am dreaming of a White Christmas' followed by 'The Road to Dundee'.

Countless songs were sung on the way making the journey go quicker before the coach pulled in to an open café at Perth. The passengers got out and drank the tea from the café while looking out at the River Tay. A few of the fans went over to the nearby pub. The Supporters Club Secretary tried to phone the Dundee club for confirmation that the game was on from a nearby telephone box. He came back and said ' The guy says it is a wee bit slippy in parts but playable'.

The Bens coaches went along the River Tay to Dundee and a sharp left turn once in the town saw a steep climb upwards. At the top of the hill a few turns were navigated before the Dundee North end ground was found. The ground was sparse to say the least with no cover whatsoever. A totally frozen pitch was found with the groundsmen throwing sand all over the ice. Surely the match will never be played thought most. The referee came out and unbelievably declared the pitch fit. In a gloomy day external light from around the ground showed a glistening ice. The teams came out the Bens in blue the home side in a redish/maroon. Benburb had a blow in that Alec Crawford was not able to play and Hugh Kennedy was to play up front. Kennedy was a very capable player and had been a good stand in for Crawford. In the event, the match was a farce with the players of both sides continuously losing their footing.

Dundee North End adapted to the conditions better and were two up in no time. The Bens finally got going towards half time and Hugh Kennedy scored a good goal to reduce the arrears.However, all hopes of a fight back were dashed soon after half time when the North end added two more quick goals. To their credit the Bens fought back well and should have had a few goals before Hugh Kennedy scored again near the end.

Final Score: DUNDEE NORTH END 4 BENBURB 2

Despite the defeat the return journey to Govan on the coach was one of song and cheer. 'Wingie' had an amazing voice as did several others who seemed to know all the words in countless songs. Most felt that the game should never have been played but as the conditions were the same for both teams there was no excuse for defeat offered. Everyone in the coach felt that had a fully fit Alec Crawford been available the Bens would have won. It must have been one of the coldest occasions everyone present had ever experienced at a football match.

Benburb returned to league action with a home game against Dunipace. The home support in a pre Christmas match were heartened with the return of Alec Crawford to the side.

BENBURB: Kerr, McFarlane, Hannon, King, Young, Watson, McDonald, Crawley, Crawford, Marshall and Murphy.

DUNIPACE: Allen, Shaw, McLaughlan, Ballantyne, Jackson, Cairns, Smith, Burns, cardwell, McWatt and Easton

The start could not have been worse when the visitors scored a goal after some unbelievably bad defending by the Bens in the first minute. However, that was as good as it got for the 'pace. Alec Crawford looked every bit the star that he was in the eyes of the Bens support. Crawford was tall with curly blond hair and every ball he received was controlled with ease. He seemed to glide past defenders and always brought his fellow team players into the game. The Bens attacked non stop until the interval and the Dunipace goalkeeper brought off a series of amazing saves. With two minutes remaining in the half Jim McDonald brought the Bens level. On half time Crawford scored for the Bens when he almost tore the net off with a rasping drive from just inside the box.

Kicking down the slope in the second half the Bens scored at regular intervals and towards the end were trying to reach double figures. Alec Crawford ran the Dunipace defence ragged and as well as scoring three probably set up at least four others. Most Bens supporters thought what a pity he was not playing at Dundee North end just a few weeks before. Marshall also scored a hat trick in an emphatic Bens win. The Dunipace goalkeeper had an inspired game and many wondered what the score might have been had he not played.

RESULT: BENBURB 9 DUNIPACE 1

St.Anthony's had a tough match in the Scottish Junior Cup 2nd Round after receiving a bye in the 1st Round. A trip to Ayrshire gave them the chance to avenge the heavy defeat from Ardeer Recreation a few seasons before.

Aided by two penalty kicks the Rec were four up at half time. The Ants did better after the break but again lost heavily to the Ayrshire club by 7 –2.

The City and District League saw Avon Villa leading the way in a tight race.

## CITY AND DISTRICT LEAGUE

| Team | Pl | W | L | D | Pts |
|------|----|----|----|----|-----|
| Avon Villa | 8 | 5 | 2 | 1 | 11 |
| Cardwadric Bluebell | 8 | 5 | 2 | 1 | 11 |
| League Hearts | 6 | 5 | 1 | 0 | 10 |
| Shettleston Violet | 6 | 4 | 1 | 1 | 9 |
| Glencairn Juveniles | 7 | 3 | 1 | 3 | 9 |
| Parkhead Juveniles | 7 | 4 | 2 | 1 | 9 |
| Penilee | 6 | 4 | 2 | 0 | 8 |
| Govan Juveniles | 7 | 2 | 1 | 4 | 8 |
| Ferndale | 5 | 1 | 2 | 2 | 4 |
| Park United | 7 | 1 | 5 | 1 | 3 |
| Parkhead Star | 8 | 0 | 6 | 2 | 2 |
| Tradeston Holmlea | 7 | 1 | 6 | 0 | 2 |
| Bridgeton Vics | 2 | 0 | 1 | 1 | 1 |
| Arden Thistle | 4 | 0 | 4 | 0 | 0 |

Govan Amateurs had a good 3rd Round win at Clyde Paper in the Scottish Amateur Cup. Charlie Petrie the centre forward was in good form and assisted with two goals from Drummond and McLeod before half time. Petrie added the third in the second half before the Paper scored a consolation goal

GOVAN AMATEURS: Cooper, McGill, McGilp, Streak, Douglas, Muir, Drummond, Kyle, Petrie, Pitt and McLeod.

RESULT: CLYDE PAPER 1 GOVAN AMATEURS 3

The Govan Juveniles side reported that no fewer than nine of their players had moved up to Junior level in the past 12 months. James Brechin was running the team.

248

Stephens reached the 4th Round of the Scottish Amateur Cup. They were drawn at home and welcomed the Stirlingshire village team of Twecher to Colla Park, Linthouse.

STEPHENS: Frew, Murray, McDermott, Bruce, Sharp, McGregor, Sim, McMurdo, Fleming, Mulholland and Johnston.

TWECHER: Stewart, Hill, Murphy, Hardie, Kirkwood, McNulty, Coyle, Duffy, Cowie, Doyle and Sluddon.

The visitors arrived late due to the freezing weather. They wore the Partick Thistle kit given to them by the Firhill management. The village side brought down two coach loads of enthusiastic supporters to Govan.

The pitch was in good condition as Twecher set the early pace with several shots. Against the run of play Craig Fleming headed Stephens ahead. However, Sluddon equalised before half time. In the second half it was one way traffic and the Stirlingshire side added three unopposed goals.

RESULT: STEPHEN'S 1 TWECHER 4

At School's football St.Gerrard's were undefeated as they entertained Camphill at Pirrie Park in the Scottish Shield 1st Round.

ST.GERRARD'S; McFadyen, Cullen, Holding, McLaughlin, Broderick, Docherty, Shiels, Stewart, Carruth, Flynn and Mackin

CAMPHILL: Logan, Arthur, Murray, Orr, Anderson, Adam, Wylie, Simpson, Somerville, McMenemy and McKerrall.

There were two quick goals with McKerrall scoring for Camphill and Mackin equalising for St.Gerrard's. Camphill got on top and McMenemy shot them into the lead. However, straight from the kick off Shiels equalised for the Saints. The second half was as exciting as the first and it was St.Gerrard's who got on top. Mackin gave them the lead and Shiels doubled it. Carruth fired in number five before an own goal gave Camphill some reward for their efforts.

RESULT: ST.GERRARD'S 5 CAMPHILL 3

Schools Results: Govan Primary School League: Greenfield 1 Sandwood 6, Drumoyne 4, Pollokshields 1, Pollokshields 1 Elder Park 4, Shawlands 0 Sandwood 8, Hillington 2 Elder Park 4, Shawlands 4 Pollokshields 1

Terrible weather prevented many games going ahead. One popular match scheduled for Tinto Park was between two Ladies teams. The Johnstone Red Rockets and Alexander's Angels. The proceeds were due to go to the Erskine Hospital Charity Fund. The frozen pitch put the match off and was re-scheduled for the spring.

Children at the Southern General Hospital received chocolate as a result of a Charity match between the Police and the Tuesday League Select.

Govan Amateurs had a tough draw in the 5th Round of the Scottish Amateur Cup against Girdle Toll from Ayrshire The match at Pirrie Park saw Charlie Petrie give Govan an early lead. However, he injured his cartilage in scoring the goal and the home side were down to ten men. The Toll equalised through Couser from a penalty kick but Govan replied immediately and Wark put them ahead after the goalie could only parry a shot. Before half time Muir had extended the Govan lead. Try as they did the Ayrshire men could not penetrate the Govan Amateurs defence and they marched on to the sixth round.

The 6th round saw another very tough draw against Muirend and despite another good performance the Govan Amateurs side bowed out 3-2.

In Schools Football Govan had three representatives in the Glasgow School's under 15's.

GLASGOW SCHOOL'S; Harrison (Kings Park), McCamley (St.Mungo), Naismith (Govan High), Barron (Crookston Castle), McLaughlin (St.Gerrard's), McCalliog (St.Mungo's), Bell (St.Mungo's), Green (St.Mungo's), Thomson (Eastwood), McGowan (Holyrood) and Brady (Lourdes).

Regular GOVAN HIGH side : Currie, Smith, Naismith, Wilson, McKenzie, Warden, McDermott, Costigan, Croll, Brown and Lockhart.

Regular ST.GERRARD'S side : Deleaney, Cullen, Broderick, McLaughlin, Eager, Folding, Shields, Stewart, Carruth, McFarlane and Flynn

Regular LOURDES side: I.Miller, T.McGlenaghan, J.Callachan, R.Houston, R.Brown, D.Brady, R.Maxwell, D.Breen, B.McNulty, A.Taylor and A.King
In the Scottish League Division 1 Dundee had at one stage opened up an 8 point gap at the top. However, Rangers were starting to show signs of consistency and the gap was closing slightly. In the Scottish Cup, Rangers 1st Round match was a midweek tie at Falkirk. Jimmy Miller put Rangers ahead before Eric Caldow headed past his own goalkeeper Ritchie for the equaliser. Early in the second half Davie Wilson scored the winner for Rangers.
Score Falkirk 1 Rangers 2
The 2nd Round saw an easy win over Arbroath. Jimmy Miller scored 3, Ralph Brand 2 and an own goal brought up a result of Rangers 6 Arbroath 0.
A 3rd Round draw sends Rangers north to a potentially difficult match at Aberdeen.
ABERDEEN: Ogsten, Bennett, Hogg, Burns, Kinnell, Fraser, Ewen, Little, Cumming, Cooke and Mulhall
RANGERS: Ritchie, Shearer, Caldow, Davis, Baillie, Baxter, Henderson, Greig, Miller, Brand and Wilson.

An all ticket 42,000 crowd saw an exciting match. Kinnell put the Dons ahead from the penalty spot after Jim Baxter fouled Little. Approaching half time Bennett clipped Brand's feet in the penalty box and referee Tiny Wharton pointed to the spot. Eric Caldow converted the kick to allow the teams to leave the field level at half time.

Rangers were awarded a second penalty but this time the giant Ogsten saved the shot. Twelve minutes from the end Ralph Brand put Rangers ahead when Ogsten and Bennett got into a mix up. With five minutes to go Little equalised for Aberdeen after good work by Cooke.

RESULT: ABERDEEN 2 RANGERS 2

If the first game was close the replay was not and Rangers ran out easy winners by a margin of 5 goals to 1. Miller (2), McMillan, Wilson and Brand scored for Rangers. Cumming replied for Aberdeen.

Result: Rangers 5 Aberdeen 1

Rangers had made progress in the European Cup and a quarter Final with Standard Liege was looming on the horizon. The Ibrox Park club had beaten Monaco in the 1st Round 3-2 at both home and away winning 6-4 on aggregate. For the 2nd Round they had to travel behind the Iron Curtain for a match against East German side ASK Vorwarts from Berlin.

Rangers won through easily with 4-1 and 2-1 victories. Standard Liege from Belgium stood in their path to a semi final place. A difficult match was expected and progress became even more difficult after the Belgian club won 4 -1 in the first leg. 76,000 mostly hopeful rather than expectant Rangers fans turned up at Ibrox for the second leg. Rangers were without winger Willie Henderson who had got caught up in Glasgow traffic on his way to the match. Alex Scott took his place.

RANGERS: Ritchie, Shearer, Caldow, Davis, Baillie, Baxter, Scott, McMillan, Miller, Brand and Wilson

With a 3 goal deficit Rangers were hoping for early goals. However, for all their first half work they had to be satisfied with just one, a cracking shot from Ralph Brand. In the second half time ebbed away and Rangers could not fashion another goal. Many of the large crowd were leaving when Rangers were awarded a penalty which was converted by Eric Caldow with 2 minutes remaining. However, it was too little too late for the 'Gers and they went out 4-3 on aggregate.

RESULT: RANGERS 2 STANDARD LEIGE 0 (AGGREGATE 3-4)

Rangers were presented with a difficult Scottish Cup Quarter Final tie away to Kilmarnock. Killie were very much a form team in Scotland and had come very close to winning titles but usually falling just short. The match at Rugby Park was a 36,000 all ticket sell out with Rangers allocated just 7,000. On the day it seemed that there were many more than 7,000 Rangers supporters in the ground which was packed to the rafters.

251

KILMARNOCK: Mc Laughlan, Richmond, Watson, Davidson, Toner, Beattie, Brown, Black, Kerr, Sneddon and Mc Ilroy.

RANGERS: Ritchie, Shearer, Caldow, David, Baillie, Baxter, Scott, McMillan, Miller, Brand and Wilson

Kilmarnock started well and took an early lead when a Brown cross was headed in by Andy Kerr. Rangers responded well and an Eric Caldow penalty had them level at half time.

Rangers took control in the second half and it was no surprise when a good move saw Ian McMillan fire home to give the 'Gers the lead. However, Killie kept plugging away and Bertie Black equalised with around ten minutes left. With most thinking a replay was on the cards, Ian McMillan went on a solo run to score and put Rangers into the Semi Finals. However, there was still time for Ralph Brand to add his name to the score sheet and end a pulsating cup tie .

RESULT: KILMARNOCK 2 RANGERS 4

Rangers were drawn to meet Motherwell in the semi finals.

The top three goal scorer's approaching the final part of the season were: Ralph Brand (Rangers) 27 goals, Alan Gilzean (Dundee) 22 goals, and Joe McBride (Partick Thistle) 21 goals.

In the Glasgow Amateur League a Govan team called Riverside were doing well. They had two brothers Billy Bowles and Andy Bowles as strikers and they scored on a regular basis.

Avon Villa were having a good run in the Scottish Juvenile Cup and were drawn at home to Arbroath Vics in the quarter finals. The match was played at Keppoch Park, Possilpark and resulted in a win for the Villa.

In the Glasgow Secondary League Harmony Row and St. Constantine's were the best placed sides from Govan.

Benburb's first home fixture for the new year arrived and they did not have Alec Crawford in the team. The Bens support were non too pleased to find out he had probably left the club. The club officials refused to give the reasons for the departure of Crawford. The fixture was against south Glasgow rivals Pollok and it was a very subdued Bens team and support that saw the Bens play abysmally in the first half and trailed 3-0. Shortly before the second half started a few officials came round to see the support to try and 'clear the air', they said informally.

It is to everyone's regret that Alec Crawford is not playing for the club. We have told the players not to feel sorry for themselves and put in a decent second half performance for everyone associated with the club. The reasons for Alec not playing we cannot give but I can assure you we would have wished him to be in the team. The Bens played much better in the second half against Pollok although they did concede a fourth goal losing 4-0.

On the Monday morning Derek went to Mc Cutcheon's newsagents in Shieldhall Road. And went to purchase a paper from Mrs. Cook the wife of the Benburb Match Secretary. She said 'Wait there a minute Derek and I will talk to you after I serve this wumin'. When Mrs Cook came over Derek said ' I am devastated Mrs Cook, Alec Crawford was my hero at the Bens and a good number of other people as well !' Mrs Cook said ' I know, we have had people coming to the door over the past few weeks asking what is going on in regard to Alec I cannot give you the reasons but please be assured no one wanted the outcome we have got. The players have promised they will put on a show at every match between now and the end of the season. They are a good bunch and the club think they will do well. Cheer up Derek, the Chookie Hens will be back !'

Benburb travelled to `in form` Rutherglen Glencairn for a 2nd Round Glasgow Cup fixture. It was a windy day with driving rain at Southcroft Park as the Bens supporters bus arrived. After the Alec Crawford affair most at the Bens expected a 'response' from the players to show they were more than a one man team.

BENBURB: Kerr, MacFarlane, Atwell, King, Young, McPhee, Mc Donald, Marshall, Fisher, B. Murphy and P. Murphy

The Bens faced the wind and driving rain in the first half and the home side, who had reached the 5th Round of the Scottish Junior Cup, attacked non stop for the first quarter of the match. However, the Bens defence held firm and approaching half time Phil Murphy capitalised on a mistake in the home defence to give the Bens the lead. On half time the Glens were awarded a penalty but the spot kick went wide. With the wind behind them in the second half the Bens were quickly on top and Phil Murphy scored the second. A memorable third goal from Bobby King with a shot from 40 yards wind assisted hit the net like a rocket. Fisher added a fourth before the end and it was a happy trip back to Govan for a good Bens support.
RESULT: GLENCAIRN 0 BENBURB 4

Maurice Young was the Benburb centre half and had a football playing career spanning 20 years. He was playing well as the closing months of the season approached as were the rest of the team. Maurice had played senior football at St.Johnstone, Stranraer and Norwich City. Another experienced defender playing well for the Bens was Bobby McFarlane a former Petershill and Scottish Junior International right back.

The Scottish Junior Cup 5th Round saw virtually all the favourites go through and some 'big' matches were certain for the quarter final.
Results: Scottish Junior Cup 5th round. Bellshill Athletic 0 Kilsyth Rangers 2, Darvel 2 Glenafton 4, Irvine Meadow 5 Maryhill Harp 0, Newburgh 4 Armadale Thistle 3, Pollok 4 Glencairn 2, Renfrew 6 Maryhill 1, Rob Roy 1 Coltness United 0, Whitburn 0 Greenock 3.

Renfrew centre forward Jimmy Rundall was scoring goals aplenty. The big Renfrew centre forward had already scored 58 goals in the season to date. Jim was a Welshman from Caernarvon. The 'frew team had their sights on Hampden Park and winning the Scottish Junior Cup. Western Road were attracting good crowds including quite a few from nearby Govan when the big matches came round.

A key player in the Rob Roy team was former Govan High pupil Martin Ferguson playing in midfield. He was having the occasional game for Partick Thistle reserves with a view to signing for the Firhill Park club.` Martin was in demand and selected to play for the Central League side. Also in the team was a tiny winger from Blantyre Celtic called James Johnstone as well as Welshman Jimmy Rundall of Renfrew.

## GLASGOW SECONDARY LEAGUE

| Team | Pl | W | L | D | F | A | Pts |
|------|----|----|----|----|----|----|----|
| Regent Star | 14 | 9 | 4 | 1 | 37 | 29 | 19 |
| Drumchapel Thistle | 12 | 8 | 2 | 2 | 35 | 26 | 18 |
| Pollok Hawthorn | 11 | 8 | 3 | 0 | 35 | 17 | 16 |
| Harmony Row | 13 | 7 | 4 | 2 | 40 | 29 | 16 |
| Rancel | 14 | 8 | 6 | 0 | 41 | 29 | 16 |
| Rutherglen Waverley | 12 | 7 | 4 | 1 | 36 | 26 | 15 |
| Market Star | 13 | 7 | 5 | 1 | 33 | 29 | 15 |
| St.Roch's | 10 | 6 | 2 | 2 | 27 | 17 | 14 |
| St.Contantine's | 11 | 6 | 3 | 2 | 27 | 11 | 14 |
| Plantation Hearts | 11 | 4 | 1 | 6 | 35 | 26 | 14 |
| Dennistoun | 11 | 5 | 5 | 1 | 36 | 30 | 11 |
| Cranhill | 11 | 5 | 6 | 0 | 21 | 24 | 10 |
| Westwood | 9 | 3 | 5 | 1 | 17 | 21 | 7 |
| Olivetti | 13 | 3 | 9 | 1 | 29 | 60 | 7 |
| Castlemilk | 8 | 3 | 5 | 0 | 21 | 29 | 6 |
| Rogany Hearts | 13 | 3 | 10 | 0 | 18 | 41 | 6 |
| Ibrox Thistle | 14 | 3 | 11 | 0 | 25 | 56 | 6 |
| Pollok | 10 | 2 | 8 | 0 | 14 | 21 | 4 |

The Govan Boys Brigade League provided great enjoyment for Derek and all the various teams. With most of the boys in the same classes it was good to preview games and get accounts of how the other matches had fared on the Monday mornings at Govan High. An eagerly awaited 'derby' match came along with the 164th BB playing the 129th BB at Bellahouston. The 129th had virtually a full strength side available as the school had no match. The pitches at Bellahouston were much better than the 50 pitches and Plantation Park. Apart from a few grassless patches in the goalmouth they were almost perfect. The match was tight and the 164th defence would rarely have played a better match.

Some of the better known players at the school were unable to stamp an impression on the game and the first half ended scoreless. The second half had the same pattern but Derek got the winning goal when he chased a long through ball and just beat the out rushing keeper to the ball and toe poked it past him. It then seemed an eternity as the ball trundled over the line chased by two back tracking defenders. So the 164th BB had completed the double over their near neighbours. However, the league title was long gone for both teams and the 164th were heading for a 3rd or 4th place league position. They had done well against the top teams with the exception of the 131st BB but dropped a number of points with draws against teams in the lower half of the league. In the Govan Primary Schools League Drumoyne entertained Shawlands at Pirrie Park.

DRUMOYNE: Hannah, McGowan, Brills, White, Martin, Gifford, Wilson, Shannon, Havard, Stewart and Rankine

SHAWLANDS: English, Ronald, Stewart, Beard, McKay, Bressley, Dewar, Murray, Blair, Clark and Ferguson.

Drumoyne opened the scoring on three minutes through Havard. However Shawlands fought back and were ahead at half time with goals from Blair and Dewar.

Shawlands had a good spell at the beginning of the second half and added three further goals through Clark, Dewar and Blair. Drumoyne refused to give up and added two further scores to their total with good goals from Havard and Shannon.

RESULT: DRUMOYNE 3 SHAWLANDS 5

Govan Primary School results: Greenfield 1 Elder Park 4, Sandwood 9 Hillington 1,
Elder Park 5 Shawlands 1, Pollokshields 1 Drumoyne 5 , Greenfield 3 Drumoyne 2, Sandwood 6 Pollokshields 0, Hillington 2 Pollokshields 0, Greenfield 1 Elder Park 4, Shawlands 4 Drumoyne 6, Sandwood 1 Hillington 2, In the 3rd Round of the Crookston Cup Govan High won 3-1 against St.Gerrard's in the local Pirrie Park derby.

In the semi finals Govan High faced a strong St.Mungo's side at Pirrie Park.

GOVAN HIGH: Bowie, Patterson, Hamilton, Fairlie, Wilson, Moan, Craig, Rawson, Blair, Greig and McCleary.

ST.MUNGO'S: Stirling, McErlane, Hughes, O'Brien, Hall and Brown, Griffin, Sherrin, Callaghan, Boyd and Fullerton

At Pirrie Park Blair gave Govan High an early lead. St.Mungo's piled on the pressure in the second half and scored a very late goal through Callaghan.

RESULT: GOVAN HIGH 1 ST.MUNGO'S 1

St.Mungo's went on to win the replay.

In the annual Glasgow v London (under 16's) match 3,500 spectators turned up at Hampden park. The match was exciting from start to finish and ended 5-5. Glasgow scored in the last minute.

In the annual match (under 17's) with Bradford it was Bradford who scored a last minute goal to salvage a 3-3 draw.

Lourdes had a good season at the oldest age group and won the prestigious Cameronian Cup with a 2-0 win over Holyrood in the Final.

Ronnie McKinnon at Rangers was becoming a popular figure around Govan. He was making a good impression at the Rangers club and the Burgh were justifiably proud. However, one group who were not always impressed with his play were the Referee's Association. Ronnie was summoned to Park Gardens to explain why he had been sent off in a match.

Ronnie was on the mat again with Willie Henderson presenting the prizes to the Govan Judo Club at Elder Park Church Hall. Both Ronnie and Donnie McKinnon were making breakthroughs into the Rangers and Partick Thistle teams respectively. St.Johnstone v Partick Thistle had a fair bit of Govan interest. Donnie McKinnon and Joe McBride played for Partick Thistle. St.Johnstone had Alex Ferguson at inside left and it was he who was the happier, scoring the only goal in a 1-0 win.

A crime that sickened most football fans in Scotland was the theft of club scarves at matches, often in the Gents near the urinals. St.Mirren fan John Jeffrey (19) was caught by other fans and Fiscal John Robertson at Govan Police Court put him on probation for stealing a scarf from a 13 year old Rangers supporter at Ibrox Park.

Dundee had a good lead at the top of the Scottish League Division 1 approaching the end of season 1961-62. However, Rangers started a remarkable run of good form and the lead started to evaporate. In early March Rangers hit the front and soon the lead was three points. The bookmakers were offering 10-1 ON that the title would once again return to Ibrox Park. Rangers had a centre forward problem for the visit to Falkirk with injuries. However, Davie Wilson was switched from the wing to centre forward and promptly scored six goals at Brockville Park in a 7-1 win.

# CENTRAL LEAGUE

| Team | Pl | W | L | D | F | A | Pts |
|---|---|---|---|---|---|---|---|
| Rob Roy | 27 | 18 | 2 | 7 | 80 | 41 | 43 |
| Johnstone Burgh | 26 | 18 | 6 | 2 | 77 | 36 | 38 |
| Greenock | 29 | 15 | 7 | 7 | 81 | 44 | 37 |
| Pollok | 29 | 14 | 9 | 6 | 76 | 60 | 34 |
| Renfrew | 25 | 15 | 7 | 3 | 67 | 50 | 33 |
| St.Anthony's | 29 | 12 | 9 | 8 | 49 | 46 | 32 |
| Vale of Leven | 28 | 12 | 9 | 7 | 67 | 56 | 31 |
| Clydebank | 27 | 11 | 9 | 7 | 68 | 64 | 29 |
| Port Glasgow | 30 | 10 | 15 | 5 | 62 | 73 | 25 |
| Dunipace | 28 | 11 | 14 | 3 | 62 | 96 | 25 |
| Arthurlie | 25 | 9 | 10 | 6 | 66 | 59 | 24 |
| Kilsyth Rangers | 29 | 8 | 14 | 7 | 54 | 68 | 23 |
| Benburb | 27 | 5 | 12 | 10 | 53 | 65 | 20 |
| Yoker Athletic | 26 | 9 | 15 | 2 | 48 | 65 | 20 |
| Duntocher Hibs | 27 | 6 | 16 | 5 | 49 | 74 | 17 |
| Gourock | 26 | 2 | 21 | 3 | 41 | 103 | 7 |

In the Scottish Cup semi finals the Old Firm were kept apart by the draw. Rangers were at Hampden Park against Motherwell while Celtic were at Ibrox Park against St.Mirren.

At Hampden Park 80,000 saw Motherwell handicapped when Bert McCann had to leave the field for a while with a leg injury. However, he returned some minutes later to huge cheers from the Fir Park support. Rangers had been the dominant force in the opening half and towards the interval took the lead with two goals. Davie Wilson managed to get behind the 'well defence and crossed for Max Murray to score. A few minutes and a repeat goal was scored again by Max Murray and he blasted in a cross from Willie Henderson who had got behind the 'well defence.

In the second half Motherwell at last got a share of the match and Bobby Roberts scored to bring them into the match. However, in the last few minutes Davie Wilson cemented Rangers win with a third goal.

Result: Rangers 3 Motherwell 1

At Ibrox Park. Celtic were wary of St.Mirren, the Paisley side having trounced them a few years previous in a semi final. However, Celtic had trounced the Buddies 5-0 just 5 days before the 'semi' in a league match. 65,000 turned up expecting Celtic to win.

However, on 8 minutes former Celt favourite Willie Fernie scored after Frank Haffey in the Celtic goal dropped a cross from Henderson. Willie Fernie dribbled through the Celtic defence before releasing Beck. The ball was fed through to Kerrigan who blasted home to double the Buddies lead on 32 minutes. A few minutes later and Beck himself got on the score sheet as he was on the right spot to beat Haffey after good work again from Willie Fernie. In the second half Celtic had all the play but were unable to get a breakthrough. Sixteen minutes from the end a lot of bottles came raining down from the rear of the terraces driving the supporters at the front terracing to climb to the safety of the track. A number of other supporters took the opportunity to invade the pitch to get the game postponed. Frank Haffey helped usher the fans back onto the terraces with the police. The match was eventually re-started and Celtic scored a consolation goal but it was St.Mirren who were destined for Hampden Park and a meeting with Rangers. Result; St.Mirren 3  Celtic 1

Duncansfield Park, Kilsyth saw a huge crowd turn up for the Scottish Junior Cup quarter final between Kilsyth Rangers and near neighbours Kirkintilloch Rob Roy. The kick off was delayed by seven minutes to allow more spectators in queue's to get inside the ground. The match was tense. Sixteen year old McIntyre fired Kilsyth into the lead and Cunningham scored a good equaliser for the Rabs.

Govan boy Martin Ferguson scored for Rob Roy from the penalty spot before Wilkie fired an equaliser for Kilsyth and it was a replay at Kirkintilloch. Another big crowd turned up for the replay and Rabs cheered their fans when Knox scored in the first minute. Kilsyth Rangers fought back and Wilkie soon had them level. The second half saw Rob Roy get on top and Joe Fascione gave them the lead. McIlwraith ended any Kilsyth chances with a third goal.

Newburgh caused a major upset when a goal in each half by Napier and Buchanan knocked out Irvine Meadow. Pollok were ahead through Harris against Glenafton but two goals from Brennan saw the Ayrshire side through 2-1.

Western Road, Renfrew had a ground record attendance of well over 9,000 for the visit of Greenock. Greenock took the lead through Samuel. Renfrew stormed back and McShee lobbed the goalie to bring them level at half time. The second half was all Renfrew being urged on by the home support. There were pitch invasions of joy as Renfrew scored three unopposed goals through Rundall (2) and Newton gave the 'frew a 4-1 victory

There was crowd trouble when a Greenock fan ran onto the pitch trying to get the game abandoned. The offender Charlie McLaughlin (30) was arrested and fined £30 by Paisley Court sheriff John Wilson. Michael Docherty (21) attacked a Renfrew fan who had a Rangers scarf on and was found guilty. His sentence was deferred awaiting reports.

Mount Ellon United were struggling in the Lanarkshire League and were without a win throughout the season. They turned up at Wishaw with just eight players. A tannoy announcement was made for any aspiring footballers to step in and make up the numbers. Three volunteers stepped forward and boots were found for them. Result:Mount Ellon United won their first match of the season.

At Bellahouston Park the match between Blairdardie and Rancel was getting a bit tardy. Angus Wylie of Blairdardie was in the thick of things and the referee warned him for some over zealous challenges. Angus got into an argument with another player and was promptly sent off. As Mr. Dempsey pointed to the dressing rooms Wylie punched him on the face and the match was immediately abandoned.

At Govan Police Court Angus Wylie was fined £5 by Fiscal Stanley Morrow. Wylie told the court. 'I am extremely sorry for what happened'. He was allowed 14 days in which to pay.

England were on their way up to Hampden Park. Walter Winterbottom the England manager and his team were invited to watch the Benburb match at Firhill Park against St.Roch's in the semi final of the Glasgow Junior Cup on the Friday evening before the match in order to ease their pre-match nerves. The choice of the Bens to ease nerves brought quite a few amusing comments from the Govan folk. 'Watching Benburb tended to make most of our supporters nervous wrecks' said some.

The Saturday morning arrived at 31 Daviot Street bright, sunny and full of optimism. Even Billy the blue and white budgie was whistling away on a diet of Trill and water. If ever a football match was anticipated with such fervour by Scots the game at Hampden Park against England was top of the list. A wounded proud nation on the back of a 9-3 pounding the previous year wanted a win. Any win, but preferably a win with a bit of style, to show that the Scots were after all good fitba' players. The English media anticipated an easy win for their country which would give them encouragement on their way to the 1962 World Cup. To the Scots this particular match was more important than any World Cup; it was personal.

To most Scots they felt that the team in dark blue had so many good players it was difficult to see how they could lose. It must have been one of the strongest Scotland teams ever to take the field. The four names around the centre of the park alone were total class probably World class. Pat Crerand of Celtic; Jim Baxter of Rangers; John White of Tottenham Hotspur and Denis Law of Turin.

The teams took to the field with the biggest roar imaginable and every Scot was tense in anticipation.

SCOTLAND: Brown, Hamilton, Caldow, Crerand, McNeil, Baxter, Scott, White, St.John, Law and Wilson

ENGLAND: Springett, Armfield, Wilson, Anderson, Swan, Flowers, Douglas, Greaves, Smith, Haynes and Charlton.

Scotland as expected started like an express train and Springett did not have to wait long for his first piece of action. In fact the entire first half was played virtually entirely around Springett and the England goalkeeper brought off a string of impressive saves. For all the Scottish dominance they only had a goal from Davie Wilson to raise the Hampden roar for. He cut in and his fierce drive hit an English defenders boot before bulging the roof of the net.

HALF TIME : SCOTLAND 1 ENGLAND 0.

At half time virtually all Scots were fearful that despite being completely in control they led by just one goal. They anticipated that the English would play better in the second period. So it turned out. England came more into the game although Springett was the keeper who was still pulling off a succession of excellent stops. Johnny Haynes saw a fierce shot hit the underside of the bar for England before Eric Caldow scored a penalty for Scotland two minutes from the end to seal a good Scotland win. Pride restored.

RESULT: SCOTLAND 2 ENGLAND 0

The Scottish Cup Final saw Govan boy Ronnie Mc Kinnon start for Rangers against St.Mirren in front of 127,000 spectators. Ronnie had after a few season's in the reserves finally claimed the centre half spot for himself and was already becoming a huge favourite with the Ibrox fans.

Some quarters of the Rangers support were comparing him to George Young as a very good centre half. The Ibrox club had been followed strongly throughout the Cup run. St. Mirren were unlikely to be any pushovers having beaten Celtic 3-1 in the semi final. RANGERS: Ritchie, Shearer, Caldow, Davis, McKinnon, Baxter. Henderson, McMillan, Miller, Brand and Wilson.

ST.MIRREN: Williamson, Campbell, Wilson, Stewart, Clunie, McLean, Henderson, Bryceland, Kerrigan, Fernie and Beck

Rangers held an edge throughout the first half but the Buddies defended stoutly. Davie Wilson had a shot which hit the post and Williamson brought out some smart saves. However, Ralph Brand got the breakthrough goal for Rangers approaching half time. Wilson went down the left and crossed for Brand to force the ball over the line.

The second half saw St.Mirren improve but a Davie Wilson goal sealed a 2-0 win for the Ibrox club. Harold Davis came through the middle and fed Wilson who shot home from the edge of the box. Try as they did the Buddies could not get a foothold on the match and the Cup went to Ibrox Park.

RESULT: RANGERS 2 ST.MIRREN 0

In the Scottish Juvenile Cup Avon Villa were making progress and took good support to Brockville Park, Falkirk for a semi final against Tulliallan Thistle. It was a happy bus back to Govan as the Villa beat the Thistle and set up a final against Lochend Hearts.

Another Govan side to reach a final was McNeil's who reached the Final of the City and Suburban League Cup with a comprehensive 5-1 win over Woodside Thistle. They had previously captured the cup in 1957. They also reached the final of the Angus Shield for the seventh successive year with a comprehensive win over Levin's United.

Rangers lost unexpectedly at home to Dundee United and then secured a late draw in the old firm match. Celtic were the better side and led through a fine individual goal from John 'Yogi' Hughes. Celtic should have been further ahead but a long punt downfield by keeper Ritchie saw Davie Wilson chase and he just beat the out rushing keeper to secure the point. However, Dundee had not given up the chase and with two games remaining the teams were now level on points.

With Rangers ahead by just goal average the last two matches of the Division 1 season would decide the title. Rangers had to travel north for a midweek match against Aberdeen and lost to a single Cummings goal. Dundee made no mistake against St.Mirren with goals from Cousins and Penman moving the Dens Parkers on the verge of the title. The final matches saw Rangers scramble a late draw at Ibrox Park against Kilmarnock and Dundee celebrated in style at Muirfield Park, Perth. Goals from Alan Gilzean and Penman took the title to Bonnie Dundee. St.Johnstone seemed in a good position to avoid relegation.

However as the results drifted in they found themselves relegated. Airdrie 1 Partick Thistle 0, Falkirk 3 Third Lanark 0, St.Mirren 4 Dunfermline 1, Raith Rovers 3 Aberdeen 1. St.Johnstone 0 Dundee 3

The Scottish Junior Cup semi finals saw Renfrew head to Firhill Park to meet Fife team Newburgh. A crowd of 10,000 with many 'Frew fans saw Newton give them an early lead. Newton dribbled through the Newburgh defence just before half time and set up Rundall for a second Renfrew goal. The second half saw Newburgh have several good spells of pressure but without reward. Rundall took his season's goal haul to 65 when he blasted home a free kick. Mowen headed a fourth goal for the 'frew near the end. Result: Renfrew 4 Newburgh 0

A crowd of around 15,000 saw Kirkintilloch Rob Roy take on Ayrshire side Glenafton at Rugby Park, Kilmarnock. Govan player Martin Ferguson was having a good season and took his place in the Rabs side. A tense match saw few chances with Cunningham giving Rob Roy the lead with a shot from 25 yards which went into the net via the post.

Glenafton piled on the pressure near the end of the match and were unlucky when a Brannon shot crashed off the crossbar. Rob Roy held on to take their place in the final.

Result:  Rob Roy  1 Glenafton  0

## SCOTTISH LEAGUE DIVISION 1

| Team | Pl | W | L | D | F | A | Pts |
|------|-----|----|-----|----|----|----|-----|
| Dundee | 33 | 24 | 5 | 4 | 77 | 47 | 52 |
| Rangers | 33 | 22 | 5 | 6 | 83 | 30 | 50 |
| Celtic | 34 | 19 | 7 | 8 | 81 | 37 | 46 |
| Dunfermline | 33 | 19 | 9 | 5 | 76 | 42 | 43 |
| Kilmarnock | 33 | 16 | 8 | 9 | 73 | 57 | 41 |
| Hearts | 33 | 15 | 12 | 6 | 53 | 49 | 36 |
| Partick Thistle | 33 | 16 | 14 | 3 | 61 | 54 | 35 |
| Dundee United | 33 | 13 | 14 | 6 | 70 | 70 | 32 |
| Motherwell | 34 | 13 | 15 | 6 | 65 | 62 | 32 |
| Third Lanark | 33 | 13 | 15 | 5 | 59 | 50 | 31 |
| Hibernian | 33 | 13 | 15 | 5 | 55 | 71 | 31 |
| Aberdeen | 33 | 10 | 14 | 9 | 59 | 70 | 29 |
| St.Johnstone | 33 | 9 | 17 | 7 | 35 | 58 | 25 |
| Raith Rovers | 33 | 9 | 17 | 7 | 48 | 72 | 25 |
| Falkirk | 33 | 10 | 19 | 4 | 43 | 68 | 24 |
| Airdrie | 33 | 8 | 18 | 7 | 54 | 78 | 23 |
| St.Mirren | 33 | 9 | 19 | 5 | 48 | 79 | 23 |
| Stirling Albion | 33 | 6 | 21 | 6 | 33 | 73 | 18 |

Last day drama. Dundee win league. Stirling Albion and St.Johnstone are relegated.

The Boys Brigade football season headed towards the end. The 164th were pleased with their league performance. The remaining games were for the annual Govan Cup. The semi finals paired them with the 281st from Drumoyne, always a tough match. They would be strengthened by several players from the Govan High 1st team. The other semi final was won by the 129th BB who knocked out the league champions 131st.

The 164th v 281st match was played at the 50 pitches and a strong wind coupled with a dry pitch made life difficult for both teams. The 164th had the advantage of the wind in the first half and attacked virtually non stop. However, a goal near half time from Robert Moffatt never really looked like it was going to be enough. So it turned out and the 281st made good use of the wind at their backs and ran out 5-1 winners. Robert Margach a near neighbour to Derek scored two of the goals.

The Final saw the 129th win the cup with a 2-0 win and the Boys Brigade football season was over. A very enjoyable experience for all concerned playing at one of the lowest levels of the football fraternity. The league did throw up some very good players and some went on to both Junior and Senior football levels.

Celtic Football Club made themselves many friends when Jimmy McGrory offered to send a team to play Johnstone Burgh at Keanie Park, Johnstone. The proceeds from the match were to be given to the Erskine Hospital Charity Fund.

Partick Thistle first team stat's showed that Donnie McKinnon and Joe McBride the Govan players in the side had missed just one game each (33 matches played each).

In addition Joe Mc Bride had scored 14 goals for the Jags.

A big crowd turned up at Cardonald to see Lourdes take on Holyrood in a top of the table clash.

LOURDES; Chiappelli, Sheridan, Chance, Campbell, McCarron, Haran, McNulty,   Slavan, Kowalewski, Breen and Taylor

HOLYROOD: Connachan, Rigby, Doherty, McLean, McManus, LePointe, Gartland, Murphy, McCafferty, Hood and Gray

Lourdes got off to a good start when Kowalewski forced the ball in the net on two minutes. A mix up in the Holyrood defence was punished by Breen to put Lourdes two up; McNulty added a third quickly afterwards. Holyrood responded with much attacking football and reduced the arrears just before half time through McCafferty. At the start of the second half Kowalewski scored a good goal to put Lourdes further ahead. Holyrood attacked non stop to the final whistle and pulled back two goals through Hood and Murphy leaving Lourdes hanging on at the final whistle.

RESULT: LOURDES  4  HOLYROOD 3

Frank McCarron the 17 year old centre half of Lourdes signed for Celtic soon after the season.

At the younger age groups some of the Govan players were making appearances for the various representative sides.

At Under 14 level Conn of St.Gerrards's and Lumsden of Kinning Park both made the Glasgow squad.

At Under 13 level Kerr of Govan High made the Glasgow squad.

A crowd of 27,000 turned up at Ibrox Park to see Scotland take on England at under 15 level. An excellent match finished 4-3 to Scotland with Peter Lorimar the key player for Scotland. Lorimar was set to become a trainee professional footballer at either Manchester United or Leeds United. Leeds were the favourites although Matt Busby the Manchester United manager had not given up.

The Scottish Junior Cup Final promised to be a good match. Much interest around Govan centred on Martin Ferguson who was to play in midfield for Kirkintilloch Rob Roy.

Martin Ferguson had played for a Central League Select against a representative team from Northern Ireland at Firhill Park. The team which won 3-2 thanks to a last minute goal from Blantyre Celtic winger James Johnstone was:

Brown (St.Anthony's), Cowie (Kilsyth Rangers), Wright (Glencairn), Ferguson (Rob Roy), McDermid (Renfrew), Taggart (Clydebank), Johnstone (Blantyre Celtic), Mullen (Shettleston), Rundall (Renfrew), James (Maryhill) and Keenan (Greenock)

Martin was signed by Willie Thornton of Partick Thistle and went over to Firhill Park on a voluntary basis to do additional training with the Scottish League Club. His playing hero was Danny Blanchflower of Tottenham Hotspur and Northern Ireland. He played for Brigade Amateurs and got selected for the Scotland YMCA side. It was during a match against England YMCA at Adamaslie Park that he was spotted by Kirkintilloch Rob Roy. The Junior club allowed him to play for Drumchapel Amateurs to gain experience. As a current member of a very successful Rob Roy side he was helping vacuum up many trophies in the world of Junior Football.

The Scottish Junior Cup Final was certain to have a good crowd. Renfrew and Rob Roy both had large followings when successful. In Kirkintilloch the Co-op branches were closed to allow the workers to go to the match. Coaches left by the dozen and supporters from USA and Canada came over to see the match. Renfrew was a town also with cup fever and a fleet of coaches were booked for the trip to Hampden Park. Harry Haddock a Govan resident and long serving Clyde captain sent the team a good luck telegram. Renfrew were Harry's previous club.

At Hampden Park 49,000 turned up to see the two Central League clubs lock horns.

RENFREW: Connelly, Collins, McMahon, Purdon, McDermid, McGrogan, McShee, Mowan, Rundall, Rooney and Newton

ROB ROY: R.McLeod, Dyer, J.McLeod, Ferguson, Loughran, Cooper, Fascione, Knox, Fleming, McIlwraith and Cunningham

Renfrew settled the quicker and took the lead on 8 minutes. A corner from Newton deceived McLeod in the Rob Roy goal and went straight into the net.

Rob Roy's two wingers Fascione and Cunningham started to get more possession and the Kirkintilloch side gradually got on top. In the second half Fleming brought the Rabs level on 55 minutes with a header. After this point play became disjointed as both sides anticipated a replay.
RESULT: RENFREW 1 ROB ROY 1
The replay drew 19,500 to Hampden Park. A dour struggle took place with both sides very defensive minded. The winner was scored by Rob Roy winger Kenny Cunningham with a shot from 25 yards.
RESULT: ROB ROY 1 RENFREW 0
Benburb Football Club received a blow when former President Ronald Cook passed away after much sterling work over the years for the club. His brother William was a current president of the club and David Cook, a nephew, the match secretary.

After the disappointments of the season Benburb had at last started to find some form. They reached the semi final of the Glasgow Cup losing 4-1 to St.Roch's after a replay.

In addition they won through a few rounds in the Kirkwood Shield to the semi finals (before losing to St.Roch's) including a 4-1 win at Petershill. The last competition of the season was the Erskine Hospital Cup which had a larger entry than normal. In the 1st Round a narrow 4-3 win was achieved at Pollok with Bobby King and Hugh Kennedy on the scoresheet. Then Port Glasgow were defeated at Tinto Park setting up a semi final with St.Anthony's. The clubs could not agree on a venue so the match was played at neutral ground; Johnstone Burgh's Keanie Park.

Although the Erskine Hospital Cup was probably the lowest in terms of importance to any outsider, for the teams involved it was important to do well as every match was virtually a local derby. The match was tense throughout and chances were few and far between. The first goal was going to win it thought most. The goal never arrived and the match was to be decided by the referee counting the corners on his notebook. Derek could not remember the actual score but thought possibly the Ants had edged it. After around 15 seconds all the players in blue jerseys were jumping in the air. The Bens had won by a single corner; the score being 6-5.

The Erskine Cup Final was played at Tinto Park on a bright sunny Saturday. The Bens opponents were Clydebank who brought a good support with them to add to a sizable Bens support.
BENBURB: Archibald, Young, Hannan, King, Nesbit, McPhee, McDonald, Fisher, Marshall, Watson and Murphy.
CLYDEBANK: Whyte, McArthur, Trotter, Bowman, Leadbetter, Taggart, Douglas, Patterson, Crawford, Maley and Nolan.

Clydebank started the better but play soon became even with both teams having chances. After the interval and kicking down the slope the Bens attacked non stop and eventually got the breakthrough when winger Jim Mc Donald burst through to fire low into the corner of the net. Near the end the same player scored virtually an identical goal and the cup was with the Bens. It was great for anyone connected with Benburb to see them lift a trophy in front of the Clubhouse. A season that promised so much at least finished with something to remember. Erskine Hospital received a good cheque as a result of football competition.

Maurice Young, now well in to the veteran stage, was offered a place for the forthcoming season at the club as a player/trainer.

RESULT: BENBURB 2 CLYDEBANK 0

Govan Salvation Army were enjoying the odd game of football. They staged a five-a- side competition at Colla Park, Linthouse, home of Stephens FC. Teams from Dunfermline and Hawick took part in the competition. The organisers were hoping that the competition could become an annual affair.

Avon Villa reached the final of the Scottish Juvenile Cup. The final was played over two matches. In the first match the Villa lost 3-1 to Lochend Hearts at Broomfield Park, Airdrie. Their cause was not helped with several players missing due to injuries. The second leg took place at Petershill Park.

AVON VILLA: Crilley, Struthers, Wallace, Alexander, Hutchison, Thomson, Best, Davidson, McGinty, Smith and Heaney

LOCHEND HEARTS: Andrew Crawford, Devine, McGovern, Dick, Black, Arthur Crawford, Dunnion, McClements, Reilly, McInally and Brown.

Avon Villa were at full strength and started brightly. However Andrew Crawford remained mostly untroubled and Lochend forced three corners in succession. On 31 minutes Reilly gave the Hearts the lead with a good shot. The Villa's hopes were beginning to disappear but they attacked until the interval.

The Villa played in spirited fashion in the early part of the second half but found the Hearts defence tough to crack. Reilly scored his second goal from a break away and the Scottish Juvenile Cup was in their grasp.

Avon Villa never gave up and scored a consolation goal near the end.

RESULT: AVON VILLA 1 LOCHEND HEARTS 2 (Aggregate 2-5)

The plight of many of the Junior football clubs was in focus as the end of the season approached. Scotland was in a worsening recession and population moves were afoot as traditional industries closed down.

Lanarkshire League side Douglas Water Thistle were on the brink but trying everything they knew to keep afloat.

Bridgeton Waverley were thought unlikely to continue. By playing at Carntyne Stadium their support was some way from Bridgeton. The committee numbers had dropped and support on the terracing was poor. However, against all odds they managed to form a reasonably strong committee and decided to carry on.

A lot of comment was made as to the decline of Duntocher Hibs FC. The Hibs had a number of good seasons which included a Scottish Junior Cup Final and a few League Championships. They had a good scouting system and young players with talent were brought on board. These players were developed at the club and several went on to play top class Senior football. These included Dick Beattie and Pat Crerand to Celtic and John Colrain to Celtic and then Clyde. It was said the trouble started when the club was doing well.

A former player William McFadden handed himself in at the police station. He said he had embezzled a lot of funds from the Duntocher Hibs football club during his period as treasurer. Once the books were examined £719 at least was unaccounted for.

The 49 year old McFadden had a wife and six children. At Glasgow Sheriff Court, Sherriff Bryden found McFadden guilty and he was sentenced to 6 months imprisonment.

McFadden was a Millwrights Labourer and his downfall came when some friends identified him as the treasurer. His friends asked if he could help them by providing short term loans. He obliged but the loans were never repaid. McFadden took to gambling to try and re-coup the losses but the situation became worse. He collected the Catering money at matches and money from the Social club.

The Bank were initially sympathetic with the overdraft but when things appeared to be going wrong took action.

Other stories of the misappropriation of collected cash then circulated and the club were struggling. In the Central League the Hibs had become a club of struggle spending most of the season one place above back markers Gourock. In Junior football supporters always took a dim view of any news on personal gain over the collective spirit of a club. Hibs` gates had plummeted and from being a safe club were now in danger of possibly going out of business.

# 1962 WORLD CUP

The 1962 World Cup was underway with England the only home nation for the trip to Chile. England did not fire on all cylinders but did qualify for the quarter finals from group 4. They achieved this on goal difference over Argentina when both sides finished on 3 points.

Group 4 Results:

Hungary 2 Tichy (17) Albert ((61) England 1 Flowers (pen—60)
Argentina 1 Bulgaria 0

England 3 Flowers (pen– 17) Charlton (42) Greaves (67)
Argentina 1 Sanfillipo (81)

Hungary 6 Bulgaria 1
Hungary 0 Argentina 0  England 0 Bulgaria 0

| Group 4 | Played | Won | Lost | Drawn | For | Agst | Points |
|---|---|---|---|---|---|---|---|
| Hungary | 3 | 2 | 0 | 1 | 8 | 2 | 5 |
| England | 3 | 1 | 1 | 1 | 4 | 3 | 3 |
| Argentina | 3 | 1 | 1 | 1 | 2 | 3 | 3 |
| Bulgaria | 3 | 0 | 2 | 1 | 1 | 7 | 1 |

| Group 1 | Played | Won | Lost | Drawn | For | Agst | Points |
|---|---|---|---|---|---|---|---|
| Soviet Union | 3 | 2 | 0 | 1 | 8 | 5 | 5 |
| Yugoslavia | 3 | 2 | 1 | 0 | 8 | 3 | 4 |
| Uruguay | 3 | 1 | 2 | 0 | 4 | 6 | 2 |
| Colombia | 3 | 0 | 2 | 1 | 5 | 11 | 1 |

| Group 2 | Played | Won | Lost | Drawn | For | Agst | Points |
|---|---|---|---|---|---|---|---|
| West Germany | 3 | 2 | 0 | 1 | 4 | 1 | 5 |
| Chile | 3 | 2 | 1 | 0 | 5 | 3 | 4 |
| Italy | 3 | 1 | 1 | 1 | 3 | 2 | 3 |
| Switzerland | 3 | 0 | 3 | 0 | 2 | 8 | 0 |

| Group 3 | Played | Won | Lost | Drawn | For | Agst | Points |
|---|---|---|---|---|---|---|---|
| Brazil | 3 | 2 | 0 | 1 | 4 | 1 | 5 |
| Czechoslavakia | 3 | 1 | 1 | 1 | 2 | 3 | 3 |
| Mexico | 3 | 1 | 2 | 0 | 3 | 4 | 2 |
| Spain | 3 | 1 | 2 | 0 | 2 | 3 | 2 |

In the quarter Finals England were paired with the holders and favourites Brazil.  Garrincha a flying winger with deformed feet gave Brazil the lead on 31 minutes but Hitchens equalised for England 7 minutes later. In the second half the Brazilians got well on top and scored through Vava on 53 minutes and again through Garrincha on 59 minutes to seal a 3-1 win.

### QUARTER FINALS
Chile 2 Soviet Union 1
Czechoslovakia 1 Hungary 0
Brazil 3 England 1
Yugoslavia 1 West Germany  0
### SEMI FINALS
Czechoslavakia  3  Yugoslavia 1
Brazil  4  Chile  2

The World Cup Final saw the talented Czech's score through Masopust after 15 minutes. The Brazilians took only 2 minutes to draw level through Amarildo. The second half saw Brazil get on top and goals from Zito (69)and Vava (78) ensured the best team in the competition won the Cup.

### FINAL
Czechoslavakia  1  Brazil  3
### 3rd/4th Place
Chile  1 Yugoslavia 0

# FOUR FANTASTIC WORLD CLASS SCOTLAND PLAYERS

Dennis Law scores at Wembley                    Jim Baxter scores at Wembley

John White Tottenham and Scotland

Pat Crerand Celtic and Scotland

Alex Forsyth 1953

Alex Forsyth

Great Benburb
Goalkeeper

Photo 11

John Baxter
Benburb & Hibernian

# CHAPTER 14
## POOR AULD BENBURB (1962-63)

The Corporation number 34 double decker bus climbs the hill at Berryknowes Road up to Cardonald railway station. Down on the large field to the right behind the railways there is a 'fitba' match going on. It is a match between the Sheriff Court staff and the Glasgow Solicitors.

Joseph Beltrami the Solicitors captain said he was not a bad player when he was at school. He was now one of Glasgow's best known solicitors. He will be supported by Eddie McGowan who has played a bit of football in his time. For the Sheriff Court team Ian Hay said 'We beat them 3-1 a fortnight ago. I play for Old Kilpatrick Juveniles in goal'.

Not too far away at Tinto Park changes are afoot and they are not changes that were pleasing the Bens supporters. Alec Crawford was not to return to the Bens and had signed for Cambuslang Rangers. Cambuslang Rangers coach was now Alec Forsyth a Benburb goalkeeping legend. Jim McDonald refused to play for the Bens although he was still on the retained list. He was on trial at Luton Town but had a preference to stay in Scotland.

Pollok were keen to sign him. The club had released Bobby King who was a favourite. Jimmy Fisher who was attracting the attention of Celtic signed for Pollok. Former Rangers and Northern Ireland centre forward Billy Simpson was now at Newlandsfield Park as trainer and coach.

Alex Crawley and Jim McIntyre were freed by the Bens and moved to Ayrshire clubs. The squad was virtually overhauled.

A bit of good news was the return to the Benburb team of Jim McCormack, a re-instatement from Dumbarton. Jack Kiernan re-signed and his army comrade John Ponesky looked a good signing at centre forward. Being army players their availability was always going to be a problem.

St.Anthony's who had a decent previous season released centre forward Jim Muir and provided J.Kerr an inside forward to Partick Thistle.

At Govan Juvenile Court a group of young footballers aged 8 to 14 years are standing in dock with their parents nearby. They had found a gate at Hampden Park open and arranged a match between themselves on the hallowed turf. They enjoyed themselves and several actually scored into the famous old wooden goal frames. The final whistle arrived from several police officers. Fiscal David Whyte said that complaints had been made and the boys were admonished.

The City and Suburban League announced a new team from Govan. Craigton Hearts were one of ten new teams to join the increasing ranks of Juvenile grade football.

Hampden Park had a good crowd of 82,000 for the new format Glasgow Charity Cup. The traditional competition between the six Glasgow senior clubs was replaced with a one off pre season prestige match. A Glasgow Select were playing Manchester United for the Cup. The turning point came in the second half with Glasgow winning 2-1. A penalty was awarded and converted by Eric Caldow. However, referee Tiny Wharton was not ready for the kick to be taken. The re-take penalty saw a save from Gaskell. Almost immediately Maurice Setters hit a good goal from distance and further goals from David Herd and Ian Moir won the cup for the visitors.

Attendances at Scottish Football matches dropped during the previous season by around half a million. Big matches could still attract big crowds but the bread and butter games were struggling to attract fans through the turnstiles at both Senior and Junior grounds.

Rangers started the season with the usual League Cup competition. A group containing Third Lanark, Hibernian and St.Mirren.

Rangers s started slowly and a defeat was suffered against St.Mirren. However, a goal rush in the last two matches, 5-2 at Cathkin Park against Third Lanark and 4-0 against St. Mirren, saw them through to the quarter finals.

Rangers won 3-1 at Dumbarton in the Quarter Final 1st leg and a 1-1 draw at Ibrox Park in the 2nd leg saw them through 4-2 on aggregate against a spirited effort from the 'Sons'.

Benburb were preparing for the new season and hopes were not high. The club support had gone down sharply after the Alec Crawford fiasco and recovered a bit towards the end. However, when Derek visited McCutcheons Post Office on Sheildhall Road for the Daily Record and comics Mrs Cook said that according to her husband, match secretary David Cook, virtually all their better players had left. A number of youngsters had joined and the prediction was for a slow start to the season followed by a pick up as the inexperienced players improved.

At Firhill there was the possibility of a Govan colony. Martin Ferguson had joined the 'Jags' from Rob Roy. Donnie McKinnon and Joe McBride were regulars in the first team. However, things did not turn out as planned. Donnie got concussed in a match and was out for several weeks. Just as he was about to return he had a bad bite on the leg by a dog. Martin Ferguson soon forced his way into the first team.

Rangers started their European Cup Winners Cup campaign against Seville in front of 60,000 at Ibrox Park. Jimmy Miller quickly had the 'Gers ahead when he moved on to a pass from Willie Henderson and fired home. Before the quarter hour mark Miller crashed a John Greig pass into the net off the underside of the crossbar. In the second half Jimmy Miller completed his hat trick and Ralph Brand made it four.

Result: Rangers 4 Seville 0

Rangers lost the 2nd Leg in Seville by 2-0 in a rough house match but progressed courtesy of a 4-2 aggregate win. Dundee lost heavily in Cologne by 4-0 but won through 8-5 on aggregate.

Benburb made a disastrous start to the season and by the time the West of Scotland matches came round they had still to record a win of any description. The only point was secured against Renfrew. The West of Scotland Cup match was away to Port Glasgow and the Bens kept up their consistent form with a 3-0 loss. St.Anthony's fared even worse with a 6-0 exit at Yoker Athletic.

A Benburb league match against Vale of Leven was one of the most amazing ever witnessed at Tinto Park. A sunny Saturday saw high flying Vale of Leven make a trip to Tinto Park for a league game. Not many gave the Bens much hope including even their most ardent supporters.

BENBURB: Archibald, Dempsey and Barrett, Kiernan, Nisbet, McCrae, McCormack, Horne, McMillan, Limond and Marshall

VALE OF LEVEN:Williams, Gallacher, Bellingham, Alexander, Buchanan, Brown, McDermid, Dennison, McLeod, Young and Murnin

The match started predictably enough when Vale kicking up the slope scored an early goal when Brown headed in a corner on 6 minutes.. Not so long afterwards they carved through the Benburb defence and a desperate hand ball gave them a penalty. The kick was saved by goalkeeper Archibald who was constantly in the thick of the action. The entire match was being played  around the Bens penalty box and it came as no surprise when the Vale added two more quick goals from McLeod before the break.

Even worse for the Bens was that two of their players were limping badly as a result of heavy challenges. As the teams came out for the second half the Bens had made a number of enforced changes due to the injured players. One wanted to come off but was persuaded to play for a few more minutes. The instructions to the two injured players could be heard from the Bens coach. ' Ther we are you two. Wan oan each wing. Jist make a nuisance of yersells'. With Vale shooting downhill against effectively 9 players the crowd were anticipating a double figure total against the Bens. The Bens switched the players around to suit. Vale peppered the Bens goal and only heroics from Archibald the goalie plus some amazingly brave defending in particular from Bobby Nisbet kept the score at three.

A long punted, desperate clearance up field saw policeman PC McMillan chasing through the middle. He out muscled  two defenders and calmly slotted home for which most of the crowd thought would be a consolation goal.

The Vale resumed the onslaught down slope to the Bens goal. They hit post and crossbar. Midway through the half the Bens managed a foray up field and forced a corner. A scramble ensued from the corner and the ball went into the Vale net.

The visitors were clearly stunned by this goal and panic set in. Even with time to control they were guilty of slamming the ball out of play. In the last few minutes following a prolonged Vale attack another long ball up field saw PC McMillan chasing the ball down the wing. With no support he ran on with the ball beat a couple of defenders and slammed the ball into the goal from an acute angle. The Bens players celebrated as though they had won the cup. The Benburb supporters were speechless and most stood with dropped jaws. It must have been the most unlikely of results ever on a football field. Bens fans thought then that just perhaps they might actually win a match during the course of the season. The comeback of all comebacks.

RESULT: BENBURB 3 VALE OF LEVEN 3

Parkhead Juniors were making a great effort to stay in business. The Helenslea Park pavillion had been badly damaged by fire and the club needed £800 to keep going. The club nicknamed the 'Heads' had won the Scottish Junior Cup no fewer than 5 times since the were founded in 1883. Appeals went out to keep the famous old club alive from John Wales the team manager. In the East End of Glasgow more news reflecting a sign of the times came with the news that the popular North East Glasgow Cup competition was finished. The organisers felt that the gates were now low and competing against television was difficult.

Jim McDonald the Benburb winger was still in dispute with the Bens. Despite much persuasion he did not want to play for the club. He had an option to play at senior level without affecting his status as a Junior player. St.Johnstone first team had injuries. They turned to Jim McDonald to play for them against East Stirlingshire. The Benburb winger had a good game and scored one of the goals in a 5-1 win for the Saints at Muirton Park, Perth. A few weeks later he signed for Pollok to the disappointment of the Benburb faithful.

In the Scottish League Division 1 Rangers had taken charge and had built up a 3 point lead from Celtic after 10 games where they remained unbeaten. However the Scottish League Cup semi final match against a strong Kilmarnock side promised to be a test.

A 77,000 crowd were present at Hampden Park for the Rangers v Killie match. On 15 minutes McIlroy headed in for Killie after Caldow had cleared off the line. Ralph Brand for Rangers was having a good game and soon equalised with a good shot. Soon after he put the 'Gers ahead. Andy Kerr was also having a good game for Kilmarnock and he equalised before half time with a snap shot past Ritchie. The second half was very even but it was the Ayrshire men who grabbed the win when Black headed in with eight minutes left.

Result: Kilmarnock 3 Rangers 2

The second Scottish League Cup semi final was at Easter Road, Edinburgh between Heart of Midlothian and St.Johnstone. The Saints started brightly and matched the hot favourites in most area's. the exception was scoring goals. Willie Hamilton gave the Hearts the lead with a good goal on 15 minutes. Towards the interval two goals from Wallace, one from the penalty spot, put the Edinburgh side out of sight. The same player completed his hat trick near the end and Hearts were on their way to Hampden Park. Poor weather greeted the teams as they came out for the Scottish League Cup Final.

HEART OF MIDLOTHIAN: Marshall, Polland, Holt, Cumming, Barry, Higgins, Wallace, Paton, Davidson, W.Hamilton and I.Hamilton

KILMARNOCK: McLaughlan, Richmond, Watson, O'Conner, McGrory, Beattie, Brown, Black, Kerr, McInally and McIlroy

Despite the poor weather over 51,000 attended the match. Kilmarnock almost scored in their first attack. The ball was played through to Black who looked well offside. The linesman did not flag and the Hearts defence were standing arms raised. However Marshall came out and made a good stop. A few minutes later Black failed to score again from close in. Hearts were playing second fiddle for the most part. However, everything changed on 24 minutes when Norrie Davidson scored for Hearts. Willie Hamilton dribbled through the Killie defence and once at the goal line crossed for Davidson to score. Before half time Marshall produced a great save as the Ayrshire men strove for the equaliser. The second half Hearts gained control and the light became very poor. The Edinburgh side were to hang on to lift the trophy.

RESULT: HEART OF MIDLOTHIAN 1 KILMARNOCK 0

The Schools football season started again. St.Mungo's were the record winners of Divisional trophies. However, in their first match of the season they were surprised by Govan High who won 2-1.

Another Govan High side travelled up to the Western Highlands in the Scottish Schools Shield and came back with a good win under their belts. Lourdes were expected to do well having won the Cameronian Cup during the previous season.

However, they crashed 3-0 in their first match. The Lourdes team was : A.Stirton, A Irvin, T.Lenaghan, A.MacNamara, R.Mallon, J.Chance, I.Miller, J.Wallace, R.Maxwell, P.Breslin and T.Traynor.

Govan Primary School League Results: Drumoyne 1 Hillington 4; Sandwood 9 Pollokshields 0; Pollokshields 1 Drumoyne 7:Greenfield 2 Sandwood 9; Drumoyne 0 Sandwood 5; Hillington 6 Greenfield 1; Greenfield 2 Drumoyne 6; Pollokshields 1 Hillington 6.

A typical Bellahouston team line up was:
V.Slater, D,MacDonald, T.Wilson, A.Miller, A.Maxwell, D.Campbell, I.Thomson, J.Dick, D.MacCallum, J.Stewart and J.Nelson

A Bellahouston team beat Hyndland team at Norwood in an exciting match. BELLAHOUSTON: Hunter, MacDougall, Kelly, Vincent, Wark, Tait, Cameron, McCabe, Murray, McCall and Thomson HYNDLAND: Mitchell, McKie, Davidson, Morrison, Stevenson, Robertson, McAlpine, Sandford, Cottingham, Milne and Ross

Hyndland scored in just 3 minutes when a shot from Cottingham beat the outstretched hands of Hunter and went under the crossbar. Bella pressure was rewarded when McCall converted a cross from winger Cameron. Bellahouston continued to be on top and Thomson ran through to put the ball under the diving goalie for the lead. The second half was different and Hyndland attacked continuously. After Cottingham had headed against the crossbar an overdue equaliser came from Ross. With two minutes to go and Hyndland looking the more likely winners a breakaway saw Thomson fire home to enable the Bella to progress into the next round of the Scottish School's Intermediate Shield.

Celtic and Falkirk supporters had poor relations with one another. The Parkhead supporters started boycotting matches at Brockville due to trouble. Relations between Falkirk and Rangers were not much better. A lot of trouble occurred in the Boys enclosure. At Falkirk Sheriff Court two youths admitted fighting during a match against Hearts. John Thomson a 17 year old labourer and Robert Hulett an 18 year old labourer were each fined £3 and £5.

A few players with Govan connections were moving clubs. Joe McBride moved to Motherwell from Partick Thistle.

At Ibrox Park discussions were going on. Liverpool manager Bill Shankly wanted to sign Billy Stevenson from Rangers. The Liverpool negotiating team consisted of Shankly, the club Chairman and a Director. After the figures were agreed Stevenson said he would like to think about it overnight. Shankly said 'Nae bother son! We will drive you home put ourselves up in a hotel in Edinburgh overnight and see you in the morning'. Billy Stevenson signed for Liverpool the next morning.

Jim McDonald the former Benburb winger had offers from senior clubs Worcester City, Cowdenbeath and Montrose. All wanted him to sign but he decided to stay at Pollok.

Gourock Juniors were struggling. They had played 14 matches and lost the lot. Scored 9 goals and let in 76 goals. Often they arrived at matches with not enough players and signed up spectators on the day to make the numbers up. Along with Benburb they were the only two sides in the Division who had not won a match.

The forthcoming fixture between the two was already being dubbed 'The Battle of the Titans'. Gourock received a letter from the Scottish Junior Football Association showing concern about the club.

Alex McConnachie the Gourock team manager said he was not unduly worried. The team had received a large number of injuries to players. In addition they had just signed some good players and things would improve. This was exactly the sort of news the Bens fans did not want to hear.

Gourock were still struggling with their team when St.Anthony's travelled to the 'tail o'the bank'. The result was Gourock 0 St.Anthony's 12 (twelve) with Ants centre forward Adams having a field day.

Gourock were drawn against a strong Pollok team in the Scottish Junior Cup 1st Round at Drumshantie Park, Gourock.

GOUROCK: Dimarco, McAteer, Brown, Warrilow, Jackson, McGrady, Campbell, Mangan, Fox, Docherty and Tyrell.

POLLOK: Buchanan, Neil, Martin, McMillan, Laidman, Smillie, Bain, McDonald, Harris, Collins and Chatwood

Jim McDonald scored in the first half for the 'lok. However, Gourock fought back and in an exciting second half won 3-2 amid much celebration. Like any self respecting top junior football club who are victims of a shock result the protest was lodged. Most of the allegations were unfounded. However, it was established that Owen Mangan had not the paperwork of re-instatement done properly and a replay was ordered.

In the replay Gourock scored first but goalkeeper Dimarco got injured. He carried on bravely although immobile and was at fault for a few of Pollok's five goals. The Newlandsfield Park side won through 5-1.

At Hampden Park Scotland hit top form against Northern Ireland with a 5-1 win. Denis Law gave an exhibition on goal scoring with four goals.

Rangers 2nd Round opponents in the European Cup Winners Cup were Tottenham Hotspur and the match was immediately dubbed another 'Battle of Britain'. The first match in London showed Tottenham to be a top class side and they secured an easy 5-2 win.

The 'Battle of Britain' Rangers v Tottenham Hotspur was shown live on Television. However, that did not prevent a full house 80,000 crowd turning up at Ibrox with the vast majority cheering the 'Gers on. Fog had prevented the first match going ahead and it was on a December night that the teams lined up for the second leg.

RANGERS: Ritchie, Shearer, Caldow, Davis, Mc Kinnon, Baxter, Henderson, McMillan, Miller, Brand and Wilson

TOTTENHAM HOTSPUR: Brown, Baker, Henry, Blanchflower, Norman, MacKay, Medwin, White, Smith, Greaves and Jones

For any chance of a 'miracle' comeback Rangers needed a quick goal. However it was the Londoners who scored after just 10 minutes. Jimmy Greaves floated past a number of Rangers defenders and put the ball past Billy Ritchie. To their credit Rangers kept plugging away and the crowd warmed to the teams effort. However the half time whistle arrived with the score line unaltered. Early in the second half Willie Henderson managed to get a good cross in and Ralph Brand equalised for Rangers. The Ibrox side piled forward in search of reducing the deficit further but were caught out with a shortage of defenders following a breakaway and burly Spurs centre forward Bobby Smith blasted a fierce shot home. Rangers continued to press forward and Davie Wilson fired home an equaliser near the end. Most thought that the draw was the least Rangers deserved but they were caught out in the last few minutes when Bobby Smith scored again.

RESULT: RANGERS 2 TOTTENHAM HOTSPUR 3

At the end of the match both teams were given great applause from an appreciative crowd. Virtually everyone in the ground expected the talented North London side to go all the way and win the trophy.

The Spurs captain Danny Blanchflower was full of praise for Rangers after the matches. 'I think they would do well in the English 1st Division. At present they are not playing consistently against good quality opposition. If they were playing in places like London, Manchester and Liverpool they would have to improve to survive After a few months they would probably reach the required standard'.

As the end of the year approached Rangers faced a tricky match at Motherwell. Joe McBride scored a first half goal for the 'well and it was only a goal near the end from Harold Davis that saved Rangers and kept their League title aspirations on track.

School's football was being badly affected by weather with most matches postponed.

Govan teams had progressed to the quarter finals in various Cup competitions. The draws threw up:

Cameronian Cup: Govan High v St.Mungo's ; Eastbank v St.Gerrard's.

Glasgow Cup; St.Gregory's v Govan High.

Castle Cup: St.Gerrard's v St.Bernard's

In the Scottish Shield Intermediate age group St.Gerrard's had progressed to the last 16 and were drawn to face Johnstone High at Pirrie Park.

Harmony Row had entered the Scottish Juvenile Cup and progressed to the 3rd round. They were paired with Clydebank Juveniles.

The day of reckoning was fast approaching with Benburb's big match with Gourock. Gourock had beaten Pollok and gained their first league point at near neighbours Port Glasgow.

Further news came that the   Bens were having serious financial problems. Mrs Cook confirmed this to Derek when he collected the papers from McCutcheon's newsagent's. She said 'Do not worry Derek, The Bens will pull through; they always do!' Heavy defeats followed to add to the already awful season. Unable to pay the players, the Bens turned to a couple of former players to help out. Alex Forsyth returned when Archibald was injured and Davie Drummond came back. One match day at Tinto Park a regular fan came over to Derek and gave him a bit of good news. The day had been as bad as ever on the pitch with the Bens getting trounced. The Govan supporters were not in good spirits as the poor old Bens chased shadows. A very well dressed man stood by one of the drainpipes under the big Enclosure. He stood alone and the water from the gutters above flowed into the down pipe and flowed then from the bottom of the pipe down the terrace to the track. The man had a fawn coat, a tie and a pair of leather shoes; totally out of place at Tinto Park. The man bringing the news to Derek and his friends said ' Dae ye see that man ower ther. He has just given the Bens a bundle of money. They reckon it wis 500 pounds. That should hopefully save the club !'.

Derek was fascinated as to what motivated the man to give the Bens the money and decided to speak to the donator. Derek said ' Hullo Mister, kin a speak tae ye!'. The man said : 'Yes of course son' Derek said ' I hear ye gave the Bens a donation; that wis very nice of ye. I wid like to thank you' Derek offered his hand and they shook hands. After watching the Bens opponents score another goal the man said ' I have always supported the Bens. .I once worked in Golspie Street. When I heard they were in danger of extinction I felt I must do something for them. I do my business down in England and am fortunately not short of a bob or two.  Unlike Rangers I think the Bens are essentially a Govan team. They do not bother with religion and all that rubbish. They always seem to attract good people to their committee and are well run. The Bens are down at the moment but they will come back. The Bens are a great club'.   The conversation lifted Derek a lot and he relayed the content of the conversation to his friends. He finished by saying 'Well I suppose for the team the only way is up. A win over Gourock is a must!'

The league matches running up to the Gourock match did not offer too much in ways of encouragement. A 5-1 reverse against Kilsyth Rangers at Tinto Park. Bens had former Third Lanark winger Ian Hilley playing and he scored the Bens goal from a penalty. Kilsyth's Jim Morrison scored four and was set to join Celtic.

Bens policeman player PC Mc Millan was selected for Glasgow Police and played at Villa Park, Birmingham against Birmingham Police.

The battle of the titans arrived with both teams without a league win all season. Benburb had two points from draws. Gourock had one point and only a few weeks previously had shipped 12 goals at home to St.Anthony's equalling the Bens record away score from a few seasons previous. Gourock turned up with virtually no supporters. The Bens support was good for the match hoping at long last to see a win. Derek and a few friends had a few fruit boxes to sit at the top of the high terracing at the top end of the pitch where Bens were shooting in the first half. A great view.

BENBURB: Fisher; Dempsey, Gibson, McMillan, Nisbet, McCann, Stewart, Gallacher, McGregor, Cairns and Atwell.

GOUROCK: De Marco, O'Hare, Brown, Warrilow, Jackson, McGrady, Hopkins, Fox, Kennedy, Docherty and Whiteside.

Benburb scored in the first minute through Gallacher and PC McMillan quickly added a second. It was all Bens but they could not add to the score before half time. In the second half they did add two more unopposed goals and the first win of the season duly arrived.

RESULT: BENBURB 4 GOUROCK 0

## CENTRAL LEAGUE—WEST DIVISION

| Team | Pl | W | L | D | F | A | Pts |
|------|----|----|----|----|----|----|----|
| Rob Roy | 17 | 14 | 0 | 3 | 60 | 19 | 31 |
| Kilsyth Rangers | 18 | 11 | 4 | 3 | 52 | 21 | 25 |
| Johnstone Burgh | 17 | 11 | 4 | 2 | 54 | 31 | 24 |
| Renfrew | 17 | 10 | 4 | 3 | 45 | 25 | 23 |
| Vale of Leven | 18 | 10 | 5 | 3 | 40 | 35 | 23 |
| Clydebank | 18 | 10 | 7 | 1 | 46 | 44 | 21 |
| Pollok | 16 | 8 | 5 | 3 | 44 | 23 | 19 |
| Greenock | 15 | 8 | 4 | 3 | 32 | 24 | 19 |
| St.Anthony's | 16 | 8 | 6 | 2 | 41 | 22 | 18 |
| Arthurlie | 17 | 5 | 7 | 5 | 33 | 41 | 15 |
| Dunipace | 17 | 5 | 9 | 3 | 32 | 45 | 13 |
| Port Glasgow | 17 | 3 | 8 | 6 | 34 | 33 | 12 |
| Duntocher Hibs | 18 | 5 | 11 | 2 | 28 | 48 | 12 |
| Yoker Athletic | 15 | 3 | 8 | 4 | 32 | 30 | 10 |
| Benburb | 16 | 0 | 14 | 2 | 9 | 62 | 2 |
| Gourock | 16 | 0 | 15 | 1 | 9 | 88 | 1 |

St.Anthony's were having a decent season apart from a dip in the West of Scotland Cup. The team always seemed to prove a thorn in the side of Johnstone Burgh A visit to Keanie Park saw the Ants again be a 'bogey' team in front of a good crowd. Centre forward McCabe scored a first half goal and the Ants held on for a 1-0 win. The Ants had it tough in the Scottish Junior Cup 2nd Round with a visit from Blairgowrie.

ST.ANTHONY'S: Brown, McGuigan, Delaney, Boardman, Doran, McGrillan, Stewart, Paterson, McCabe, Armour and Gillan

BLAIRGOWRIE: Sidey Warrander, Rodger, Harley, Donaldson, Cargill, Barclay, Miller, St.John, McMurdo and Brown.

The visitors attacked from the start and Brown was in constant action with some smart saves. The Ants scored from a breakaway when McCabe set up Gillan. The score remained the same until half time. In the second half it was much the same as before. Each side found the net once and St.Anthony's were through to Round 3.

RESULT: ST.ANTHONY'S 2 BLAIGOWRIE 1

Benburb were unable to build on the Gourock win. The next match saw heroics from goalie Eddie Archibald and centre half Bobby Nisbet keep a good Clydebank side to 7-0 at Kilbowie Park. Derek's uncle Jack who lived at Clydebank and was a life long Benburb supporter said 'This is the worst Bens team I have ever seen!!'.

Benburb were given a tough match at Lanark United in the second round of the Scottish Junior Cup. However the win over Gourock had given them a lift in that they were capable of winning a match and they were hopeful of at least forcing a replay.

LANARK UNITED: Newlands, Shankly, McLean, Barr, Bryden, Woods, Gourlay, Lowe, Nicholl, Valentine and Sneddon.

BENBURB: Archibald. Dempsey, Atwell, McCormack, Nisbet, Gibson, Horn, Mc Millan, Marshall, Cairney and Stewart.

The Bens took a surprisingly good support to Lanark filling one coach and others going on the team bus as well as travelling down by cars and trains. They did not have long to wait to cheer a goal as PC Mc Millan blasted home in the Bens first attack. The conditions were terrible as was the referee who seemed to be the worst 'homer' the Bens support had ever seen. Even Mrs. Cook was getting annoyed as he gave every decision to the home side. Despite this Benburb remained on top and should have been well ahead at half time. In the second half the home side improved and cheered on by their support started to pile on the pressure. The pressure told and they got the equaliser. However, the Bens responded well and looked the more likely side to win when out of the blue the referee awarded Lanark a penalty near the end. No one in the ground knew the reason. The penalty was scored and the Bens were out; a great effort thought the Bens folk. RESULT: LANARK 2 BENBURB 1

The weather running up to the New Year had been bitterly cold and many matches were falling victim to the freezing conditions. Rangers made a great effort to get the 'Old Firm' match at Ibrox Park on. As New Years Day arrived, both uncles Robbie and Jack plus Derek went to the Old Firm match. Rangers were clear favourites to win against a young and struggling Celtic team. The game was in doubt but most were surprised to see the teams run out to play on what was effectively a sheet of ice with sand on top. Harold Davis ruled the roost in midfield and Rangers ran riot. Davis, Wilson, Miller and Greig scored for the Ibrox side in one of the easiest wins in an Old Firm match.

The Celtic end was near deserted long before the end and but for some amazing misses from the normally dependable Ralph Brand, Rangers could have scored many more. Both Uncles agreed that the game should not have been played and that Celtic were poor throughout and threw the towel in early on.

Benburb had a team manager and he was enthusiastic. Colin Cooper an Aberdonian signed eight new players. Included in them was Eddie Mulheron as well as signing Bobby Nisbet on a permanent basis. Maurice Young was to become a coach to a number of young Govan footballers who had joined. Derek and his uncles thought ' Things are looking up !'.

However, little football was played over the coming weeks as the UK experienced one of the worst winters ever.

In the City and Suburban League McNeil's a consistent Govan side led the way approaching the half way point. However, Maitland were putting in a strong challenge to their title aspirations.

## CITY AND SUBURBAN AMATER LEAGUE– 1st DIVISION

| Team | Pl | W | L | D | F | A | Pts |
|---|---|---|---|---|---|---|---|
| McNeil's | 8 | 6 | 1 | 1 | 20 | 11 | 13 |
| Maitland | 6 | 6 | 0 | 0 | 26 | 4 | 12 |
| Argyle Chair Works | 8 | 4 | 1 | 3 | 27 | 13 | 11 |
| JCBS | 6 | 3 | 1 | 2 | 17 | 8 | 8 |
| Bloomvale | 9 | 4 | 5 | 0 | 19 | 19 | 8 |
| Marinite | 10 | 3 | 6 | 1 | 18 | 46 | 7 |
| Woodside Thistle | 9 | 3 | 6 | 0 | 17 | 20 | 6 |
| Bevin's United | 8 | 1 | 6 | 1 | 16 | 31 | 3 |
| Dorset Rangers | 6 | 1 | 5 | 0 | 11 | 15 | 2 |

Scottish football received a boost from Dunfermline football club. Manager Jock Stein was none to pleased with the refereeing in the 1st Leg of the Inter Cities Fairs Cup against Valencia. The Spaniards won 4-0 and that seemed to be that. However an amazing night of football saw the Pars pull back the deficit and win 6-2 levelling the aggregate scores. Unfortunately Valencia won the play off.

Benburb drew 2-2 against Gourock after being two up at half time through Wilson and Stewart. The Bens games were starting to become close even against the top teams in the league. At Greenock they lost narrowly against the strong Greenock side

At Tinto Park they almost pulled off a win against Johnstone Burgh. However, they did not get too much luck and lost 1-0.

John Cooper had a policy of signing up young local players and things were definitely looking up for the Bens. In came Eddie Mulheron (Nitshill Royal Victoria) a top class player and Johnny Whitelaw Bellahouston Academy a Scottish Schoolboy International,

Eddie Wilson (Linthouse Amateurs), Archie McGrory (Camphill United), Bobby Nisbet ( Glendale Thistle) who joined earlier confirmed to the Bens.

Most of the Bens team were young Govanites, full of pace and enthusiastic. The average age of the team was just 20 and that included 25 year old Jim McCormack. The smiles were returning to the Bens fans faces who anticipated the end of the weather enforced break.

The atrocious weather continued and few football matches were able to beat the weather. The temperatures were recorded at minus 28 degrees on the Fahrenheit scale. Completely to everyone's surprise Benburb managed to get a match on at Tinto Park against Port Glasgow. A large number of helpers plus some expertise from the Ibrox groundsmen saw the Tinto Park pitch passed fit for play. Benburb had a lot of new faces in their side.

BENBURB: Archibald, McGrory, Mulheron, Mc Cormick, Nisbet, Cairney, McIntyre, Gibson, Ashe, Donnelly and Wilson.

Bens dominated the first half but could not score. The Port managed to score twice in the second half and take the points with a 2-0 score line.

The harsh continuing winter meant that little football was played for almost three months. St.Anthony's were drawn away at Whitburn in the Scottish Junior Cup and the fixture was delayed almost continuously due to frost. Eventually the match went ahead. The Ants got off to a good start helped by an own goal. However, the east of Scotland side piled on the pressure and equalised before half time before going on and scoring the winner. Result Whitburn 2 St.Anthony's 1.

Rangers matches resumed and they were moving steadily to another league title. Partick Thistle had been the main challengers but a surprise 1-0 home defeat to Queen of the South at a vital stage of the season left the door open for Rangers.

## SCOTTISH LEAGUE DIVISION 1

| Team | Pl | W | L | D | F | A | Pts |
|------|----|----|----|----|----|----|----|
| Rangers | 19 | 15 | 1 | 3 | 56 | 17 | 33 |
| Partick Thistle | 20 | 14 | 3 | 3 | 40 | 19 | 31 |
| Kilmarnock | 22 | 12 | 5 | 5 | 61 | 30 | 29 |
| Aberdeen | 21 | 12 | 5 | 4 | 47 | 25 | 28 |
| Celtic | 22 | 11 | 6 | 5 | 47 | 24 | 27 |
| Hearts | 17 | 9 | 2 | 6 | 43 | 21 | 24 |
| Dundee United | 20 | 8 | 5 | 7 | 44 | 32 | 23 |
| Queen of the South | 22 | 9 | 10 | 3 | 27 | 45 | 21 |
| Dunfermline | 18 | 9 | 7 | 2 | 33 | 26 | 20 |
| Dundee | 20 | 7 | 7 | 6 | 38 | 29 | 20 |
| Third Lanark | 21 | 7 | 8 | 6 | 40 | 44 | 20 |
| St.Mirren | 25 | 6 | 12 | 7 | 30 | 53 | 19 |
| Motherwell | 21 | 5 | 9 | 7 | 38 | 40 | 17 |
| Falkirk | 21 | 11 | 7 | 3 | 42 | 45 | 17 |
| Clyde | 22 | 5 | 14 | 3 | 31 | 57 | 13 |
| Airdieonians | 21 | 6 | 14 | 1 | 29 | 58 | 13 |
| Hibernian | 18 | 3 | 10 | 5 | 22 | 40 | 11 |
| Raith Rovers | 22 | 2 | 18 | 2 | 23 | 81 | 6 |

Former St.Constantine's player Michael Cassidy moved up to Junior level and joined Neilston. Michael had the distinction of always being selected for away matches at whatever club he played at. He owned a Dormobile which had seating for 14.

At Cumnock Juvenile Court a mother had taken the law into her own hands. Her 16 year old son, an avid Rangers supporter, had stolen £3 and 6 shillings from a milk roundsman. The mother, on finding out, tore up his ticket for the Rangers v Spurs match and stopped him going to Ibrox Park until he had paid back all the money he had stolen. Provost H.Turner and the court smiled as he admonished the youth.

# GLASGOW CORPORATION -YOUTH LEAGUE

| Team | Pl | W | L | D | F | A | Pts |
|------|----|----|----|----|----|----|----|
| Crookston Castle | 8 | 8 | 0 | 0 | 32 | 5 | 16 |
| St. Gerrard's | 6 | 0 | 0 | 0 | 27 | 6 | 12 |
| Arden | 8 | 4 | 2 | 2 | 31 | 21 | 10 |
| Burnbrae | 9 | 4 | 4 | 1 | 26 | 31 | 9 |
| Penilee | 8 | 4 | 4 | 0 | 22 | 27 | 8 |
| Gowanbank | 9 | 3 | 5 | 1 | 27 | 27 | 7 |
| Carnwadric | 6 | 2 | 4 | 0 | 16 | 19 | 4 |
| St.Bernard's | 8 | 1 | 7 | 0 | 5 | 19 | 2 |
| Govan | 6 | 0 | 6 | 0 | 9 | 40 | 0 |

In the Corporation Youth League St.Gerrard's made a good start and with Crookston Castle held 100% records. Govan watched from the back of the field.

George Duncan was a Bellahouston Academy winger who stepped up to Rangers. He had several games in the Rangers first team and always performed well. However with Alex.Scott and Davie Wilson as competition he did not get the chances he deserved and after being freed moved to England. Initially he played for Southend United before moving north to Chesterfield. George was hitting top form and several clubs from the higher English Leagues including Blackpool were taking notice.

John Fraser Wilson the Chairman of Rangers Football Club died at the age of 74. He was in business as a Stevedore since 1920 and was once on the Govan Parish Council. He got elected onto Glasgow Corporation for Kinning Park West in 1925 and later he elected to represent Camphill as a Progressive member. John Wilson had stuck steadfastly behind Willie Woodburn the Rangers centre half suspended sine die and eventually got the ban lifted. He joined Rangers in 1947 and became chairman two years later.

The long and harsh winter of 1962/63 brought many demands for a review of the Scottish Football season. The clubs were mostly inactive from late November to early March. The clubs leading for change were Kilmarnock, Motherwell and Dunfermline. Rangers and Celtic were opposed to change and by the time the vote came it was clear there would be no change. The motion would have required a two/thirds majority to succeed. In the event it lost by two/thirds 25 votes to 12.

The clubs tended to follow the lead of the 'old firm'

Former Benburb goalkeeper John Gallacher had the misfortune to break his foot when he slipped on the ice. This meant he would be out action for a while leaving his club Ayr United in difficulties.

Frank Haffey the Celtic goalkeeper who hailed from Copland Road left Glasgow Sherrif Court and immediately shook hands with the man who had been charged with assaulting him. The man was a Celtic fan and he ran on the pitch after 72,000 watched Real Madrid beat Celtic in a friendly match. Daniel Main made for Frank Haffey to congratulate him on the excellent match he had played. However when the police intervened he gave them a barrage of abuse. Main of Castlemilk was fined £10. Big Frank was largely unperturbed.

Former Benburb player Mike Jackson who did well at Celtic moved on to St. Johnstone.

Charlie Gibson a youngster who was on Rangers radar signed for Benburb. Just four players from the early season squad remained. Ian Archibald the goalie, Bobby Nisbet at centre half, captain wing half Jim MacCormack and inside right Ian Horn. Benburb also signed a young powerful centre forward Jim Ashe from Camphill United amid good reports. His father Jimmy Ashe had played at top level with Third Lanark and St.Mirren.

A player who played for Benburb in their early formation years passed away. Jimmy Reckord became a Pollok fan but always liked to talk about his Bens days. The big freeze was putting paid to Bens matches. However, coming up they had an exciting game at Tinto Park against the league's best team. Most of the Bens folk could not wait for it. Could the young team beat one of the best Juniors teams in Scotland for some years?

Rangers started their Scottish Cup campaign with an away match at Airdieonians. They were gifted a penalty on seven minutes when Airdrie's centre half Thomson picked the ball up in his own penalty box assuming an offside decision. Brand scored from the spot. The goal knocked the stuffing out of the 'diamonds' and goals from Wilson (3), Brand, Thomson and Henderson at regular intervals brought up a 6-0 win for the 'Gers.

Rangers next opponents were East Stirlingshire at Ibrox Park. A bitterly cold midweek match saw the 'Shire score twice through Sandeman and Coburn. However, Rangers put in seven of their own from Brand (4), Wilson, Miller and McLean and moved on to the next round courtesy of a 7-2 win.

A trip to Dundee in the quarter finals saw a game of two penalties. Dundee took the lead in the first half through a Penman penalty. In the second half Ralph Brand scored from the spot to enable a replay at Ibrox Park. The replay saw Dundee mostly the better side and Alan Gilzean scored twice. However Rangers made the most of fewer chances and progressed courtesy of a Hamilton og, Brand (2) 1– a penalty. Result Rangers 3 Dundee 2.

The much anticipated Benburb v Rob Roy match arrived. John Cooper said 'We feel we have a good chance of a win'. His son John Cooper was playing for the Rabs who were unbeaten. With such a long break it seemed like the start of a new season and a good crowd turned up for the game.

BENBURB: Archibald, McGrory, Mulheron, McCormack, Nisbet, Cairney, McIntyre, Horn, Ashe, Gibson and Wilson

ROB ROY: R.McLeod, Dyer, J.McLeod, Reid, Loughran, Cooper, Moy, McIlwaith, Fleming, Knox and McGowan.

Bens young team started brightly and soon had the Rabs on the back foot. Horn and Gibson had good efforts well saved by McLeod. Benburb attacked non stop against a good defence.

Totally against the run of play Fleming scored for Rob Roy on 35 minutes; the first shot they had in the first half. The second half followed the same pattern for a while with Bens on top. However, Rob Roy had their first decent spell and added two more goals. The score line was farcical but Bens kept plugging away and got a brilliant consolation goal when Eddie Mulheron blasted into the net from distance.

RESULT: BENBURB 1 ROB ROY 3

The following week the Benburb Supporters bus leaving Greenfield Street was packed. A trip to Dunterlie Park to play Arthurlie gave the Bens the chance to do well against a team not on the Rob Roy class. A special interest to the Benburb support was a recent signing for Arthurlie from Johnstone Burgh. Alec `Peachie` Patterson. He got the usual warm welcome from the Bens support who remembered the Burgh v Bens matches.

'Away ye go ya big mug Patterson !!'. 'Yer a clown Peachie!'

Alec Patterson was a lawyer and played for Johnstone Burgh since they were formed. He was a no nonsense type of centre half which did not always endear himself to the opposition. However, he was also a very good footballer and started many Burgh moves with his foresight and skill from defence.

However, he had little chance to shine for Arthurlie against Benburb. Jim Ashe was proving to be a handful and scored a hat trick in a remarkable 5-1 win for the Bens. The supporters coach was happy on its way back to Govan. Next up was an away game just down the road at St.Anthony's. It proved to be very even but Doris scored a second half goal for the Ants and it proved to be the winner. The same player had missed a penalty in the first half.

Benburb were to conclude their matches with a fair number of wins and the best was 3-0 at Kilsyth Rangers. A disastrous start had given way to a considerable amount of optimism.

The England v Scotland match at Wembley duly arrived. Scotland were confident of doing well and took an enormous support south. Some observers thought that the Scottish support could have been as high as 25 to 30,000 amongst the 100,000 crowd.

ENGLAND: Banks, Armfield, Byrne, Flowers, Norman, Moore, Douglas, Greaves, Smith, Melia and Charlton.

SCOTLAND: Brown, Hamilton, Caldow, MacKay, Ure, Baxter, Henderson, White, St.John, Law and Wilson

With the game barely ten minutes old Bobby Smith and Eric Caldow collided and it was immediately evident that both were hurt. The stretcher was called for Eric Caldow who was taken off with a broken leg. Bobby Smith resumed after treatment for England but was hobbling. Davie Wilson dropped back to left back and played well. Scotland seemed undaunted by the setback and scored twice in two first half minutes. First Jim Baxter dispossessed Jimmy Armfield and strode on before unleasing a shot into the roof of the net.

Barely had the Scottish celebrations died down when they had a second. Willie Henderson was upended in the penalty box and in the absence of penalty taker Eric Caldow; Jim Baxter scored from the spot.

The second half saw an improved England come back at the Scots and a nervous final 10 minutes was provided when Bryan Douglas scored. Scotland held on to a famous win and took the Home International Championship with maximum points.

RESULT: ENGLAND 1 SCOTLAND 2

At Plantation Park a large number of spectators had gathered around the touchlines for the last sixteen match in the Scottish Juvenile Cup. Tradeston Holmlea were in top form against Kirkton from Dundee and ran out easy 7-0 winners. In the following round Holmlea travelled to Fife and beat Crossford with the only goal scored.

In the Scotland Amateur team former Bellahouston Academy player Andy Roxburgh who was playing for Queen's Park was selected.

School's football was decimated throughout the winter. The Schools football group decided the league's as they were before the big freeze started would stand as they were. The Govan school's did not do too well out of the arrangement and just two progressed to the play off's in the 5 age groups. Division 1 (oldest) St.Gerrard's and Division 4 Lourdes. The ground of former junior side Shawfield was purchased for Schools Cup finals. Roseberry Park was an excellent venue for this purpose being a decent standard ground.

Govan High Former Pupils were fortunate that despite the Main School Building being burned down they were able to continue training at the nearby Dysart Street Gym.

# GLASGOW SECONDARY LEAGUE

| Team | Pl | W | L | D | F | A | Pts |
|---|---|---|---|---|---|---|---|
| Harmony Row | 7 | 7 | 0 | 0 | 26 | 8 | 14 |
| Rancel | 9 | 6 | 1 | 2 | 26 | 12 | 14 |
| Pollok Hawthorn | 7 | 5 | 1 | 1 | 18 | 18 | 11 |
| Drumchapel Thistle | 7 | 4 | 2 | 1 | 34 | 14 | 9 |
| St.Constantine's Juv. | 9 | 3 | 5 | 1 | 10 | 20 | 7 |
| Castlemilk YC | 9 | 2 | 6 | 1 | 13 | 30 | 5 |
| Botany Hearts | 6 | 1 | 3 | 2 | 11 | 21 | 4 |
| Pollok Juveniles | 10 | 0 | 9 | 1 | 15 | 30 | 1 |

As well as heading the league, Harmony Row reached the 6th Round of the Scottish Cup where they had a replay against Shieldhall.

With summer approaching, Derek was able to get football matches with any number of teams at the 50 pitches. At the internal annual Fairfields football competition he managed to get the odd match. Also he played for a couple of Boys Brigade and Boys Guild teams usually on the wing. On occasions the referees were late or failed to show and Mr.Donnelly, who was well into his seventies and walked with difficulty, stepped in. He was rarely able to hobble out the centre circle but no one seemed to bother. The 50 pitches still had football pitches which were Spartan. Half ash down the middle of the pitch grass down to the sides. No nets or corner posts and the lining was difficult to pick out. The only water was one push button well where the players would line up to dig out the grit from their legs and sip a small bit of water. The changing rooms still had no proper floor and no lighting which made life awkward in evening matches which finished late.

The Scottish Cup semi finals saw Rangers play Dundee United at Hampden Park and Celtic play Falkirk. Barring a freak result the first old firm final in 35 years was on the cards.

At Hampden Park Rangers were comfortable winners over Dundee United. In front of a 55,000 crowd Jimmy Millar scored mid way through the first half and quickly added a second. Dundee United responded by scoring twice in quick succession through Gillespie and Mitchell. Ralph Brand put Rangers ahead again and further goals from Millar and McLean enabled the first half of the old firm to take their place in the final.

Result: Rangers 5 Dundee United 2

Celtic were given the lead through Johnny Divers who had a short spell at Benburb against Raith Rovers. Frank Haffey somehow drop kicked a clearance straight to Raith's McDonald who promptly sent the ball back straight into the net. Early in the second half Celtic were awarded two penalty kicks and Dunky McKay fired them in. Chalmers and Brogan brought the Celtic score up to five before Gilfillan scored a late second goal for the Rovers. Result: Celtic 5; Raith Rovers 2.

The Scottish Junior Cup saw a strong surge from the Ayrshire clubs. No fewer than five reached the quarter final. The quarter finals saw Irvine Meadow beat Bellshill Athletic 4-0 and establish themselves as favourites. Bonnyrigg Rose picked up the baton as the sole East of Scotland challenger by beating Whitburn and progressed to the semi final.

Glenafton had a good win at Pollok before facing Cumnock in the quarter finals. A 5-0 rout of the 'Nock' took them forward to the semi final. Winger Billy Paton scored three and the others were scored by Danny McCulloch. Craigmark Bruntonians edged past Ardeer Recreation to take their place as the final semi finalist in an all Ayrshire affair. Craigmark had another all Ayrshire semi final against Irvine Meadow at Rugby Park, Kilmarnock. The Meadow proved too good and were easy winners with 3-0 scoreline.

The second semi final at Firhill was a very close affair with two evenly matched sides. The crowd was disappointing but not the enthusiasm of the teams. Bonnyrigg Rose and Glenafton served up a good match. The Glens had the better of the first half and deservedly led 1-0 at the break. The Rose came back in the second half and equalised. No team was able to get the winner so a replay was required. Result: Glenafton 1; Bonnyrigg 1

The replay was at Firhill Park again and the game was exciting. The heavy rain kept the crowd well down. Duncan Hoogerbeets of Bonnyrigg opened the scoring on 10 minutes and chances came on a regular basis at both ends. In the second half Danny McCulloch shot high into the net to equalise and the match progressed to extra time. It seemed that Billy Paton had secured the Glens a place in the final when he scored in the first half of extra time. However, with time running out the Rose threw everyone up and a Scott shot which was going wide was deflected into his own net by a Glens defender. Result: Bonnyrigg Rose 2 Glenafton 2 (after extra time 1-1)

In the second replay at Firhill Park a goal with just a few minutes remaining from Danny Mc Culloch set up an all Ayrshire Scottish Junior Cup final. The match was in the balance at 2-2 with extra time looking certain. Result: Glenafton 3 Bonnyrigg Rose 2.

Roseberry Park was officially opened by the Glasgow Schools FA and renamed 'New Roseberry Park. The ground was opened by Mr.Bob Kelly the Celtic chairman. Mr.Kelly also gave permission for St.Gerrard's to play St.Mungo's at Celtic Park in the Schools Division 1 League decider.

Rangers were heading to a league title and were having a good run in the Scottish Cup. They reached the Final and a match against their fiercest rivals Celtic. A bit of Govan interest in the match was Frank Haffey in goal for Celtic. Former Benburb player John Divers also played for Celtic. Former Govan High pupil and Bens player Ronnie Mc Kinnon was centre half for Rangers. The road to the Final

2nd Round   Airdrieonians  0 Rangers 6   Celtic 3 Heart of Midlothian  1
3rd Round  Rangers 7 East Stirlingshire 2  Celtic 6 Gala Fairydean  0
4th Round  Dundee 1 Rangers  1    St.Mirren 0  Celtic  1
Replay  Rangers 3  Dundee 2
Semi Final  Rangers 5  Dundee United 2   Celtic 5 Raith Rovers 2
FINAL TEAMS:
RANGERS:  Ritchie, Shearer, Provan, Greig, Mc Kinnon, Baxter, Henderson , Mc Lean, Miller, Brand and Wilson
CELTIC: Haffey, Mac Kay, Kennedy, MacNamee, Mc Neil, Price, Johnstone, Murdoch, Hughes, Divers and Brogan

Rangers started as favourites in front of a 134,000 crowd and took the lead when Ralph Brand converted a Willie Henderson cross. Celtic improved and Bobby Murdoch was left clear in the penalty box to drive home the equaliser with a low shot. The second half was a tense affair but no further goals were scored.
RESULT:  RANGERS 1 CELTIC 1

For the replay Rangers made one change with Ian McMillan replacing George McLean. Celtic made two changes with Bobby Craig replacing Jimmy Johnstone and Stevie Chalmers coming in for Frank Brogan.
If the first game was close the replay was not. Over 120,000 turned up to see Ralph Brand give Rangers the lead with an identical goal as the first game. Willie Henderson crossed and Brand swept home.  Rangers remained on top and Ralph Brand had a fierce shot  partially stopped by Frank Haffey only for Davie Wilson to tap home. The second half saw a lot of Celtic pressure but they were to concede a third goal. A speculative shot from Ralph Brand eluded Frank Haffey and the Scottish Cup was Ibrox bound.
RESULT: RANGERS 3 CELTIC 0

John Cooper the Benburb manager was a spectator watching his son John play for Rob Roy against Chelsea at Adamslie Park. The London club sent a team up to show gratitude for the transfer of Joe Fascione.

In London there was a Youth tournament. Scotland qualified from the group stages and met Greece in the quarter finals. A rough house match took place with two Greeks getting sent off as Scotland went on to win 4-0. Tough right back for Scotland Malcolm McKenzie had his name taken which meant he could not play in the semi final against a very strong England side. Scotland gave England their toughest match before the hosts had a Wembley final against Northern Ireland. England won 4-0 a score which flattered them as the Irish had played well. Most observers thought that the top three could well be doing well in the 1966 World Cup and in particular England who did not concede a goal throughout the competition. Top three: 1 England 2 Northern Ireland 3 Scotland

In terms of rough house matches the Scotland match against Austria fitted the bill. The match was a 'friendly' but had to be abandoned after a rumpus between the referee and the Austrian team. 94,500 turned up for the match and Scotland were winning 4-1 when the match was abandoned on 79 minutes. The referee stopped the game because he felt the Austrians who were enraged would damage some Scottish players.

Austria had a player sent off as they protested at Davie Wilson scoring Scotland's second goal on 25 minutes. Nemec was sent packing but refused to go to the dressing room. Eventually he was led away by officials. In the second half Denis Law added two more goals for Scotland before Hof committed a bad foul on Willie Henderson. Hof was sent off and the rumpus which followed saw the referee abandon the match.

The Scottish Junior Cup Final saw Irvine Meadow line up against Glenafton Athletic at Hampden Park. It was the first Scottish Junior Cup Final between two Ayrshire sides since 1886-1887. The crowd was expected to be affected by circumstances beyond the control of the Scottish Junior Football Association. Due to the long freezing winter ;one of the worst in living memory; a full programme of Scottish Senior level matches were scheduled. Normally the fixtures would have been completed some weeks previously. The crowd of 21,384 was respectable and would probably have been in excess of 40,000 under normal events.

GLENAFTON ATHLETIC: Niven, Caldwell, McLean, Moffat, McKenzie, Murray, Maley, Brennan, Black, McCulloch and Paton
IRVINE MEADOW: Prentice, Miller, McVean, Dickie, Curran, Murray, Walker, Bingham, Garvie, McIntyre and Paterson

The Glens started the better and took the lead when Moffat took a pass from McCulloch and hit a shot into the roof of the net in 9 minutes. Danny McCulloch was ruling the roost in midfield and the Glens had a few half chances. The New Cumnock fans were in fine voice. Irvine eventually started to get a foothold in the match a equalised when Patterson dribbled through the Glenafton defence before flicking home.

Glenafton started the second half in the same fashion as the first and Black fired inches wide. Hookey Walker on the right wing had a few opportunities to get things going for the Meadow but the attacks broke down.

Generally it was all Glenafton and a number of half chances came and went. However when Millar fouled Maley in the box mid way through the second half the referee awarded a penalty. Moffat stepped up but hit the ball wide of the post. Glens continued to press for the winner. However, in the last few minutes Irvine Meadow stole the match when McIntyre scored the winner on a rare attack.

RESULT: GLENAFTON ATHLETIC 1 IRVINE MEADOW 2

After the match the winning goal scorer and veteran John McIntyre announced his retirement from the game. Afterwards Irvine Meadow FC hired a special bus and drove through the streets of Irvine with the Scottish Junior Cup.

Benburb had a team of young talented players. The supporters had taken them to their hearts. However, the expression 'tapping up' soon came to have a meaning.

Celtic had two of Bens youngsters playing as 'Newmen' in a match. They were Archie McGrory the right back and Charlie Gibson the inside right. Jim Ashe the centre forward seemed a class act and with Johnny McIntyre scored freely for the Bens. The latter, a winger, had scored 4 goals in two matches. Eddie Mulheron was signed by Clyde after a number of faultless games for the Bens. The feeling was that Eddie belonged at the top level of Scottish football. Left half David Cairnie was signed by Falkirk.

A Kirkwood Shield Select team included two Benburb players in a Charity match at Newlandsfield Park against a Rangers team. The Select won 6-3. Eddie Mulherron and Bobby Nisbet were the Benburb players.

Bobby Nisbet at centre half was rapidly becoming one of the most popular players at Tinto Park. He was outstanding every match and endeared himself to the Bens support by saying he would never leave Tinto Park. Bobby could have played at senior level football and was requested to attend countless trial matches.

Jim Ashe, Eddie Wilson and Ian Horn all got good offers and manager John Cooper had little option to let them go. A bit of good news was that Benny Murphy who was an immensely popular player in previous times at Tinto Park was to return. Benny was to be de-mobbed from the Army and was still very fit. He was looking forward to helping the Bens.

John Cooper was unperturbed about losing so many players having built a good side from nowhere. He said ' We will be bringing in some good exciting young players for next season. It will take them time to gel but they will come good.

Scottish Junior Football was struggling and a number of the more established clubs were in danger of folding altogether.

Bridgeton Waverley, who Benburb had beaten 3-1 in the Scottish Junior Cup Final of 1934 at Ibrox, folded. They had been playing at Carntyne Racetrack some distance from Bridgeton. Always a popular and seemingly established Junior football club their end was surprisingly sudden.

Parkhead looked to be in danger of folding when their pavilion at Helenslea Park was burned down. The small committee put a fantastic effort in to raise between £600 and £800 to re-build the damaged structure. Team manager Jock Wales was over the moon and looking forward to continuing until the end of the season and re-building a team for 1963-64. Then disaster struck when the re-built pavilion was again burned down by fire. Arrangements were made to continue until the end of the season and complete the fixtures. A committee meeting in June 1963 saw an analyses of the situation facing the club. A decision was taken to close the 'Head' down. In their time the team had produced countless players which subsequently went on to Senior football.

Wishaw Juniors were in trouble. A fire had gutted their pavilion, training hall and committee rooms and things looked bleak. A determined effort from Chairman Willie Martin and his committee saw alternative arrangements being made and they pledged that Wishaw would not be without a Junior side.

Gourock improved before the end of the season. They finished bottom with seven points, some eight points behind Benburb who were second bottom. However, as it looked like the 'tail o' the bank' side were odds on to finish pointless the seven points were seven more than expected. At the halfway point in the season they signed some good players who now were in demand by other clubs. When manager John Toner arrived at Gourock station for a match at Drumshantie Park against Kilsyth Rangers, he found that a number of his players were having 'trials' with other clubs. He had just 7 players. He saw four young fit looking youths nearby and went over to ask them if they fancied a game.

They explained they were rugby players but together they were up for the challenge. All gave their best efforts but two of the 'rugby playesr' had to be carried off leaving Gourock with just nine players. In the event they plugged way and even managed to score a goal. The problem was Kilsyth scored eight of their own to secure an 8-1 win.

In Lanarkshire Mount Ellon United departed after a grand effort to keep going..

A bit of good news for the Junior Football world was that a new team would finally start playing on a more regular basis. East Kilbride Thistle had signed up players and was looking forward to the season starting.

293

Although the top positions in the Schools football were given as the positions as at 31st December 1962, some league football was allowed to continue.
Govan High had an exciting match against Victoria Drive at Pirrie Park.
GOVAN HIGH: McDonald, Frew, Seddon, Crawley, Wilkie, Turner, Sheriff, Clark, McGregor, Kerr and O'Donnell.
VICTORIA DRIVE: Hamilton, Duncan, Stewart, McCreight, Stevens, Fulton, Anderson, Martin, Sewell, Dobbie and Breadley.
Anderson scored an early goal for the 'Drive' and centre half Stevens came up to score two more in quick succession. Right on half time McGregor pulled one back for the 'High'. In the second half Govan piled on the pressure and goalkeeper Hamilton made some good saves. However, he could do little when Turner scored with a good shot from the edge of the box. With time running out the 'High' snatched a deserved equaliser when Kerr scored with a low drive.
RESULT: GOVAN HIGH 3 VICTORIA DRIVE 3
The Glasgow school's under 16 team had one Govan High player for the match against London. McLaughlin of St.Gerrard's played at centre half.
St.Gerrard's lost in the Final at Celtic Park against St.Mungo's in the Division 1 decider.
Tradeston Holmlea were drawn against Germiston Star in an all Glasgow Scottish Juvenile Cup semi final at Petershill Park. The winners were expected to be the winners of the competition.
The Holmlea were also in contention for reaching the play offs for the league. The top two on the Glasgow West Juveniles played off against the to two of the Glasgow East Juveniles. City and District Juvenile positions as they approached the home straight of fixtures.

| Team | Pl | Pts |
|---|---|---|
| League Hearts | 19 | 32 |
| Tradeston Holmlea | 19 | 31 |
| Avon Villa | 20 | 28 |
| Shettleston Violet | 18 | 27 |
| Glencairn Juveniles | 17 | 26 |

To reach the semi finals Tradeston Holmlea's path was as follows:
1st round—Balloch United—scratched
2nd Round—Park United (a) 4-2
3rd Round—Hillof Beath Hawthorn (a) 2-2
Replay Hill of Beath Hawthorn (h) 4-2
4th Round—Kirkton (h) 7-0
5th Round—Crossford (a) 1-0

The semi final saw Germiston Star score after 4 minutes. Tradeston Holmlea fought back and were unlucky not to level by half time. However, in the second half non stop pressure brought them two goals and the 'Lea ' were in the Scottish Juvenile Cup Final.

The Final was over two legs and a long trip to Aberdeen Donside for the first match of the Final was arranged. Holmlea looked in trouble at one stage and trailed 3-1 in the second half. However, a collapse by the home defence late in the match saw Tradeston return with a 6-3 win. The second leg saw a 2-1 win and Tradeston Holmlea were the Scottish Juvenile Cup winners courtesy of an 8-4 aggregate win.

Final teams:

TRADESTON HOLMLEA: McGurr, Smith, Kidd, Ross, McAuley, Craig, Campbell, Anderson, McQuade, Dallas and Rankine

ABERDEEN DONSIDE: Simpson, Youngson, Rae, Stephen, Pirie, Martin, F.Morrison, C.Morrison, Rattray, Anderson and Greig.

Tradeston is of course not technically in Govan being the next burgh along towards Glasgow. However, the team played all their home matches in Govan and the bulk of their players probably came from Govan.

The Juvenile FA announced that it would be mandatory for clubs to provide nets for forthcoming season 1963/64. At the 50 pitches there were many arguments about whether a goal was scored ' That wis in !'. Naw it 'wisnae'.

Rangers were sued for the accident on stairway 13 at Ibrox Park when two spectators were killed and many others injured. Sam Smith (32) sued for £200. 'He was at the Rangers end and was about two thirds the way down when a barrier broke.

He fell forward and felt a sharp pain in his knee. An ambulance man and a spectator helped him back up the stairway when he found he had been injured by a spike from the broken barrier. Smith said that as he was going down the stairs people were trying to hold back. Those at the back kept pushing and there was considerable pressure. He agreed that the handrail was not designed as a crush barrier. Accident inspector John Campbell (57) said the foot of the barrier was about 33% decayed. In conclusion a sum of £123 was agreed to be paid to Mr.Smith.

Harmony Row had a free scoring forward line of Brown, Waters, Shaw, Iuster and McKenzie who ,had scored over 100 goals between them. The team had won the league and the only defeat was in the Scottish Secondary Juvenile Cup semi final against Denny Juveniles. The score was 1-0.

The Row had also reached the final of the Glasgow Secondary Juvenile Cup and faced Cranhill Juveniles at Lochburn Park, Maryhill. Cranhill Social Club were proud of their teams achievement and win, lose or draw a good Social evening was to be laid on for the team.

The teams were:
CRANHILL: J.Short, Duncan, Greenwell, Ward, Marshall, Patrick, I.Short, McMenemy, Duthie, Lennox and Stewart.
HARMONY ROW: Smith, Clark, Paterson, McMillan, Rossan, Hendry, Waters, Hunter, Shaw, McKenzie and Brown
  No trace could be found for result.
  Storm clouds were gathering over Cathkin Park home of Third Lanark. The club had a new stand built. However, what they did not realise was that the brand new tip up seats were rented and not bought. A deal for the rent of the seats amounted to around £80 per week. Bill Hiddleston, whose son once played for Benburb, was the new owner and making his presence felt. Mr.Robert Spence the Vice Chairman of Third Lanark Football Club resigned. He said 'I leave without any disagreement and purely for business reasons. Mr. George Foster would continue as Chairman.

  The resignation of Mr. Spence was the sixth since Mr.Hiddleston took over in December 1962. A number of other staff left the club including George Young the team manager soon after Mr.Hiddleston arrived.

  The season finished on a high. Scotland had a three match tour. They lost surprisingly to Norway 4-3 with Denis Law scoring all the Scotland goals. They lost 1-0 to Eire in Dublin. A trip to the Bernebeu Stadium in Madrid looked a daunting prospect. However, Scotland showed what they were capable of and won 6-2. Spain scored first through Adalardo but two quick goals from Denis Law and Davie Gibson had Scotland in front.

  Frank McLintock scored the third and Davie Wilson added a fourth. Right on half time Velosa pulled a goal back for the Spaniards. The second half saw further goals from Willie Henderson and Ian St.John
RESULT: SPAIN 2  SCOTLAND 6

# CHAPTER 15
# THE FINAL WHISTLE (early 1963– 64)

With a recession and the Govan shipyards struggling, a move to England was on the cards for Derek's family. However, some early season football was followed ardently.

Rangers were put in the same group as Celtic in the Scottish League Cup and opened the fixtures at Parkhead. Rangers won 3-0 with two goals from Jim Forrest and followed this up with 5 wins and a draw in the League Cup section matches in a group which included Kilmarnock and Queen of the South. Rangers repeated the 3-0 score line against Celtic at Ibrox Park with Wilson a Brand penalty and Forrest getting the goals.

In the quarter final, East Fife pushed Rangers all the way at Methil and the Ibrox side were lucky to scrape a 1-1 draw. Forrest got Rangers goal, Dewar for East Fife. A penalty goal from Ralph Brand and a second from Jim Forrest gave Rangers a 2-0 win at Ibrox Park and a 3-1 aggregate victory over gallant East Fife.

The Semi finals saw Rangers play Berwick Rangers at Hampden Park. Just 16,000 turned up and saw Davie Wilson give Rangers a 16th minute lead. There was a shock on 35 minutes when Ken Bowron equalised for Berwick. Brand restored Rangers lead before half time and Jim Forrest scored a third to give the 'Gers a 3-1 win and a place in the Final.

Morton had caused a major surprise in knocking out Hibernian after a 1-1 draw at Ibrox Park. They had a 4th minute lead through Adamson but Martin equalised mid way through the first half. That is how it stayed to the end and extra time could not separate the sides. The replay was a tight match but Morton won through with the only goal scored courtesy of an Alan McGraw penalty.

Rangers European Cup journey ended at the first hurdle.

The first match at Ibrox Park saw a spirited performance from Rangers; only a late goal from Puskas separated the sides. However, in the second leg the Spanish side brushed Rangers aside by the margin of 6-0; winning 7-0 on aggregate.

Derek and a number of his friends do not visit Ibrox Park on such a frequent basis. Many of Rangers games are becoming predictable against sometimes part time opponents. The expression ' two in each half!1 is born indicating that Rangers seem to score two goals in each half in a number of games.

However, one team which is matching them win for wins is Kilmarnock and is already evident the Rugby Park side will have a say on who wins the title.

Up and coming Morton reached the Final of the Scottish League Cup. A crowd of 105,000 turned up including a considerable number from Greenock.
RANGERS: Ritchie Shearer, Provan, Greig, Mc Kinnon, Baxter, Henderson, Willoughby, Forrest, Brand and Watson
MORTON: Brown, Boyd, Mallan, Reilly, Keirnan, Strachan, Adamson, Campbell, Stevenson, Mc Graw and Wilson.

Morton gave the match everything they had. They were long odds underdogs but were not going to go down easily. For the first half they battled for everything and reached the match mid point scoreless. The second half saw Rangers superior fitness start to tell and Jim Forrest gave them the lead. The same player soon added a second before Alex Willoughby scored and put the game well beyond Morton at 3-0. Two late goals from Jim Forrest brought his personal tally on the day to four.

RESULT: RANGERS 5  MORTON 0

St.Anthony's like Benburb are struggling and the small support the Ants had all but evaporated. The gates at the three Govan teams grounds have dropped. A number of reasons were put forward. Television, recession and better entertainment elsewhereseemed to have changed peoples habits.

Benburb once again had many new faces with the manager continuing his policy of giving young local players a chance.

Not surprisingly many of the promising young players they had were snapped up by other clubs who could afford to pay better money. Notwithstanding that the Bens managed a better start than the disastrous beginning to the previous season. They were in good spirits as they travelled the short distance to the tight Newlandsfield ground by the River Cart and Pollok. The pitch was in poor condition with a mixture of ash and thin strands of grass.

BENBURB: Archibald, Sutherland, Johnstone, Murray, Nisbet, McGowan, Ross, Hainey, Caldwell, Gallacher and Devon.
POLLOK: McLean, Dickie, McColl, McDonald, Neil, Smellie, Stewart, Sellars, Querns, James and Hastie.

The Bens had many very talented young players. They were athletic and skilful. However, their lack of experience often caught them out; especially corners and free kicks. Benburb attacked from the start but had to wait until mid way through the half when Caldwell scored. However, Pollok soon equalised only for Mc Gowan to restore the Bens lead. Pollok equalised again before half time. Benburb were the better side in the second half but could not force the winner against one of Pollok's not so good sides.

RESULT: POLLOK  2  BENBURB  2

Scottish football got a boost when two players were selected for the Rest of the World team. Denis Law and Jim Baxter both played in the Rest team in the England 100 year celebration match.  England won the match 2 goals to one.

# CENTRAL LEAGUE

| Team | Pl | W | L | D | F | A | Pts |
|---|---|---|---|---|---|---|---|
| Johnstone Burgh | 10 | 7 | 1 | 2 | 37 | 9 | 16 |
| Greenock | 10 | 6 | 2 | 2 | 20 | 10 | 14 |
| Vale of Leven | 10 | 6 | 2 | 2 | 26 | 16 | 14 |
| Kilsyth Rangers | 10 | 5 | 2 | 3 | 28 | 21 | 13 |
| Rob Roy | 10 | 6 | 3 | 1 | 22 | 18 | 13 |
| Port Glasgow | 9 | 5 | 2 | 2 | 22 | 17 | 12 |
| Yoker Athletic | 10 | 4 | 3 | 3 | 17 | 22 | 11 |
| Arthurlie | 9 | 4 | 4 | 1 | 13 | 13 | 9 |
| Clydebank | 10 | 3 | 4 | 3 | 20 | 22 | 9 |
| Dunipace | 10 | 2 | 3 | 5 | 26 | 28 | 8 |
| Renfrew | 10 | 4 | 6 | 0 | 22 | 23 | 8 |
| Benburb | 10 | 3 | 6 | 1 | 20 | 22 | 7 |
| Duntocher Hibs | 10 | 1 | 4 | 5 | 15 | 20 | 7 |
| St.Anthony's | 10 | 2 | 5 | 3 | 16 | 25 | 7 |
| Pollok | 10 | 0 | 4 | 6 | 13 | 22 | 6 |
| Gourock | 8 | 0 | 7 | 1 | 13 | 41 | 1 |

Rangers were getting the better of the old firm matches and won three in a row. Two in the League Cup and one in the League. The matches saw a fair bit of crowd trouble. The Ibrox League Cup match.
RANGERS: Ritchie, Shearer, Provan, Greig, McKinnon, Baxter, Henderson, Mc Lean, Forrest, Brand and Wilson
CELTIC: Haffey, Mc Kay , Gemmell, Clark, Mc Neil, Price, Gallacher , Turner, Divers, Chalmers and Jeffrey.

Govan interest was maintained with the inclusion in the teams of Ronnie Mc Kinnon, Frank Haffey and John Divers facing each other directly. Celtic were the better team in the first half but a cross from Bobby Shearer was headed in by Davie Wilson to put the Ibrox side ahead. A number of Celtic supporters were arrested after the goal  and dragged out of the terracing by policemen. The second half saw Rangers gain a grip on proceedings and they were awarded a penalty which Ralph Brand coolly converted. Jim Forrest scored a third and this prompted a considerable amount of trouble in the Celtic end as the Rangers following chanted 'Easy, Easy'.
RESULT : RANGERS 3 CELTIC 0

Following the trouble of the previous match a number of high powered people gathered around the players entrance as the teams took to the field. Scot Symon –Rangers, John Lawrence– Rangers, Jimmy McGrory-Celtic, Bob Kelly-Celtic and the Glasgow Lord Provost Peter Meldrum. All appealed for good behaviour.

Celtic were the better team in the early stages and it was no surprise when Stevie Chalmers shot in a goal off the inside of the post. Rangers came more into the game but were thwarted by some smart saves from Frank Haffey. In the second half Rangers pressed for the equaliser and it arrived when McLean made a good run and, taking Forrest's pass, squeezed the ball past Haffey. Soon afterwards Rangers went ahead when Ralph Brand scored and Rangers held on for the two points.

RESULT: RANGERS 2 CELTIC 1

At Muirton Park, Perth they had a small Govan colony. Mike Jackson (former Benburb and Celtic) and Alex Ferguson (former Govan High and Queens Park) played in the same team. Both were beginning to get more regular games and in the case of Alex Ferguson more regular goals. One eventful match saw them lead 1-0 in a match against Hearts. Hearst equalised but the Saints goalie got injured. After a delay Alex Ferguson put on the gloves and bunnet and took over in goal. The outcome was he had a few good saves but Saints lost 4-1. Derek watches more Benburb matches. The team has a number of young players but these are being out muscled by the more experienced opponents most weeks. Top of the league Johnstone Burgh visit Tinto Park and bring a huge support. The 'Burgh had 13 coaches at least in the car park and one double decker. With the attraction of playing good opposition there is also a good support for the Bens side which had a number of Govan players.

BENBURB: Stewart, Johnstone, Sheddon, Gallacher, Nisbet, Mc Gowan, Dearie , Mc Ghee, Caldwell, Gibson and Devon.

The Burgh were on top early on and took the lead on the quarter hour mark. Bens hit back and played well. Some slick moves had the Burgh defending for long periods and it was no surprise when McGhee forced the ball home after a corner. In the second half with the Bens kicking downhill the Govan side forced the pace and went into the lead stunning the Johnstone support. However, it was the travelling fans who had the last laugh when two late goals gave them the spoils. An excellent match where the Bens support thought ' Why can the team not play like this every week'.

RESULT: BENBURB 2 JOHNSTONE BURGH 3

*Derek is destined for a life in England. On the day of departure he is walking past Drumoyne Primary School. The boys are picking the teams for football via the scissors/stones/paper method Immediately memories went back to some years previous when in the Drumoyne School playground. Farewell Govan !!.*

# Ants reject ...Bens hero

Nostalgia goes hand in hand with Hampden Park and when Govan man Tommy Dearie stepped on to the hallowed turf recently it was an occasion for the memories to come flooding back.

For Tommy was the man who scored the goal that brought the 1936 Scottish Junior Cup to Tinto Park in the replay against Yoker Athletic.

After drawing the first game 1-1, Tommy's goal was enough to take the Cup to Govan.

However, on this return visit to Hampden, there was no crowd, no noise and there weren't even nets on the famous goals. But nevertheless it was a proud Tommy as he showed Benburb's team boss, Tommy Douglas, the very spot where he scored his winner 44 years ago.

"I remember it all very clearly," said Tommy. There was a bit of a goalmouth scramble and I got a foot to the ball and prodded it into the net."

Tommy was wearing the number 11 jersey that day and by coincidence Bens boss Tommy Douglas wore the shirt in his playing days at Tinto Park.

The football writers at that time predicted that "Dearie will be the man Yoker will have to watch." Unfortunately for the Holm Park side, they let Tommy prove the press was right.

St. Anthony's unwittingly played a big part in Bens' 1936 Cup win, without realising it at the time.

It was the Moore Park club which discarded Tommy and he switched his allegiance to Govan's other Junior aide.

It was just a year after the Cup Final that Tommy was selected to play in a trial for the national Junior side and his instructions were: "If you want to play a trial for Scotland, bring your boots, white knickers, towel and hose."

The match was held at Council Park, Campbeltown, and Tommy had to meet the bus in the centre of Glasgow at 7.30 in the morning. Kick-off was at 3.30 and poor Tommy didn't get home until 7 p.m. the following evening!

Forty years later, Bens will still be pinning their hopes on the No. 11 jersey.

This time it's Eddie McKim, the most prolific scorer in the Junior game, who Bens will be looking for to put the ball in the net.

And no one will jump for joy like Tommy Dearie, who will be the Bens' guest at Hampden, if the number 11 jersey again helps to bring the Scottish Junior Cup back to Govan.

## EARLY EXITS

The Bens were knocked out of two major cups early in the season. In the Lang's Trophy they won only two of their eight group matches and then lost 2- at home to Irvine Meadow in the Whyte and Mackay West Scotland Cup.

Their Drybrough C. campaign survived a lit

---

Photo 15

Printed in December 2021
by Rotomail Italia S.p.A., Vignate (MI) - Italy